KUDRUN

with *The Book of King Otnit*
and *The Book of Wolf Dietrich*

KUDRUN

with *The Book of King Otnit*
and *The Book of Wolf Dietrich*

Edited and Translated, with an Introduction, by
William T. Whobrey

Hackett Publishing Company, Inc.
Indianapolis/Cambridge

Copyright © 2025 by Hackett Publishing Company, Inc.

All rights reserved
Printed in the United States of America

28 27 26 25   1 2 3 4 5 6 7

For further information, please address
 Hackett Publishing Company, Inc.
 P.O. Box 44937
 Indianapolis, Indiana 46244-0937

 www.hackettpublishing.com

Cover and interior designs by E. L. Wilson
Composition by Aptara, Inc.

Cataloging-in-Publication data can be accessed via the Library of Congress Online Catalog. Library of Congress Control Number: 2024945643.

ISBN-13: 978-1-64792-210-8 (pbk.)
ISBN-13: 978-1-64792-211-5 (PDF ebook)
ISBN-13: 978-1-64792-212-2 (epub)

The paper used in this publication meets the minimum requirements of American National Standard for Information Sciences—Permanence of Paper for Printed Library Materials, ANSI Z39.48–1984.

CONTENTS

Introduction	ix
The Book of Kudrun	**1**
Chapter 1: No Heading	1
Chapter 2: How Hagen Was Taken Away by the Griffin	9
Chapter 3: How Hagen Came Aboard the Ship	13
Chapter 4: How Hagen Was Received by His Father and Mother	17
Chapter 5: How Wate Traveled to Ireland	23
Chapter 6: How Sweetly Horant Sang	38
Chapter 7: How the Young Women Viewed the Ships and How They Were Taken Away	45
Chapter 8: How Hagen Pursued His Daughter	49
Chapter 9: How Wate, Morunc, and Horant Returned Home	56
Chapter 10: How Hartmut Courted Kudrun	58
Chapter 11: How Herwig and Hartmut Came for Kudrun	61
Chapter 12: How Herwig Fought against Hetel and How Kudrun Was Given to Him	62
Chapter 13: No Heading	66
Chapter 14: How Hetel Sent Out Envoys from Herwig's Land	71
Chapter 15: How Hartmut Took Kudrun by Force	74
Chapter 16: How Hilde Sent Out Envoys to Hetel and Herwig	78
Chapter 17: How Hetel Arrived at the Wulpensand to Rescue His Daughter	82
Chapter 18: How Ludwig Killed Hetel and Fled in the Night	85
Chapter 19: How the Hegelingen Returned to Their Homeland	89
Chapter 20: How Hartmut Returned Home	91
Chapter 21: How Kudrun Had to Do the Wash	100
Chapter 22: How Hilde Fought to Save Her Daughter	103
Chapter 23: How They Arrived at the Anchorage and Marched into Ormanieland	109
Chapter 24: How Kudrun Learned of Their Arrival	111
Chapter 25: How Ortwin and Herwig Arrived There	114
Chapter 26: How Herwig and Ortwin Returned to the Army	126
Chapter 27: How Hartmut Identified the Nobles' Standards for Ludwig	128
Chapter 28: How Herwig Killed Ludwig	135

Contents

Chapter 29: How Hartmut Was Taken Prisoner	140
Chapter 30: How They Sent Out Envoys to Hilde	145
Chapter 31: How the Four Kings Celebrated in Hilde's Land	155
Chapter 32: How the Others Went Home	157

The Book of King Otnit — 159

Chapter 1: No Heading	159
Chapter 2: How Otnit Found His Father Alberich When He Gave Him His Armor	168
Chapter 3: How Otnit Waged War for a Lady Overseas	181
Chapter 4: How Suders Was Razed	189
Chapter 5: How the Town Surrendered and [They] Went On to the [Next] Town	195
Chapter 6: How the Muslim Sent Dragon Eggs to His Son-in-Law Otnit	208
Chapter 7: How Otnit Was Killed by the Dragon	211
Chapter 8: No Heading	216

The Book of Wolf Dietrich [*Version A, fragment*] — 219

Chapter 1: No Heading	219
Chapter 2: How the King Returned and Saw the Child	222
Chapter 3: How the Child Was Rescued and Secretly Given Refuge	225
Chapter 4: How the Lady Lamented Her Child, Not Knowing Where He Was	230
Chapter 5: How the Captive Berchtung Was Brought to Trial	233
Chapter 6: How Saben Quit the Land on Account of His Great Disloyalty	238
Chapter 7: How Hug Dietrich Died and Saben Gained Favor	241
Chapter 8: How Wolf Dietrich Fought Against His Two Brothers and Defeated Them	247
Chapter 9: How Wolf Dietrich Lamented His Liegemen, Berchtung's Sons	252
Chapter 10: How He and His Eleven Sons Were Besieged	255
Chapter 11: How His Sword Broke on the Dragon, and It Carried Him into the Mountain	260
Chapter 12: How He Defeated the Robbers in the Forest	265
Chapter 13: How He Heard Lady Liebgart Lament Her Dear Husband	267

Chapter 14: How He Found a Dead Knight Who Had Been Left by the Dragon	270
Chapter 15: How He Brought the Dead Knight's Wife to a Peasant and Gave Her Over to Him, Along with the Child	272
Chapter 16: How the Horse Drove the Dragon Away While He Slept	272
Chapter 17: How His Sword Broke on the Dragon, and It Carried Him into the Mountain	274
The ending of Wolf Dietrich A *according to the* Dresdener Heldenbuch (k)	276
Placenames in Kudrun, Otnit, *and* Wolf Dietrich A	279
Personal Names in Kudrun, Otnit, *and* Wolf Dietrich A	286
Family Tree for Main Characters in Kudrun	292
Manuscripts Containing Kudrun *and Versions of* Otnit *and* Wolf Dietrich	293
List of Texts in the Ambraser Heldenbuch	295
Selected Bibliography	296

INTRODUCTION

The High Middle Ages, especially the time around the year 1200, was for German literature a time of extraordinary productivity and genius. The early virtuosity of Heinrich von Veldeke's vernacular retelling of the story of Aeneas, the Arthurian tales of Hartmann von Aue, the monumental *Parzival* of Wolfram von Eschenbach, the masterpiece that is Gottfried von Strassburg's *Tristan and Isolde*, along with the hundreds of courtly love poems still extant from this period, give witness to a movement, one might even say a literary program, of amazing breadth and depth. The emergence of the poet as celebrity represented an early recognition of vernacular literature as a cultural and especially dynastic instrument with the power to change the way people thought about art and authority and the role that language played in both.

Along with these works by writers well known to their readership, we have in the *Nibelungenlied* an epic narrative from around 1200 by a poet who, despite the growing fashion of literary personality, declined to name himself. The ownership of heroic storytelling was communal, that is, it was by definition a narrative tradition that precluded individual authorship. There is growing consensus that the text of the *Nibelungenlied* in its assorted forms was most likely the work of a succession of poets or redactors rather than a single person. The various versions of this ancient story of Siegfried, Gunther, Kriemhild, Brunhild, Hagen, and other characters whose names reach back in part to the Germanic Migration Era (around 200 to 500 CE), had by 1200, however, become part of a nascent and growing book culture. In the concluding remarks of his important study of vernacular epic in the Middle Ages, Jan-Dirk Müller characterizes the *Nibelungenlied* as the prototype of a new genre of "literized" (*literarisierten*) epic narration.[1]

One or two generations later, sometime most likely between 1230 and 1240,[2] another epic narrative joined this emerging book culture. The text we now call *Kudrun* has since its rediscovery by German philologists in the early nineteenth century stood in the shadow of the earlier *Nibelungenlied*, but the text deserves to be reexamined as a unique witness of its own time. It was written by a poet who also chose to remain anonymous, and it shared with the *Nibelungenlied* a poetic form that was purposefully anachronistic, which is to say it attempted to take on the guise of orality while already being read and reworked in written form. The central protagonist is a woman, a young princess named Kudrun, who is both the desired object and guarantor of a line of heroic, dynastic succession. Although

---

1. Jan-Dirk Müller, "*Episches*" *Erzählen*, 400.
2. Estimates of the date of composition vary from 1210 to 1250. See Störmer-Caysa, 661, and Bartsch/Stackmann, 1965, vii–x.

Introduction

men, warfare, and a culture of conflict dominate the narrative, it is Kudrun, like Kriemhild in the *Nibelungenlied*, who drives events to their final resolution. There can be little doubt that *Kudrun* was written with an understanding of and deep appreciation for its predecessor's artistic merit and central place in epic narrative, but its poet also sought to navigate a changing artistic climate and readership in what was at the time of its writing already recognized as a postclassical era.

The *Kudrun* story revolves around extraordinary individuals who seek to make their mark in a society in which conflict and reconciliation have become increasingly consensus-based and law-bound. In the story's traditional setting, the seed of conflict is the propagation of dynastic power by way of interclan marriage. The hero seeks out the most beautiful woman of royal lineage with whom he can increase his own standing, which is characterized as honor. Conflict is fueled by competition and rivalry, and violence is the prevailing means to resolve it. Here the violence most often takes the form of grand military campaigns and invasions, both by land and by sea. The setting is primarily northern Europe, in what is a fairly ahistorical and loose arrangement of petty kingdoms around Denmark and the North Sea, but the rival parties also include a decidedly non-European lord named Siegfried. As leader of much of North Africa and the eastern Mediterranean, this character represents a European worldview that had fully incorporated the broader conflict between the Christian West and the Muslim East. In fact, the stage on which these conflicts play out is virtually global, in that the interaction of various kingdoms in their quest for dynastic supremacy is basically unrestricted by time or distance. Other actors may be far away, but that rarely constrains the ability to engage with them.

Along with *Kudrun*, a substantial text in its own right of 1,705 strophes, or 6,820 lines (the *Nibelungenlied* consists of 2,379 strophes),[3] also presented here is a translation of two shorter texts that have much in common with *Kudrun*. These are the stories of two heroes, Otnit and Wolf Dietrich, and their struggles, triumphs, and setbacks in a world where the hero still strives to control his own fate. In various versions the tales formed a single story; that is, the *Wolf Dietrich* text, at least in its earlier form, served as the continuation and resolution of the tragic tale of Otnit. In this format the two texts combined make up a total of 1,203 strophes, which is certainly within the range of what we might call a longer heroic narrative, especially considering that the *Wolf Dietrich A* version remains a fragment. The texts' composition can be dated, most unassuredly, to around the same time as *Kudrun*, perhaps a bit later, but also around 1240. Here, too, Otnit and Wolf Dietrich find themselves caught up in the need to justify their claims to dynastic rule, whether that claim is through marriage or is contested by rival siblings. The conflict is projected onto a series of military campaigns,

---

3. According to the Heinzle edition (2015). The three main manuscripts all have different total strophe counts.

but this time the protagonists are mainly Christian and Muslim, and the battles are very much like those that were being waged in the Levant at the time these stories were written. In fact, Otnit's main opponent is one of the few historically recognizable characters in the story, a certain Muslim king of Syria named Machorel, a corruption of the name of Saladin's brother and heir, Sultan al-Malik al-Adil (1145–1218). Although as heroic epic these stories find themselves outside of historical time and space, there is a realism, especially in the description of warfare, that is likely reflective of the experience of some of the readership and perhaps even of the poets themselves.

WOMEN AND THE NEW HERO

What follows is not meant to be a comprehensive interpretation but rather some thoughts on a few aspects of epic narrative, specifically concerning the role that women play in this narrative and how this is linked to the emergence of a new hero type. The *Kudrun* poet was clearly influenced by both the tradition of vernacular epic narrative and the way in which that tradition was exemplified in the *Nibelungenlied*. His audience wanted more of the same, and yet the ground was shifting under all of them. The notion of "source" was in flux as the new book culture expanded its reach into every secular court in Europe. This was both a function of the movement of centers of reading and writing from monasteries and church schools to universities and secular capitals and also the sense that writing in the vernacular could be an equivalent truth proposition to Latin and its clerical centers. We want to address the central question of what it meant to be "heroic" in the middle decades of the thirteenth century. How much had *Kudrun* and *Otnit/Wolf Dietrich A* moved away from the norms set around 1200 by the *Nibelungenlied* toward a new understanding of the hero and his place in a culture of books, that is to say, in competition with the courtly romance?

Our texts concern themselves primarily with the question of dynastic stability, that is, the longevity of familial power. This can be achieved through the intermarriage of powerful clans, each of which can be a partner in maintaining a system of hereditary rule meant to secure honor for the ruler, the land, and its people. Honor is maintained through strength, and interclan or tribal alliances are defined in terms of the strength they are able to project across borders. The notion of dynastic power politics and military strategies was in the thirteenth century still very much connected to individuals and their extended family, but increasingly the Realpolitik of large military operations became the means to honor through collective strength. Families were judged not only by the military might they could bring to bear but also by their reputation, or what was said about them. This was subsumed under the general concept of honor in a

Introduction

society that placed a great deal of stock in the relationship between leaders, both male and female. Strong men, or heroes, aimed to maintain or increase power as expressed through courageous action, and strong women aimed to maintain or increase the cultural preeminence of the court as expressed through joy.

The bridal quest is the common theme shared by all three of our texts, a theme as old as the story of Abraham sending a representative to his homeland to find in Rebekah a bride for his son Isaac (Genesis 24). The theme is also central to the *Nibelungenlied*, a fact somewhat obscured by the complexities of the plot and its subplots. Siegfried travels to Worms for no other reason than to win Kriemhild as his wife. His father even advises that he take an army with him, but the hero insists on going it alone with a small company of men, *in recken wîse*, that is, as appropriate to a hero (*NL* 57,3). Gunther likewise travels with Siegfried to Brunhild's homeland with the hope of surviving three deadly challenges and winning the grand prize, Brunhild. It is only later that Siegfried brings in an army from his Nibelungen lands. In *Kudrun*, the high status and stability of familial dynasties must be secured by a union in which the extreme beauty and reputation of the bride-to-be is deemed to be a value-added proposition by two generations: the parents and their grown children. This is to say that the generation in power must ensure its own claim to power by ensuring the next generation's equal or greater worth. Hagen, once in power, denies his daughter Hilde to any suitor out of hand by executing all who would dare deem themselves worthy. The bridal quest therefore becomes a life-and-death challenge for those who, by marrying his daughter, would seek to benefit from an alliance with one of the strongest men alive, known far and wide as the "Terror of All Kings." This establishes both the means and the end in a quest that is by definition worthy of heroic effort, even though Hagen himself had found a bride quite easily, namely, in Hilde from India, with whom he was stranded on the griffin's island and who then lived at his court.

Their daughter, also named Hilde, is described as "beautiful beyond measure" (*K* 199,2a), her beauty spoken of in distant lands. As powerful nobles begin to vie for Hilde's hand, they are killed by Hagen out of "arrogance" (*K* 201,2b), but pride or arrogance (*übermuot*), as the narrator says, is a quality that once found in one man is certain to be found in another (*K* 203,2–3). Young King Hetel of Hegelingen is by implication such a man, as he calls his advisors together to come up with a plan to travel to Ireland and win Hilde as his wife. The best chance of success lies in overwhelming military strength and deception, both of which are provided by loyal vassals and clever counselors. When Hetel later finds himself in a situation similar to Hagen's, and his daughter Kudrun, Hagen's granddaughter, becomes the object of the attention of three suitors, Siegfried of the Moors,[4]

---

4. This is an anachronistic term that was imprecisely used to refer both to Muslims in general and inhabitants of North Africa more specifically.

Introduction

Herwig of Seeland, and Hartmut of Ormanie, he likewise denies them her hand. The pattern of military campaigning and deception is repeated until Herwig proves in a tactical standoff in the Battle of the Walays Shore that he is worthy of Hetel's approval. Subsequently Kudrun is kidnapped by Hartmut, and her father, Hetel, is killed by Hartmut's father, Ludwig. Kudrun is held prisoner in the land of Ormanie for fourteen years. The final military campaign, promoted and financed now by Kudrun's mother, Hilde, succeeds in freeing Kudrun, and peace is eventually restored in a reconciliation secured through a series of marriage alliances.

The story of Otnit is similarly motivated by the challenge of a bridal quest, this time in the context of an actual crusade that takes the hero from Italy to Messina and on to Syria. His opponent, the father, and the prize, his daughter, are both Muslim, and so the ensuing military invasion of Outre-mer, as the Levantine lands across the Mediterranean Sea were called, by Otnit's army is suggestive of contemporaneous events. The fortress of Mount Tabor in Galilee was eventually captured by Christian forces in 1229, but the failed siege in 1217 against Sultan al-Malik al-Adil was a stinging defeat for the crusader movement. Otnit first succeeds with the help of his father, Alberich, in defeating the Muslim army and taking Suders (Tyre), but his forces are thwarted at Mount Tabor. It is only through subterfuge that Alberich manages to coax the princess out of the fortress. Otnit's victory is pyrrhic, however, as Machorel manages to stay in power while Otnit and his bride-to-be hasten to return to safety in Lombardy. This, of course, leads to an ongoing threat once the dragon eggs sent by Machorel hatch near Otnit's home and his kingdom falls victim to their terror campaign. It remains for Wolf Dietrich, a Greek son of the king of Constantinople who is cheated out of his inheritance, to avenge Otnit's death and take his wife, Liebgart, as the prize for his single-handed heroic defeat of the dragons.

What does all this say about the role of the hero and, perhaps more importantly, the role of women in this hero's world? How have these two poles of dynastic power moved beyond both the traditional epic quest for individual validation and the courtly romance's goal of societal harmony? Is there an element of social critique expressed through a reinterpretation of the definition of heroic action? The older generation, that is, Wate, Fruote, and Hagen, along with Ilias of Russia, Otnit's uncle, seems at first to represent the traditional, solitary hero. Yet even though Hagen demonstrates his unique gifts as a young child by single-handedly defeating a supernatural creature on an otherworldly island, as a young king in Ireland he is described as a typical leader who goes to war by invading the lands of his enemies, has mercy on the poor when doing so, and defeats other nobles guilty of being arrogant (*K* 195). He is a terror, a devil even, to his enemies, but his daughter is the proverbial apple of his eye. His life at court is described as pleasant and joyful (*schône* and *frô*; *K* 197,1), and it should be remembered that

Introduction

even as a boy returning home from his island exile, Hagen managed to reconcile the enmity between his father and the count of Garadie. Hagen becomes, in front of our own eyes, a conventional ruler.

The hero in our texts is primarily a military leader, not a lone wolf. The next generation of younger men who go out to find a bride and bring her home are skilled at assembling vassals and allies into a large military force that can invade a foreign land and impose its will on the enemy. There are four distinct military operations and culminating battles in *Kudrun*: the Battle of the Walays Shore, the Battle of Matelane, the Battle of Wulpen Island, and the Battle of Cassiane. Similarly, opposing armies clash in *Otnit* in the Battles of Suders (Tyre) and Mount Tabor, and in *Wolf Dietrich A* Wolf Dietrich and Berchtung gather a large army to invade Greece, which results in the ensuing meeting engagement between the two armies and finally Saben's siege of Lilienport. Military campaigns in *Kudrun* and *Otnit/Wolf Dietrich A* are portrayed in great detail and realism. Whether through siege warfare or open battle, the tactics as described accurately reflect the state of warfare in the thirteenth century. The detail of battle is realistically rendered, for example, in Hartmut's last stand outside his castle, where his knights dismount, have their horses led away, and fight on as infantry, or the scene of Hetel's beach landing on Wulpen Island, with the initial launching of arrows and missiles, then the fight through the waves to secure a foothold on the shore. These men are all outstanding fighters, and they meet each other in combat, not as solitary knights in search of adventure but rather as kings and commanders at the head of their armies.

The young kings in *Kudrun* are complex and multifaceted characters, especially in their contradictions. Rather than view them as tragic or misguided heroes, we should more properly understand them as good men who find themselves in no-win situations. They work within an older honor-shame-vengeance system that often produces the opposite of the desired result. The case of Hartmut will illustrate the point. There is little doubt that he is a courageous and handsome noble, powerful and in all other ways worthy of Kudrun's hand (*K* 623,1–2). At first he sends out ambassadors to present his case, but they are quickly dismissed by Hetel. The reason given is that Hartmut's father, Ludwig, was once a vassal to Hagen, and so any union between the two families would be on unequal terms. Hartmut then journeys to Ireland with a small retinue of kinsmen to make his case in person. He appears at court as a typical *Minneritter*, or knight in the service of courtly love, and is generally acclaimed by everyone. In fact, his feelings of love even seem to be reciprocated by Kudrun, but still he is rejected both by Kudrun and her mother, even to our own narrator's (supposed) surprise (*K* 623,2b). He leaves the Irish court to plot revenge for his dishonor and shame. This vengeance takes the form of a military campaign against Hetel's capital, which is left defenseless as Hetel is away supporting his son-in-law Herwig's battle against Siegfried. Hartmut kidnaps Kudrun and brings her to Ormanie against her will, where she suffers abuse for fourteen years at the hands of the evil Queen Gerlint. In the end, however, it is Hartmut, although defeated in battle, who saves Kudrun's life from his mother's attempt to have her killed in order to deny Herwig the fruits of his victory. This was, in fact, the second time he saved her life, the first being when he pulled her out of the water after his father had tried to drown her (*K* 961). Hartmut is caught between his professed desire to win Kudrun without bloodshed and warfare (*K* 755,3a) and his vow to use any means necessary to achieve his goal (*K* 591,2–3). Herwig is obliged to use his army (*K* 640,4) where kindness (*liebe*) alone had failed to convince Hetel of his worthiness as Kudrun's suitor (*K* 633,4).

Otnit is introduced as a powerful lord, feared both for his conquests and military might (*O* 4,1), but in reality he is a somewhat hapless, inexperienced young leader who relies on the advice of his uncle Ilias and his father Alberich in most things. Otnit is certainly not a hero in the tradition of a Siegfried, and he explicitly states that he doesn't believe he can win his bride overseas without a large army (*O* 122,2). In contrast, the narrative of his solitary quest for adventure, following the pattern of the romance's lone knight, is a rather unmotivated episode clumsily inserted just after preparations for leading an army to win his overseas bride are finalized. He has a vision or dream of some sort (*O* 73,1) and tells his mother that he has set his heart on a quest, or *aventiure*. He subsequently meets his father, but the resulting contretemps is more slapstick than heroic. At the end of the story, as he and his wife rule amid the dragon terror in Garda, Alberich refuses his aid, with the result that Otnit falls asleep on his hunt for the dragon, making him an easy dinner for the dragon's young. His successor, Wolf Dietrich, a tremendously strong and accomplished warrior, defeats this same dragon and its brood but must likewise fulfill his role of leading an army to reclaim his birthright. His military exploits tend toward unacceptably high casualties and an inability to see the larger, strategic picture, but we know from the Dresden manuscript (k) that Wolf Dietrich ultimately invades Greece and Constantinople and defeats his enemies.

These impulsive and somewhat inconsistent young heroes attempt to act and react to insult and injury within the conventional framework of an honor-shame culture. When dishonored, the proper response is vengeance, but in *Kudrun*, vengeance brings about a host of unintended consequences. In fact, it calls into question the ability to achieve the intended goal at all. The problem is that the hero fails to consider the other side of the equation: the reaction of the woman he hopes to marry. Hartmut is haunted by the fact that he and his father killed Kudrun's father and many of her kinsmen. His question then becomes, how can a woman have any affection for someone who caused the death of so many of her loved ones (*K* 1016,1–3)? The other suitors are equally frustrated in their strategies for success. Siegfried attacks his

Introduction

successful rival Herwig, not necessarily in the hopes of winning Kudrun but mostly out of spite for having lost in his own bridal quest. Herwig, after Hetel's rejection, simply returns home, gathers an army of three thousand, and invades Hegelingen with the intention of winning Kudrun through force of arms (*K* 640,4; *K* 646,4). He succeeds when Kudrun, fearing for her father's and Herwig's lives, calls for a truce. Yet he also fails when told by Kudrun's mother that he must wait a year for the marriage to be consummated. Finally, we see in Otnit a hero-type who must rely on the help of others. His strength and military might fail him, and it is only through Alberich's tricks that his future wife agrees to leave her family and marry. Otnit makes his final stand against Machorel and prepares for death, only once again to be saved by his father and uncle, who literally arrive with the cavalry at the last minute. But Alberich, too, in his rebuke of Ilias of Russia's mayhem, must pose the question: "How will a beautiful woman find happiness with the man who took her father's life?" (*O* 418,1–2). In the end, however, Otnit can only express regret for not having killed his wife's father when he had the chance (*O* 533).

Women in *Kudrun* represent the means to subverting the traditional heroic type, thereby enabling a new kind of hero to emerge alongside them. Across the generations in our story it is the queen who is at first the object of desire and then the true dynastic actor. Uote first urges Sigebant to show more courage in public feasts. It is she who has to remind her husband to control himself in his public show of grief when Hagen is abducted. Hilde, Hagen's daughter, leads Hegelingen with a strong hand after her husband's death. She becomes the main proponent of vengeance for Hetel's death and the motivating energy behind the military expedition to free Kudrun (*K* 929). Gerlint is very much the driving force behind her son Hartmut's aspirations in love and war. Her abuse of Kudrun can be seen as a function of her fundamentally evil nature but also as a desperate measure to help her son to greatness.

Kudrun speaks for all women when she says that if she were a man she could take up the sword herself (*K* 1033), and in saying so she echoes Kriemhild's complaint.[5] In her betrothed husband Herwig's absence, she takes the lead and convinces her father to help defend her lands in Seeland against Siegfried's attack. When she herself is kidnapped, Kudrun suffers the consequences of her father's rejection of and insult to Hartmut and his clan. She retaliates with the tools at her disposal: constancy, suffering, and love. Kudrun becomes a living martyr, one worthy of a visit, almost an annunciation, by an angel. Survival becomes the goal, but it is survival with honor, and so Kudrun comes to represent the ethos that will propel her generation and the next into a peaceful and just future. Her

---

5. In the *Nibelungenlied* (*NL* 1416), Kriemhild says that if she were a knight, she would certainly have made the trip to Etzel's court earlier, implying that she would have had more courage than her brothers if she were a man. In the *Klage* the narrator defends Kriemhild's actions by stating that had she been a man she would have avenged Siegfried's death many times over (*KL* 126–33).

reconciliation of the warring parties through marriage alliances brings the cycle of violence to an end. In this she succeeds where men have not. Suffering (*leid*) is replaced by love *(liebe)* in very practical terms. This is not the same as *minne*, or service in the name of an ethereal love, that has so enthralled the male nobility. Rather, it is a love that aims to subvert and redefine honor as the just and peaceful rule of people and lands. This is echoed in two of Kudrun's most faithful companions. Ortrun, Hartmut's sister, becomes a friend to Kudrun, initially with the aim of bringing her around to her brother's way of thinking but then as an ally at a very hostile court. She as well as Hildeburg represent humility in service. This very Franciscan quality is a new feature in the subversion of male heroics and the time-honored rule of an eye for an eye. Humility is not the same as submission. It finds strength in reconciliation and success in peaceful coexistence.

What about the women in *Otnit/ Wolf Dietrich A*? First and foremost we have Liebgart, who remains unnamed until the continuation of Wolf Dietrich's story. She is the Muslim daughter of the ruler of Syria and Jerusalem. Her great beauty and high status are legendary, her distance from Lombardy challenging, but it is the fact that her father has killed every one of her suitors, as did Hagen, that seems to make the prospect of her as a bride most appealing to Otnit (*O* 11,4). Her part in Otnit's adventure seems at first rather submissive. She is the object, the prize, the hero's quest, and this is the role she plays. She is devoted to her father but also willing to declare Otnit the winner and to become his wife and accept baptism. In Lombardy, Liebgart plays the role of a conventional queen, always with the knowledge that she is a stranger, a guest in her new land, and that her family and supporters are far, far away. This aspect of medieval exogamy usually comes to the fore with the death of the husband, although this is not always the case, as, for example, when Hilde, originally from Ireland, remains a powerful queen after Hetel's death. Liebgart, however, is disinherited and ostracized after Otnit is killed by the dragon. She remains in Garda but without power or influence, left to suffer in solitude, as we are continuously reminded at the end of several chapters. But she survives, and in doing so she represents a hopeful future in which her rightful place is restored and justice returned to the kingdom. In the story of Wolf Dietrich, it is his mother who plays the dominant female role. She is also unnamed, known only as the queen of Greece, but she fights for her rights with Berchtung of Meran's help. With Wolf Dietrich sidelined, she is likewise exiled by her two older sons and Duke Saben. She ultimately seeks refuge in Lilienport with Berchtung and Wolf Dietrich. Her fate remains unknown in the fragment found in the Ambras manuscript, but we can gather from the Dresden manuscript's ending that she most likely dies along with Berchtung before Wolf Dietrich can return to Greece to free them.

One particular attribute assigned to certain heroes is that they are *wise*. This adjective has a broad range of meaning, from our modern concept of wise

Introduction

to clever, cunning, shrewd, experienced, and resourceful. Generally the term denotes experience and common sense, a kind of practical wisdom developed over time. It is often contrasted with the young (*tumben*) and describes a kind of wily ability to see three moves ahead. The men so characterized most often are Wate and Fruote, the grizzled old warriors of the Danes, with Ludwig and Herwig less frequently so described. Hagen as a child is deemed *wîse* even in his youth (*K* 162,4b). In *Otnit* the term is more sinister in tone, as only non-Christians are characterized in this way. In *Wolf Dietrich A* it is Berchtung alone who is "wise." Women are almost never pronounced wise or clever. In *Kudrun* there are three examples, in the other texts none. First, Hagen is raised by wise women (*K* 23,3a), which most certainly means experienced and conservative. Second, Hilde, Kudrun's mother, is pronounced very wise in ensuring that those who memorialize the fallen in the Battle of Wulpensand are well cared for (*K* 949,4b).

It is Kudrun herself, in a very curious couple of strophes, who is declared both wise and not so wise. Before Kudrun is forced to wash clothes on the beach, Hartmut hits on the idea that his sister Ortrun might be able to convince Kudrun to become his wife through kindness and persuasion. Kudrun befriends Ortrun and in a short time is restored to health through good food and drink. The poet remarks that Kudrun was then (*dô*) not so wise or clever (*K* 1046,4b). Kudrun repays this kindness with a rudeness toward Hartmut that causes his mother to intervene and demand that Kudrun serve her, which she then readily accepts as a condition of her misfortune (*K* 1053, 1055). In agreeing to wash laundry in order to earn her keep, Kudrun is characterized ten strophes later as very wise (*K* 1056,4b). This same chapter (21) begins with a strophe stating that Ludwig will lose the battle against Herwig in the end because Kudrun was forced to become a washerwoman (*K* 1041,4). In hindsight, then, Kudrun is wise to have accepted hardship and humiliation, but unwise to have accepted friendship from Ortrun and the better living conditions this brought with it. Most translators and editors have struggled with this apparent paradox (see my note on line 1046,4 for more details). For the men mentioned above, *wîse* denotes their experience and shrewd action. As we have seen, this kind of wisdom does not usually lead to success. For Kudrun, the same adjective denotes a recognition of her circumstances and a determination to accept her fate. She is unwise in accepting anything that would ameliorate her suffering. By accepting her humiliation, Kudrun guarantees Herwig's victory and her own freedom. A peaceful future is achieved and guaranteed not by men through heroic, that is, violent and vengeful, action, but rather by a woman through reconciliation and partnership.

Introduction

MANUSCRIPT TRANSMISSION

Along with thirteen[6] other Middle High German texts, *Kudrun* shares the slightly dubious and somewhat frustrating distinction of being transmitted in a single manuscript from the early sixteenth century, a manuscript written on parchment leaves some sixty or more years after Gutenberg's invention of printing with movable type. This transmission is dubious because it might lead to the conclusion that our text, along with some others, was rarely copied and hence exceptionally unpopular, perhaps already from the time it was composed. Given the complex state of medieval communication networks, such a conclusion would be, however, not at all self-evident. This transmission is frustrating because it does not allow us as editors, translators, or readers to compare our text with any other exemplar that might provide a better representation of its thirteenth-century form. In fact, given the late transmission, we don't have a text in Middle High German at all, but rather in a form of early modern German with Bavarian or Austrian features.

The other two texts presented in this book, *Otnit* and *Wolf Dietrich*, are almost always transmitted together and extant in various versions in sixteen other manuscripts dating from the first half of the fourteenth century to the late fifteenth century. For *Otnit*, an earlier manuscript from the first half of the fourteenth century thankfully preserves the text as well, but the version of *Wolf Dietrich* translated here, like *Kudrun*, exists only in this one manuscript from the early sixteenth century. It remains unfinished and breaks off after 606 strophes, although estimates put the likely total for a complete version at around 860 strophes.[7]

This exceptional manuscript is commonly referred to as the *Ambraser Heldenbuch*, which we might render in English as the "(Castle) Ambras Book of Heroes." *Heldenbuch* is a term that refers to several such late medieval literary collections, and the term itself supplies our manuscript with its title (*Tabula des Heldenpuchs*). Ambras refers to its repository at the castle of that name near Innsbruck, Austria, where it was kept from at least 1596 until 1806, when it was moved for safekeeping to Vienna during the Napoleonic Wars. Its more formal catalog number is Cod. Ser. nova 2663 of the Österreichische Nationalbibliothek in Vienna,[8] where it has been deposited since the end of World War I. The existence of the manuscript was first announced in 1816, and the text was first published in two volumes in 1820 and 1825 by Friedrich von der Hagen and Alois Primisser, the son of the custodian of the Ambras collection.[9] Two hundred years later, the

---

6. In some cases, Hartmann von Aue's *Erec* is included. However, *Erec* is also preserved in part in another three manuscript fragments, unlike the fourteen works that have no other manuscript transmission whatsoever outside of the Ambras manuscript.
7. Kofler 2009, 14.
8. It is also known as manuscript A for the *Kudrun* text.
9. Primisser announced the discovery of the manuscript in 1816 in Büsching's *Wöchentliche Nachrichten*, I, 389, and provided a table of contents in 1817 in the same publication (III, 174–81).

xix

Introduction

entire manuscript is now available in a beautiful eleven-volume edition, with both allographic and diplomatic texts and full-color, high-resolution images.[10]

The entire manuscript contains twenty-five texts, four of which are incomplete and, as mentioned above, fourteen of which are unique to this manuscript.[11] The composition of this collection has been the subject of much debate, but it is generally agreed that there seem to be three main sections, or kinds of texts, gathered here. First are seven texts most often thought to be representative of what we today generally call courtly romances. This includes the only nearly complete version of Hartmann von Aue's *Erec*, which one might imagine to have been a fairly popular work, as were Hartmann's other texts. This group of seven is followed by a set of eight works, including our three texts, that might be characterized as heroic or epic narratives. These include *Dietrichs Flucht*, *Die Rabenschlacht*, the famous *Nibelungenlied* and its epilogue the *Klage*, followed by *Kudrun*, *Biterolf*, and then the A versions of *Otnit* and *Wolf Dietrich*. Finally, there are ten shorter tales, including a fragment of Wolfram von Eschenbach's *Titurel*.

One thing all these works have in common is that they were written in the late twelfth or first half of the thirteenth century and would have originally been available in parchment manuscripts, most likely from the late thirteenth or fourteenth century.[12] In other words, this manuscript from the early sixteenth century was intent on gathering together particularly early texts on parchment, while ignoring pretty much anything from the fourteenth century on, likely to be on paper. The search for a broader concept of the manuscript's project, especially one that pertains to the kind of literary collecting done in the early sixteenth century, still yields more questions than answers. To call it simply a "Book of Heroes" does it only partial justice in light of the current state of medieval genre studies.

The manuscript was written by a single person, namely, Hans Ried, a Tyrolean government official who worked to complete the book between 1504 and 1515 or early 1516[13] at the behest of none other than Emperor Maximilian I, the so-called last knight. This deluxe codex was anachronistically written entirely on parchment, not paper, in three columns of text in a very neat and consistent calligraphic hand that can be described as chancery script or early Fraktur.[14] Initials, alternating in blue and red ink and done by a later hand, mark the beginning of individual strophes, while very large illuminated initials, usually seven lines tall, and titles in red ink mark the start of chapters (*aventiuren*). The margins are also rich in illustrations. Among them is a female figure standing next to a tablet with

---

10. *Ambraser Heldenbuch: Gesamttranskription mit Manuskriptbild*, edited by Mario Klarer, 11 vols., 2022.
11. For a complete list of these texts, see page 295.
12. This important point was highlighted by Ingeborg Glier in her book *Artes amandi*, 391.
13. The manuscript was still incomplete in the summer of 1515 but completed before Hans Ried's death in the spring of 1516. See Bäuml, 9.
14. Schneider, 81; Bäuml, 29–30.

the date 1517 (fol. 215r), which helps secure the dating for the illustrations if not the entire codex. The link between the images and the texts is not direct, however, which is to say that the purpose of the illustrations is primarily decorative, although there are interesting botanical images as well as a few human figures that have some meaning beyond mere beautification.[15] Notable among these is the dragon depicted on folio 212v with a broken sword on its back. This image illustrates the *Wolf Dietrich* text and the (misplaced) Chapter 11 title ("How His Sword Broke on the Dragon, and It Carried Him into the Mountain"), which does not, however, correspond to the text on that page.

The question of Ried's sources is fraught, and only a single manuscript has to date been identified as a direct source for one of Ried's texts, namely, a small fragment of the *Nibelungenlied* dated to the end of the thirteenth century.[16] The other source manuscripts are all presumably lost. The notion that Ried copied from a single manuscript, itself a collection of chivalric and heroic tales or *Heldenbuch*, has generally been discounted, although some would believe that the "heroic" second section (works 8 to 15) might still have been sourced from a single book.[17]

Another important manuscript that deserves attention in the context of the *Otnit* text is also deposited in the national library in Vienna, and that is Cod. 2779, otherwise known as the Windhagen manuscript, or for our *Otnit* text simply manuscript W. This manuscript is dated to the first half of the fourteenth century and was written on parchment. The manuscript was copied by four different hands in a Gothic *textualis*, and the text of *Otnit* (beginning fol. 71v) is presented in three columns, each line the length of a half-line of verse, with the beginning of a strophe indicated by an initial. There are no chapter headings. The manuscript is presumably missing a significant number of leaves, given that the last work, Heinrich von dem Türlin's *Diu Crone*, is incomplete. An entry in the codex points to an early ownership by the Turs family in 1358, and an *ex libris* identifies Joachim Enzmillner, Baron (*Freiherr*) of Windhag, as the book's owner in 1656. In 1784 the manuscript was incorporated into the Viennese court library. The Windhagen manuscript is a collection of texts that includes the *Kaiserchronik*, Hartmann von Aue's *Iwein*, short stories from the Stricker, among others, and the version of *Otnit* associated with *Wolf Dietrich A*. The Windhagen manuscript has most recently served as the *Leithandschrift*, or lead manuscript, for Walter Kofler's 2009 *Ortnit* edition.[18]

---

15. Domanski, 145–69.
16. Berol. Mgq 792, Biblioteka Jagiellońska, Krakow.
17. Stackmann 2000, xi. See also Stephan Müller, 88–98.
18. The Ambras manuscript (A) is the *Leithandschrift* for the 2013 Reclam edition by Fuchs-Jolie, Millet, and Peschel. The text version of *Otnit* in manuscript W is 589 strophes long as opposed to 597 in manuscript A.

Introduction

While the Windhagen manuscript's version of *Otnit* is closely related to the text in the Ambras manuscript, which was copied some two hundred years later, the text in W was not a direct source for Hans Ried's work. This earlier exemplar does allow us, however, to scrutinize Ried's work in light of a very similar Middle High German text that dates to probably only a hundred years after the work was originally composed. One of the most striking features of manuscript W is that *Otnit* is not followed by the story of *Wolf Dietrich*, which makes it unique among the manuscripts that contain some version of *Otnit*. Each of these thirteen other manuscripts, including the Ambras Book of Heroes, includes both texts as a pair. The absence of a *Wolf Dietrich* story in manuscript W is frankly a mystery. The ending of Otnit's story in manuscripts AW clearly refers to Wolf Dietrich as Otnit's widow's future husband and dragon slayer (although not by name), and to the fact that he was as yet unborn (*O* 596). Furthermore, there appears in the Windhagen manuscript to have been space originally left blank after *Otnit*, which was later filled in with devotional texts.[19]

One other late medieval manuscript in the transmission of this pair of texts should be mentioned: the so-called *Dresdner Heldenbuch*, now in the Dresden State Library as Mscr. M 201, or manuscript k for our two texts. This manuscript contains eleven works in total, including an abridgement of the A versions of *Otnit* and *Wolf Dietrich*. It was written in Nuremberg in 1472 by two scribes, one of whom was Kaspar von der Rhön. The manuscript greatly redacts and shortens both the *Otnit* and *Wolf Dietrich A* texts, from 597 to 297 strophes, or *lied*, for the former and to just 334 for the latter,[20] so that its main usefulness is in filling in the ending of the *Wolf Dietrich A* story missing from the Ambras manuscript.[21]

EDITIONS AND TRANSLATIONS

The editorial history of *Kudrun* begins with the aforementioned 1820 publication by von der Hagen and Primisser, which was the first edition of all the texts of the Ambras manuscript in their sixteenth-century form. The nineteenth century saw a considerable number of subsequent editions and translations of varying quality and approaches, guided primarily by the assumption that a text written down almost three hundred years after its composition must have gone through multiple redactions, additions, and copies that resulted in considerable corruption.[22] Adolph

---

19. Fuchs-Jolie et al., 677.
20. The *Otnit* text runs from folio 1r to 43r, *Wolf Dietrich A* from folio 44r to 91r.
21. For a synopsis of the ending according to the Dresden manuscript, see pages 276–78.
22. In fact, Karl Stackmann still considered the text to be in parts "quite debased" or "corrupted" ("sehr verwahrlost"); 1965, lxxxix.

Introduction

Ziemann in 1835 was the first to attempt to transform Hans Ried's language into a normalized Middle High German of the thirteenth century. This soon became the standard approach, which is to say almost every subsequent edition presented *Kudrun* in an (artificial) form it might have had when it was first written. This remained a common philological method well into the twentieth century, with the search for the "original" text always at the forefront, even if that meant linguistically reverse engineering a sixteenth-century text by some three hundred years. The 1845 edition of Karl Müllenhoff went even further and reduced the text to its "genuine" parts, or strophes, presenting them as separate stories completely detached from their state in the manuscript. As late as 1953 Henrik Becker engaged in an equally misguided effort to rewrite the epic by including only "genuine" strophes in his *Warnlieder* ("cautionary tales") edition, which was itself an attempt to present a text in terms of the feudal class system that certain enlightened (i.e., socialist) medieval poets had warned against.

The Karl Bartsch edition of 1865, also in an anachronistic Middle High German, mostly followed the manuscript's original strophic order, although the order of some strophes was rearranged to improve the narrative flow wherever that seemed appropriate.[23] The Bartsch edition became the standard, and its revision by Karl Stackmann in 1965, reissued in 2000 in the Altdeutsche Textbibliothek series to replace the Symons/Boesch edition of 1883 and 1954, still serves as the basis for most of the work on *Kudrun* today. The 2010 Reclam edition by Uta Störmer-Caysa uses the Bartsch/Stackmann text as its foundation. This editor did, however, later question her own decision in the matter, conceding that a text closer to Ried's language might have been more appropriate for a modern edition.[24] Two other nineteenth-century editions of *Kudrun* deserve mention for their thoroughness, namely, Ernst Martin's of 1872, which includes many valuable revisions and notes in the second edition of 1902, and Paul Piper's work of 1895, published as part of Kürschner's Deutsche National-Litteratur series. Franz Bäuml's diplomatic edition of the Ambras manuscript text for *Kudrun* in 1969 offered the first (since von der Hagen) accurate rendition of the early modern German version, but it is thanks to the work of Mario Klarer that we now have both an allographic and diplomatic edition of the original text, with original in this case being defined as Ried's text alone, since this is in fact the only text that exists.

A brief review of the editorial work on the *Otnit* and *Wolf Dietrich* texts shows a similar pattern. As part of the Ambras manuscript, these two works appeared in the von der Hagen/Primisser edition's first volume of 1820, alongside *Kudrun*, *Biterolf*, and *Rosengarten*. This was quickly followed by an 1821 edition of *Otnit* by Franz Mone, whose *Leithandschrift*, however, was a paper manuscript from

---

23. Wisniewski, 3, posits that the scribe (Hans Ried) was so irritated by the repetitious strophe beginnings that he would skip some accidentally, only to insert them later in their incorrect order.
24. Störmer-Caysa, 575.

Introduction

around 1420 in Heidelberg.[25] We now recognize that this was part of the branch of the manuscript stemma that transmitted the later D version. This was followed by Friedrich von der Hagen in 1855 with an edition of *Ortnit* and *Wolf Dietrich A*, the first text being based on both the Ambras and Windhagen manuscripts, the second of course appearing only in the Ambras manuscript. The best edition of the nineteenth century for both texts was the work of Arthur Amelung and Oskar Jänicke that appeared in 1871, and this was to become the foundational work for all subsequent editions. Hermann Schneider released an edition of *Wolf Dietrich A* in 1930, but there was little other significant activity until Walter Kofler's edition of both texts in 2009. This was followed quickly in 2013 by a new Reclam edition, this time with Hans Ried's text in the original along with a modern German translation. Both texts have also been included as volume 10 in Mario Klarer's monumental edition of the Ambras Book of Heroes.

Early German translations of *Kudrun* date to 1839 and 1840 with efforts by Albert Schulz and Adelbert Keller. One of the better verse translations of the nineteenth century is that of Ludwig Freytag, whose *Gudrun* is dated 1888. The standard translation, however, became that of Karl Simrock in 1843. Simrock was, of course, the leading translator of all things Middle High German in the middle of the nineteenth century, and in fact his verse translation of *Kudrun* remained in print well into the twentieth century, when it was reworked by Friedrich Neumann for Reclam in 1958. Simrock's was followed by many more translations in the nineteenth century, and the twentieth saw its fair share as well. Most notable among these might be Joachim Lindner's 1971 translation, published along with beautiful woodcuts by the Polish artist Maria Hiszpanska-Neumann, the 1995 work of Bernhard Sowinski for Reclam, and finally the 2010 edition and translation by Uta Störmer-Caysa, also for Reclam. It should be noted that several of the editions mentioned previously contain extensive notes that often function as a translation aid or as translations in their own right. This would include the 1902 Martin edition, Piper's edition of 1895, and Stackmann's 1965 revision of Bartsch. A thesaurus-like glossary and index for *Kudrun* was published in 1994 by Klaus Schmidt.

English translations are not lacking, and it was a flurry of activity and interest in the text in the late 1980s and early 1990s that gave us three different translations of *Kudrun* into English: by Brian Murdoch in 1987; Winder McConnell in 1992; and Marion Gibbs and Sidney Johnson in the same year. All three are prose translations. The Murdoch translation is perhaps the freest in terms of its prose, and the back cover of the paperback edition conveys this best by characterizing the translation as "lively." McConnell's efforts some five years later thankfully turn to the manuscript text as well as the Bartsch/Stackmann edition of 1965, and in several cases the translator questions certain editorial choices and argues

---

25. Heidelberg, Universitätsbibliothek, Cpg 365.

instead for the meaning conveyed by the original manuscript text. His footnotes are helpful in providing the sense that the translation stems from a manuscript, with all its flaws and inconsistencies, and not just an "improved" edition. The Gibbs/Johnson translation that also came out in 1992, and hence is independent of McConnell's work, is probably the most faithful to the original text. The strophes are numbered at fairly regular intervals, something sorely missing from the McConnell translation, although the endnotes tend to be more difficult to access than McConnell's footnotes. An earlier translation by Margaret Armour in 1928 is still worth consulting. There is a verse translation done in 1889 by Mary Pickering Nichols that unfortunately suffers from a "medievalization" of the language that makes it almost unreadable.

Relatively few translations in German or English exist for *Otnit* and *Wolf Dietrich*. Karl Simrock, in his "Little Book of Heroes" (*Das kleine Heldenbuch*), was the first in 1859 to present a verse translation titled "King Ortnit's Sea Voyage and Death" (*König Ortnits Meerfahrt und Tod*), along with a translation of *Wolf Dietrich B* in two main sections titled "Hugdietrich" and "Wolfdietrich." Another notable early verse translation of *Ortnit* was by Karl Pannier in 1877. It wasn't until 2013, however, that a new German translation of both works was published in a dual-language edition for Reclam. The situation for English translation is even more meager. Aside from a couple of fragmentary and paraphrased versions from the nineteenth century, there is only a single prose translation of the two works into English by John Wesley Thomas from 1986, whose translation of both texts is based on the 1871 edition by Amelung and Jänicke. His *Wolfdietrich* translation is of the B version, however, so there is in fact no English translation to date of the A version. This book presents the first.

FORM AND STYLE

The poetic form and style of *Kudrun* speak to its liminal position between two eras. The one is the distant past that connects the poem to a heroic, Germanic time and the many abuses to which those labels subjected it in later scholarship and cultural appropriation. The other is the postclassical period of Middle High German literary activity, a time that looked on the accomplishments of the previous generation as both groundbreaking and unrivaled. The *Kudrun* poet clearly saw himself in the shadow of the masterpiece that was the *Nibelungenlied*, but he also understood that work as only one link in a long and rich tradition. The *Kudrun* poet chose to follow that tradition in form but to move beyond it in style and content. His attempt at presenting traditional material in a traditional form but with new meaning is generally judged to have been only partly successful. The perceived inconsistencies, the seams tying different stories together that are anything but seamless, and the repetitive and rather flat nature of certain

Introduction

rhetorical devices have left critics to disparage the work as lacking poetic merit. Finding himself at the threshold of a burgeoning book culture, the poet was perhaps too optimistic in his ability to please an audience that longed for more traditional, we might even say "oral" material, while still trying to accommodate a fresh taste for the new book style that was sweeping a readership enamored of the romances and courtly poetry that were in fashion.

The *Kudrun* text has generally been divided into three main parts by most editors: the stories of Hagen, Hilde, and Kudrun. This is a division based solely on content and is not supported by any formal textual evidence. The *Kudrun* text is arranged in the Ambras manuscript in what we should best call chapters, the same kind of *aventiure* divisions that organize the *Nibelungenlied*. There are thirty-two of these in total, and all of them except two have a heading or title. The very first does not, since it also functions as the beginning of the entire text, which is titled in red ink "This is the Book of Kudrun" (*Ditz puech ist von Chautruon*). This is followed by a large, nine-line-tall decorated uncial initial to introduce the text. The subsequent chapters are not numbered but rather introduced, again in red ink, with the word *Abentheur* or *Abenthewr* and a short title describing the content of the chapter that follows. Chapter 13 has no title marking but is introduced by a four-line illuminated initial. There is no explanation for this, most likely scribal, lapse. Given the 1,705 strophes in the text, the average chapter length is 53 strophes, or roughly 212 lines, but chapter length can range from 10 strophes (the last chapter) to 168 strophes (Chapter 5).

The chapter divisions function mostly to indicate a passage of time or change of place. Typical opening lines of chapters for a temporal shift include: "one evening" (372); "The next morning" (440); "As evening approached" (488); "At the time" (587); "They refrained for several years" (617); and "After having waited a long time" (1207). Some chapters begin by announcing a narrative shift of subject or place: "Let us now take our leave" (67); "Let us now leave this tale" (563); "Now let us move on" (630; 951); "We will now put aside" (1071); "Now we will end our talk . . . I want to let you hear" (1165); and "Now we'll hear a story" (1335). Two of the early chapters begin with the typical introduction of a main character, such as Sigebant (1) or Hetel (204), while certain others begin by introducing the name of the relevant main character for that episode. A few simply begin *in media res*: "Hetel and Ludwig held their sharp swords" (880); "They sailed to that same forest" (1142); "He thought to himself" (1441); and "Wate was raving mad" (1494). The chapter divisions emulate the practice of thirteenth-century book epic of dividing content into "adventures." They do not function as convenient breaks for the reader, whether as an individual or in front of an audience of listeners. Furthermore, the theory that various chapters were further subdivided into three, four, or five parts put forward by Bostock has failed to convince or encourage further such lines of inquiry.[26]

---

26. Bostock, 521–25.

In examining the basic building blocks of *Kudrun*, we immediately recognize the four-line strophic form of the *Nibelungenlied*, with its eight half-lines, pairs of which are divided by a caesura, or metrical boundary. In fact, of the poem's 1,705 strophes, some hundred use a form and meter, mostly in the earlier sections, that are identical to the so-called *Nibelungen* strophe.[27] Our poet offers a variation as his primary form, however, namely, a meter that relies more heavily on secondary stress endings, and a final, eighth half-line with five stresses instead of four. To illustrate this, we will first look at the standard *Nibelungen* strophe. Each half-line has three stressed syllables, while the very last, or eighth, half-line has an additional fourth stressed syllable. Pairs of long-lines form a rhymed couplet with a scheme of AABB, with the occasional internal rhyme between alternating half-lines. A typical *Nibelungen* long-line can be represented metrically as follows:

$$(x) \mid x´\ x \mid x´\ x \mid x´\ x` \parallel x´\ x \mid x´\ x \mid x´\ - \mid$$

The last, or eighth, half-line with an additional stress would appear as follows:

$$\ldots x´\ x` \parallel x´\ x \mid x´\ x \mid x´\ x \mid x´\ - \mid$$

Initial half-lines (*Anvers*) usually end in a stress followed by a secondary stress (x´ x`), and the half-lines following (*Abvers*) typically end in a primary stress followed by a stop or pause (x´ -).

The *Kudrun* strophe is similar, but with a few key differences. The strophe tends to use secondary stress endings in the final half-lines of the third and fourth lines, thus retaining the single stressed endings only at the end of the first and second lines. Put another way, the first two lines of the *Kudrun* strophe are exactly the same as the *Nibelungen* strophe, whereas the third and fourth lines both end with a secondary stress, and the final half-line has five instead of four stresses. For purposes of illustration, the following translation of *Kudrun*'s first strophe, which is by necessity rather free, attempts to demonstrate these principles in English.

```
       x    |  x´   x  | x´  x | x´  x`   ||  x| x´   x  | x´    x  | x´ - |
         There ónce grew úp in Íreland      a míghty kíng and fámed.
        x | x´ x |  x´     x | x´ x  x`   ||  x | x´   x | x´    x  | x´ - |
         His gíven náme was Sígebànt,      his fáther Gér was námed.
     x |   x´   x  |  x´    x    | x´ x x` || x  | x´   x|    x´      x   |    x´  x` |
         His móther wás named Úotè,      and wás a quéen most spléndìd.
  x´      x | x´   x  | x´ x   x`  || x´   x  | x´   x | x´    x | x´    x | x´ x` |
     Thánks to hér good cháractèr    tó that míghty mán her lóve was súitèd.
```

---

27. Of the first 390 strophes, 60 (or 15 percent) are of the *Nibelungen* variety.

Introduction

As with all such strophic forms, the total number of syllables in a line varies considerably, and the rhyme and meter scheme are not always, or even usually, perfectly executed. Variations, some might say imperfections, are sometimes blamed on later redactors or less skilled revisers, but it is fair to say that the poet was probably less concerned with a perfect execution of form than we might be. In fact, the imperfections might have even suggested to an audience more of an oral form than a written one.

This strophic form is furthermore characterized by the blocklike function of each strophe, which is to say that each is very much a single, self-sufficient unit of four lines. Enjambment between strophes in *Kudrun* is extremely rare.[28] The extra stress, or actually two stresses, of the final half-line further emphasizes the finality of the strophe. In addition, it is common for the beginning of each strophe to be signaled by an upbeat adverbial *dô* or *dâ*, which has been retained in this translation despite, or in a sense because of, its purely formulaic nature. A full 490 strophes, close to 30 percent of the total and spread fairly evenly throughout the work, begin in this way, and they are often clustered in three, four, or even five consecutive strophes. The oral, or aural, features of such a device are evident, although the constant use of a "filler" element at the beginning of a line or sentence seems to us the sign of either a lazy or an unimaginative poet. What we see, however, is a poet attempting to imitate certain features that intentionally, and rather inelegantly, signal the traditional form of his subject.

The organizational and metrical structure of *Kudrun* follows convention, especially with regard to that most popular work of its kind, the *Nibelungenlied*, while not hesitating to inject a modicum of innovation. The stylistic characteristics of *Kudrun* likewise tend to accommodate the expectations that a contemporary readership would have of the subject. For example, formulaic epithets are common, with heroes and villains alike often characterized or introduced by a typical descriptor, such as wild, old, wise, noble, evil, or worthy. Another prominent characteristic of heroic epic is that much of the narrative unfolds in direct speech. The formulaic introduction of direct speech with the verb form *sprach* (consistently translated here as "said") occurs over five hundred times throughout the text. In fact, more than seven hundred strophes, over 40 percent of the total, contain some direct speech at least in part. Most direct speech is introduced with the formula *dô sprach* or *sprach dô*. This formula makes up more than half of all occurrences, and these appear mostly at the beginning of the strophe. Personal pronouns, proper names, or epithets and titles, such as "the noble king said . . ." or "the bold knight said . . .," sometimes function to identify the speaker. The phrase *dô sprach aber*, literally "then (he/she) said again," is meant to indicate a reply and has been translated as such.

---

28. There are only six cases in total: between strophes 73–74; 257–58; 274–75; 467–68; 1326–27; and 1539–40.

Introduction

Direct speech seems to be limited mostly to single strophe utterances, but there are times when a speech can run on for a considerable number of lines.

The manner of speech is rarely indicated, but adverbs do accompany the main verb on occasion.[29] Indirect or reported speech, on the other hand, is quite rare, and only a handful of examples can be listed.[30] This is also true in the use of the verb *fragen* (to ask), as almost all cases of a character asking a question are reported as indirect speech.[31] Interior speech or thought is virtually nonexistent.[32] Protagonists act through speech in ways that are open and public, and the reader or listener is in this way as much a participant as is any character in the story. The reader is witness to heroic speech and in this way participates in the timeless quality of the narrative.

There are some seventy instances in *Kudrun* in which the poet inserts himself as a first-person narrative voice, either in the singular *ich* or plural *wir*. There are first the highly formulaic and repetitive instances where the poet simply says to his reader "I will tell you that" or "I want to tell you" (*ich wil iu sagen daz* or *daz wil ich iu sagen*), the variation depending on whether he needs a primary or a secondary stress to end the line. Other such fillers include "as we hear tell" (*sô wir hœren sagen*) and "as we told you before" (*als wir iu sageten ê*). Then there are expressions of feigned unknowing, with phrases such as "I (we) can't tell you" (*ich kan iu niht bescheiden*), "I wonder . . ." (*mich wundert*); "I don't know" (*ich enweiz* or *daz is mir ungewizzen*); or "we don't know or haven't heard about it" (*des wizzen wir niht mære noch habens niht erfunden*). These phrases impart a sense of narrative authenticity, as the poet struggles with supposedly inadequate or very old sources. Finally, another group of first-person insertions denotes authorial conjecture or opinion. The most common verb here is "to think" or "to guess" (*ich wæne*) or variations thereof, such as "I know" (*ich weiz*) or "I believe" (*ich geloube*). In most cases the use is formulaic, and the fact known is usually fairly inconsequential. Of course, the poet can know whatever he chooses to represent as known, but acknowledging the unknown connects him to his readers as participants in the more complex and sometimes contradictory

---

29. A total of thirty-three cases of *sprache* with an adverb or adverbial phrase can be identified: *lachende* (laughing; 220,4); *lûte* (loudly; 236,1); *trûrende* (sadly; 278,1); *schône* (calmly; 448,1); *mit sorgen* (with concern; 718,2); *offenlîchen* (openly; 1038,1); *vîntlîchen* (hatefully; 1052,1); *trûriclîchen* (sadly; 957,1; 1223,1); *mit listen* (shrewdly; 945,1; 1284,1); *schiere* (quickly; 1366,4); *gezogenlîche* (politely; 120,2; 153,1; 335,1; 438,1; 815,2; 1486,1); *mit zorne* (angrily; 242,1; 447,2; 1467,2; 1491,1), *in zorne* (in anger; 133,1; 1386,1; 1406,1; 1517,1, Bartsch/Stackmann 1515,1), *zornicliche* (angrily; 1035,1; 1342,2); *sorgende* (with concern; 1512,2, Bartsch/Stackmann 1510,2*)*; *in tobeheite* (beside himself; 1522,3); *weinende* (crying; 1066,1; 1387,1; 1525,1)
30. 171,4; 459,2–3; 585,3–4; 603,2–3; 840,3; 1114,1–2; 1626,1.
31. 233,1; 678,3; 774,3; 1112,1; 1483,3. There are only two occurrences of a direct question: 346,1; 1235,2.
32. One example is 707,4 with the phrase "they thought" (*si dâhten*).

Introduction

narrative flow. There are, however, a few cases of seemingly authentic authorial commentary, especially toward the end, as in "I think King Hetel was not well disposed toward Hartmut" (606,4); "I think that God himself avenged that insult against him" (845,4); "I think never before was there such peacemaking as what that young woman achieved" (1644,1); "I think that God cared for many of them after their hardship" (1692,4); and "I think they were not completely free of envy" (1702,2).

Other syntactic features can be especially challenging for both the reader and the listener as well as the translator. Most annoying perhaps is the frequent use of pronouns within the same line or strophe without a clear referent. In a few cases where it is possible to make a distinction, a proper name has been added to the translation for clarity. In other cases, the apparent confusion has been left standing. The *Kudrun* poet's frequent use of anacoluthon and related syntactic patterns (anastrophe, parataxis, apo koinou, and others) that disrupt the natural flow of a phrase or line makes it very hard to put an English sentence together in a structure that doesn't sound stilted or contrived. While it might be argued that such contortions are often necessitated by meter and rhyme, they can also be viewed as distinctive stylistic features intended to demonstrate the poet's finesse and agility with words and their arrangement. More times than not this translation has tried to follow the poet's syntactic meanderings in the hope of demonstrating how the original syntax works within the strophic form. This admittedly can make for a somewhat disjointed, even inelegant translation at times, but this more literal approach hopefully demonstrates the quality of the original more honestly. This is particularly difficult in a prose translation, where the urge to smooth out these features by connecting lines and half lines with an "and" or a "but" is strong. The frequent use of the semicolon in the translation is an attempt to overcome this difficulty by maintaining a style that, while it may seem abrupt in prose, resists the impulse to link independent clauses with a conjunction or to chop up a series of half lines into short sentences.

The form and style of *Otnit* and *Wolf Dietrich A* are in many ways similar to *Kudrun*. In the Ambras manuscript, the tale of *Otnit* opens, as does *Kudrun*, with a kind of book title in red ink, "King Otnit's Book Begins" (*Künig Ottnides Puech hebt sich an*), followed by a large illuminated initial. *Wolf Dietrich* begins similarly in the same manuscript with the title "This Is the Book of Wolf Dietrich, How He Was Born and Took the Lady Who Was Otnit's Wife as His Own" (*Das ist Wolffdiettrichs puech wie Er geporn ward Vnd die frauen nam ze weibe die Otnides was*). The beginning of *Wolf Dietrich* in the Ambras manuscript is situated, however, in the middle of folio 205v, unlike our other two texts that begin at the top of a separate, recto page. This is likely a further indication that *Wolf Dietrich* was considered by the scribe, Hans Ried, to be a continuation of *Otnit*, in which the final line reads: "If you want to hear the story, it will begin straightaway." It is also important to note that both texts are divided into similar kinds of chapters, or *aventiuren*. *Otnit* has eight of them, *Wolf Dietrich A* has seventeen. The length of each chapter in *Otnit* is quite in line with *Kudrun*. The average length of a chapter in *Otnit* is 75 strophes while in *Kudrun* it is 53, and similarly the first and last chapters of *Otnit* have no chapter titles or headings.

In this particular aspect of textual organization, we have some disparities in *Wolf Dietrich A*, however, even though the two texts are very similar in overall length (*Otnit* has 597 strophes; *Wolf Dietrich A*, which is unfinished, has 606 strophes). The first eleven chapters in *Wolf Dietrich* seem to follow the pattern of *Otnit* and *Kudrun* quite well, with a somewhat shorter average chapter length of 46 strophes, whereas the first sign of a major break in form and style occurs at strophe 506 with the beginning of the twelfth chapter. Chapters 12 to 17 are each quite short, with an average length of just 17 strophes, the longest being only 32 strophes.

Unlike *Kudrun*, the chapters in both *Otnit* and *Wolf Dietrich* tend to end with a formulaic line, generally along the lines of "So ends another chapter of Otnit's story" (*Otnides abentewr is aber aine hin*, O 212,4; O 287,4) or for *Wolf Dietrich* "The poor queen is living still in Garda in her misfortune" (*noch lebt auf Garte in sorgen die arme künegein*, WDA 33,4), or some line containing the word *sorge(n)*. Strophes 503 and 505 of *Wolf Dietrich A* are a bit confusing in this practice, as both close with the typical end-of-chapter phrasing (which is why Schneider ends his edition with 503), but the chapter heading in the manuscript precedes strophe 506.

Aside from this general conformity in the use of chapter divisions, the basic strophic form of both *Otnit* and *Wolf Dietrich* is also comparable, but not identical, to that of *Kudrun*. Each strophe consists of four long lines, the half-lines divided by caesura. As outlined above, the *Kudrun* strophe ends with its eighth half-line having five stressed feet and a secondary stress ending (the *Nibelungen* strophe ends in four stressed feet and a stressed ending). Both the *Otnit* and *Wolf Dietrich* strophes end with a half-line of just three stresses, with a secondary stress ending for the sixth and eighth half-lines. This metrical scheme is often referred to as the *Hildebrandston*, so called because it is constructed in the same meter and rhyme as a ballad from the sixteenth century about that eponymous hero. Again, a loose translation of the first strophe of *Otnit* mimics this meter and rhyme:

```
    x    | x´ x | x´    x | x´    x` || x | x´    x  | x´  x | x´ - |
     There wás a bóok discóvered,    at Lóndon, ín the tówn.
         x | x´ - | x´ - | x´    x`  || x    | x´    x |  x´      x | x´ - |
          Its scrípt whát wónder,    thereín did leáves abóund.
    x |    x´    x  |   x´        x | x´x` ||  x    | x´    x | x´  x | x´ x` |
      The Múslims thróugh their évil,    they díd the códex búry`.
    x   |   x´    x  | x´      x  | x´  x`  ||  x  | x´ x | x´    x    | x´ x` |
      Now sháll we fróm this vólume    gain éntertaínment mérry`.
```

Introduction

Enjambment is more commonly employed than in *Kudrun*,[33] and the utilization of an adverbial *dâ/dô* to introduce strophes is quantitatively amazingly (coincidentally?) similar to *Kudrun*.[34] Likewise, direct speech dominates strophic content, but to an even greater extent than in *Kudrun*. In fact, over 75 percent of all strophes in *Otnit* contain some direct speech, making for a poem that is almost exclusively presented in the voices of its protagonists. *Wolf Dietrich A* is remarkably similar in this regard, with some 71 percent of strophes containing direct speech across the entire work, and 74 percent to strophe 506, at which point a different redactor began his work. Interjections by the narrator are virtually nonexistent.[35]

The final aspect of form and style that deserves some mention is the hard break at strophe 506 in *Wolf Dietrich A*, already mentioned above with regard to chapter length. The final 101 strophes that we have in the Ambras manuscript of this text are distinctly inferior stylistically, and there can be no doubt that a later redactor was at work here, presumably with the intent of finishing the story, although even that seems to have been unsuccessful. Without listing all the deficiencies in this last section, one particularly striking aspect is the numerous formulaic uses of authorial utterances, almost as if the redactor was at a loss for words and had to resort to his handy store of throwaway phrases. Most common is a version of "as I (we) have gathered" (*als ichs vernommen han* or *als wir das han vernomen*) or "as we have been told" (*als uns das ist gesait* or *als uns das ist bekannt*). Another phrase that includes the reader or listener is "this I make known to you" (*das tuon ich euch bekannt*). There are, in fact, eighteen occurrences of these kinds of half-lines in only 101 strophes, sometimes twice in a single strophe. There is nothing comparable in frequency or phrasing used by the primary poet of the first 505 strophes.

THE TRANSLATION

The Bartsch/Stackmann edition of 1965[36] provided the basic text for this translation of *Kudrun*, alongside the 2010 Störmer-Caysa Reclam edition, which

---

33. There is a total of seventeen cases of enjambment between strophes in *Otnit* (3 percent), sixteen in *Wolf Dietrich A* (3 percent), versus six in *Kudrun* (0.3 percent).
34. There are a total of 171 occurrences of strophes beginning with *dâ/dô* in *Otnit* (29 percent of 597 strophes) and 140 in *Wolf Dietrich A* (23 percent of 606 strophes, less common between strophes 506–606).
35. In *Otnit* these come at the very end, 597,2 and 597,4; in *Wolf Dietrich A* there is no use of an authorial "I" or "we" before strophe 506 and only one instance in which the narrator addresses his audience directly (87,2).
36. The later reprints of 1980 by Brockhaus and 2000 by Niemeyer are essentially identical to the 1965 edition, except that Stackmann's very useful introduction from 1965 was deleted from the 2000 edition.

itself relies on Bartsch/Stackmann. There is no doubt that some strophes appear out of order in the manuscript, either because of a defect in the source or error by the scribe, and editorial reordering has often attempted to impose a more logical narrative flow. This translation, however, follows the original manuscript order with regard to the numbering of strophes, with a notation of the Bartsch/Stackmann numbering if it differs. In recognition of the heavy-handed nature of past editorial emendations, text that is not in the original manuscript and not necessary to the meaning is omitted, even though it has been added by an editor either for reasons of meter or to fill a perceived imperfection in the manuscript's transmission. In other words, the manuscript trumps the edition unless meaning is compromised. When editorial emendations from the Bartsch/Stackmann edition are included in the translation, they are placed within square brackets. This is a fairly radical departure from common practice, but given the fact that two of our three texts are found in only a single manuscript, I felt it important to distinguish the numerous emendations from the original text, not necessarily to show that the manuscript was defective but rather to emphasize the large number of interventions made by our texts' editors.

Given the affinities between *Kudrun* and the *Otnit/Wolf Dietrich A* texts, most of the comments above hold true for the approach to the latter pair as well. The Kofler edition of 2009, based on the older Windhagen (W) manuscript's text for *Ortnit*,[37] provided a welcome update to the Amelung/Jänicke edition of 1871 as well as the Schneider edition of *Wolf Dietrich A* from 1930. The present translation is based primarily on the Ambras (A) manuscript text as presented in the *Otnit* and *Wolf Dietrich A* edition of 2013 by Fuchs-Jolie, Millet, and Peschel, which takes Kofler's edition and its readings into account while maintaining the primacy of manuscript A. Finally, the high-quality digital copies of manuscripts AW available online and the 2022 edition of all three works by Klarer[38] have made it possible to consult both manuscripts directly when necessary.

A few words on names and their pronunciation might be helpful, as this can sometimes be a bit challenging for English speakers. I have opted to use the more common spellings of names, such as Kudrun instead of Gudrun or the manuscript's *Chautruon* or its many variations, Hartmut instead of Hartmuot, Siegfried instead of Sifrit. Where there was a good English equivalent I have used it, especially with peoples such as the Franks, Moors, Danes, Greeks, and Frisians. Names with stressed diphthongs, such as Uote and Fruote, are a bit trickier. They could be monophthongized to Ute and Frute, but to little benefit,

---

37. Kofler opts for the spelling "Ortnit," since this is the predominant Windhagen manuscript spelling.
38. These are in volumes 8 and 10, respectively, of his "comprehensive transcription" (*Gesamttranskription*) of the Ambras manuscript. Klarer also opts for the "Ortnit" spelling in his volume as a concession to the accumulated weight of editorial and scholarly practice over more than a century.

Introduction

I think. Then there are the vowels more generally, especially "i" and the perennial "ie" and "ei" confusion between German and English. A name like Liebgart or Dietrich is always pronounced with the long "e" sound in English, as in "Leebgart" or "Deetrick." The same holds true for the "i" sound in Irolt, Ilias, Sigebant, or Ortwin, which will either be a short or long "i" as in "bit" or "beet," never as in "bite." Perhaps the most difficult for English speakers will be the personal name Wate, a major character after all. While an English pronunciation like "wait" is tolerable, the Middle High German can better be approximated with the British pronunciation of "water," with an "a" sound as in "father," but without the final "r." The final "e" should be pronounced, even if only as a kind of "uh" or schwa sound. The same holds true for Fruote,[39] with the final "e" pronounced, i.e., not like "fruit."

There is lastly the question of Otnit or Ortnit, with or without an "r." The practice in this translation has been to use Otnit without "r" consistently when it comes from or refers back to the Ambras manuscript. Ortnit with "r" has become commonplace in literature and scholarship, but it is used here only when referring specifically to such scholarship's practice. I have chosen to separate the names Wolf Dietrich. They are spelled as a single word in most editions, but only sometimes in the Ambras manuscript, and separation emphasizes that "Wolf" is an epithet, not a birth name or a double name, and that the character is often called "the Wolf Dietrich," meaning something like "Dietrich of the wolves."

As for placenames the variation in the manuscript(s) is greater, and so it is sometimes more difficult to settle on a spelling. For those names that are almost certainly related to modern names and actual places, the English spelling is used, as in Constantinople, the Danish March, Frisia, Garda, Greece, Jerusalem, Lombardy, and Ireland, to name only the most common. I have chosen to use the name "Daneland" instead of Denmark so as not to confuse the reader with the modern country by that name. Many names are sheer fantasy, and for these the spelling is closest to that used in the manuscript. As for the debate concerning Nortland, Hortland, or Ortland, and Ormanie, Normandie, or Hormandin, this is addressed in the notes. The most common manuscript spelling is used for Ortland and Ormanie, since these lands are also to a great extent fantasy lands. There is no evidence, either internal or external, that would justify conflating Ormanie with the historical area or duchy of Normandy. Finally, the Ambras manuscript's opening strophe of *Otnit* substitutes the city of London for the more appropriate Levantine town of Suders (Tyre, in present-day Lebanon), which is the Windhagen manuscript reading. There seems to be little reason for keeping London, as it plays no role whatsoever in the story, but I have retained

---

39. Interestingly, the name is related to the character Frodo Baggins in J. R. R. Tolkien's *Lord of the Rings*. Both names share an etymology with Old English *froda*, meaning "wise" or "experienced."

it nonetheless as an authentic representation of the Ambras manuscript's (mis) reading of *Lunders* (O 1,1).

A few concluding words are in order concerning the overall approach of this translation to its source. Any translation should aim to be both accurate and readable, but I would posit a third goal, and that is that any translation should aim to be honest. Fidelity not only to the text but also to the intent of its poetic form can help the reader gain a better appreciation for the original, including its defects. Karl Pannier, in his 1877 translation of *Otnit*, explained to the reader that he wanted to deliver a translation "with skin and hair,"[40] even to the point of having something "wooden" about it. It is my hope to accomplish something similar. The *Kudrun* text and the poet who created it have been much criticized for lacking poetic or even artistic merit. It is true that this work along with others like it from the time around 1230 or 1240, including *Otnit* and *Wolf Dietrich*, are not the great masterpieces that even their own authors recognized in the generation that preceded them. Too often modern translations, especially in prose, tend to smooth over the rough spots in such works, creating the impression among a modern readership that all medieval texts were more or less equally good, or at least equally readable. The challenge therefore comes when translating a work that has distinct deficiencies, both metrically and stylistically, in how best to convey these in a way that works in the target language.

All translation is compromise, and so too is this translation. I have decided to answer the questions posed above with a mix of solutions. The first is to offer a line-by-line translation for the first chapters of *Kudrun* and *Otnit* in order to show the reader that what is being translated is in fact poetry, and that form matters. This is not meant to provide any kind of word-for-word equivalency but is rather a way to demonstrate the patterns and formulas used in such a work. Such devices can of course only be approximated in another language, but nonetheless it is hoped that at least this approximation of original form will prove useful. The rest of the text is done in prose, as this is the modern standard and allows for a fuller transmission of meaning than something constricted by verse form.

Most important is the retention of a kind of strophic format, and so each strophe is separately numbered. This should allow for easy comparison with an edition of the German original, and it should also make the internal organization of this structural element more evident. The reader may often be frustrated by the poet's labyrinthine style and repetitive or formulaic modes of expression, but this is the tradition that is being emulated, and the "feel" of the poem comes back to life once these rough spots are accepted as part of the overall poetic landscape. For example, the rhetorical device of marking the beginning of a strophe with an adverbial *dô* or *dâ* is consistently imitated. The word has a wide range of adverbial

---

40. Pannier, 5. The original German phrase *mit Haut und Haar* means something like "completely," "lock, stock, and barrel," or "warts and all."

Introduction

meanings in context, but the repetitious nature of this device is most often mimicked by an imprecise "then." If recognized as such, the irritating overuse of this marker can be understood as an important aspect of epic form. Only in rare cases is an added "but" or "and" used to smooth transitions between phrases or lines, and a semicolon often serves to bridge the disjuncture between short independent clauses. Other formulaic features, including the straightforward and simple introduction of direct speech, are meant to foreground the narrative presence of the protagonists, which allows the poet to recede into the background. Ultimately, it is this translator's hope that the reader will gain some appreciation of the importance of this text's epic form and why the poet felt it important to emulate such a form as a way to foreground the ancient, even heroic lineage of his tale.

THIS IS THE BOOK OF KUDRUN[1]

PART I: HAGEN

Chapter 1 [1–66]

[1] There once came of age in Ireland a mighty highborn king.[2]
His [name was Sigebant,[3] his father's][4] name was Ger.
His mother was named Uote, and she was queen.
Given her noble character, her love well suited that mighty lord.
[2] Ger, the mighty king, this is known to all,
was served by many castles; he held the lands of seven lords.
There he had his knights, four thousand or even more,
and with these every day he was able to gain both wealth and honor.
[3] Young Sigebant was called to come and live at court,[5]
where he would learn, should he have the need,
to gallop with a lance, to wield a sword and spear,
so that when facing the enemy he would be all the more successful.
[4] He continued to mature until he took up arms.
In the ways of heroes he was fully skilled,
for which both friends and family would rightly praise him.
The noble hero never found any of this to be a burden.

---

1. The book and chapter titles are taken directly from the manuscript, with the chapter numbers added. Chapter 1 has no separate title (nor does Chapter 13). The division of the work into three parts (Hagen, Hilde, and Kudrun) is a modern editorial construct.
2. The opening line, *Ez wuohs in Irlande ein rîcher künic hêr* (1,1), mimics the introduction of Kriemhild in the *Nibelungenlied*: *Ez wuohs in Burgonden ein vil edel magedîn* (*NL* 2,1). The introduction of Siegfried in the *Nibelungenlied* is similar: *Dô wuohs in Niderlanden eins vil edelen küneges kind* (*NL* 20,1), as is the introduction of Brunhild (*NL* 329,1). Finally, King Otnit is introduced with this *ez wuohs* formula in much the same way (*O* 3,1).
3. The manuscript inexplicably leaves out this critical piece of information, which is clearly missing given the next line's reference to the mother, Uote, who is Sigebant's mother, not Ger's. A young prince like Sigebant could also be referred to as a "king," which explains why we seem to be dealing with two kings in the first and second strophes.
4. Words or phrases not found in the manuscript but added or emended by the editors Bartsch/Stackmann (1965/2000) are placed in square brackets. Only those editorial emendations deemed necessary to make sense of the original text have been adopted here.
5. This foreshadows his son Hagen's "coming to court" at the age of seven, an event that marked the transition in a young boy's upbringing from the women's domain to the men's.

[5] A short time later death tore them apart,
as happens still to noble folk, [to] everyone's misfortune.
There is evidence of this in every sovereign realm,
which each and every day we must fearfully await.
[6] Sigebant's mother assumed her place as a widow,
which is why the famed and upright hero declined to seek
the love of a woman to be his lawful wife.
Noble women of royal birth yearned for Sigebant.
[7] His mother counseled the mighty man to take a wife
and so bring honor to himself and to his lands,
to him and to his family, after such great sorrow.
After his father's death, he would come to know both joy and great happiness.
[8] His mother's advice made good sense to him.
He did just what she said, as is proper among kin.
He had one woman courted [for him], the best among the leading families.
She was at home in Norway;[6] to this end his family eagerly supported him.
[9] She was then engaged to him, as we've been told.[7]
Her retinue consisted of many a beautiful young woman
and seven hundred men from the land of Frideschotten.
They gladly accompanied her, since they respected the young king.
[10] With honors due a virgin bride, those who went with her
brought her to his lands, as befitted a mighty king.
Those who wanted to see her hastened to set out.
The roads were packed for more than three and a half miles.
[11] Everywhere and all along the roads
the throng of people [trampled over] flowers and fields.
It was at the time of year when everything's in bloom,
and when in the forests, too, the birds sing their sweetest song.[8]
[12] Many cheerful youngsters rode beside her.
Plenty of pack animals carried [sumptuous garments],
which her attendants brought from their homeland.

---

6. Manuscript A reads: *in Horwage* (8,4a). As with many place-names in *Kudrun*, it is often hard to know if there is a scribal error at work or if the name is simply meant to represent a place of fantasy. Real geographical names have typically been assigned by previous editors when it seemed appropriate, but their accuracy is far from certain.

7. Still unidentified (until 42,4), Sigebant's bride from Norway is named Uote, the same as Sigebant's mother.

8. Springtime, or the season of Pentecost, was the time for not only travel but also large court festivities, and the season was evocative of love in courtly poetry.

At least a thousand were loaded with valuables and garments.[9]
[13] The lovely young bride was received with great decorum
at the border of two lands, to where a strong wind
had driven her down across the ocean waves.
She was given lodging, which the young king had ably arranged.
[14] The courtly woman was received with equestrian games,[10]
[which] were finally brought to an end with considerable effort.
The lady was then escorted into Ger's own lands.
She grew in authority there and was later known far and wide.
[15] However anyone might serve her, it was quickly done.
The riding horses were outfitted with expensive saddlecloths
that hung down to their hooves, all the way to the grass.
Ah, the ruler of Ireland, his spirits soared to great heights.
[16] When it came time for him to kiss the lovely bride,
a crowd gathered around him with considerable difficulty.
Many a great buckle could be heard clanging
in the collision of shields; they weren't able to get out of each other's way.
[17] On the following morning a message was sent ahead,
saying how she was to arrive in the sovereign's land,
where she would wear the crown beside [that] brave man.
She later became queen and earned much acclaim from that hero.
[18] No one thought it proper that he should lie with her,
since she was a queen and he not yet a knight.[11]
First he had to take up the crown over powerful and noble lords.
His relatives helped him do so; he later enjoyed great fame and praise.
[19] Five hundred warriors were knighted alongside him.
Everything they desired they were freely granted,
whether horses [or] clothing or different kinds of armor.
The young and noble king was absolutely unwavering in his honor.
[20] He ruled in Ireland from that time on for many days,
during which his lofty honor was never diminished.
He punished the deserving and avenged the poor;
he was at all times magnanimous and an exceptional hero in his own right.
[21] His estates provided him with great wealth.

---

9. A noble young woman engaged to be married could bring her own household into the marriage, as well as a dowry.
10. This is the *bûhurt*, a kind of war game for mounted knights, where one team, or "army," would ride out against another, with an ensuing melee that was meant for show. Usually the "combatants" were unarmed. It stressed horsemanship and elegance over combat.
11. Although consummation of a marriage usually preceded the actual wedding ceremony, here we have a social mismatch that threatens the court's honor. Although heir to the throne of Ireland, Sigebant is crowned only after he is knighted.

His wife the queen was of the mind that,
if she could have ruled the lands of thirty kings
and had authority over them, she would have given them all away.[12]
[22] After three years' time, as we hear tell,
she became pregnant with the king's child.
The child was baptized and since then called
by his name, Hagen. His story is well known to all.
[23] They raised him lovingly and had him well cared for.
If he took after his ancestors, he would surely become a brave warrior.
He was cared for by wise women and many a beautiful girl.
For his father and his mother he was an absolute joy to behold.
[24] Then he grew to be seven years of age.
He was often seen being led by warriors.
He scorned the company of women and cherished that of men.
Later he was taken from them; he was abducted and carried far away.
[25] Wherever the boy saw weapons there at court,
he recognized them easily, and it was often the case
that he wanted to wear a helmet and suit of armor.
These [were] later taken from him; all his hopes were shattered.
[26] One day Sigebant was sitting on some steps.
His wife the queen was chatting with him
underneath a cedar tree. "We are rich in honors,
but I'm curious about something that I can't keep to myself."[13]
[27] He asked her what it was. The noble woman said,
"It pains me a great deal, in my heart and in my soul,
that I see you so seldom, and this is what causes my pain,
in the company of your bold heroes, which would give me joy to behold."
[28] Then the noble king said, "Why is it
that you want to see me with my warriors?
Please tell me why this is, mighty queen.
To fulfill your wish I will gladly make a greater effort."
[29] She said, "There is no one alive more powerful,
who has so many castles and such far-reaching lands,
silver and gemstones along with heavy gold.
We don't act accordingly, which is why I'm unhappy living like this.

---

12. Largesse and generosity were the most important hallmarks of good kings and queens. The more one gave away, the greater the reciprocated honor and social recognition.
13. This episode is reminiscent of the famous scene in Hartmann von Aue's *Erec and Enite*, where Enite informed her husband that his inaction outside the bedroom had led to their social decline. This act of *verligen*, or failing through inertia, can only be countered by *arbeit*, or the exertion and hardship that a knight must publicly endure. Sigebant's reaction to his wife's criticism is very different than Erec's, however.

[30] "When I was still unmarried and living in Frideschotten,
dear king, please don't take offense at what I'm saying,
there each day I watched my father's men
striving for great acclaim, which I've never seen happen here."
[31] She said, "A king so mighty, as everyone proclaims,
and I hear the same of you, should invite [guests] more often.
He should often ride in equestrian games with his heroes,
so that he might gain distinction for his land and for himself.
[32] "Those powerful lords are in the wrong
who gather together great wealth beyond measure
and then refuse to share it with their warriors.
How will they be compensated for the grave wounds they receive in battle?"
[33] Then the noble king said, "My lady, you do me wrong.
I would like to remain steadfast in the hope
that my heart never turns away from one thing:
may I always be instructed in how a noble lord should act."
[34] She said, "Then you should summon lords to your land
with the promise of receiving riches and fine garments.
I will also send out messengers to my relatives.
I'll offer them my goodwill, so that we may then be less discontented here."
[35] The king of Ireland said to his wife,
"I'll gladly follow your advice, [since] often in the past
festivals have been declared at a lady's behest.
I will invite my relatives and yours to come here to court."
[36] Then the queen said, "That makes me very happy.
I for my part will give away dresses to five hundred ladies
and outfit sixty-four young girls with rich clothing."
When the king heard this, he said that he would readily agree.
[37] Since he had promised a festival, eighteen days later
he had all his friends and family informed,
those who readily wanted to travel to Ireland,
that they should wait for the end of winter and the arrival of summer.
[38] He had benches made, as we hear tell,
from wood that was brought out of distant forests.
He had benches made for sixty thousand warriors.
The king's stewards and cupbearers were in charge of the preparations.
[39] They all began to arrive by many different routes;
those who came to court were well cared for.
In the end they came to the king from [every] land.
Eighty-six thousand in all arrived honorably at court.
[40] Things to wear were brought out from the host's coffers;

everyone who wanted something was given more than enough.
In addition, they were given shields and horses from Ireland.
The noble queen enriched many with fine clothing.
[41] She gave away rich garments to at least a thousand women,
as well as to the girls, what was suitable for children,
with decorative trim and gems and fine fabrics.
The lovely ladies looked splendid in their radiant garments.
[42] All those who wanted them were given beautiful clothes.
People saw horses prancing, their reins held by squires;
they brought along bright shields and fine spears.
Uote, worthy and noble, sat in a place of honor at the windows.
[43] Then the host allowed his guests to begin their games;
many a [helmet's] luster was darkened because of it.
The praiseworthy ladies were seated close by,
so they could easily see whatever the heroes accomplished.
[44] The war games dragged on, as so often happened;
the host was intent on being seen among his guests.
His wife, the queen, praised him profusely for that,
as she was seated nearby, up on the ramparts.
[45] After he rode alongside them, as was fitting for a ruler,
he brought to an end, and did so without discredit,
the considerable exertions of his dear guests,
after many honors. Then he presented them to the ladies.[14]
[46] Fair Uote then began to greet
both strangers and friends alike. By doing so
she gained the goodwill of many, who gladly saw her as well.
None of them had occasion to scorn Uote's gifts.
[47] Knights and ladies could be seen together.
They were all well aware of the host's intentions,
that he wanted to honor them at his festivities.
As evening approached he allowed the esteemed guests to ride out again.
[48] The festival lasted until the ninth day.
The chivalrous manners on display in the king's company
were hardly disappointing to traveling entertainers.[15]
They had plenty to keep them busy, because they wanted to benefit as well.
[49] Horns and trumpets sounded out loudly.

---

14. Permission had to be granted by the male sovereign for any knight to be in the company of a woman at court.

15. These itinerate poets and musicians, usually translated as "minstrels" (*varnde*, literally "travelers"), were an important way to display publicly a court's cultural acumen. Here it might also be a nod from this work's own poet to his professional colleagues.

Flutes and harps, whatever they played there,
strumming and singing, they performed with gusto,
piping and fiddling; their take in fine clothing was all the greater.
[50] On the tenth morning, now listen to this strange tale,
after all their joy many had much to lament.
During the festivities a new turn of events unfolded;
after their great happiness they sank into heart-wrenching despair.
[51] As the host was happily sitting with his guests,
one of the minstrels approached. He did so with real zeal
and played better than anyone, who would have believed it,
with such great skill that even noble lords gave him their undivided attention.
[52] Then a charming girl took him by the hand,
the young son of the host from Ireland.
They were joined by ladies who properly looked after him,
and by the host's kinsmen, [who] raised him as his family wished.
[53] From the host's hall could be heard a great clamor;
there was constant laughter almost everywhere.
Young Hagen's guardians got much too close,
so that they lost sight of the young girl [and] the child.
[54] The host's misfortune was soon upon him;
it would cause him and Lady Uote great pain.
The wicked devil had sent into the kingdom
his emissary from afar. It would end badly for them all.
[55] It was a fierce griffin[16] that came flying toward them.
Just as King Sigebant had raised the boy with love,
now on his account he suffered great misfortune.
He would have to lose his young son because of that fearsome griffin.
[56] Dark shadows were cast where its wings carried it,
as if it were a cloud. It was fearsome indeed.
Engrossed in all the merriment, they noticed not a thing.
The young girl and the child stood all alone in front of the hall.
[57] The griffin's might brought down the trees in the forest.
When the noble girl saw the winged creature in flight,
she saved herself and left the child behind.
This astonishing event can only be explained as something truly wondrous.
[58] The griffin plummeted downward and took hold of the child

---

16. Griffins are mythical creatures with the body of a lion and the wings and head of an eagle that can be found in many Near Eastern and Mediterranean cultures as early as 3000 BCE. Although during the Middle Ages the griffin developed aspects of positive religious, even Christologic symbolism, here it is clearly depicted as a monstrous, evil beast allied with the devil.

The Book of Kudrun

in its claws. It did this to demonstrate
that it was ferocious and filled with evil intent.
Since then heroes both gallant and good have had to bemoan these events.
[59] The child began to scream out loud; he was overcome with fear.
It carried him to great heights with its tremendous strength.
Then it soared up into the sky toward distant clouds.
This brought the ruler of Ireland to tears.
[60] Sigebant's friends were seized by pain and sorrow;
they ardently lamented the death of the child.
The king and his wife were grief-stricken.
Everyone all around mourned for that noble child.
[61] Because of this anguish the grand festivities
had to be halted. The griffin had accomplished this
with its vast strength. With great regret
they all had to part ways; they were heartbroken.
[62] The host wept profusely; his shirt was wet with tears.[17]
The noble queen then said to him politely
that he should stop his lament, that everyone must die.[18]
It will be done as God in heaven has commanded.
[63] The guests wanted to leave, but the queen said,
"Truly, noble heroes, you should remain here at court,
and don't refuse our silver and gold.
This we have to offer; we are much indebted to you."
[64] Then the men in turn bowed to her. They all expressed
high [praise] and thanks. The host ordered
rich fabrics brought in; they were still uncut.
Some of them had been brought there from far-off lands.

---

17. The question is whether this kind of behavior was considered appropriate on the part of a ruling king, commander in chief, and knight. Public displays of grief by men were not considered effeminate per se, but as the queen's reaction tells the reader, it is she who appears more concerned about social status and her husband's uncontrolled, and therefore excessive, mourning. Her reaction to the loss of her son seems cold, but we have here a reminder that it is often the female sovereign who is mindful of the court's reputation.

18. Most translators follow Bartsch/Stackmann's gloss and translate this half-line (62,3b) in a generic sense, that everyone must die. Both Störmer-Caysa and Lindner offer different translations. Lindner reads 62,3b and 62,4 as direct speech: "'And even if everyone were dead, everything would be done as God from heaven commanded'" ("'Und wenn auch alle tot wären | alles muß sich vollenden, wie Gott es vom Himmel gebietet'"); Störmer-Caysa translates 62,3b as indirect speech: "he should stop his lament, [as if] the entire populace had died" ("er möge aufhören zu klagen, das ganze Volk sei gestorben"). An alternate reading then to the standard translation of line 62,3 might be: "he should stop lamenting as if everyone had died." Line 62,4 can be read either as direct or indirect speech.

[65] [He] also gave them horses, for travel and for war.[19]
The horses from Ireland were very tall and strong.
They were given red gold and silver unmeasured.
The host had his guests well and generously cared for.
[66] Then the queen said farewell to many women
and many of the highborn girls, such that they were
honored by her gifts. They were impressively dressed.
The festivities came to an end, they departed from Sigebant's realm.

Chapter 2: How Hagen Was Taken Away by the Griffin [67–113]

[67] Let us now take leave from how they departed and resume the story with the swift journey of the ferocious griffin and the noble child. His relatives were inconsolable on his account. [68] He was still alive, because that was God's will, but he was terribly frightened, seeing that the old griffin was carrying him to its young. When they came face to face, he was in grave danger indeed. [69] As soon as the old griffin arrived at the nest, it released the child from its claws and dropped him to its young. One [of them] grabbed him. That it didn't devour him, that was a sign of God's great mercy. [70] They wanted to tear him apart and rip him with their talons, so listen to this marvelous tale of the peril he faced and how that lord of Ireland managed to stay alive. One of the young ones took him far away in its claws. [71] It flew from tree to tree with the child; the griffin regarded its own strength a bit [too] highly. It rested on a tree limb but was too heavy and fell to the ground, when it would rather have been back in its nest. [72] Thanks to the griffin's fall the child escaped its grip, and the little castaway hid himself in the brush. He hadn't eaten a thing; he was weak from hunger. Later he came to the aid of several beautiful women in their exile.

[73] God works in mysterious ways—this can well be said. Thanks to the griffin's strength, it had previously come to pass that the daughters of three kings had been carried there. They were close by, but no one can explain to you[20] [74] how they managed to stay alive for so long, except that God in heaven had mercifully cared for them. Hagen wouldn't have to stay there alone; the child found the lovely young women inside a cave. [75] When the ladies spotted him crawling around the mountain, they at first thought he might be a wild dwarf or maybe

---

19. Horses were bred for all sorts of tasks. Packhorses, or *mære*, were able to carry heavy loads as well as people. Travel horses, here *zelter*, were chosen for their comfortable gait and often used by women, whereas *marc* were war horses chosen for their height and strength, able to carry an armored knight at a full gallop.
20. One of the very rare cases of enjambment in *Kudrun*.

some sea creature that had come up from the deep. When he approached them later, they received him with kindness. [76] Hagen caught sight of them; they fled back into the cave. Their hearts were filled with terror and dread until they discovered that he was a Christian. With his constant efforts he later freed them from their suffering.

[77] Then the oldest one said, "How dare you come to us, since we were given this refuge by God in heaven. Go back to your companions in the wild sea. We suffer here from strife and agony."

[78] Then the noble child said, "Let me stay with you, if you might believe that I'm a Christian. One of the fierce griffins carried me here to this rock. I want to stay with you; surely I won't survive on my own."

[79] Then they lovingly welcomed the little boy; later they came to appreciate his service. They asked him where he was from, but he was not inclined to talk while he suffered so from hunger.

[80] Then the noble child said, "I'm very hungry. Would you share with me your water and your bread? I've had nothing to eat for three days now, since the griffin carried me here for more than a hundred miles."

[81] Then one of the ladies said, "It so happens that we've not seen our cup-bearers or our stewards, those who would bring us food, for some time now."[21]

They lived by God's grace and were clever beyond their years. [82] They soon began to search for herbs and other plants. They wanted to feed Sigebant's dear child themselves, and so they brought together the kinds of things they had been living on. It was a strange kind of food that the young women gave him. [83] He was compelled to eat the plants because of his hunger. Suffering a pitiful death is a terrible thing. He lived there with the ladies for many a day, during which he kindly served them. [84] They had to be watchful, though, I will tell you that. [He] came to know misfortune at an early age, but it came to pass that these young people, amid their cares, experienced strange things outside their cave.

[85] I do[n't] know from where, sailing across the sea, a great crusading fleet came to the rocky cliffs. They were overwhelmed by the strong surf, and the homeless young women became ever more distraught. [86] The ships broke up in pieces, and all aboard were lost. After this occurred, the old griffins soon appeared and carried many of the dead back to their nest. [Many women] were deeply distressed by questions about their fate.[22] [87] After they had given the

---

21. This statement is meant to be highly ironic, even humorous.
22. Manuscript A reads: *des frage vil sorgen gewan* (86,4). This line has been deemed fragmentary by all editors, and two main interpretations have been offered. Martin (1902): that Hagen became distressed (with *frage* perhaps a scribal error for *Hagen*), or Symons/Boesch (1964) and Bartsch/Stackmann (1965/2000): that women were distressed at not knowing the fate of their men (a common trope). Murdoch translates: "These events were soon to lead Hagen into danger" (8); McConnell: "Many women were later in great distress" (10); Gibbs/Johnson: "Many women were distressed when their questions about the missing men went unanswered" (8).

Chapter 2: How Hagen Was Taken Away by the Griffin [67–113]

young griffins something to eat, the old griffins again flew from their nest, I don't know which way, [out to] the open sea. On the mountain they had left behind a ruthless resident.

[88] Hagen saw that people were still lying on the beach, those who had drowned. They were crusaders. He thought he could find their food there, so he crept silently down to the shore, on account of the griffins. [89] Once there he only found a solitary man with weapons, but he would suffer much grief from the griffins because of it. He stripped him of his chain mail; he was not ashamed to do so.[23] He found a bow and other weapons lying next to him. [90] Next the little boy put on the armor himself. Up in the air he heard a rustling of the wind; the little prince had been too slow. When the old griffin appeared, Hagen was already too far away from the cliffs. [91] Filled with rage, the griffin plummeted down to the beach. Its former lodger, the one left at home, it would have very gladly devoured on the spot, but bold [Hagen] proved himself to be a great hero. [92] With only a child's strength he drew back on the bow and released many a solid arrow, but he couldn't pierce the griffin. How could he save himself now? He then took up the sword; he heard the ladies weeping and wailing. [93] [Although he] was unskilled, [he] fought fiercely enough. He cut off one of the griffin's wings right at the shoulder and injured it severely on one of its legs, so that it was unable to get away. [94] Hagen had won the victory; the other one was dead. The next one arrived quickly, bringing even greater danger. He killed them all, the young ones and the old. God in heaven helped him; he alone certainly didn't have such strength.

[95] After he had accomplished this great miracle, he told his ladies to come out of the cave. He said, "Come and enjoy the fresh air and sunshine, now that God in heaven wishes to grant us great happiness."

[96] They welcomed [him] most kindly, and the ladies promptly kissed him again and again on the mouth.[24] Their overlord lay there dead. What could prevent them now from going anywhere at all on the mountain? [97] Now that he had freed them from these great worries, the exiled castaway learned to shoot well, so that birds in flight could not escape him. He learned to do whatever he pleased once he started thinking about his plight. [98] He soon became quite bold, both reckless and cautious at once. How he learned to run and jump from the animals! Like a wild panther he ran over the rocks. So he raised himself, alone, he had no family. [99] Often he went down to the shore for something

---

23. Stripping the dead of armor and weapons on the battlefield was common practice, but not something that kings or high nobles engaged in. His lack of embarrassment signals how far Hagen is from the court and from his own social milieu.
24. Being kissed on the mouth was not necessarily an overtly erotic act, but in most cases it acknowledged the high social class of the recipient. Here Hagen has been accepted into the circle of nobility, although the irony of doing so on a deserted island is rich.

to do. There in the waves he saw all the wild fish. He could have caught them, if only he could have made use of them, but his kitchen had no fire, something that frustrated him every day. [100] From his encampment he would go out into the forest, where he would see all kinds of animals, wild and fierce. Among them was one that wanted to devour him. He killed it with his sword, it fell victim to his wrath. [101] It was like a kind of dragon.[25] First he skinned it and then gained great strength, he thirsted for its blood. After he had drunk his fill, he became even stronger and came to know many things. [102] The hero wrapped himself [in] the animal's skin. He next came upon a lion that was very close by. It was unable to flee from him—that's how fast he ran toward it. The hero didn't harm it but embraced it with kindness instead.[26]

[103] The animal he had previously killed, he wanted to carry it back to his dwelling. The ladies now regularly benefited from his kindness. Their hearts and spirits were raised by this strange meal. [104] They didn't have a fire, but they had plenty of wood. He struck lots of sparks on a hard stone cliff, and what they had lacked before they now had in plenty. There was no one else to do it; they had to cook the meat themselves.[27] [105] After they had eaten their meal, their strength increased. Their senses, too, were enlivened through God's power. Their appearance became more attractive and even admirable, as each [of them] had been [at home] in their father's land. [106] Fierce Hagen now had the strength of twelve men,[28] for which he gained high praise during his lifetime. He and the young women were greatly dismayed, however, that they would have to stay in that wasteland forever.

[107] Then the women asked to be escorted to the shore. They were ashamed to go out, because the clothes they were wearing were so shabby. They had made them themselves when young Hagen found them in their wretched state.

---

25. The name of this mythical beast, the *gabilûn*, is a borrowing from Old French *caméléon* and related to MHG *gampilûn* (*Parzival* 383,2). It is usually translated as a chameleon or lizard. The text says that the animal in question is "similar" to a chameleon. Neither translation does justice to the fact that the animal in question is very much like a dragon, in that its blood confers wisdom and great strength, as it did for Siegfried, or Sigurd, who immersed himself in the blood of the dragon he killed, while also tasting its blood and roasted heart, from which he learned the language of the birds.
26. Another knight, Iwein, was famous for saving and then befriending a lion. Since the lion is never mentioned again in this text, this reference might have been inserted simply as a nod to the reader's knowledge of Arthurian lore. A similar insertion, with little consequence, is made at the end of the story of *Wolf Dietrich A*, where the hero saves a lion from a dragon (*WDA* 600–601).
27. This seems a fairly inappropriate complaint, given that the young people are stranded with little hope of rescue, but it emphasizes how far removed they are from civilization, and how self-reliant in everyday affairs they had to be, something unbecoming of royalty.
28. This number seems to have been a somewhat common multiplier of strength. Otnit also had the strength of twelve (*O* 6,3; *O* 106,1; *WDA* 548,2). Wolf Dietrich gained the strength of one man each year. Hagen had the strength of twenty-six men (254,3), as did Wate (1469,1–2).

[108] For twenty-four days they wandered through the forest. Early one morning the young man spied a heavily laden ship. It was coming from Garadie.[29] The dispossessed women suffered from their hardships. [109] Hagen yelled out loudly; he wasn't discouraged no matter how much the wind whipped up the waves. The ship's rigging began to creak, and as they came closer to land, they feared the wild mermaids, seeing the women there standing on the beach. [110] The master of the ship hailed from Salme. He had known Hagen and his family a long time. He was their neighbor, but the one from Ireland, the son of Sigebant, went unrecognized by any of the pilgrims. [111] The count ordered his helmsman to steer clear of the shore. The castaway man prayed that he might be rescued by God's mercy from that desert island, and the others were reassured when he so boldly invoked Christ's name. [112] The count himself with eleven men jumped into a skiff. It seemed to him a long time before he could discover the truth about whether they were forest sprites or fierce sea creatures. He had never in all his life seen such marvelous beings.

[113] He then asked, before he set foot on the strand, "Are you children baptized? What are you doing here?"

He saw that their beautiful figures were covered with fresh moss. They implored the strangers to let them travel with them.

Chapter 3: How Hagen Came Aboard the Ship [114–50]

[114] Before boarding the ship, they were given clothes[30] that the pilgrims had brought with them to that land. Despite their modesty, they had to put them on. They were extremely embarrassed, but their grief came to an end. [115] Once the beautiful women had been brought aboard, the proud and noble knights came to greet them. They graciously received the highborn daughters of nobility, even though earlier [they] had mistaken them to be fierce and monstrous. [116] Then they spent the night with them on the water. The young people were unsettled by their strange surroundings. I think they would have been wise to consider all this an honor. The Count of Garadie ordered that they be given a good meal. [117] After they had eaten and he had sat down to join them, the count asked

---

29. Manuscript A reads: *Karade* (108,3b). There is some echo here perhaps of the Arthurian *Karidoel* in Wolfram von Eschenbach's *Parzival* (280,2), or *Karidôl* from Hartmann von Aue's *Iwein* (32).
30. These were clothes for men, as the "pilgrims" described here are actually crusading warriors. Wearing men's clothing would have been uncourtly, indeed shameful for the young women, who were still mindful of courtly norms and protocol.

them to tell him who had brought [such] beautiful women so far across the sea.[31] The young people were upset by his questioning, as well as by their suffering.

[118] Then the eldest among those sitting there said, "I come from distant lands, sir, this you should know, from splendid India, where my father was king as long as he lived, where sadly I will never wear a crown."

[119] Then the middle one said, "I come from far away. A fierce griffin seized me in Portugal. The one who called me his child was lord of that land, a ruler most powerful, both near and far."

[120] The youngest among them, who sat next to the count, said most courteously, "Sir, I say this to you. I am from Iserland, where my father was lord. I am sadly all too far away from those who cared for me."

[121] Then the noble knight said, "God has done well, even though he chose not to let you stay with your families. You have been mercifully rescued from great danger, since I found you beautiful young women here on this shore."

[122] Whatever he might have asked about how they had escaped a horrible death from the griffins that carried them to their nest, it was useless. They had suffered many things but never spoke of them.

[123] Then the mighty count turned to the young man. "My friend and companion, let me hear from you, now that the ladies have told me their stories. I would very much like to know where your homeland or your kinfolk are."

[124] Then fierce Hagen said, "I will gladly tell you. One of the griffins also carried me here. My father's name was Sigebant. I'm from the kingdom of Ireland and have been with these ladies a long time under difficult circumstances."

[125] Then everyone asked, "How is it possible that you survived so long among the griffins?"

Young [Hagen] said, "That was God's merciful will. I stilled both my courage and resolve at their expense."

[126] Then the man from Garadie said, "Tell me this.[32] How did you overcome this danger?"

"I killed the old ones and the young ones. Not one survived among those that made me fear for my life."

---

31. Manuscript A reads: *woheer sy* <u>*recht schoene*</u> *bracht zu dem see* (117,3). The normalized and emended Bartsch/Stackmann text reads: *wer si (sô) rehte schœne bræhte zuo dem sê*, whereby *schœne* has been translated almost unanimously as the object. McConnell translates: "who had brought <u>such beautiful women</u> to these shores" (14). An alternate translation for *rehte schœne* is offered by Störmer-Caysa (2010): "who would have brought them <u>so far</u> out to sea" ("wer sie so weit aufs Meer gebracht hätte").

32. The count changes his address of Hagen at this point in the conversation from the formal you (*ir*) to the informal you (*du*), signaling perhaps a desire to make Hagen feel more comfortable, or to disarm his suspicions.

[127] Then everyone said, "You are strong indeed. You will soon be celebrated by men and women alike. A thousand of us would never have been able to destroy them. You were blessed."

[128] The count and his crew were afraid of this young man. He was incredibly strong, which later caused them problems. They wanted to disarm him with some kind of trick, but he angrily resisted. To be sure, they soon regretted his arrival.

[129] Then the count replied, "Fortune has been kind to me after all the great adversities I've experienced. And if [you] are from Lord Sigebant's clan there in Ireland, I will take you as my hostage. [130] Luckily you fell into my hands, that I can tell you. Your relatives have done me much harm in the land of Garadie, which is so close to them. They killed and captured my heroes in a hard-fought battle."

[131] Then young Hagen said, "I'm blameless for what they've done to you. Take me to them now and I believe I can reconcile their hate and your enmity. Kindly let me hope to be reunited with [the] people I know."

[132] The count said to the young man, "You are my hostage, and these pretty young women will serve me at court. I will keep them in my lands to my honor."

It seemed to Hagen that this talk would bring him harm and humiliation. [133] The young man said angrily, "I refuse to be held hostage. No one ought to demand this should he want to stay alive. My good seafarers, if you take me back to my country I'll gladly reward you for it. I'll pay with treasure and with garments. [134] You expect my ladies to become your attendants. They can survive very well without his help. If anyone here is sufficiently clever, listen to my counsel. [Turn] your sails so that we head toward Ireland."

[135] The crew wanted to seize him; their captain ordered it done, but he was already eye to eye with them, and they found themselves in danger. Grabbing them by the hair, he threw at least thirty into the water. His physical strength became sorely apparent to those pilgrims. [136] If the kind young women hadn't intervened, he would have killed the hero of Garadie as well. They were all the same to him, rich or poor. Those same seafarers now had to change course for Ireland. [137] They made haste so as not to lose their lives, for they had reason to fear young Hagen's wrath. For seventeen days they labored tirelessly. They were all afraid of him, because they could see how violent he was.

[138] As he approached his father's land, and since the many large towns were well known to him, he recognized a towering castle near the water. He made out three hundred tall spires, all strong and solid. [139] Inside were Lord Sigebant along with his noble wife. The pilgrims had to fear for their lives, for if the Irish king became aware of them, he would kill them all. Hagen prevented this, to his credit.

[140] Then that distinguished man said to the foreigners, "I'll gladly try to resolve this, even though I don't hold sway in this land. I will send out messengers

The Book of Kudrun

and try to end this ancient enmity between you and the king. [141] Whoever now wants to earn a great reward from me, whoever gladly delivers and conveys this message to the king, to him I will give the finest gold. Surely my father and my mother will also reward him richly."

[142] He told twelve of the pilgrims to ride out. "Now ask the king," said the young man, "if he should want to see Hagen, his son, the one on whose account he was made to suffer so terribly by a griffin. [143] I know full well that the noble king will refuse to believe it. So ask my mother to agree that she will acknowledge that I am her son if she sees a golden cross on my chest."[33]

[144] The envoys rode out to the nearby land, where in a great castle Lady Uote and Sigebant reigned. He realized that men from Garadie were approaching. They were his enemies, which is why the ruler and his people grew angry. [145] He demanded to know how they dared ride into his land.

Then one among [them] said, "We were sent here by your son, young Hagen. He's very close by. If anyone wanted to see him, it could very quickly be accomplished."

[146] Then Lord Sigebant said, "There's no need for you to lie. The child was taken in a way that has often aroused the deepest emotions in my heart."

"If you don't believe us, then ask your wife the queen. [147] He was often enough very close to her. Did he have a golden cross on his chest, and would that reveal the truth about this man? Should you both agree, then you may rightly declare [him] to be your child."

[148] This was reported to Lady Uote. She was overjoyed at the news, before this she often grieved. She said, "We should go to where we can find the truth."

The ruler commanded that horses be prepared for him and his closest companions.

[149] Quickly then one of the pilgrims said to fair Uote, "If you would heed my counsel, my lady, I'll advise you what to do. You should bring along dresses for the lovely girls; they will do you much honor. They are his young companions."

[150] Luxurious dresses were brought along with the lady, and many bold men escorted the queen. Hagen had already come ashore on the beach, and the men from Garadie were seen alongside the castaway.

---

33. This red-gold cross is most likely a birthmark in the shape of a cross, but others believe it is a cross hanging around his neck. Störmer-Caysa translates "around my neck" ("um meinen Hals"). Martin's (1902) note on this "golden cross" gives numerous literary examples to support the notion of a birthmark.

Chapter 4: How Hagen Was Received by His Father and Mother [151–203]

[151] As he saw these women and men approaching, Hagen wanted to go out to meet them. He wanted to see who was coming to greet him. His family and friends crowded all around, as they should.

[152] The king welcomed him to his land and said, "Are you the stranger who sent for us and declares the noble queen to be his mother? If this story is true, then I will be elated beyond all measure."

[153] Uote the Fair said most courteously, "Order these people here to make room for us. I can easily see if this one deserves the crown here."

She recognized the true signs,[34] and they welcomed the young hero most lovingly.

[154] With tears in her eyes, she kissed him on the mouth. "Before this I was ill; now I am completely well. You are welcome, Hagen, my only child. Now all those here with Sigebant can place their hopes in you."

[155] The king came closer, his joy was great, and his heart, filled with love, caused his eyes to overflow with an abundance of hot tears. By rights he lovingly held the child in the highest regard.

[156] The exiled strangers were introduced to Lady Uote. She gave them all sorts of garments, gray and multicolored, costly materials with fur linings that suited them well. Their fears were assuaged by King Sigebant's wife. [157] The beautiful women were dressed as it best suited them. Before that they had been much ashamed, until they were outfitted [with] sumptuous robes. The sovereign and his heroes received the young women attentively.

[158] Hagen requested that the king and his men show the men from Garadie mercy, for his sake, that he should forgive them all injury and fault, and so young Hagen secured a pardon for the pilgrims. [159] Then the king renounced his enmity with a kiss, and they restored to them all that they had lost.[35] This brought them great benefits and honored Hagen as well. From that time on they were never again to be enemies of Ireland's king. [160] Then the foreigners were told to carry to the beach, under Hagen's surety, their food stores and their clothing, so that they might rest there for fourteen days. The proud pilgrims had Hagen to thank for that.

---

34. This refers most likely to the aforementioned birthmark in the shape of a cross, although the manuscript reads "signs" (*bilde*) in the plural, not a single image or "cross."

35. The king, urged on by Hagen's entreaties, engages in a ceremonial act of peacemaking. The kiss of peace sealed what was probably a formal oath renouncing all hostilities and promising reparations for past damages. It is unclear here if the reparations were meant to make good losses from the previous war, or if they included Hagen's killing of the thirty sailors who were part of the pilgrims' party.

The Book of Kudrun

[161] Then they made a great noise riding back from the seashore. At Balian castle throngs of people came out on account of the strange news, that the son of that powerful king was still alive. No one could believe it. [162] Hagen didn't leave his ladies unattended. He made sure that they could bathe at any time and served the lovely young women most discreetly. They were given luxurious clothing. He was wise beyond his young years. [163] He soon matured into a full-grown man, and he practiced with heroes the ancient arts that knights were meant to master, with deeds and with action. He later came to rule in his father Sigebant's lands. [164] After fourteen days they allowed those sea-weary heroes staying with them to depart. The sovereign gave them gifts of gleaming gold, as he wanted to make them steadfast allies for the sake of his son's love.

[165] Young Hagen learned what was expected of heroes, such that he never needed to be ashamed [in front of] other warriors.[36] Beautiful women applauded that. His munificence came to be so great that no one could believe it. [166] Moreover, he grew to be so bold, as we've been told, that he dared to avenge his friends' injury. He maintained his honor in all manner of affairs, which is why throughout the land stories and songs were heard about that hero. [167] He grew up in a wilderness, that noble young prince, among the wild animals, and so with a single bound he could catch whatever creature he wanted. It seems he and his ladies experienced many strange things there by the sea.[37] [168] His proper name was Hagen, but later he was called the "Terror of All Kings."[38] This is how he was known in every kingdom on account of his strength. Hagen the bold readily profited from his name.

---

36. Manuscript A reads: *von*, which has been emended by Bartsch/Stackmann to *vor*. McConnell offers a translation based on the original reading: "from many a warrior at Sigeband's court" (19). Sowinski takes another approach to the emended *vor*, translating it not in locative terms but figuratively as "Hagen learned . . . better than other warriors" ("Hagen lernte . . . besser als mancher andere," 32).
37. This strophe encapsulates Hagen's youth, as it might have been recounted by the previously mentioned stories and songs.
38. There has been much commentary on this epithet and the word *valant*. The word's primary meaning is "devil" or "Satan," although its etymology is unclear. Hagen's epithet has been translated variously: "devil among kings" (McConnell, 20); "Devil-King" (Murdoch, 15; Armour, 25); "Devil of All Kings" (Gibbs/Johnson, 15); "Teufel aller Könige" (Sowinski, 33); "Teufelskönig" (Lindner, 36; Freytag, 30). Only Störmer-Caysa steers clear of the "devil" reference with "Schrecken aller Könige" (59). The term, when applied to monstrous creatures or people, can extend its range of meaning to "devil-like," while in Hagen's case the epithet is clearly reputational. I have chosen to follow Störmer-Caysa's lead with "terror" (*Schrecken*), given that Hagen is never equated with the devil or any netherworld character. He is most often given the epithet *wild* (twenty-five times), translated here as "fierce," a description shared with the griffin that carried him off and the island to which he was taken. Other adjectives describe him as a typical epic hero: *küene* (bold), *jung* (young), and *stark* (strong). His "devilish" traits are therefore mostly linked to his wildness in battle and the treatment of his enemies, in contrast with Hartmut's mother, Queen Gerlint, who is often described as *ubel* (wicked or evil) as well as a *vâlantinne*, or she-devil.

Chapter 4: How Hagen Was Received by His Father and Mother [151–203]

[169] His family advised him to take a wife. There was a woman very nearby; no one was more beautiful in all the world, anywhere on earth. She had looked after him herself; in fact, he had grown up alongside her under difficult circumstances. [170] Her name was Hilde, and she was from India. She had often shown [him] her affection under great duress, there where he first found her inside a cave. In all the lands he desired no one more than her.

[171] His father encouraged him to be knighted promptly, along with a hundred of his comrades. He would give a thousand marks[39] to every four companions for horses and equipment. Brave Hagen said he would do this most willingly. [172] Then the king let it be known throughout the other kingdoms when this would occur, and so they were informed. His great generosity was wholly confirmed after that. The festival was to be held in one year and three days' time.[40] [173] Fighting men who wanted to attend made their preparations. They had shields crafted that shone in bright colors; costly saddles were fashioned as well. Breast girths and bridles were skillfully adorned with gold. [174] They were to be encamped on a wide-open field, all the great king's guests. He made sure they wanted for nothing, and accommodations were made over a wide area. His guests could be seen arriving in the land from all directions. [175] The foreigners who were to be knighted with him, he had them all outfitted, which certainly pleased them. A thousand warriors came from foreign domains into that realm, and he enriched them all with horses and clothing.

[176] Hagen said to his kinsmen, "You have advised me that I should become king. That suits me all the more if I might love with all my heart [the one who] wears the crown beside me. I'll not relent until I've compensated her [for her] suffering."

[177] They said, that is, his men were asking who would lead his heroes on their way to court. He said, "It is Lady Hilde, from the land of India, who will greatly honor me and my supporters in all the world."

[178] It was pleasing to his mother when she heard this, to his father as well, that [she] should be crowned. She had all the attributes that would bring the land honor. At least six hundred brave men or more were knighted alongside him. [179] According to [Christian][41] rites they were both anointed and crowned. Without delay, Hagen and Lady Hilde rode out at the head of the procession. Plenty of splendid equestrian games[42] with the king's men were on display.

---

39. The "mark" is a standard of weight, not currency, that gained prominence in the eleventh century. Standards varied somewhat, but it was equivalent to about 250 grams.
40. The seemingly gratuitous extra three days may be just that. It is possible that the extra days were thought to be a kind of grace period, "or a bit longer," not to be taken literally.
41. Manuscript A reads: *nach siten sittlichen* (179,1a), "according to ritual rites" or "courteous courtesies," which seems redundant. *Sittlichen* has been emended by Bartsch/Stackmann and others to *kristenlichen*. It is assumed that Hilde is a Christian.
42. See note 10 above.

[180] Lord Sigebant himself rode out; he was in great spirits and paid little attention to how much treasure he was spending. Once they had finished riding around as befitted knights, the royal court's many stewards were kept especially busy. [181] They set up all the seating, wide and long, benches and tables. After Mass was sung, Lady Uote rode to court, and with her many other ladies. The young knights were happy to watch [them] pass by.[43]

[182] As King Sigebant sat next to Lady Uote, and Hagen next to Hilde, people were saying how fortunate he was to have such a dear child. Their retinue endeavored to break many a lance within view of the tables. [183] After the king of Ireland finished his meal, the flowers and grass were completely trampled to dust by his many guests, who rode around making a great noise. Those who were up to it all joined in the melee.[44] [184] Twenty-four knights assembled on the field, armed for battle. This was all splendidly performed, and they demonstrated many a well-executed joust. Beautiful women looked on; anything else would have been bad form. [185] Sigebant's son himself rode out for the equestrian games. His beloved was watching, and she certainly didn't disapprove. If she had served him in strange lands before, he eagerly rewarded her for it now. He was a hero in his own right. [186] There with the king, riding through the dust clouds, were seen a dozen and more[45] who were also kings. They were vassals of his, Christians and non-Christians,[46] and Sigebant and Hagen were both faithfully served by them. [187] The festival lasted [a long time], and everyone was greatly amused by the melee and the crush, the shouts and the noise. The host bid his guests to end [their] exertions, and they were invited to take their seats next to the ladies.

---

43. This male pastime, *frouwen schouwen* or "watching the ladies," is famously mentioned in a poem by Hartmann von Aue (*Minnesangs Frühling* 216,29 or XV) as something in which the poet himself has little interest.
44. This somewhat loose translation of the verb form *buhurdieren*, from the aforementioned *bûhurt*, is meant to convey the chaotic nature of large groups of men riding around simulating the confusion of battle. This was different from the jousting (*tjoste*) described in the following strophe, which was much more organized. The distinction between the two forms of mock battle is important. Although the order of the strophes could be questioned, Hagen's participation seems to be limited to the large maneuvers, not the individual jousting between two opponents.
45. The text specifies *zwelf unde drî*, or twelve and three, which is not necessarily meant to be a precise amount but rather means "a dozen and some additional." It is possible that the number three was simply chosen for the rhyme (*bî/drî*).
46. The original Middle High German is *heiden*, which can refer to non-Christians generally or more specifically to Muslims. In the past this term has most often been translated with the antiquated and pejorative English "heathen." Here the term is translated as "Muslim" when it seems to be the most obvious meaning, as with Siegfried and his people from the land of the "Moors," and "non-Christian" when the meaning is most likely more generic.

Chapter 4: How Hagen Was Received by His Father and Mother [151–203]

[188] Lord Sigebant said in the presence of his peers, "To my son Hagen I give my lands, the citizenry and towns, near and far. All my men will have him as their sovereign."

[189] Once Lord Sigebant had renounced the crown, Hagen enfeoffed[47] towns and lands with much good intent. To those about to receive them, he seemed so exceptional that they were glad to accept them from him. [190] As proper under feudal right, many a hand was extended to the young king.[48] Treasure and clothing, too, he gave to his guests from near and far. Such a generous noble's festival would profit even the poor.

[191] At court were the ladies who had come with him to that land. One of them was sent for, she was told to appear before Lady Hilde and the king. She was from Iserland and was as beautiful as one might wish. [192] A young nobleman desired her; he had seen her with the queen, which is why he could well claim that she had every right to wear a crown. She was Lady Hilde's companion, and she later received a great land as a reward. [193] Then the guests parted company, as did the king and his men. The noble maiden was later escorted to the nobleman's kingdom of Norway. Following her great suffering, her position was now most agreeable.[49]

[194] Then Hagen held court in Ireland. Whatever he found among the people to be unlawful, they had to pay him dearly for it. Within [a single] year he had eighty or more beheaded. [195] After that he led an army into the land of his enemies. To spare the poor he avoided setting fire to the land, but whenever a noble was found to be overly proud, Hagen razed his castles and avenged himself with terrible mortal wounds. [196] Wherever he fought a battle, he proved himself to be a good knight. He put the haughty heroes in their place in his realm, both near and far.[50] He was known as the "Terror of All Kings," which subdued his enemies.

[197] This hero lived a good life; he was certainly happy. The lady from India gave this warrior a beautiful daughter named Hilde, after her mother. This part of the story is well known. [198] Fierce Hagen had the child raised in such a way

---

47. This technical term translates the verb *lihen*, or "to loan," which is to give a vassal a fief, that is, the use of land and property in return for military, economic, and administrative service.
48. As part of the formal ceremony, a handshake or a clasping of the vassal's hands between the lord's hands confirmed the oath of vassalage.
49. This refers in a rather unspecific way to the unnamed third young woman from Iserland mentioned in the previous two strophes.
50. Manuscript A reads: *in sein vorgetane nahen und verren* (196,3). The line is assumed to be corrupt, given its metrical shortfall and the fact that *vorgetane* is otherwise unattested. Bartsch/Stackmann offer various suggestions for emendation, while leaving the original reading in their text. Bartsch's first edition (1865) offers a clue to a solution, dropped in later editions. The earlier gloss raises the question: "perhaps a corruption of *vogetîe*?" ("vielleicht entstellt aus *vogetîe*?"). Störmer-Caysa picks this up (585n196,3), assuming a loanword from *praefectura* and a dropped "r" abbreviation. This explanation is adopted here in the translation "realm."

The Book of Kudrun

that the sun hardly ever shone on her or the wind hardly ever touched her. She was watched over by noblewomen, and his relations did likewise, the ones he could trust the most. [199] Within twelve years the lovely girl grew to be beautiful beyond measure, which was widely known. Highborn and powerful nobles considered how they might contend for fierce Hagen's daughter's love.

[200] One of these lords ruled near the Danish March,[51] in the land of Walays.[52] When he heard this, [that] she was [so] beautiful, he tried very hard to win her. Hagen was contemptuous and relieved him of his life and honor.[53] [201] No matter how many ambassadors were sent to win that worthy maiden, Hagen had them all killed on account of his arrogance. He didn't want to give her to anyone who was weaker than him. This story about the king was heard told everywhere. [202] He had at least twenty or more envoys hanged,[54] all those who were sent to win his exceptional daughter. Those who couldn't avenge this were outraged. Many were told about this and no longer wanted her as their wife. [203] Still there were brave men who would not give up. When someone is overly proud, so the saying goes, there will always be someone who thinks just as highly of himself. Hagen's troubles would only grow as a result of their service to love.[55]

---

51. This translation of *Tenemarke* avoids the conflation with modern Denmark, as it refers to an unspecified march, or border area, with the Danish lands, or Daneland. It could be similar to the border territory established north of the Eider River by Charlemagne around 810 to defend the empire from Danish incursions.

52. The manuscript's *Walays* is impossible to locate. Wales would not make sense geographically.

53. If this is an early reference to Hetel from Walays, then we must infer that it was his messenger, not Hetel himself, who was killed.

54. These executions broke every norm and convention concerning the inviolability of the office of envoy or legate and would have been considered criminal acts.

55. Manuscript A reads: *von ir hohen mynne* (203,4a). The concept of *hohe minne*, literally high or elevated love, is translated here and elsewhere in the text with the help of the term "service," which was by the thirteenth century inextricably linked to what is usually termed "courtly love."

PART II: HILDE

Chapter 5: How Wate Traveled to Ireland [204–371]

[204] A hero[56] once came of age in Daneland.[57] His family ruled there at Stormarn in a border region, this is known by all, and they raised him honorably. Ortland[58] served him as well. He was unquestionably powerful and imposing. [205] One of his relatives, whose name was Wate, held towns and lands from [this] man, and because he was his kinsman, Wate raised him correctly.[59] He taught him to be virtuous, he had him looked after at all times. [206] The lord of the Danish March was Wate's sister's son,[60] Horant the worthy. He later served Hetel the king so well that he thought it fitting that [he] should wear a crown. He rewarded that hero with a kingship of his own.[61]

[207] Mighty Hetel ruled in Hegelingen, which was close to Ortland. I want to tell you this: he had there in his possession eighty or more castles.[62] Those responsible for them served him daily with great honor. [208] He was sovereign in Frisia over water and land,[63] and Diethmers and Walays were in his possession. Hetel was prosperous and had many kinsmen. He was also determined and daring, and he often lay in wait for his enemies. [209] Hetel was an orphan, and

---

56. Although not mentioned by name until a little later (206,3), the hero introduced here is Hetel, the king of Hegelingen, a realm that included the Danish March, Horant's land. Horant is therefore Hetel's vassal.
57. The original is *Tenelant*, not to be equated with present-day Denmark, although it is basically in the same geographical region.
58. Manuscript A throughout reads: *Ortlant, Hortlant,* or *Nordlant*. Editions and translators have usually emended this to an ahistorical *Nordland*, or Northland. Unless a definite identification with some real or otherwise attested place-name can be made, this translation uses the manuscript as an orthographic guide, given that most place-names in *Kudrun* are not to be equated with actual geographical or historical names. See the excursus by Störmer-Caysa (645–47) for more detail.
59. This relationship is called fosterage. Young boys, usually around the age of seven, would go to live with a male relative, often the mother's brother or close family friend, and stay until sometime in his teens, when he would return home.
60. Wate is described here as Horant's uncle. The sister-son relationship was particularly important for the education of young boys in the Middle Ages. It was also a typical fosterage relationship, although Wate is not specifically named as Horant's foster father.
61. This refers to the kingship of *Tenemark*, not Hetel's own kingship. It was common to have several "kings" within a larger kingdom, all of them still tied to a single king through bonds of family and vassalage. Horant continued to serve as Hetel's vassal even though Hetel had made him the sovereign of his own land, which was then enfeoffed to Horant.
62. Middle High German *burc* (plural *bürge*) can mean "castle" or "town" or both, since villages or small towns were often part of the castle complex outside the walls.
63. This most likely includes any islands that would be "over the water" from the mainland. This land and its islands are most likely part of what is now Friesland along the German North Sea coast.

The Book of Kudrun

this meant that [he] should take a wife. Both were lost to him, his father as well as his mother; it was they who had left him the land. Otherwise he had many supporters, but he was tired of living with them.

[210] So his best counselors advised him to pursue a love that was suitable. The young man said, "I don't know anyone who might be a worthy queen of the Hegelingen, who could be brought into my household."

[211] Then Morunc, the young man from Nifland, said, "I know of one, so I've heard, who is more beautiful than anyone else in the world. We should do our utmost to see that she becomes your beloved."[64]

[212] He asked who she was and what her name was.

He said, "Her name is Hilde, and she lives in Ireland. Her father's name is Hagen, and he hails from [Ger's] clan. If she came to this land, you would be forever joyful and happy."

[213] Then Lord Hetel said, "But I've been told that whoever attempts to win her reaps her father's fury, and for that reason many a nobleman has died. I wouldn't wish such a death on any of my supporters."

[214] Then Morunc replied, "Send people to Horant's land and have them bring him back. He knows all of Hagen's customs; he's seen them for himself. Without his help this could surely never succeed."

[215] Hetel said, "I will do as you advise, since she's [so] beautiful. If she is to be the prize, then you'll have to be a part of this as well. I firmly believe that you can succeed at anything. You will be rewarded and honored if she becomes the lady of Hegelingen."

[216] Soon he had messengers sent to Daneland, where they found Horant, Hetel's cousin.[65] He asked that brave man to report to him within seven days, should he want to serve. [217] [Horant] was so committed to his loyal service that after the envoys had arrived and he had heard their message, he gladly complied with whatever was requested of him. For this he later suffered hardship and great danger. [218] He quickly traveled to court with sixty of his men. After the hero had taken leave of his home, he hastened to discover the cause in which he could honorably serve that brave man. [219] He arrived in that land on the seventh morning. He and his companion were elegantly dressed. The king went out to meet the brave warrior, when he saw bold Fruote alongside the man from the Danish March.

---

64. Manuscript A reads: *daz sy euch zu ainer* <u>trauttine</u> *werde* (211,4b). The meaning of *triutinne* is generally linked to a romantic or sexual relationship, ranging from "friend" to "lover" to "wife."

65. Manuscript A reads: *neven* (216,2b), a term that is not synonymous with modern "nephew" but includes a range of relationships (Latin *nepos*), especially sister-son (nephew) or mother-brother (uncle). It is similar to modern German *Vetter*. Here it most likely refers to a kind of cousin, since it is probable that Hetel and Horant are roughly the same age, since both are described as young.

[220] It was welcome news that they had arrived, the king was happy to see them. This relieved him of some [of his] worries, those that troubled him. He laughed and said, "You are most welcome, cousin[66] Fruote."

[221] Then Fruote and Horant reported to the [king].[67] He asked how things stood at home in Daneland, so they both said to him, "We only recently fought hard battles and dealt many grievous wounds."

[222] He asked where they had journeyed for these battles. They said, "Portugal,[68] that's where we fought. That noble and powerful king left us no choice, he was harassing us daily along our borders."

[223] Then young Hetel said, "Let's leave that aside. I don't think old Wate will want to give up the march at Stormarn, where he has his seat. Anyone who might take a castle from him may well receive his eternal reward."[69]

[224] The heroes went to take their seats in a great hall. With youthful exuberance, Horant and Fruote began speaking about the love of noble women. The king enjoyed listening and gave them a good reward in return.[70]

[225] Hetel then questioned Horant, "If [you] have any information, please let me know, what is the situation with Lady Hilde, the young queen?[71] I want to offer her my service and send envoys to convey my message."

---

66. Also *neve*, as with Horant.
67. The Bartsch/Stackmann edition postulates an insertion of *fürsten*, but there is evidence of a more common usage of the formula with *künic*. This appearance refers to a formal gathering before the king in the great hall, not the initial meeting.
68. Manuscript A reads: *Portigal* (222,2a), as in 119,2. Geographically speaking, this seems highly unlikely if we think of this as modern-day Portugal. This is a good example of how the *Kudrun* poet's geography is meant to be more fantastical than real.
69. Manuscript A reads: *dannckh hab er des ymer der im ain purg angewünne* (223,4). The normalized Bartsch/Stackmann text reads: *danc habe er des immer, der im eine burg an gewinne*. This line has been variously understood by translators and editors. The Bartsch/Stackmann note wants the line to be read ironically, in the sense that "it would really take a great knight who, etc." ("das müßte schon ein herrlicher Ritter sein, der usw."). Murdoch follows this and translates: "You would have to be a very bold warrior indeed to capture one of *his* castles" (20). Others are more literal and focus on the nature of the reward (*danc*), e.g., McConnell: "Anyone fortunate enough to capture a castle from him would have good reason to be happy" (26); Gibbs/Johnson: "Anyone who can wrest a fortress away from him surely deserves credit!" (20); Sowinski: "He will get his reward, who takes a castle from him" ("Der wird seinen Lohn empfangen, der ihm eine Burg abnimmt," 42). Absent from all of these is any consideration of the adverb *immer* (always), i.e., the reward would be forever.
70. It is worth speculating on whether this could have included some sort of recitation or even musical performance in the *Minnesang* style. The reward, or *miete*, would be appropriate to such an interpretation and would not necessarily exclude the nobility, given that some known poets were of high rank. Horant is of course well known for his musical mastery and singing voice, as will become evident later on.
71. A young princess was often referred to as a queen, without any assumption of sovereign authority. The title stressed her royal lineage.

[226] Then the brave man said, "In this matter I'm well informed. I've never met a young woman more beautiful than the eminent Hilde from Ireland, fierce Hagen's daughter. She's truly well suited to be a queen."

[227] Hetel then asked, "Could it ever come to pass that her father [might give] me that beautiful woman? If he deemed me worthy, I would love and serve her, and I would forever be indebted to whomever helped me win that maiden."

[228] "That could never come to pass," said Horant. "No one goes to Hagen's land as an envoy. I [myself] wouldn't be in any great hurry. [Whoever is sent there] ends up condemned to death by [hanging]."[72]

[229] Then Hetel replied, "My desire for her is great. If he [hangs] one of my messengers, then Hagen himself, the king of the Irish, will have to die. As brazen as he is, his ruthless attitude will be his undoing."

[230] Then Fruote said, "If Wate would agree to be your ambassador to Ireland, we might well succeed in bringing the lady back to you, unless we were mortally wounded and stabbed through the heart."

[231] Hetel the mighty said, "Then I will send emissaries to Stormarn. I have no doubt that Wate will gladly travel [wherever] I ask him to go. Have Irolt and his men come to me from Frisia."

[232] The envoys rode swiftly to the land of Stormarn, where they found Wate the bold with his heroes. They presented the king's message that he should appear before him. Wate wondered what the king of Hegelingen wanted from him.

[233] He asked if he should take his helmet or chain mail and some of his men with him. One of the envoys said, "We didn't hear anything about needing armed men, just that he wanted to see you."

[234] Wate was ready to depart. He left to his people the land and the towns. Once he had mounted his horse, no more than twelve of his men accompanied him.[73] Wate, the most bold of men, began his journey to court. [235] He arrived in Hegelingen. After the brave man had reached Campatille, brave Hetel was greatly pleased and rode out to greet him. He thought about how he should properly receive his old friend Wate.

[236] He greeted him eagerly, and the lord shouted out, "Sir Wate, you are welcome. It's been a long time since I last saw you, since we sat together, when we tested ourselves in battle against our enemies."

---

72. Manuscript A reads: *den haysset man da slahen oder haben* (228,4). This has been emended by Bartsch/Stackmann to read: *den heizet man dâ slahen oder hâhen* (228,4b). The difference between the two, *slahen* and *hahen*, is that the former (related to "slain") could mean execution by the sword or some similar method, generally granted to the nobility. Hanging was common for the average criminal with a view to deterrence. This could also just be a tautology.

73. This number represents a very small contingent that still essentially leaves the protagonist traveling on his own, in *recken wîse* as a "solitary hero," not as a military commander. In the *Nibelungenlied*, Siegfried rides to the Burgundian court at Worms with only eleven other companions, having rejected his father's advice to take an army (*NL* 58–59).

[237] Wate answered him, "Good friends should gladly be together, then they can prevail all the more easily against their powerful enemies."

He took him by the hand and did so most affectionately. [238] They both went to sit down, away from the others. The king was powerful, and Wate was renowned and supremely confident in all his dealings. Hetel was thinking about how he could get him to go to Ireland.

[239] Then the young man said, "I sent for you because I need an ambassador to go to fierce Hagen's land. I don't know of anyone who would suit me better than you, Wate, my dear friend. You are a most persuasive envoy."

[240] Then old Wate replied, "Whatever I should entreat on your behalf and to your honor, I will very gladly do so. You can trust me. I will settle the matter for you, [. . .],[74] unless I'm killed in the attempt."

[241] Hetel said, "All my supporters advise me, if Hagen the strong would be willing to give me his beautiful daughter, that she should become queen in my land. This is my greatest hope."

[242] Wate said angrily, "Whoever told you that wouldn't be the least bit sorry to see me dead. Surely no one other than Fruote of the Danish March put you up to this, having me bring fair Hilde to you. [243] The lovely young woman is closely guarded. Horant and Fruote are the ones who've been saying that she's so beautiful, but I won't rest until you have me and both of them enthusiastically in your service."

[244] Hetel wanted to send for both of them right then. Several of his friends were informed that they should appear at court before the noble king. That was the end of their[75] private conversation. [245] Wate, the very bold, when he saw Horant and also Fruote, said right away, "May God reward both of you heroes that my honor and my journey here to court are occasionally such a great concern of yours. [246] You seem quite keen that I should be an envoy, but the two of you will have to come along with me. This is how we will serve the king to remain in his favor. Anyone who endangers my welfare should share the consequences."[76]

[247] Then Horant said, "I will gladly travel there. Even if the king were to excuse me, I wouldn't want to avoid taking on such adversity, where I might meet beautiful women, the source of honor and joy for me and my kinsmen."

[248] "We should," said Lord Fruote, "take seven hundred men with us on this journey. Lord Hagen treats no one with real honor. He won't fancy himself quite

---

74. This first half of the final line is defective. Bartsch/Stackmann have conjectured *nach iurwerme willen* (to your liking).

75. This most likely refers to Hetel and Wate, who were sequestered by themselves and had a close relationship, since Wate had raised Hetel.

76. There is a similar scene in Gottfried von Strassburg's *Tristan and Isolde* (8523–44). King Mark's councilors suggest to him that Tristan go alone on a bridal quest to win Isolde in Ireland. Mark calls them out and accuses them of wanting Tristan dead. The nobles end up reluctantly accompanying Tristan. McConnell mentions this in his note (28n50).

so daring should he mean to use force, and he'll be obliged to forgo his arrogance. [249] Your Majesty, you should make ready for the sea voyage a ship of cypress trees, solid and seaworthy, that can safely transport your troops. The sides should be adorned with silver buckles.[77] [250] And procure the food supplies that will be needed. Have helmets skillfully crafted, along with sturdy armor to take with us, so that we may all the better win fierce Hagen's daughter. [251] My cousin Horant, who is a clever man, should stand in his sales booth, which I gladly yield to him, selling clasps and bracelets to the ladies, and gold and precious stones. [This way] we can more easily gain their trust. [252] We should take weapons and clothing with us to sell. Since the situation with Hagen's [daughter] is so dangerous [that] no one can win her without a fight, Wate should choose those he'll take along on this journey himself."

[253] Then old Wate said, "I don't know how to sell things. My property never just sits there. I've always shared with heroes, and that's my custom still. I'm not suited to selling little trinkets to pretty women. [254] Since my nephew Horant recommended me, he knows full well what the situation is with Hagen. His strength is equal to twenty-six men. If he discovers our true purpose, we'll be hard pressed to leave again. [255] Your Majesty, make haste and order that our ship's decks be covered with planks. Below decks should be full of tough warriors who'll help us fight if fierce Hagen decides not to let us go quietly. [256] About a hundred of them should take along arms and armor to Ireland, and my nephew Horant, along with two hundred men, will stay around the sales booth. That way the pretty ladies will flock to him. [257] Furthermore, three solid cogs[78] should be built to transport horses and supplies, staying close by, so that in a year's time we'll still have enough of them. We should tell Hagen that we barely escaped from Stormarn, [258] and that [we] have fallen into disgrace with King Hetel. With our generous gifts we should often go see Hilde and Hagen at court; that way the king will grant us his permanent pledge of safety. [259] We should tell everyone that we've been banished. Fierce Hagen will then quickly sympathize with me. They will accommodate us as exiled foreigners. That way Hagen will make sure we want for nothing in his land."

[260] Hetel asked the heroes, "When could you depart from here, my dear friends?"

---

77. Manuscript A reads: *von silber weysse spangen sullen <u>seule</u> werdenn geslagen* (249,4). The precise meaning of the original text is in dispute. The point of contention hinges on the meaning of *seule*, which would normally be some kind of column or perhaps mast. Somehow affixing or fastening these with metal buckles or clasps doesn't make sense. Martin emends to "they should be fastened/affixed/joined" (*suln si werden beslagen*), with "they" presumably referring back to the cypress trees. McConnell (29) and Murdoch (22) opt for "masts," while Gibbs/Johnson (22) translate with "freeboards." The actual construction of the ship refers to sides (*wende*) fastened with silver (264,4).

78. These were tall, square-rigged merchant or supply ships, common in the Hanseatic League and able to transport large amounts of goods over long distances.

They said, "As soon as winter gives way to summer, we'll be fully equipped and then return to court. [261] In the meantime whatever we need should be well crafted: sails and rudders, the cogs and galleys[79] that we will sail, so that the ocean swell can't harm us."

[262] Lord Hetel said, "Go back now to your own land. Don't squander your money on horses or clothing. Anyone who goes with you, I'll be sure to outfit them such that any lady would be honored to take notice of you."

[263] Wate took his leave and rode back to Stormland. Horant and Fruote returned immediately to the Danish March, where they were lords. They had [no] intention of renouncing their service to King Hetel. [264] Then Hetel let it be known at home what he wanted. His ship builders and carpenters were kept busy enough; they constructed his ships in the best way possible. The sides were joined to the frame with silver rivets. [265] The masts were made solid and sound, and the rudders were wrapped with bright gold, glowing red as fire. The king was very wealthy. Before they departed, they prepared [themselves] magnificently for the journey. [266] Their anchor lines were brought from Arabia, a considerable distance, so that no one before or since could have found any as good anywhere. They sailed all the better from Hegelingen on the ocean waves. [267] Then sails were fashioned day and night; the king ordered them to make haste. [They] chose the best silk they could find from Abalie, and those tasked with making them were busy at all hours. [268] Who would believe us that the anchors were made out of fine silver? The king's ambition and intent were fixed on the service of love. He kept many a man exceptionally busy since he was in such a hurry. [269] The ships were secured with planks and beams against the weather and against attack.

They quickly sent for those who wanted to win that beautiful woman. No one was summoned except for those the king could trust completely. [270] Wate rode from Stormarn to where Hetel was staying, his horses burdened with silver and clothing. He led four hundred men with him from there. Hetel, the worthy, gained many bold guests. [271][80] (272) Intrepid Morunc rode out from Frisia; he brought two hundred warriors. The king was told that they had come with helmets and chain mail. Irolt also arrived promptly. They were, after all, from Hetel's clan. [272] (271) Horant, that bold man, came riding from the Danish March. Hetel gained there a thousand or more dedicated emissaries[81] whom he was eager to send out. Had he not been so wealthy, he could never have accomplished all this. [273] Irolt of Ortland had prepared himself so that, had the king not given

---

79. This was a general term for a warship.
80. All major editions and translations have reversed the manuscript order of strophes 271 and 272. This translation maintains the original manuscript order for all strophes according to Bäuml (1969), with an appropriate notation as to the editions' revisions and the Bartsch/Stackmann edition's strophe numbers in parentheses.
81. This is an ironic use of the term *boten* (messengers), as Hetel is sending out an army of thousands to deliver his message of courtship.

The Book of Kudrun

him his equipment, his heroes and he were well outfitted and had little need to ask for anything wherever they went.

[274] The king greeted them all as was proper and fitting. He kindly took Irolt by the hand; he went to where he saw old Wate sitting. When the time was right for the heroes to leave the realm, [275] then everyone was told to pay close attention,[82] to make sure that whatever they took would be sufficient. The heroes saw for themselves that their ships were impressive. Hetel [shrewdly][83] sent his emissaries off to win fair Hilde. [276] Two new galleys, strong and sturdy, as well as two cogs, set out to sea, [along with] the best ship that anyone in that land had ever seen on the ocean waves. [277] They were ready to leave. Their horses and gear had been loaded onto the ships. Wate counseled [King Hetel that until] they returned, he should be of good spirits, because they all served him willingly.

[278] The king said sadly,[84] "I entrust to you the younger ones, who depart here in my service with trepidation. For your own honor's sake, lead the inexperienced heroes daily by your example."

[279] Wate said to the king, "Whatever happens out there, here at home you should make sure that your resolve does not waver wherever honor is called for. Protect the homeland. The young ones will not want for my leadership."

[280] Fruote, the bold, was in charge of the treasure of gold and precious stones and many other things. The king was happy to do whatever was asked of him. If Fruote wanted one of something, the king gave him thirty. [281] A hundred men were chosen to hide inside the ship, since the young woman was to be won through deception, in case they had to fight. The king gladly promised them substantial rewards. [282] They took all kinds of people with them, knights and squires, three thousand men in all, as if they had left their land and been forced into adversity.

Hetel said to the heroes, "May God in heaven grant his protection."

[283] Horant said to the king, "Have no fear. When you see us return, you will behold a woman so beautiful that you'll be glad to welcome her."

The king was happy to hear it, but their return was still a long way off. [284] He gave many of them their leave with a kiss. The young king was saddened

---

82. Manuscript A reads: *da hiess man allenthalben vil klaine nemen war* (275,1). Störmer-Caysa has a unique translation for this line: "they dispensed everywhere with checking to see if they had everything" ("da verzichtete man überall darauf, überprüfen zu lassen, ob sie alles hätten"). Bartsch/Stackmann, on the other hand, translate the phrase in question in their gloss: "to ensure carefully" ("sorgfältig dafür sorgen").

83. McConnell goes back to the manuscript's reading *lustlich* (275,4b) instead of the Bartsch/Stackmann emendation *listecliche* and translates "gave his men a most pleasant send-off on this trip" (31). Martin emends to *costliche*, resulting in an alternate translation: "sent . . . at great expense."

84. McConnell reads the manuscript's *trawrende* (278,1a) as *trawende*, which he translates "with hope, confidence, having faith" (31n56). There is no compelling argument for emending the original text in this way.

on account of their hardships; he always feared for their safety. The king was inconsolable on their account.

[285] They were fortunate to have a wind out of the north fill the heroes' sails, as they had hoped. Their ships set out smoothly as they left the land behind. Those who knew about hardship instructed the inexperienced men. [286] It's difficult for us to know, nor can we recount, where they were able to rest over the course of thirty-six days there on the high seas. They all swore solemn oaths to watch over those who traveled with them.[85] [287] Whatever their purpose out there on the stormy seas, they still sometimes suffered from harsh conditions. Aside from that they were able to [rest][86] from time to time. Whoever goes to sea must deal with such adversities. [288] The sea carried them some thousand miles to Hagen's castle at Balian. As we hear tell, he had ruled brutally in Poland,[87] but these are just foolish lies. That's not the way the story goes.

[289] When the men from Hegelingen came closer to Hagen's castle, they were spotted, and the people all wondered from which kingdom the waves had carried them. They were handsomely dressed. [290] They quickly secured their ships by dropping anchor; their sails were hurriedly lowered. It didn't take long before the news was reported in Hagen's castle that foreigners had arrived. [291] They left the ships and carried to the beach whatever people needed. People found anything they wanted for sale there. They were hardly poor, but regardless how much money they had, they weren't there to buy anything. [292] Pretending to be merchants, the men were seen standing on the shore, sixty or more of them, all well dressed. Fruote of the Danish March was the leader of the group. He was also more expensively dressed than any of the others.

[293] Due to the arrival of these wealthy foreigners, the magistrate[88] of the town of Balian, along with his townsfolk, rode out to where they met the cunning merchants. They[89] were on their best behavior.

[294] The magistrate asked them from where they had sailed across the sea. Brave Fruote replied, "Our land is far away. We are merchants and have wealthy nobles aboard our ship."

---

85. This most likely refers to the previous strophe, where the older men now swear among themselves to protect the younger, inexperienced warriors.
86. Manuscript A reads: *rewe* (287,3a). Bartsch/Stackmann emend to: *ruowe* (rest). McConnell argues for keeping the original reading (32n58), meaning "concern." He translates: "they entertained serious concerns as to how it might all turn out" (32). Gibbs/Johnson translate: "but they also had periods of calm on occasion" (25).
87. This seems absurd, although again we should not equate this land with present-day Poland (the manuscript has *Polay*). It may, in fact, be a scribal error for the previous *Balian*.
88. McConnell (33n59) states that this is in fact Hagen, in his role as judge (*richtære*). This is not convincing, given the fact that in 295,4 Wate and the others are taken to see the king in his palace.
89. Manuscript A reads: <u>die gehabten sich so sy peste kunden</u> (293,4b). The relative pronoun *die* could refer either to the preceding merchants or the townsfolk, although it most likely refers to Fruote and his men, i.e., the "merchants." See McConnell (33n60) for a more detailed discussion.

[295] Lord Wate asked the lord of the land for assurances. People could see from his imposing manner that he [could be] harsh with those he ruled. The foreigners were brought to Hagen, the king, along with their account.

[296] He said, "My protection and my peace, this I will grant. Whoever troubles these foreign gentlemen will pay with the rope. They can rest assured, nothing will happen to them in my land."

[297] They gave the king costly treasures worth at least a thousand marks. He hadn't asked for even a penny's worth, but they wanted to show that what they had was well suited for knights and ladies. [298] Lord Hagen was very grateful and said, "[And should] I live only three days hence, what you have given me will be recompensed, my guests, in such a way that I would forever be disgraced should they be lacking anything."

[299] The king handed out what had been presented to him, including bracelets that would certainly please the lovely ladies. Expensive belts, headbands, and rings, all these were eagerly given away by the sovereign. [300] His wife as well as his daughter quickly recognized that such costly gifts had seldom been offered by any other merchants in the king's land. Before anything else, Horant and Wate sent their gifts to the court. [301] Sixty heavy uncut silks, the best that could be had, and forty select silks were carried onto the beach. Purple cloth and Baghdad brocade were insignificant by comparison. They gave away a hundred bolts of linen, the best they had with them. [302] Measured out along with the costly silks that were taken to court, rich fabric linings were provided as well. It could have been forty or more. If acclaim can be bought, then their gifts surely honored them. [303] They also brought twelve Castilian[90] mounts, fully saddled, as well as some mail shirts and fine helmets. These were accompanied by twelve shields, inlaid in gold. Hagen's guests were generous indeed.

[304] Horant and Irolt, the strong, rode to court with these gifts. The king was told—he was again brought news about his guests—that they were landed nobles. That was obvious based on their gifts. [305] They were escorted to court by some twenty-four men, those whom they had brought with them. They were quite striking and were outfitted, or so it seemed to King Hagen's men, as if they were to be knighted that same day.

[306] One of his men said to the king, "Sire, receive these valuable gifts that are presented to you, and please don't let the foreigners go unthanked."

As wealthy as he was himself, he thanked the guests profusely. [307] He said, "I gladly thank them, as I am obliged to do so."

---

90. Horses from Castile, in north-central Spain, were considered especially valuable warhorses, given their Andalusian and Arabian pedigree.

Chapter 5: How Wate Traveled to Ireland [204–371]

His chamberlains[91] were ordered to report there; they were told to pay special attention to the clothing. After they had carefully inspected them, they were astonished by these gifts. [308] Then one of the chamberlains said, "Sire, I tell you, here stand many chests made of silver and gold, adorned with precious stones, all rare and valuable. What they have given you surely amounts to twenty thousand marks."

[309] The sovereign said, "May these guests be blessed. I will share all this with my men."

The king provided for all; whoever wanted anything from him, he gave each one of them what he wanted.

[310] The host had the two young men, Irolt and Horant, sit next to him. He started by asking them from where they had come to that kingdom. "Guests have never conferred such admirable gifts on me in my life."

[311] Then brave Horant said, "I want to tell you, sire, may it please you, this is what we have to lament. We are men banished from our own country. A mighty king has [avenged] his great injury on us."

[312] Then fierce Hagen said, "What is his name, on whose account you had to leave your towns and lands? I see you as the kind of men, if he had any sense—you seem to me to be so worthy that he should gladly have wanted to keep you."

[313] He asked the name of the one who had banished them, on whose account they were in such dire straits that they sought out foreign kingdoms in their flight.

[. . .][92] "We will certainly tell you who it is. [314] His name is Hetel from the land of the Hegelingen. His power and might are as strong as his own hand. [He] has taken from us much happiness, so that by rights we are disheartened."

[315] Then fierce Hagen said, "Things have turned out well for you. What he took from you will be completely restored. Unless I lose everything that is mine, you needn't ask the king of Hegelingen for anything that is his." [316] He said, "If you men want to stay here with me, then I will share the lands I have with you and honor you in ways King Hetel never did. Whatever he took from you, I will give you ten times over."

[317] "We will gladly stay here with you," said Horant of the Danes. "We're afraid that if Hetel of Hegelingen finds us here in Ireland, since he surely knows the sea routes, I worry all the time that he will seek to kill us."

---

91. These were officers (Latin *camerarius*; Middle High German *kamerære*) in the household responsible for the care and storage of furnishings, clothing, and other valuables necessary for the management of a castle or estate. They were often nobles in their own right responsible for managing financial matters, including payments and collections.

92. This line is metrically too short and clearly deficient. Bartsch/Stackmann simply fill with a formulaic phrase: *dô sprach der degen Hôrant* (313,4a), "then the warrior Horant said . . ." This is, of course, logical but purely speculative, and rather than create an entire half-line out of nothing, the line and its translation stand here as written in the manuscript.

[318] Lord Hagen said to these comrades, "Come to the right decision and make yourselves comfortable. Lord Hetel would never dare harm you here in this land, as it would bring great dishonor on me."

[319] He quickly had them lodged in the town. Fierce Hagen told his own citizens to show them every honor they could. The sea-weary heroes could be seen enjoying their rest. [320] The people of the town fulfilled his command, and the very best houses (this was all done willingly), more than forty were cleared out for the men from Daneland. The citizens themselves moved out. [321] They brought large quantities of goods to the shore.[93] Those left in hiding often felt that they would rather fight hard battles than wait for good fortune to win fair Hilde. [322] The king had his esteemed guests asked if they would share his bread and his wine until they received royal lands from him.

Fruote of the Danes said, "That would embarrass us all. [323] If King Hetel favored us as he should, and even if we were to make a diet of silver or gold, we would still have so much at home that we could often enough satisfy any appetite for more."[94]

[324] Fruote had a roof erected for his booth. Such an amazing thing had never happened before in any other land, that merchants sold such precious goods so cheaply. They could have sold everything in a single day. [325] Those who wanted bought gems and gold. The king was appropriately grateful to his guests. If someone wanted anything of theirs without paying, they were often inclined to grant such requests. [326] Whatever anyone said about these bold men, about Wate and Fruote, what was done there in magnanimity was greater than anyone could have imagined. They were determined to gain honor. This was reported to the noble women at court. [327] Poor people could be seen wearing their clothing, and people who had lost everything had their debts paid and canceled. The young queen often heard these stories from her chamberlain.

[328] She said to the king, "My dearest father, send for your worthy guests to appear at court. They say that one of them is such a strange man that, if it were possible, I should want to see him."

[329] The king said to the young woman, "That can easily be done. I'll let you have a look at his manners and his conduct."

At that point Hagen was still unacquainted with him. The women could hardly wait to see how old Wate behaved. [330] The king invited his guests and summoned them, if they had a shortfall or needed anything at all,[95] to come to

---

93. Störmer-Caysa notes (591n321,1) that this must refer to gifts received from Hagen. While this is possible, it is also possible that the goods to be sold are still being moved onto the beach.
94. Gibbs/Johnson translate this line literally: "that we could often overcome great hunger by eating it [silver and gold]" (27). Murdoch takes a more figurative approach: "that we should always be able to satisfy even the greatest of hungers" (28).
95. Störmer-Caysa has a distinctive translation: "they should come even if they lacked nothing and needed nothing" ("zu kommen . . . wenn es ihnen auch an nichts fehlte und sie nichts bräuchten").

court and share a meal with him. Fruote of the Danes, both bold and clever, advised that they accept. [331] The men from Daneland prepared for court, so that no one could criticize their attire. Those from Stormarn, Wate's retinue, did the same. He himself was definitely deemed to be a [great] swordsman. [332] Morunc's men wore fine cloaks and robes from Campalie. Glowing red like fire, jewels set in gold were seen gleaming on the surface. Irolt, the bold, was well attended as he went to court. [333] Fearless Horant, none would disagree, was the best dressed of all. They were seen to be wearing cloaks both long and broad and light in color. These bold Danes all looked most impressive indeed.

[334] No matter how mighty and proud Hagen was, he went out to greet them. The noble queen arose from her seat when she saw Wate, but he wasn't in a laughing mood. [335] She said courteously, "May you be welcome. I and my lord the king have heard that you are heroes wearied by hard battles. Now the king shall be mindful of his glory and his honor with you."

[336] They all [bowed before her]; their behavior was respectful. The king asked them to be seated, as one does with guests. They were served the very best wine to drink that could be had in any royal hall in all the world. [337] They sat down amid lighthearted banter, as the noble queen left the room. She asked fierce Hagen to allow her to invite the formidable heroes to the women's quarters for conversation. [338] The king quickly agreed, as we've been told, and the young queen was very pleased. The young women attended to their gold jewelry and clothes; they wanted to see how the foreign retinue would behave. [339] While the elder Hilde sat next to her daughter, the lovely young women wanted to make sure that anyone observing their own behavior would say nothing but that each of them, too, was a queen.

[340] Then old Wate was asked to appear before the young lady. As old and grey as he appeared, she still had the good sense to be careful in her youthful judgment. The young queen courteously went to greet Wate. [341] She received him first. [She might have had regrets if she had had to kiss him.][96] His beard was substantial, his hair was interwoven with all sorts of costly threads. She asked them both to be seated, Wate and Fruote of the Danish March. [342] The imposing men stood in front of their seats. They were familiar with proper etiquette and had accomplished much in their lives in many a tough battle. The heroes were lauded for that; they received the highest acclaim. [343] Lady Hilde and her daughter, in a humorous mood, asked Wate if he enjoyed sitting with pretty women or if he would [rather] fight in hard battles.

Murdoch, on the other hand, translates: "pressed them to see whether they wanted for anything" (29), and Gibbs/Johnson render similarly: "in case they were lacking anything" (28).

96. This Bartsch/Stackmann insertion to repair a deficient strophe is based on a similar scene in the *Nibelungenlied*, where Ruediger's daughter is afraid of kissing the grizzled Hagen (*NL* 1665–66).

[344] Then old Wate said, "One does seem better to me. Although I've never sat so comfortably next to pretty women, it would be preferable that I, along with brave warriors, if it had to be, could fight hard battles."

[345] The lovely young woman laughed out loud. She could tell he was uncomfortable around pretty women. That led to [more] good-humored teasing there in the room. Lady Hilde and her daughter spoke with Morunc's men. [346] She asked about the old gentleman, "What's his name? Does he have people, castles, and lands somewhere? Does he have a wife and children in a castle? I imagine that they see little tenderness at home."

[347] One of the men said, "A wife and children he has back home. Property and life he has risked for honor; this is well-known about him. He has been a bold warrior his entire life."

[348] Irolt said of the bold man that no king had ever gained such an exceptionally bold warrior in all his lands. "As easy-going as he seems, he really is a legendary hero in his own right."

[349] Then the queen said, "Sir Wate, this is my advice: since King Hetel exiled you here from the Danish March, you should stay here. There is no one so powerful that he could drive you away from here."

[350] [He] said to the queen, "I once had my own lands. There I gave away horses and clothing to whomever I wanted. If I should now serve as a liegeman, that would be difficult for me. I'm [never] away from my homeland for more than a year."[97]

[351] The king was constantly offering valuable gifts. These exceptional men were resolved to take not even a mark from anyone. Lord Hagen was powerful, and their pride made him angry. [352] They departed then from there. Fair Hilde offered that they would at any time have permission at court to visit the women's quarters. They would suffer no dishonor.

Then brave Irolt said, "We were offered the same in our own lord's land."

[353] They appeared before the king, where many knights were gathered, and there they saw all manner of games. Some played chess, others parried with shields. They didn't yield to fierce Hagen as much as was usually the case. [354] As was customary in Ireland, people often played games for fun, and Wate participated and gained the friendship of the king. Horant of the Danish kingdom was often seen having fun for the sake of the ladies' affection. [355] Lord Wate and Fruote, both formidable and brave knights, were just about the same age. Their

---

97. Manuscript A reads: *von den meinen erben belib ich ymmer jares frist staete* (350,4). There is general agreement that the second half-line is corrupt. The word *immer* has been almost universally emended to *nimmer*, since the original hardly seems to make sense given the context, i.e., Wate arguing that it would be difficult for him to swear vassalage to Hagen because he is always away from home for more than a year at a time.

grey hair was woven through with gold. Wherever fighting men were in demand, they proved to be most valiant.

[356] The king's retinue carried their shields, staffs, and bucklers[98] at court. They often trained in defense and fought with swords, and they threw spears at sturdy shields. These young heroes were tireless. [357] King Hagen asked Wate and his men if they were as proficient in defending with the shield [in] their lands as they were in the kingdom of Ireland, the way his warriors handled [them]. At this Wate smiled scornfully. [358] Then the hero from Stormarn said, "I've never seen it. If someone were to teach me, for that I would stay here an entire year until [I] had mastered it. Whoever the teacher might be, I would gladly reward him."

[359] Then the king said to the foreign guest, "I'll have my best master teach you, out of affection for you, so that you can execute three moves whenever there is a fight in a tough battle. It might prove useful to you at some point."

[360] Then a master swordsman arrived. He began to instruct Wate, the most bold, and soon learned to fear for his life. Wate defended himself like an expert fighter. Fruote of the Danes had a good laugh over that. [361] What saved the master swordsman was that he sprang around like a wild leopard. That fine weapon rang out often in Wate's hands, and sparks flew off the shields. The master had his fencing student to thank for that.

[362] Then fierce Hagen said, "Bring me my sword! I'd like to have some fun with the man [from] Stormland. Let's see if I can't teach him four of my attacks and have him thank me for it."

Old Wate agreed right then and there. [363] The foreign guest said to the king, "Give me your pledge of security, Lord Hagen, that you won't try to kill me. If you wounded me I would be embarrassed in front of the women."

Wate knew how to defend himself, better than anyone might have guessed. [364] Hagen suffered so from the "unskilled" man that he started to smolder like a doused fire. The master faced the novice, who was remarkably strong, but the host gave his guest plenty of tough blows in return. [365] People were keen to watch on account of their strength. The king immediately recognized Wate's expertise. Hagen would have become enraged had his honor not been on the line. Of what was shown of the two men's strength, Hagen revealed more of his.

[366] Wate said to the king, "Let's get serious about this fight of ours. I've learned four of your attacks; now I'd like to return the favor."

---

98. A buckler shield (*buckelære, buckeler*) has been variably described as both a small round shield that was lightweight and highly maneuverable and therefore ideal for training, where the opponent would not wield the full force of his sword, and, as in the Bartsch/Stackmann gloss, a large shield with a central boss. Training with large or full-sized shields would be the sign of mature swordsmen who could withstand a strong blow and combatlike conditions.

He paid him back like some wild Saxon or Frank might.⁹⁹ [367] Once they had given up any restraint, the hall echoed with their blows. Whatever else they might have done would have succeeded.¹⁰⁰ Their parries were so violent that the pommels of their swords broke off.

[368] They both went to sit down, and the host said to his guest, "You said you wanted to learn? I've never seen anyone whose student I would rather be in such skills. Wherever such things are done, [you] are surely famous in the arena."

[369] Irolt said to the king, "Sire, it happened that you were able to test each other. We've seen this before in our ruler's land. It's common for us that knights and squires practice like this every day."

[370] Then Hagen replied, "And if I had known that, I wouldn't have taken up a shield and sword. I've never seen a student learn so quickly."

Many a noble mother's son laughed at what was said. [371] Then he allowed the guests to spend their time doing whatever they wanted. The men of Ortland agreed with him on that, and when they became bored, they hurled stones and took to throwing spears.

Chapter 6: How Sweetly Horant Sang [372–439]

[372] They were fortunate one evening to have the bold man from the Danish March sing, and with such a wonderful voice that everyone was enthralled. Even the birds stopped their singing because of it.¹⁰¹ [373] The king listened

---

99. This is most likely an anachronistic reference to two well-known Germanic tribes that were prominent in the Migration Era and known for their ferocity in battle. A reference to wild Saxons recurs in 1503,4.

100. Manuscript A reads: *was sy annders taten in mocht sein wol gelungen* (367,3). The normalized Bartsch/Stackmann edition reads: *swaz si anders tæten, in möhte sîn wol gelungen*. Translators have found various solutions to this line. Murdoch translates somewhat loosely: "It would have been better if they had indulged in some other pastime!" (32); McConnell: "These were clearly two warriors who would have been successful at anything they undertook" (39); Gibbs/Johnson: "They could have succeeded in whatever else they might have undertaken" (31). The difficulty presents itself in the first half-line, and the crux seems to be the meaning of the subjunctive "would do" (*tæte*) and the scope of "whatever" (*swaz*). One solution takes the subjunctive to mean the two fighters should have done something else to be successful, i.e., they were not going to be successful against each other. The other solution assumes that they would have been successful both at their swordplay as well as anything else they might have undertaken, i.e., they were two heroes who were successful at whatever they did.

101. The notion of a human voice so beautiful that it can mesmerize animals, and by extension all of nature, goes back to the myth of Orpheus. Ovid writes in *Metamorphoses* 11,1: "with his songs, Orpheus, the bard of Thrace, allured the trees, the savage animals, and even the insensate rocks, to follow him." Another Germanic hero who was a great singer and musician was the "fiddler" (*videlaere*) Volker, most prominently featured in the *Nibelungenlied*. In the final battles at Etzel's court, as total destruction loomed, Volker comforted his fellow warriors with his songs (*NL* 1833–35) and then wielded his "bow," that is, his sword, to slay the enemy (*NL* 1976).

Chapter 6: How Sweetly Horant Sang [372–439]

with delight, as did all his men, and Horant the Dane gained many [friends][102] because of it. The elder queen also enjoyed listening to him. It drifted through the window where she was sitting near the castle wall.

[374] Then fair Hilde said, "What is this I've just heard? The finest melody[103] I've ever heard from anyone in all the world has reached my ears. Were it God in heaven's wish that my courtiers could do likewise."

[375] She sent for him, the one who had sung [so] well. When she looked upon that noble man, she thanked him profusely that the evening had passed by so blissfully for her. The hero was well received by Queen Hilde's ladies-in-waiting.

[376] Then the queen said, "Let us hear the melody that I heard from you this evening. Make it a gift to me every evening that I might hear you sing, and accordingly your reward will be great."

[377] "My lady, if it is your wish and you thank me for it, I will sing for you at any time songs so lovely that whoever listens closely will forget his sorrows, and if he is attentive to my sweet melody his cares will disappear."

[378] He said he would serve her gladly, and with that he left. His singing gained him a high [reward] in Ireland. He had never been so richly rewarded at home; the man from the Danish March had also served Hetel in this way. [379] As the night came to an end and dawn arrived, Horant began to sing so that all the birds in the bushes fell silent from his sweet singing. The people sleeping there soon awoke. [380] His song sounded lovely, ever higher and more beautiful. Hagen heard it himself. He was sitting next to his wife, and they left their room to go out onto the rampart. The foreign guest was fortunate; the young queen had heard it as well. [381] Fierce Hagen's daughter and her ladies were sitting and listening, and the birds forgot their songs there at the royal court. The heroes, too, heard how exquisitely the man from the Danish March sang.

[382] Then he was thanked by women and men alike. Fruote of the Danes said, "My cousin should give his inappropriate songs[104] a rest, those I hear him singing. Who is served by such an inappropriate dawn song?"[105]

---

102. Manuscript A reads: *da von Tene Horant der freude vil gewan* (373,2). Bartsch/Stackmann and all other editions emend *freude* (joy) to *friunde* (friends). Martin (1902) justifies the emendation in his note (p. 86) by citing a parallel construction in 354,2 with the same verb (*gewinnen*). McConnell stays with the original text and translates: "which gave the Dane great joy" (40).
103. The technical term translated here as "melody" is *wise*.
104. The technical term used here for songs is *doene* (singular *dôn*), as in 381,3; 384,1; 387,4.
105. Fruote's criticism is aimed specifically at the *tagewise*, or *Tagelied* in modern German, *alba* in Occitan or Provençal, "dawn song" in English. The theme of infidelity and the lovers' fear of being discovered in the morning by the woman's husband was indeed controversial and considered illicit in some circles. It is possible that Fruote here represents an older generation's critique of a new fashion. It is also possible that Fruote's condemnation is directed more generally at the singing of songs at dawn.

The Book of Kudrun

[383] Then Hagen's heroes said, "Sir, don't you agree that no one is so ill that it might not profit him to hear the voice that comes out of his mouth?"[106]

"Would that it be God in heaven's wish," said the king, "that I could do the same."

[384] After he had sung three songs, all those listening thought it not too long at all. They would have [deemed] it only the blink of an eye had he sung as long as it takes to ride a thousand miles. [385] When he had finished singing and got up from his seat, the young queen, who was being dressed for the morning [in] a bright robe, was happier than ever. The noble young woman sent for her father Hagen. [386] The lord quickly went to where he found the young woman. The girl's hand lovingly rubbed her father's chin and pleaded with him. She said, "Dear Papa, please have him sing more often."

[387] He said, "Dear daughter, if he wanted to sing for you in the evening, I would give him a thousand pounds. But my guests are so proud that his songs will likely not ring out for us here at court."

[388] No matter how much she pleaded, the king departed. Horant, though, cleverly concentrated on singing[107] more gallantly than ever before, and the sick and the well were unable to turn their attention anywhere else. [389] The animals in the forest left their grazing. The insects that should crawl in the grass, the fish that should swim in the water, they all stopped in their tracks. He certainly knew how to put his talent to good use. [390] Whatever he [sang][108] there, no one thought it too long. Even the choir chants of the monks seemed less dear. The bells didn't ring out as they once had. Everything that heard him yearned longingly for Horant.

[391] Then the fair young woman sent for him in secret so that her father wouldn't find out, and no one was to tell her mother Hilde that he was secretly

---

106. This could either be a direct response to Fruote's criticism or addressed to Hagen, who answers with his own praise of Horant's talent.
107. Manuscript A reads: *des vliss sich aber <u>weyse</u> Horant daz er nie | gesang so riterliche* (388,2–3a). The normalized Bartsch/Stackmann edition reads: *des vleiz sich aber wîse Hôrant, daz er nie | gesanc sô ritterlîche*. The note to the text in Bartsch/Stackmann translates *wîse* as "song, melody" (*Lied, Melodie*) but also acknowledges that Martin (1902) could be right with his emendation to *anderweide* (once again). Almost all translators essentially agree that Horant here begins to sing again, this time in an especially "chivalrous" or courtly manner. For example, McConnell translates: "Horand, however, again put so much into the performance of his song that he had never before sung more magnificently" (41). Störmer-Caysa, however, takes *wîse* in its meaning of "clever, intelligent" and translates: "Again Horant focused and was so clever to sing as chivalrously as never before" ("Wieder achtete Horant darauf und war so klug, so ritterlich zu singen wie nie"). I have adopted this interpretation since it emphasizes Horant's conscious effort to win over the court with his almost magical abilities.
108. Manuscript A reads: *was er da <u>dienen</u> mochte* (390,1a). Bartsch/Stackmann emend *dienen* (serve) to *dænen* (sing). McConnell chooses to stay with the original text and translates: "However he entertained through his melodies" (41), which seems to try to accommodate both options.

Chapter 6: How Sweetly Horant Sang [372–439]

in her chambers. [392] A willing chamberlain earned the messenger's reward. What she gave him in pay was red gold, gleaming and costly, the weight of twelve bracelets, provided that the master of song was in her room that evening. [393] He arranged it in secret. Horant was happy that he had won such goodwill there at court, since he had traveled from foreign lands for the sake of her love. She held him in her favor on account of his talent. [394] She told her chamberlain to stand in front of the house, so that no one would enter after Horant, until she had heard all the songs that he sang. There were no other men there except for him and young Morunc.

[395] She invited the hero to be seated. "Let me hear," said the noble woman, "what I heard before. That's what I want most, because your voice, more than any other pleasure, is the crown jewel of all entertainment."

[396] "If I dared sing for you, oh fair maiden, that is, if your father King Hagen wouldn't take my head for it, I would not refuse to serve you wherever I could. If only you were close to my lord's land."

[397] He began a song from Amile. No Christian had ever come to know it before or since, as he himself had heard it on the wide-open sea.[109] This is how Horant, that brave and good man, served at court.

[398] When he had finished singing that sweet melody at court, the fair maiden said, "My friend, I thank you." From her hand she gave him a gold ring of incomparable value. She said, "I gladly reward you, for you I do this most willingly."

[399] She gave him her hand as a pledge that if she ever became queen and ruled a land, he would never be banished farther away than her castle, where he could always stay with honor. [400] Of all the lady offered him, he wanted none of it, except for a belt.[110] "People will confirm this about me, that I can look after it with care.[111] I will bring it to my lord, and he will be most pleased by my news."

---

109. This could imply some otherworldly or mystical origin of the song, or it could point to a geographically and culturally remote source such as the Arabic Mediterranean. Amile is not otherwise attested but is similar to other place-names in the text's pseudo-African realm: Alzabe, Abali, and Abakie.

110. This is reminiscent of Siegfried taking Brunhild's belt (*gürtel*) as a souvenir of his sexual conquest in the *Nibelungenlied* (*NL* 680).

111. This is a particularly difficult line, most likely corrupt, and translations and suggestions for emendation differ considerably. Manuscript A reads: *daz ich sy behalten mag vil mynneklich* (400,3). The normalized Bartsch/Stackmann edition reads: *daz ich † sî behalten †, maget vil minnecliche,* marking the phrase *sî behalten* as a crux and emending *mag* (may) to *maget* (maiden). McConnell has tried to use the original text for the first half-line but the emended for the second: "If I might be allowed to keep this, lovely Lady" (42). Störmer-Caysa has an extensive note on these lines (592–93n400,2–4) and argues that Hilde's gifts (ring and belt) to Horant indicate that she is in fact pledging herself to him, not to his lord. Her alternate translation in the note reads: "people will say to me that I may keep them for myself / that I may look after them" ("Darüber wird man mir

[401] She said, "Who is your lord, what is his name? Does he have a crown, does he have his own land? He surely has my favor for your sake."

The bold man of the Danes said, "I've never known a king so powerful." [402] He said, "If we are not betrayed, fair maiden, I will gladly tell you how my lord took leave of us when, for your sake, my lady, he sent us here to your father's town and land."

[403] She said, "Let me hear what your lord would convey to me from your land. If it is my will as well, I'll make sure you know it before we part."

Horant was afraid of Hagen and was uneasy being there at court. [404] He said to the lady, "He wants you to know that his heart belongs to you, without reservation. Let him enjoy your favor, my lady. For you alone he has forsaken all other women."

[405] She said, "May God reward him for his regard for me. If he is worthy of me, then I will be his wife,[112] provided you sing for me every evening and every morning."

He said, "That I will do gladly, you needn't worry about that." [406] He said to fair Hilde, "Most noble maiden, my lord has at his court on any day twelve who can sing much better than I can. As sweet as their song is, though, my lord sings best of all."

[407] She said, "If your dear lord is so talented, then I wouldn't want to dissuade him from the notion that I might reward his desire for my love. If I dared do so in spite of my father, I would gladly follow you there."

[408] Then brave Morunc said, "My lady, seven hundred soldiers are at the ready. They freely share joy and hardship with us. If you join us on the journey home, you need have no fear that I would abandon you to fierce Hagen." [409] He said, "We want to obtain permission to leave. You should ask Hagen to grant you a request, my pure and noble maiden, that he and your mother might come see our ships, with you as well," said that good man.

[410] "I will do so most happily, if my father allows it. You, too, should ask the king and his men if I and my ladies may ride down to the shore. Should my father agree, then let me know three days beforehand."

[411] The head chamberlain had the right to be in her presence regularly. This bold man was at that moment bringing a message to the lady when he discovered the two heroes, who feared for their lives. [412] He said to Lady Hilde, "Who are these two sitting here?" The two heroes had never felt so vulnerable. He said, "Who gave you two permission to come to the women's quarters? Whoever allowed this has surely betrayed you."

---

sagen, dass ich sie für mich behalten / dass ich sie behüten kann," 592). I have tried to make the best sense possible out of the original text.

112. The original is *ligen bî*, i.e., literally to lie with, the sexual act that would consecrate the marriage.

[413] She said, "Don't be angry; they mustn't be harmed. Unless you want to make things difficult for yourself from now on, quietly bring them back to their lodgings. They would otherwise gain little comfort from the fact that one of them can sing so chivalrously."

[414] He said, "Is this the fellow who can sing so well? I know someone just like him. A king never had a better man. My father and his mother were siblings on their father's side. He was a fine, accomplished warrior."

[415] The young woman asked, "What was his name?"

He said, "He was called Horant and [came] from Daneland. Even though he didn't wear a crown, [he] deserved one. Even though they're all unknown to me now, we had a good life there with Hetel."

[416] Then Morunc recognized the man who, at home in his own land, had been exiled. He couldn't help himself; his eyes welled up and sadness took hold of him. The queen looked on the man with sympathy.

[417] The chamberlain also saw that the men's eyes were moist. He said, "Dear lady, I want to tell you that these are my kinsmen. Please help save them, these two heroes. I will be their guardian." [418] The men were apprehensive, but their hearts were moved. "If I dared do so in front of my lady, I would kiss them on the mouth, these two warriors. It's been a long time since I've been able to inquire about Hetel from Hegelingen."

[419] Then the young woman said, "If they are your kinsmen, then these foreign guests are all the dearer to me. Go tell my lord who these heroes are, so that they don't so quickly take to the ocean waves."

[420] Then the two outstanding knights took him aside. Morunc told the chamberlain what he had in mind, that they had come to that land on account of Lady Hilde, [and] how King Hetel had sent them there to win Lady Hilde.

[421] Then the chamberlain said, "Two things are important to me: the king's honor, and how I can keep the king from killing you. Once he realizes that you want this maiden, you'll never leave here alive."

[422] Then brave Horant said, "Listen to what I tell you. In three days' time we'll ask for permission to depart, saying that we want to leave this land. The king will want to present us with treasure and clothing. [423] Please support us in this request, we want only this: that with all due courtesy Lord Hagen allows us to return to the ships, and that he and my lady, his wife the queen, come to see the ships themselves. [424] Should we be successful, our worries will be over, and all our hard work will have paid off. If the noble young lady rides down to the shoreline, we will reap the reward from King Hetel at home."

[425] Then the shrewd man brought them away from the house, and the king remained unaware of what had occurred. They quickly returned to their lodgings and had good cause to be grateful for such loyal service there at court. [426] They secretly told old Wate that the noble maiden wholeheartedly loved Hetel of

the Hegelingen, their kinsman.[113] They discussed with that brave man how they could bring her home.

[427] Then old Wate said, "If she were to step outside the gate, and if I were to see [her] just once there beyond it, then no matter how much we'd have to fight the castle guards, the young queen would never return to her father's house."

[428] This bold plan was kept strictly confidential, and they secretly prepared themselves for their return voyage. They also informed the warriors hiding in the ships, who were glad to hear it, since surely they were tired of waiting there. [429] They brought everyone who was needed together, and they conspired in whispers among them, so that many in Ireland would come to suffer greatly. Those from Hegelingen steadily sought honor, no matter how much Hagen had to suffer. [430] On the fourth morning they rode to court. The foreigners were dressed in completely new clothes, all well tailored to order. They were ready to depart, and they asked the king and his men for permission to leave.

[431] Lord Hagen said to the foreigners, "Why are you leaving my realm? I've directed all my attention to how I might make my land and my kingdom appealing to you. Now you want to go and leave me here without your company."

[432] Then old Wate said, "The ruler of Hegelingen has sent for us. He's willing to do whatever it takes to bring about a reconciliation. Those we left behind miss us very much as well, which is why we're in such a hurry."

[433] Then fierce Hagen replied, "Then I will miss you. Now agree to accept my horses and my clothing from me, gold and precious stones. I want to repay you for your impressive gifts, so that people can't criticize me in this regard."

[434] Then old Wate said, "I'm too wealthy to take your gold with me. Since our kinsmen have gained us mighty Hetel's favor, he would never forgive us this offense. [435] But there is one thing, Your Majesty, that we ask of you. It would be an honor for us if you would agree, that you yourself might take a look at how we are provisioned. We would not have run out of the very best food for three years. [436] We will give it to anyone who wants it, since we are leaving. May God protect your honor and your person here. We leave you now; we can't stay longer, but we would like to be accompanied to the ships by an escort of the highest rank. [437] Your fair daughter and my lady, your wife, should come see our anchorage. That would honor us most, and should [this] honor be granted us, noble King Hagen, then we ask nothing else of you."

[438] The host courteously said to the guests, "If you won't change your minds, then tomorrow morning I will have a hundred horses saddled for the girls and ladies. I will accompany them and gladly look over your ships."

---

113. The phrase *ir friunt* could mean either "their kinsman," with "their" referring to Horant and Wate, or "her kinsman," referring to Hetel as Hilde's future kinsman. Murdoch, McConnell, and Gibbs/Johnson all agree with the first option. Bartsch/Stackmann, in their gloss, choose the second option.

[439] Taking their leave in the evening, [they] rode to the water's edge. They offloaded the best wine in the cogs to the beach, along with most of the victuals, and so their ships became lighter. Fruote of the Danish March was very clever.

Chapter 7: How the Young Women Viewed the Ships and How They Were Taken Away [440–87]

[440] The next morning, after early Mass, the young women and ladies, those whom Hagen wanted to escort to the shore, vied to put on their best dresses. Alongside them rode some thousand fearless men from Ireland. [441] The foreigners had heard Mass in Balian. The king didn't know that things were about to turn out so badly for him. The departure of the foreigners meant a complete loss of honor for his daughter. [442] When they arrived where he could see the ships, Lady Hilde and her attendants were helped down on the sand, and the lovely women were then able to board the ships. The sales booths were set up, where the queen could find all sorts of marvels. [443] Lord Hagen saw for himself everything that was on the counter, the many tiny treasures, all of which were quite expensive. [After] he and his retinue had surveyed things, the young women were allowed to look and were encouraged to take their fine bracelets.

[444] The king had boarded one of the cogs to have a look around. Before the door of the booth was even open, Wate had already raised all the anchors from the seabed. The women were then gently segregated as quickly as possible. [445] Wate paid no attention to anyone's displeasure; he didn't care what happened to the merchandise on the counters. The elderly queen was separated from the young maiden, and the men in hiding clambered out. King Hagen was furious. [446] People looked on as they raised the sails. Those who were thrown off the ships got a bit wet and floated like birds there in the water near the shore. The elder queen was in agony over her lovely daughter.

[447] When fierce Hagen saw the armed men, the hero flew into a rage and cried in his anger, "Bring me my javelin, quickly. Anyone I can get my hands on will have to die."

[448] Lord Morunc said calmly, "Don't be too hasty. However many pursue us to do battle, we'll hurl them into the sea. [Even if] a thousand of your heroes are armed, we'll give them a cool, wet resting place."

[449] When bold Hagen's men weren't ready to give up, the seabed started to sparkle; there was heavy fighting. Swords were drawn and spears were launched. The oars were thrown into the water; the cogs were seen pulling away from the shore. [450] Wate, always bold, jumped from the beach onto a galley, making his armor clang. He rushed to follow Hilde with fifty of his warriors. The proud citizens were eager for a fight. [451] Then brave Hagen appeared fully armed, with a sharp sword that was strong and heavy. Wate had almost delayed too long. The

hero was in a rage; he raised his javelin. [452] He yelled out loudly, urging everyone to hurry. He spurned his people on relentlessly to see if he could catch up with his foreign guests. They had done [him] great harm; he wanted to slay and hang them all. [453] He quickly gathered a large army, but he couldn't pursue them over the open sea. The ships proved to be unseaworthy and unprepared as [they] were launched, and these defects were reported to Hagen. [454] He didn't know what else to do, so he ordered the shipbuilders along with other men to come to the shore to make completely new, seaworthy ships. Everyone reported to him who could; he acquired many skilled, accomplished men. [455] They left Ireland on the seventh day. Those whom King Hetel had sent out after Lady Hilde added up to not more than a thousand men,[114] but [Hagen] had gathered three thousand heroes to chase after them.

[456] The bold Danes sent Hetel a message. They informed him that they were bringing Hagen's daughter to his land, to his great honor. I don't think they imagined that they would still have more hardships to overcome.

[457] Hetel, the sovereign, said cheerfully, "My cares have vanished, and I'm glad that my heroes endured such adversity in Hagen's realm. I was constantly worried about those who had left my court. [458] If you aren't deceiving me, my dear messenger, and if you aren't lying that you saw the young woman with my kinsmen there in that kingdom, I will richly reward you for this news."

[459] "I tell you without deception that I saw the maiden, and that she was terribly afraid. The queen said, even though they were many miles away from there, 'I'm worried that my father will chase after us in his ships.'"

[460] He had the messenger paid with gifts worth a hundred marks. The knights there were provided with helmets and swords and many a solid shield. They came from Hetel's townships as they prepared for their arrival at court. [461] All those he could gather together, he hoped he could assemble his men in the field with such great honor that a king's daughter would never have been more worthily received. [462] As much as they hurried, those who were supposed to come, it wasn't nearly enough to bring together all the people that were needed, which concerned them a great deal. Nonetheless he brought together a thousand or more of his followers to greet Hilde. [463] They were smartly outfitted, as it should be, the poor along with the rich, in gleaming armor. They wanted to escort the lady home to their land, and the proud, stately heroes were excited about their journey. [464] As they were preparing to leave, they heard a great clamor. Before their departure, they could see many people along the road, on the hills and in the valleys, as Hetel raced to where he would see his lovely lady.

[465] Old Wate, the hero from Stormland, had come ashore in the march of Walays. The sea-weary heroes all disembarked there. They provided

---

114. Compare this with line 282,2, where the number is three thousand.

Chapter 7: How the Young Women Viewed the Ships and How They Were Taken Away [440–87]

accommodations for Lady Hilde there in their allies' houses. [466][115] They wouldn't have believed it, the men from Daneland, unless they had seen it with their own eyes, that Hagen and his men would appear there on the shores of Walays, coming for noble Hilde. The men from Ortland were happily spread out on the beach. [467] They put up tents right there on the strand for old Wate's men. Life was good. Very soon thereafter they received the latest news. The stately heroes were told that Hetel of Hegelingen had arrived [468] and was coming for his darling, both he and his men. The beautiful young women were hoping they would be taken to their new home with honors; they didn't expect another battle. [469] They had everything they needed, food and wine. The local people who were supposed to attend to them gave the guests whatever they could. What they needed and what they wanted, they made sure there was plenty.

[470] Hetel was coming into that region with those he had previously gathered together, into his father's demesne.[116] They approached so splendidly in gleaming armor that the foreign guests were happy to see them. [471] The men of Hegelingen rode out onto the fields, where the hearty heroes engaged in equestrian games, enjoyed by the younger ones, to gain chivalrous acclaim. Fruote of the Danes appeared, and clever Wate rode with him. [472] Hetel saw them from a distance, and he was thrilled. He spurred his horse for sheer joy, that famous and brave hero, until he saw the two best men he had sent to Ireland, along with that worthy expedition, to bring back fierce Hagen's daughter. [473] Then they were happy to see that praiseworthy hero as well. Day after day, their joy only increased. Before this they had endured much distress in foreign lands, Wate and his companions. King Hetel now compensated them for their privations.

[474][117] (475) With joy in his heart, in his kinsmen's presence, King Hetel said, "My dear emissaries, I was overwrought with worry for you heroes, that all my troops had ended up in Hagen's dungeon."

[475] (476) Then old Wate said, "Nothing of the sort happened. I've never heard tell of such great power as mighty Hagen exercises in his realm. His troops are extremely confident; he is a hero in his own right."

---

115. Symons/Boesch (1964) and Piper (1895) place this strophe after 468 for the sake of continuity and narrative flow. The first Bartsch edition (1865) inexplicably places 466 after 489, while subsequent editions (e.g., 1885) place it after 468. The Bartsch/Stackmann edition reverses this and keeps the strophe in its original manuscript order, as presented here.

116. The term used is *erbe*, or "inheritance," and refers to the concept of *erbland*, which literally means "heritable land." It is best translated with the originally French word "demesne," that is, land not enfeoffed to vassals, but instead under the direct control of the sovereign and his heirs. It is also translated as "homeland" and "crown land."

117. Symons/Boesch (1964) and Bartsch/Stackmann move the original strophe 476 up before the original strophe 474. Most other editions do likewise, except for Martin (1902). Lindner's translation also does not change the original order. I have kept the original manuscript order, with the Bartsch/Stackmann strophe number in parentheses.

The Book of Kudrun

[476] (474) He kissed both of the grizzled old men out of love. The king enjoyed there a sight more welcome than any [he] had seen in a long time, if ever. I believe that that brave man had not in recent times experienced anything more agreeable.

[477] "It was an auspicious moment that anyone even thought of him, whoever advised you, so that we've now brought you the most beautiful woman, without exaggeration, believe me, that I've ever seen with my own eyes." [478] Then the noble knight said, "Our enemies are fearless, and Hagen is ruthless, so see to it as quickly as you can that he doesn't catch us here in this borderland. His extreme pride will cause us real trouble."

[479] Wate and Lord Fruote, too, both bold and brave heroes, took King Hetel's men with them to where they could behold fair Hilde that very same day. Later many helmets were to be smashed over gleaming shields. [480] The noble maiden traveled with an impressive entourage.[118] The men of Hegelingen with the king dismounted from their horses on the grassy field, and the noble retinue was in a joyful mood. [481] Irolt of the kingdom of Ort[119] and Morunc of Frisia, both of these brave men led fair Hilde by the hand to where they saw the king. Her excellence was worthy of a crown; there she meant to receive the hero. [482] Accompanying her were twenty or more maidens, all dressed in white linen, I'm sure of it. You could see these highly esteemed young women wearing the very best silks, and they were delighted by it all. [483] With all the proper courtesies, that handsome man greeted the one who would later become his queen, that lovely young woman, the object of his desire. He embraced her shapely body and kissed her tenderly.

[484] Then he received each of the other fine maidens. There was one among them who could well have been born into a royal clan; she came from an important family. She was one of the women who had for so long been held by the griffins. [485] Her name was Hildeburg, and Lady Hilde, Hagen's wife, had cared for that outstanding woman with honor. She was born in and from the land of Portugal. She had seen many foreign peoples, and she longed [for her] own kinsmen. [486] Hetel greeted the young women courteously, but they weren't out of harm's way yet. They thought themselves free from hardship, [but] the next morning, just as the new day dawned, they had to contend with great danger. [487] The noble retinue was greeted by all, and they sat down with Hagen's child

---

118. Manuscript A reads: *under ainem schönen huote* (480,1a). Bartsch/Stackmann and Martin translate *huote* with "hat" (*Hut*). Murdoch agrees and translates: "fine head-dress" (42); McConnell likewise: "beautiful headdress" (49); and Gibbs/Johnson the same (41). Sowinski translates *huote* as "marvelous protection" ("herrlichem Schutz," 87). Lindner is similar: "with a splendid retinue" ("mit einem stattlichen Gefolge," 91). I take the word *huote* here to refer to the coterie of young ladies-in-waiting that serve, watch over, and "protect" Hilde. This is supported by 482,1.
119. Manuscript A reads: *von Hortrich* (481,1a).

among the bright flowers under sumptuous silk pavilions. Hagen was coming ever closer, which was to cause them much suffering.

Chapter 8: How Hagen Pursued His Daughter [488–562]

[488] As evening approached, Horant from Daneland, that bold warrior, saw something he readily recognized, a cross on a sail along with an image of heraldic arms. Old Wate had little love for these kinds of pilgrims.

[489] Morunc cried out loudly to Irolt, "Go ask King Hetel what he wants to do now. I can see Hagen's coat of arms on a great sail. We've been caught napping, and we really did depart from him on fairly bad terms."

[490] The news was reported to Hetel that his father-in-law from Ireland [had] brought with him to that shore many cogs and also [many] galleys. [Wate and Fruote] both took up counsel with the king.

[491] Then Lady Hilde, that fair woman, heard about it. The noble and generous one said, "Once he comes ashore here, my father will with his own hands inflict on many a fine woman what no one in the world can imagine."[120]

[492] "We will surely prevent that," said brave Irolt. "If he flew into a rage, I would refuse a mountain of gold just so that, once the battle begins, I could see my uncle Wate fight fierce Hagen."

[493] Then the lovely young women began to cry and lament.[121] The ships were tossed about; an evening wind had brought many heroes to the march of Walays. In hard-fought battles, they gave them blood-red graves.[122] [494] Wate ordered Lady Hilde to stay in one of the cogs. Quickly shields were positioned all around the ship in order to protect the young women from all sides. There were a hundred or more knights there to defend the ladies. [495] Then all those on the beach prepared for battle, those who had accompanied Hilde and had kidnapped her from Ireland, to the king's harm. Many perfectly healthy men were in danger of losing their lives.

[496] Hetel could be heard shouting out to his men, "Defend yourselves, brave warriors! Whoever has never won gold, I will give it away in unmeasured

---

120. The Bartsch/Stackmann edition comments that this refers to Hagen's killing of the women's men in battle and not any direct harm done to the women. The note by Gibbs/Johnson on this line (158n51) agrees with this reading.
121. It seems that the women have already been put back on the ships to protect them from Hagen's approaching fleet (see 494).
122. Manuscript A reads: *gaben sy in die pluot varben selde* (493,4b). There are two pronouns in this half-line, one the subject, the other the object. It is therefore not clear who is doing what to whom, but based on the context and the fact that the receiving side is offered a resting place (*selde*), it would seem that Hetel's forces, given their position on dry land, would give Hagen's arriving forces a new, blood-red resting place on land. Murdoch (43) and McConnell (52) agree.

handfuls. All of you, remember this: here is where you make a stand against the Irish!"

[497] With all their battle gear they formed up on the beach. The whole land of Walays was plunged into war in those times [by those] brave heroes. Enemies and friends alike were intent on holding the same territory.[123] [498] By now Hagen had arrived. Facing them on the beach, spears were thrown there by brave heroes' hands. Those in formation on the sand defended themselves vigorously against the men from Ireland. This caused ever more wounds to be inflicted. [499] How unusual it is to give up one's daughter to someone who would repay him with a firestorm of blows on hard helmets, especially in the sight of beautiful women. Fair Hilde now sorely regretted running away with the foreigners. [500] There they stood, under the exchange of solid spears, those under their shields who wanted to inflict grave wounds on each other through stout chain mail. The water was stained with their life's blood. [501] Hagen cried out loudly to his comrades, and the waves resounded—he was that strong—that they should help him seize the shore and inflict grave wounds. This they were eager to do; for this their weapons were tested in battle.

[502] Hagen had made his way right up to the beach.[124] Swords rang out loudly. Hagen met up with Hetel, standing right at the water's edge, there on the shore. He had gained this position with splendid and courageous deeds. [503] Hagen jumped out into the water with tremendous fury; that exceptional warrior waded up to the shore. There they could see arrows being shot at him as if it were a snowstorm. This was done by the troops from Hegelingen. [504] Then a great clamor arose from the clanging of swords. Those who wanted to kill [him] had to dodge and duck his blows. Hetel, the mighty, came up to his father-in-law. Fair Hilde broke down in tears because of it. [505] It was a real miracle, as the books tell us, that as strong as Hagen was, the lord of the Hegelingen stood toe to toe with him. As they drew ever closer to each other in the fight, solid helmets could be heard ringing out. [506] The battle wasn't going to be decided quickly. Bold Hetel was wounded by Hagen. His kinsmen joined in along with Wate of Stormland. Irolt and Morunc were brave warriors in their own right.

[507] Then brave Fruote arrived, and along with Wate and his troops a thousand brave heroes surged forward with him there. Hetel's kinsmen from the Hegelingen inflicted many wounds; the invaders lay scattered on all sides.

---

123. Manuscript A reads: *wolten alle sein an ainen selden* (497,4b). This is another case of the use of the word "grave or resting place" (*selde*). Störmer-Caysa translates: "wanted to rest next to each other" ("wollten alle nebeneinander ruhen"). Bartsch/Stackmann gloss this line and translate: "at one and the same place" ("an einem und demselben Ort"), i.e., everyone wanted to control the same area. Sowinski translates similarly: "pushed toward the same place" ("drängten auf denselben Platz").

124. The assumption here is that Hagen and most of his men are still approaching the beach in their ships, ready to jump into the water once their keels have hit the sand.

Chapter 8: How Hagen Pursued His Daughter [488–562]

[508] By then Hagen's comrades had also courageously gained a foothold on land. The men of the kingdom of Ireland came up to the beach against their worthy opponents. There helmets were smashed; they struggled with determination to win back the ladies. [509] Hagen spotted young Hetel near him. From that point on the men from Daneland and from Hegelingen wounded many there. Others urged old Wate to force his way toward fierce Hagen. [510] Powerful Hagen broke through the throng. His sword cut harshly; he intended to avenge the kidnapping of those lovely young women. Many a mail coat was struck; he had been grievously disgraced. [511] Avenging his insult with the sword was not enough. Flung backward by [his] javelin, many a noble knight would never recount at home the tales of how he had won victories in battle.

[512] Then Wate came up swiftly, a noble and brave knight, to where he could see the blood of his kinsmen flowing from gleaming mail coats slashed by swords. Five hundred of his kin, those who had come to his aid, lay around him already dead. [513] By then the invading and friendly troops were completely intermingled; the noise there was deafening. Wate and Hagen pressed forward toward each other. Those able to get out of the way considered themselves fortunate. [514] Then the king rained down great blows on old Wate; he brought his strength to bear. Many brave men saw sparks flying off the helmets like flashes from a smithy's fire. With their powerful hands they could cleave helmets in two. [515] Then old Wate bore down, and the shoreline shook. The women were barely kept away from all the fighting. After King Hetel's wound was dressed and bound, he asked where he might find his kinsman Wate. [516] He found his kinsman there with the "Terror of All Kings." The man from Stormland defended himself such that tales could be told [about] both of them, how bold Wate stood his ground in mortal combat with Hagen. [517] Hagen's javelin, the one he carried in battle, shattered on Wate's incredibly tough shield. There was no better swordsman in [all the] world; Wate would not give ground to Hagen.

[518] Then he gave King Hetel's man, bold Wate, such a blow on [the] head that blood from the wound ran out of the helmet. The winds began to blow cooler; it was nearly evening. The entire army was engaged in battle. [519] Wate angrily returned the deadly stroke that[125] covered him in beads of blood. He crashed down on Hagen such a blow that his sword blazed brightly on the helmet's braces. In front of his eyes, daylight turned to night. [520] Then Irolt, the hero from Ortland, was also wounded. Although many lay nearby, dead by

---

125. Manuscript A reads: *Wate galt mit zornne den grymmen ferchschlag | das pluotiger zähere so vil auf im lag* (519,1–2). The normalized Bartsch/Stackmann text reads: *Wate galt mit zorne den grimmen verchslac, | daz bluotiger zehere sô vil ûf im lac.* Störmer-Caysa, in her note (595n519,1 f.), disagrees with Bartsch/Stackmann's interpretation of *daz* in the second line as a conjunction ("so that") and interprets *daz* as a relative pronoun referring back to the blow that Hagen received, translating: "from which so many tears of blood lay on him" ("von dem so viele Bluttränen auf ihm lagen").

his hand, he was unable to separate old Wate from [Hagen]. The women wept terribly, as they heard the mighty crash of swords.

[521] Fair Hilde cried out in misery to Hetel, the warrior, that he might bring her father out of danger from the grizzled Wate. He ordered his troops to follow his standard-bearer into the grueling melee. [522] Mighty Hetel fought vigorously. He reached old Wate, but that only angered the hero. The king called to Hagen, "For the sake of your own honor, bring this fighting to an end, and let no more of our friends die."

[523] Hagen asked loudly, enraged as he was, who it was that wanted him to end the battle. The brave hero replied, "It is I, Hetel of the land of the Hegelingen, who sent his dear kinsmen so far away to win Lady Hilde."

[524][126] (528) Then the proud one said, "Since I now know that they came for her with great daring, your heroes have only confirmed your honor. You managed to win my daughter with great cunning."

[525] (524) Hetel pressed even closer, as some still do, wanting to break up the fight. [Even though] Wate the bold [was] still furious, they moved apart, whereupon Hagen and all his men promptly stepped back as well. [526] (525) Lord Hetel took off his helmet. The call for an end to the fighting was heard all around. Hilde's father declared the battle to be over. The women had not heard such welcome news in a long while. [527] (526) Then everyone who had been fighting laid down their arms. Many of them rested, and many were in pain from the grave wounds they had received in battle. Many were found there who would never suffer pain again.

[528] (527) Then King Hetel left the field along with fierce Hagen. He said to the warrior, "Since I want honor for your daughter Hilde, then you, too, should want for her that she wear a crown where she has gained many splendid heroes."

[529] Hetel sent out couriers to call for Wate. They had heard a long time ago that Wate had learned healing from a forest woman.[127] The legendary Wate had restored many to health. [530] After removing his armor and treating his own wounds, he picked out a potent herb and a box that contained a dressing. Hilde, the fair queen, fell prostrate at his feet.

[531] She said, "Wate, dear friend, save my father! Whatever you would have me do, I will do it, and help his warriors who are lying on the field. I believe [you]

---

126. The order of this and the next four strophes has been rearranged in the Bartsch/Stackmann edition, the edition's strophe numbers are in parentheses, the original manuscript order in square brackets. There is good reason to think that this strophe (524 in the manuscript) is out of place, since it is Hagen who is speaking, rather than Hetel or Wate.

127. The term *wilden wibe* (529,3b) could refer to a number of types of women who were adept in the healing arts and lived "wild," which usually meant alone in the wilderness or forest. Among these were herbalists, hermits, healers, magicians, witches, or even various sorts of forest creature, half woman, half animal. Bartsch/Stackmann gloss: "woman adept in magic" ("zauberkundige Frau"). Murdoch translates with an alliteration: "wise-woman of the woods" (46).

can [heal] those who wanted to help my father. [532] You mustn't forget those from Hegelingen, Hetel's supporters. They have drenched the sand with blood as if it were rain. I'll only ever remember [the suffering] of this journey."

[533] Then old Wate said, "I'm not [their] doctor, and I refuse to do anything until such time as mighty Hagen negotiates a reconciliation with my Lord Hetel. Until then I am obliged to stay away from them."

[534] Then the noble woman said, "If only I dared go to him, but sadly I've wronged my father greatly, and I don't dare go to see even my closest relative. I think that he and all his men would refuse my greeting."

[535] Hagen was asked, "Hero, with your permission. If you wouldn't mind, your fair daughter would like to see you, the young queen. She would like to see to your wounds, if you are agreed."

[536] "I'll gladly see her, whatever she's done. I would also enjoy greeting her. Why should I not, here in this foreign land, accept her welcome? King Hetel can grant me and my daughter full compensation."

[537] Horant of the Danish March led her by the hand, along with [that] warrior Fruote and accompanied by just one maiden, to where she found [the king], to see to her father's wounds. Whatever Hetel might have wanted from her, she grieved for her kinsmen.

[538] When he saw her and Hildeburg coming toward him, Lord Hagen jumped up from his seat and said, "You are welcome, daughter, Hilde, great princess. I cannot do otherwise; I greet you most gladly."

[539] He didn't want to let the child see his wounds. They were bandaged for him, and he asked the noblewomen to stand back. Wate worked quickly to treat the king, so that the young woman would stop her crying. [540] When the medicine, roots and herbs, had been applied, he was relieved of suffering from his grave injuries. Once Wate had finished bandaging King Hagen's wounds, his daughter came back to him, where she found her father completely restored. [541] The master of healing was kept busy indeed. If he had wanted to gain wealth in that great military campaign,[128] then camels[129] could not have carried it all away. I've never heard anyone tell of such great skill. [542] Right away he healed Hetel of the Hegelingen, and after that all the others, whoever was found there. Those who could not be healed by any other treatment, he was able to save. He kept them alive and completely well.

---

128. Wate, as a nobleman, would not sell his services, as a university-trained doctor might.
129. The Middle High German word for camel is *olbent*. This originally meant "elephant" (Greek ἐλέφας, Latin *elephantus*) but was later used for "camel" as another kind of (similarly?) exotic animal from Africa.

[543] Then they wanted to get the young women away from there. Hagen said to Hetel, "We [should] stay somewhere else while the battlefield is cleared of all the dead. They hardly expected this day to come."[130]

[544] Hetel asked Hagen to accompany him back to his country. He was reluctant to agree, but he soon learned that the man from Hegelingen ruled wealthy lands. Along with his precious daughter, he later proudly rode to the capital. [545] The young heroes sang as they prepared to leave; those still alive were fortunate. They had left there, both poor and highborn, some three hundred dead. They lay there in a pitiful state, mutilated by sharp swords. [546] The battle-weary heroes rode into the realm, where everyone they met was filled with joy. But the kinsmen of those who lay there dead, they could find no joy. They had every reason to grieve. [547] Hilde traveled home with Hetel. Some who were far from home[131] cried. Afterward she made herself comfortable in that country. Lady Hilde was crowned by a mighty king, which was to the Hegelingen's honor.

[548] [Hetel][132] had accomplished what he wanted. Old and young alike carried their swords to the court; the foreign guests did likewise there, along with that mighty lord. Her father Hagen rightly praised Lady Hilde's wedding feast. [549] With herself so honored, the highborn woman sat there in the bridal seat. People say that five hundred brave men were knighted there. Fruote of the Danish March acted again as chamberlain. [550] Hagen had seen the great wealth for himself. Hetel's comrades had told him before that [he] was lord over seven wealthy lands. They made all the poor there happy and then sent them home to their dwellings. [551] Then King Hetel gave silver and clothing, horses and red gold to those from Ireland, so that they could hardly take it all away from his castle. He won [them] over as friends, which honored Lady Hilde greatly.

[552] On the twelfth morning they departed from the land. The horses of the Danish March, whose manes reached down to their hooves, were [led] to the shore. The foreign guests were glad that they had come to know Hetel. [553] The seneschal and marshal accompanied Hagen, as well as the cupbearer and

---

130. Manuscript A reads: *sy haben irs tages erpiten heer vil kaume* (543,4b). The normalized Bartsch/Stackmann text reads: *si habent ir tages erbiten her vil kûme*. The Bartsch/Stackmann gloss discusses various meanings, first: "they did not suppose that this would be their death day" ("sie haben nicht damit gerechnet, daß dies ihr Todestag sein würde"), or second: "they could hardly wait for this to be their death day" ('kaum erwarten können"), i.e., as warriors or martyrs they were in heaven and had thrown off the physical body of a corrupt world.

131. The term used is *waise* (orphan). McConnell has a long note (56n87) that discusses how the young women from Ireland could be considered orphans, now that they were being taken to a new home. Bartsch/Stackmann's gloss, however, argues that the term refers only to those young women who had lost their fathers in battle. See 557,4, which supports McConnell's reading.

132. Manuscript A reads: *Hagen*. Either Hagen or Hetel could be correct, in that Hagen was pleased that his daughter was married to a worthy man, and Hetel, of course, got to take Hilde home with him.

Chapter 8: How Hagen Pursued His Daughter [488–562]

chamberlain.[133] [He] had never been as well served at his own estate, by those who were so employed. That Hilde was queen there pleased fierce Hagen. [554] Meals and lodging were had along the way. Hagen and his heroes were so well cared for that they could certainly say at home that Hetel's followers bestowed every honor [on them].

[555] Hagen took Hildeburg in his arms. He said, "Take care of Hilde, for the sake of your great loyalty. The women will be easily confounded amid such a large retinue. Act with kindness, so that you may be the example of courtesy."

[556] "Sire, I will do so gladly. As you well know, I suffered much along with her mother, without ever losing her for one moment as a friend. [I] accompanied her for many a mile before she ever chose you as a husband."

[557] He told all the others to go on ahead to court. When the women could not stop their crying, he commended them to the sovereign by his own hands. He said, "Be kind to them, these lovely children are all strangers here." [558] He said to his daughter, "Wear the crown such that I and your mother never hear it said that someone hates you. You are rich and powerful, and if you allowed someone to speak ill of you, it would harm your good name."

[559] Hagen kissed Hilde and bowed before the mighty king. He and his men never saw the land of Hegelingen again. They lived too far away from them. Lord Hagen embarked and sailed back to Balian. [560] When he was sitting at home with her mother, the elderly queen, Hagen said that he could not have given his daughter to anyone better. If he had had more daughters, he would have wanted to send them all to Hegelingen.

[561] Fair Hilde praised almighty Christ for that. "That we have succeeded so well with our daughter makes me happy in every way, in heart and soul. How is her household faring there, along with gracious Lady Hildeburg?"

[562] Then Lord Hagen said, "The people and the country, these they have become accustomed to, and such dresses were never worn by ladies-in-waiting here with us. We have to leave her there; many mail coats were shattered for her sake."

---

133. These four traditional court offices are introduced early on in the *Nibelungenlied* (*NL* 11). From the thirteenth century on they became more and more ceremonial, with the actual responsibilities delegated to other courtiers and clerks.

PART III: KUDRUN

Chapter 9: How Wate, Morunc, and Horant Returned Home [563–86]

[563] Let us now leave this tale. I want to tell you about Hetel's clan, those who lived in that country, how they paid him taxes for towns and land. They all came to court when Hetel and Lady Hilde sent for them. [564] Wate rode back to Stormarn, Morunc to Nifland; Horant of the Danish March brought his heroes to the coast to Gyfers, because there he was their lord. They defended their homes there, their sovereign's name was known far and wide. [565] Irolt held great power in Ortland. He was lord there and so was all the better able to serve Hetel well, both near and far. The king was so outstanding, a better lord they'd never known. [566] Since he wanted to increase his prestige, wherever Hetel heard about beautiful young women of noble lineage in his land, he brought them to his castle as part of his household. In every way [she] wanted, they served fierce Hagen's daughter.

[567] The king ruled most happily together with his wife. Their life was such, and everyone knew this, that he would have given up the world for her sake. His kinsmen had never known a more beautiful woman. [568] Over the next seven years, Hetel fought three wars, in truth. Those who threatened his honor day and night, wherever they could manage it, were often dealt great losses by brave Hetel. [569] He founded towns and governed his land in peace according to the right of kings. He performed great deeds, so that it was said of him in faraway foreign kingdoms that he never wavered. He was a tribute to his name. [570] Hetel's reign was highly praised, and rightly so. Wate, who was very clever, never neglected to visit his lord three times during the year. He served him loyally both near and far. [571] Horant of the Danish March also came to court often. He brought the household precious stones and apparel, gold and silks. Whatever women should wear, he brought from Daneland and gave to anyone who wanted something. [572] The liege service, which the king's men performed for King Hetel, secured for him greater honor than other men enjoyed. Lady Hilde, that noble and powerful queen, made it all complete.

[573] Hagen's daughter Hilde bore King Hetel two children. When that had come to pass, they had them properly raised. It was reported all around that the land and its towns would not be without an heir. [574] The one child became a brave man and was named Ortwin. He was entrusted to Wate, who raised the boy so that his conduct was grounded in great virtues. He was educated from an early age; he became a famous man in his own right.

Chapter 9: How Wate, Morunc, and Horant Returned Home [563–86]

[575] The fine-looking daughter was called Kudrun the Fair of the land of the Hegelingen. He sent her to the Danish March to be raised by her closest relatives. This is how they served Hetel; in this they were ever attentive. [576] Now the young woman grew up and was so beautiful that men and women alike sung her praises. People knew about her far beyond her own land. She was named Kudrun and was raised in Daneland. [577] She was of an age when she would have carried a sword had she been a knight.[134] For this very reason, powerful lords coveted her noble love, but many of those who courted her suffered harm as a result. [578] As beautiful as Hetel's wife Hilde was, Kudrun was much more beautiful, even more so than her grandmother Hilde from the kingdom of Ireland. Kudrun was every day more highly praised than other beautiful women.

[579] Hetel denied her to a king who ruled in Alzabe. When he heard of his rejection, he was deeply offended, as he believed he was so powerful that no one else's conduct and virtue were more worthy of praise. [580] His name was Siegfried, and he ruled in Moorland.[135] Widely known for his courageous deeds, he was a king with authority over seven great kings. He longed for Hilde's daughter, because people spoke of her great honor. [581] He and his comrades from Ikaria, his armed retinue, often won much acclaim there when the ladies watched them. They often practiced deeds of chivalry there in front of Hetel's castle. [582] When Hilde and her daughter went into the great hall, they often heard loud noises in front of Wigaleis's[136] house, when those from Moorland were showing off in their chivalric finery, and their shields and lances rang out loudly.

[583] A noble knight could not have acted more properly. She thought very highly of him, and did so often, no matter how darkly complected his skin appeared.[137] He would have gladly shared her love, but no one gave her to him as

---

134. This is essentially another way to say that she had reached adulthood. A man could be knighted around the age of eighteen into his early twenties.
135. This indistinct, fictional territory has both African and Arabic characteristics. Originally the Latin term *Mauri* referred to the littoral region of northwestern Africa and the Mediterranean, what is today northern Morocco and western Algeria. Later, the term was used by Christians to refer to Islamic peoples on the Iberian Peninsula following the conquest of 711, and during the crusading period to refer to Muslims generally. The Middle High German word *moere* is here translated throughout with the admittedly outdated English word "Moor," although the generic reference is to any North African or Muslim.
136. This character plays no role in the story, but based on the context here he is one of Hetel's men. He is further mentioned in 715,1 and 759,1. The name itself alludes to an Arthurian character, Wigalois, the eponymous hero of Wirnt von Gravenberg's romance (c. 1210–20). Wigalois was Gawain's son and so was clearly a part of the inner circle of Arthurian lore. The name-dropping here may serve no other purpose than to place our text within this broader context of chivalric heroes.
137. The complexion of this hero's skin clearly places him in an African orbit. Siegfried's coloring is revised later when we are told at the end of the story that he had one European parent and that he had blond hair (1664,2–3).

his wife. [584] He complained excessively, and he was very angry that traveling all that distance had been a waste of time. Because of this he threatened Hetel with torching his entire kingdom. Those from Moorland expressed their great disappointment. [585] It was Hetel's pride that denied him his child, and that was the end of any amicable cooperation between them. He said that if ever the right time came, he would not hesitate to act against Hetel's interests. [586] They departed then from the land of the Hegelingen. Thanks to all this a noble knight would come to harm a long time after these events occurred. They did whatever they could to harm Herwig.[138]

Chapter 10: How Hartmut Courted Kudrun [587–616]

[587] At the time, people in the land of Ormanie heard stories acknowledging that no one was more beautiful than Hetel's daughter, noble Kudrun. There was a king named Hartmut, and he pledged all his love to her. [588] He was encouraged in this by his mother Gerlint, and the young ruler later followed her counsel. His father's name was Ludwig, from the land of Ormanie.[139] Once they were in agreement, they sent for the aging king. [589] The elderly Ludwig rode to see Hartmut; everything he had in mind was shared with him. When he heard the stories from young Hartmut, there was cause for concern, but the brave man still thought it commendable.[140]

[590] "Who told you," said Ludwig, "that she was so beautiful? Even if she ruled all the world, she's not so close to us in her capital that we could try to win her. Many envoys could lose their lives along the way for the sake of her love."

[591] "Nothing could be too far away," said Hartmut then. "Wherever a sovereign lord seeks a woman's hand and property to be his for always, he does so until the very end.[141] So please agree with my plan, I ask that envoys be sent to her."

---

138. This seems to be an almost extreme case of foreshadowing. Herwig isn't mentioned again until Chapter 11 (617,3), where he makes a very brief appearance of only three strophes, before becoming the main protagonist of Chapter 12 (630,2).
139. Manuscript A reads: *von Normande lanndt* (588,3b). There has been speculation here that Ludwig and Hartmut might actually rule over separate lands, one Normandy, the other Ormanie, but that distinction is not upheld in later spellings of the same realm.
140. Manuscript A reads: *doch preyszt im͚ der degen guote* (589,4b). The normalized Bartsch/Stackmann text reads: *iedoch prîste im si der degen guote*. The Bartsch/Stackmann gloss states that *si* refers to *mære* in the previous line, i.e., the stories. Lindner (1971) has an alternate translation: "no matter how much the young man praised Kudrun" ("wie sehr der junge Recke Kudrun auch pries," 111). Lindner takes *der degen guote* to be Hartmut, not Ludwig, and *si* is Kudrun, not the *maere*. Most translations, however, take the *es* in *ims* or the emended *si* to refer to the idea generally.
141. Manuscript A reads: *wo eines lanndes herre leib und guot | wirbet im ze state das weret unns an das ennde* (591,2–3). The normalized Bartsch/Stackmann text reads: *swâ eines landes herre lîb unde guot | wirbet im ze stæte, daz wert unz an daz ende*. The gloss in Bartsch/Stackmann interprets the phrase *leib und guot* as a circumlocution for wife, i.e., her self and her property. Bartsch (1885) even

[592] Then the elderly Gerlint from the land of Ormanie said, "Command that letters be written. Treasure and also attire I will gladly give the envoys who shall deliver the petition. Tell them to find out how to locate Kudrun the queen."

[593] Then Ludwig replied, "Do you know how her mother Hilde was taken from Ireland, or what happened to those brave men on their journey? These people are arrogant, Kudrun's kinsmen will treat us with contempt."[142]

[594] Then Hartmut replied, "If I had to lead a large army to her over land and sea, I would gladly do so. I'm of a mind to never give up until I have won fair Hilde's daughter."

[595] "I will gladly help make it so," said Ludwig. "You may rest assured that I will send along twelve pack animals loaded with my silver, so that this petition may all the more readily lead to honor."

[596] Hartmut chose sixty of his men to send after that lady. They were well prepared with equipment and rations and a good escort. The elderly Ludwig was a clever man. [597] When they were equipped with everything they needed, brave Hartmut and Lady Gerlint could be seen going to meet them with sealed letters. They sent the proud retinue out from the land. [598] They rode as hard as they could, day and night, until they came to where they were supposed to present the petition from the land of Ormanie with which they were entrusted. Meanwhile Hartmut was filled with thoughts both pleasant and painful. [599] At least a hundred travel days over water and land caused them hardships, until they had determined in what region the land of the Hegelingen was located. The horses grew weary before they were able to deliver the letters. [600] In the end, they finally reached the Danish March by sea. They had endured much before they discovered that place and saw the king. They requested an escort; they were sent the most excellent men.

[601] This was reported to Horant, who was a cultured man. They[143] also discovered that the story that had been told about Hetel and Hilde was not at all made up, and that people in their land could often be seen armed with helmets and shields. [602] Horant ordered the escort to show the foreign guests the way from Daneland and to lead them, that is Hartmut's kinsmen, to where they could appear at court. The heroes made every effort to do so. [603] When the envoys were seen arriving in Hegelingen, they carried themselves in such a way that everyone said they must be wealthy, whatever their purpose there. The king was soon informed at court of all the news. [604] The men from Ormanie

---

asks in a note if there should be an emendation of *lip* to *wip*. At the end of the sentence, the context might support a translation of 591,3b as: "he does so to the ends of the earth."
142. Manuscript A reads: *Chaudruon mag auch sy verschmahe* (593,4b). The normalized Bartsch/Stackmann text reads: *Kudrunen mâgen <wæne> sî wir smæhe*. McConnell has a long note on this strophe (63n100) and translates the last half-line according to the manuscript reading: "Kudrun herself may even scorn our envoys" (63).
143. This refers to the envoys.

were given lodgings, and people were sent to serve them attentively. The king didn't know what they wanted in his realm; on the twelfth morning he sent for Hartmut's envoys. [605] Among them was a count, who was especially courteous. The clothes they wore were thought to be very expensive, and they rode the best horses that could be found. They arrived to see the king at court in the best way possible. [606] The host and his men all greeted them kindly, but once he understood that they were in love's service, they were rewarded by being treated very badly. I think King Hetel was not well disposed toward Hartmut. [607] After the letters were read by someone who could do so, the king became angry that worthy Horant, a brave and mighty warrior, had given them an escort, without which they would have had to leave the king all the worse for wear.[144]

[608] Then King Hetel said, "It was unfortunate for you that King Hartmut sent you here. You will have to pay for that, brave and noble envoys. Hartmut's petition has offended me and Lady Hilde greatly."

[609] Then one of them said, "He wants us to tell you that, if he pleases the maiden, and if she wants to be queen in Ormanie and rule over all his supporters, Hartmut, who is wholly without dishonor, would be well deserving."

[610] Then Queen Hilde said, "How could she be his wife? My father Hagen gave one hundred and three castles in Karadine to his father in fealty. My family could then hardly accept fiefs from Ludwig's hand.[145] [611] Ludwig ruled in Frideschotten, and then he earned the hatred of King Otto's[146] brother, who is also a vassal of my Lord Hagen. He became [his] enemy, and for that he was hard pressed by the king. [612] Now tell Hartmut this: she will not become his wife. May that brave hero never pride himself in believing that my daughter would love him. You should direct him somewhere else where he might win a queen for his realm."

[613] The envoys were distraught. They didn't deserve the ordeal of having to travel back to faraway Ormanie for so many days in sorrow and dishonor. Ludwig and Hartmut were distressed by their efforts and complained mightily.

---

144. The sense is that Horant, as their escort, was the guarantor for their safety, and so Hetel had to be mindful of this in his treatment of the messengers.
145. Hilde refers to some time in the past when Hagen enfeoffed Ludwig with 103 castles in Karadine. The name of the land has been emended to Garadine in Bartsch/Stackmann and Martin, since it makes no sense that Ludwig should have property in Siegfried's Moorish land or that the name should be confused with the Garadie that is home to the count who rescues Hagen from the griffins' island. This Garadine/Karadine is not mentioned again as a land given to Ludwig or to Hartmut, his son. We don't know the circumstances of how Ludwig came to be Hagen's vassal, except that it means that Hartmut cannot be of the same social standing as Kudrun and her family.
146. The Symons/Boesch edition argues against this name in a gloss on the line. It seems inserted merely to satisfy an internal rhyme of half-lines (Frideschotten: Otten), and there is no other mention of this name in the rest of the text.

[614] Then young Hartmut said, "Can you tell me if you were able to see Hagen's granddaughter? Is Kudrun as beautiful as the accounts I've been told? May God humble Hetel for being so hateful toward me."

[615] Then the noble count said, "I can certainly tell you that whoever sees that lovely woman will be enthralled. They will praise her virtues above all other maidens and women."

Then Hartmut said, "I cannot go on without her."

[616] Then Lady Gerlint complained tearfully. She said promptly, "Oh, my dear child, that ever we sent our envoys after her.[147] I wish I could live long enough that I might see her in these lands."

Chapter 11: How Herwig and Hartmut Came for Kudrun [617–29]

[617] They refrained for several years from sending messengers. There were new tales told, the story [is] absolutely true, about a young king whose name was Herwig. He was often seen winning acclaim, which is still how brave men are recognized. [618] He wanted to see if the beautiful maiden would take him as her lover; he tried often, with great effort and wealth. But even if the young woman had agreed, King Hetel was opposed. [619] No matter what the hero did or however many envoys were sent, they were threatened there. That made him furious. His proud heart was weighed down by despair, and he made it clear that he wanted to be with Kudrun.

[620] It so happened, however it may have come about, that knights and maidens there in the land of Hegelingen, and beautiful ladies, too, caught sight of proud Hartmut.[148] Hetel didn't want to believe it. [621] When the battle-tried man arrived in that country, the highborn foreigners remained unrecognized. Hartmut and his kinsmen, those heroes, were served attentively, and he hoped that the maiden would still become his queen. [622] Noble women watched him as he went to greet Lady Hilde in the most courteous manner possible. They could tell from mighty Hartmut's demeanor that he rightly desired to serve highborn women in noble love. [623] He [was] quite tall, handsome and gallant, generous and bold. I don't know why he deserved to be rejected by the beautiful and regal daughter of Hetel and Lady Hilde, but it caused Hartmut much heartache.

[624] He finally caught sight of the one his heart desired, and many a furtive glance was exchanged. He secretly sent her a message, so she would know that

---

147. Her lament may well be that envoys were sent instead of Hartmut and an army. Gerlint is later characterized as a she-devil (629,4), so this lament is likely about not being tough enough or about being shamed by Hetel.

148. This seems to be a rather abrupt shift to, or perhaps insertion of Hartmut's character, after the introduction of Herwig. Chapter 12 resumes the narrative with Herwig.

his name was Hartmut, and that he came from the land of Ormanie. [625] Then she sent a reply to the brave man saying she was sorry, she certainly wanted him to live, that noble maiden, but that he should leave the court straightaway if he wanted to escape her father and all his men with his life. [626] She saw that he was handsome, and so she followed her heart, even though his envoy had been shamed and sent away. The one for whom his heart yearned fancied him, even though she had rejected Hartmut's advances. [627] So the well-mannered foreigner departed, carrying with him the great burden of how he might take vengeance on Hetel for that affront, but not lose that beautiful young woman's favor in doing so.[149] [628] This is how Hartmut departed Hegelingen. His confidence rose and fell as to whether he could accomplish his pursuit of that woman. Subsequently many helmets were smashed on her account. [629] When he arrived back home, where he had left his father and mother, Hartmut, now enraged, began to prepare for a great military campaign. Gerlint, that old she-devil,[150] was constantly goading him on.

Chapter 12: How Herwig Fought against Hetel and How Kudrun Was Given to Him [630–67]

[630] Now let us move on from how he fared. Bold Herwig, just like Hartmut, also yearned for Kudrun, the noble one. With the support of all his kinsmen, he diligently pursued that maiden. [631] He was her neighbor and had territory next to hers. Even if he had petitioned her a thousand times a day, he would have met with nothing but arrogance [and] rebuke. But no matter how much they opposed him, he did later marry Kudrun. [632] Hetel told him to stop pursuing his daughter. Herwig angrily sent a reply later to the king that he would not hesitate to confront him with shields, so that he and the queen, Lady Hilde, would suffer because of it. [633] I don't know who counseled him in this. Herwig gathered three thousand bold men who were his supporters. With these he dealt out much harm there in Hegelingen to her,[151] whom he had simply wanted to win for himself with kindness.

[634] Then the men from Stormland didn't think it was true; those in the Danish March were also unaware. Later Irolt learned, there in the kingdom of

---

149. This typifies the new hero's dilemma: how to exact revenge on a father without losing the daughter's affection.
150. The original epitaph is *valentinne* (female devil). In 738,1 she is called *tiuvelinne*, a variation on the theme of evil. Refer also to the note on line 168,2.
151. Manuscript A reads: <u>der</u> *die er in sein dienst* (633,4a). The *der* has been construed as both singular and plural. McConnell's note (68n106) makes the case for the singular, i.e., Kudrun, or "to the one," instead of all the Hegelingen as a people. Gibbs/Johnson agree. Murdoch, however, translates as a plural: "the very people" (56), i.e., "to them."

Chapter 12: How Herwig Fought against Hetel and How Kudrun Was Given to Him [630–67]

Ort,[152] that bold Herwig had attacked Hetel in force. [635] When Hetel found out that Herwig was by then fearlessly approaching with his army, he spoke to his men as well as to the queen. He said, "What do you say to that? I hear we're being invaded by a foreign army."

[636] "What can I say about it except what is good? It seems to me not unfair that a knight does in love or misery what people praise as honorable. How can he fail? Herwig is worthy and clever. [637] But we should make sure," said the noble woman, "that he doesn't threaten our heroes' lives here. I've heard it said that he is approaching your fortifications with heroes to make your daughter reward him."

[638] The king and his men were slow to react, and so Herwig went on the attack. In the cool, early morning he and his foreign host reached Hetel's castle. He later achieved great things there.

[639] While the [men] were still asleep in Hetel's hall, a watchman called down into the castle, "Everyone up and out of bed! A foreign army has arrived. To arms, you heroes! I can see many helmets gleaming."

[640] They jumped out of bed and lay there no longer. Whoever was inside there, commoner or noble, had to be concerned for his honor and his life. This is how Herwig pursued his wife by means of war. [641] Hetel and Lady Hilde had gone to the window. Herwig had gathered an army around him that had its home at the foot of a mountain in Galays, which mighty Morunc of the Walays March knew well. [642] Hetel watched as they pressed toward the gate. Kudrun's father would not have wanted to be on the outside, no matter how fearless he was. The foreigners enraged him; his people were ready to defend him. [643] There were a hundred or more armed men inside. The sovereign fought as well, and did so with enthusiasm. His troops were bold, but that [didn't] hold the enemy back. Mighty Herwig inflicted terrible losses on Hetel. [644] Often mighty Herwig hammered a fiery wind on helmets. The king's child, fair Kudrun, was a witness; she was delighted by the sight of it. The hero seemed worthy to her, which caused [her] both joy and pain.

[645] Hetel was resolute and wielded his own weapons. He excelled both in physical strength and resources, but the king acted rashly.[153] He engaged Herwig too late, so that they could clearly see the battle even from the castle. [646] When they wanted to close the gates, they discovered that their retreat made it impossible. They streamed back through the gate along with the enemy. Herwig's only

---

152. Manuscript A reads: *von Horriche* (634,3b).
153. Manuscript A reads: *der wirt der tet <u>unrechte</u>* (645,3a). There is some discussion as to the kind of *unrechte* (wrong) meant here. Gibbs/Johnson translate most literally: "he was not doing the right thing" (56), with a note (160n68) discussing the moral or tactical root of the error. Bartsch/Stackmann, in a gloss, argue that Hetel was fighting someone who had not wanted to fight him in the first place. My translation favors the tactical, not moral, failure, given the explanation that immediately follows, i.e., that Hetel had assembled his troops with too little room to maneuver. See also McConnell (69n108).

goal was a beautiful woman's reward. [647] Hetel and Herwig ran to the head of their troops, those two brave knights. The rims of the shields they held in their hands began to light up with sparks. It didn't take long before the two recognized each other. [648] When King Hetel recognized how bold proud Herwig was, he said to him in the heat of battle, "Those who discouraged me from accepting this warrior as kin did not know him. He strikes deep wounds [to the bone]."

[649] Fair Kudrun watched and heard the clamor of battle. Good fortune is often round like a ball.[154] Since that woman could do nothing to stop it, she wished that both her father and the foreigner could have what they wanted.

[650] She called out to him from the great hall, "Hetel, my lord father, now blood is streaming from the mail coats, the walls have been splattered with it. Herwig is a dangerous opponent. [651] For my sake I want you both to call a truce. Take the time for heart and limbs to recuperate from the fight, so that I can ask you both where Lord Herwig's closest kinsmen come from."

[652] Then the noble knight said, "A truce is impossible unless you, my lady, allow me to come before you unarmed. Then I will tell you about my kinsmen. If I'm granted security during [this] time, then you may ask me whatever you wish."

[653] The battle was halted out of love for that woman. The battle-weary warriors took off their mail coats and washed off the rust from the armor with water. Then they were presentable again, and everyone was happy that they had survived. [654] Herwig went to see Kudrun with a hundred of his heroes and found she was [of] two minds. Kudrun from the land of Hegelingen, along with other ladies, received him, but the noble and brave knight didn't trust them completely. [655] The stately young woman asked the foreigners to be seated. Herwig's courage soon made him very popular, and through his courtesy he found favor with them both. Hilde and her daughter were advised to end all enmity without [delay].

[656] Herwig said to the lady, "I've been told, [you]'ve since had regrets on account of my efforts,[155] that you are ashamed of [me] because of my low birth. The highborn are often happy among the poor."[156]

[657] She said, "What woman, so well served by a hero, would be ashamed of him and reject him? Believe me," said Kudrun, "I'm not ashamed. You've never

---

154. The Wheel of Fortune is a common motif in medieval literature. It is sometimes represented as a ball that can randomly roll this way or that, as in Gottfried von Strassburg's poem (*MF* XXIII/I), or as a seesaw that goes back and forth, up and down.

155. Manuscript A reads: *doch het es* <u>mich</u> *gerawen von meiner arbait* (656,2). The Bartsch/Stackmann edition marks the entire line as a crux and emends to: † - *doch hêt es* <u>iuch</u> *gerouwen von mîner arbeit* - †. The line seems to be an interjection into the *daz-* clause of the next line. Lindner translates according to the original version, with *mich*: "and I was hurt by that, given my serious entreaty" ("und das tat mir weh nach meiner ernsthaften Werbung," 124). All other translators accept the emendation to *iuch*, i.e., that Kudrun now has regrets, not Herwig.

156. This line sounds proverbial.

Chapter 12: How Herwig Fought against Hetel and How Kudrun Was Given to Him [630–67]

known a woman who cherishes you more than I do. [658] If my closest family members agree, then I would want to be with you, just as you wish."

He gazed at her with love in his eyes. She declared publicly, without evasion, that he had won her heart. [659] That bold warrior requested permission to ask for her hand. This he was then granted by Hetel and Hilde. They both wanted to hear if [their] beloved daughter favored the proposal or not. [660] He very quickly came to know how she felt. The brave hero stood before the young woman as if painted by a master's hand on a white wall.[157] This is how that famous man appeared.

[661] "Should you give me your love, fair maiden, I will always act with all my heart as you wish. My towns and my kinsmen will all serve you, my lady, such that I shall never regret it."

[662] She said, "I'm happy to confess that I hold you in great esteem. With your service here today, you[158] have earned that I should end the enmity between you and my family. No one [can] begrudge me that. You shall always be happy with me."

[663] Hetel was brought to the queen, and this ended the conflict. He was later followed by the very best men the king had from the land of Hegelingen. This put an end to all his grievances. [664] Hetel asked her, upon his men's advice,[159] right then, whether she wanted to marry Herwig, that brave and noble knight. The fair woman said, "I can imagine no better husband."

[665] Right then she was formally pledged to the man who would make her his queen. He would experience joy and suffering on her account. Then she was given to him as his wife. It happened very soon after the battle fought by many good men. [666] He hoped he could take the young woman away with him, but her mother would not allow it. This would cause him great hardship at the hands of unknown warriors. Hilde said that she wanted to prepare [her] better for the coronation.[160] [667] Herwig was advised that he should leave her there, so that he might over the course of the year divert himself with other beautiful women

---

157. The original is *weyssen wennde*, or "on a white wall." A similar reference is made in the *Nibelungenlied* (*NL* 286, 1–3) to Siegfried as a painting on parchment.
158. Here Kudrun switches to addressing Herwig with the informal *du*.
159. The future bride's public agreement to marry is a ceremonial act meant to demonstrate the suitability of the match, especially in terms of social compatibility. Kriemhild is likewise asked, or rather prompted, to agree to a marriage with Siegfried in the *Nibelungenlied* (*NL* 612–13).
160. Hilde's intent may be to prepare Kudrun for her coronation or for her role as queen of a foreign land. Unfortunately the motivation for this major delay in consummating the marriage between Kudrun and Herwig remains unclear and weak, although it generates a crisis the consequences of which turn out to be most significant.

elsewhere.[161] The men from Alzabe[162] heard about this and plotted to attack Herwig.

Chapter 13 [668–724][163]

[668] Then Siegfried, the king of Moorland, gathered troops and ordered ships to be procured. Wherever he found them, he had them well armed and supplied with weapons and rations, to Herwig's harm. He secretly gathered his supporters around him. [669] He ordered twenty large ships built. I think that those he called up were not pleased that he wanted to conduct a military campaign against Seeland.[164] [The expedition was to start] at the end of the long winter. [670] He gathered eighty thousand heroes in all, the land of Alzabe was emptied of its people. The kings of the Moors pledged to support the war. Some were absent; others obeyed the king's command. [671] He ordered that war be declared on [See]land, which offended the lord there. He had every right to object, because he had done nothing to earn the mighty kings' hatred. He ordered that the border and his castles be even more closely guarded. [672] He complained to his supporters, wherever he found them, that his realm was about to be put to the torch and laid waste. Whatever he had to spend, he gave out for military service. Those who wanted to be paid were satisfied enough.[165] [673] In the month of May they arrived from across the sea, those heroes from Abakie and from Alzabe, as if they had wanted to conquer the whole of the earth. Many among them were vain, but they were later ground into the dust. [674] They left only scorched earth in Herwig's lands. Whatever support he had gathered from allies, he had them ride out with him to fight bitter battles. They paid with their lives for their reward in gold, silver, or jewels.

[675] The warrior from Seeland was disheartened by his losses. He was a hero in his own right. Oh, how he could fight, until he made the battlefield fertile with the dead. The old were made young again, but many hearty men were left maimed. [676] The war lasted a long time; many men lay dead. Noble Herwig

---

161. This advice, although likely made by Herwig's own men and meant to support Hilde's argument for delaying the marriage, seems gratuitous, in that there is no motivation either in the text or in tradition that a husband should engage in a year's worth of romantic dalliances to pass the time. Störmer-Caysa has an extensive note (600-601n666 f.) on the weak motivation for Hilde's delay. The delay serves to bring about the conflict between Herwig and Siegfried and so may have no other purpose than to motivate the necessary crisis.
162. These are Siegfried's men.
163. This chapter, although clearly indicated in manuscript A with a large initial "D(ô)," has no title.
164. This is Herwig's land.
165. This seems to indicate that some of the troops were mercenaries, or perhaps reluctant vassals that wanted to be paid upfront.

suffered grave setbacks, and he had to retreat to his border regions. The entire country was in flames; he informed Kudrun the queen of this. [677] He sent out couriers to ride to Hetel's country. Those he sent out shed some tears along the way. They were received by Hetel and told him the news; they told the mighty king about all the needless suffering. [678] Even though he could see how [they] behaved, he received them as friends should be received in a foreign land. He asked them how they had made it out of their lord's realm, since the castles had been razed and the entire march was ablaze. [679] They said then, "We left there with some difficulty. Night and day Herwig's men are paying for their reward with their lives. They strive tirelessly for honor; many of their women can be heard crying."

[680] Then King Hetel said, "Go see my lady.[166] Whatever she commands, it shall be done. If she asks us to avenge the destruction in her land, then we will gladly support you. Herwig's injury will be fully avenged."

[681] Even before the envoys had gone to see that fair maiden, the people there clearly saw how they suffered. Noble Kudrun thought she could wait no longer, so she sent for them. She lamented that her land and honor had been lost. [682] The envoys appeared before her. It was out of loyalty that the noble young woman sat there and cried. She asked how they had left her dear husband, whether he was still alive when they had departed there.

[683] Then one of them said, "We left [him] in good health. Since we departed from there, we have no knowledge of how the men [from] Moorland have dealt with him. Many of them have been killed; they did nothing but pillage and burn. [684] Now hear, noble maiden, what my lord bade us tell you. He and his heroes are in grave danger. They fear every day that they will lose life and honor. My Lord Herwig is now putting your fidelity to the test, dear [lady]."

[685] Kudrun arose from her seat, that fair maiden. She reported all the damage done to the king, both that her people were being slaughtered and the castles razed. She asked her father Hetel to ride to King Herwig's aid.

[686] She embraced her father with tears in her eyes, "Help, noble king! My suffering will be all too great if your men don't quickly come to the aid of my friends. Surely no one else can make this right."

[687] "I will let no one prevent me, I tell you this, from going [to] Herwig as soon as possible. [I] will put an end to your great losses as best I can, and I will send for old Wate and for the others. [688] He will bring all the men he has out of Stormarn. Once Lord Morunc hears how things stand in that country, he will send us at least a thousand brave heroes. The enemy will discover that we are willing to respond with force. [689] Horant of the Danish March will lead three thousand knights in the campaign. Irolt will assemble all the troops under his

---

166. This refers to Kudrun. She is being treated here as a queen with full rights to demand vengeance for the attack on her husband's land.

banner, and her brother Ortwin will come as well. Then my daughter can praise our support."

[690] Couriers rode out quickly, sent by that young woman. They knew of no help nearby.[167] All who wanted to ease her suffering with their support, she showed them great honor. She knew how to welcome heroes, so all the more warriors rallied to her.

[691] Hilde, the young woman's mother, said in support, "Whoever volunteers to help your friends in the service of arms when they leave here will receive a portion of everything we gain."

[692] Then the arms chests were opened. They carried to court plenty of armor, which they knew to be inside, well fastened with steel. Many white-silver mail coats were brought for the heroes, and the young queen was encouraged by that. [693] The sovereign gave horses and tackle to a thousand heroes. They were led out of the stables, as often happens when men ride out to war on long journeys. Of those the king owned, he was determined to leave very few at home.

[694] The sovereign then took leave of his wife. Hilde and her daughter began to cry, but they were pleased to see the heroes riding with him. They said, "May God in heaven grant that you win glory and honor."

[695] When they arrived at the castle gate, they heard many squires in front of it singing. They imagined the plunder that would come from hard fighting. They still had far to ride; the enemy was nowhere near them. [696] Very early on the third morning, old Wate linked up with them with a thousand heroes. On the seventh morning, Horant arrived from Daneland with the four thousand that fair Kudrun had requested. [697] From the Walays March came brave Morunc. He wanted to fight to gain the love of beautiful women. He brought—this is [true]—two thousand well-armed men who all rode on with good cheer. [698] The queen's brother, that brave man Ortwin, led some four thousand or more across the ocean waves for his sister. If those from Alzabe had known, they would have been very afraid. [699] By the time [they] came to the aid of Herwig and his men, he had already endured setbacks. Whatever he undertook, he and his brothers in arms often suffered great casualties, and the enemy had advanced up to his castle gate. [700] Great suffering was caused by these kings' kinsmen, as

---

167. Manuscript A reads: *sy westen nicht so nahes* (690,2a). Bartsch/Stackmann indicate a likely corruption of the text and offer various interpretations, essentially that the messengers had to seek help from afar, since they knew of none nearby. Störmer-Caysa offers another possibility in her translation: "They knew nothing about what was so close to them" ("was ihnen so nah war, davon wussten sie nichts"), i.e., Hartmut's future attack, which was close in time, not in distance. There is also some argument to emend the plural verb form *westen* to the singular *weste* to refer to Kudrun (Bartsch/Stackmann gloss; Gibbs/Johnson, 160n72; McConnell, 74n113).

they breached the [gates][168] and razed strong castles. This is what comes of treachery and great arrogance. Whoever acts in this way is never accorded good for it.[169]

[701] The couriers hurried back; Herwig was informed of this. The enemy, urged on by their hatred, went on the attack, often late at night or early in the morning. It soon became evident that Herwig's allies were advancing from all directions. [702] When the men from Karadie[170] heard this, they were troubled. Two kings were there whose efforts ended in dismal disappointment, as mighty Hetel pursued them from far away with his legendary heroes. [703] Because they were allies,[171] they prepared to defend themselves.[172] The army from Moorland gave the impression that they would retreat from no one in battle. Those who wanted to confront them would be rewarded with many hardships.

[704] Wate the bold arrived with a large force. Fair Kudrun had sent her husband Herwig a great contingent of knights. However they fared there, they would later leave in good cheer.[173] [705] Although the men from Moorland were [Muslims], they could not be overrun. It was clear to see that they were among the best in all the world; they often gave their opponents a ruinous resting place. [706] Herwig of Seeland wanted to avenge his losses on the men from Alzabe. For this the armies on both sides would have to suffer. Many of their kinsmen would often be sorely wounded, and King Hetel was greatly troubled because of it. [707] When they finally clashed, those I've spoken about, with all their forces, the men suffered without [joy][174] and agonized constantly about what would happen to them at night. They wondered, "How will we survive until morning?"

[708] They fought three battles against the Moors, but the towns were spared according to the rules of chivalry. They opposed each other sharply with swords

---

168. Manuscript A reads: *herten* ("hard," an adjective paired with strong), but *porten* has been proposed by Bartsch/Stackmann and others, meaning either "gates" or "harbors." Martin emends to *warten* ("towers") but misread the original as *horten*.
169. The portrayal of "heathen" knights, i.e., Muslims, often acknowledges their courage in battle (e.g., 705) but also emphasizes their arrogance and vanity (e.g., 673,4). This is the case in the *Nibelungenlied*, where some of Etzel's non-Christian troops are characterized in much the same way (*NL* 1885).
170. This is Siegfried's land.
171. Manuscript A reads: *freunde* (703,1a). This is emended by Bartsch/Stackmann to *frevele* (conceited, overconfident). McConnell argues for the original text, since "these two kings, who were fighting for Siegfried, being friends or allies, prepared to defend themselves . . . against the onslaught of the approaching Hegelings" (75n114). I've chosen the original text as well.
172. This refers to the Moorish forces.
173. McConnell argues against an emendation of the original *froelichen* (happily) to Bartsch/Stackmann's *unfroelichen* (unhappily), since "this engagement would conclude on a happy note for the Hegelings" (75n115). I agree.
174. Manuscript A reads: *freunde* (friends or allies), which is emended by Bartsch/Stackmann to *freude* (joy or happiness). The original reading is also plausible, i.e., Siegfried's forces could not rely on reinforcements from other allies.

and spears; they did not seek quarter, which only increased their wounds. [709] The enemy and friendly forces would not cease their constant fighting. Because of that their best men were left lying on the battlefield, as they did not want to stop. This was reported to noble women, who cried beyond measure.

[710] Wate the bold, how he fought there in battle! He was very clever, and he often inflicted great suffering and destruction on the foreign enemies. He was always seen with his heroes, next to the very best of them. [711] Horant of the Danish March was definitely brave. How many solid helmets he cleaved with his own hands! He also rarely forgot the bright mail coats. They owed him a debt; he thinned out the enemy's dense masses. [712] Morunc the daring often stretched his hand out over the shield's rim with bold courage. He would not retreat from the men [of] Moorland, those noble and mighty kings. On them he avenged the injury to Herwig. [713] Hetel the mighty, because his fair daughter had sent him out to Herwig's realm to make peace, conducted himself accordingly. Whoever wanted to live would have to leave his border lands in peace. [714] Herwig himself fought better than anyone else, there before the gates and on the field. His face was drenched in sweat under the chain mail. Many of those who hoped to force him back were knocked unconscious. [715] Wigaleis the valiant inflicted pain on the enemy. Fruote of Daneland fought with such chivalry that he deserved the gratitude and honor he received. [He] was skilled in battle; never before had they seen such a formidable old warrior. [716] Ortwin the young, the hero from Ortland—many voices said of him that no one in the battles had so fully proved himself with a bolder hero's hand. They frequently said that he inflicted the most terrible wounds.

[717] They had fought bitterly now for twelve days. Hetel's heroes could often be seen near the king relentlessly smashing gleaming shields, so that the proud Moors regretted their military campaign. [718] On the morning of the thirteenth day, before early Mass, [Siegfried][175] said with concern, "Look at how many of our brave men are lying here. The king of [See]land is leaving nothing undone in the service of love."[176]

[719] He took counsel with those from Karadie, how happy they were to do so, as well as those from Alzabe, to ride to a fortified place where they could save themselves, so that the worthy enemy would not find them all dead. [720] They withdrew from the battle to a defensible place, with a large river flowing along one side. As they were riding to where they intended to withdraw, their

---

175. The speaker is not identified in the manuscript. Manuscript A reads: *Morlannd*, which refers to Siegfried, so that he could not be the intended speaker in the original text. Instead, Bartsch/Stackmann insert Siegfried as the speaker and change Moorland to Seeland, so that Herwig becomes the object. This makes sense given the pronoun that starts strophe 719 clearly refers to Siegfried. McConnell (76n118) argues that the original text is correct.

176. The term is *hohe minne*. See note 55 above.

Chapter 14: How Hetel Sent Out Envoys from Herwig's Land [725–52]

adversaries could be seen harassing them, wanting to give them no rest. [721] The king of the Moors rode to face Hetel. Everyone could plainly hear that whatever fighting he had done before was just the start, now that he had found the one who had inflicted such grave wounds on his kinsmen. [722] Hetel of Hegelingen and Lord Siegfried gave their all in high-spirited combat. The gleaming shields in their hands were shattered; the king of the Moors had to give way to the man from Daneland.

[723] Then the men from Daneland set up their siege camp. There is little doubt that thanks to this the bold enemies later found themselves in a precarious position. However secure their fortified place was, they would have rather been at home. [724] Once they were besieged by enemy forces, the arrogant heroes were unable to engage properly in acts of chivalry whenever they were challenged.[177] They defended their stronghold as best they could.

Chapter 14: How Hetel Sent Out Envoys from Herwig's Land [725–52]

[725] Then Hetel sent a message home that they needn't worry. He had the fair and noble women informed that they had been successful in battles and in skirmishes, the old as well as the young. They should await them with optimism. [726] And he let it be known that they were conducting a siege, [he] and all his men, there where they served fair Kudrun and Herwig of Seeland. They were doing everything they could every day with their own resources.

[727] Fair Hilde accordingly wished Herwig and all his men the best of luck, that they would have success as their honor demanded. "May God grant," said Kudrun, "that they bring our friends home safe and sound."

[728] Then the men from Stormarn refused to allow those from Moorland and Alzabe a way out to the sea. They had to hold out where they were in great danger. With Wate and Fruote they had the worst of neighbors. [729] Hetel swore oaths that he would never withdraw and leave the field to them until he and his troops had taken the men from the Moorish kingdom prisoner. They[178] behaved rashly. Their military campaign would later cause them grave harm.

[730] Hartmut's scouts had been sent there from the land of Ormanie with nothing but ill intent. They were constantly observing everything that happened;

---

177. The "heroic" response was individual, not collective action. It was particularly "unheroic" to be unable to respond to challenges with individual feats of arms and displays of courage.
178. The "they" (*si*) in this line is not clear. It could be the armies from Moorland, or it could be Hetel and his armies, thereby projecting a future tragedy, i.e., Hartmut's abduction of Kudrun. See the detailed discussion in McConnell (78n121). Based on the context, the most likely answer is that Hetel's army is too focused on the immediate threat posed by Siegfried's forces and not on the defense of their own homeland.

they had nothing but ill will for Hetel in his battles and in skirmishes. [731] They saw that the king of Karadie, the lord of the noble Moors, was surrounded day and night and unable to withdraw, which caused him great harm. No reinforcements came to his aid; his lands were too far away. [732] The scouts returned to the land of Ormanie, those men that Ludwig and Hartmut had sent out. They reported at home the good news that Hetel and Herwig were fully engaged in the war.

[733] The ruler of Ormanie thanked them for the welcome news. "Could you tell me how long it might be that the men from Karadie will stay in [See]land[179] with their enemies, or when they will have fully avenged their insult?"

[734] Then [one of] the messengers said, "Your Majesty, it is true. They will have to stay for more than a year. The men from Hegelingen will not let them escape. They've been surrounded in such a way that they have no access to any of the roads."

[735] Then daring Hartmut of Ormanie said, "How such high hopes free me [from cares]! Since they[180] are busy with their siege and have to fight, we should ride to Hegelingen before Hetel returns."

[736] Ludwig and Lord Hartmut were in agreement that if they had ten thousand at hand, they could take Kudrun away from there before Hetel returned to Hegelingen with his men. [737] Old Gerlint was especially intent on how she could take vengeance on Hetel for shamefully refusing to give his daughter to her son Hartmut. She hoped that both Wate and Fruote would [hang][181] for it.

[738] Then the she-devil said, "You can have plenty of money. If you want to ride out, then I will give the troops my silver and gold, and take it away from the women. I couldn't care less if Hetel and Hilde now had regrets."

[739] Then Lord Ludwig said, "We should discuss whether to launch a campaign with my warriors from Ormanie.[182] I trust that I can gather twenty thousand men in a short amount of time. Then we can take Kudrun away from there."

[740] Then young Hartmut said, "If only it might happen that I should see Hilde's daughter here. I would give up an entire kingdom to make it possible that we might affectionately [be] together."

[741] They took to planning at all hours of the day how it might be accomplished that Ludwig could gather an army with which to invade Hegelingen. How could Hilde have known that this would mean her downfall? [742] By whatever means she could, Ludwig's wife was determined that Kudrun herself

---

179. Manuscript A reads: *Sturmlannde* (733,3b).
180. This pronoun could refer either to Hetel's or Siegfried's forces, but most logically it would be the engagement of Hetel's forces that prevented him from defending Hegelingen. See Störmer-Caysa (602n735,3) for further discussion.
181. Manuscript A reads: *haben*, which is emended to *hâhen* (hang) by Bartsch/Stackmann.
182. Manuscript A reads: *von Hormandin* (739,1a).

Chapter 14: How Hetel Sent Out Envoys from Herwig's Land [725–52]

would come to be contented with Hartmut in Ormanie. She truly did everything in her power so that he might hold her [in] his arms.

[743] Ludwig said to his son Hartmut, "Consider this, good sir. We will have problems gathering the people together from the villages. Son, provide for those coming from afar;[183] I will provide here at home for my heroes."

[744] They handed out ample provisions here and there, the likes of which had not been seen even in Swabia:[184] horses and pack animals, saddles and shields. I think they enjoyed doing so; Ludwig had never been so generous. [745] They quickly prepared themselves for a long journey. Ludwig recruited capable ships' crews who were well acquainted with the sea routes. [. . .][185] They had to exert themselves on the waves to earn such high pay. [746] Everything was prepared with considerable care. They let it be known across the country and along the roads that Ludwig and Hartmut were ready to depart their land, but they were still concerned about how they were going to get to Hegelingen. [747] When they came to the coast, they found ready there the ships that would take them to the foreign shore. They had been well built with Gerlint's wealth. Neither old Wate or Fruote knew anything about this. [748] They crossed the ocean with twenty-three thousand men. Hartmut was tormented by his yearning for Kudrun, and he acted accordingly. With all his kinsmen he launched a great military campaign against King Hetel. [749] They arrived sometime later, however they managed to do so. Many a mother's son was in peril because of it. The waves carried them along the Ortland shore before Hetel found out, where they could make out Hilde's castle.

[750] Hartmut's army arrived at that time about twelve miles' distance from the open sea, in the land of Hegelingen, close enough for them to see the palace and towers of fair Hilde's castle. [751] Ludwig of Ormanie[186] gave the order to cast anchor there on the sandy bottom. He ordered all of them to disembark as quickly as they could. They were so close that they feared the Hegelingen would discover them. [752] After they had carried them out of the ship, they put the many shields and solid helmets in order. They made themselves ready for battle and sent out their messengers. They wanted to see if they could find any allies in Hetel's lands.

---

183. This (*gesten*) could refer to mercenaries or to foreign warriors already living in their realm.
184. Swabia (*Schwaben*) was an important and wealthy duchy, especially during the period of Hohenstaufen rule from 1138 to 1254.
185. Manuscript A begins the line with: *den lonet er on masse* (745,4a). This is left out completely in the Bartsch/Stackmann edition for metrical reasons, where the line starts: *si muosten arbeiten . . .* McConnell includes the original beginning of the line in his translation: "he rewarded them most generously for their service" (80).
186. Manuscript A reads: *von Hormandine* (751,1a).

Chapter 15: How Hartmut Took Kudrun by Force [753–809]

[753] Hartmut ordered his messengers to ride out. Fair Hilde and her dear daughter were quickly informed that, if it could be agreed, he would do for Kudrun's love whatever it took to satisfy them both. [754] If she loved him, as he had previously proposed (he often thought of how much he longed for her), then he would serve her always as long as he lived. He intended to give Kudrun his father's inheritance. [755] If she did not agree, then he would turn against her. He tried to attain what he wanted from that lovely young woman by bringing her to his country without going to war. This was bold Hartmut's hope.

[756] "If she does not accept," said Hartmut then, "then tell her that no amount of money could prevent me, before I depart from here, from treating fair Kudrun to a parade of warriors. [757] My able envoys, you should tell her this as well. I will never travel back across the wide ocean, and I would rather let myself be hacked [to pieces], than have that young woman from Hegelingen not return with me. [758] If she refuses to say that she will comply, then she will see me and my warriors advancing to attack. I will leave twenty thousand heroes lying dead, to the right and left of the road that leads to Hegelingen castle. [759] Since [Hetel] followed Wigaleis's advice, along with old Wate,[187] we had no choice but to undertake this long journey here to Hegelingen, which will result in many orphans. I want to put an end to this."

[760] It was time, and the envoys rode off quickly after receiving Hartmut's instructions, to a great castle named Matelane. Lady Hilde lived here. Her daughter, the young queen, was incredibly beautiful. [761] He had sent two distinguished counts there; he had brought them with him across the sea from Ormanie, to offer his service to Hilde with conviction. He didn't want to turn back; he didn't want to renounce his service to her. [762] Hilde should bequeath the young woman to him. He prized that lady above all others; he was still passionately devoted to serving love. She should have every advantage of being so highborn; he would never waver in his service to her.

[763] Those who protected the ladies were informed that a delegation from Ormanie was riding there to Matelane to present a formal petition. Lady Hilde told them to keep still. Kudrun[188] was alarmed at that. [764] Hilde's officeholders

---

187. Bartsch/Stackmann and other editions insert Hetel's name here, where manuscript A has none. There is no evidence that Wigaleis played any role in advising Hetel to support Herwig's fight against Siegfried. Furthermore, there seems to be no compelling logic that Hartmut was then left with no choice but to attack Hetel's home during his absence. It was a move calculated to take advantage of Hetel's, and therefore Kudrun's, vulnerability.

188. Manuscript A reads: *diu wol getane* (the beautiful or handsome one) and so is not specific as to whether this is Hilde or Kudrun. Most editions and translators take this to mean Kudrun, and in line 771,4, Kudrun is described as *diu wol getane*. McConnell extracts a bit more from the text

Chapter 15: How Hartmut Took Kudrun by Force [753–809]

opened the castle gates, so that whoever arrived would not have to wait. The gates were opened wide, and Hartmut's emissaries were allowed to enter Matelane. [765] They asked to see Hetel's wife. The guards allowed[189] it, those tasked with protecting the beautiful queen, as required by the king's honor. They were never left alone, noble Hilde and Kudrun.

[766] Once Hartmut's men arrived at court, fair Hilde greeted them right away. Noble Lady Kudrun did the same out of courtesy. The noble and good woman loved bold Herwig very much. [767] Regardless of how distressed they felt, refreshments were offered to the messengers before they spoke. Lady Hilde allowed them to sit in her and her daughter's presence. What did they want there? asked the queen. They should tell her everything. [768] Most courteously they arose from their seats, the entire delegation, as envoys still do. They reported what they wanted there in the land of Hegelingen, that their Lord Hartmut had sent them there to ask for fair Kudrun's hand.

[769] Then the noble maiden said, "I reject this petition. Bold Hartmut will not stand alongside me in front of both our followers wearing a king's crown. The one whose goodwill I gladly reward is named Herwig. [770] I am promised to him. I took an oath to him as my husband, he took me to be his wife. I wish for that warrior all the great honor he could ever receive. I don't want any other man to love for the rest of my life."

[771] Then one of the envoys said, "My [Lord] Hartmut wanted us to tell you that if you don't do what he demands, you will see him with his warriors at Matelane in three days' time." The lovely woman laughed at that.

[772] The envoys wanted to depart. They were heard asking for leave, the two distinguished and noble counts. Lady Hilde commanded, even though they were strangers to her, that they be given rich gifts, which they refused to accept. The envoys were cunning in their embassy. [773] Hetel's men, this the envoys were told, did not at all fear their hatred and enmity. If they did not want to drink King Hetel's wine, then he and his warriors would be served blood instead. [774] Then the envoys returned with this message to the place from which Hartmut had dispatched them. He came up to meet them and asked how things had gone, whether noble Kudrun had happily received them and his petition.

[775] One of the envoys said to the noble, "You were refused. The distinguished woman already has a husband, whom she loves in her heart above all

---

than is actually there: "Lady Hilde asked them to refrain from saying more, for the young maiden was frightened by the news" (81–82). Murdoch has: "and the beautiful Kudrun became nervous" (67); Gibbs/Johnson: "and Lovely Kudrun was terrified at that" (67).

189. Manuscript A reads: *die helde sich des werten* (765,2a). Gibbs/Johnson read *werten* as "refused" (68), Murdoch (67) and McConnell do likewise (82), but German translators (Simrock, Sowinski, Störmer-Caysa, Lindner) read this as *gewährten* in modern German, or "allowed."

other men. If you don't want to drink her wine, then you will be paid in hot blood."

[776] "What shame!" replied Hartmut. "This reply stabs me in the heart. I don't need any better friends, [than] those who will now help me fight."

Then everyone on the shore rose up. [777] Ludwig and Hartmut angrily mustered their army together under raised banners. From Matelane they could see their standards flying at a distance. That fair woman said, "What luck, here come Hetel and my husband!"

[778] They realized that it was not the king's standard. "Ah, what a great tragedy is about to transpire here today! Fierce foreigners have come to take Lady Kudrun. We will see many a solid helmet smashed before the day's end."

[779] The men from Hegelingen reassured Hilde, "Whatever Hartmut's followers do here today, we will repay with many grave wounds."

The queen ordered the castle gates to be locked immediately. [780] Hetel's bold men did not want to obey. The defenders of the land had their lord's battle flag raised; Hetel's warriors wanted to rush out of the castle to defeat the worthy opponent. [781] The gate's barriers, which should have all been closed, were opened on account of their overconfidence. They were unconcerned that Hartmut was observing them. When the first of the enemy rushed in, the last were not far behind. [782] With swords held high, a thousand or more men could be seen [assembled] in front of the gate. Hartmut came at them with a thousand men of his own. They dismounted on the field and had the horses quickly led away. [783] They had in their hands long lances with sharp tips. Who could have prevented the battle then? They drove back the proud castle guards with terrible wounds. Just at that moment, Ludwig of Ormanie appeared with his men. [784] The women were alarmed when he rode up. They could clearly see his banners everywhere, some three thousand men with each of them. The bold men came filled with rage, however they would depart from there.[190] [785] They were all soon fully engaged on all sides. Warriors more bold had never been seen from any land than those defending Hetel's home. They knew how to mete out wounds and fought bravely against Hartmut's heroes.

[786][191] (787) Bold Ludwig, the ruler from Ormanie, struck red sparks from hard shield rims with his fearless courage, which he held in his heart. His comrades in arms were exceedingly bold themselves. [787] (786) Just when the castle guards thought they were safe, Hartmut's famous father from Ormanie came

---

190. McConnell offers another possible interpretation, i.e., that Ludwig's and Hartmut's forces departed from Matelane happy with the result that they had captured the castle and Kudrun: "The Normans had come to Hegelingenland in great anger, however [happy] they may have been when they eventually left" (83–84n130).

191. The order of this and the next strophe has been reversed in Bartsch/Stackmann for reasons of narrative flow.

riding up to the fray with his heroes. He intended to support Hartmut—that was apparent throughout the day. [788] The proud castle guards regretted that they had ignored the order from Hilde, that beautiful woman, Hetel's wife. Because of that they saw shattered shields, and many men lost their lives. [789] Ludwig and Hartmut had both approached each other by now. They could plainly see that the defenders wanted to secure Lady Hilde's castle; they surged forward with raised shields to bring their standards into the castle. [790] Whatever was thrown or shot from the walls, they paid little attention, their bravery was incredible. They didn't care how many dead they saw; many heroes were seen brought down by the large rocks.

[791] Ludwig and Hartmut breached the gate; they left many mortally wounded men out front. The young woman began to weep because of it. Even greater casualties were sustained inside Hetel's castle. [792] The king of Ormanie was elated as he and his men carried his kingdom's banner into King Hetel's great hall. The flag was flown high above from the battlements, which dismayed the most noble queen. [793] I wonder what would have happened to the enemy if Wate, that fiercest of men, had seen how Hartmut's heroes, along with Ludwig, roamed through the hall that way, where they took fair Kudrun captive. [794] Wate and Hetel would have prevented it, had they been told. They would have struck helmets with strong swords, and it would never have happened that Kudrun was taken as a prisoner to Ormanie. [795] Of the people left there, all were demoralized. The same would be true today. Whatever valuables were at hand, those who wanted to steal something took it out of the palace. This you can believe, all of Hartmut's heroes became rich.

[796] Hartmut, the daring, went up to Kudrun. He said, "Noble maiden, you have always despised me. My men and I should now also despise taking anyone prisoner in this place. We should kill and hang them all."

[797] Then she said nothing except, "Oh, dear father, if only you knew that your daughter was being taken out of your land by force, then I, poor queen, would be spared this injury and shame."

[798] After they had taken the treasures and wardrobes, Hilde was led outside by her pale hand. They wanted to burn lovely Matelane to the ground. The men from Ormanie weren't concerned about what might happen to them as a result. [799] Hartmut ordered that the castle remain intact. He was in a great hurry to leave the land before King Hetel and his kinsmen were alerted. They were assembled with a large army in the Walays March.

[800] "Stop the plundering," replied Hartmut. "I'll provide for you from my father's wealth at home, and we'll have an easier time crossing the sea."

Ludwig's power over her made Kudrun suffer. [801] The castle was razed, the town set ablaze.[192] The highest-ranking people had been taken prisoner. Sixty-two women, all lovely maidens, were taken away from there, and noble Hilde was heartbroken. [802] How forlorn they left the ruler's wife there! The queen rushed to a window opening so that she [could] look down on the young women. They left behind many other beautiful women to suffer in that land. [803] Wailing and crying could be heard all around. They were all miserable, as Hilde's daughter and her household were taken out of the land, something that would later harm many a worthy knight's child. [804] Hartmut took the hostages with him to the shore. The ruler's land was left scorched and ruined. Everything had gone according to plan, and he took Kudrun and Hildeburg away with him as prisoners. [805] He knew very well that Hetel was fighting a war in a faraway land, so he set sail and left the coast. He had only just departed from the Hegelingen when Lady Hilde sent Hetel and his followers the news. [806] With what great lament she told the king that his knights at home had been killed! Hartmut left them to die lying in their own blood. His daughter was taken prisoner, and along with her he took many beautiful women.

[807] "You messengers, tell the king that I am utterly alone. Things have gone badly for me. Mighty Ludwig has returned to his land full of conceit. A thousand or more men lie pitiably in front of the gate."

[808] Hartmut, in the space of three days, had quickly boarded his ships again. His warriors had looted and pillaged whatever they could carry. King Hetel's troops had been decisively defeated. [809] How they went on from there, who could tell you? Their sails could be heard stirring and billowing as they headed away from the king's land, toward a deserted island called the Wulpensand.

Chapter 16: How Hilde Sent Out Envoys to Hetel and Herwig [810–46]

[810] Hilde, that most noble woman, was focused with all her heart and her mind on how to send her envoys to the king. Heartbreak and suffering had been caused [by] Hartmut; he had left her to witness the desolation. [811] The lady informed her husband and Herwig that their daughter was a prisoner. Their heroes were dead and had left her alone in misery. Their gold and jewels had been taken away by the men from Ormanie. [812] The envoys rode hard and raced through the land; the lady had sent them off in her great distress. On the

---

192. This seems in direct contradiction to what had just been ordered by Hartmut in 799,1. It is impossible to say if he was overruled in this by his father, Ludwig, as implied in line 800,4, or if this is simply an inconsistency.

Chapter 16: How Hilde Sent Out Envoys to Hetel and Herwig [810–46]

seventh morning they arrived where they could see, in their great distress,[193] the Hegelingen ensconced near the Moors.

[813] Every day they practiced their knightly skills, and different kinds of games could be heard that kept them from getting bored there in the camp. They could see people running and jumping and frequently throwing spears.

[814] Then Horant, the warrior from the Danish March, spied Hilde's envoys riding toward them in that country. He said to the king, "We're going to get some news. God grant that something terrible [hasn't happened] to us heroes at home."

[815] The king himself went out to where he saw them. He spoke courteously to the disheartened envoys: "You are welcome, dear sirs, here in this land. How fares my lady Hilde? Tell us who sent you here."

[816] He said, "It was my lady, she sent us here. Your castles have been razed; your land has been put to the torch. Kudrun has been taken away along with her household. I don't think your land can recover from such great destruction." [817] He said, "I have more to lament—great suffering compels us. At least a thousand of your kinsmen and your troops lie dead. Your riches have been taken off to a foreign kingdom; your treasury is looted. This is shameful to such brave heroes."

[818] He asked who had done this—what his name was. One of the envoy's men said to the king, "The one is named Ludwig of Ormanie. The other is named Hartmut. They came with heroes to attack us."

[819] Then Lord Hetel said, "Because I refused to give him my lovely daughter. I knew full well that the king of Ormanie was in vassalage to Hagen for his land. This is why Kudrun could not have been honorably matched with him. [820] We should keep this news from our enemies. We must lament in secret with our supporters. Let us now quickly bring our kinsmen together. The brave men at home could not have fared worse."

[821] Then Herwig was called to come to court, with followers and kinsmen and other king's men. When these good warriors arrived at court, they saw King Hetel in a miserable state of mind.

[822] The ruler of Hegelingen said, "I have much to lament, and I have to share my troubles with you in confidence. My wife Lady Hilde has namely informed us that Hegelingen is in a terrible state. [823] My realm is torched, my castles razed. Our defenses at home were unfortunately too weak. My daughter is a prisoner; my kinsmen, who defended land and honor for me at home, are dead."

---

193. This could refer either to the envoys or the men from Hegelingen. Some editors (Bartsch, Piper, Martin) remove 812,4a altogether. Line 815,2a supports the reading that the envoys were distressed.

The Book of Kudrun

[824] Then tears ran from Herwig's eyes because Hetel's eyes were already moist from crying. Everyone else did the same when they saw them crying. No one who was close to the king could be cheerful.

[825] Then old Wate said, "Keep quiet about this. Whatever disaster has just befallen [our] friends, we can recover later with great satisfaction. Hartmut's and Ludwig's relatives will be hurled into great unhappiness."

[826] Hetel then asked, "How can [that] happen?"

Old Wate said, "We will offer [an end to hostilities] to those from Moorland, the king and his troops. We will lead our warriors to fair Kudrun, your daughter."

[827] Wate knew how to give wise counsel. "We will engage[194] with the enemy tomorrow morning and make it clear to them in no uncertain terms that their army will never escape this place unless we allow it."

[828] Then bold Herwig said, "This is good advice. So prepare yourselves today, and tomorrow we will show them how we deal with the enemy. However we remove ourselves from here, I grieve terribly for the women."

[829] They prepared themselves for battle with horses and arms. They would never have gone against old Wate's counsel. When morning came they began the attack against the men from Abakie. This brought them glory and honor. [830] The banners everywhere were carried into the melee; many perfectly healthy men were killed there. The men from Stormland loudly cried, "Forward!" Those they wanted to defeat were all the more eager for [battle].

[831] Irolt cried out over the rim of his shield, "Are you ready to treat with us, you heroes of Moorland? My lord, King Hetel, commands that I ask you. Your lands are far away; here you squander wealth and kinsmen."

[832] Siegfried, the king of Moorland, answered, "Should you achieve victory, you will gain valuable hostages. I won't negotiate with anyone unless I do so with honor. If you [think] you can defeat us, then many more will die on both sides."

[833] Then brave Fruote said, "If you pledge to stand by us in support, we will let you leave our lord's lands, never again to wage war."

The men from Karadie stretched out their hands to secure the peace. [834] So they were reconciled, as I told you. The men approached each other with good cheer. Those who were once enemies now offered their support. Their enmity was resolved, and they discussed a campaign against Ormanie. [835] Only then did Hetel convey to the king of Moorland the terrible news he had received from his messengers. If he would help him punish Lord Hartmut for his disgraceful actions, he would be forever in his debt.

---

194. Manuscript A reads: *wir mit den gesten werben sullen morgen frue* (827,2). Translators have interpreted the verb *werben* differently. Störmer-Caysa has "to negotiate" (verhandeln); Martin (1902) has the same; Sowinski translates "to fight" (kämpfen). Bartsch/Stackmann gloss: "to deal with" (verfahren), which is adopted by Murdoch, McConnell, and Gibbs/Johnson.

Chapter 16: How Hilde Sent Out Envoys to Hetel and Herwig [810–46]

[836] Then Lord Siegfried of Alzabe said, "If we knew where to find them, they would suffer."

Then old Wate said, "I know that their likely sea route is not far away at all. We can surely catch up to them at sea."

[837] Hetel said to them all, "Where can I get ships here? Although I'd like to attack them, how is that possible? If I could make myself ready at home to go and seek them out in their land, then I could avenge both insult and injury."

[838] Then old Wate said, "There is an answer to that. God acts with power and might as he sees fit.[195] I know there are, very close to us here in this land, seventy good ships at anchor with plenty of supplies. [839] They have transported pilgrims across the sea.[196] We have to take the ships, whatever the consequences. The pilgrims will have to wait patiently for us on the shore until we have either reconciled with or defeated our enemies."

[840] Wate the bold was eager to depart with about a hundred warriors; the others followed. He said he wanted to buy provisions if they would sell them.[197] For this many of his kinsmen would die, and he would also suffer for it [later]. [841] Those they encountered on the shore,[198] this I know is true, were three thousand strong, I think, and maybe more. They couldn't prepare themselves for battle in time, as the king and his large army came right up to them. [842] Regardless of what they did, everything that Wate didn't want, their silver and their clothing, was offloaded. He ordered that their provisions be left on the ships. He said, "You'll be compensated as soon as we can return."

[843] The pilgrims complained and cursed, as they had every right. Whatever they told him about their situation, he paid no attention. Wate, the most bold, insisted in all earnest that they had to give up their transports and other ships. [844] Hetel was unconcerned whether they could ever traverse the sea with their cross again. From their armed contingent he took five hundred or more of the best men that could be found. Of these, very few came back safe and sound to Hegelingen. [845] I [don't] know if Hetel and his men paid for the fact that these foreign citizens were treated so poorly, that they had to part there in that foreign

---

195. The meaning of the second half-line seems unclear in Manuscript A: *als es umb in stat* (838,2b). Bartsch (1865) originally emended to *al daz in bestât*, but the Bartsch/Stackmann edition marks the crux and retains the original text. Störmer-Caysa translates "as he is" ("als er ist"), i.e., powerful.
196. There is some disagreement as to whether these are pilgrims, crusaders, or both. According to 841,3 they seem to be armed. See also 844. Out of three thousand, at least five hundred were good soldiers. They may be mostly pilgrims with an armed escort, as was common.
197. Some translations take this as indirect speech directed toward the pilgrims, i.e., "he said to the pilgrims," followed by direct speech. See Lindner, McConnell, and Murdoch. Others stick more closely to the text.
198. These are the pilgrims.

land. I think that God himself avenged that insult against him.[199] [846] They departed as quickly as they could. Hetel and his men enjoyed fair winds. They sailed after their enemies, wherever they could find them, and wanted to avenge their insult and injury.

Chapter 17: How Hetel Arrived at the Wulpensand to Rescue His Daughter [847–79]

[847] Now King Ludwig and also Lord Hartmut had remained with their troops near the shore to get some rest, there on the deserted island. As many men as they had, they still weren't able to use that to their advantage. [848] It was a large island and was called the Wulpensand. There the men from Ormanie, from King Ludwig's realm, made themselves and their horses comfortable. Their respite only made their later injuries harder to bear. [849] Those most noble hostages from the land of Hegelingen had been escorted onto the deserted beach. [They] could be seen acting as befitted their situation, those lovely young women. They were unhappy to be with the enemy. [850] There were fires visible all along the shore, as the men from distant lands made themselves comfortable. They thought they could stay there with those lovely women (this would be their downfall) for seven nights or more. [851] While these men lay in a remote anchorage, Hartmut and his kinsmen had to give up [hope] that they could stay there for seven days to rest with those lovely women. [852] They were far away from Matelane [with] Kudrun, that stately woman, and Ludwig's men, relaxed as they were, had no reason to expect that Wate and his followers could ever cause them harm.

[853] Then the lookout spotted a ship with large sails traveling out on the open sea, and he had the king informed. Lord Hartmut and all his men could see the crosses on the sails; they thought that these were pilgrims. [854] Soon they saw three large ships underway, along with nine impressive cogs. These were carrying men over the waves who had never before worn a cross for God's honor on their surcoats. The men from Ormanie would have to suffer because of that.

[855] They approached so closely that their helmets could be seen gleaming aboard the ships. Ludwig and his men were filled with fear and great distress. "Be on guard!" [cried] Hartmut.[200] "My bitter enemy has arrived!"

---

199. This is one of the few moralizing strophes by the narrator. Pilgrims were a class of people expressly protected by the church and secular law. The comment offers a rationale for impending doom with Wate's and Hetel's rough treatment of the pilgrims and expropriation of their vessels. Although very rarely "preachy," here the author presumes that the insult is avenged by God himself.
200. Manuscript A reads: *wolauf Hartmuot* (855,4a). Bartsch/Stackmann insert *rief dô* (called then) before Hartmuot. McConnell (91n139) stays with the manuscript's ambiguity and assumes that Ludwig is crying out to Hartmut, and so includes him in the exclamation: "Be on your guard, Hartmut" (91).

Chapter 17: How Hetel Arrived at the Wulpensand to Rescue His Daughter [847–79]

[856] They hurried toward the shoreline, and the oars could be heard creaking in the hands of many men. Those standing on the beach, the old and the young alike, didn't know what to do except to prepare to defend themselves. [857] Ludwig and Hartmut carried their shields in their hands. In the past they had returned to their own land more peacefully, but now their rest had mostly betrayed them. They had assumed that their enemies, that is, Hetel, had no kinsmen left.

[858] Ludwig cried out loudly to all his men—what he had previously done was child's play. "Now it is time that I fight brave heroes. I will make all those who dare stand under my banner wealthy men."

[859] Hartmut's standard was carried down to the shore. The ships were so close that the men on the beach could have reached them with their spears. I think that old Wate kept his shield at the ready. [860] No one ever defended a land so resolutely, as the men from Hegelingen stormed onto the beach. They fought relentlessly with spears and with swords. They traded blows until they grew weary of such exchanges. [861] They had formed up all along the shoreline. Never before, when the wind blows from the Alps, had snow fallen so heavily as when the missiles left their hands. Even if they had wanted, no one could have averted that catastrophe. [862] There was an exchange of spears; it took a long time before they gained a foothold. Old Wate vaulted into the enemy throng—they were that close to him. He was enraged, and they could well see his intentions. [863] Ludwig of Ormanie charged at Wate. He launched a sharp spear at the man, so that the splinters flew high into the air. Ludwig was bold, but then Wate's contingent arrived. [864] Wate struck Ludwig, slashing through his helmet, so that the sword's blade grazed his skull. [He] had under his chain mail a precious silk shirt from Abalie. Without it he surely would have died.[201] [865] Ludwig just barely escaped with his life and had to retreat from the field. Wate was a dangerous opponent when he was out to vanquish the enemy. Many a fighter was seen laid low by his hand.

[866] Hartmut and Irolt charged at each other. Their weapons rang out on each other's helmets, so that it could be heard throughout the ranks. Irolt was most courageous, Lord Hartmut was bold as well. [867] Herwig of Seeland, a famous and brave hero, was unable to reach the shore, so he jumped into the water. He stood in the waves up to his armpits. Herwig came to realize how difficult love's service really was. [868] His enemies wanted to drown this brave warrior in the sea. Many solid spears could be seen shattering against him; he

---

201. There is some speculation among translators about this line (864,4). Murdoch and Gibbs/Johnson (162n88) believe that the silk undergarment must have included a hood, worn over the head, that protected Ludwig "by a hair's breadth" (Murdoch, 166n2). This seems to be a stretch, no matter how thick the silk might have been. It may simply refer to a shirt that protected the rest of his body from other wounds as well. The Symons/Boesch edition notes that the silk shirt likely was "strengthened" by sewn-on holy relics, similar to the protection offered by the hero's baptismal shirt in *Wolf Dietrich A* (*WDA* 430–35). Sowinski agrees (314n864,3 f.).

was in a hurry to get ashore and reach his enemies. The suffering of many a warrior was avenged there. [869] Once they had a foothold on the beach, they could see the sea turn the color of blood from those who had died, streaming all around them in a reddish hue, so far out that no one could have thrown a spear beyond it. [870] Heroes had never before known such strife. Never before had so many heroes been hurled to the depths. There were enough of the uninjured who drowned to found a kingdom.[202] I think that those who caused them such harm died all around them.

[871] Bold Hetel was fighting for his dear child, he and his kinsmen. Injury and suffering were dealt all around by foreigners and friends alike. Many doomed to die were found there on Wulpensand. [872] Their feats of arms surpassed all expectations, the men from Ormanie and those from the land of Hegelingen. The bold Danes could be seen fighting magnificently. Whoever wanted to live had to avoid them at all cost. [873] Ortwin and Morunc dominated the field with such great honor that there were few better able to inflict injury with their bravery. They inflicted many wounds, these two heroes and their comrades. [874] The proud Moors, as I've heard, disembarked from their ships and advanced toward their enemies. Hetel expected to have their support in the fight. They were bold heroes; blood could be seen flowing through stout helmets. [875] The leader they had—how could he have been more bold? On that day [he] bloodied many a mail coat's gleam. He was rightly a famous and brave hero in tough battles. How could old Wate and Fruote have been any bolder? [876] The spears had all been spent, on this side and that. Ortwin and his comrades advanced [without fear].[203] On that day many helmets were shattered by them. Kudrun cried bitterly, as did all the other women with her.

[877] The fierce battle lasted the entire day. The troops were eager to engage; the melee was immense. Courageous heroes had to suffer greatly, as Hetel's allies wanted to win back his daughter. [878] The evening approached ever closer, and the king was to suffer even greater losses. Ludwig's men did what was expected of them, since they didn't know where else to turn. They inflicted [grave wounds] and so protected the queen. [879] From the early morning until darkness made them quit, the battle caused them much agony. Without shame they did all they could, the old and young alike, until King Hetel was able to force his way over to the king of Ormanie.

---

202. This refers to those who died in the sea by drowning, i.e., they were not able to reach the shore to fight on land. The Bartsch/Stackmann gloss references a definition of *erben* that can mean "to bequeath, to bestow," along with the more common definition of "to inherit." The implied meaning is that so many men drowned that they could have given away, or put together, an entire country with their combined lands.

203. McConnell (93n142) rejects Bartsch/Stackmann's emendation *frevelichen* (fearlessly) of the original *froelichen* (happily) and translates: "advanced into battle with high spirits" (93).

Chapter 18: How Ludwig Killed Hetel and Fled in the Night [880–918]

[880] Hetel and Ludwig held their sharp swords high in the air. Each of them recognized what kind of man [the] other was by his strength. Ludwig then killed Hetel. Heart-wrenching stories were later told about that. [881] When the lord of Matelane was slain, that stately woman learned of it. Surely then they heard fair Kudrun and all her ladies lamenting. There was no distinction:[204] people on both sides were saddened. [882] When terrible Wate became aware of the king's death, he bellowed like a wild boar.[205] Helmets could be seen glowing like a red sunset from his quick strokes. He and all his men were consumed by rage. [883] Whatever the brave heroes did, what good did it do? The island was soon drenched in hot blood. The men from Hegelingen weren't interested in a truce. There on Wulpen Island they wanted to bring Kudrun home. [884] The men from Walays avenged the king's death [in] battle. The men from the Danish March supported those from Hegelingen and from Ortland in their hour of need. The glorious heroes shattered good swords in their hands. [885] Bold Ortwin wanted to avenge his father, then Horant and his heroes arrived with a great host. The day was ending and night was upon them, while the heroes were inflicting more grim wounds than ever.

[886] One of the men from the Danish March ran up to Horant, his sword ringing out loudly in his hand. He mistook him as one of the enemy. Then Horant dealt him [a great blow]; the bold warrior mortally wounded him. [887] After he had killed his own kinsman, Horant had the dead man's banner taken to join his own.[206] He then recognized him by his voice, the man he had struck down with his great strength. Horant grieved for the dead man.

[888] Herwig cried out loudly, "This is murder! Now that we no longer have the light of day, we're killing everyone, the enemy as well as our own. If this goes on until morning, not even a third will be left alive."

---

204. The meaning of the phrase *ez wart gescheiden kûme* (881,4a) is in some doubt. The Bartsch/Stackmann edition offers two possibilities: the first follows the previous line that there was no stopping the women from their lament, there was no end to it; the second takes the view that it was hardly possible at the point of Hetel's killing to separate the two sides. Sowinski offers a third possibility, which I have adopted, by translating: "it could hardly be distinguished" ("es ließ sich kaum unterscheiden," 156), i.e., the sadness felt on both sides was indistinguishable or equally great.
205. Manuscript A reads: *er begunde limmen sam ain swein abent rot* (882,2). Most editors have deleted *swein*, placing a period after *limmen* (roared) and then continuing to line 882,3 with the phrase *sam ain abent rot*. I have followed McConnell (95) and the manuscript by retaining *swein* and starting the new sentence with *abent rot*.
206. The sense is probably that he had the unidentified warrior's captured pennant or flag taken as a trophy. He only later recognized who that warrior was, perhaps through some dying declaration. An alternate possibility is that Horant recognized his mistake and then made sure that his relative's banner was still visible by taking it to where his own banner could be seen.

[889] Wherever bold Wate could be found in the melee, anyone was ill advised to force his way toward him. No one near him could withstand his boundless rage. He led many to a place where they would stay forever. [890] They had good reason, though, to withdraw until daytime. On both sides the troops lay about mortally wounded, killed by the enemy. The moon also provided no light. The day had ended; the attacker and all his men were robbed of their victory. [891] The embittered men reluctantly ended the fighting. Wearied to the bone, they separated themselves. They remained close enough to each other to see the gleam of their helmets and shields in the firelight.

[892] Ludwig and [Hartmut] from Ormanie came together to confer privately. The king spoke to his retinue, asking why he should remain so near to bold Wate, who wanted to kill [him].[207] [893] He instructed them shrewdly, "Lie down on the ground, with your heads on your shields, and make a lot of noise.[208] This way the men from Hegelingen won't suspect that I might try to get you out of here."

[894] Then Ludwig's kinsmen and vassals obeyed him. Drums and trumpets could be heard, as if they had conquered the land for themselves. Ludwig revealed his great cunning. [895] They heard all around them an outcry and lament, and the young women were told to stop their tearful outbursts. If they didn't stop, they would drown all of them. Whoever they could hear, they would throw her into the sea. [896] Whatever they could gather up was carried out. They left the dead lying there where they had fallen. Many friends were gone—that was a heavy burden. They left behind some of their empty cogs. [897] With this great ruse they made it out to sea, the men from Ormanie. The women were pained that they had to remain silent as they left their relatives behind. The heroes who remained there on Wulpen Island knew nothing of this.

[898] Before dawn they were well on their way, those whom the men from the Danish March planned to attack. Wate had the call to battle blown on his horn. He wanted to advance toward those he intended to kill. [899] On horse and on foot, the army from Hegelingen was seen marching down to the shoreline, searching for the ones from Ormanie, Ludwig and his men, whom they wanted to attack. By then they were far away from there. [900] They found the ships empty. Clothing was strewn about, all of which could be seen lying around there on Wulpensand. They found many abandoned [weapons]. They had overslept

---

207. Gibbs/Johnson translate this in the affirmative as "informed his troops that he was going to remain there and fight with valiant Wate because he wished to kill him" (80).
208. These instructions seem to be contradictory. Either the men should pretend that they are sleeping or they should pretend to be celebrating a victory. The next stanza seems to indicate that the noisemaking was the actual ruse. It is possible that the order is somewhat reversed, which is to say that the noisemaking should have come first and then the warriors would have pretended to sleep. Störmer-Caysa (607n893,1–4) imagines that two separate groups are meant, one that feigns sleep and the other that makes noise. See notes on this section in Gibbs/Johnson (162–63) and McConnell (96n150).

Chapter 18: How Ludwig Killed Hetel and Fled in the Night [880–918]

any chance of being able to defeat them. [901] When Wate was told all this, he was deeply troubled. [He] fervently lamented King Hetel's death, and the fact that he was unable to exact revenge on Ludwig himself. Many helmets lay there shattered, which many good women lamented at home.

[902] Angry as he was, how sorely Ortwin lamented his brave warriors there! He said, "Get up, you heroes, so that we might still catch them, before they get away. They're still close to the coast."

[903] Wate, that old man, wanted to do as he said, but Fruote first checked the direction of the wind. He said to the men, "What's the use of rushing around? Listen [to me] carefully—they're at least thirty miles[209] from here. [904] And we don't have enough fighting men left to ensure that they would suffer losses from our pursuit. Don't reject my counsel too lightly," said Fruote. "What more do you want? You surely won't catch them. [905] Now make sure the wounded are carried to the ships. Search for the dead who have been taken from us and have them buried along the deserted shore. They have many friends here; they should profit from that."

[906] All of them stood there wringing their hands. If they had suffered only the one setback, having lost the young queen—but what were they going to tell Lady Hilde now? [907] Then Morunc said, "Nothing would come of it,[210] except that we alone would suffer pain and heartbreak. We will earn little reward when we bring her the news that Hetel has been killed. I would rather steer clear of Lady Hilde."

[908] Then they searched the entire beach for the dead. Those who were Christians, of all who were found there, the hero from Stormarn had them brought together. They conferred with the younger men where they should put them.

[909] Then Ortwin advised, "We should bury them here. We should make sure that they are forever memorialized after their passing with a magnificent monastery, and that every family contributes a part of the cost."

[910] "You have given good counsel," said the man [from] Stormland. "Their horses and equipment should of course be sold, of those who have died, so that poor people can have some benefit from their property after their passing."

[911] Then Irolt said, "We should also bury those who have harmed us. Or should we leave them to the ravens and ferocious wolves to devour here on the island?"

---

209. The phrase is formulaic for "a great distance." Martin (1902, 203) gives many other examples.
210. Manuscript A reads: *und wurde ir nu nicht mere* (907,1b). I have followed Störmer-Caysa in this translation, against Bartsch/Stackmann and others. She relates the phrase back to the futile attempt to catch up with Ludwig's army, i.e., the "it" is the proposed pursuit of Ludwig. See her endnote (607n907,1).

The Book of Kudrun

Then wise men advised that they not leave anyone lying there.[211] [912] After they had found some respite from their suffering, they buried the king, who had found an honorable death for the love of his family there on the shore. Whatever [their] names were, the same was done for men from every land. [913] Each one of the Moors was separated from the others. The same was done for the men from the land of Hegelingen, as well as those from Ormanie. Their graves were marked; they were all set apart. They were both Christian and Muslim. [914] They were kept busy until the sixth day. They had no free time, but the retainers never stopped thinking about[212] how they might lead the men from Hegelingen out of their great sin and their misdeed into God's graces.[213] [915] They heard so many masses read and sung there that God had never been so well served anywhere else on behalf of the fallen in any other land. Later on many of the clerics were left there on the island with the dead. [916] Those charged with caring for them also stayed.[214] They were told to write down what had been given to them, some three hundred hides of land.[215] They became hospitalers.[216] The news that a monastery had been founded there spread far and wide. [917] All those who had lost their kin there made their oblations, women and men, for the sake of the souls of those they had buried. It later became so wealthy that it had at least three hundred tenants.[217] [918] Now may God have mercy [on those] who lie there, as well as the others in that land. Those who were still fit took their leave from the Wulpensand. Each one of them returned home after his ordeal to his lord's land.

---

211. Manuscript A reads: *daz sy der <u>Cristen</u> ainen nicht ligen liessen* (911,4b). Most editions have emended this line to exclude the word *Cristen* (Christians), presumably for metrical reasons, but the text supports the notion that the burial of non-Christians would have been of secondary concern. Nonetheless, the lines of this strophe and the next two indicate that warriors on both sides were spared the dishonor of having their corpses despoiled by scavengers, and that each individual warrior deserved a separate grave and memorial.

212. Simrock and Lindner translate along the lines of Murdoch's note (167n3 for ch. 18), "that they had no time for anything *except* to consider the expiation of the guilt." An alternative might be: "They had no free time. The retainers never stopped thinking about how they . . ."

213. This is a reference to the theft of the pilgrim ships and the involuntary enlistment of the best soldiers from the pilgrim fleet.

214. These are the monks and probably the lay brothers of the new monastery.

215. The monastery's endowment would have been documented and witnessed in a written charter. The exact measure of the Middle High German term *huobe* is difficult to determine. It is related to the German *Hufe* and may have defined something on the order of up to thirty fertile fields of a specific dimension. It is translated here with the English term "hides," which was, although etymologically related, not the same measurement. See Murdoch's note on hides (167n4).

216. The term "hospitalers" does not necessarily refer to the chivalric order (the Knights of St. John) commonly referred to by the same name, although Störmer-Caysa (607n916,2–4) claims that it might. Many monastic orders and towns and communities were engaged in running, staffing, and managing hostels and hospitals.

217. Tenants were essentially considered vassals to the monastery. The monastery would have received specific income or taxes from these tenants.

Chapter 19: How the Hegelingen Returned to Their Homeland [919–50]

[919] Hetel's kin had left many behind at death's lair, and brave [men] had never before returned home to their land in such great despair. Later fair women could be seen crying and wringing their hands. [920] Ortwin, who came from Ortland, didn't dare appear before his dear mother, fair Hilde, because of the pain of loss and dishonor. She waited every day for them to bring Lady Kudrun back. [921] Wate rode into Hilde's realm with trepidation. The others didn't dare go. His strength and his own hand had provided little protection in the bitter battles. He didn't believe he could regain Hilde's favor anytime soon. [922] When people reported that Wate had arrived, many were apprehensive. They knew from times past that whenever he returned from battle there was much noisemaking; he had always done so. Now everyone was silent.

[923] "Ah, woe," said Lady Hilde. "What has happened? Old Wate's men are carrying broken shields. The horses are struggling and weighed down. They're all downtrodden. I would like to know where the king is."

[924] Just a short time after she had said this, people were seen running to where they saw Wate. They wanted to find out about their dear friends, but he gave them the news that made each of them miserable.

[925] Then Wate from Stormarn said, "I can't keep it from you, and I'm not going to lie to you. They're all dead."

Old and young alike were shocked. Never before had anyone witnessed such a mournful assembly.

[926] "Ah, woe, what agony," said the king's wife. "That my lord's life has been ripped from me, mighty Hetel, that my honor has vanished, that I have lost both. Surely I will never see Kudrun again."

[927] Knights and young women then tormented themselves with unbecoming grief. The king's wife lamented her husband so intensely that the hall shook. "Woe is mine," said Lady Hilde, "should King Hartmut profit from this."

[928] Then bold Wate said, "Lady, take leave of your lament. They're not coming back. In the days to come, when the next generation grows up in this land, we will make Ludwig and Hartmut suffer as well."

[929] Then the grieving woman said, "Ah, if only I could live that long. I would give everything I have to that end, that I might be avenged, however that might happen. That I, God's poorest, might see my daughter Kudrun."

[930] Wate said to Hilde, "Lady, take leave of your lament. In the next twelve days we will summon all your warriors, however many we can gather, and plan a campaign, so that [those in] Ormanie will be defeated." [931] He said, "My Lady Hilde, this is what happened. I robbed some pilgrims of nine of their ships. We should return them to these poor people so that when we fight again we will have more success."

[932] Then the grieving woman said, "I agree. I'm determined to compensate them for their losses. Whoever robs from pilgrims has committed a grave sin. They should be given three marks of my silver for every one of theirs."

[933] The ships were returned, as the lady commanded. Before a single pilgrim had left the shore, they were all so well compensated that they cursed no one, and Hagen's daughter was left blameless.

[934] The next morning bold Herwig arrived from Seeland, where he found Lady Hilde crying bitterly after her husband's death. Wringing her hands, she nonetheless received the hero courteously. [935] Moved by the lady's tears, noble Herwig began to cry as well. Then the young man said, "They did not all die, those who supported you there and did so gladly. Many of the enemy paid dearly for that. [936] My heart and my body will never rest; Hartmut will have to pay that he dared take my [wife] from me and slaughter our heroes. I will pursue him relentlessly until I seize his throne."

[937] As unhappy as they all were, they rode to the town, all the way to Matelane. The queen let it be known that those who wanted to remain loyal need not avoid the queen because of what had happened to them. [938] Then the men from Frisia and from Stormland arrived. She also summoned the men from the Danish March.[218] Morunc's heroes arrived there from Walays. The men from Hegelingen rode with them to fair Hilde's capital. [939] Then her son Ortwin arrived from Ortland. She lamented his dear father, as she should. The heroes entered into secret counsel with their lady, and the mighty heroes agreed to launch a military campaign.

[940][219] (942) Then old Wate said, "It can't be done until we see that those who today are still children here are able to bear arms, these many noble orphans. They will remember their kinsmen and eagerly help us in this campaign."

[941] Then the queen said, "When might that be? If my dear daughter is to remain captive all that time with the enemy there in a foreign land, then I, miserable queen, will have lost all my joy."

[942] (940) Then Fruote of the Danes said, "It can't happen until we have a full complement of able men, that we embark on a campaign from here, no matter how many the enemy gather together there."

[943] Then the queen said, "May God let us see that day. For me, a poor woman, that day is too far off. Whoever thinks about me and about poor Kudrun, [I believe that] he will be moved to compassion on our account."

[944] They asked to take their leave. Then the noble woman said, "Whoever is concerned about me, may he be blessed. You bold warriors, may you come to my aid and organize our expedition as best you can in the meantime."

---

218. This is Horant and his men.
219. Most editions reverse manuscript strophes 940 and 942. McConnell leaves the strophes in their original order.

Chapter 20: How Hartmut Returned Home [951–1040]

[945] Then Wate said shrewdly, that aged and bold hero, "My lady, we should turn our attention to the dense forest. Since we are confident about our military campaign, you should command that each land produce forty cogs."

[946] She said, "So then I will order twenty solid ships to be built on the coast, strong and seaworthy, and I will have them outfitted, of this I have every confidence, so that they will safely bring my supporters to meet the enemy."

[947] Then they wanted to take their leave. The ruler of Moorland [went] with all due courtesy to where he found the lady. He said, "I should be notified of the exact point in time when they will depart, so that I don't need to be summoned again."

[948] She let them depart on amiable terms. After all their tribulations, the brave guests and beautiful women could be seen in mourning. Day and night they planned what the men from Ormanie could hardly have imagined. [949] When they had returned to their own lands under a cloud of grief, it was arranged that those who prayed for the dead on the Wulpensand be sent food, that they might remember them to God. Lady Hilde was very wise. [950] In addition, she had a large church constructed; after that she had the monastery and hostel built as well. I believe that it became well known in many lands because of those buried there. Later it was called "At the Wulpensand."[220]

Chapter 20: How Hartmut Returned Home [951–1040]

[951] Let us now move on from what was happening with them or what the monks were busying themselves with. We should let [you hear] about Hartmut, how he brought many noble and worthy young women home. [952] When they had departed, as we told you before, the many men who had been mortally wounded in the battle had to be left behind with their injuries. Many orphans have had to mourn that excessively in their lands since. [953] They sailed across the sea in real distress. In the evening and the morning, many brave men were ashamed, the old and the young alike, that they had fled, even though they had otherwise been successful.

[954] They were approaching Ormanie, Ludwig's realm; the experienced mariners recognized it. When in their misery they saw their homeland, one of them said, "We're coming up on Hartmut's castle."

[955] Then the winds helped them reach the king's land. The men of Ormanie were glad there and then that they had been able to return to their children and their wives, although they had thought before they might have to remain behind, dead. [956] Ludwig, that nobleman, caught sight of his castle. The man from

---

220. It was traditional to found a church or monastery in commemoration of victory in a military battle. Perhaps the best-known example is Battle Abbey near Hastings, which William of Normandy founded in 1070 and was completed in 1094.

Ormanie said to Kudrun, "Do you see this castle, my lady? You should be happy. If you are well disposed to us, we will reward you with a prosperous land."

[957] Then the noble maiden said sadly, "To whom should I be well disposed? My happy disposition is regrettably now so far removed from me, I think much too far,[221] that I will remain miserable all the days of my life."

[958] Then Ludwig replied, "Don't be sad. Love Hartmut, he's a pleasant man. Everything we have, we will offer you. You could enjoy honor and bliss with that man."

[959] Then Hilde's daughter said, "Why don't you leave me alone? I would sooner be dead than accept Hartmut. Even if his father's lineage allowed him to pursue my love,[222] I would rather die than take him as a lover."

[960] This speech insulted King Ludwig. He grabbed her by the hair and flung [her] into the sea. Bold Hartmut quickly prevented her demise by saving the noble maiden from the strong waves before his father's eyes. [961] Hartmut ran up as she was beginning to go under. She would have drowned had that brave man not grabbed hold of her blond braids with his hands. That's how he pulled her out; he could not have prevented [her] death any other way. [962] Hartmut, that brave man, pulled her into a small boat. Ludwig knew how to treat beautiful women badly. She sat there in her shirt after he dragged her out of the water. This kind of behavior was new [to her]; just thinking about it upset her greatly. [963] Then all those lovely young women cried together; none of them was happy. What could have been worse for them than having the king's daughter punished so severely? They thought to themselves, "They will do [even] worse things to us."

[964] Then Lord Hartmut said, "Why would you drown my wife, fair Kudrun? She means as much to me as my own life. If anyone other than Ludwig, my own father, had done this, I would have been furious; I would have taken his life and honor."

[965] Then Ludwig replied, "I have reached old age without reproof, and I would like to continue to live as befits my honor until the end of my days. Tell Kudrun not to take her anger out on me."

[966] The messengers had arrived in good spirits. [They] informed Lady Gerlint of her son Hartmut's loving and good and willing service, and that she should receive the many brave knights at the shore. [967] He also let it be known that the maiden from Hegelingen had arrived from across the sea, the one for whom Hartmut had longed painfully even before setting eyes on her. When Gerlint heard this, I think surely she had never been so pleased.

[968] Then the worthy envoy said, "My lady, you should appear outside the castle down below, where you can receive the ladies in their sorrow with a loving

---

221. Bartsch/Stackmann indicate 975,4a as a crux. Although the meaning is fairly clear, it is thought in the edition's gloss to be an insertion (*Flickstelle*) designed to establish an internal rhyme.
222. This refers back to Ludwig's vassalage to Hagen; see 610,2–3.

welcome. You and your daughter should both ride [down] to the shore. [969] You should also bring with you down to the water young women and ladies and brave knights, there where the exiled[223] woman will be in [the] harbor. You should greet her household affectionately."

[970] "I will do so gladly," said Lady Gerlint. "It will give me great joy that Hetel's child has arrived here in this land with her household. I want always to see that Hartmut is happy with her."

[971] The horses were made ready, as were the tack and blankets. The young queen was happy and cheerful,[224] now that it would come to pass that she might see Kudrun, who had so often been spoken of with high praise in her father's land. [972] Then they searched in the chests for the very best attire they could find there and that anybody owned. Hartmut's heroes were meticulously dressed, and the king's retinue rode out of the castle with great pomp and ceremony. [973] On the morning of the third day, women and men, all of the retinue that Gerlint [and] Ortrun had brought together, were fully prepared for the joyous reception. They rode out of the castle without lingering for long in the courtyard.

[974] Then all who had been away arrived in the harbor. Everything they brought was unloaded and carried away. They had happily returned to their land; only Kudrun and her household arrived in sorrow. [975] Valiant Hartmut led her by the hand. If it had been possible, she would rather have refused. Surely the poor woman accepted his service for honor's sake. From then on he did it quite gladly, along with however else he could serve her. [976] She was accompanied by sixty young women, who looked as if they should have been escorted from their homes with high honors. They were well known in many kingdoms, but their great ordeal had left them in misery. [977] Hartmut's sister was accompanied by two noblemen as she worthily welcomed Hilde's daughter. With tears in her eyes the homeless maiden kissed the ruler's daughter, then Ortrun took her pale hands in hers.

[978] Ludwig's wife wanted to kiss her as well, but that upset the young woman. She said to Gerlint, "Why do you come so close to me? Why would I kiss you? You don't need to welcome me. [979] It was your scheming that made me, poor woman, suffer such heartache and disgrace in constant uncertainty.[225] There will regrettably be more."

---

223. The term *ellende* has a broad range of meanings. At its core is the concept of exile or abandonment and its related attributes, such as separation, punishment, confinement, and misery. In this instance the word describes Kudrun's captivity far from home and the related suffering this causes her. See also, for example, 977,3; 989,1; 994,4.
224. This is Ortrun, the young daughter of King Ludwig and Queen Gerlint. She is mentioned by name in 973.
225. Manuscript A reads: *es warn ewr rate daz ich vil arme maid | auf michel unstete vil manige hertzenlaid | mit schanden han geduldet* (979,1–3a). The phrase in 979,2a, *auf michel unstete*, has been taken by editors and translators either to complete the half-line 979,1a (*es warn ewr rate*) or to

The Book of Kudrun

After this the queen tried hard to gain her favor. [980] She also greeted each of the women individually. Lots of people appeared and made a great noise. A great many pavilions were raised there on the beach, with silk ropes, for Lord Hartmut and his men. [981] The people were kept busy until they had unloaded everything they brought with them. Kudrun was distraught that the men [from] Ormanie were lingering around her [ladies].[226] She was seen being pleasant to no one except Ortrun. [982][227] They had to spend the entire day on the beach, and her eyes filled with tears, regardless of what others did. Her eyes and fair cheeks were seldom dry. Hartmut often comforted her, but her melancholy persisted a long time. [983] Ortrun was in no way hostile to her, given Kudrun's virtues. Regardless of what others did, she was happy to be with her and loved being there [for her] in her father's land, but the poor young woman was sad and missed her family. [984] As could be expected, the knights and squires were happy to show people at home what they had brought back from Hegelingen. How joyfully they were welcomed, since they hadn't been expected to return anymore.

[985] When [they] had recovered from the wind-swept seas, no matter what the people there did,[228] Hartmut's army was dispersed to the far corners of the realm. Some were seen laughing, while others were wringing their hands. [986] Then noble Hartmut also departed from the area. He brought Kudrun to a strong castle, where she had to remain longer than the young woman wanted. She suffered there from fear and worry. [987] After the noble maiden, who was to be crowned there, took up residence in the castle, the lord told everyone that they should always serve her eagerly. She would make them all wealthy, without exception.[229]

---

follow the *daz-* clause of 979,1b directly. Murdoch translates the lines: "It was at your instigation that I, poor wretch that I am, have had to suffer great hardships, heartaches and shame" (87). Gibbs/Johnson translate the phrase: "and face so much uncertainty" (88). Störmer-Caysa, however, takes the phrase as a disjointed part of the main clause, and so translates: "it was your counsel to renounce all trustworthiness, which caused me, poor, poor maiden, to suffer great pain and shame" ("Es waren Eure Ratschläge, jede Verlässlichkeit beiseitezulassen, nach denen ich armes, armes Mädchen sehr viel tiefen Schmerz und Schande erduldet habe").

226. McConnell opts for the original manuscript text *menige* (many) rather than the emended *megeden* (maidens) and translates line 981,4: "to see so many Normans all around her" (104).

227. The Symons/Boesch edition moves 982 after 983, but the Bartsch/Stackmann edition does not. Lindner follows Symons/Boesch, while others follow Bartsch/Stackmann.

228. Manuscript A reads: *was do die leute taten* (985,2a). Murdoch offers a different translation: "though pressed to stay by the local people" (87); McConnell has: "regardless of what the other Normans on the beach wished to do" (105); Gibbs/Johnson translate: "in spite of all that the people, some smiling, some wringing hands, tried to do to detain them" (88).

229. Manuscript A reads: *sy machtens all zehannt* mit guot reiche (987,4b). The normalized Bartsch/Stackmann edition emends and reads: *si machtes allesant mit guote rîche*. McConnell (105n159) states that the original text reverses the subject and has Kudrun being made wealthy with gifts, a reading that Murdoch supports: "She was offered rich gifts" (87). McConnell himself, however, argues for the correctness of the emendation and translates: "but would shower them all with riches" (105).

Chapter 20: How Hartmut Returned Home [951–1040]

[988] Then old Gerlint, Ludwig's wife, said, "When will Kudrun take Hartmut, the young and mighty king, into her arms? He can claim equally high birth. If she were willing, that need not trouble her."

[989] Kudrun overheard this, that homeless maiden. She said, "Lady Gerlint, how would you like it if someone forced a man on you who was the cause of so many of your kinsmen's death? It would surely upset [you] to serve him."

[990] "What no one can change," said the king's wife, "should rightly be put behind us. Now love this man. I swear on my life that I will reward you for it always. If you want to be a queen, I will gladly give you my own crown."

[991] Then the angry woman said, "I will not wear it. You can't tell me enough about his great wealth to make me ever want to love that man. I don't want to be here; every day I long to be gone from here."

[992] The young lord of the land, brave Hartmut, was hurt by that speech, which seemed to him unkind. He said, "If I can't win over the noble lady, then she should also not expect goodwill from me."

[993] Then noble[230] Gerlint said, "Those who are wise shall lead the young and ignorant. If you permit me, Lord Hartmut, to instruct her, I believe that I can oblige her to moderate that pride of hers."

[994] "I gladly hand things over to you," said Hartmut then. "However it might work out for me, take the lovely maiden into your tutelage according to her and your honor. The young woman is far from home. Lady, you should educate her gently."

[995] Before [he] left, the young king left fair Kudrun in the care of his mother. The young queen was greatly distressed by that. She didn't want to accept Gerlint's instruction, regardless of what she did.

[996] Then the she-devil said to the fair maiden, "If you don't want [joy],[231] you will have grief. Take a look around. Who can save you from this? You will have to heat my room and tend to the fire yourself."

[997] Then the noble maiden said, "I can do that. Whatever you tell me to do, I will do it all until God in heaven turns my misfortune around. But my mother's daughter never had to tend the fire [for her]."

[998] She said, "As long as I live, you'll have to do things that other queens have never done before. I'll make you regret your great arrogance. Before the day is through you'll have to leave your ladies. [999] You think you're so special,

---

230. McConnell follows the manuscript text *edel* (noble) in 993,1a, whereas editors have emended this to *übele* (evil). It seems that "noble" could still be correct, used in a highly ironic sense, even though Gerlint's most common epithet is clearly "wicked."
231. The manuscript, as McConnell points out (106n162), has *freunde* (friends) in 996,2a, which would still make sense, as in "if you will not accept us as your friends" (106). The Bartsch/Stackmann edition emends to *freude* (joy). The juxtaposition of *freude* and *leit* is most likely correct in this case.

as I've heard told. That will be the cause of much misery for you. I'll make you regret your stubbornness; I'll chasten and break you of your high-mindedness."

[1000] Wicked Gerlint angrily returned to the court. She said to Hartmut, "Hetel's child has no respect for you and your family. Before I have to listen to more of that, I'd rather never set eyes on her again."

[1001] Then Hartmut said to his mother, "My lady, regardless how the girl behaves, please treat her with kindness so that I can thank you for it. I've hurt her so much that she may well refuse my service."

[1002] Then the queen said, "Whatever people do with her, she won't listen to anyone. She's so obstinate that she'll never agree to be your lawful wife unless she's forced. We'll resort to that, too, before she gets away with it."

[1003] Then that outstanding man from Ormanie said, "My lady, [if] you are devoted to me, then show it and act accordingly, and instruct [her] in such a way that the queen does not lose all regard for me."

[1004] The wicked she-devil angrily returned to where she had left the Hegelingen household. She said, "You women will have to go to work. What I command, let not one of you refuse."

[1005] Then they were separated, those lovely young women, so that they had to remain apart for a long time. Those who had been highly honored duchesses were made to wind yarn.[232] From then on they lived under difficult circumstances. [1006] Some of them had to spin and comb flax for her. They had come there from noble circumstances and knew how to work with gold thread and silk and affix precious gems. They had to toil under harsh conditions. [1007] The one [who] should have been foremost at court was ordered expressly to make the other women carry water [to] Ortrun's chamber. She was named Heregart. Her nobility didn't give her the least advantage. [1008][233] (1009) She was the daughter of a lord, who had towns and land. She had to stoke the oven with her white hands when Gerlint's ladies went to their rooms. She was never shown any appreciation when she served them in this way. [1009] (1008) There was another one among them from Galicia, whose misfortune had driven her there from Portugal. She had come from Ireland with Hagen's daughter to the Hegelingen. Afterward she became a household servant in Ormanie. [1010] Now listen to how strange this great suffering was. Whatever the lowliest among them[234] told her to do, she had to comply with whatever was ordered done. She gained no advantage there in Ormanie by virtue of her noble relatives. [1011] This most

---

232. The technical term *garn winden* has to do with the entire process of spinning yarn that included washing, beating, combing the wool, spinning the yarn with a drop spindle, and then winding the wool thread. This was all very labor-intensive and usually the work of laborers and peasants.

233. The Bartsch/Stackmann edition reverses this and the next strophe. The manuscript order would indicate that Heregart is the subject of strophe 1008, whereas strophe 1009 clearly introduces Hildeburg. McConnell retains the manuscript order, as is the case here.

234. This refers to Gerlint's ladies.

Chapter 20: How Hartmut Returned Home [951–1040]

degrading work, this is all true, was done by these women for three and a half years, until Hartmut returned to his homeland from three military campaigns. The dispossessed were in servitude the entire time.

[1012] Hartmut ordered that he be taken to see his beloved. It was readily apparent that the noble woman very rarely had any comfort or good food. She was being punished for the fact that she lived so virtuously.

[1013] When she approached him, the young king said, "Kudrun, lovely lady, how have you been since I and my warriors departed from our realm?"

She replied, "I've had to work in service; thanks to your sin it is my shame."

[1014] Then Hartmut replied, "Why did you do this, Gerlint, dear mother? I left [her] in your care to watch over her, in the hope that her great sorrow would in all things be eased in this land."

[1015] Then the she-wolf said, "How could I treat her any better, Hetel's daughter? You should know this: I was unable, with appeals or prohibitions, to prevent her from cursing you and your father and your whole family."

[1016] Then Hartmut replied, "That's because of [her] great suffering. We killed her relatives, along with many knights. [We made] noble Kudrun an orphan; my father killed her father. She can be wounded by careless talk."

[1017] Then his mother replied, "Son, this much is true: if we pleaded with Kudrun for thirty years, even with lashes and beatings I couldn't get her to sleep with you. There's no way anyone could force her."[235] [1018] She said to Hartmut, "I will gladly treat her well and ever better."

At the time the bold man didn't realize that it would end up worse than ever for Kudrun. No one could protect the poor woman from that.

[1019] Then she went back to where she found her sitting. She said to Kudrun from Hegelingen land, "If you don't improve your attitude, pretty girl, you'll be made to dust the seats and benches with your hair. [1020] I'm here to tell you that you'll have to clean my chamber thoroughly three times a day and keep the fire going inside for me."

She said, "I will do all that before I love anyone except my betrothed."

[1021] She willingly did everything she was told to do, that noble maiden. She left nothing undone. A full seven years in foreign lands she suffered this great hardship. She was not deemed to be a royal heiress. [1022] As the ninth year approached, the hero came to realize—Hartmut was astute—that it was a disgrace for him and his family that he ruled a kingdom but still did not

---

235. The Bartsch/Stackmann gloss on strophe 1018 speculates that some strophes might be missing between 1017 and 1018 in the manuscript. Gibbs/Johnson have a similar note (164n102). There are no gaps in the manuscript, however.

wear a crown.[236] [1023] He returned from battle, he and his men. He had won acclaim through his great courage. It was then that he thought he should become engaged to fair [Kudrun], whom he wanted to have as his wife more than any other woman. [1024] Once he had settled in, he had her brought to him. Gerlint didn't allow her to wear any decent clothing and beat her.[237] Whatever the hero did, the young woman paid little attention, since she remained steadfast in her high honor. [1025] Then his relatives advised him, whether his mother liked it or not, that he should make the lovely maiden bend to his will any way he could. He could still look forward to many pleasant times with that lady.

[1026] Following his relatives' counsel, he went to where he found her in a room. He took her by the hand. He said, "You should love me, most noble and highborn maiden, and be a queen. My heroes will serve you admirably."

[1027] Then the lovely maiden said, "I have no intention of doing that. Wicked Gerlint causes me such suffering that I have no desire for any man's love. I loathe you and all your kin with every fiber of my being."

[1028] "I'm sorry about that," said Hartmut. "If I could serve you, I would compensate you for whatever my mother Gerlint has done to hurt you, to both our honor."

Then the noble maiden said, "I will never trust you again."

[1029] Then young Hartmut from Ormanie said, "You know full well, Kudrun, that I command this land and the towns and the citizens. Who would take me to the gallows if I forced you to be my lover?"

[1030] Then Hetel's daughter said, "I would call that a crime. I've never had to worry about such a thing before. Other lords would say, if they heard tell about this, that a granddaughter of Hagen's was a concubine[238] in Hartmut's realm."

[1031] "What do I care what they do?" said Hartmut then. "If it pleased only you alone, my lady, then I would become king and you would be queen."

---

236. As an unmarried heir, he did not have the right to take his father's crown while his father was still alive. If he had been married, then his father could have bestowed the crown on him and "retired."

237. Manuscript A reads: *Gerlint die sluog sy* (1024,3a). The normalized Bartsch/Stackmann text emends and reads: *Gêrlint diu übele*. McConnell comments on this (109n166) and retains the original text in his translation: "Gerlind had not allowed her to wear fine clothes and had beaten her" (109). Gibbs/Johnson translate with the emendation: "Wicked Gerlint did not allow her to wear any decent clothes" (91).

238. The Middle High German term is *kebese*, which is often translated in English as "concubine" (Murdoch; Gibbs/Johnson) or "a kept woman" (McConnell). The concept of legitimacy in the eyes of society is key to the dispute between Kriemhild and Brunhild in the *Nibelungenlied*. Kriemhild accuses Brunhild of being a *kebse* because Siegfried, and not her husband Gunther, took Brunhild's virginity (and with it her extraordinary strength). In translations of this scene (*NL* 838–51), the term has been translated with a variety of words, including mistress, consort, paramour, concubine, harlot, and whore.

Chapter 20: How Hartmut Returned Home [951–1040]

She said, "You needn't worry that I'll ever want to love you. [1032] You know very well, Lord Hartmut, how things stand. How your daring recklessness has harmed me, when you kidnapped me and took me away from there, what your warriors did to harm my father's men. [1033] [You] also know, this pains me greatly, that your father Ludwig killed my father. If I were a knight, he could never approach me without being armed. Why then should I sleep with you? [1034] It [was] until now custom that no woman would have to take a husband unless they both consented.[239] That was most honorable."[240]

Fair Kudrun grieved terribly for her father.

[1035] Then Hartmut said angrily, "I couldn't care less what they do to you, since you won't consent to wear a crown with me. You will find what you seek; that will surely be [your] daily reward."

[1036] "I will earn that reward as I have done up to now. Whatever I can do for Hartmut's men and Gerlint's women, since God has forsaken me, I will gladly suffer it all. I am weighed down by care."

[1037] They wanted to try another way. They told fair [Ortrun], a lovely young woman, to come to court. She, along with her household, was to persuade poor Kudrun with her gentility to show more goodwill.

[1038] Then brave Hartmut said openly, "I will make you wealthy, sister, if you help me and make high and mighty Kudrun forget her great suffering, so that she stops complaining so much."

[1039] Then young Ortrun of Ormanie said, "I will serve [her] always, along with all who are here, so that she might forget her pain. I will bow my head before her. I and my young ladies will serve her always, as if we were her bondwomen."[241]

[1040] The stately young woman thanked [her] for that. "That you would want to see me crowned next to Hartmut the king, and that I should live in honor, this I will repay you with loyalty. Still my exile here remains a great hardship."

---

239. McConnell (110n168), quotes from Frances and Joseph Gies, *Marriage and the Family in the Middle Ages* (1987), 137–38, that Roman law and the church fathers required the active consent of both parties to a marriage.

240. Murdoch (169n13) suggests that the second half-line (1034,3b) may not be a part of Kudrun's speech but rather a comment by the narrator.

241. The Middle High German term used in the text is *eigen*. This is equivalent to the modern German term *Leibeigenschaft*. McConnell translates as "servants" and Murdoch and Gibbs/Johnson as "vassals." The term is better equated with the concept of serfdom or indentured servitude, in which an unfree person was bound to work on the manorial land and not free to leave, but could not be sold as a slave.

Chapter 21: How Kudrun Had to Do the Wash [1041–70]

[1041] Then Kudrun was offered towns and land. Since she didn't want them, soon after she had to wash clothes every day, from morning into the night. Thanks to this, Lord Ludwig was deprived of victory when he fought Herwig.

[1042] Then Kudrun was asked to get up from her seat, and the noble maiden was told to go with Ortrun to get some rest and drink some good wine. The outcast said, "I don't want to be queen. [1043] You know very well, Lord Hartmut, regardless of what you want, that I was given to a king with binding oaths to be his lawfully wedded wife. Unless he is dead, I will never be with another man."

[1044] Then Lord Hartmut said, "You suffer needlessly. Only death can separate us now. You should remain on friendly terms with my sister. She will soften your suffering; I fully trust that [she] can do so."

[1045] Hartmut wanted to believe that her stubbornness would be moderated if his sister shared with her in equal parts whatever she might do. They both clearly still thought they might succeed with her. [1046] Kudrun welcomed whomever offered her service. Ortrun lived near her, and her coloring turned rosy in just a short time because she drank and ate well. All of this was made available to her. The poor woman was not so clever then.[242] [1047] Whenever the king greeted her and was nice to her, it made little difference to her. She thought of the suffering that she and her household endured in foreign lands. She struck back at Hartmut with harsh words for her abuse.

[1048] She did this for so long that the king became irate. He said, "My Lady Kudrun, I am of the same rank as Lord Herwig, whom you have most honorably[243] taken as your lover, but often you reproach me all too harshly. [1049] If you would stop, it would be good for us both. It hurts me immeasurably when

---

242. The meaning of this line has led to considerable debate. Manuscript A reads: *da was die arme nicht so weyse* (1046,4b). Just the opposite is declared in 1056,4, i.e., that Kudrun was indeed very clever. Aside from a possible scribal error to explain the line, it seems difficult to square the two statements, that she was at once not clever but then later very clever. McConnell includes an editorial note in his translation: "the poor woman was, however, not so 'wise' [as to change her mind]" (111). Gibbs/Johnson translate: "but the poor woman was not that sensible" (93) and speculate in a note "that Kudrun was not 'sensible' enough to dissimulate so that she might continue to enjoy a better life" (164n104); Murdoch translates: "but poor Kudrun was not sure how to respond to this treatment" (93), also with a note (169n2). Martin (1902) has an interesting take on the line in his gloss: "she didn't possess the wisdom to choose this life" ("sie besass nicht die klugheit, dies leben zu wählen"), and in parentheses indicates that the meaning is ironic. This would be similar to McConnell, who puts "wise" in quotes. Finally, the Bartsch/Stackmann gloss on the line interprets the meaning to be that Kudrun was not clever or wise enough to feign a more friendly attitude in order to enjoy a better life.

243. The Bartsch/Stackmann gloss suggests that *für michel ere* (1048,3b) could mean something like "instead of the great honor" ("an Stelle der großen Ehre"), i.e., that she has chosen Herwig instead of the great honor she could enjoy as Hartmut's queen. Murdoch agrees with this reading (93), but McConnell (111) and Gibbs/Johnson (93) do not.

Chapter 21: How Kudrun Had to Do the Wash [1041–70]

someone does you harm, and in doing so burdens your heart and your mind. No matter how much you hate me, I would still make you queen."

[1050] Hartmut went to urge his men to protect the realm and his honor in all respects. He thought to himself at times, "Everyone hates me so much that I need to make sure I'm not on the losing side."[244]

[1051] Wicked Gerlint ordered her into service, the one whom she never allowed into the ladies' chamber. The woman who by all rights should have been sought out among the offspring of lords was instead to be found among the poor.

[1052] The old she-wolf, filled with hate, said to her, "I want Hilde's daughter to be in service to me, since, in her wickedness, she deems herself to be so unyielding. Now she'll have to serve me in ways she would have never done otherwise."

[1053] Then the noble maiden said, "Whatever I must do in service, I do so willingly and with my own hands, day and night.[245] I will do so diligently at all times, since my misfortune does not allow me to be with my family."

[1054] Then wicked Gerlint said, "You will carry my clothes down to the beach every day, and you will wash them for me and my household, and you will take care that no one ever finds you idle."

[1055] Then the noble maiden said, "Almighty wife of a king, please arrange that I be taught, so that I can learn how best to wash your clothes. I should not have any pleasure; I would rather you punished me even more. [1056] Make it so that I am taught, since I am to do the wash. I'm not too good for it; I would want to do it well. Since this is how I will earn my meals, I will not refuse anyone."

Poor Kudrun was very clever.[246]

[1057] Then Gerlint had a washerwoman, the one who would teach her, carry the clothes down to the beach with her. This was the beginning of her wretched and dreadful service. No one intervened, and Gerlint tormented highborn Kudrun. [1058] There below Ludwig's castle she was taught to be of service to heroes in this way, so that no one could wash their clothes better in the land of Ormanie. Her young ladies were never more sad than when they saw her toiling

---

244. Manuscript A reads: *man hazzet mich so sere daz ich an dem schaden icht werde erfunden* (1050,4). Gibbs/Johnson translate: "She hates me so much that I may suffer damage as a result" (93; see also 164n105). Despite the note, it's not quite clear why the subject would be changed. Leaving the subject "one" (*man*), expressed here with a generalized "everyone," makes the threat much more universal, possibly even from within Hartmut's realm or his own court.

245. Manuscript A reads: *was ich dienen mag | mit willen und mit hennden nacht und tag | daz soll ich vleissiklichen tuon in aller stunde* (1053,1b–3b). Störmer-Caysa has a different translation here (see 611n1053,1–4): "Every service that I am prepared to do day and night and can undertake with my own hands, I will do diligently at any time" ("Jeden Dienst, den ich bei Tag und Nacht bereitwillig und mit eigener Hand ausfüren kann, werde ich jederzeit geflissentlich tun"). The point is that Kudrun reserves for herself the right to say what she is willing to do.

246. Compare with 1046,4.

away on the beach. [1059] There was one among them, who was also a king's daughter. However much they all lamented, it was nothing in comparison with her. This hardship hit all of them especially close to home, when they saw their noble lady so sadly doing the wash.

[1060] Then Hildeburg, that young woman, said with devotion, "It should grieve all of them, may God hear our lament, all of those who came to this land with Kudrun. They hardly expect any rest, but now she herself is standing on the beach washing."

[1061] Gerlint heard this. She said to her cruelly, "If you want your lady to not have to work, then you will at all times help her with this work."

"I would gladly do it in her stead," said Hildeburg, "if someone allowed me. [1062] For the sake of God almighty, my Lady Gerlint, don't leave her alone. She is the child of a king. My father also wore a crown, but I will do it nonetheless. Let me wash alongside her, [whether] things go well for us or not. [1063] I feel sorry for her, even though I suffer myself, because of the high honor that God has bestowed on her. The most powerful kings of old were her ancestors. Her work here is unbecoming, but being with her will never be a burden to me."

[1064] Then wicked Gerlint said, "Then you will suffer often. No matter how hard the winter is, you will have to wash clothes in the snow and in the icy wind, even if you would rather spend time in the heated rooms."

[1065] She[247] could hardly wait for it to be evening. That was a solace to noble Kudrun. Lady Hildeburg went to her in one of the rooms; they both heartily complained about their work.

[1066] Crying, highborn Hildeburg said, "Surely your great hardship pains me deeply. I asked the she-devil that you not be left alone on the beach to do the washing. I will carry [the burden] with you."

[1067] Then the exile said, "May Christ reward you, that you are so saddened by my suffering. If you want to wash with me, that will make us happy and make the time go by, and it will make us feel better."

[1068] Then she was permitted to carry the clothes, bereft of all joy, down to the beach to wash with her in her great misery. Regardless of what anyone else did, these two still had to do the wash. [1069] When her household had the chance, they would start crying whenever they saw [them] standing there on the beach washing. This they all sorely lamented, even though they had their own privations, more than anyone else in the world. [1070] This lasted for so long—this is all true—that they had to do the wash for five and a half years, providing white clothes for Hartmut's heroes. Women never had it so bad; they could be seen outside the residences in a pitiable state.

---

247. The Bartsch/Stackmann gloss states that this is Hildeburg. Most translators make this explicit by adding her name.

Chapter 22: How Hilde Fought to Save Her Daughter [1071–1141]

[1071] We will now put aside how they served these men and women. Lady Hilde never stopped thinking about how she could devise a plan to rescue her dear daughter from the land of Ormanie. [1072] She had ordered seven strong ships, solid and seaworthy, to be built there on the seashore, twenty-two [cogs], all new and well outfitted. They were fully supplied with whatever they needed. [1073] She had forty galleys on the sea, which she cherished above all. She was waiting for an army that she could send out. She had procured rations for them as best she could; she rewarded her heroes, to her credit. [1074] The time came when she was no longer prepared to delay the sea voyage to those who suffered so terribly from their many privations in foreign lands. Fair Hilde had her messengers well outfitted with clothing.

[1075] It was around Christmas when she announced the time had come to go out and avenge Hetel's death. She commanded that all her relatives and her vassals be told that her dear daughter was to be brought back from there. [1076] Then she sent her messengers first to Herwig, so that he and his men should be reminded that they had sworn long ago to undertake a military campaign against those[248] who had left many a highborn orphan in Hegelingen. [1077] Then Hilde's envoys hurried toward Herwig's realm. He knew well why they'd been sent there. He went out to meet them where they had been seen. He greeted them attentively as they presented him with Hilde's message.

[1078] "You know very well, sir, how things stand with the oath that warriors in Hegelingen swore. Lady Hilde is relying on you more than anyone else. Kudrun's misery rightly touches no one more."

[1079] That noble knight said, "I know how things stand, that Hartmut with his insolence captured my beloved [because] she rejected him and chose me as her betrothed. That is also why my Lady Kudrun lost her father, Hetel. [1080] Envoy, tell her that I am at her service. Hartmut will surely never be forgiven that he has kept my lady captive for so long. This arduous task concerns me more than anyone else. [1081] You should tell her and her household, envoy, that I will ride to Hegelingen twenty-six days after Christmas with three thousand men."

They didn't stay any longer; Lady Hilde's messengers departed from there.

[1082] Then Herwig prepared himself for the coming battle, along with those who had often done the same. He equipped men for the journey who wanted

---

248. Manuscript A reads: *von den* in *was bestan daz den Hegelingen manig reicher wayse* (1076,4). The Bartsch/Stackmann gloss on the line states that *von den* refers to "the enemy, namely the Normans, from whom etc." ("Feinden, nämlich den Normannen, von denen usw."). Störmer-Caysa, in her note (612, incorrectly listed as n. 1067,4) disagrees and claims that *von den* refers back to Herwig, whom Hilde blames for the defeat of the Hegelingen, and translates: "because of whom . . . many noble orphans stayed behind" ("durch die . . . viele vornehme Waisen zurückgeblieben waren").

The Book of Kudrun

to ride with him during the harsh winter, those who would fight alongside him. [1083] Fair Hilde was in dire need of help. She had [her supporters] in the Danish March informed that the brave men should wait no longer, those who wanted to march to Ormanie to save fair Kudrun. [1084] She had Horant told that he should remember that he was the king's kinsman, [so that] he and his men would have compassion for her dear daughter. She would rather die before Kudrun lay in Hartmut's arms.

[1085] Then the bold man said, "You should tell Lady Hilde that I will avenge this with many [a woman's] lament. I will gladly come to her aid, along with all my household. Because of this many mothers' children in that land will be heard crying out. [1086] In addition, you should tell my lady that I will gladly come to her aid in a few days' time, and that I am optimistic about this war. I will provide ten thousand of my heroes from the Danish March."

[1087] The messengers wanted to take their leave and went to the march in Walays, where they found Morunc, that powerful margrave,[249] along with his men. He was happy to see the envoys and welcomed them most kindly.

[1088][250] (1090) Then Irolt spoke, "Since I know well that [I] should ride to Hegelingen land in seven weeks with my warriors, however many I can provide, I do so most gladly, whatever the outcome might be for my men."

[1089] Then Morunc let it be known in Holzanland that Lady Hilde had sent for her supporters. The brave men were told that there was to be a war. The news was passed on to bold Fruote of the Danish March. [1090] (1088) Then the worthy knight said, "I will gladly travel to where we can win her back. It's been thirteen years since we swore to undertake a campaign against Ormanie, after Hartmut's allies ran away from us with Kudrun."

[1091] Wate was also supportive, the hero from Stormland—he provided aid. Even though he [had] not [been] visited by the queen of Hegelingen's messenger,[251] he hurried as best he could to bring as many brave knights as possible. [1092] Then they all prepared themselves for the campaign. Wate there in Stormarn was well supplied with a thousand heroes, his vassals and kinsmen. With these he intended to attack Hartmut of Ormanie.

[1093][252] The captive women were poorly cared for by Gerlint, except for Lady Hergart, which was the name of [one] of them. She was served in love

---

249. The term *marcgrâve* denotes a count or noble responsible for defending a border area (*marc* or march).
250. The Bartsch/Stackmann edition switches manuscript strophes 1088 and 1090. The edition conjectures a break in the text after 1089. Supposedly Fruote's answer and the messenger's visit to Irolt are missing.
251. This may or may not be intentional, since Wate was the leader of the unsuccessful expedition to rescue Kudrun fourteen years prior.
252. The Bartsch/Stackmann edition notes that these two strophes, 1093 and 1094, are almost certainly in the wrong position in the manuscript. Gibbs/Johnson (164n110) state that 1093 and

Chapter 22: How Hilde Fought to Save Her Daughter [1071–1141]

by the king's cupbearer; she wanted to become a powerful duchess. [1094] Fair Hilde's daughter cried often about this. It later came to harm that same lady greatly that she did not want to share their burden with them. Whatever happened to her on that account was of no concern to Kudrun.

[1095] The people were working hard, as I've already told you, but there was little relief from all the hardship that those in Hegelingen land often endured. The heroes suggested that they call for Kudrun's [brother]. [1096] The messengers rode with all speed to Ortland.[253] There they found the young warrior in a grassland near a wide river, where there were many birds. The king was hunting skillfully there with his falconer.

[1097] He saw the messengers approaching and promptly said, "People are riding there who were sent to us by my Lady Hilde, you bold heroes. She must be thinking that we've forgotten about the campaign."

[1098] He let the falcons fly and [rode] swiftly out to where he soon had reason to be concerned. He greeted the messengers, who quickly told him that they had witnessed how the queen wept constantly. [1099] They informed him of her devotion, loyalty, and affection and asked what the warrior thought about that, and which of his men he would bring with him. They would launch the campaign toward [Ormanie from] Hegelingen.

[1100] Then Ortwin said, "You have spoken correctly. I will lead from here a great and massive army with brave heroes, with twenty thousand men. These I will lead there, even if none of them ever returns."

[1101] Men from all over could be seen riding into the land, those whom Lady Hilde had summoned. How the heroes endeavored to serve her well for honor! Sixty thousand or more came for her sake. [1102] Lord Morunc of Walays [had] on the sea some sixty strong cogs, solid and seaworthy. He wanted to take however many people they could carry across the waves to Hegelingen to bring Lady Kudrun back. [1103] Great ships were also brought there from Ortland. With admirable care, their horses and attire and everything else were outfitted for the war, their helmets and their weapons. They carried excellent armor for their knights. [1104] They estimated from the shields how many there might be coming to the aid of fair Hilde, to bring back the noble maiden from the kingdom of Ormanie. They counted seventy thousand, to them Lady Hilde gave expensive gifts. [1105] Whoever had arrived, or whoever came to the court, the unhappy lady never neglected to go out and meet them and greet each one. Those extraordinary men were given some amazing things. [1106] Hilde's ships were so well provisioned that, even if they had set sail early the next day, the worthy guests would have thought it [appropriate]. She didn't want to let

---

1094 appear to be an interpolation, and the translation places these in brackets. Murdoch places the two strophes in Chapter 20 of his translation, between 1010 and 1011.
253. Manuscript A has *Nortlant* (1096,1b).

them go until they wanted for nothing. [1107] Lady Hilde had the weapons loaded onto the ships, along with many robust helmets made of steel. Gleaming breastplates[254] for five hundred men, beyond what they already had, she had these loaded as well. [1108] Their anchor lines were made of good, strong silk. Their sails were substantial, and with them they would travel from the land of Hegelingen to Ormanie, those anxious to bring Kudrun back to Lady Hilde. [1109] Their anchors were not constructed of iron, but as we hear tell were cast of bronze from bells. They[255] were joined with Spanish brass, so that the brave heroes would not be threatened by magnetic stones.[256] [1110] Fair Hilde presented Wate and his men with many gold armbands. Many of these heroes would lose their lives because of it, when he took the Hegelingen to bring the fair lady back from Hartmut's castle.

[1111] Hilde adamantly appealed to the men from Daneland, "As you have fought in tough battles until now, I will honorably reward you. Follow my standard-bearer; he can lead you best." [1112] They asked who that was, so she told them. She said, "That is Horant, from Daneland. His mother was mighty Hetel's sister. If you trust [him] in this, you should not leave his side in battle. [1113] You should also not forget my dear son. That hero [is] especially daring. He has only just grown to be a man in his twenty years of life.[257] If someone threatens him, then help him, brave warriors, to escape."

[1114] They would gladly do so, if they were near him, they all said together. He would return home to his land uninjured if he followed them. That hero Ortwin, in his youthful exuberance, was pleased. [1115] There were so many amazing things carried and loaded onto the ships that no one could really tell you all about it. They took their leave to set out on their difficult mission. Fair Hilde prayed that Christ in heaven might accompany them. [1116] Many went with them whose fathers had been killed. The worthy orphans did not want to accept their loss. Many of the women there in Hegelingen wept, wondering when God in heaven would bring their dear children back again. [1117] They could bear no more of this and didn't want the people to go on lamenting. They made their way from there with a joyful noise. As they went down to the ships, the brave knights could all be heard singing. [1118] After the men had left that place, many women could be seen standing in the windows. They accompanied them with their eyes as far as they could, from the castle at Matelane, as the heroes got

---

254. This is more properly termed the mail coif (*halsperge*), which can be also a metonym for the entire chain mail coat.
255. This may refer to the aforementioned anchors, but it would make more sense to think of the ships being joined, that is, constructed, with brass rivets.
256. So-called magnetic stones, even mountains and islands, were thought since antiquity to attract ships containing iron to hazardous coastlines and their doom.
257. As McConnell (117n172) and Murdoch (170n5) point out, there is a chronological problem here if Ortwin actually fought at the Battle of Wulpensand thirteen or fourteen years prior.

Chapter 22: How Hilde Fought to Save Her Daughter [1071–1141]

underway. [1119] The masts creaked; a strong wind had come up, and all the sails billowed. Many a mother's child traveled in the hope that they would win honor. There was much to be won, but they would have much to suffer for it.

[1120] I really don't know everything that happened to them, except that the king of the land of Karadie[258] traveled with his army to meet these warriors. From his own land he brought with him at least ten thousand eager fighters. [1121][259] On the Wulpensand, where the battle had taken place, those from every land had set themselves the goal, all of them equally, to assemble together again. Their monastery was prosperous; old and young alike had made gifts. [1122] Of those who left the ships and the harbor, many now returned from their father's grave with such anger that it would prove challenging, they now realized, for those who [had been] their enemies in battle.[260] [1123] The king of the Moors was well received. He brought twenty-four cogs filled with men, along with plenty of rations, enough to last them twenty years. They were intent on attacking them in Ormanie.

[1124] They shoved off from the shore as best they could with their ships. Later they experienced great hardships out on the open sea. What good did it do now that old Wate and Fruote of the Danes led them? [1125] They encountered southerly winds that drove them out to sea,[261] that noble retinue, and this caused them great distress. They couldn't have reached the ocean floor with a thousand lines. Almost all their best sailors soon shed tears and lost hope. [1126] Hilde's army was stuck near the mountain at Givers. Regardless of how good their anchors were, the magnetic stones had drawn them into the Dark Sea.[262] Their sturdy masts were all bent and bowed.

[1127] When the troops cried and complained, old Wate said, "Drop our heavy anchors all the way into the endless depths. People tell stories about certain places—I'd rather be in any of them now. [1128] Since our lady's army is adrift here, and we've come so far out onto the Dark Sea, long ago as a child I heard tell seafaring stories that in the mountain at Givers a great kingdom was founded.

---

258. This is Siegfried.
259. The Symons/Boesch edition (and Piper, 1895) rearranges the order of strophes 1121–23. The Bartsch/Stackmann edition keeps the manuscript order. Symons/Boesch 1121 = Bartsch/Stackmann 1123; 1122 = 1121; 1123 = 1122.
260. Manuscript A reads: *der in schedlich in streite ware* (1122,4b). All editions emend *ware* to *wære*, and translators render this as past indicative or past subjunctive. Only Störmer-Caysa translates in the present subjunctive: "that he would be their enemy in battle" ("dass er im Kampf ihr Feind sein würde").
261. Sailing in the open seas, beyond the sight of land with its potential safe harbors and reference points, was especially hazardous throughout the Middle Ages. The proper handling of sea currents and prevailing winds was largely based on experience and luck.
262. According to the Bartsch/Stackmann gloss, this *vinster mer* represented a particular sea, perhaps in the far north. It could also have had some connection with the Black Sea, marking the boundary with the East.

[1129] People live in comfort there. Their land is so rich that the rivers flow with silver instead of sand. That's what they build their castles [with]. What they use as stones is the very best gold. Certainly they are anything but poor. [1130] I [heard] even more told, God works in mysterious ways, that whoever is brought to the mountain by the magnets, and whoever can wait for the winds of the land, will be rich forever, along with all his kinsmen for all time. [1131] Let's have something to eat and see if good fortune awaits us,"[263] said Wate, that clever man. "Then we can fill our great ships with precious gems. If we return with all that, then we can happily stay at home."

[1132] Then Fruote of the Danes said, "Before this dead calm ruins me and my comrades here, I would swear a thousand oaths to forever forgo [riches] to escape from this mountain with fair winds."

[1133] The men who were Christians said their prayers. After the ships had been held in one spot for four days, I think, or even longer, the Hegelingen feared they would never get away from there. [1134] The fog lifted more and more, as God commanded. The waves began to stir, delivering them out of their misery. They saw the sun appear through the great darkness, a westerly wind came up, and their suffering was over. [1135] It drove them swiftly past the mountain at Givers some twenty-six miles, and they humbly recognized God's intercession and help. Wate and his troops had come all too close to the magnets. [1136] Next they entered into an ocean current. They were forgiven their sins; in fact, they were rid of most of their cares. God did not want them so burdened. The ships now sailed straight toward the land of Ormanie.

[1137] Then a different complaint was quickly raised. The ships' sides were creaking, and their ships started to roll and pitch heavily on the ocean waves. Brave Ortwin said, "We're paying a high price for our honor."

[1138] Then a sailor cried out, "Ah, ah, what a disaster! That we didn't meet our deaths at the mountain of Givers! Whoever is abandoned by God, how can he save himself? You proud heroes, the sea is heaving and raging again."

[1139] Then bold Horant of the Danish March shouted, "Get hold of yourselves, you warriors. I know well that this gust will harm no one; this is a wind from the west."

The king of Karadie and his retinue were gladdened by this news.

[1140] Daring Horant climbed up to the crow's nest; he saw a great many waves. He let his eyes roam across the horizon. Then that nobleman said, "You can rest easy now, we're not far from Ormanie."

---

263. Manuscript A reads: *essen wir die speyse ob unns gelinge wol* (1131,1). Störmer-Caysa offers an alternative translation of this line: "If we happen to be successful, then we can eat up our rations" ("Wenn es uns gut gelingen will, können wir den Vorrat aufessen"). Sowinski (316n1131,1) speculates that the line may be proverbial: "let's wait and see what happens" ("warten wir ab, was kommt").

Chapter 23: How They Arrived at the Anchorage and Marched into Ormanieland [1142–64]

[1141] The command went out to all the fleet to furl their sails. They saw there on the water a mountain in front of them, and also an expansive forest in front of the mountain. Wate told his heroes to set a course in that direction.

Chapter 23: How They Arrived at the Anchorage and Marched into Ormanieland [1142–64]

[1142] They sailed to that same forest at the foot of the mountain. The bold men had to proceed with stealth. They lowered their anchors down to the sea floor and bivouacked in the forest, so that no one would notice. [1143] To get some rest, they left the ships and went ashore. My, what a great many pleasant things they found there. Fresh cold streams flowed in [the] forest down from the mountain. The sea-weary men enjoyed it all. [1144] Where the men were to camp comfortably, brave Irolt climbed a tree, the tallest one of all. He looked intently to see where they should go from there, and then he beheld the kingdom of Ormanie.

[1145] "Cheer up, lads," the young man said. "My worries have disappeared, now that I've seen seven royal residences and a great hall. We'll be in Ormanie before noon tomorrow."

[1146] Then wise Wate said, "Go and carry the shields and weapons and your battle gear onto the shore. Get to work and tell your squires what to do.[264] They should exercise the horses, and have them secure the armor and helmets with straps. [1147] If for some of you a piece of equipment, that is, part of your armor doesn't fit, take my advice. My Lady Hilde sent five hundred breastplates along with us. These we will give to this company of brave knights."

[1148] The horses were quickly brought ashore to join them. Whatever kinds of rich blankets and caparisons they found, the knights and squires tried them out on their horses to see which ones fit. Everyone took the one that was right for him. [1149] The horses were exercised all along the shoreline, all the way up and down. Some were discovered to be stocked up[265] and unable to run. They had been standing too long; Wate had them cooled down right away. [1150] They lit their campfires. Good, hearty food, the best they could get there on the seashore, was prepared for those foreigners far from home. They knew that there was no respite to be had nearby. [1151] That night they were able to rest until the next day. Wate and Lord Fruote held counsel with the king. They went to discuss in

---

264. Manuscript A reads: <u>tuet euch selbe unmüessig</u> die knechte haysset dienen (1146,3). McConnell notes (121n175) that Murdoch has a "very different interpretation" of the first half line: "rest yourselves" (102).

265. This is an equine technical term. When horses have been stabled for too long, their legs may swell up due to impaired circulation, making walking and especially running very difficult until they have been carefully exercised.

109

private there on the secluded beach how they could repay those in their own land who had destroyed their castles.

[1152] "We should send out scouts," said Ortwin, "who can find out about my sister and the other captives, if the young women are still alive. When I think about her, heartache overwhelms me."

[1153] They debated who it was who could be their scout and bring them intelligence, where the young women could definitely be found there in that land, and who could keep his spying concealed from the enemy.

[1154] Then brave Ortwin of Ortland, a hero in his own right, said, "I will be a scout. Kudrun is my sister, from the same father and mother. Among all these brave men, there is no better scout."

[1155] Then King Herwig said, "I will be the other. I will live or die alongside you. The maiden was your sister, but she was given to me as my wife. I will never spend a single day not in her service."

[1156] Then Wate said angrily, "Outstanding heroes, that would be childish. I advise you most faithfully not to do this. Don't be offended, but if Hartmut found you, he would have you hanged on the gallows."

[1157] Then King Herwig said, "For better or worse, a friend should help a friend in need. I and my friend Ortwin will not give up. Whatever may happen to us, we have to find Kudrun."

[1158] Since they both wanted to join in the scouting mission, they had their kinsmen and vassals brought together, so they could tell them never to forget their most sacred [oaths] to both of the warriors.

[1159] "I remind you of your fealty," said Ortwin then. "If we are found out, if we are taken prisoner, and they want to exchange us for ransom, sell off lands and castles. Don't let that deter you. [1160] Listen, brave warriors, to what we say to you. If we are not meant to live and we are killed, then you should not forget to avenge your grievance, you proud heroes, with swords in King Hartmut's lands. [1161] We ask one more thing of you, you brave and noble knights, regardless of the hardships you heroes might encounter, that you not abandon the captive women before you've ended the fight. They have put their faith in you."

[1162] They swore fealty to the lord with their hands, the very highest-ranking among them, that they did not want nor did they intend to see their own land again until they could bring the captive women back from Ormanie. [1163] Those devoted to them lamented (they all greatly feared Ludwig's hostility) that they couldn't send out other scouts. Many of them thought, "No one can prevent their deaths now." [1164] They discussed the matter and argued all day long. By then it had grown late, and the sunlight was hidden behind the clouds toward Gustrate. That was why Ortwin and Herwig had to wait even longer.

Chapter 24: How Kudrun Learned of Their Arrival [1165–1206]

[1165] Now we will end our talk of these brave men. I want to let you hear how things were for the ones who should have been joyful but now had to do laundry in a foreign land. Kudrun and Hildeburg spent all their time washing clothes on the beach.

[1166] It happened during a time of fasting[266] around midday that a bird came swimming along. Kudrun said, "Oh dear, pretty bird, I feel sorry for you, that you have to swim around so much on the water," said the noble maiden.

[1167] A heavenly angel of God answered her in a human voice, as if it were a person: "I [am a] messenger from God, and if you know how to ask, noble, highborn maiden, then I will tell you about your relatives."

[1168] When the young woman heard the voice, she didn't want to believe that the wild bird had become so tame and was able to speak. She heard its voice as if it had come out of a human mouth.

[1169] Then the heavenly angel said, "You should rejoice, most noble maiden; great gladness will be yours. If you want to ask me about the land of your kin, then I am your messenger, as God has sent me here to comfort you."

[1170] Noble Kudrun fell down onto the sand, just as [she] would pray to God with outstretched arms. She said to Hildeburg, "How greatly we are honored, that God would have mercy on us, and we need not be sad anymore."
[1171] Then God's poorest said, "Since Christ sent you to comfort us homeless women in this land, please let me hear, dearest messenger, does Hilde still live? She was poor Kudrun's mother."

[1172] Then the heavenly one said, "I will tell you. Hilde your mother was well when I saw her, as she sent out to you in this land an army greater than any widow or kinsman has ever sent out for the sake of family."

[1173] Then the noble maiden said, "Heavenly messenger, please do not be irritated; I want to ask you more. Does Ortwin still live at all, the king of Ortland, and Herwig, my beloved? This is news I would love to hear."

[1174] Then the heavenly angel said, "I will gladly reveal this to you. Ortwin and Herwig are very well. I saw them on the waves out on the sea. The courageous warriors were sailing together as one."

[1175] She said, "Now tell me more. Do you know whether Irolt and Morunc are coming to this land, heavenly messenger? I would like to ask this. I would like to see them very much. They were also kinsmen of my father Hetel."

[1176] Then the heavenly messenger said, "I will tell you this. Irolt and Morunc, I have seen them. They willingly serve you, lady most fair. When they

---

266. Murdoch (104) and Gibbs/Johnson (104) have speculated that *in einer vasten* (1166,1a) might be the Lenten season. Gerlint states in 1192,2 that Palm Sunday is approaching.

arrive here in this land, they will shatter many helmets." [1177] Then the heavenly angel said, "I must leave, may God preserve your honor; I still have much to do. It is also beyond my station to say more."

He disappeared before their eyes, which the young women lamented very much.

[1178] Then Hilde's daughter said, "I'm saddened beyond measure. What I wanted to ask about has been denied me. I charge you in Christ's name, before you go away, to release me, poor, poor queen that I am, from misery."

[1179] He hovered before her eyes as before. "Before we take our leave, yours and mine, however I may serve you, that shall not displease me. Since you have asked in Christ's name, I will tell you everything about your kinsmen."

[1180] She said, "I would like to hear, should you know, if Horant of the Danish March is coming here, along with his heroes, who left me in such misery? I know that he is daring, and that I, poor maiden, might profit from him."

[1181] "Your cousin Horant is coming to you from the Danish March to wage a great war, he and his warriors. He will be carrying Hilde's standard in his own hands, when the Hegelingen arrive in Hartmut's land."

[1182] Then Kudrun replied, "Can you tell me, does Wate of Stormarn still live? If so, I wouldn't complain. We would all rejoice if it happened that we could also see old Fruote under my [mother's] standard."

[1183] Then the angel replied, "Wate of Stormarn is coming for you to this land. He holds in his hand a solid rudder in the same ship with Fruote. You couldn't ask for better allies in a time of war."

[1184] Then the angel wanted to leave them again, when God's poorest said, "I'm still troubled. I would very much want to know when it might be that I, an outcast, might see my mother Hilde's messenger."

[1185] The angel answered her, "Joy is at hand. Two messengers will come to you tomorrow morning. They are so worthy that they will not deceive you; whatever news they bring you will not in any way be untrue."

[1186] Then the heavenly messenger had to leave them. The homeless women asked no other questions. They were lost in thoughts both pleasant and burdensome, about the men who would help them, where that worthy retinue was. [1187] That day they washed the clothes more slowly. They talked about the heroes who had been sent there from Hegelingen by mighty Hilde. The women waited anxiously for Kudrun's kinsmen. [1188] The day drew to a close; the captive women wanted to go home, but they were angrily reprimanded by wicked Gerlint. There was rarely a time when she was[n't] angry with the noble servants.

[1189] She said to the women, "Who gave you permission to take your time washing the fine linens and other clothing? You've been lazy bleaching my white fabrics. If you aren't careful I'll make sure that you have something to cry about."

Chapter 24: How Kudrun Learned of Their Arrival [1165–1206]

[1190] Then Lady Hildeburg said, "We do what we can. You should treat us, dear lady, with the respect we deserve. We, the poor house servants, are often freezing. If the weather were warmer, we could wash more for you."[267]

[1191] Then Gerlint replied to them harshly, "You shouldn't waste time regardless of the weather, but instead wash my linens from morning till night. As soon as the day dawns, you should be gone from my chambers. [1192] We will soon have a feast day; you know that very well. Palm Sunday is approaching; we'll be welcoming guests. And if you don't give my heroes clothes that are white, then washerwomen will never have had it so bad in a king's palace."

[1193] They left her and took off the wet clothes they had been wearing. They should have been treated better, but any kind of sympathy for them was completely lacking. They were unhappy about that; their meal consisted of rye bread and water. [1194] The poor servants wanted to go to sleep. Their beds were not soft. Both of them wore nothing but two soiled nightshirts. This is how wicked Gerlint treated them; she let them sleep without a pillow on hard benches. [1195] Poor Kudrun slept very uncomfortably. They both could hardly wait until the day came, and they barely slept at all. They were probably thinking about when the birds would bring the brave knights [to them].[268]

[1196] When the new day arrived, noble Hildeburg from the land of Galicia, who had slept uncomfortably all through the night, went to the window. It had snowed, and the poor women were miserable and fearful. [1197] Then the outcast woman said, "We should go washing. Unless God prevents it, the weather is so bad that if we wash today, completely barefoot, they'll probably find us dead before evening."

[1198] She was hopeful, though, and indeed it did happen that she would see Hilde's messengers that day. When they thought about them, those lovely maidens, about those who would bring them solace and joy, they were not so heartbroken.

[1199] Then Hilde's daughter said, "Friend, please ask wicked Gerlint if she would allow us to wear shoes down to the water. She can see for herself that if we go barefoot, we'll certainly freeze to death."

[1200] They went to find the king and his wife. There with her arms wrapped around Ludwig was wicked Gerlint. They were both still asleep. They didn't dare wake them; poor Kudrun regretted that.

---

267. Manuscript A reads: *waren warme winde wir wüeschen offte ewch destmere* (1190,4). Störmer-Caysa comments in her note (616n1190,4) that the striking alliteration may be an attempt to invoke an older epic style.

268. This might be a reference to birds showing ships at sea the way to land. As stated in the Bartsch/Stackmann gloss, it could also be a reference to birds as the heralds of the new day.

[1201] She heard them complaining in her sleep as they stood there. She scolded the lovely women. She said, "Why haven't you gone down to the beach to wash my clothes, until the rinse water is clean and clear?"

[1202] Then the foreign woman said, "But I don't know where to go. Last night there was a heavy snowfall. Unless you want us to suffer death,[269] we will certainly die today if we aren't wearing shoes on our feet."

[1203] Then the she-wolf said, "I don't think that's possible. You'll have to leave as you are, for better or for worse. If you don't hurry with the wash, I'll make sure you regret it. What do I care if you die?"

Both of the poor women cried. [1204] Then they took the clothes and went out. "May God grant," said Kudrun, "that I can remind you of this."

With their bare feet they trudged through the snow. The noble maidens suffered because of their captivity. [1205] As was their routine, they went down to the beach. They stood there and washed the clothes as always, what they had carried down to the shore. Their high hopes were of little use to them now. [1206] They often looked out over the water with longing glances, to where the noble messengers should come from, the ones who had been sent to the noble household servants by the mighty queen from her land.

Chapter 25: How Ortwin and Herwig Arrived There [1207–1334]

[1207] After having waited a long time, they saw out on the sea two men in a small boat, and no one else. Lady Hildeburg said to noble Kudrun, "I see two men rowing out there; they look like they may well be your messengers."

[1208] Then the woman rich in misery said, "Oh dear, wretched me! Inside I'm filled with both joy and pain. If they are Hilde's messengers, and they find me here like this, washing on the beach, I could never endure such shame. [1209] I, God's poorest, don't know what I should do. My dear friend, Hildeburg, give me your advice. Should I run away from here or let them find me here in this disgraceful condition? I would rather remain a servant forever."

[1210] Then Lady Hildeburg replied, "You see how things stand. You shouldn't leave such crucial advice to me. I gladly share in everything you do. I will stay with you and suffer evil or good."

[1211] Then they both turned around and ran away. In the meantime the two men were so close that they could see the pretty women washing on the shore. They could plainly see that they were about to leave the clothes behind.

---

269. Manuscript A reads: *ir welt unns dann des todes gerne puessen* (1202,3). All editors add *en-* before *welt*, making it negative, with a meaning like "unless you don't want us to suffer death." Sowinski (211) translates in the original sense: "Do you want to punish us here with death?" ("Wollt Ihr uns etwa hier mit dem Tode strafen?"), as does Lindner (224).

Chapter 25: How Ortwin and Herwig Arrived There [1207–1334]

[1212] They jumped out of the skiff and called out to them, "You pretty washerwomen, why are you in such a hurry? We are friends[270]—this you can surely tell. If you run away from this place, you may well lose all that fine linen."

[1213] They acted as if they hadn't heard, but they understood everything they said. Lord Herwig spoke out a bit too loudly. He didn't know the truth, that he was standing so close to his beloved.

[1214] Then the ruler of Seeland said, "You lovely girls, please let us hear whose clothes these are. We ask without malice. Do this in honor of all maidens, you lovely ladies, and please come back to the shore."

[1215] Then Lady Kudrun said, "I would otherwise be ashamed, since I am a maiden, but you asked me in the name of other maidens' honor. That is to your benefit," said the highborn woman, "[even though] I'll surely shed tears because of it."

[1216] They came forward in their shirts, which were both wet. These most noble women had seen better days. They shivered on account of the cold, those poor servants. They were shabbily dressed, and the cold winds of March were blowing. [1217] It was the season when winter retreats, and the birds compete in wanting to sing their songs again after the days of March. The poor destitute women were seen there in the snow and ice. [1218] They saw them coming back, with their hair in tangles. Even though they both had attractive faces, their hair was disheveled from the March winds. Whether it rained or snowed, the noble girls were miserable. [1219] The sea was covered with floating ice that was starting to melt. They were terrified. Their lovely bodies shone from beneath their shirts as white as snow. Not knowing what was going to happen frightened them.[271]

[1220] Noble Herwig wished them a good morning, those miserable girls. They were in dire need of that, since their mistress was incredibly cruel. "Good morning, good evening," these were rarities for the lovely [maidens].

[1221] "Please let us hear," said Lord Ortwin, "whose fine clothes these are here on the beach, and for whom do you wash? You're both so beautiful. How

---

270. Manuscript A reads: *wir seins freunde leute* (1212,3a). Bartsch/Stackmann emend to: *wir sîn fremede liute*. McConnell accepts the emendation from friends to foreigners, although he speculates (128n179) as to how the original could be correct in certain contexts. Herwig and Ortwin say they are friends, but they don't know yet to whom they are speaking. If instead they say they are foreigners, they may elicit some sympathy, but also possibly fear.

271. Manuscript A reads: *in tet die unkunde wee* (1219,4b). McConnell's note (129n180) on this half-line takes issue with the Bartsch/Stackmann gloss on *unkunde*: "living among foreigners; . . . or more likely: that they didn't know who the foreigners were" ("der Aufenthalt unter Fremden; . . . oder wohl eher: daß sie nicht wußten, wer die Fremden waren"). McConnell believes that the unknown foreigners are the Normans [Hartmut], not the messengers, whereas a general sense of "uncertainty" (Ungewissheit) as proposed by Störmer-Caysa in her translation seems more reasonable.

can he treat you so poorly? May God in heaven punish him for that. [1222] You really are so beautiful, you could wear a crown. If you were both blessed in terms of birthright, then you should be rulers of a land, held in high honor. Does he, for whom you do such menial service, have other beautiful washerwomen?"

[1223] Then the beautiful maiden said sadly, "He has many who are more beautiful than we are. Ask now what you want to know. We have the kind of mistress that we will surely suffer if she sees us from the ramparts speaking with you."

[1224] "Don't be troubled. Here, take our gold. Your reward will be four solid gold bracelets, so that you, fair ladies, are not upset. We give them to you gladly, to tell us what we want to know."

[1225] "May God keep you and your bracelets. We won't accept any reward from you," said the maiden. "Now ask what you want to know. We have to go. If we are seen with you two, then I will regret it with all my heart."

[1226] "Whose patrimony is this, along with this prosperous land and all these strong castles? What is his name, he who has you perform such lowly service without any clothes? If he wanted honor, then [no] one should praise him for this."

[1227] She said, "One of the lords is named Hartmut. Extensive lands and strong, solid castles serve him. The other is named Ludwig, of the kingdom of Ormanie. He is served by many heroes, who rule admirably in their lands."

[1228] "We would very much like to see [them]," said Ortwin. "Could you inform us, dearest fair maidens, where we might find both of the lords in their land? We have been sent to them, and we are part of a king's retinue."

[1229] Highborn Kudrun said to the heroes, "I left them this morning in the castle, lying in their beds, along with four thousand of their men. I don't know for sure if they've gone out riding in the meantime."

[1230] Then King Herwig said, "Could you please tell us, what[272] is the reason that these bold heroes are [so] troubled, that they have [so] many heroes with them all the time? If I had that many in my castle, I could conquer a kingdom."

[1231] "We don't know anything about that," said the young women. "We don't know how far the lords' Crown lands extend. There is a land far away that is called Hegelingen. They are constantly afraid that they will send them bitter enemies from there."

[1232] Then the fair maidens were shivering from the cold. Lord Herwig said, "Could it be possible, if you lovely women would not think it a disgrace, that you, noble maidens, would wear our cloaks here on the beach?"

[1233] Then Hilde's daughter said, "May God keep you and both your cloaks. May no one ever see me wearing men's clothing."

---

272. Manuscript A reads: *von wem* (of whom, by whom; 1230,2a), which is emended by Bartsch/Stackmann to *von wiu* (why).

Chapter 25: How Ortwin and Herwig Arrived There [1207–1334]

If the men had only known that far worse had happened to them.[273] [1234] Herwig often looked at the young woman. She seemed [to him] so beautiful, and had such a lovely figure that his heart was filled with sighs. She seemed very much like someone else, of whom he thought often and lovingly.

[1235] Then Ortwin, the king of Ortland, replied, "I would ask both of you maidens if you are aware of a group of captives that came into this land. There was one among them named Kudrun."

[1236] Then the young woman said, "I am well aware of them. A foreign household arrived here a long time ago. They were brought into this realm during a great war. The captive women came to this land in anguish." [1237] She said, "The one you seek, I have seen her endure great hardship, I can tell you that."

Of course, she was one of those whom Hartmut had brought there. This was Kudrun herself. She remembered the story better than anyone else.

[1238] Then Lord Herwig said, "You see, Lord Ortwin, if your sister Kudrun is alive anywhere, in any land at all anywhere on earth, then she must be the one. I've never seen anyone who resembles her so."

[1239] Then King Ortwin spoke, "She is very lovely, but she is not in any way similar to my sister. I still think of the time when we were both young, when no more beautiful woman could be found in all the world."

[1240] When the bold man said his name, that he was called Ortwin, she looked at him again, poor Kudrun. She wanted very much to know if it really was her brother. If so, all her miseries would come to an end.

[1241] "Whatever your name is, you are worthy of praise. I knew someone who was very much like you. His name was Herwig, and he was from Seeland. If that hero were still alive, he would free us from this harsh captivity.[274] [1242]

---

273. There are as many interpretations of this obscure line as there are translations. Manuscript A reads: *mohten sy sich erkennen so war in offt und dick geschehen laider* (1233,4). Part of the problem is the referent of *sy*: is it the two women or the two men, or all of them? The Bartsch/Stackmann text, marked as a crux, offers this gloss: "if they had been able to judge their situation, then they would have recognized that they often had to suffer worse than now, when they were supposed to wear men's clothing" ("wenn sie ihre Lage hätten beurteilen können, dann hätten sie erkannt, daß ihnen oft Schlimmeres geschehen war als jetzt, da sie Männerkleider tragen sollten"). Störmer-Caysa in her translation suggests a different approach: "if they could have recognized each other, then the evils which they had often experienced would have been worse" [than wearing men's clothing] ("Hätten sie einander erkennen können, dann wären für sie Übel, die sie oft erlitten hatten, schlimmer gewesen"). Sowinski offers yet another solution: "if they could recognize each other, their suffering would be even greater" ("Könnten sie sich erkennen, wäre ihr Leid noch größer," 217).

274. Manuscript A reads: *so erleset er unns von disen starchen panden* (1241,4b). The normalized Bartsch/Stackmann edition reads: *sô erlôste er uns von disen starken banden*. Störmer-Caysa explains (618n1241,4) why she translates this half-line in the past tense: "he would have (already) freed us from this arduous captivity" ("hätte er uns aus dieser schweren Gefangenschaft befreit"). All other translators use the present subjunctive (would free us).

The Book of Kudrun

I am also one of them who was captured [by] Hartmut's army in the war and brought across the sea. You seek Kudrun. You do so in vain. The maiden of Hegelingen died as a result of her great suffering."

[1243] Then Ortwin's bright eyes filled with tears, nor could Herwig keep from crying. When she told them that fair Kudrun had died, the heroes mourned greatly.

[1244] When she saw them both crying there in front of her, that most miserable maiden then said to them, "You are behaving as if you brave heroes were related to noble Kudrun."

[1245] Then Lord Herwig said, "I will surely mourn for her to the end of my days. The maiden was my wife. She was betrothed to me with binding oaths. Since then I've been bereaved of her thanks to old Ludwig's scheming."

[1246] "Now you're lying to me," said the poor woman. "I've often been told that Herwig is dead. All the world's joy I would gain if he were still alive, because he would have taken me away from here."

[1247] Then the noble knight said, "Take a look at my hand, and if you recognize the gold ring, then my name is Herwig. With this ring I was engaged to marry Kudrun. If you are my lady, then I will lovingly[275] take you away from here."

[1248] She gazed at his hand on which a ring shone brightly. There in the gold of Abalie was set a stone, the very best in the world that [she] had ever set eyes on. Fair Lady Kudrun had once worn it on her own hand.

[1249] She laughed with joy. The maiden said, "I recognized the gold ring full well; it used to be mine. Now you should look at this one, which my beloved sent me when I, poor woman, was happy in my father's land."

[1250] He looked at her hand. When he saw the gold ring, noble Herwig said to Kudrun, "You, too, were born of nothing less than a royal family. After all my pain and sorrow, I have found my joy and happiness."

[1251] He embraced the noble woman in his arms. Their circumstances meant joy and pain for them both. He kissed, I don't know how often, the highborn queen and the lovely maiden Hildeburg. [1252] Ortwin started asking the noble woman—she was ashamed because it was a painful subject—whether she couldn't serve in the land in some way other than always washing clothes on the beach.

---

275. Manuscript A reads: *minneclich* (1247,4b). Bartsch (1885) originally emended this adverb to *meinliche* (forcefully), which Piper (1895) followed. The Symons/Boesch edition (1964) emended to *gewalticliche* (violently). The Bartsch/Stackmann edition has the original. Murdoch translates: "for the sake of that love" (111).

Chapter 25: How Ortwin and Herwig Arrived There [1207–1334]

[1253] "Tell me, dear sister, where are your children, those that you've had with Hartmut up to now, that they leave you washing here on the shore? If you are to become a queen,[276] then you are ill served here."

[1254] She said to him, crying, "Why would I have children? Everyone who is close to Hartmut knows full well that he was never able to command me to be with [him]. Since then I've had to endure this hardship."

[1255] Then Lord Herwig said, "We can definitely say that things have gone well for us on this journey, so that we could never have had [more] success. Now we should hurry, so we [can] take her away from the castle."

[1256] Then brave Ortwin said, "I don't think that's possible. And if I had a hundred sisters, I would leave them to die rather than slink around in foreign lands and abscond with those my bitter enemy had taken from me in battle."

[1257][277] (1260) Then the hero of Seeland said, "I'm afraid that if we're discovered, they'll take the ladies far away (which is why we're disguised), so that we'll never lay eyes on any of them again."

[1258] (1261) Then Ortwin replied, "How can we leave the noble household here? They have long persevered in this foreign kingdom. They would give up hope. All of her ladies should benefit from being with my sister Kudrun."

[1259] (1257) Then brave Herwig said, "Are you out of your mind? I will take my beloved away from here. We will do everything we can for our lady."

Then brave Ortwin said, "I would sooner that I and my sister be hacked to pieces."

[1260] (1258) Then the unhappy woman said, "Whatever did I do to you, dear brother Ortwin? I've never acted in any way that should cause me to be reproached. I don't know what you, sir, want to punish me for."

[1261] (1259) "I'm doing this, dear sister, not because I hate you. Your ladies-in-waiting will all the more surely be rescued. I can't take you [from here] except in an honorable manner. You will [still] be with noble Herwig, your beloved."

[1262] They went to the boat, and the fair woman lamented. She said, "Oh dear, poor me. My suffering is without end. To those who were always my comfort, should I now be so loathed that they won't save me? My good fortune is far, far away."

---

276. The Bartsch/Stackmann gloss on this line points out that if Kudrun were already Hartmut's wife, then she would already be a queen, and if she were his concubine, then she could not in the future become queen.

277. The following five strophes have been rearranged in the Bartsch/Stackmann edition in an attempt to make the flow of the dialogue more logical. The original manuscript order has been retained here.

The Book of Kudrun

[1263] The valiant men were quick to leave the shore. Poor Kudrun called out to Herwig, "Once I was the highest; now I am deemed to be the lowliest. To whom do you leave me, and how will I, poor orphan, be consoled?"

[1264] "You are not the lowliest; you will be the highest. Most noble queen, say nothing about my visit. Before the sun rises tomorrow morning, I will return to this castle with eighty thousand heroes; on that I give you my word."

[1265] They left as quickly as they could. There was a parting among family as difficult [as] any family parting could be; this I know to be a fact. They followed the emissaries with their eyes as long as they could.

[1266] The highborn women had forgotten all about the wash. Wicked Gerlint was well aware of the fact that they had been standing idly on the beach below. She was enraged by that; she was angry and irritated about her laundry.

[1267] Then Lady Hildeburg, the maiden from Ireland, said, "My queen, why do you leave these clothes lying about, and why are[n't] you washing Ludwig's men's clothing? If Gerlint finds out, she'll beat us more than ever."

[1268] Then Hilde's daughter said, "I'm too highborn for that, that I should ever wash for Gerlint again. I refuse to do such menial service from now on. I was kissed by two kings, and they were happy to embrace me in their arms."

[1269] Then Hildeburg replied, "Please don't be upset if I give you some advice. We should bleach the clothes some more, so that we don't take them back to the rooms looking so grey. Otherwise our backs will be covered with lashes."

[1270] Then Hagen's offspring said, "I deserve joy, solace, and happiness. If someone were to beat me with switches the whole time until tomorrow morning, I think I would survive. Of those who treat us so harshly here, many will have to die. [1271] Now I'll carry these clothes to the water. They should have the benefit," said the noble maiden, "that I can now act like a queen. I'll throw them into the waves, so they can float away from here."

[1272] Regardless of what Hildeburg said, Kudrun carried off Gerlint's linen. [She] became angry and threw them into the water with her own hands. They floated for a while—I don't know if they were ever seen again. [1273] Then the night was approaching; daylight was fading. Hildeburg carried a heavy burden up to the castle. She was carrying various garments and seven fine linen cloths. Ortwin's sister went alongside her empty-handed. [1274] It had grown late by the time they reached Ludwig's castle. There they saw wicked Gerlint standing out front waiting for her servants. She greeted the noble washerwomen with harsh words.

[1275] "Who gave you permission to be late?" said the king's wife. "Both of you will have to pay dearly for strolling around on the shore so late in the evening. It's not appropriate for a king's wife to have to see you in her

Chapter 25: How Ortwin and Herwig Arrived There [1207–1334]

chamber."[278] [1276] She said, "Tell me this instant, why are you acting like this? You refuse to speak to mighty kings, whom you hate, but you spend the evening gossiping with some lowly attendants. If you want to gain honor, this is not the way to do it."

[1277] Then the highborn maiden said, "Why do you falsely accuse me? Wretched woman that I am, I never intended to speak to anyone, no matter how noble he was, except for my own family, to whom I should be able to speak by rights."

[1278] "Shut up, you spiteful woman![279] You're calling me a liar? I'll avenge myself tonight and make you pay, so that you'll never again vent your anger so loudly. Before I'm done your back will have to suffer for it."

[1279] "I would advise against that," said the highborn maiden. "You should never again punish me with a lashing. I'm of a higher rank than you and all your kin. That kind of unseemly punishment might now be something you regret."

[1280] Then the she-wolf said, "Where are my linens, that you would have your hands folded so calmly and casually in your lap? With my last breath I'm going to teach you what it means to serve."

[1281] Then Hagen's offspring said, "I left them lying down there by the water. When I tried to carry them up to the castle, they were too heavy for me. If you never see them again, believe me, I couldn't care less."

[1282] Then the she-devil said, "You won't get away with this. Before I go to bed, you will know what misery is."

She had thorny branches broken off and tied into a switch. Lady Gerlint was not going to forgo this unseemly punishment. [1283] She had her tied to a bed-post and didn't allow anyone else to be present in the room. She wanted to flog the fair woman's skin from her limbs. The ladies who knew what was going to happen began to cry inconsolably.

[1284] Kudrun said shrewdly, "I will tell you this. If I'm going to be beaten with this switch tonight, and if I'm ever seen in the company of mighty kings and wearing a crown, then [you] will most definitely reap your reward. [1285] So that you might willingly release me from this punishment, I will agree to love the man I have so far rejected. I will make the kingdom of Ormanie my home. Should I ever gain power, I will do what no one would imagine."

[1286] Then Lady Gerlint said, "Then I would forsake my anger. And if you had lost a thousand linens, I would excuse that. It will be to your benefit if you choose to love Lord Hartmut of Ormanie."

---

278. Manuscript A reads: *es zimbt nicht kueniges weibe daz sy euch sehe in ir kemmenaten* (1275,4). Sowinski translates very loosely: "You are no longer worthy of staying at the queen's court" ("Ihr seid es nicht mehr wert, am Hof der Königin zu bleiben," 224). Murdoch translates, equally loosely: "You are not fit to enter the chambers of a queen" (113).

279. The original is *uble galle* (1278,1a). Murdoch translates as "spiteful bitch" (114).

The Book of Kudrun

[1287] Then the fair maiden replied, "I want to make amends.[280] I can't endure all these tortures. Have the king of Ormanie brought to me, and whatever he demands of me I will do from now on."

[1288] Those who overheard this conversation hastily ran off. They told valiant Hartmut all about it. Some of his father's men were sitting next to him. Someone told him the news, that he should go see Kudrun.

[1289] He said to him openly, "I claim the messenger's reward. Fair Hilde's daughter has agreed to serve you and wants you to come to her chamber. She no longer rejects you; she has reconsidered for the better."

[1290] Then the noble knight said, "There's no need to lie. If your news were true, I would reward you with three strong castles as well as fertile acreage and sixty golden armbands. Surely I would live happily forever more."

[1291] Then one of his companions said, "I heard the same thing. I want a share in the reward. You are to come to court. The noble maiden said that she would gladly marry you. If you agree, then she would become queen here in the land."

[1292] Hartmut thanked the messenger. He jumped up from his chair for joy. It seemed to him that God had given him the gift of love. He went to the maiden's chamber filled with joy. [1293] There the noble young woman stood in her wet shift. With tears in her eyes she greeted him then. She approached him and stood so close to him that he wanted to take Kudrun into his arms.

[1294] She said, "No, Hartmut, don't do that yet. People will surely criticize you for it if they're watching. I'm a poor washerwoman. That would dishonor you. You're a mighty king. How could it be appropriate that I embrace you? [1295] I'll allow you [to do so] most willingly, Hartmut, when I stand crowned in front of your brave men. Then I will be queen; then I won't disgrace you. Then it would be appropriate for us both; then you may embrace me."

[1296] In a show of great courtesy, he stepped back a bit. He said to Kudrun, "Maiden so lovely, now that you have decided to marry me, I will reward you highly. You may command me and my friends to do as you wish."

[1297] Then the young woman said, "I've never felt so relieved. If I, God's poorest, would have something to command here, my first order would be, after such great hardship, that before I go to bed I should have a nice bath prepared. [1298] My second order would be that my ladies be brought to me quickly,

---

280. Manuscript A reads: *ia wil ich mich erholen* (1287,1b). The Bartsch/Stackmann gloss for *mich erholn* offers: "to make good a past error, to correct a mistake" ("Verfehltes wiedergutmachen, einen Irrtum berichtigen"). Sowinski translates very differently: "I first need to recuperate some" ("Ich muß mich erst etwas erholen," 226). Störmer-Caysa (620n1287,1) comments that *erholn* with the reflexive can mean both "to restore, to make amends" (wiederherstellen, wiedergutmachen) as well as "to recuperate" (sich erholen). She suggests that Kudrun is intentionally ambiguous in her statement.

Chapter 25: How Ortwin and Herwig Arrived There [1207–1334]

wherever they can be found among Gerlint's women. None of them should be left in their bedrooms."

[1299] "I will gladly make that happen," said Lord Hartmut.

Then the noble maidens were all found in their rooms. They went to court with their hair in a mess and in shabby clothes. Wicked Gerlint was heartless and imprudent.[281]

[1300] Then sixty-three appeared before Hartmut. Noble Kudrun said most courteously, "Please take a look, mighty king. Do you think this is honorable? How have these women been treated?"

Then he replied, "This will not happen to them again."

[1301] "Do this for my sake, Hartmut," said the noble woman. "Let all of my ladies who have been so mistreated have a bath tonight. Do as I ask. You will see them for yourself when they are dressed in beautiful clothes."

[1302] Hartmut, that outstanding knight, answered her, "My dear Lady Kudrun, if any of the clothing that your attendants brought here with them has been ruined, they will be given the very best that can be found anywhere. [1303] I will gladly see them with you when they are dressed."

The bath was quickly and diligently prepared. Some of Hartmut's relatives became chamberlains. They all hurried to serve her, [so that] she might later grant them her favor. [1304] Then the highborn woman was properly bathed, along with her ladies. The very best dresses that anyone could have were brought for each of them. The lowest-born of them would have pleased a king. [1305] After they bathed they were brought wine, the likes of which none better could be had in Ormanie. The very best mead was brought to the ladies. How could Lord Hartmut have known how he would be thanked for that?

[1306] The lovely ladies were seated in [a] great hall. Lady Gerlint told her daughter Ortrun that she should get [dressed],[282] along with her own ladies, if they wanted to socialize with Hilde's daughter and her ladies. [1307] Noble Ortrun immediately got dressed. She happily went to where she found Kudrun. Old Wate's kinswoman [went] to greet [her].[283] When they were together, everyone

---

281. Manuscript A reads: *die ubl Gerlint was <u>umbeschaiden</u>* (129,4b). The Bartsch/Stackmann gloss suggests "inconsiderate" (rücksichtslos) for *umbescheiden*. Störmer-Caysa translates *unbescheiden* with "unwise" (unklug).

282. Manuscript A reads: *das sy sich darzu <u>schaiden</u> solte mit ir iunckfrawen* (1306,3). The normalized Bartsch/Stackmann edition emends the original *schaiden* (to depart) to *kleiden* (to get dressed), while marking lines 1306,3–4 as a crux. McConnell translates: "that she should leave [her chamber]" (137), retaining the original manuscript reading. He justifies his decision in a note on the line (137n188).

283. The Bartsch/Stackmann gloss expresses surprise at this mention of a familial relationship between Wate and Kudrun. Wate was, of course, related to Hetel, Kudrun's father (205,1; 515–16). He fostered him and was most likely his uncle. Wate is also described as an uncle to Horant and Irolt. He may well have been Kudrun's great-uncle on her father's side.

saw them happy and joyful. [1308] Adorned with fine red gold, they kissed each other. Their faces were gleaming as well, but they were of two minds. Ortrun, the mighty queen, was happy to see that the noble washerwoman was so beautifully attired. [1309] Then the poor woman was happy, as we have said, that she would see her noble kinsmen so soon. The highborn ladies sat [there] enjoying each other's company. To look at them often would have made any sad heart glad.

[1310] "Bless me," said Lady Ortrun, "that I have lived to see that you want to stay here with Hartmut. As a reward for your good intent I will give you my mother Gerlint's crown, which I should inherit."

[1311] "May God reward you, Ortrun," said the maiden. "Whatever you ask of me, I will do gladly. You often cried over my own heartache. I will never cease to serve you loyally every day." [1312] The noble maiden said with childlike guile, "You should send out messengers, my Lord Hartmut, into the kingdom of Ormanie, if it pleases them, to your closest supporters, that they all come here to court. [1313] When there is peace in the Crown lands, this I say to you, then I will wear a crown with you in front of your heroes, so that I can recognize those who want me as their lady.[284] I will let your warriors greet me and [my] kin."

[1314] It was a cunning ploy. However many [messengers] he found, at least a hundred or more, he had sent out. This way there were fewer of the enemy when the Hegelingen sought out Hartmut. That was the maiden's intent.

[1315] Then Lady Gerlint said, "My dear daughter, you should part company now. When tomorrow comes, you can be together again as propriety allows."

Then she bowed to Kudrun and prayed to God he might protect her. [1316] Hartmut left as well. She was sent cupbearers and stewards; there was little need to call for them. The stately and noble maidens were [well attended] there. The captive women were diligently served with drink and food.

[1317] Then a very pretty maiden from Hegelingen said, "We are often saddened when we think about it, that we have to stay with those who brought us here, much to our dismay. We never thought something like that would happen."

[1318] She began to cry, there where her lady sat. Once the other girls saw this, they reflected sadly on their own great misfortune, and many of them wept. Highborn Kudrun just laughed. [1319] They thought they would have to stay forever. Their lady was not inclined to stay willingly for even four more days. It happened soon after that Gerlint was secretly informed of this. [1320] Kudrun

---

284. Manuscript A reads: *daz ich das muge erkennen wer mein beger ze frawen* (1313,3). The Bartsch/Stackmann gloss translates: "so that I know how powerful my husband is" ("damit ich weiß, wie mächtig mein Gatte ist"). Sowinski (230), Murdoch (117), and McConnell (137) all translate along the same lines. Gibbs/Johnson offer a somewhat different interpretation: "in order that I may discover what kind of a man desires me as his wife" (116). Störmer-Caysa, however, translates: "so that I see who wants to have me as their queen" ("damit ich sehe, wer mich zur Königin haben will"). The *wer* (who) can refer either to Hartmut or to a more general collective of Hartmut's nobles.

Chapter 25: How Ortwin and Herwig Arrived There [1207–1334]

began to laugh more than was appropriate, given that she had never been happy in fourteen years. The wicked she-devil heard all about this. She called Ludwig to her; she was deeply troubled.

[1321] Then she quickly went to where she found Hartmut. She said, "My son, throughout this land some misfortune will befall the people who live here. I don't know what Queen Kudrun was laughing about. [1322] However it may have happened or however she heard it, secret messengers were sent to her by her friends. You will need to defend yourself against this, noble, highborn knight, so that you don't lose life and honor on account of her friends."

[1323] He said, "Let it be. I'm pleased to allow it; she should have every happiness with her ladies. Her closest relatives reside far away. How could they attack me by surprise? I don't think I need to worry about them anymore."

[1324] Kudrun asked her household if her bed had been prepared; she wanted to go to sleep. This one night she was released from all her cares. King Hartmut's chamberlains escorted the maidens. [1325] The pages of Ormanie carried lights for them. They had never served her prior to that occasion. They found some thirty or more clean beds prepared, where the highborn daughters of knights could lie down. [1326] On them lay blankets from Arabia of many different colors and sumptuous coverlets as green as clover, embellished with fine lace edging. In the firelight the gold from the precious silk shone red [1327] in the gleaming fabric. Underneath were linings made from the furs of various sea animals. Hartmut imagined that he [was] dear to that lovely woman from Hegelingen. He didn't know what was to come, what suffering her kindred would bring him.

[1328] Then the noble maiden said, "You should all go to sleep, you, Hartmut's heroes. We want to be left in peace, I and my ladies, and be alone tonight. Since we came here we've not had anything like this."

[1329] Whoever didn't belong there was seen leaving, the old and the young. Hartmut's men left the ladies' chamber and hurried off to their rooms. The poor women were well supplied with mead and wine.

[1330] Then Hilde's daughter said, "Close the door for me."

Four strong bolts were lowered into place. The building was so substantial that whatever was done there, no one outside could hear or understand what was happening in the room.

[1331] Then they first all sat down and drank the good wine. The most highborn of them said, "You should all be joyful, all my dear ladies, after your terrible suffering. Tomorrow I'll let you have a look at what you most want to see. [1332] Today I kissed my husband Herwig, as well as my brother Ortwin. Think about this: should one of you want me to make her rich and carefree, then she should take heed to tell us at the end of the night when morning comes. [1333] Her reward will not be trivial; joyful times are coming. I will readily give her large and strong castles, along with many hides of land. These I will acquire when the time comes that I'm made queen."

[1334] Then [they] all went to sleep. They were in a joyful mood. They knew that many brave knights were coming who would save them from their terrible troubles. This is what they hoped for, that they would see them the next day.

Chapter 26: How Herwig and Ortwin Returned to the Army [1335–65]

[1335] Now we'll hear a story we haven't heard yet. Ortwin and Herwig quickly came to the place where they found their comrades, there on the remote beach. The heroes from the land of Hegelingen ran up to greet them. [1336] They welcomed the scouts and asked them to share the news they had brought, holding nothing back. They asked bold Ortwin, who was sent out on that mission, "Is Kudrun still alive in King Ludwig's land?"

[1337] Then the noble knight said, "I can't talk to each of you separately, so I'll have to keep you waiting until our closest allies are here beside me. Then we'll let you hear what we saw in front of Hartmut's castle."

[1338] This was passed on to the heroes. A great many arrived, and they were surrounded by a large company of knights. Then Ortwin said, "I now bring you news that I and my friends could do without, if only that were possible. [1339] Now listen to the strange events that occurred. My sister Kudrun, I saw her and [also] Hildeburg, the maiden [from] the kingdom of Ireland."

When he told them this, some of them thought it was a lie. [1340] Then some of them said, "You can stop with the tall tales. We've been thinking about her now for a long time, how we could bring her back from Ludwig's land. Ortwin and his men are still suffering from the injury and insult."

[1341] "So ask Herwig, he saw [them], too, and in circumstances that could not have been more painful to us. Now think about this, all you kinsmen, is this not dishonorable? We found Hildeburg and Lady Kudrun doing the wash on the beach."

[1342] Then all the kinsmen there wept. Wate, ancient of men, said angrily, "You're all acting like a bunch of women, and you don't even know why. This is not how heroes behave. [1343] If you want to save Kudrun from her misfortune, then turn those white clothes red, the ones she washed there with her own white hands. This is how you can serve her, how she can be rescued from her captivity."

[1344] Then Fruote of the Danes said, "How can we manage to invade her land before Ludwig's men and Hartmut's heroes discover the fact that Hilde's troops are in their midst, among them in Ormanie?"

[1345] Then old Wate replied, "I can answer that. I believe I can deal with them best on the embankments, should I live long enough to get that close to them. You heroes, leave this place and march on to Ormanie! [1346] The breeze is fresh, and the moon is full and shining brightly tonight. I'm feeling confident about this. Now get up off the beach, you excellent heroes, so that before the day dawns we stand in front of Ludwig's castle."

Chapter 26: How Herwig and Ortwin Returned to the Army [1335–65]

[1347] They were soon hard at work because of Wate's command, until they loaded their horses and equipment onto the ships.[285] They hurried, as best they could, through the night to reach land. Before it turned light, they were on the beach in front of the castle. [1348] Wate ordered the entire army to use stealth, to take up positions quietly along the shore. The sea-weary heroes were allowed to lay down their shields; some of them rested their heads on them.

[1349] "Whoever wants a victory in the morning," said old Wate, "should [not] get too comfortable. We've been keenly looking forward to this expedition, so that when [morning] comes, you brave warriors should leave nothing undone. [1350] And I want to tell you something else. Up and down the ranks, whoever hears my horn sounding out loudly should prepare himself at that moment for battle. When I signal the morning's dawn, let none of you delay. [1351] When I signal for the second time you should all saddle up, mount your horses, and stand at the ready until I have chosen the time for the assault, so that no one's efforts will be in vain."[286]

[1352] They said that they would gladly do as he commanded. How many noble women he would divorce [from their joys] with deadly wounds [in] that terrible battle! They all anxiously awaited the coming of the next [day].

[1353] "When I signal for the third [time], my dear comrades, you should be fully armed and mounted. Still, you warriors should wait for me, until you see me fully armed, riding behind fair Hilde's battle standard."

[1354] Then the tired men lay down along the shore. They were very close there to Ludwig's great hall. It was night, but they could still all see it. The proud and famous heroes lay there without making a sound.

[1355] By now the morning star had risen in the sky, when a lovely maiden went to stand at a window. She looked out, anticipating that it would be morning. By doing this she hoped to earn a great reward from Lady Kudrun. [1356] Then the noble maiden caught a glimpse of the morning's first light. And toward the glistening water, as expected, she saw gleaming helmets and many shining shields. The castle was surrounded; the whole countryside sparkled with weapons.

[1357] Then she went back to where she found her lady. "Wake up, noble maiden! The whole countryside and this strong castle are surrounded by the enemy. Our friends at home haven't forgotten us poor women."

---

285. Apparently they were making the attack at night by sea, with landings on the beaches near the castle.

286. Manuscript A reads: *daz niemand da sein arbait verliese* (1351,4b). The Bartsch/Stackmann gloss for *sin arbeit verliese* has: "come too late, lose track of time" ("zu spät komme, die Zeit verpasse"). Sowinski translates accordingly: "no one should be late for it" ("niemand darf die Zeit dazu verpassen," 237). Murdoch (120) is much the same. Gibbs/Johnson translate: "so that no one wastes any effort when the right time for the attack comes" (120). McConnell translates: "No one should be caught unprepared when it is time to attack" (141). I have followed Störmer-Caysa's version of this: "in which no one's efforts should be in vain" ("an dem niemandes Mühe umsonst sein soll").

The Book of Kudrun

[1358] Highborn Kudrun jumped out of bed; she was in a hurry to get to the window. She thanked the maiden for reporting this news. She became rich because of it. On account of her great suffering, she anxiously watched out for her friends.

[1359] Then she saw the broad sails bobbing on the waves. The noble maiden said, "My pain is just beginning. Oh, that I, God's poorest, was ever born. Many gallant men will lose their lives today."

[1360] When she said this, most of the people were still asleep. Ludwig's watchman cried out with a loud voice, "Get up, you proud warriors! To arms, my lord, to arms! You brave men of Ormanie, I think you've been asleep too long."

[1361] Gerlint heard this, Ludwig's wife. She left the old king lying there asleep and quickly ran to the ramparts by herself. When she saw the large enemy host, the she-devil was terrified beyond measure.

[1362] She ran back to where she found the king. "Wake up, Lord Ludwig! Your castle and your land are surrounded by an enormous enemy army. Your men will pay dearly today for Kudrun's laughter."

[1363] "Be still," said Ludwig. "I want to see for myself. All we can do now is wait to see what happens to us."

He quickly went into the great hall to have a look. He was going to receive guests that day who were not altogether trustworthy.[287]

[1364] Then he saw large banners waving outside his castle. King Ludwig said, "We really should alert my son Hartmut. These are probably pilgrims[288] standing outside my town and castle, wanting to buy provisions."

[1365] Hartmut was awakened. When he was informed, the brave man said, "Don't be troubled. I know the standards of nobles from twenty lands. I think, though, that our enemies want to avenge their old grievance."

Chapter 27: How Hartmut Identified the Nobles' Standards for Ludwig [1366–1440]

[1366] He left all his men lying there asleep. Ludwig and Hartmut went together to take a look out the window. When they saw the armies, Hartmut said straightaway, "They're posted a bit close to my castle. [1367] These are no pilgrims, dear father. It could very well be Wate and his kinsmen, the hero of Stormland, along

---

287. Manuscript A reads: *er het des tages geste, <u>der er ubel mocht getrawen</u>* (1363,4). The second half-line has various translations. The Bartsch/Stackmann gloss reads: "for whom he was not prepared" ("auf die er nicht gefaßt war"). Sowinski translates: "whom he assumed would do their worst " ("denen er das Schlimmste zutraute," 239). Gibbs/Johnson translate: "and it was better that he did not trust them" (121). Murdoch is more free in his translation: "he had guests that day who were hardly welcome" (121). The narrator's comment itself is ironic.

288. The text uses the term *pilgerîne*, but given the armed nature of the "guests," even Ludwig can't imagine that these are just poor pilgrims. Most translations render this as "crusaders."

Chapter 27: How Hartmut Identified the Nobles' Standards for Ludwig [1366–1440]

with the man from the kingdom of Ort.[289] I see a standard waving over there that seems to fit that [description].[290] [1368] It's made of brown material; it comes from Karadie. Before it yields, heroes will have to suffer. In the middle is placed a head made of red gold.[291] I could well do without such bold foreigners here in our land. [1369] The ruler of the Moors brings us a good twenty thousand men. These are very [bold] warriors, as far as I can see. They want to win much honor in battle at our expense. I see another standard over there with even more heroes gathered around it. [1370] That flag belongs to Horant, coming from Daneland. I see Lord Fruote next to him, I know him, and Lord Morunc from the land of Walays. He's brought many of the enemy here to our shores this morning.[292] [1371] I see another one with bright red bars running through it, in a saw-toothed pattern.[293] Heroes will be hard-pressed by this. It belongs to Ortwin, the

---

289. Manuscript A reads: *von Hortreichen* (1367,3b). Ortwin is referred to later as *von Hortreiche* (1371,3). This could refer to Irolt, although he is also mentioned later in 1374,1. The order of lords and their corresponding standards seems somewhat muddled in the manuscript.

290. Manuscript A reads: *dort sich ich wagen ain zaichen das mag sein dem mare vil wol geleichen* (1367,4). This line seems most logically to refer to the previous line, but Sowinski reads *moere* (Moor), as opposed to the emended *mære* (telling, description) and so connects the banner to Siegfried and the next strophe.

291. Heraldic devices with the head of an African warrior or king are thought to have originated during the Crusades. One example from the fourteenth century, and most likely earlier, is the coat of arms associated with the bishops of Freising. The district (*Landkreis*) of Freising has retained this in its crest. Another example from the town of Lauingen goes back to the fifteenth century.

Freising   Lauingen

292. Manuscript A reads: *der hat unns vil der veinde wider morgen gefueret zu dem sannde* (1370,4). Störmer-Caysa is the only translator who takes the emended text *wider morgen zuo dem sande* to mean "eastern shore" (Ostküste).

293. This is known as a "fess" in heraldic terminology, a bar running horizontally or diagonally across a shield or flag. From Latin *fascia* (not the same as *fascis*, or bundle, cf. fascist). More than one fess is termed "bars." The points (*örter*) could refer to what is known as a fess or bar dancety, a zigzag pattern. Murdoch has it as a "barry indented" (173n2). Gibbs/Johnson (166n127) point to the coat of arms of the Counts of Scheyern-Wittelsbach (yellow zigzag). The blue-and-white arms of Bavaria, from the Wittelsbach family, are another variant of diagonal pointed lines.

Scheyern-   Bavaria/
Wittelsbach Wittelsbach

The Book of Kudrun

lord of the kingdom of Ort.[294] We killed his father. He's not here with friendly intentions. [1372] Over there [I] see a banner that is whiter than a swan. You can see golden images on it. My mother-in-law[295] Hilde sent that across the sea. The hatred of the Hegelingen will become obvious before the day turns to night. [1373] I can also see another broad banner waving, made of sky-blue silk. I'm telling you, that one is brought to us by Lord Herwig of Seeland. Arranged on it are flowers of the sea.[296] He wants to avenge his injury. [1374] Lord Irolt is also here among us, that I can say for sure. He's bringing many of the Frisians, as far as I can see, and also the Holzan men. They are splendid heroes. An assault is close at hand, so arm yourselves, warriors in the castle! [1375] Now forward, all my men," said Hartmut. "I won't grant this tough foe the honor of riding up so close to my [castle]. We will greet them in front of the gate with sword blows."

[1376] Then the men still lying down jumped out of their beds. They called out for their shining battle gear to be brought to them. They wanted to help the king defend the kingdom. About four thousand men diligently prepared themselves within. [1377] Then Ludwig and Hartmut, too, armed themselves. The captive women thought it both good and not good. They didn't have a safe place to go to in the castle. One of them said, "He who laughed before will have to cry now."

[1378] Lady Gerlint suddenly appeared, Ludwig's wife. "What are you going to do, Lord Hartmut? Why would you want to lose your life here along with all these heroes? The enemy will surely kill you if you meet them outside the castle."

[1379] Then the noble knight said, "Mother, please leave. You can't order me and my men around. Go command your ladies—they will gladly comply—how they should set gems and work gold into silk. [1380] Then you can," said Hartmut, "make Kudrun and her ladies go wash, as you did before. You [thought] that she was bereft of friends and family. Today you can see for yourself how our guests will soon thank us."

[1381] Then the she-devil said, "That is how I served you, thinking I could compel her. Now you should listen to me. Your castle is strong enough; order your gates closed. That way your enemies will have little to show for their journey here. [1382] You know full well, Hartmut, that they hate you; you killed their kinsmen. Now be all the more on guard. You don't have anyone outside the castle

---

294. Manuscript A reads: *von Hortreiche* (1371,3b).
295. The original term is *swiger* (1372,3a). This implies that at least Hartmut assumes that he is as good as married to Kudrun, or the term could be an ironic acknowledgment that any marriage is now out of reach.
296. An example of a coat of arms with sea flowers is from the town of Tegernsee.

Chapter 27: How Hartmut Identified the Nobles' Standards for Ludwig [1366–1440]

who is your kin or ally. The proud Hegelingen have brought [twenty] against one.[297] [1383] You should think about this, my dear son. You have here in this stronghold bread and wine and good food to last a whole year. But if someone were taken prisoner, they would hardly allow him to be ransomed."[298] [1384] Then Ludwig's wife again counseled the warrior. "Defend your honor, don't lose your life. Command that the crossbows fire from the windows, to inflict grave wounds and make their friends at home weep. [1385] Command that the best catapults be pulled into position against this host. The castle is full of warriors. Before I let you cross swords with the enemy, I and my ladies will bring the stones to you in white linen."[299]

[1386] Then Hartmut said angrily, "Lady, leave, now. What can you counsel? What good is having a mind of my own? Before I allow myself to be trapped in this castle, I would rather die outside among Hilde's troops."

[1387] Then the old king's wife said, crying, "I'm only doing this so that you can better protect yourself. Whoever is gathered here today underneath your standard should trust us to reward him. [1388] Now arm yourselves," said Gerlint. "Stand next to my son and hammer their helmets until the fiery sparks fly. Stay close to this man today. You should greet the enemy with mortal wounds."

[1389] "My lady is right in what she tells you," said Hartmut. "You brave men, whoever does so willingly and goes with me today to help fight the enemy, however many grown men die, I will make all your orphans rich."

[1390] Ludwig's men, one thousand and one hundred strong, armed themselves there. Before they left to sortie from the king's gate, he organized the castle's defenses. They left another five hundred brave knights behind. [1391] Then they unlocked the bolts to four castle gates. They had everything they needed, down to the last spur. Those who wanted to help the young king in battle, three thousand of them were seen mounted with their helmets securely fastened.

[1392] The battle was soon engaged. The hero from Stormland sounded a horn, which, because of his strength, could be heard at least thirty miles away from the shore. The men from Hegelingen started to rush to Hilde's standard.

---

297. Manuscript A reads: *die stoltzen Hegelinge bringent ye wider ainen* (1382,4). No specific number is provided. The number "twenty" [times] is an emendation in the Bartsch/Stackmann edition based on a conjectured 4,000 defenders (1376,4) against 80,000 attackers (1264,4), although by strophe 1390, the number of defenders is down to 1,600, only to go to 3,000 mounted knights outside the walls in strophe 1391. Symons/Boesch insert the number "thirty" [times] as a formulaic representation of a large number.

298. If someone were captured outside the walls, Hartmut would not be able to ransom him, much less have himself ransomed. Gerlint is arguing that the leaders of the Hegelingen forces would not abide by the code of chivalry and allow captured nobles to buy their freedom.

299. This is another extreme argument made by Gerlint that offered to make the ladies in the castle a part of the active defense force by hauling rocks for Hartmut's catapults. The white linen would be their own robes, which were meant to remain spotless.

[1393] Then he sounded it a second time. He did this so that every warrior would mount up and the squadrons would move into their positions. Never before in battle had such a magnificent old [swordsman] been seen. [1394] He signaled a third time with such great force that the shore quaked and the [waves] echoed the sound. The cornerstones of Ludwig's castle could have been shaken loose. He commanded Horant to carry Hilde's standard to the front. [1395] They were very afraid of Wate. No one made a sound. A horse was heard neighing. Herwig's beloved stood above on the ramparts. The brave [men] who would fight against Hartmut could be seen riding calmly in formation. [1396] Now Hartmut and his men also came forward, well armed and equipped, through the gates. The helmets of friend and foe shone through the window frames. Hartmut was not alone there either.

[1397] [The] army advanced on the castle from four [directions]. All of their armor was a silver color, and the gleaming of bright shield rims could be seen. They feared Wate as much as a ferocious, wild lion. [1398] The Moorish heroes were seen riding apart. They launched strong missiles; many a point was broken. When they launched the attack against the men of Ormanie, fiery sparks could be seen flashing from their weapons and mail coats. [1399] The men from the Danish March rode toward the castle. Irolt, who was very strong, began to organize at least six thousand men at the foot of the wall. These were brave heroes; this would harm Ludwig greatly. [1400] Then Ortwin rode out separately with his men; he led at least eight thousand. They would bring destruction to the land of Ormanie and to its inhabitants. Gerlint and Ortrun stood at the ramparts and wept. [1401] Then Lord Herwig arrived as well, Lady Kudrun's husband. He caused many a lady to suffer great pain as he began to fight for his heart's beloved. The helmets could be heard ringing out loudly from the solid swords. [1402] Finally old Wate appeared with his men. The hero was in a sinister mood, they could tell. Without lowering his spear, he rode right up to the gates. That troubled Gerlint, but Kudrun was grateful to him for it.

[1403] Then Hartmut could be seen riding at the front. Had he been an emperor, he could not have acted more resolutely. His entire armor shone brightly in the sun; his supreme confidence was as yet unbroken.

[1404] Then Ortwin, the king of Ortland, caught sight of him. He said, "Can someone who recognizes him tell [us], who is this warrior? He looks by all appearances as if he wants to gain a whole kingdom from us by himself."

[1405] Then one of them said, "That's Hartmut. Among those who know their heroes, he's a brave knight. In fact, he's the same man who killed your father.[300] He's certainly courageous and valiant in all battles."

---

300. There is general agreement that this statement is wrong. Ludwig killed Hetel (880,4; confirmed later 1433,4). One can only speculate as to the reason for the discrepancy.

Chapter 27: How Hartmut Identified the Nobles' Standards for Ludwig [1366–1440]

[1406] Then Ortwin said angrily, "He owes me. He will most surely have to pay today for what we lost on his account. This we win back here. There's nothing Gerlint can do to help him ever come back alive from this place."

[1407] Then Ortwin set his sights on Hartmut. Even though he didn't know [him], still he spurred the flanks of his horse, which took off at a run. Hartmut charged at Ortwin. They both lowered their spears, and sparks were seen flying off their chain mail. [1408] Neither one failed to strike the other in the exchange. Ortwin's powerful horse went down on its hindquarters. They couldn't withstand the kings' great rage; King Hartmut's charger was also seen to stumble. [1409] The horses jumped back up, and the kings' swords rang out mightily. They were to be congratulated on having opened the battle with such chivalry. They were both bold; each would give no ground to the other.

[1410] Both their contingents charged with lowered spears, much to the harm of the young men. They could be seen inflicting grievous wounds on impact, those brave knights. They were all admirable and struggled mightily to gain honor. [1411] A thousand[301] of Hartmut's men began to advance against the same number of Wate's fighters. The lord of Stormarn made them regret it. Whoever collided with him soon forgot about advancing. [1412] Then Herwig's force became entangled with ten thousand men who attacked them fiercely.[302] They were intent on meeting their deaths there rather than letting anyone drive them out of the land. [1413] Herwig was a brave man; how ardently he fought! With his resolve he ensured that the fair maiden would favor him all the more. How could he imagine how successful he might be? Kudrun, that young woman, saw it all.

[1414] Then the elder Ludwig gathered his forces against the men from Daneland. He carried in his hand a great sword. He stood there every bit a lord, but he and his warriors had advanced too far beyond the gates. [1415] Along with the Holzan men, bold Fruote killed many. He was certainly accomplished. Morunc, the young man from the land of Walays, was seen enriching the soil with the dead in front of Ludwig's castle. [1416] Young Irolt was a brave knight and struck hot battle blood out of chain mail. Wate's kinsmen fought under Hilde's standard. Faces were seen to go white; they were definitely thinning out the ranks.

[1417] Then Hartmut and Ortwin faced each other as once before. The wind has never driven snowflakes as swiftly as [those] heroes swung the swords in their hands. Hartmut was again hard pressed by the king of Ortland. [1418] Young

---

301. Manuscript A reads: *tausent wider tausent* (1411,1a). Murdoch translates: "Thousands upon thousands" (125), whereas all other translators have: "a thousand against [*wider*] a thousand."
302. Manuscript A reads: *Da was unnderschuttet des Herwiges schar | mit zehentausent mannen* (1412,1–2a). Sowinski takes this to mean that ten thousand of Herwig's forces were interspersed with the others ("Dann waren Herwigs Scharen mit zehntausend Mann zwischen die Feinde gedrungen," 247). Lindner assigns the ten thousand to Herwig's army as well (262). All others interpret this to mean that ten thousand enemy forces attacked Herwig's army, except that Hartmut didn't have ten thousand men.

Ortwin was definitely skilled. Hartmut, strong as he was, struck him through the helmet, so that his bright hauberk was covered in blood. Bold Ortwin's men were unhappy to see it. [1419] Then there was a great melee; the ranks became disorganized. They were striking great wounds through chain mail. They could see many a head brought low by swords. Death let it be known that he robs people of their good friends.

[1420] Then Horant of the Danes saw that Ortwin was wounded. He asked right away who had injured his dear lord in battle. Hartmut laughed. They weren't that far apart.

[1421] Ortwin answered him, "Hartmut did this."

That brave warrior Horant handed off Hilde's standard, with which he was able to win great honor to the detriment of his enemies, and pushed forward toward Hartmut.

[1422] Hartmut heard a great clamor all around him. He saw copious amounts of blood streaming out from the wounds of many, down to the ground. The bold warrior said, "I'll make them pay for this injury to my heroes."

[1423] Then he turned around to where he could see Horant. Because they were both courageous, sparks soon flew off their chain mail in front of their eyes. The edges of the swords in their hands were bent on the helmets' braces. [1424] He wounded Horant, as had happened to bold Ortwin, so that [a] red river flowed from his chain mail, caused by Hartmut's hand. He was so incredibly skilled, who could have hoped to take his lands? [1425] [Many] solid shields were hacked to bits in this time of terror, by men on both sides with their keen swords. With these they struck at each other with great fervor. Hartmut defended himself most honorably. [1426] Ortwin's and Horant's comrades were keen on getting them out of the throng, so that their grave wounds could be bandaged. They hastened to do just that. Then they rode back, where they fought even harder.

[1427] Now let us leave them to proceed as they see fit. Who is gaining an advantage or who is losing, that is still undetermined there in front of Ludwig's castle. His troops defended themselves fervently; the invaders were also intent on [honor]. [1428] It's impossible to tell you about all of them equally. Many of those who are remembered there were killed. Many swords were heard ringing out in all directions. It was impossible for some time to distinguish the prudent from the daring. [1429] Wate did not stand idly by, I'm sure of that. He greeted many of them by ending their lives, those who lay shattered before him by his own hand. The brave knights' kinsmen from Ormanie wanted to avenge them.

[1430] Now Herwig arrived on the scene, as we are told, to confront Ludwig with a great force. There he saw old Ludwig fighting fiercely, and he and his warriors struck down many men under his standard.

[1431] Herwig shouted out loudly, "Does anyone know who this old man is? He has by his own hand wounded everyone here so terribly with his great courage that beautiful women will have to weep."

[1432] Ludwig, the ruler of Ormanie, heard this. "Who is it there in the throng who asked about me? I am called Ludwig, from the kingdom of Ormanie. Whenever I can fight the enemy, I will do so without fail."

[1433] Then King Herwig said, "You have earned, since your name is Ludwig, my hatred. You once slaughtered many of our heroes on the beach. Hetel was also killed by you; he was a bold hero in his own right. [1434] You harmed us even more before you left there, which we still lament to this day. This was the cause of much heartache for me. You robbed me of my wife. There on the Wulpensand you left many of my heroes dead. [1435] I am called Herwig. You took my wife from me. You must give her back, or one of us must die because of it, as will many other men."

Then King Ludwig said, "You are too great a threat to my land. [1436] You've made your confession to me needlessly. There are many more here from whom I've taken property and kinsmen. This much you should know: I will make sure you [never] kiss your wife again."

[1437] After saying this they rushed at each other, these two mighty kings. Whoever gained any advantage did so with difficulty. Given the peril they were in, brave men could be seen running toward them from both their standards. [1438] Herwig was skilled and definitely bold. Hartmut's father struck at the young king, who started to stagger under Ludwig's hand. He wanted to deprive him of his life and his lands. [1439] If Herwig's men, who had quickly come to his aid, hadn't been right next to him, [he] would never have escaped from Ludwig with his life intact. This is how the elder Ludwig made himself loathed by the younger man. [1440] They came to Herwig's aid and saved his life. Once he had regained his footing after his fall, he immediately looked up to the ramparts to see if the love of his heart was standing there.

Chapter 28: How Herwig Killed Ludwig [1441–93]

[1441] He thought to himself, "Ah, what just happened to me? If my Lady Kudrun saw what happened, if we ever enjoy the day when I can embrace her, then she'll judge me when I'm lying close to my wife. [1442] The grizzled old man knocking me down is something I'm greatly ashamed of."

He ordered his standard carried toward Ludwig and his men. They pressed forward to the enemy; they didn't want to let him escape. [1443] Ludwig heard a great deal of commotion behind him, so he turned around to face him farther down below. Swords could be heard ringing out on many helmets. Those alongside him were shocked by both men's rage. [1444] They ran at each other on the battlefield to fight, where blow rang out against blow in the struggle. All the men who died there, who could know how many? Ludwig yielded the victory in his fight against Herwig. [1445] Kudrun's beloved struck Ludwig under his helmet's rim with a solid blow. He wounded him so seriously that he was unable to continue, and so Ludwig awaited a bitter death at his feet. [1446] He struck him once again with a powerful blow, and the king's head tumbled from his shoulders. This repaid him for the fact that he himself had fallen. The king was dead, and many fair eyes welled up because of it.

[1447] Ludwig's heroes wanted to carry the standard back inside the castle after he had been slain. Still they were too far away from the gate. The standard was captured; many of them had to stay behind with their lord. [1448] Then the castle guards saw how he lost his life. Men and women could be heard weeping; they knew that the mighty old king had been killed. Kudrun and her household, filled with fear, remained there at court. [1449] At the time, Hartmut hadn't yet heard the news that he'd been killed, along with many brave knights, his father and others who were their kinsmen. He heard loud wailing and lamentation coming from the castle.

[1450] Then Hartmut said to his men, "Return now with me. Many of them are lying here, those who wanted to kill us in this hard fight. Go back to the castle so we can wait for a more favorable time."

[1451] They wanted to follow him; they turned to where he had gone. They fought their way out with great effort, where they had been faced by a determined enemy. Blood ran everywhere, at the hands of Hartmut and his men.

[1452] "You have served me so well, you kinsmen and my vassals, that I will be glad to share my patrimony with you. Now we will ride together to my castle to rest. The gate will be opened for us, and we will be served mead and wine."

[1453] They had left many men behind. Had the land been theirs to rule, they could not [have] fought any harder in the battle.[303] They wanted to get to the castle, but Wate kept them at bay with a thousand of his heroes. [1454] He had moved up to the gate with a great force, to where Hartmut and his men wanted to go. They were unable to move forward; they failed completely. They could see a great many stones being thrown down from the walls. [1455] They were shooting at Wate and his heroes so fiercely, it was as if a rainstorm had come down from the sky. Wate paid little attention to who lived or died. All his resolve was focused on how he could achieve victory.

[1456] Then Hartmut saw him in front of the castle gate. He said, "The debts we incurred in the past are truly coming back to haunt us today. Those still not wounded must take care; many dead lie here already. [1457] That I ever earned

---

303. Hartmut's offer to share his demesne or crown land with his vassals is largely symbolic. The sentiment expressed is that men will fight harder for land in which they actually have a stake rather than strictly out of a sense of duty to their feudal lord.

Chapter 28: How Herwig Killed Ludwig [1441–93]

so many strong enemies is now causing me a great deal of difficulty. Wate and his men, I see them there at the castle gate, slashing away with their swords. If he becomes the gate guard, I don't expect much good will come of it. [1458] Men, see for yourselves. The walls and the gates are completely surrounded; many heroes stand before them. They have blocked the way in all directions. Kudrun's supporters want to gain victory at any cost. [1459] You can recognize this for yourselves, just as I have. We will suffer the loss of comrades. However it came to pass, I can see the sovereign standard of the Moorish kingdom flying in front of the gates. My heroes are resisting it with determination. [1460] There at the second gate I can see my enemies. The wind is blowing the jagged banner. Lord Ortwin is there, Lady Kudrun's brother. He wants to serve ladies here. Before his rage cools, many a helmet will be smashed here. [1461] I see Herwig standing there at the third gate. Some seven thousand men followed him there. He's vying for his heart's delight with acts of chivalry. Lady Kudrun will be glad to see that today, as will her bold ladies.

[1462] "I've been too slow in coming to a decision. Now I don't know where I should go with my warriors, since old Wate is fighting at the fourth gate. My retinue inside will wait a long time for their friends. [1463] I can't fly, I don't have wings. I can't go under the ground either, no matter what happens to me. We can't escape our enemies by [marching] to the sea. I'll tell [you] exactly what my best recourse is. [1464] There is no other way, you brave and noble knights. Dismount to the ground and strike hot blood out of that bright chain mail, and do[n't] be discouraged."

They got down from their saddles and drove the horses [to] the rear.

[1465] "Forward now, you storied heroes!" cried Hartmut. "Advance to the castle! For better or worse, I have to make my way to old Wate. Whatever may happen there, I have to try to get [him] to move away from the gate."

[1466] They advanced with swords held high, Hartmut the bold and all his men. He faced off against dreadful Wate; that was to the hero's honor. Swords could be heard ringing out, and even more brave knights died there.

[1467] When Wate saw Hartmut pressing toward him (Lord Fruote carried the banner), the hero said angrily, "I can hear the sound of solid swords coming ever closer to us. Dear cousin Fruote, don't let anyone force you away from the gate."

[1468] Wate charged at Hartmut with great fury, but the fearless man did not try to evade him. A cloud of dust darkened the sun. Their strength was unabated; Hartmut and Wate fought mightily for honor. [1469] What good did it do to say that old Wate had the strength of twenty-six men?[304] Young Hartmut, the lord of Ormanie, responded to him with chivalry. Just as the foreigners fought, he tried to do the same with his men. [1470] He was also a warrior and held his own in

---

304. Hagen is also said to have the strength of twenty-six men (254,3).

The Book of Kudrun

the fight. The dead were lying all around the hill.[305] It was a real miracle that Hartmut was not killed there by Wate. The warrior was filled with rage.

[1471] Hartmut heard Ludwig's wife screaming loudly; his mother Gerlint mourned the death of the king. She offered a great reward so it would not go unavenged, so that someone would murder Kudrun along with all her household. [1472] Then a traitor, who coveted the prize, ran to where the women from Hegelingen were sitting together, causing the gracious women to tremble with fear. To earn the large reward he intended to kill them all. [1473] When Hilde's daughter saw that a naked sword was raised against her in anger, she had good reason to lament that she had been taken so far from her family, and if Lord Hartmut had not seen it, she would have lost her head. [1474] She almost lost her composure, she screamed so loudly, as she was about to die. She was trembling with fear. The other women did likewise, those who stood with her at the windows. You could see them gesturing wildly.

[1475] Brave Hartmut recognized her voice and wondered what was wrong. The brave hero saw a vile man standing there with a sword, as if he wanted to attack them.

The hero quickly called out, [1476] "Who are you, you coward? What makes you want to murder these young women? If you strike even one [of them], your life will be forfeit. Your entire family will surely hang for it."

[1477] The man ran away; he feared his wrath. In the meantime the king almost lost his own life as he saved that woman, God's poorest, out of loyalty. Because he saved her from a gruesome death, he was himself in danger. [1478] Ortrun of Ormanieland, the young queen, appeared straightaway before Lady Kudrun, wringing her hands. The highborn young woman fell down at her feet; she lamented her father Ludwig sorely.

[1479] She said, "Have mercy, noble, highborn woman, so many of my kinsmen have been killed here, and remember what it was like when your father was killed. Noble queen, now I have lost mine here today. [1480] Just look, noble maiden; this is a catastrophe. My father and most of my kinsmen are dead. Now brave Hartmut faces Wate and is in grave danger. If I were to lose my brother, I would forevermore be orphaned. [1481] And let it be recognized," said the noble woman, "when no one else among those here cared about you, you had no other

---

305. Manuscript A reads: *der perg von den todten lag allenthalben vol* (1470,2). There have been varying interpretations of this line, differing in whether there was an actual hill on which the men were fighting, or that the dead men were stacked so high as to make a hill. Most translate in the first sense. Some others take the second meaning. Störmer-Caysa translates: "there were mountains of dead lying all around" ("ringsum lagen Berge von Toten"); Murdoch: "the dead lay in a vast mound all around them" (130); Lindner: "so that a mountain of dead had piled up around both of them" ("so daß sich um beide ein Berg von Toten häufte").

Chapter 28: How Herwig Killed Ludwig [1441–93]

friend except me alone. Whatever was done to you, I always had to cry for your sake."

[1482] Then Hilde's daughter said, "You did so often. I don't know how I can stop the fighting. If I myself were a fighter and could carry arms, I would gladly intervene, so that no one would kill your brother."

[1483] She cried out of fear. She pleaded with her until Lady Kudrun stepped up to the window. She waved her hands and wanted to know if anyone from her father's land was there.

[1484] Herwig, a noble, brave knight, answered, "Who are you, young lady? Who asks us this? There is no one from Hegelingen nearby. We here are from Seeland. Tell us now, dear maiden, how can we serve you?"

[1485] Then the royal kinswoman said, "I would like to ask kindly if you could stop this. There has been enough fighting here. I would forever be in his debt, if someone could assure me that he could rescue Hartmut from old Wate for me."

[1486] Then the hero of Seeland said politely, "Now tell me, noble maiden, what is your name?"

She said, "My name is Kudrun, and I am Hagen's kin. As powerful as I once was, I see very little here that brings me joy."

[1487] He said, "If you are Kudrun, my dear wife, then I will gladly be at your service always. It is I, Herwig, and I took you as my companion, and I will show you that I would gladly release you from every care."

[1488] She said, "If you want to serve me, outstanding knight, then don't be angry or think ill of me. The noble maidens here are pleading fervently with me to have Hartmut removed from the fight with old Wate."

[1489] "I will gladly do that, my dearest lady." Herwig shouted loudly at his warriors, "Carry my standard [toward] Wate."

Herwig and all his [men] could be seen urgently pressing forward.

[1490] He had achieved a difficult task for his lady. Herwig shouted loudly at old Wate. "Wate, dear friend, allow this terrible fight to come to an end. The lovely maidens request this of you."

[1491] Wate said angrily, "Lord Herwig, be gone! If I now do what women say, where would that get me? If I spare the enemy, I do so at my own peril. I will not obey you in this; Hartmut must pay for his crimes."

[1492] For the love of Kudrun, Herwig leapt between the two of them. Many swords rang out. Wate was enraged; he would make it difficult for anyone who [dared] separate him from his enemies in battle. [1493] He gave Herwig, who had wanted to end the fight, a masterful blow, and he lay stretched out in front of him. His men rushed in and helped him separate himself. Hartmut was taken prisoner there in front of Herwig and all his men.

Chapter 29: How Hartmut Was Taken Prisoner [1494–1560]

[1494] Wate was raving mad. He advanced toward the gate in front of the great hall. From all directions the sound of weeping and swords clanging could be heard. Hartmut was taken prisoner; after that his heroes were doomed to defeat. [1495] Then along with the king, eighty brave knights were seized. The others were all killed. Hartmut was led to their ship and securely bound, but this was not the end. They still had more ordeals to endure. [1496] No matter how often they were forced back from the castle by spears and arrows, Wate seized the castle with merciless assaults. After that the gates were torn right off their hinges. Noble women wept because of it. [1497] Horant of the Danish March carried Hilde's standard. Many of the warriors followed him—he had plenty there—past the great hall to the strongest of the towers that the Hegelingen could see.

[1498] The castle had been taken, just as I told you. Those they found inside were deathly afraid. Many of the men could be seen looking for plunder. Wate, the merciless, said angrily, "Where are the squires with the sacks?"

[1499] Then many lavish rooms were entered by force. A great uproar came from within; the invaders were not all of one mind. Many of them kept fighting; others were on the hunt for more treasure. [1500] They took from the castle, as we hear tell, more than what two ships could carry, of fine cloth and silk, of silver and gold, if anyone wanted to load [it] onto their ship for the open sea. [1501] No one in the castle had reason to be happy. The citizens of the land were butchered. Men and women alike were killed within; many a child in its crib lost its life.

[1502] Irolt the strong yelled at Wate, "What the devil have these little children done to you? They're not guilty for what happened to our kinsmen. For God's sake, have mercy on these poor orphans."

[1503] Then old Wate said, "You're like a child yourself. Those crying in their cribs, do you think it would be right for me to let them live? Should they grow up, I wouldn't trust them any more than a wild Saxon."[306]

[1504] Blood ran out of the rooms in all directions. Their friends who witnessed it, how it upset them! Then highborn Ortrun, greatly troubled, arrived to where she saw Kudrun. She was afraid of [even] greater mayhem.

[1505] Then she bowed her head in front of the fair maiden. She said, "Lady Kudrun, have mercy on my great misfortune and let me live. Unless your virtue prevents it, I will die here at the hands of your friends."

---

306. Saxons had a reputation during the Migration Era and later as great sea raiders, with their homeland along the North Sea coast. They were also considered "wild" in the sense that the continental Saxons remained pagan until Charlemagne's campaigns against them in the late eighth century. Gibbs/Johnson (167n137) take Saxons to be representative of "any foreigner" or enemy.

[1506] "I will do all I can to save you, if I can by rights, because I wish for you both honor and all good things. I'll make sure you are reconciled. You will keep your life. Come stand next to me with [your] maidens and women."

[1507] "I will do so most gladly," said young Ortrun.

She later saved herself along with thirty-three young women. Sixty-two warriors were standing alongside the women. If they had not fled, they would have been slaughtered by the invaders.

[1508][307] (1516) Then wicked Gerlint also hurriedly arrived there. She submitted herself as a bondswoman at Hilde's daughter's feet. "Save us, queen, from Wate and his men. It is entirely up to you; otherwise I think that I have met my end."

[1509] (1517) Then Hilde's daughter said, "Now I hear you pleading that I should show you mercy. Why should I agree to that? You never wanted to grant a single thing I asked for. You were cruel to me; for that I should despise you."

[1510] (1508) In the meantime, old Wate noticed them. He quickly came up to them, gritting his teeth, with eyes ablaze and a long beard. Everyone there was terrified of the hero of Stormarn. [1511] (1509) He was covered in blood; his clothing was soaked. As much as Kudrun wanted to see him, she'd have preferred that he had not come to her in such a rage. I think none of them would have received him out of fear.

[1512] (1510) Only Kudrun, the noblewoman, went up to Wate. Hilde's faultless daughter said with concern, "Wate, [you are] welcome. How happy I would be to see you, if only so many people weren't coming to harm on your account."

[1513] (1511) "With thanks, noble maiden. Are you Hilde's daughter? Who are these women next to you?"

Kudrun replied, "This is highborn Ortrun. You should spare her, Wate. These women are terrified of you. [1514] (1512) The others are the poor women that Ludwig's army took across the sea from Hegelingen along with me. You are completely soaked in blood; don't come too close to us. Whatever you can do for us, we poor women would be grateful."

[1515] (1513) Wate went on to where he found Herwig and Ortwin, the king of Ortland, Irolt and Morunc, and also Fruote of the Danes. They were still engaged in killing brave knights.

[1516] (1514) Hergart,[308] the young duchess, came rushing up. "Most noble Kudrun, please have mercy on me, a poor woman. Remember that we were part of, and that I am still in your household. May that be to my advantage, lady."

[1517] (1515) Lady Kudrun said angrily, "You should stand aside. Everything that we poor women had to endure, you made no protest and paid little attention.

---

307. The order of strophes is changed significantly at this point in the Bartsch/Stackmann edition.
308. She was previously mentioned in strophe 1093 as having sided with Gerlint.

The Book of Kudrun

Now it is I who couldn't care less if things go well or badly for you. [1518][309] But [come] closer to me here among the younger women."

Old Wate was still searching for his archenemy, where he might find wicked Gerlint. The she-devil and her household were with Lady Kudrun.

[1519] Wate resolutely walked up to the great hall. He said, "My Lady Kudrun, send Gerlint down here to me along with her companions, who made you do the wash, along with her kinsmen who killed many of our men at home."

[1520] Then the gracious woman said, "They aren't here."

Wate, in his anger, came closer to them. He said, "If you don't quickly point out the right one to me, then friend and foe alike will all have to die."

[1521] He became enraged; they could see that. A pretty young woman pointed him to the spot with her eyes. That's how he recognized the wicked she-devil. He said, "Tell me, Lady Gerlint, would you like to have any more washerwomen?"

[1522] He grabbed her by the hand and hauled her away. Wicked Gerlint began to lose heart. Beside himself, he said, "Mighty queen, my young lady will never again have to wash your clothes."

[1523] When he brought her to the doorway of the hall, they looked to see what he intended to do with her. He grabbed her by the hair; he needed no one's consent. His rage was out of control—he cut off the queen's head. [1524] All the women screamed; they couldn't help themselves. Then he came back to them.

He said, "Where are the others who are called her kin? Show me who they are. None of them is so noble that I wouldn't dare take her head."

[1525] Then Hetel's daughter said, crying, "For my sake spare those who came to me to be reconciled and now stand with me. This is noble Ortrun and her household from Ormanie land."

[1526] Those for whom she had won clemency they let stand aside.

Wate asked bruskly, "Where is my Lady Hergart, the young duchess, who took the king's cupbearer here in this land, for the sake of courtly love?"[310]

[1527] They didn't want to point her out, but he stepped closer. He said, "Even if you held sway over the entire kingdom, who would believe that you could be so arrogant? You did little to serve your lady Kudrun in this land."

[1528] They all cried together, "Pray let her live!"

Then old Wate spoke, "That won't happen. I'm the chamberlain; I'm the one to discipline women."

---

309. The Bartsch/Stackmann edition marks a lacuna or disturbance of the strophic order at this point.

310. The term in question is *hohe minne*, usually translated here either as "service for love" or the more common "courtly love." It is difficult to determine if the concept itself is being criticized as the motivation for Hergart's disloyalty to Kudrun. Her motivation seems to have been a desire for power and comfort, along with simple survival. But she meets a bad end for sleeping with the enemy, and so *hohe minne* here is clearly not proffered as a legitimate excuse.

Chapter 29: How Hartmut Was Taken Prisoner [1494–1560]

He cut off her head. The others hid behind Kudrun.

[1529] Everywhere else the fighting had ceased. King Herwig came into Ludwig's hall with his fighting companions, all the color of blood. When Lady Kudrun saw him, she greeted him lovingly. [1530] That brave man quickly removed his sword from his side and tossed his armor onto the back of the shield. He went, still discolored by the iron, to stand before his lady. For the sake of her love he had that day cut his way across the battlefield. [1531] Then Ortwin, the king of Ortland, arrived as well. Irolt and Morunc took off their armor [in order] to cool off without their mail coats. They wanted to go to the ladies; the heroes had been anticipating just that. [1532] After the heroes from Daneland[311] had stopped fighting, they put down their shields and their weapons. They took off their helmets and walked up to the young women. Kudrun greeted them both with a tender welcome. [1533] Irolt and Morunc immediately bowed before the lovely young woman. How quickly it became obvious that she was happy to see that noble retinue! Hilde's daughter of Hegelingen land was content.

[1534][312] (1535) Then the lords and their men reached an agreement. Now that Cassiane, that great castle, had been taken, all other castles in the land were subject to them. Old Wate recommended that the towers and great hall be razed.

[1535] (1536) Then Fruote of the Danes said, "That must not happen. My dear lady must stay here for a while longer. You should have the dead removed from the rooms. This will be to the benefit of all these heroes here in this land. [1536] (1537) The castle is very strong, large, and well made. Have the blood washed from the walls so that the lovely ladies are not upset. We will conquer the rest of Hartmut's homeland with our army."

[1537] (1538) They followed Fruote in this; he was definitely wise. Many brave knights were carried out of the castle, cut to pieces with mortal wounds. They brought the dead they found in front of the gates down to the shore. [1538] (1539) They committed four thousand or more to the waves. That was a gruesome task.[313] Fruote advised them to do so. What they had yet to accomplish was still undone. Queen Ortrun was being held captive in Ludwig's castle [1539] (1540) along with sixty-two men and thirty ladies. They had been made hostages along with her.

Then [the queen][314] said, "I want to protect them, since they accepted my peace. Wate can do what he wants with his own hostages."

---

311. This refers to Horant and Fruote.
312. The Bartsch/Stackmann edition presumes a lacuna or disturbance of the strophic order at this point.
313. Manuscript A reads: *das was ein ungenade* (1538,2a; Bartsch/Stackmann 1539,2a). Störmer-Caysa's rather understated translation reads: "that was not a friendly treatment" ("das war keine freundliche Behandlung").
314. Manuscript A reads: *daz maidin* (the maiden; 1539,2b). The Bartsch/Stackmann edition emends to: *diu künigîn*. This is Kudrun.

[1540] (1534) The king of [the] Moors was made most welcome, as is appropriate for brave men after such exertion. The brave man was thanked by the [lady][315] for having traveled so far from Karadie on that expedition. [1541] Then Horant, the hero from Daneland, was entrusted with whatever other prisoners were found there in Cassiane. He was entrusted with Kudrun, with her and all her ladies. He was a close relative, so he could be relied on all the more. [1542] He was given command of the forty strong towers and sixty large halls that stood next to the sea, along with three great palaces. [He] was the lord of all therein. Lady Kudrun, the queen, had to stay with him a while longer. [1543] Then a guard force was formed for the ships on the water. Hartmut was brought back to Cassiane to join the rest of his family, where the pretty ladies were being held captive along with the heroes. [1544] They were guarded so that no one could escape, and a thousand bold men were left there as well, who along with the Dane were to protect the women. Wate and bold Fruote were still keen on smashing more shields.

[1545] Then they prepared to move out with thirty thousand men. Fires were ordered to be set everywhere, and every corner of their homeland began to burn. Only now did noble Hartmut fully realize the extent of his loss. [1546] The heroes from Stormarn and Daneland razed strong castles wherever they found them. They plundered as much as anyone could gather together, and many pretty women were taken prisoner by the Hegelingen. [1547] Before Hilde's supporters returned from their campaign, they demolished twenty-six castles. They were exceedingly proud and pleased with their expedition; they brought Lady Hilde a thousand or more hostages. [1548] Hilde's standard was seen carried openly across Ormanieland and back to the shore, where they had left that noble highborn maiden. They wanted to leave that place; they didn't want to stay any longer.

[1549] Those who had been left behind in Hartmut's hall rode out of the castle down to meet their friends. They happily greeted the older and the younger men. The men from Daneland asked, "How did [you] lads make out?"

[1550] Then King Ortwin said, "We did so well that I will always be grateful to my comrades. We avenged ourselves with our foray so successfully that whatever they did to us, we paid back a thousand [times] over."

[1551] Then old Wate said, "Who do we want to leave behind? Who can govern these lands for us? Now ask fair Kudrun to come down here. We should depart for Hegelingen and let Lady Hilde see what we've brought home for her."

[1552] Then all of them, old and young, said, "We want to leave the Danes Horant and Morunc here. They'll stay here with a thousand bold men."

---

315. Manuscript A reads: *gedanncket von den frawen* (1540,3a; Bartsch/Stackmann 1534,3a). Bartsch/Stackmann emend to the singular *der frouwen*. McConnell retains the plural and translates: "thanked by the women" (158). Armour (1932) does likewise (192).

They had to agree with them; the nobles led many a hostage away. [1553] After they had decided to return to Hegelingen, they loaded supplies onto the ships, some they had taken and some that were theirs. The men who had collected war trophies wanted to show them off at home. [1554] Then Hartmut was told to come out of the hall, that brave man, along with five hundred men, who were prisoners and had been captured there. They later spent many long and difficult days with their enemies. [1555] Ortrun was also brought along, that highborn woman, with her household, to endure great hardship. When they departed from the land and friends, they could imagine how it had been for Kudrun and all her ladies. [1556] They led the prisoners away from there, and the captured castles were given over to Morunc and Horant. When the others left, they stayed in Ormanie with at least a thousand bold men.

[1557] "Now I humbly request," said Hartmut, "something for which I was willing to risk life and property,[316] that you let me go free here in my father's kingdom."

Old Wate said, "We'll do our best to keep you close. [1558] I don't know why it is that my nephew does this for someone who would have gladly robbed him of life and property, that he has him taken with him to his own home. If he allowed it, I would quickly make sure that his chains never bothered him again."[317]

[1559] "What good would come of it," said Lord Ortwin, "if you killed everyone here in this land of his? Hartmut and his household should have better prospects. I want to bring them home honorably to my mother Hilde."

[1560] They brought considerable plunder to the ships, along with gold [and] jewels, horses and clothing. They succeeded in what they had hoped to accomplish. Many of those who had previously complained were now heard singing.

Chapter 30: How They Sent Out Envoys to Hilde [1561–1666]

[1561] [The] Hegelingen army got underway full of joy. Of those they had brought with them across the sea, more than three thousand had to stay behind, either dead or wounded. Each one was silently mourned by his friends. [1562] Their ships sailed smoothly; they enjoyed fair winds. Those who had taken

---

316. Manuscript A reads: *darumb wolt ich setzen leib und gut* (1557,2). This line has been translated variously, especially with regard to verb tense and mood. Störmer-Caysa translates: "for which I wanted to wager life and property" ("wofür ich Leben und Besitz hatte einsetzen wollen"); McConnell: "I will offer my life and my property as security" (160); Gibbs/Johnson: "and I will surrender my life and my property" (138); Murdoch: "I shall place my life and all that I own at your disposal" (138); Sowinski: "I would offer life and property as security" ("dafür würde ich Leben und Gut als Sicherheit setzten").

317. In other words, he would kill him.

The Book of Kudrun

[plunder] were high-spirited. However they accomplished it, they sent out their messengers, who brought the news back to the land of Hegelingen. [1563] They hurried as best they could, I can tell you that much. They arrived back home in I don't know [how] many days. Lady Hilde had never before heard such welcome news, when they informed her that King Ludwig had been killed.

[1564] She said, "How are my daughter and her ladies?"

"Lord Herwig is bringing back his beloved to you. Brave heroes need not accomplish more than this. They are bringing Ortrun and her brother Hartmut as prisoners."

[1565] "This is wonderful news," said the noble woman. "My heart and my life were tormented by them. When I see them, I will punish them for it. I suffered much grief in public and in private. [1566] You messengers, I will reward you for telling me what has relieved me of such terrible grief. I give you my [gold] and do so by rights."

They said, "Noble lady, you can quite easily make us rich. [1567] We're bringing back great quantities of what we looted there. [None] of us refuses you out of disrespect. Our cogs are heavily laden with bright gold. We left it on our journey with many trusted chamberlains."

[1568] Lady Hilde started making preparations when she heard [this], for her many welcome guests who were about to arrive: refreshments and food and chairs along with the benches where they could sit. Of course she knew how to organize everything properly. [1569] The people of Matelane were kept busy enough. There on the field and on the beach, carpenters were summoned. They were in a great hurry so that Herwig and noble Kudrun could reign honorably.

[1570] I can't tell you if they had any problems out at sea. Ortwin's army traveled back to Matelane in six weeks. They brought Kudrun back, along with many exceptional young women. [1571] By the time they arrived—we are told this truthfully—their military campaign had lasted a whole year. It was the month of May when they brought their hostages back. Now they returned with a great noise as they remembered their hardships. [1572] When their cogs were seen off Matelane, they could hear loud sounds from trumpets and trombones, flutes and horns, and the beating of drums. Old Wate's ships had entered an anchorage. [1573] Then the men from Ortland also arrived. Lady Hilde and her household rode out from the castle of Matelane to greet them on the beach. Kudrun arrived then as well, where [many] an exceptional woman could be seen. [1574] They dismounted from [the] horses there on the beach, Lady Hilde and her household. Famed Irolt led fair Kudrun by [the] hand. Even though Hilde knew them, she didn't know each one of them individually.

[1575] She could see at least a hundred ladies in her household. "Now I don't know," said Lady Hilde, "whom I should receive as my dear daughter. I can't make her out. My friends are welcome, those who have landed here on this shore."

Chapter 30: How They Sent Out Envoys to Hilde [1561–1666]

[1576] "This is your daughter," said brave Irolt.

Then she approached her more closely. Who could calculate in treasure the joy that they felt when they kissed each other? [Their] grief vanished completely.

[1577] Lady Hilde received Irolt and all his men. Wate bowed deeply before her.[318] "Welcome, hero of Stormarn. You have served me well. Who could reward you if not by giving you a land and a crown?"

[1578] Then he said to the lady, "Whatever I can do to serve you, I am willing to do until my dying day."

She kissed him out of friendship; [she] did the same [with] Ortwin.[319] Herwig arrived as well, along with his proud and worthy men.

[1579] He led young Ortrun by the hand. Kudrun next asked her mother kindly, "Now, my dear lady, please kiss this highborn maiden.[320] She afforded me ample service and honor during my captivity."

[1580] "I don't want to kiss anyone I don't know. Who are this lady's kinsmen, or what are their names, whom you have asked me to kiss so kindheartedly?"

She replied, "This is Ortrun, the young maiden from the kingdom of Ormanie."

[1581] "I will not kiss her. Why do you advise me to do this? It would be more to my liking if I had her killed. Her kinsmen have surely caused me much grief. What I have shed here in tears was a delight to her supporters."

[1582] "My lady, this fair maiden has never counseled," replied Kudrun, "anything that would hurt you. Consider, dear mother, how much guilt I would bear if my family were to commit murder. Let the poor woman have your sympathy."

[1583] She didn't want to comply. Kudrun started to cry and plead with her mother. She said, "I don't want to see you crying like this anymore. If she did indeed serve you, then she will benefit from it here in this land."

[1584] Then fair Hilde kissed Ludwig's daughter. She later also greeted many other ladies for Kudrun's sake. Lady Hildeburg, who had done the washing with her, arrived from that foreign land. Lord Fruote led her by the hand.

---

318. Manuscript A reads: *Wate sich vil tieffe naigen began* (1577,2). It is clear that Wate is bowing before Hilde, which would seem the appropriate gesture, given that she is his sovereign and queen. The Bartsch/Stackmann edition emends to: *Waten si vil tiefe nîgen began*, which reverses the order, with Hilde bowing to Wate. This might seem appropriate given Hilde's gratitude to Wate for freeing her daughter and exacting revenge on her enemies. Most translators follow this emendation. McConnell translates according to the manuscript: "Wate bowed deeply to her," with a note (162n205). I have done likewise.

319. Manuscript A reads: *da kusset sy in vor liebe also tet auch Ortwein* (1578,3). The Bartsch/Stackmann edition emends to: *dô kuste si in vor liebe; alsô tete(s) ouch Ortwînen*, again reversing the order, with Hilde kissing Ortwin as opposed to the other way around in the manuscript. The difference is probably inconsequential. McConnell has an extensive note on this line (162n206).

320. Kissing was considered a sign of peace and reconciliation as well as affection.

[1585] Then Kudrun replied, "My dearest mother, please greet Hildeburg. Is there anything better than a friend's loyalty? Gold or precious jewels, whatever a kingdom possesses, that is what Hildeburg alone should be given."

[1586] Then the queen said, "It has been reported to me how she endured both good and bad with you. I won't be happy wearing this crown until I have rewarded her faithfully for how she served you."

[1587] After she kissed the young woman, as she did the others, Lady Hilde said to Fruote, "There is no shame in coming down to greet you and your fighters. You men are all welcome here in Hegelingen land."

[1588] They dutifully bowed before her. When their salutation was done, the king of the Moors could be seen noisily arriving with his warriors on the shore. The most distinguished among them sang a song from Arabia.

[1589] Lady Hilde waited until they had reached the beach. She respectfully welcomed the ruler of Karadie. "You are welcome, Lord Siegfried, a king from Moorland. I am forever in your debt that you helped right the wrong done to me."

[1590] "My lady, I [do] so gladly, wherever I can serve you. Now I return to the lands which have been mine for a long time, since my youth, when I first rode out to attack Herwig. I will never again wage war against him."

[1591] Then they unloaded the cogs and carried onto the beach many of the things they had brought with them to that land.[321] . . . could be seen running toward Herwig. [1592] Lady Hilde rode onto the field with her guests. There in front of Matelane they found shelters and pavilions decorated with [gold].[322] Many a bench could be found there; in this way they were served respectfully. [1593] Lady Hilde had ordered that they be escorted into the land without having to provide sponsors or pay guarantees. There had never been a better host in any kingdom than the noble widow. Her guests paid nothing for wine or food. [1594] Then the weary men rested until the fifth day. Even though everyone there was treated well, Hartmut was still burdened with worry, until the young women asked Lady Hilde for a reconciliation.

---

321. There is a lacuna here in the manuscript. Three lines in the middle column of fol. 164r are left blank in the manuscript, possibly to be filled in later. The missing text is limited to this particular strophe, however. This is the only blank space in the manuscript's text of *Kudrun*, indicating that there must have been either a lacuna or corruption in the source manuscript or some considerable differences between multiple sources. See Klarer (2022, 8:608–9) for a view of the manuscript.

322. Manuscript A reads: *von walde gezieret manig sedel reiche* (1592,3). The Bartsch/Stackmann edition emends the first half line to: *von golde gezieret*. McConnell notes (164n208) that the original *walde* makes sense as benches carved from wood if the half-line is read with the rest of lines 3 and 4, and not, as the emendation does, with the previous line 2 and its "golden" pavilions.

Chapter 30: How They Sent Out Envoys to Hilde [1561–1666]

[1595] Her daughter and Ortrun went to where she was. She said, "My dear mother, consider this, that no one should repay hatred with evil.[323] You should spare King Hartmut for the sake of your virtue."

[1596] She said, "My dear daughter, you should not ask this of me. I have suffered great harm on his account. My dungeon will make him pay for his arrogance."

Along with sixty young women, the ladies fell down at her feet. [1597] Then Ortrun said, "My lady, let him live. I guarantee that he will gladly serve you. Please deal mercifully with my brother. It will be to your honor if he should once again wear his crown."

[1598] All of them together cried because he was being held captive and in heavy chains. Their eyes filled with tears for Hartmut's sake, the king of Ormanie. He and his men were bound with very strong shackles.

[1599] Then the queen said, "Stop your crying. I will allow them to come to court unfettered. They must promise me that they will not try to escape and swear oaths that they will not leave this place without my permission."

[1600] The noble hostages had their chains removed. Kudrun secretly had the heroes bathed and nicely dressed and brought to court. They were brave men, which increased their prospects for success. [1601] Then Hartmut was seen standing among the men. People thought that no other man was more handsome. Despite all of his worries, he carried himself as if he had been painted with a brush. [1602] Then the ladies looked at him with admiration, and consequently he began to gain more trust. The enmity they bore was fully reconciled; they completely forgot that their warriors had once fought each other. [1603] Herwig considered how he might depart the land of the Hegelingen with honor. Weapons and clothing he had brought to the horses; his pack animals were loaded up. Lady Hilde heard about this, but she denied him permission to leave.

[1604] She said, "My Lord Herwig, you should stay here. You have done so much to bring me happiness that I am forever in your debt. Please don't go. Before my guests depart, I want to celebrate with my friends."

[1605] Then Lord Herwig replied, "My lady, it is well known that everyone who sends their kinsmen off to other kingdoms would like [them] to come back again. They can hardly wait for us to begin our journey home."

[1606] Then Hilde replied, "Grant [me] here and now this honor and joy. This would make me happier than anything. Most noble King Herwig, grant me this one reward, that my dear daughter might wear her crown alongside a poor woman like me."

[1607] He was reluctant to agree. She asked and asked again. The prisoners were to benefit from this later. When he replied that he would do it gladly, Lady Hilde was [filled] with great joy. [1608] She made sure the heroes were given even

---

323. Compare with Paul's letter to the Romans, 12:17: "Do not repay anyone evil for evil."

better seats. Later many warriors sat next to her with honors at a festival which has since been praised far and wide. Lord Herwig ordered that fair Kudrun be crowned. [1609] Of those who had come with him, no one departed until the festivities at Matelane had begun. For that event Hilde attired sixty or more lovely ladies. Her acclaim and her honor were important to her. [1610] At least a hundred women were given fine dresses. Those who had been brought to the land as hostages were not forgotten; each one of them was dressed as well. Fairest Hilde worked miracles with her generosity. [1611] Irolt was made chamberlain. He had to return quickly to their land; he was soon found. Wate, the hero of Stormland, was made seneschal. They also sent for strong Fruote of the Danish March.

[1612] He was to be made the cupbearer. The hero said to her, "I will gladly comply, my lady. If you want that I should do so, then grant me the fiefdom with twelve mighty banners. Then I'll be lord of Daneland."

Lady Hilde laughed graciously at that.[324] [1613] Then the queen said, "That is not possible. Your kinsman Horant is lord in Daneland. You should be cupbearer in his place, as his friend. Since he is still in Ormanie, you should remember him here at home."

[1614] The servants were told what to do. Lady Hilde had them give away what had long stayed in chests and closets, many a rich silk cloth. Chamberlains fetched them; they were distributed generously. [1615] There was no one of a rank so low that he was not given a good robe. If they also brought a foreigner with them to the land, I don't know what they were thinking. There were at least thirty thousand that they had brought from Ormanie. [1616] Anyone who wanted to clothe them all, where would he get it from? Even if the kingdom of Arabia were his to rule, I don't think anyone there could have found better clothing than what was given to the guests there. That was also done at Lady Kudrun's bidding.

[1617] As the lovely woman was sitting with the guests, she sent for Ortwin. She did this because she wanted to encourage him to seek Ortrun's love. Ludwig's daughter was also seated there next to Kudrun. [1618] The hero of Ormanie[325] went to her rooms. Many of the young women greeted Ortwin respectfully. His sister got up from her seat and took him by the hand; noble Kudrun took [him] aside from the courtly gathering.

---

324. The Bartsch/Stackmann edition has a long gloss on the use of banners as symbols of vassalage. Historically, banner-fiefs were granted to princes of the empire and represented the right to enfeoff those territories to their own vassals. An interesting example cited is Ottokar's acceptance of the Kingdom of Bohemia in 1276 with thirty-five banners.

325. Manuscript A reads: *Normandinen* (1618,1a). Bartsch/Stackmann emend this to *Nortriche*. While one would normally think of Hartmut as the hero of Ormanie, or Normandie, Ortwin could be granted this title as one of the victors of the campaign in Ormanie, Hartmut's land.

Chapter 30: How They Sent Out Envoys to Hilde [1561–1666]

[1619] She said, "My dear brother, listen to me. I want to give you this counsel out of faithful devotion. If you ever want to win joy in your life, however you can achieve it, you should seek to love Hartmut's sister."

[1620] Then the bold knight said, "Do you think that would be proper? We aren't the best of friends, Hartmut and I. We killed Ludwig. Whenever she thinks of that and is lying next to me, I think it would upset her."

[1621] "You should strive to ensure she doesn't do so. I give you this counsel with the most faithful devotion that I've ever felt for anyone in the world. You will be happy with her should she become your wife."

[1622] Then the noble knight said, "If you know her well enough to believe that people and land should serve her, if you say she is cultured, then I will gladly seek to love her."

Then Kudrun replied, "You will surely never experience an unhappy day with her."

[1623] He told his friends about this. Lady Hilde was against it, until he also let Herwig know about it. He faithfully urged him to agree.

He also told Fruote about it. He said, "You should marry her. You will gain many a brave warrior through her. [1624] The hatred that we've borne should be reconciled. I'll tell you how we can accomplish this"—this is what daring Fruote said. "We should have Hildeburg betrothed to King Hartmut."

[1625] Worthy Herwig faithfully spoke in support. "I gladly advise that the young woman should do this. She will be the sovereign [lady] of Hartmut's lands. He has under him at least a thousand castles."

[1626] Fair Kudrun spoke privately with noble Hildeburg; she wanted to ensure her well-being. She said, "Dear friend, if you want me to reward you for how you have served me, then you can wear a mighty crown in Ormanie."

[1627] Then fair Hildeburg said, "It pains me that I should love someone who never at any time [held] me in his heart or thoughts. Should I grow old with him, we will surely argue all the time."

[1628] Then Lady Kudrun said, "You will avoid that. I will quickly call for Hartmut to be summoned, to see if it would please him that I release him from his bonds along with his men and send him back home to his country. [1629] Should he thank me, I will promptly advise him that he should serve us [all the] more in the future. I'll ask him if he wants to pursue a love that can secure me and my kinsmen as allies."

[1630] Hartmut was summoned, the king of Ormanie. Fruote went with him to where proud young women were sitting in a room next to Hilde's daughter.[326] They would later forget much of their ordeal because of their lady's mediation.

[1631] When Ludwig's son went through the hall, no one, not the highest or the

---

326. This probably refers to Ortrun and Hildeburg, who are in Kudrun's company.

lowest born, failed to rise from her seat out of respect for him. He was utterly courageous, and he was dignified and noble.

[1632] Then Kudrun, that lovely young woman, asked him to take a seat. Not one of them denied him her greeting. Then Hilde's daughter said, "Sit down next to my friend, Hartmut, the one who used to wash your heroes' clothes."

[1633] "You wish to reproach me, mighty queen. Whatever was done to make you suffer, I was saddened by it, too. My mother kept it from me all that time, so that I knew [nothing], nor did my father and all his heroes."

[1634] Then the young woman said, "It can't be avoided; I have to speak with you alone, Hartmut. No one should hear this except for you and me."

Then Hartmut thought to himself, "God grant that she's well intentioned."

[1635] She allowed only Fruote to go with them. The handsome woman said to the king, "If you choose to do what I advise you, Hartmut, if you do so willingly, you can free yourself from all your cares."

[1636] "I know you to be a virtuous person," said Hartmut then, "that you would only advise what is honorable and good. In my heart I know of no reason that I should not do what you counsel, noble queen."

[1637] She said, "Then I happily suggest that you save your life. I and my family, we will give you a wife with whom your land and your honor will be preserved. And no one will think about our enmity any longer."

[1638] "So tell me, my lady, whom will you give me? I would sooner die than love someone that would cause my kinsmen at home to be ashamed. I would rather be condemned to death."

[1639] "I want to give Ortrun, your sister, to my dear brother as his wife. You should take Hildeburg, the noble queen. You won't find a more excellent maiden anywhere in the world."

[1640] "If you can arrange this as you've told me, that your brother Ortwin will honestly take that fair maiden Ortrun to be his wife, then I shall take Hildeburg, so that we may always live in peace."

[1641] She said, "I have succeeded in having him promise, if you should agree, that he will return to you the land and also your inheritance and castles as well. So it should please you to have Hildeburg as queen."

[1642] He said, "I gladly pledge to do so," and pledged by her hand. "As [soon] as my sister is crowned with the king of Ortland, I will not object to letting fair Hildeburg bestow and confer fiefs with me."

[1643] After he had pledged this, the highborn woman then said, "I would like to create even more alliances, so that we may always have security. We will give the man from Karadie Herwig's sister[327] as his wife."

[1644] I think never before was there such peacemaking as what that young woman achieved. The excellent, bold heroes had gathered together. Fruote of

---

327. She remains unnamed throughout the text.

Chapter 30: How They Sent Out Envoys to Hilde [1561–1666]

the Danish March had organized everything, so that Ortwin and the Moorish king were summoned. [1645] They came to court wearing exceptional clothing. Lady [Kudrun]³²⁸ made sure that Wate was informed. Irolt was also told the same thing. They went off to discuss things, and the heroes provided praiseworthy counsel.

[1646] Then old Wate said, "[Who] can make peace until Ortrun and Hartmut go before Lady Hilde and throw themselves at the noble queen's feet? And if she alone approves, then we can bring everyone together."

[1647] Then noble Kudrun said, "I can tell you this, that she is not hostile toward them. You can see that they are wearing the same clothes that my mother gave me and my ladies. I will gladly make peace; the captives can trust me in this."

[1648] Then Ortrun was brought into the circle,³²⁹ and so was Hildeburg, that stately woman. Ortwin and Hartmut took them to be their wives.

"It is my wish," said Lady Hilde, "that there be peace forevermore."

[1649] Ortwin lovingly pulled the young woman out of the circle. A golden ring he gave to the queen, to fit her white hands. With this her great suffering was brought to an end. [1650] Then Hartmut, too, embraced the young woman from Ireland. Both of them placed a gold ring on each other's hand. There was nothing about her that he didn't like. Hartmut and Hildeburg were since then inseparable in faithfulness.

[1651] Then Hilde's daughter said, "My dear sir, is your homeland close enough to us here that your sister, however it might be done, could be brought to my mother's land for the king of Karadie?"

[1652] Then King Herwig said, "I can tell you this. If someone were in a hurry, it could be done in twelve days. Whoever wanted to bring the young woman here to this land would have a hard time of it, unless I sent my own envoys with them."

[1653] Then Hilde's daughter said, "I gladly ask you to do so. By doing this you will guarantee yourself much enjoyment.³³⁰ My mother will make sure you

---

328. Manuscript A reads: *Hilde* (1645,2a), emended to *Kudrun* by Bartsch/Stackmann. McConnell retains the manuscript text, stating in his note that "there is no reason to believe that Hilde does not continue to have a part to play in the process!" (168n211).
329. Germanic rituals often involved some sort of community circle (*rinc*), in which vows or oaths were proclaimed in public. Heroic epic echoed this ancient ritual. In the *Nibelungenlied*, Siegfried and Kriemhild were placed inside a circle of family and friends to exchange their wedding vows (*NL* 614–15). A similar scene is enacted when Siegfried swore an oath to deny that he had claimed to be the first to sleep with Brunhild (*NL* 859–60). Finally, Ruediger's daughter and Giselher were betrothed inside a circle (*NL* 1683).
330. Manuscript A reads: *so brueset ir euch selber maniger hande spil* (1653,2). The normalized Bartsch/Stackmann text reads: *sô brüevet ir iu selben maniger hande spil*. The gloss on the line translates: "then you will provide yourself with much pleasure" ("so bereitet ihr euch selbst großes Vergnügen"). Sowinski translates along the same lines (289). Störmer-Caysa has a very different

have clothing and provisions. Now bring the lady to us, so that I can faithfully praise you for it."

[1654] Then Lord Herwig said, "Where would she get her wardrobe? The lord of Karadie ravaged my land and razed my castles. I lost all her possessions."

Then the king of the Moors said that he would ask for her even in a simple shift.

[1655] Herwig sent a hundred men to bring her back. He ordered his men to make haste during the voyage. He asked Wate to ride with them, along with daring Fruote. It was a difficult task for them, but they did it for that brave man. [1656] They hastened on, as fast as they could, day and night. When they found the young woman, Herwig's heroes were barely able to prevent Wate from resorting to force. Along with twenty-four ladies they brought her out of her residence. [1657] Wate was her escort from the castle down to the shore, where he found two galleys and two cogs. They boarded one of them; they were in a great hurry. The wind came to their aid; they arrived back in twelve days. [1658] When they brought the young woman to Hegelingen land, the knights thought about how they might rush to meet that beauty there on the beach, and [they] rode out with their banners. They had upheld their oaths, those who had sworn to support the noble lady's betrothal.

[1659] How could a welcome by noble young ladies have been any better? The fair maidens went out to meet her, along with noble Hilde and the rest of her ladies. Even though her land had been ravaged, Herwig's sister did not come alone. [1660] At least three hundred men accompanied Hilde from her residence. As King Herwig started the journey to greet her, he rode in many a contest[331] to honor her. All the others did the same; proud heroes' shields could be heard crashing together. [1661] The four kings rode out to meet her. When they had come together, the heroes argued over how they all looked, and which woman was the most beautiful. They praised everyone's qualities, and this brought the matter to a close. [1662] Then Lady Kudrun promptly kissed her and the others. They went down to the shore where they found a pavilion made of the finest silk, and they took their places underneath it. Herwig's sister wondered what they were planning to do.

---

translation: "Then you can announce various games of your own accord" ("dann mögt Ihr von Euch aus verschiedene Spiele ankündigen"). McConnell: "you yourself can enjoy the celebrations" (169); Murdoch: "you will be able to enjoy the festivities too" (146); Gibbs/Johnson: "you will secure all kinds of happiness for yourself" (146).

331. The Middle High German term is *puneiz*, which comes from the French *pougneis*, which stems from the Latin *pungere*, to prick, sting, then stab or thrust. This was a type of tournament or equestrian game in which two sides or teams tried to unhorse the opponents in a mock battle formation. Similar to the *bûhurt*, here the knights were usually armed with blunted weapons, which could still result in casualties.

[1663] The king of Karadie was summoned to appear. They said to the lady, "Will you have this man? He will make you sovereign of nine kingdoms."

She saw standing with him many praiseworthy knights with dark skin. [1664] His father and his mother were not of the same race. The hero's complexion was as light as a Christian's.[332] His hair lay on his head as if it were spun gold. She would have been unwise had she not granted him her love. [1665] But she was slow to pledge herself to him, as is true of most young women.

Then he was offered her love, and the brave man said, "She is so pleasing to me that I will not fail to serve the lady, so that I might take my place in this beautiful woman's bed."

[1666] Then they were betrothed, the knight and the young woman. On that day they could all hardly wait for night to fall. It so happened that they all enjoyed a wonderful wedding night. The daughters of four kings were anointed in front of the heroes there at the coronation.

Chapter 31: How the Four Kings Celebrated in Hilde's Land [1667–95]

[1667] Then the kings were anointed as well, as was their right. Five hundred or more warriors were made knights. That splendid celebration took place in Hilde's land, [at] Matelane, next to the castle by the seashore. [1668] Then fair Hilde gave all her guests something to wear. Ah, how old Wate rode in front of the stands, as did Irolt and Fruote, those warriors from Daneland! Many lances could be heard shattering, which the heroes lowered in their hands. [1669] Since there was no wind, the dust made it seem like night. The praiseworthy heroes were not interested in whether the fair ladies' precious clothing was soiled. They engaged in various equestrian games there in front of the stands at Matelane. [1670] They didn't want to leave the young women there, so they were soon brought away with fair Hilde to the large castle windows, where the men could admire them. There with the four queens were at least a hundred young women in beautiful attire.

[1671] The traveling entertainers had to display their talents that day. Whatever each one could do, how gladly he showed it off! The next day[333] after early Mass, after God had been worshipped, they saw the warriors ride out again. [1672] What else could there be than joy and excitement? The great hall often resounded with various melodies. This all went on for three whole days. The noble household was hardly ever not kept busy.

---

332. This statement is contrary to 583,3, where Siegfried is described as dark-skinned.
333. Manuscript A reads: <u>untz</u> *and den anndern morgen, nach fruemess zeiten* (1671,3). McConnell retains the manuscript's *untz* (until), which Bartsch/Stackmann and others strike, and so translates: ". . . continued into the early hours of the morning. After early Mass . . ." (171, with n. 216).

[1673] Then one of the openhanded nobles made his way to court.[334] He had heard that the traveling entertainers all wanted to become rich—at least that was their aspiration. He eagerly made things even better for the minstrels. [1674] It was the ruler of Seeland who tossed out the first gifts freely with his own hand, so that everyone who witnessed it or heard about it later thanked him for it. Lord Herwig gave away at least a thousand pounds of his red gold there. [1675] In addition, his kinsmen and his vassals gave away clothing. Some people acquired horses with good saddles, even though they had never ridden before. Ortwin took notice; they all tried to outdo each other in generosity. [1676] The king of Ortland gave away such expensive clothing that if anyone has since worn better, we don't know or haven't heard about it. He and his men were very soon standing there without any clothes. [1677] No one could calculate how expensive the clothing was that the men from Moorland, as we've been told, left behind there, including many good horses. Those to whom they wanted to give something could not have asked for better.

[1678] Young and old alike became rich with goods. Hartmut could be seen acting as if he hadn't been made destitute, that young and noble king. He was known to be so generous that no one gave away more. [1679] He and his friends who accompanied him, who had also been hostages, how easy it was for them to get what they wanted, or what someone wanted from them! Hartmut and his men were happy to confer it all on the people. [1680] Fair Kudrun was very devoted to Hildeburg of Ireland, who had often carried the clothes down to the beach where they did the wash. I think she did not neglect to encourage Hartmut's devotion to Hildeburg. [1681] She had so much treasure brought to him from her room, and as could be said of anyone she wanted to reward, the young queen was so well disposed toward him that [he] could in turn give away clothes and heavy gold.[335]

[1682] They saw the Stormarn men rise from their seats with such good attire that a king or a king's vassals at no time ever wore anything better. Those who wanted a gift from them were not left waiting. [1683] Wate himself gave away such a magnificent robe that a king had never been seen wearing a better one. It was draped with a costly net, made of gold and jewels, which the hero had brought to court with him. [1684] On each strand of the net was set a precious stone, whatever they were all called, but it was clear that they had been cut and polished in the land of Abalie. The heroes took Wate and his heroes by the hand. [1685] All those who saw what happened there had to admit that it was true, that brave Wate's gifts were far superior to anything a king could give. Whoever

---

334. The Bartsch/Stackmann gloss states that this *einer* (one) is Herwig. This would link strophes 1673 and 1674.
335. Manuscript A reads: *daz sy ze gebene hette wat und golt das sware* (1681,4). The Bartsch/Stackmann edition emends the *si* to *er* (he). This changes the subject from Kudrun to any male noble to whom the queen was well disposed, including Hartmut. McConnell retains the original *si*, and so translates: "the young Queen must have been very kindly disposed to whomever she wished to give such fine clothes and heavy gold" (172, with n. 218).

received any of these would long possess a great fortune. [1686] Irolt made it clear what his intentions were, that he was not concerned with the value of anything. Fruote of the Danish March was Hilde's chamberlain. He served his lady in ways that were recounted for a long time to come.

[1687] Then they wanted to depart; the festival had come to an end. Hartmut was allowed, as it was appropriate for him, to negotiate with his enemies under his lady's peace. They later returned home in a better state than anyone could have imagined. [1688] Lady Hilde graciously allowed them to depart. She and her daughter, along with all the household of the castle, accompanied Hildeburg. When they were ready to go, Lord Hartmut took his leave. [1689] Lady Hilde provided an escort both on land and on sea. In addition they acquired a splendid army, which Ortwin and Lord Herwig sent back with them. They returned to their land with at least a thousand of their followers. [1690] Everywhere the ladies could be seen kissing each other. Some of them said their goodbyes there as if they would never see each other again. Ortwin and Lord Herwig escorted them down to their cog. [1691] Irolt was responsible for the escort back to their country. The king[336] ordered him to be sure to inform Horant of the Danish March how they parted. Later he brought many famous warriors back with him. [1692] I don't know at what point, whether later or sooner, their sails began to appear before Cassiane. All the people there were genuinely happy. I think that God cared for many of them after their hardship.

[1693] Irolt informed Horant in Ormanie land why the kings had sent him there along with them. He said, "It is right that we leave this land to these men; they are happy to be home. I can hardly wait to get back to my own country myself."

[1694] They welcomed Hartmut and returned his land to him. How he ruled the land is unknown to me. Horant and his friends were in a great hurry as they departed from there, so they could quickly return to the Danish March. [1695] We take leave now of their journey and want to point out that no warrior or his kinsmen ever took better leave of a festival. The men from the land of Karadie stayed on in high spirits.

Chapter 32: How the Others Went Home [1696–1705]

[1696] They did not stay there in Hegelingen any longer. They took Herwig's sister to Alzabe with great pageantry. They had been very successful there. Once they were on their way, the proud knights sang out in joy. [1697] Lady Hilde sent them all off in friendship. Even though Herwig's men had arrived with great wealth, she did not let anyone go without a gift from her. If someone were that generous today, it would surely be considered a miracle.

---

336. Störmer-Caysa (628n1691,2) identifies this as Ortwin.

[1698] Lady Kudrun said to her mother, "Bless you. Console yourself concerning the fallen. I and my lord will always serve you, so that you are never burdened with sadness again. You will profit from Herwig's kindness."

[1699] Then the queen said, "My dear daughter, if you want to make me happy, then your messengers should visit me here in Hegelingen three times a year. I don't think I could live here [like this], even [without] great adversity."[337]

[1700] Then noble Kudrun said, "Mother, it will be done."

She and her ladies looked back on Matelane and left with laughter and with tears. Their troubles were now at an end; no one before had seen such a pretty sight. [1701] Then they brought handsome horses, fully saddled, with golden bridles and narrow breast straps, to carry her and her ladies. I think that the ladies were of a mind to not stay any longer. [1702] Those riding with loose hair[338] adorned with gold, I think they were not completely free of envy[339] when they departed from Ortrun and her ladies. If someone had been better off, Kudrun would have been displeased. [1703] Ortwin's beloved thanked noble Kudrun. It was because of her that her brother Hartmut had regained the land of Ormanie.

"May God reward you, Kudrun, that I am now forever free from care."

[1704] She also thanked her mother Hilde, that she would wear the crown in Ortland [with] Ortwin, the king, and that she would be the sovereign lady there. The queen said that she had forever renounced any animosity. [1705] Ortwin and Herwig both swore together that they would forever be faithful to each other, that they would worthily carry out their royal office with great honor, and if anyone wanted to do them harm, that they would both pursue and punish them.

THIS IS THE END OF KUDRUN

---

337. Manuscript A reads: *on michel ungemute getrawe ich ymmer hie gedingen* (1699,4). The Bartsch/Stackmann edition emends the line: *ân michel ungemüete getrouwe ich (sus) nimmer hie gedingen*, changing the adverb *immer* (always) to *nimmer* (never). McConnell stays with the manuscript reading and translates: "I believe that I can continue on here now without much sorrow" (175, with n. 223). Gibbs/Johnson translate as emended: "Otherwise I don't think I'll manage to survive here without a great deal of misery" (151). Murdoch accepts the emendation but translates quite loosely: "otherwise I shall not be able to contain my impatience for news" (151). The difference in meaning is, of course, considerable. Queen Hilde is either triumphant and hopeful for the future, or she is still for some reason fearful of how her life might still be ruined.

338. Only unmarried young women could appear in public without their hair up and covered.

339. Manuscript A reads: *ich wane die des hasses icht warn frey* (1702,2). The Bartsch/Stackmann gloss translates in the negative: "they were not free of hatred" ("sie waren nicht frei von Zorn"). Störmer-Caysa does not have the negative: "I believe they were free from all hatred" ("ich glaube, die waren frei von jedem Hass"). Gibbs/Johnson interpret the motivation behind the departure differently: "those young girls . . . were not best pleased to be leaving Ortrun and her maidens" (151), with a further explanation in a note that "presumably the young women were sorry to be taken away from this joyful social gathering" (169n155).

KING OTNIT'S BOOK BEGINS[1]

Chapter 1 [1–69][2]

[1] There was a book unearthed at London,[3] in the town.
It was a wonder of writing, made up of many a leaf.
Muslims,[4] because of their wickedness, had buried it.
Now we can be pleasantly entertained by this book.
[2] Whoever would be joyful and amused,
let him have this book sung or read to him,
about a kingdom by the name of Lombardy.
It needn't be ashamed of its name in any royal house.

---

1. The title in the Ambras manuscript (hereafter referred to as manuscript A), in red ink, reads: *Künig Ottnides Puech hebt sich an*; the Windhagen manuscript's (W) heading, also in red ink, reads: *Hie hebet sich an dc bůch das da haisset kaiser Ortnit*, "Here Begins the Book That Is Called Emperor Ortnit," and goes on to include the text of the first line and a half, which is repeated then in normal black script. This book title highlights both the alternate spellings of the eponymous hero's name and his rank as either king or emperor. Manuscript A spells the main character's name consistently without an "r" (*Otnit, Ottnit, Otneit, Otneidt*). According to a note in the most recent Reclam edition (Fuchs-Jolie, Millet, and Pesche, 2013, 614n1; for the sake of brevity hereafter referred to simply as the Reclam edition), twelve of seventeen manuscript witnesses containing one version or another of the story likewise do not spell the name with an "r." Among the notable exceptions with "r" (*Ortnit*) are manuscript W and the *Dresdener Heldenbuch* (manuscript k).
2. There is no separate first chapter indicated in manuscripts AW. Line 69,4 does end with a reference to such a chapter, or *abentewr*, in the same way that other chapters end, and so a first chapter is inserted into the text here as an indication that what follows can be considered the first of eight chapters.
3. Manuscript A reads: *Lunders* (London; 1,1b); manuscript W reads: *Suderz*, which is the capital of Machorel's kingdom in Syria. The name likely corresponds to the city of Tyre in present-day Lebanon. *Lunders*, or London, is probably a scribal error, but manuscripts a and b, which contain the D version of *Wolf Dietrich*, also use this place-name. There are two narrative logics at work here. For the book to have been buried by non-Christians it is most logical to name a site in a Muslim city. For a book to be found by Christians, it is most logical for that site to be in a Christian land.
4. The original Middle High German word *haiden* is translated throughout based on context rather than the generic and pejorative English "heathen." Since Otnit's story unfolds very much in the guise of a crusade against Islamic territory (Suders, or Tyre) and its ruler (Machorel, or al-Malik al-Adil), this translation will use the term "Muslim" accordingly. There are two exceptions in *Otnit*. In the first instance (203,4), Otnit returns to his castle unrecognized and taunts his subjects by telling them he is a "wild heathen." In the second instance (225,1), Ilias of Russia is referred to once as a *haiden*. Editors have changed this to "Russian," but the reading in both manuscripts AW is clear, even though the reason for this appellation is unclear.

[3]⁵ There once came of age in Lombardy a mighty and powerful king.
There was at that time no other king his equal
in any of the Italian⁶ lands. This was made evident
over the course of his entire life by how strongly he ruled.
[4] Everyone had to fear the king as well as his army.
He had conquered the lands from the mountains to the sea.
They had to pay him tribute, those who ruled alongside him.
They all had to fear his decrees and his threats.
[5] For his dignity as a king he was praised.
His name was Otnit; he was experienced in battle.
Brescia and Verona were under his dominion.
He was served in Garda daily by seventy-two liegemen.
[6] In his virtue he sought to gain true dignity as a king.
His vassals helped him vanquish other lands.
He had the strength of twelve men, that marvelous, bold man.
The might of Rome, as well as the Lateran,⁷ served him.
[7] Once that noble man had grown to maturity,
his counselors advised him to take a wife
who would suit him and be his lady
and rule over Lombardy with honor as its queen.
[8] Then the noble king said, "Advise me, kinsmen and vassals,
you who are the ones I value most in my land,
where I can find a wife to be my companion,
so that I need not be ashamed [of]⁸ her lineage."⁹
[9] They gathered in council for five whole days
and could in all honesty not tell the king

---

5. The third strophe is typical for the introduction of a character in heroic epic, with its *ez wuohs* formula. Compare this with similar strophes in the *Nibelungenlied* (*NL* 2,1: Kriemhild; *NL* 20,1: Siegfried) and *Kudrun* (*K* 1,1: Sigebant).
6. The geographical reference is to *alle lant ze Walhen* (3,1a). The term *Walhen* refers to Romance-language–speaking lands, at this time primarily France and Italy. In this context the term most likely refers to the area of northern Italy.
7. Otnit is apparently so powerful that he is served by both the ancient imperial and ecclesiastical centers of the West, a possible commentary on the continuance of imperial Roman rule and the primacy of secular rule over the Roman church.
8. Words or phrases not found in manuscript A but added or emended in the Reclam edition (2013) are placed in square brackets. Only those emendations necessary to make sense of the original text have been adopted.
9. Manuscript A reads: *vor irem geschlechte* (before her lineage; 8,4b). Kofler (2009) and the Reclam edition opt for the manuscript W reading: *von*. As noted in the Reclam edition (615n8,4), the manuscript A reading would imply that Otnit is concerned about his own lineage in comparison with his future wife's. This could be a valid reading, given his insecurities and self-doubt in his campaign to win a wife overseas. Lines such as 12,4 make this less likely, however.

where they might find a wife whom he could take with honor,
so that they would later not come to regret their advice.
[10] Then Margrave[10] Helmnot of Tuscany said,
"Those kings who rule around us are under your authority.
We can find no land on this side of the sea
where a king is so powerful that he is not subject to you."
[11] Then King Ilias of the Russians said,
since after Otnit he was the highest ranking there,
"I know of a lady who is beautiful and highborn;
no man has ever asked for her hand and not lost his head."
[12] Then King Otnit said, "So tell me more,
dear Uncle Ilias, why is that so?
Who are her kinsmen? Who is this lady?
Could she rule with honor over Lombardy as queen?"
[13] "I'll tell you her father's name; he is called Machorel,
born at Mount Tabor. His skin is the color of a Moor.
More Muslims serve him than all of Christendom.
In Jerusalem this lord wears the king's crown.
[14] "Suders in Syria is his capital city.
Anyone who has ever asked for that lady's hand
has had to give up his life for the queen's sake.
What more do you want to know? She can't ever be yours anyway.
[15] "She shines above all other ladies, just as good gold
outshines plain lead. That you may believe.
She shines above all other women as does a rose.
There was never a young woman so beautiful, and she is of high repute."
[16] Then King Otnit of Lombardy said,
"Now help me achieve this, if you all cherish me.
I will forfeit this kingdom of mine;
I will lose my life, or she shall be my queen."
[17] Then the king of Russia said, "May God have mercy
that I ever mentioned these stories to you today,
which have been resurrected to bring about your death.
I would gladly advise against this, since you are my sister's son."
[18] "Whoever advises against this will forever lose my favor.
I have for a long time amassed silver and gold.
I will now spend the treasure on building a great army.
God's will be done; I must travel to her across the sea."
[19] "When you arrive at Mount Tabor, take a look at the ramparts.
He's affixed seventy-two heads on them,

---

10. This title (*marggrave*; 10,1a) denotes a count given authority over a border region or march.

which he severed from the envoys for that lady's sake.
That I ever thought of her, may God have mercy on me,
[20] "that because of this such great suffering will now be mine."[11]
Then the king of Lombardy said, "How much he must love his child.
He should act faithfully according to his laws
and give her to a man. That way he has a daughter and a son."
[21] "He's well advised to do so, but he thinks otherwise,
and I'll tell you why he won't do it.
He means to do something he ought to be ashamed of.
When her mother dies, he wants to take his daughter.
[22] "He would like to see the lady's mother dead,
so that his beautiful daughter might become his dear wife."
"May God prevent that," said King Otnit.
"I will not rest until she comes to lie by my side."
[23] Then King Ilias of Russia replied,
"Since you have your heart set on this,
then this voyage will be the [day of judgment][12] for many Lombards.
Nevertheless I will help you as best I can."
[24] "Whoever helps me with this voyage will forever gain my favor.
I will share my silver and my gold with him as well,
along with land and towns, people and property.
I will be forever grateful to whomever does this willingly,
[25] "to him I will always be favorably inclined as long as I shall live.
May God grant me grace and good fortune,
that I may convert this Muslim from his sinfulness,[13]
and bring back the fair maiden here to Christianity.
[26] "Dear comrades-in-arms, we must take to the sea.
May God grant us grace so that we might succeed.
Any Christian man who dies, I give him this consolation.
His cleansed soul will be redeemed forevermore.
[27] "Now don't be discouraged; march on in joy.

---

11. Amelung's edition (1871) reverses lines 20,1 and 20,2. Thomas (1986) follows this and reads line 20,1 as spoken by Otnit. He translates both lines: "Why should his fondness for his child cause me so much distress?" (2).

12. Manuscript A reads: *fünffzigk tag* (fifty days; 23,3b). According to the note in the Reclam edition (616–17n23,3), this is a hapax legomenon whose meaning is unclear. It may refer to the fifty days before Easter, i.e., the Sunday before Lent, or the period of Pentecost. Five and fifty are prominent numbers throughout the text. Manuscript W, on the other hand, reads: *ein suentach* (*suontac*), which can be translated as "Judgment Day" or "Doomsday" (Thomas, 1986,2). This reading has been adopted here.

13. Manuscripts AW read: *daz ich den haiden irre seiner unrainikeit* (25,3). Thomas translates: "as to prevent the heathen's wicked deed" (2).

We'll put out to sea with a large contingent of knights.
Whoever wants to help me now should keep this in mind.
With a happy heart," said King Otnit,
[28] "we will kill the Muslims, those who are [not] Christians."
Then Ilias of Russia said, "You are my sister's son.
By rights I will risk life and limb for you.
I will provide you with a thousand[14] knights and myself as well."
[29] Then the Lombard said, "You have in short order
made it very clear to me what it is that you owe me.
The support of faithful friends is truly a blessing,
and if God allows me to return, I will make your kingdom even greater."
[30] Then Engelwan, the Burgrave[15] of Garda, said,
"You have in this castle seventy-two vassals.
You were born to be placed above them as their superior,
and they will grieve terribly should you be lost to them there."
[31] His brother, bold Helmnot, said angrily,
"You have no idea why you ride to your death for this woman.
You should more appropriately stay here in your own lands.
The daughter of a rich and noble lord could also be your queen."
[32] Then the Lombard said, "You can't deny me this.
If you fear for your life, then swear me no oath.
Surely you've often heard," said King Otnit,
"that a worthy man's legacy lies in any land."
[33] Then the seneschal,[16] their father Huteger, said,
"We realize that you are serious; we won't try to dissuade you.
Here in this castle, seventy-two liegemen will give you
each a hundred knights, if you won't excuse them."
[34] Then the Lombard said, "That is a friend's counsel.
That this castle of Garda has so many knights!
They were always my vanguard when I needed support.
They will guard the border region," said King Otnit.
[35] "Lords, counts, free men, and noble liegemen,
all I have in my land, aside from those in Garda,
those who are willing to undertake this voyage with me,

---

14. Amelung emends to five thousand, although manuscripts AW both clearly say one thousand. This is likely done to match Ilias's five thousand men mentioned in 46,2a.

15. Engelwan and Helmnot, two of Otnit's vassals, are given the title of kings in manuscripts Wk. A burgrave (*burggrave*, 30,1b) is a count responsible for the defense and administration of one or more castles (*burc*) and attendant territory.

16. This court office, also known as steward, was originally responsible for the domestic administration of a royal household. The position later became mostly ceremonial but still represented an important position among the counselors of a king or lord.

we will travel to distant lands. This I cannot leave."
[36] Then Margrave Helmnot of Tuscany said,
"So take as a tribute from me five thousand bold men.
These I will send with you, sire, across the fierce sea.
If I sail with you, then there will certainly be more."
[37] "May God reward your gift," said King Otnit.
"You have contributed to a praiseworthy campaign.
You have supported me without being asked or reminded.
For your loyalty, I place in your hands both people and lands.
[38] "Mighty and virtuous lord, with you they will be safe.
When I depart from my land on this precious campaign,[17]
you will have authority over Garda and all my honor.
I also entrust my mother to you, sir, and to your loyalty."
[39] Then Duke Gerebant of Troia said,
"I will contribute, sire, to your campaign
my five thousand heroes; may this be satisfactory to you.
And if you like, I will sail with you myself to win the queen."
[40] Then the Lombard said, "I don't require that of you.
You have made a great contribution, whatever happens to me,
in that you have provided me with so many proud men.
You should defend the lands[18] here at home yourself."
[41] Then Zacharis, the Muslim from Sicily, said,
"I am a member of your council;[19] you are my sovereign lord.[20]
What you ask of others, I give to you without being asked.
I will provide an ample tribute whenever you wish to travel by sea.
[42] "When you want to sail from the coast out to sea,
I will provide you with twelve ships loaded with rations
and with the best wine that a king was ever given.
Depart whenever you wish; I will give you enough to last three years.
[43] "I will make a great contribution, mighty King Otnit,

---

17. This line is missing entirely in manuscript W.
18. The note in the Reclam edition (618n40,4) interprets manuscript A's *Heugeburges* as a hapax legomenon and place-name, possibly synonymous with medieval references to Monte Gargano. The translation in this edition reads: "You should stay here at home and defend the Heugeburge [Heu mountains]" ("Du sollst hier daheim das Heugeburge halten"). Manuscript W reads: *des her gebirges*. Kofler takes this to mean *herberge*, or "army camp" (Heerlager), i.e., "stay with the troops at home." Thomas translates: "dwellings" (3).
19. Manuscripts AW read: *ich sitz(e) in dem gedinge* (41,2a). Thomas seemingly takes a variant from other manuscripts (ec) and translates: "I am under your protection" (*in diner gewalte*), going against both manuscripts AW and Amelung.
20. The metaphor used here is a tree, with Otnit sitting on the highest branch. A literal translation would be "you are my highest branch" (*du bist mein obristes reis*, 41,2b).

silks and velvet for twenty thousand heroes,
rich cloths of gold weave and brocade.
All this I will give to you and twenty thousand heroes."
[44] Then the Lombard said, "I will also lead across the sea
thirty thousand heroes and even more men.
You should be mindful of this. I want to travel free from care.
May God protect those I leave here at home.
[45] "Keep this in mind, you heroes, and be forewarned,
I won't take anyone who does not have battle armor,
even if he is a noble knight or of equal rank.
No one will accompany me if even a finger is left unprotected."
[46] Then the king of Russia said, "I will lead across the sea
five thousand valiant heroes, shining like the snow
in their bright coats of mail rings, without a spot uncovered.
Wherever I plant my banner, they will not waiver."
[47] Then Margrave Helmnot of Tuscany said,
"I will provide you with many well-bred Castilian horses.
Five thousand valiant heroes I have already pledged.
My fealty to you[21] will be suspect if even a foot can be seen
[48] that is not covered and shielded by mail rings."
Then Duke Gerebart of Troia replied,
"Nocera and Benevento are subject to me,
so I will also send you five thousand men
[49] "in gleaming mail rings, noble and highborn,
those I have chosen for you as the very best in my land."
"All of you have provided me," said King Otnit,
"with fifty thousand[22] warriors for the hard fight against the Muslims.
[50] "If I could find another hundred thousand, I would pay for them myself.
Whoever stays behind will never find favor with me again."
Then some were seen coming forward for the pay and reward,[23]
while others were eager to join on account of their adventurous spirit.

---

21. Amelung and Kofler prefer the manuscript W reading: *so gesweich mir dein trewe* (Renounce your fealty to me; 47,4a), to the manuscript A reading: *so gesweche dir mein trewe*, used in this translation.
22. Manuscript A reads: *fünfzigktausent* (fifty thousand), manuscript W reads: *funf tausent* (five thousand; 49,5a). Amelung emends to fifteen thousand, which would be the sum total for the previous three noblemen.
23. Manuscript A reads: *durch habe und auch durch got*, "for pay and also for God" (50,3b); manuscript W reads: *guot* (property, wealth). Both readings make sense, but the W reading is preferred to fit the rhyme with *muot* in the next line, and because of the formulaic nature of the pair *habe und guot* (Reclam, 620n50,3).

[51] They all willingly supported that mighty and powerful king.
Many of them never saw Lombardy again.
Horses and armor were distributed there.
They risked their lives for the sake of riches.
[52] Many young squires were knighted by him.
"I'm glad," said the Lombard, "that people desire wealth.
There is a tower in Garda that contains my coffers.
It is filled with treasure from the floor to the ceiling."
[53] But he gave so much away that there was nothing left.
Those who watched over his estate made certain to account for
thirty thousand shields and just as many suits of armor.
They were all made ready so that nothing was lacking.
[54] "Nephew and lord," said King Ilias,
"since you have so much treasure and such great virtue,
along with such great standing, now choose for yourself a man
who can give you counsel. To whom do you entrust this honor?"
[55] Then the Lombard said, "I am your sister's son.
Since all the other nobles are under my authority,
I will choose you as my father. You are my father.[24]
The citizens and my person are entrusted to your fealty."
[56] "I'll tell you this," said the Russian, "if you sail out to sea
you will certainly be lost, you and all your army.
The wind is unfavorable; it is not the right time for going to sea."
"I will depart when you command it," said King Otnit.
[57] "When May appears and turns to bright summer days,
then ask your friends to tell their heroes
to prepare themselves, come what may,
so that we can take to the blustery sea when the birds sing."
[58] Then King Otnit of Lombardy said,
"Since all my happiness and joy depend on you,
then pledge me your fealty, as you have promised me.
I want to be worthy of this,[25] should I live so long."
[59] They swore their fealty and assured him
that they did so most happily. The king was glad of it.
The winter and its short days seemed long to the king,
for love and the maiden's beauty pleasantly tormented him.

---

24. There is no mention of Otnit's father in the opening strophes of the story. In 76,2–3 his mother claims to have no other relatives except Otnit and his uncle Ilias. It is unusual to refer to a chief counselor and military commander as "father" (Reclam, 620n55,3), but in this case it is in keeping with the common role of the mother's brother, or child's uncle, as a foster father or comparable paternal figure.
25. Manuscripts AW read: *das wil ich verdienen* (58,4a). Thomas translates: "I'll repay you" (5).

[60] They were pleased with everything he required of them.
They took their leave and departed from Garda.
With feelings of affection, he granted them all leave to go.
Excellence and honor followed that king to his grave.
[61] Then they all left him except for one man,
the Muslim[26] from Apulia—he did not want him to go—
and also the king of Russia. These two he had chosen
as the best of those who were in his land.
[62] Then the Lombard said, "May God let me live
long enough to thank you for what you have given me,
virtuous Muslim, for what I never asked of you.
And if you were to become Christian, I would consider you my brother."
[63] "Don't think of me as a Muslim. My fealty is constant
whether or not I serve you more than Christians do.
My fealty is unwavering, whatever you may need.
I serve you as gladly as someone who's been baptized."
[64] Then Ilias of Russia said, "The time is drawing near.
You can trust him completely. Ask the Muslim to tell you
where you can find the ships that he wants to give you.
So that you can make your plans, ask him to tell you the place."
[65] Then the wise Muslim said, "Where else could it be
that he will find the ships than in Messina,
in my kingdom and in my best port,
where all mariners depart from and return to?"
[66] Then the Apulian said, "Now let me go, sire,
if I am to complete and secure your ships,
so that you may find them just as I have promised."
Then the Lombard said, "I gladly grant you leave."
[67] "I also want to depart for Russia," said King Ilias.
"It's been almost a year since I've been home.
I would like to see my wife and my children at home.
I need to inspect the heroes I promised you."
[68] "God bless you both," said King Otnit,
"and may you be rewarded for your fealty,
that you so readily undertake what I ask and command.
I don't dare keep you any longer. May God bless you."
[69] So without further ado he gave them both his leave.
I think the stories of the maiden's beauty weighed on his mind.
His love for her very nearly made him take leave of his senses.
So ends one chapter of Otnit's story.

---

26. Manuscript A reads: *heyden*, (heathen; 61,2a); manuscript W reads: *herren* (lord).

Chapter 2: How Otnit Found His Father Alberich When He Gave Him His Armor [70–212][27]

[70] His mother, that loving woman, said respectfully, "[You are] taking a great risk with your life. You should rightly get your friends' advice. Things seldom go smoothly if they are done without counsel."

[71] "Mother and sovereign lady," said King Otnit, "please don't oppose my resolve or will to fight. Whatever you ask of me, lady, it will be done, but even if I had a thousand mothers, I wouldn't stay for their sake."

[72] "I don't want to dissuade you," said the queen. "Father and lord, man and little child,[28] since you are so passionate about this, I won't stop you. May God grant you good fortune and keep you safe."

[73][29] Then the Lombard said, "A dream came to me. My dear chamberlain, bring me my battle armor."

The loving woman said with sadness, "Son, you won't rest until you forfeit your life."

[74] Then the Lombard said, "Lady and mother mine, it's impossible for a man to be forever without misfortune. The one to whom I entrust myself, he must protect me. I've been idle too long; I want instead to go on an errant quest.[30]
[75] I haven't been out in search of adventure for a long time. Mother and sovereign lady, you should want what's good for me, since I've never crossed you—at least I don't think I have. And if you forbid me to go on this journey, I will go nevertheless."

[76] Then the lady said respectfully, "You are my beloved child; you are the only kinsman now left to me, along with my brother, your uncle Ilias, the king of the fierce Russians, who has always been faithful to you."

[77] "Bring me my ringed chain mail," said the daring hero. "I must ride out into the forest to seek adventure. My [heart] is free from care; I should have success. A worthy man should try his luck in all things."

---

27. Manuscript W marks the beginning of this chapter at the previous line, 69,4, with a large initial "O" (*Ortneides*; three lines high). There is no chapter title or other special marking as there is in manuscript A.
28. This address by the queen to her son is unusual. The term "father" must obviously be taken figuratively, and it may be appropriate under the guise of Otnit as a *pater familias* of his land and all his subjects, including his mother. She recognizes in her address that Otnit has both royal as well as familial rights and obligations. In 79,3a, however, she addresses him with the more conventional "son and lord." Otnit addresses his father Alberich in the same, more appropriate manner (227,1a).
29. Strophes 73–75 are missing entirely in manuscript W. Indeed, the sudden shift from preparation of a crusade to the pursuit of some vague vision is abrupt and may represent in manuscript A some attempt at patching together a transition.
30. The original text is *irre varen* (74,4b), which evokes an aimless journey without a real destination.

Chapter 2: How Otnit Found His Father Alberich When He Gave Him His Armor [70–212]

[78] Then his dear mother said, "You long for a life of strife. But if you seek adventure, I will make my contribution, so that you might be all the more beholden to me. If you leave me now, I will give you this small ring."

[79] "Mother and lady, I swear this oath to you: I will never give it to anyone, should that upset you."

"Son and lord, now take this gold ring. But if you give it to someone, you will lose my favor forever."

[80] When the Lombard saw the little ring, he examined it carefully. He laughed and said, "Now I would really like to know, my dearest mother, how could you be so fond of this little ring?"

[81] "The ring is precious, even if it seems worthless to you. You seek adventure, since this is what your heart desires. If you want to ride into the wilderness, never part with it. You will find adventure, brought about by the ring's stone. [82] You must believe me when I say that you should never part with this little ring, even if kingdoms could be yours. The gold does not have much value, but the stone is so powerful that it will confer on you fifty thousand marks this year alone. [83] When you ride out from Garda, keep to your left hand,[31] over fallen trees and over mountains, along the rock wall, and look out for a linden tree that stands beneath the mountain, where a cool fountain flows out from the rock wall. [84] The linden tree is green; under it is a broad meadow. Five hundred knights could find pleasant shade under that linden. If you go beneath the green linden, you'll agree with me. If you are meant to find adventure, it will happen there."

[85] Then the Lombard bowed to his dear mother. She said, "You should not hide the ring, my son. Wherever you go, let it be seen openly. If you are meant to find adventure, it will lead the way."

[86] Then the Lombard rode out fearlessly from the castle of Garda, without any of his men. Those loyal to him and among the worthy were sorry that he didn't want anyone to accompany him. [87] Then he avoided the open country, as his mother had told him, and turned toward the wilderness, away from roads and paths. [He] held his hand and the ring toward the sun and rode across untrodden ground along the rock wall down to the valley. [88] Then he arrived at a meadow next to the Garda lake. There flowers and clover had sprung up across the heath. The birds sang beautifully; he listened to their sweet sound. He'd stayed awake throughout the night; the long ride had disheartened him. [89] The sun shone through the clouds heralding the morning. He often looked at the gold ring and its stone. He noticed that the green grass past the meadow was trampled; he saw that little feet had made a small path. [90] He followed the same path along the rock wall to where he found the cool fountain and the linden tree. He saw the green heath as well as the linden's bough. It hosted many a worthy guest among its branches. [91] On them the birds competed loudly in their singing.

---

31. In chivalric romance, this is often the "sinister" direction that leads to (mis)adventure.

"I think I've taken the right path," said King Otnit. He dismounted from his horse and led it by the reins. His heart rejoiced that he had found the linden. [92] He looked at the linden for a long time. He laughed and said, "God in heaven only knows, you are a beautiful roof. Never did such a sweet fragrance spring from any tree."

As he peered beneath the branches, he saw a little boy. [93] He was stretched out in the grass, but the Lombard couldn't make out who it was. He was wearing the [best][32] attire that anyone young or old ever had in all the world. [94] His outfit was adorned with precious jewels.

When he found the child all alone under the green linden, "My goodness, where is your mother?" said King Otnit. "You're lying here under this tree completely unattended. [95] You're wearing clothing suited for a knight. I don't want to startle you. How very hesitant I am.[33] I don't dare do you any harm; you're such a beautiful child. Might God in heaven grant that you were my son. [96] You seem to be about the size of a four-year-old child. If I took you with me, what good would it do to force you? I would gain little honor, seeing as no one is watching over you. My goodness, where is your mother, my dear little child?"

[97] His clothing was made entirely of silk and gold. He stood there and stared at his body and his hair. He thought that the child was quite beautiful, as was his attire.[34] It was by virtue of that remarkable stone that he saw him lying there. [98] He carried it on his hand, set in a ring. He stood there where he lay; his heart was moved.

He said, "Your great beauty and your clothing are so precious. Even though I've found you all alone, you haven't been abandoned. [99] I've traveled through the night to seek adventure; now gracious God has brought me to this linden tree. Since I've traveled here in search of adventure, and I haven't happened upon anything else, you'll have to come with me." [100] He tied up his horse securely to a branch of the linden. He said, "I'd like to find out if anyone is with you. When are you going to wake up?" the Lombard shouted.

The little one let on that he wasn't soundly asleep. [101] He wanted to carry him to the horse like a child. For that he got a hard punch in the ribs. The little

---

32. Manuscript A reads: *allerhertisten*, (hardest; 93,3b); manuscript W reads: *pesten* (best), which in this case seems preferable, given that the clothing is later described as silk and gold (97,1), not armor.

33. Most editions take the second half-line to be a question: *wie bin ich so gar verzait?* (95,2b). While this is possible, even a rhetorical question seems stylistically out of place here. I follow Simrock's lead in reading the half-line as Otnit's comment on his own lack of determination. Simrock (1859) translates: "I don't have the courage" ("ich habe nicht den Muth"). In fact, the entire speech is more internal monologue, since the "child" is apparently still asleep.

34. Manuscript A reads: *in dauchte hart schöne das kind und auch sein dach* (97,3). Thomas translates: "both the child and the roof over it seemed charming" (7), but *dach* here likely refers to his clothing, a kind of covering, or "roof," for the body.

Chapter 2: How Otnit Found His Father Alberich When He Gave Him His Armor [70–212]

boy punched the grown man with his fist. His strength made it impossible for him to carry him.

[102] Then the Lombard said, "Whoever spares his enemy and angers his friend has not taken good care of himself. He may well suffer great harm from both. Ignoble enemies and slight wounds are nothing to be ashamed of. [103] Why are you being so obstinate?" said King Otnit. "Where do you get such strength in that body of yours? You want to get away from me, and there's not much I can do about it."

The big man crossed himself often as he wrestled with the little one. [104] The big man was angry; the little one was delighted. The one laughed out loud; the other was not amused. Eventually the grown man gained the upper hand. The little one was betrayed by his own arrogance and cleverness. [105] Because of his great contempt he forfeited the prize, and if he hadn't laughed he wouldn't have been overpowered. The grown man took the little one and threw him to the ground. It was his own fault that this is what [Otnit] wanted to do.[35] [106] That massive man had the strength of twelve men, but he could hardly hold on to the little one so that he didn't get away. Just as the little one had been bested by the bigger one, [Otnit] reached for his sword and wanted to give him a blow [107] out of anger that would have taken his life.

"Stop!" said the little one. "You should sooner strike a woman. If you want to punish me and then kill me,[36] you will gain little honor. You should make me your prisoner instead."

[108] Then the Lombard said, "Truly, I will not. I would be forever disgraced if people see you as a prisoner. I couldn't dare tell others about what happened to you; no one would believe me if I killed you here. [109] If I take you with me as a prisoner, people will make fun of me because I'm a grown man. Everyone would

---

35. This is a difficult line. Manuscript A reads: *das kam von <u>seinem</u> schulden, daz es sein wille was* (105,4); manuscript W reads: *daz chom von <u>seinen</u> schulden, daz iz sein wille waz*. This has been emended by the Reclam edition to: . . . *von <u>den</u> schulden* . . . , a change not supported by either manuscript. The Reclam edition then translates: "the reason for this was that he [Otnit] simply wanted it" ("das hatte seinen Grund darin, dass er es einfach wollte"). Kofler retains the original line but is unsure as to the referents for the possessive pronouns *seinem* and *sein*, Otnit or Alberich. In his note he chooses the more likely option: that Otnit has imposed his will on the dwarf ("Am naheliegenderen ist, dass Ortnit dem Zwerg seinen Willen aufzwingt"). Pannier (1877) translates: "It was his [Alberich's] own fault because he laughed" ("Er hatt' mit seinem Lachen sich selbst verschuldet das"). Simrock is completely different: "The winner [Otnit] took the prize because he forgot to gloat" ("Dem ward des Sieges Ehre, weil er zu spotten vergaß"). Thomas translates very loosely: "It was his own fault that he was seized and thrown down on the grass" (8). My translation is informed by both of these ideas and takes the possessive pronoun in each half-line to refer to the most logical candidate in this interaction.

36. Manuscript A reads: *wilt du mich sere schelten und darzuo ze tode schlahen | des has du lützel ere* (107,3–4a); manuscript W reads: *wil du mich ser schelten und dar zu ze tod erslachen | dez hastu luezel ere*. Thomas translates: "you won't gain any honor by killing me after having insulted me" (8).

say, 'This is a discredit to Otnit, that he would take such a small child prisoner to gain fame.' [110] If my sword should strike you, you will die. No man has ever brought me into such difficulty; you would dishonor me if I let you live."

"Truly," said the little one, "you must have mercy on me." [111] The diminutive creature fell down at his feet. He said, "Let me live, King Otnit—you are all powerful! As a sign of my affection, I will give you such exquisite armor that no one in the world has any so strong. [112] Fifty thousand marks in gold is this armor's worth. Along with the mail coat I will give you a sword that can destroy ringed mail as if it had never been made of steel. There is no helmet so strong that it can't be damaged by its blow. [113] Along with the mail coat there are mail leggings.[37] No ring is lacking in anything; my craftsmanship is evident in every piece.[38] If this ringed chain mail should become yours, be respectful. There is nothing imperfect about it; it is made of pure gold. [114] I don't think there is any as good in all the world. I took it from a land called Arabia. The gold is without imperfection, and it shines like a mirror. I took it from a mountain called Caucasus.

[115] "Along with the gleaming mail rings I will give you a shield so solid and so strong, should you accept it from me, that never did a missile or sword penetrate or slash, nor did the heat of fire ever damage it. [116] I will tell you the name of the sword: it is the color of light. However you may use it in battle, it will never splinter. The blade is called Rose, if I am to use its proper name. Wherever swords are drawn, you need never be ashamed of this one. [117] Along with all this hardware, I will give you a head covering the likes of which has never been seen on any knight's head. The man who wears this helmet is always safe. You can also see his head from more than half a mile away."

[118] Then the Lombard said, "Since you're handing out such great gifts, I will release you, but only if you tell me who you are."

The little one replied, "I am a wild dwarf. In Lombardy many a valley and mountain serve me."

[119] "So tell me your name," said the mighty king.

"If you want to call me by my name, just say Alberich."

The Lombard said, "You won't be set free, and your armor and your sword won't help you either, [120] nor will anything else that you've promised to give me. None of it will help you or keep you alive. I will cut off your head here under the linden tree unless you help me win a beautiful queen."[39]

---

37. Chain mail protection for the legs (*baingewant*) at this time probably referred to the more complete protection provided by mail hose or leggings (French *chausses*), as opposed to greaves, which protected the shin but were usually made of leather or later plate armor.

38. Manuscript A reads: das ist ninder ringk, so <u>scheinet</u> insondere mein handt (113,2); manuscript W reads: Da ist ninder rinch so <u>chlainer</u> in smit mein selbes hant, "There is no ring so small that I didn't make it with my own hands."

39. Manuscript W reads: *magedein* (maiden; 120,4b).

Chapter 2: How Otnit Found His Father Alberich When He Gave Him His Armor [70–212]

[121] "Who is she, the one you want?" replied Alberich. "Is she a queen rich in beauty and wealth? If she may with honor be called your wife, then I will win this lady for you, or my life is yours."

[122] "Her father has many lands across the sea. I wouldn't dare try to win her without an army to claim her. Her father is so sinful that he will give her to no one. No man has dared to court her who didn't pay with his life. [123] He's a powerful king and rules over all Muslim peoples;[40] he has great authority over all kings across the sea. He lives at Mount Tabor—that's where he's at home."

"I know him very well," replied Alberich. [124] "If you set me free now," said the bold man, "then I will deliver what I've promised you."

The Lombard said, "I don't think that's going to happen. You'll never be set free unless you first provide guarantees."

[125] "You're making me pay a high price," said the bold fellow. "You demand guarantees of me, but I don't have any. You should be mindful of God," said the little man. "Let me go; I will do what I've promised you."

[126] Then the Lombard said, "No one is being let go until I see the gleaming mail rings with my own eyes."

"Truly," said the little man, "they will never be yours as long as I remain a prisoner in your custody."

[127] "So then recommend what is best for us both," said the mighty king.

"I'll explain it to you," replied Alberich. "Let me go on my honor, and I will act only in your best interest."

"No," said the Lombard. "First I need to see the mail rings."

[128] "Let me go on my honor; you'll be happy you did. You can readily let me go; I'm a king just as you are. My friends tell me that I'm faithful. However many lands you own, I have three times as many.[41] [129] You have great authority above the ground, but I have all that I want below it. I give silver and gold to whomever I like. A man will become wealthy should I favor him with my loyalty. [130] Now let me go," said the little one. "I'll swear an oath and pledge you my fealty and promise that I will [never] lie to you," replied Alberich.

"I'll take a chance on your loyalty," said the mighty king then.

[131] He pushed the little one away from him. He stood there politely, using courteous language, as prisoners do.

---

40. The original is *haidenschaft*, or literally "heathendom."
41. The entire line in manuscript A reads: *wie vil du hast der lande -: dann dein drei!* (128,4). The second half of this line is difficult. The Reclam edition stays with this reading, and its note on the line interprets the three words as an anacoluthon, with each syllable stressed in mimicry of oral speech. It then translates literally: "like three of your kind!" ("wie drei von deiner Sorte"). Manuscript W provides more context and reads: *swie vil du hast der lande, ich han mer danne dein drei*, "As many lands as you have, I have more than your three." Thomas translates: "Moreover, your many lands are less than a third of mine" (9).

The Lombard said, "Since you stand there as my prisoner,[42] now go and quickly bring me what you promised."

[132] The little one said politely, "Grant me one request, for the sake of the dignity of all kings, before I step away from you."

Then King Otnit said, "What is this request?"

The little one said politely, "It is not to your disadvantage."

[133] "So let me hear already what it is that you want."

The little one said politely, "I made up my mind earlier that I would like to be forever in your service and become your vassal. For the sake of the dignity of all kings, give me your ring."

[134] Then the Lombard said, "Truly, I dare not. I would gladly give it to you, but it is strictly forbidden. Anything else that you might ask for, I would grant you. I would gladly give it, but I cannot be without it."

[135] Then the little one replied, "What good is it to you? What good is a kingdom if you don't have a generous heart? Why are you so concerned about this little ring? If I had asked you for your horse, I would have never received it."

[136] "I would rather give you a castle or a land than now give you this gold ring on my hand. Why are you so obsessed with having this gold ring? I would gladly give it to you, but I made a promise. [137] My mother gave it to me; I swore her an oath. I'm afraid that if I gave it to you I would lose her favor."

"My goodness," said the little one, "what good is your size and your manly strength if you're afraid of a woman? [138] Why are you so afraid of a woman's lashing? I believe that you might never recover from such wounds."

"She hasn't beat me with a switch in a long time, but my mother is so dear to me that I would gladly forgive her. [139] My heart aches when I see her saddened. You can make fun or get angry, but I really won't give it to you."

"Truly," said the little one, "you really shouldn't give it to me. I'm afraid that if you gave it to me, your mother would beat you. [140] I don't believe a little ring was ever more cherished by a king. Can you at least let me have a look at it, on my honor?"

He said, "Since you're so eager to have this gold ring, promise on your honor that you'll give it back to me."

[141] He wouldn't let him have it, so Alberich had to swear an oath. He grabbed his hand; [Otnit] didn't dare resist. As soon as he snatched the ring from his hand the little one disappeared, and he couldn't see him anymore.

[142] Then the Lombard said, "Tell me, where did you go?"

The little one said angrily,[43] "It's none of your concern where I am. You gave up a little ring from your hand. You can't change that now, no matter how long

---

42. Manuscript A reads: *seit du gefangen stast* (131,3b); manuscript W reads: *ungevangen* (unfettered, unrestrained).
43. Manuscript W reads: *mit zuchten* (courteously; 142,2a).

Chapter 2: How Otnit Found His Father Alberich When He Gave Him His Armor [70–212]

you live. [143] When you first caught me, and [you laid eyes on me],[44] that good fortune happened on account of this very stone. I would have to serve you always if you still had the ring. Now be on your way to wherever; you won't get the ring back."

[144] Then King Otnit of the Lombards said, "Let me have the benefit of your being a king, since I relied on your fidelity. All the wealth that I still have, that could all be yours."

[145] The little one said politely, "You're not thinking straight. What your father and your mother advise you, that is good. Where have you ever seen someone give up a game already won? The stone is so valuable to me that I won't give it back to you."

[146] Then the Lombard said, "So then I've lost it. If you were to bring me the armor and the sword that you promised, then some of what you said would still be true."

"I couldn't care less," said the little one, "about anything you say."

[147] Then the Lombard said, "I've been treated badly. If I could chase you down, or if I could see you, you'd have to pay for what you promised me, or I'd grab one of your legs and slam you against this rock."

[148] "What do you want with all these rings?"[45] replied Alberich. "Or why is a fool granted such great royal power? I'll give the rings to someone who needs them more than you."

[Alberich] then threw some huge rocks at him. [149] Then he angrily pulled his horse's saddle girth tighter. He wanted to ride off; he mounted his horse in anger. The mighty king rode off in a grim mood.

"Sir, good man, stay!" replied Alberich. [150] "For whom do you want to leave your dear little ring? Or who will gain your mother's favor for you again? You shouldn't want to lose it; the stone is so precious. Oh, how sorry I am for the blows your mother will give you."

[151] Then the Lombard said, "I'll take it as it comes. I've been so dear to my mother that I'll gladly suffer whatever she does to me. We're so close that she surely won't beat me to death."

[152] "I want to give you something more to hope for," replied Alberich. "Give me your word of honor, mighty and powerful king, that you won't get angry no matter what I say about your mother or whatever else I may say, and I'll give you back the ring."

---

44. Manuscript A reads: . . . *und dich mein auge sach*, ". . . and I laid eyes on you" (143,1b), which is most likely the inferior variant, since Otnit is able to see Alberich because of the stone, not the other way around; manuscript W correctly reads: *und mich dein aug an sach*.

45. The use of the word "ring" or "rings" is multivalent throughout the text. Rings of various types play a key role in realizing Otnit's destiny. Here the rings refer to the chain mail armor Otnit has been promised.

175

[153] Then the Lombard said, "I'd sooner let you keep your gold, and if you go on speaking with such malice, you'll never gain my favor. You might slander that virtuous woman so terribly that, if I knew where to find you, I'd take your life."

[154] The little one said politely, "Good for you, blessed child! You have the kind of loyalty that looks out for other people."

The Lombard said, "All right, so I'll hold my tongue regardless of what you say. Are you going to say something anytime soon?"[46]

[155] "I will only speak the truth about your mother. You may be angry for [awhile], but you won't be mad forever. I'll sugarcoat it for you so that you'll want to pay attention. Promise me on your honor that you won't hurt me because of it."

[156] Then the Lombard said, "I give you my word of honor that I won't be angry with you for as long as we both shall live. A man can sometimes say too much of the truth,[47] but you can talk all you want, and I'll listen to the end."[48]

[157] The little one said politely, "It is so pledged. I'm counting on your sincerity. Look, here is your ring."

The Lombard said, "I'm grateful to you. I don't care what you blabber on about, as long as I have the gold ring back."

[158] The Lombard was crafty and also the stronger of the two. He had to give him back his gold ring, then [Otnit] threw him to the ground and sat down beside him. "Now talk, you wicked soul. Before I let you go this time, you're going to tell me what you know."

[159] The Lombard stuck the gold ring back on his finger. Now he could finally see the little one. He wouldn't let go of him. The wild schemer said, "Your Majesty, you're filled with rage. Now be mindful of your promise. What is it that you pledged?"

[160] Then the Lombard said, "My friend, I won't hurt you, and my heart is happy as long as my eyes can see you. Your life is worth even more to me than this little ring. Tell me everything you know about my dear mother."

[161] "I promise you that your mother is free from all fault. I believe there is no other woman in Lombardy as virtuous. But she did do certain things in days gone by. Just think about who your father might be. She was with two men."

---

46. Manuscript A reads: *wann wilt du auch heute sagen?* (154,4b). Amelung emends to *wenne wilt die wârheit sagen*, "when will you tell the truth," even though manuscript W reads: *wenne wildu eu heut sagen*. Thomas follows Amelung's emendation in his translation: "but will it be the truth?" (11).

47. Thomas translates: "A man is permitted to say much if it is true" (11). This follows manuscript W's and Amelung's *also vil* rather than manuscript A's *allze vil* (156,3b).

48. Manuscript A reads: *daz ichs immer hören wil* (156,4b); manuscript W reads: *daz ich sein nicht horen wil*, "until I don't want to listen to you anymore." Amelung and Thomas follow the latter reading.

Chapter 2: How Otnit Found His Father Alberich When He Gave Him His Armor [70–212]

[162] Then he grabbed his knife; he would have grabbed his sword. The little one would have been glad to be let go. [Otnit's] face turned white and then bright red. He said, "Say no more and spare me this anguish."[49]

[163] "I'm not at all afraid," said little Alberich. "Be mindful of your pledge, mighty and worthy king. Your heart and your feelings go back and forth, but please be so faithful as to do me no harm. [164] I seem very small to you, and you loom over me, and you tower over all kings more like a giant's kin. The limbs on the two of us are not at all alike, but however big you may think you are, you're still my child."

[165] Then the Lombard said, "Now you've told a lie. If I wasn't breaking a promise, and if it wasn't rude—my heart is near bursting—and still I don't dare harm you."[50] He said angrily, "But am I really your son?"

[166] The little one said politely, "You are my little child."

"My mother will have to burn at the stake for this, that someone other than my father lay with her first. And if I find her in the castle at Garda, she won't live to see another day."

[167] The little one said angrily, "You've taken leave of your senses. Your rank is elevated even higher with me as your father. You don't even recognize your own luck and good fortune. You have your towns and lands by my design. [168] I lay with your mother for the first time during the green month of May, around midday. She cried hot tears, the first time I forced myself on her. You shouldn't blame her; it happened without her consent. [169] I heard your father and your mother praying devoutly, according to ancient custom in their reverent[51] manner, that God might grant them a little child. Your father, and your mother, too, prayed fervently for this. [170] As loving as they were to each other, I can honestly say that the lady was not going to get a child from that man. She was so decent, though, that she didn't seek out anyone else. They both lamented fervently that their land would be left without an heir. [171] So I thought to myself, 'And what if her husband dies? Then this exceptional lady will immediately be banished.

---

49. Manuscript A reads: *er sprach, nu sag nicht mere und lasse mich on not* (162,4); manuscript W offers a close variation of the same. Thomas translates: "'Have no fear,' said the Lombard, 'you may go. But say no more'" (12). It is unclear from where in the text the first part is taken.

50. These two lines, 165,2–3 and especially 165,3b, have challenged translators. Manuscript A reads: *bräch ich nicht mein trewe und wär nicht ungezogen | mein herze ist ungefüege <u>und getar dir doch nicht getuon</u>*; manuscript W reads essentially the same. Thomas translates very loosely: "I am furious but can't do anything without being ill-bred and breaking my word" (12). The Reclam edition translates: "If I weren't breaking my loyalty and weren't rude | my heart is out of control—and yet I don't dare do anything to you" ("Wenn ich nicht meine Treue bräche und wäre nicht ungezogen | mein Herz ist aus den Fugen—und wage dir doch nichts zu tun!"). Pannier translates 165,2 much like the Reclam edition, but then interprets 165,3b very differently: "you wouldn't get away" ("du kämest nicht davon"). Finally, Simrock (1859) translates 165,3b ironically: "I would gladly give you your reward" ("gern zahlt' ich dir den Lohn").

51. Manuscript A reads: *wirdiclichen* (worthily; 169,2b); manuscript W reads: *traurichleichen* (sad).

The land would have to live with misfortune forevermore.' Then I made her my wife, may God forgive me.

[172] "One day she was sitting on her splendid bed. She was weeping for a dear child; her eyes were wet with tears. No one was allowed to be with her in her chambers, since she was crying. She wouldn't let anyone enter. [173] Then I stood in front of the bed and listened to what she said. I was able to overpower her because she couldn't see me. No matter how much she resisted, she still became my wife. Now you should love me,[52] small as I am, as much as two kings.[53] [174] I believe I could conquer more than you and all your army, even though no king dares defend himself against you."

The Lombard said, "I have to accept this. Whatever I might do, it would have happened anyway."

[175] "Now sit down a spell and keep your little ring. I will deliver on the promise I made to you. I don't want to lie to you, on my honor. I will bring you the chain mail rings on top of your shield."

[176] Just as quickly as the little one disappeared into the mountain, he came back from the forge carrying that marvelous handiwork, a new shield completely covered by mail rings of gleaming gold, just as a man should properly wear them on his body. [177] Clearer than a fountain and brighter than a mirror, he put the mail rings down on the ground, and along with the armor a solid, shining helmet. It was made to be so strong that no sword could cut through it.

[178] Then the Lombard was happy about his rings of mail. He could hardly look at them, their reflection was so bright. "I think this must be a miracle," said the bold man. "I can barely see the mail rings on account of their brilliance."

[179] When he looked at the mail rings, there was no steel present. They were unusually large, golden, and as big as a finger. After examining them, he put them on for the first time. The rings lay down evenly; the man was glad to see it. [180] They were neither too long nor too short, too broad nor too narrow. He cheerfully jumped up and down in them. The helmet was fixed with braces all around. As bright as light, a carbuncle glittered on every side. [181] In the middle of all this there was a diamond. The strap was inlaid with gold thread; he fastened the helmet.

"May God reward you for your gift," said the mighty king.

"Are the mail rings to your liking?" replied Alberich.

[182] "In all my life I've never been presented with such attire."

---

52. Manuscript W reads: *nim mich* (take me; 73,4a), as opposed to manuscript A: *minn mich* (love me).
53. There is considerable disagreement on this line. Manuscripts AW read: *für zwaier künige leib* (173,4b). The Reclam edition translates: "as the embodiment of two kings" ("für die Verkörperung zweier Könige"). Thomas translates: "as the equal of two kings" (13). Kofler paraphrases in his gloss on the line: "Alberich is more useful to Ortnit (on account of his strength) than two kings" ("Alberich nützt Ortnit (aufgrund seiner Stärke) mehr als zwei Könige").

Chapter 2: How Otnit Found His Father Alberich When He Gave Him His Armor [70–212]

"Long before I even saw you, I thought this would be yours. Now I have properly adorned your person, Lombard. If you want me to serve you, don't anger the woman. [183] I'll make this pledge to you. If you anger your mother, then we will part ways forevermore."

The Lombard said, "I will gladly comply with your demand. Before I anger her, I would sooner anger God. [184] May God reward my mother, from whom I have this gift. I will rely on your mercy in all things. My heart will never oppose your will. My mother will profit from you her life long."

[185] The Lombard, now contented, reached for his horse. The little one wanted to hold his stirrup,[54] but the Lombard said, "I'll stay here the entire day if that's the only way I can forestall your vassalage."

[186] With great resolve he tightened the saddle girth. The wild man stepped aside until he had mounted. The Lombard said, "Hand me the shield."

"I can see," said the little one, "that you intend to leave me."

[187] [Before] he took up the shield, he examined his sword. He said, "I'm well equipped to face the dangers of battle. If anyone had this Rose and fled, he would forever bring shame on himself."

He found his name[55] inscribed on both sides of the blade. [188] The sheath was made of gold; the belt was made of silk with gold thread woven throughout. What was above the hilt, the sword's pommel, was a carbuncle the size of three fists.[56] [189] He secured the shield around his neck and then wanted to leave him.

"May God bless you," replied the little man. "You shouldn't avoid me from now on, whenever you need me. You can never fail to find me as long as you have the ring."

[190] The Lombard turned away and rode into the forest. He was lighthearted and filled with joy.[57] He said, "Now I am finally well prepared for battle. Where can I go to test my armor and my sword?"

[191] He rode back along the path next to the rock wall. He was discouraged because he couldn't find anyone to fight. He said, "Am I not meant to see this sword work miracles? No one will do battle with me. Surely it will happen in front of the castle."

---

54. The feudal act of holding a stirrup was a symbolic gesture of vassalage, originally performed by a *strator* (Latin), or groom, for a nobleman. By declining this act, Otnit recognizes Alberich as his equal and not his liegeman.
55. Kofler claims that this would be the name of the sword, *Rose*, not the name of the new owner. According to his gloss (52), owners' names were not engraved on the blade of a sword until the sixteenth century. But in this text *Rose* is clearly feminine, and *seinen namen* can only refer to Otnit.
56. Manuscript W reads: *zwaier feuste* (two fists; 188,4b). Amelung emends even further, down to one fist (*einer*).
57. Manuscript W reads: *sorig* (worry, care), but this has been emended by all editors to manuscript A's reading: *freude* (joy; 190,2b), which is a more logical complement to his "mood" or "heart" (*muot*) being "light" (*ringe*), i.e., "carefree."

[192] He continued to ride on seeking battle until the third day. He denied himself any rest out of sheer arrogance. Then the Lombard said, "I'm a man who's cursed, that I have no one to fight as I would like."

[193] The people who relied on him had abandoned hope, and those who wished him only ill had ceased to mourn him. Garda and the entire land were filled with dreadful anguish; they all alike thought the king was dead. [194] His mother was weighed down by a dreadful burden. No one could console the noble queen, who suffered so terribly for her child, that virtuous woman. If he hadn't come back soon, she would have died. [195] On the fourth morning the Lombard rode up to the castle of Garda, onto the broad, green field. As the morning star broke through dark clouds, his helmet and his armor shone just like that star. [196] The stranger was completely unknown to the watchman. His armor shone as if it were the break of day. He rode out in front of the castle of Garda onto the green field. He held his horse's reins closely; it was now growing light.

[197] He vigorously bounded up to the castle moat, as if he had wanted to storm the walls. The guard said, "Even if you blaze brighter and charge more fiercely, no one will let you in."

[198] Then the Lombard said, "Open the gate for me now and tell all the leading citizens that their lord is here."

The guard shouted loudly, "Why is everyone still asleep? It's been four days since my lord left this place. [199] A bold man stands here beneath the castle walls; he's ablaze from his head down to his feet. He says that he's my lord, as I heard him declare. He's likely escaped from the devil and come straight out of hell."

[200] Amid her cares, the noble queen awoke. She peered out the window, where she saw the bright light. She said, "[Look], that man's burning like a candle! My son's chain mail rings aren't nearly as precious."

[201] Those who were in the castle, both men and women, went out on the ramparts to see this wonder. The burgrave[58] said, "My lord, who might you be? You must first give us your name before we let you in."

[202] His voice was transformed, his speech loud; a confounding noise came out from under his helmet.

The burgrave said, "So tell us, sir, who you are."

The Lombard said, "It is I, your lord, Otnit."

[203] "Who gave you this armor and this brilliant helmet, along with that new shield? My lord did not have these things."

The bold man said, "I will tell you the truth. I'm a fierce heathen, and I've killed your lord. [204] There are seventy-two liegemen here in this castle. They should avenge the injury that I've inflicted on their lord. The Lombard named and numbered each one of them for me. I will wait at the gate, should any of you want to avenge him."

---

58. This is Engelwan.

Chapter 3: How Otnit Waged War for a Lady Overseas [213–87]

[205]⁵⁹ Then the burgrave said, "Truly, it must be done."

At first the poor queen beat her own breasts. Their lord's death was painful to those who were most loyal. He donned his mail rings, which were white as snow. [206] Enraged, he threw the gate wide open. On the drawbridge they drew two impressive, sharp blades. Bold though the burgrave was, still the stranger infuriated him. He⁶⁰ shredded the rings off him as if they were rotten matting. [207] He defended himself as best he could against his liege lord, but his sword was worthless, and he couldn't make a dent in the rings. He struck him down at his feet; he could have easily killed him.

The Lombard said, "Somebody take him away from here."

[208] If he hadn't shown him mercy, he would have taken his life. In the meantime, his brother⁶¹ came along, fully armed.

The Lombard said, "That's enough fighting. May God forgive me that I struck him down today. [209] Now I can be certain that you are all loyal to me. Please forgive me this unseemly behavior. It is I, Otnit."

Now they finally recognized him and let him enter.

The Lombard said, "Where is my mother?"

[210] Then straightaway the lord was well received, and the people showed him where he could find his mother. The lady recognized him immediately, now that his head was uncovered. The lady, out of love, was at first overcome with tears.

[211] Then he went up to the wounded man, who lay beaten there before him. "Ah, woe, that I gave you even one blow today. May God have mercy. You must forgive me; I will recompense you for as long as I live."

[212] "Tell me," said his mother, "who gave you this armor?"

"I rode out as you told me, along the rock wall. There I profited greatly from your help, for which I am grateful to you."

So ends another chapter of Otnit's story.

*Chapter 3: How Otnit Waged War for a Lady Overseas [213–87]*⁶²

[213] His mother asked him repeatedly, "Where did you get this armor?" He told her everything that happened from the beginning. "I can't deny it,"⁶³ said

---

59. This entire strophe is missing in manuscript W.
60. This is Otnit.
61. This is Helmnot of Tuscany.
62. Manuscript W marks the beginning of this chapter at 212,4 with a large initial "O" (*Ortneides*; three lines high). There is no chapter title or other special marking.
63. Manuscript A reads: *ich mag dirs nicht gelaugen* (I can't lie to you; 213,3a); manuscript W reads: *ich mach dirz nicht gelauben* (I don't believe you).

the noble woman. "I place my life in your merciful hands." [214] She hugged and kissed him until they were on good terms again.

The time for his military campaign approached, but he stayed in Garda until the end of the year. Those who would go to war with him all began arriving. [215] He entrusted his mother and the land to the burgrave;[64] the nobles swore him their allegiance. He quickly prepared himself along with his comrades-in-arms and took leave of his mother. He traveled with his heroes[65] to the port of Messina. [216] There the Muslim received him affectionately; he had prepared the ships for him. [Otnit] quickly departed from there. The ships had been loaded with supplies for three years. They weighed anchor and sailed away from the shore.

[217] Then the Lombard and his army traveled with joy. He arrived across the sea on the twelfth morning.[66] A mariner climbed to the top of the crow's nest. He saw the castle at Suders and the Muslim's capital city.

[218] He called out in a loud voice, "What's going to happen to us now? I've seen the vast land of Syria and the town of Suders. We're very close to it, and it would be good to sail past so that we can be unafraid."

[219] Then the captain who commanded the fleet said, "I don't think I have any good advice to give you. The wind is taking us too close. We'll never get away like this." He said to his crew, "Furl the sails!"

[220] Then the Lombard said, "Are you sure that we've taken the right route to the land of Syria? And if you don't tell me the truth, it will cost you your life. I'll give you twelve golden armbands as a messenger's gift."

[221] "You've sailed directly to Suders and its port. I advise you against going ashore here. I think we've sailed too close to the town. There are many war galleys in the fortress of Suders."

[222] Then the Lombard said, "I'm not familiar with this place. As much as I'd like to move on, I don't know where else to go. The one I chose as master of this expedition, who was supposed to advise me, I've sadly lost him. [223] I should turn back. What good has this journey done me? I've sadly proven myself unworthy for this campaign."

He was completely incapacitated by his feelings of despair.

"You need to get ahold of yourself," said Ilias of Russia.

[224] Then the Lombard said, "I'm sorry, but I can't. Now may God have mercy that I lived to see this day. The one who should help me in my need is too far away. Sadly I forgot all about him."

---

64. Manuscript W reads: *margraven* (margrave).
65. Manuscript W reads: *holden* (loyal [men]).
66. This is an exceptionally swift passage. The 1,200 or so miles distance could have been completed in twelve days under the very best conditions, but the journey would most commonly have taken some twenty to thirty days, or even more in bad weather. See Norbert Ohler, *The Medieval Traveller*, trans. Caroline Hillier (Woodbridge, UK: Boydell, 1989), 98–101.

Chapter 3: How Otnit Waged War for a Lady Overseas [213–87]

[225] The heathen[67] said angrily, "But you have all these men who have come to your aid. They're all here with you. You have at your disposal, for combat and for battle, a force of thirty thousand men, all well equipped in bright ringed chain mail."

[226] "I've lost the very best," said the mighty king.

Miserable, he looked around. Next to him stood Alberich. The Lombard was so strong and happy again that he forgot his cares. He shouted loudly, [227] "Father and lord, who brought you here? Right now I just want to laugh. I would have never guessed."

He picked him up in his arms and kissed him a thousand times over.

The little one said courteously, "Hero, you are unaware [228] of the great loyalty I hold for you. You readily abandon me, but I will not abandon you. You forget about me all the time, but I never forgot about you. Welcome me however you like, I'm here with you again."

[229] Then the Lombard said, "For God's sake, enlighten me. Tell me, on your honor, where have you been hiding?"

"Up there on the main mast, I was sitting in the crow's nest. I would have showed myself, except that I wanted to test you."

[230] Then the Lombard said, "You are welcome. That I found you here will always be to my benefit. I felt completely lost the whole time I was without you."

"Who were you muttering to?" said Ilias of Russia. [231] "You could easily lose your life over this. Curse this woman! I regret before God that I ever mentioned her name to you."

The Lombard said, "I have some good news for you."

[232] "Tell him on his honor," replied Alberich, "that I want to help you win the mighty queen. I know him to be so faithful that he won't bear you a grudge. If both of you know about me, that will be all the better for you."

[233] Then the Lombard said, "Uncle, come here. You'll be happy to hear I have good news. You thought I was muttering to myself before. If you want to hear the story, come here to the two of us."

[234] "Tell me," said the Russian, "who's with you there? You're making my hair turn grey with your muttering."

The Lombard had just asked the Russian to step over toward the little one and the big one. [235] Then the captain of the ship called out, "Save yourselves! I think the mighty king is in for trouble. If you want to fight the Muslims on the

---

67. The reference is clearly to Ilias of Russia, but his identification as non-Christian is odd. Both manuscripts AW read: *haiden*, but other manuscripts in the D version do not. Kofler emends to *Reuzze*, Amelung to *Riuze*, Thomas translates "Russian" (16). There are aspects of Ilias's actions that are "unchristian," such as the massacre of women and Christian troops at the Battle of Suders and his refusal to baptize those who are willing to convert (330–37), but he later helps Alberich baptize Otnit's bride (481,4).

water, prepare yourselves for battle. An army is quickly bearing down on you. [236] They're coming with Greek fire;[68] the odds are not in your favor. If they torch our ships, we'll drown beneath the waves."

The two mighty kings stood there anxiously.

"I can give you good counsel," replied Alberich.

[237] "A good friend's advice was always good in times of trouble."

Ilias of Russia began to make the sign of the cross.[69] "Who is it who gives us this counsel and advice? Don't you want to cross yourself, Otnit, my nephew? [238] He's one or the other, either the devil or God. Tell me, are you a demon? If not, I'll follow your command."

The Lombard said, "Actually, he's a dwarf. He's well acquainted in the world with many a valley and mountain."

[239] "Truly," said the Russian, "I hear what you're saying, but if I'm going to believe it, I'll have to see it first."

The Lombard said, "Can't you hear him?"

"I don't know what it means until I see it with my own eyes. [240] It may be some sort of spell cast by magic."

"If you want to see him, take this ring and put it on your finger, then you can see him."

The Russian laughed out loud once he saw the little one.

[241] He said with tender words, "Where do you come from, little child? Oh dear, that your family is so far away."

"As small as I may seem to you, this you can believe: I have lived to see more than five hundred years. [242] You should both do as I say; that will benefit you both. Whoever acts according to a friend's advice and purpose will be held blameless should he not succeed. One friend can teach the other what he doesn't know. [243] A king can tell a lie if his life is in danger. The right speech has often enough prevented death.[70] Whoever asks you to say where these ships come from, say that you want an escort and that you're a merchant."

---

68. The term *wilde feur* describes the infamous Greek fire used to such terrible effect in naval battles, as it could not be extinguished by water. Made of various ingredients including naphtha and quicklime and in use in the Byzantine Empire from around the start of the eighth century CE, Crusader forces in the centuries that followed associated this weapon with militaries from the East, especially Islamic naval forces.

69. This could also simply refer to the act of "blessing oneself," something not necessarily only a Christian act. In 269,2 Machorel's action is described using the same term, and he "blesses himself" (*segnete sich*), which clearly refers to a non-Christian act of blessing or protecting oneself from evil.

70. Manuscript A reads: *gefüege rede gehöret vil dicke für den todt* (243,2). Interpretations of this line vary considerably. The Reclam edition translates: "Proper speech often enough leads to death" ("Eine Rede nach Fug und Recht führt oft genug in den Tod!"). Pannier translates differently: "Proper speech has protected many from death" ("Gefüge Rede schützte schon manchen vor dem Tod," 42). Simrock translates in much the same vein. Thomas translates: "suitable words are much to be preferred to death" (17). *Gehœret* with the preposition *für* can mean "to help against" or

Chapter 3: How Otnit Waged War for a Lady Overseas [213–87]

[244] Then the Lombard said, "That advice is useless. I would gladly speak with them, but I don't know their language. I've never learned it," said the mighty king.

"Then I'll have to teach you," said Alberich. [245] "If you show yourself to be grateful, I'll give you a stone that can teach you their language. There is no language, if your tongue holds the stone in your mouth, that you won't understand, regardless what someone says to you."

[246] "How can I believe," said King Otnit, "that God has given a stone such great ability that I can understand all peoples with its power? You should be ashamed of yourself for lying all the time."

[247] "Be still," said the little one. "You condemn me too harshly. God can make of this stone, and of the earth, whatever he wants. There is surely nothing he can't do. You should have faith in that," replied Alberich.

[248] He opened his mouth and hid the stone. He said, "I will test its amazing powers."

It seemed to him that he could understand what everyone said. The Lombard went over to the ship's railing.

[249] Then the captain cried out, "What will happen to us? There are at least forty war galleys out on the water! Whatever they have in mind, they're approaching quickly. Whoever can speak to them should tell them what's going on."

[250] The war galleys glided swiftly through the water. Their sails, white as snow, gave out a loud sound that surrounded the ships. Otnit laughed, and the galley captain said, "Tell me who you are!"

[251] Then the Lombard said, "I'm a merchant. I've brought many costly trade goods with me."

He motioned for his people to hide themselves below deck, with their helmets and shields, so that none of them could be seen.

[252] "Who ordered you to come so close to this fortress?" said the captain. "You should steer clear."

"I want to come even closer, with my person and with my goods. It's said that whoever brings trade goods won't be harmed by you. [253] I bring from Carolingian lands the very best cloths that I could find in all the towns of the French and Italian lands. I've loaded and filled my ships with them. Now provide me with an escort and take me to shore. [254] This land will be all the better for it. Help me get to the town wall; I don't want any trouble."

"Whoever brings so many goods will be welcomed," said the galley captains and sailed back toward land.

"to protect," as in Erec 5989, *dâ für (ge)hœret kein list* (no ploy will protect against that). Manuscript W has a completely different text: *nu volget meiner lere und laistet mein gepot*, "Now follow my instructions and obey my command." Kofler follows this reading, Amelung instead adopts the manuscript A reading.

[255] There the town constable was waiting for them. He asked them to make their report and wait there.

They said, "Sir, he has filled his ships with garments and would like an escort, if we will provide one. [256] They say that whoever brings goods to trade should be safe here. This should be granted to them, guaranteed on penalty of death."

The town magistrate said, "I will be sure to prevent them from being harmed. I will escort them myself."

[257] Then he commanded that he be given one of the war galleys. He took at least forty trumpeters with him. He had a flag and a cross tied to the top of the mast to show them that they were guaranteed safe passage.

[258] Then the sailor sitting in the crow's nest cried out loudly, "Be of good cheer below; our fortunes are improving. We are being allowed to bring our ships in peaceably. The master of the town is going to escort us himself."

[259] The magistrate led all the Muslims himself. From the upper deck of the galley the trumpets sounded loudly, and he welcomed the foreigners kindly and escorted them into the harbor.

He said, "Whenever you like, come ashore in your skiffs."

[260] They remained at sea during the day until night.[71] Otnit had gathered all his ships together.

"Now counsel and advise us, dearest Alberich, how we should take the town," said the mighty king. [261][72] "The gate is wide open; I don't think anyone will resist us. When everyone is asleep, we'll move in with our army. We'll make them pay for the fact that they are all Muslims. We will kill them ourselves, their women and their children."

[262] Then the little one said wisely, "Who taught you such deceit? It would be an evil thing for you as a king to deliberately attack your neighbor without first declaring war. It would be disgraceful."

[263] Then the Lombard said, "He'll have to accept it from me. This Muslim is so ill tempered that no one dares declare war on him. I won't send a messenger there hoping for his mercy. If I do him any injury, he'll certainly know about it."

[264] "Truly," said the little one, "that would be to your dishonor. Rather than have you condemned for this, I will be your envoy. This should be done with honor. Why are you so apprehensive? If you are in agreement, I'll declare war on him at once."

---

71. Manuscript A reads: *den tag unz an die nacht* (260,1b); manuscript W reads: *den tach und die nacht*, "through the day and the night," but it makes more sense that Otnit and his army would attack at night, which is confirmed in 261.

72. Otnit continues speaking in this strophe, even though it seems as if he is answering his own question.

Chapter 3: How Otnit Waged War for a Lady Overseas [213–87]

[265] Then the Lombard said, "I would be forever grateful for that. I will gladly thank you for it, if it turns out as you say. Should I wait for you here?" said the mighty king.

"I'll be back tomorrow."

Alberich left him. [266] He demonstrated to him that he was indeed a dwarf. The wild man was acquainted with both valleys and mountains. He knew [what] castles there were in the Muslim country. He arrived at Mount Tabor before the day had dawned. [267] There he sat down on a rock outside the wall and could hardly wait until it had turned day, when he could deliver the message he had been asked to deliver. The Muslim came out onto the ramparts of the wall above him. [268] He went out to get some air on account of the fragrant breeze; he had left his subterranean rooms because it was so hot.

The little one said politely, "Who is that standing above me? If I may be so bold as to ask, then please answer me. [269] Where is the lord of this house?" he said.

"Here I am." The Muslim was afraid, and he blessed himself fervently. "What is speaking there, that I can't see it?" He said, "Are you the devil? What are you doing here?"

[270] "Not I," said the little one. "I'm another kind of messenger. My master and my God sent me here."

"I'm not interested in your god's message. Whatever he wants from me, I couldn't care less. [271] I don't give a damn about your god's demands. I fear only Apollo and my Muhammed. I serve them gladly, these are my gods."

"So tell me," said the little one, "how long do you want to be damned? [272] That you don't believe in [him], that easily leads nowhere, that you don't fear the one who is all powerful,[73] the one who created you as a human being. Muhammed and Apollo, where is their heavenly kingdom?"

[273] "They are wherever they want to be," said the Muslim. "They often bestow joy on me and my fellow believers."

The little one said cleverly, "You have the mind of a child. I'm stronger than your gods all by myself."

[274] Then the Muslim replied, "Now let me know, tell me what you want, why have you been sent here?"

"My master sent me to you for this reason: that you might give your daughter to a mighty king."

[275] He tore at his beard with both hands. "Ah, woe!" said the Muslim, "that I was ever born! No man ever asked for my daughter's hand that I didn't have his head chopped off on the spot."

---

73. Manuscript A reads: *dem man gewaltes gicht* (272,2b); manuscript W reads: *den man gewaltich sicht*, "who is powerfully seen or evident."

[276] Then the little man replied, "Your talk doesn't interest me. Things have often been done that won't be anymore. I'll tell you openly that if you don't give him the maiden, he will come after you with an army. He hereby declares war on you."

[277] The old Muslim wailed loudly and said, "That such a disgrace should befall me in my lifetime! No man has ever dared declare war while I was alive. Now that I hear it said, I have to cry out to the gods. [278] Believe me, if I could get my hands on you, and even if you reigned in heaven, I would slam you against a wall."

He threw a large rock down into the moat. He wanted to kill the little one by stoning him to death.

[279] The little one said angrily, "What good is your defiance? Give him your daughter, or he'll attack you with his army. Before you know it, you'll see it here before you. He'll take her by force and string you up in front of the gate."

[280] The Muslim screamed so loudly that mountain and valley and the entire castle shook with the sound. Those asleep in the castle were awakened by it. They arose to see what great wonder had just occurred.

[281] "I think you've taken leave of your senses," said the queen.

"Not I," said the Muslim. "Someone is asking for my daughter's hand. A voice has angrily declared war on me. I'm unable to avenge myself, may that be decried before Muhammed." [282] He said to his fellow Muslims, "Encircle the castle moat so that he doesn't get away. You should surround him."

The Muslims all jumped down to the field below. They hit and struck out where Alberich was standing. [283] The little dwarf was hiding behind the Muslim's back. "King, you should command that they stop their shooting. I'm confident that I can hide from arrows and spears. If they keep aiming for me, they're likely to hit you."

[284] The Muslim said angrily, "Cease fire, stop shooting. How do you think you'll hit someone you can't see? Whatever he rants about all day, I'll just have to endure it."

The little one replied, "What shall I tell the king?"

[285] "That God will condemn the two of you for my sake. I don't believe you: give it to me in writing."

Alberich said, "Since I can't give you a letter on the spot, you'll have to accept this instead," and he slapped him on the cheek.

[286] All the people heard it, that's how loudly his slap rang out. The Muslim went into a rage, he had to be tied up because of his raving. The daughter and her mother fell to their knees in prayer. They all lamented their disgrace to Apollo and Muhammed. [287] At that point Alberich had finished delivering his message. He left the wall and returned to the mighty king. They tried to hit him with their spears, but by then he was already gone.

So ends another chapter of Otnit's story.

Chapter 4: How Suders Was Razed [288–346][74]

[288] Then he arrived back at the ships before nightfall. The Lombard said, "What news have you brought me?"

"I bring you bad news concerning the queen.[75] If you don't win her in battle, she will never be yours. [289] I made her father so angry that he had to be tied up."

The Lombard said, "So give us your counsel."

"If we seize the fortress, we will control the entire land.[76] I trust that I'll be able to lead you to the beach in skiffs. [290] The night is dark now; the moon[77] is hidden from sight. The guards on the walls are not paying attention. We will quietly row up to the shore in boats. They're not expecting an attack from the sea. [291] I also trust that I can silently steal the boats for us, and all of you should remain quiet and keep this properly secret."

The two kings agreed with the little man. He made off with five hundred boats down by the castle wall. [292] The men guarding the boats were completely fooled; they thought the waves[78] had taken them out to sea. Each of them said, "I don't know where my boats are. The chains all break, and the wind takes them away."

[293] They all jumped from the ships down into the boats, which came to them empty and then quickly went back. In the morning they all found their boats again. They had carried thirty thousand heroes during the night to the beach. [294] They jumped out of the boats and onto the sand. All of them were glad that they[79] had been released. Otnit of Lombardy and Ilias of Russia disembarked from the boats onto solid ground.

[295] Then the Lombard said, "Now help us, Alberich, so we can destroy the town to the ruin of the mighty king."

---

74. Manuscript W marks the beginning of this chapter at 287,4 with a large initial "O" (*Ortneides*; three lines high). There is no chapter title or other special marking.

75. Manuscript A reads: *ich bringe dir böse märe von der künigin* (288,3); manuscript W reads: *ich pringe dir suezzeu mer von der chuniginne leip*, "I bring you pleasing news about the queen." Kofler's note asserts that this is an ironic remark given Otnit's desire to attack the town.

76. This line (289,3) could be Otnit or Alberich speaking. Among the editors and translators, almost all opt for a continuation of the previous line, with Otnit speaking, even though he has just asked Alberich for advice. Only Simrock reads the line as the beginning of Alberich's reply, and to me this makes the most sense, given that Alberich goes on to detail how the fortress will be captured, i.e., with a night landing on the beaches.

77. Manuscript W reads: *den vanen niemen sicht*, "the banner will not be seen" (290,1b). Kofler adopts the manuscript A reading: *manen*, "moon."

78. Manuscript W reads: *veinde* (enemy).

79. Kofler's gloss takes the "they" (*si*) in 294,2a to refer to Otnit's men, not the boats, i.e., that the men were glad to be "free" and on land again.

"You can easily see," said the little one, "that the gate is open. I can't give you any advice as far as the battle is concerned."

[296] Then the Lombard said, "You don't need to say anything else. Ilias of the Russians, take my battle flag. No one else is worthy of carrying it in his hand. It would not be right to give it to anyone else."

[297] "You should excuse me from this, nephew Otnit. I brought five thousand heroes here to this battle, and I must properly direct and lead them. Such a large contingent needs its own commander."

[298] Then the Lombard said, "I can't excuse you from this, since I brought you with me for support. We can both fight under a single bright banner. Those we brought here won't forsake us now."

[299] "Only God knows that," said the Russian. "Give it to me."

He hoisted up a large[80] flag on which a golden lion of fiery red gold shown forth. The two kings led many men to their deaths.

[300] They were well prepared by the time dawn broke when a Muslim on the wall called out in a loud voice, "Everyone up, get up, all of you! A fortune in merchandise has arrived. Whoever goes to buy something will quickly lose his life. [301] He will pay dearly for it, as will his children's children. There are at least thirty thousand knights at the walls, in bright chain mail rings as white as snow. This fortune in goods will ruin us all."[81]

[302] Many a Muslim in the town was terrified. The sun and the day arrived to their downfall. Many were lost to that exchange in goods. Otnit forced his way through the gate and sounded his battle horn. [303] The Muslims formed up; there was great commotion and noise. They quickly gathered from every part of the town. At least sixty thousand Muslims assembled in front of the palace, where the constable, their commander, was situated. [304] He rode out against the invaders with a great host. Otnit fought courageously alongside the Russian. They all maneuvered in formation in that dreadful fight. The Lombard cried out, "*Che Chevalier Otnit!*"[82]

---

80. Manuscript W reads: *swartzen* (black).
81. The use here of the term *koufschaz* (wares, goods) is highly ironic. It can mean both the actual goods for sale or the activity of buying and selling, as in mercantilism. Since Otnit's army has "sold" itself as a company of merchants, the watchman's statement refers on one level to the fact that the "merchants" have arrived with their wares, seeing full well that they are warriors, and on another level that the "trade" about to begin is one of life and death. In *Kudrun*, a similar metaphor of selling is used when King Ludwig thinks that an army surrounding his castle is actually a group of pilgrims looking to buy goods (*K* 1364), or for the "exchange" in swordplay (*K* 860,4).
82. A battle cry from the Old French, meaning roughly "Here, Knights of Otnit." Both manuscripts AW misunderstood this and wrote nonsense words: manuscript A: *tschatsouilier*; manuscript W: *schachza valyr*. The Middle High German transliteration of the Old French could read "Zâ, Schevaliers!" Thomas translates: "To me! Chevalier Ortnit!" (22).

[305] Then Ilias of Russia charged into the masses. They knew[83] who were the Christians and who were the Muslims. So many Muslims appeared that they stopped the advance of the king's banner. He pushed on to the middle of the palace. [306] Then the Lombard wounded many a Muslim. They had led him there from the shore to their own detriment. Whomever that monstrous man struck with the point of his sword lay dead before him. [307] The Muslims all retreated before that bold man. No one dared face him at the front of the formation. He took many a bold Muslim's life, but his own men were not without losses. [308] He struck a great many gaping holes on both sides. The Russian covered his back and carried the flag behind him.

"Leave the heroes to fight on!"[84] cried Alberich. "The Muslims are getting away from you, mighty king. [309] Unfortunately the gates have all been left unattended. They've opened those that were closed. See if you can't turn this around, King Otnit. They're burning your ships and everything in them."

[310] The Lombard was mounted on a fast Turkish horse. Along with his heroes he pushed back through a gate to the outside. The Muslims shrank back from his mighty army. He killed a good many of them and drowned them in the sea. [311] After the Lombard had left the Russian to go down to the shore, Ilias was left in dire need of his support against the Muslims. He suffered a great many casualties, which he deeply regretted. He lost five thousand heroes and was struck down himself.

[312] The little man came riding up on a Turkish horse. He said to the Lombard, "You've fought enough here. Turn around at once and avenge your anger. You've lost the king of Russia and his heroes."

[313] Then the Lombard said, "Uncle Ilias, may God have mercy that I was not at your side. I will be forever heartbroken after your death."

He angrily turned around and came to his aid. [314] At that point the Russian had given up on his support. He saw him lying there pitifully among the enemy troops. He had defended himself as long as he could. Now help came swiftly; that's how he was saved. [315] He was still clutching the banner with one hand, his sword in the other, when he found [him] lying there. He had succumbed to many hard blows. He found him lying there unconscious, and yet he wasn't wounded at all. [316] Otnit took the sword in his hands and threw the shield onto his back. Now he really put his sharp blade to the test. He lashed out wildly

---

83. Manuscript A reads: *wisste* (305,2a); Manuscript W reads: *enwest* (didn't know). Either reading makes sense in the tumult of battle.
84. Manuscripts AW read: *lasse die helde streiten* (308,3a). Thomas translates: "Warriors, stop fighting!" (22), misreading *lasse/lazze* (manuscripts A/W) for "stop." The meaning is rather that Otnit should let those warriors who are under Ilias's command and engaged in the city continue the fight, but he is needed elsewhere with other forces to save the ships. It's not entirely clear how the Muslim forces are burning the ships, but they may be stranded on the beach and left unguarded.

at friend and foe alike. The one they had previously pressed now had plenty of room.

[317] The [bold][85] Russian spoke most mournfully, as he saw his nephew above him through his helmet's visor. "May God have mercy that I was ever born. What I held most dear I have regrettably lost."

[318] The bold man was happy that he had found him alive. He quickly pulled him up off the ground by the hand. "This journey could not be made without losses. I will certainly compensate you for it, if you think you'll recover."

[319] "How can you compensate me for the losses I've suffered? All my men lie before us, hacked to pieces." The Russian said miserably, "I will certainly recover, but cursed as I am I don't know what purpose my life has now."

[320] "A man must be prepared to lose," said King Otnit, "his life and his men if he goes into battle. He has to accept whatever he loses there. It seems to me that you're unable to fight on.[86] Let me take the banner."

[321] "No," said the Russian, "I'll be all right in a minute. The dead we see here will certainly be avenged. I will continue to support you; you should give me the flag. I'll avenge my men or you'll see me die here today."

[322] The Muslim army was standing by and waiting for them, when they could put their manly strength to the test again.

The Lombard said, "We have to go after them again. It would be unforgiveable to leave these dead here unavenged."

[323] They charged at each other, their formations became enmeshed, and bright mail rings turned the color of blood. The invaders gained the victory again over the defenders. Many a Muslim could be seen lying at the Lombard's feet. [324] They had hurled many a dead man to the ground. The Muslims hid themselves; no one fought them.[87] They had laid low many a dead man on the field.

"Against whom do I fight now?" said Ilias of Russia.

[325] "Before you go on complaining like that, I'll show you a thousand Muslims," replied Alberich, "who are in hiding, if you want to avenge your men."

"Gladly!" said the Russian. "Sir, show the way!"

[326] Then the little one led him into a rock wall, where he found at least a thousand Muslims holed up inside. He kicked down the lock and door with his foot. "Cursed Saracens, you'll have to come out now!"

[327] Then they fell down at his feet. "Lord, let us live! We submit ourselves to your God's mercy."

---

85. Manuscript A reads: *kunig* (king; 317,1b); manuscript W reads: *chune* (bold).
86. Manuscript A reads: *ich wän, du magst* <u>nicht</u> *streiten* (320,4a); manuscript W reads: *ich wen, du mocht streiten*, "I think that you can fight on."
87. This could either mean that the Christian forces (no one) did not engage the enemy (them), since they were hiding, or that the Muslim forces (no one) were intent on hiding and therefore did not engage the Christians (them). Thomas translates: "the rest hid and no one opposed them" (23).

"Gladly," said the Russian, "and you'll pay me back for my men. I'll clear the way with this broom.[88] [328] I'll impose a penance that you won't easily escape. You'll look just like those others who lie there. Those I strike down with this broom today will have to perform penance until Judgment Day."

[329] He dragged every one of the enemy into the light of day. He grabbed them by the hair; he cut off their heads. He killed all of them, until he could find no others. If he had found more, he would have killed them himself as well.

[330] Then he made his way back through the dead. He came into a vaulted chamber full of women. They fell down at his feet. "Lord, now spare our lives! You will gain little honor if you slaughter us poor women."

[331] "You're all the same to me, women and men. You must compensate me for those I've lost."

He took them by their hair and did the same to them. The little man was furious and became incensed with the Russian. [332] The little one quickly left him, from inside the rock wall to the battlefield of the fallen, where he found Otnit.

"Your uncle is butchering women. You should be ashamed of that. Those who want to become Christians, he's taking their lives."

[333] The Lombard angrily ran to where the Russian stood. He said, "Have you lost your mind? Damn you! These women are innocent, the ones you've killed. You should remember that you also came from a woman. [334] If you want me to continue to serve you in any way, then do this for my sake and put your sword away. Your way of thinking [is] foolish. Come, help me baptize those who want to become Christian."

[335] The Russian said angrily, "I couldn't care less about that. Leave me in peace with your baptisms. The ones I lead to water will suffer for it.[89] If they're left to me to baptize, I'll put them in the ground."

[336] Then he was barely able to persuade him to sheathe his sword and leave the poor women in peace. The mighty king baptized those who wanted to become Christians, and little Alberich eagerly helped him.[90] [337] The Russian angrily made his way back onto the battlefield. Every wounded man who got up, he knocked back down. Christians and Muslims alike, he kicked them in the teeth. Those who could have recovered, he made unwell.

---

88. Manuscript A reads: *mit disem besemreise wil ich schlahen den ban* (327,4); manuscript W reads similarly: *mit disem pesem reise wil ich eu zeslachen den pan*. The broom is a metaphor for a sword, as it clears the way or makes a path. According to the Reclam edition note on the line (632n327,4), there are multiple meanings available for *ban* (path or death or banishment), any one of which could fit the context here. According to Kofler, the line could be read: "with this rod of correction I will free you from exile" ("Mit dieser Zuchtrute befreie ich euch von dem Bann").

89. Manuscript A reads: *die werden ungesunt* (335,3b); manuscript W reads: *daz tun ich dir wol chunt*, "this I tell you with certainty," which is essentially just an interjection and filler.

90. Manuscript A reads: *im*, which would refer back to Otnit; manuscript W reads: *und half in des vil vaste*, "them," i.e., Alberich helped the Muslims who are being baptized.

[338] The little one said angrily to the Lombard, "We won't have any rest from this troll[91] all day. He could at least leave the Christians alone. Some of them could well be healed, but instead he takes their lives."

[339] Then King Otnit replied angrily, "Uncle, you don't seem to want to give up your fight. What are you avenging on the men who died for our cause? By all rights, you really are the son of some kind of monster."

[340] Hardly had the Russian been dissuaded from this indecent behavior, when he suddenly thought of other indecent deeds. He went to the Muslim place of worship, where he found their false gods. He carried the shrines outside and smashed them against a wall.

[341] Then the Lombard said, "May God give you some sense of sanity. How much longer today do I have to guard against your indecency? Go ahead, have your way, do whatever you think best. You won't change your bizarre way of thinking on my account."

[342] "Follow me, Lombard," replied Alberich, "and let's go search among the dead; that is proper. Those in this army who have a chance of recovery, we'll send them out in boats to the ships at sea."

[343] Then they went and searched for those who had been injured. They found among the Christians fewer than five hundred men who could recuperate. These he sent out on the water. The suffering was a terrible torment for the Lombard.

[344] "I tell you," said the little one, "you've endured great harm. Unfortunately, many were brought here to find their death. Your Majesty, if you would like, now sound your horn.[92] You may laugh or cry, but still you've lost nine thousand knights."

[345] "May God let me make amends," said King Otnit, "that so many dead lie here who were in my service. Evening is approaching; I can do no more. We'll have to stay here until daylight tomorrow. [346] Look," he said to the Russian, "what good would my anger do me? As monstrous as I could become, they would still have been lost. Long military campaigns are distinguished by loss. Another one of my misfortunes is over."

---

91. Manuscript A reads: *trolle*; manuscript W reads: *tievel* (devil). The Reclam edition note (632n338,2) on the word *trolle* comments on two different meanings. The word is apparently not attested until the fifteenth century. One meaning, that of a kind of kobold or mischievous little person, is northern European in origin and still in use. The other meaning is a southern German dialectal word connoting a "crude, vulgar, uncouth" person (brute, churl, goon).

92. The purpose of sounding the horn in this particular case is unclear. It was not a retreat. Perhaps it signaled a regrouping or a victory.

Chapter 5: How the Town Surrendered and [They] Went On to the [Next] Town [347–483][93]

[347] The town was occupied and guarded during the night. Everything that the Lombard and the Russian wanted done, the Muslims did gladly, whatever the king ordered. They surrendered themselves and the town to his mercy.

[348] So they spent the night up to the next day untroubled. The Lombard said, "I don't want to remain in this town any longer. Let's go, it's time. We will go on to take Mount Tabor," said King Otnit. [349] "Let's go, bold Russian, and avenge our anger, and avenge the men we've lost. The fallen will always have a place in my heart. I will never forget them unless the queen is mine."

[350] Those who were still with them wasted no time. Many a white mail coat and many a bright helmet, hard steel rings they donned. They marched from the fortress onto the broad green field.

[351] Then the Lombard said, "Let's go, my men. I will fight now with every ounce of my strength.[94] I must either conquer the town or lose my life. I will never rest until that woman is mine. [352] I command those who have followed me to this point. Ilias of Russia, take my battle flag. Sixteen thousand heroes will follow us up to the moat. The Muslims won't dare deny us the town in battle."

[353] The Russian spoke unhappily: "I don't know where I should go. In Italian lands I would know my way, and I could lead the men on the right roads. They would get lost here following me. I myself don't know where I am."

[354] "If you want to follow me," replied the dwarf, "then I will lead the heroes through hill and dale, up to the top of the mountain, where Mount Tabor lies."

"May God in heaven reward you," said King Otnit.

[355] "Order that I be given your horse, the one being led there. I'll carry the banner into the king's land. If they ask you, those who are riding with you, who is carrying your banner, tell them I'm an angel."[95]

[356] The Lombard handed the horse over to him and happily lifted him onto it. He made quite a spectacle; he held the banner securely. Then he rode to the front of the army, where he showed the heroes the unguarded roads.

[357] The Italians crossed themselves often, and all of them said, "Mighty and powerful [king], when will you make the sign of the cross? Don't you see the

---

93. The first town refers to Suders, just captured, and the second, unspecified town to which they travel is Mount Tabor. Manuscript W has no chapter title or marking.
94. Manuscript A reads: *nu ich ze leben han*, literally "what I have to live" (351,2b); manuscript W reads: *nu ich ze geben han*, "what I have to give." Kofler, in his gloss on the line, interprets this to mean: "now that I have the (necessary) means" ("da ich über die [nötigen] Mittel verfüge"), meaning that he is confident in his army.
95. This scene closely resembles the angel of God leading the Israelites out of Egypt, especially Ex. 23:20: "Behold, I send an angel before you, to guard you on the way and to bring you to the place which I have prepared" (see also Ex. 14:19, 33:2).

miracle that has been bestowed on you? Who is that on your horse holding your banner?"

[358] The two mighty kings laughed genially about that. They alone could see him, and otherwise [no] one else. "It is the angel of God," said King Otnit, "escorting us to Mount Tabor. [359] You should remember this. Those who perish here, he will lead up to heaven. You should not spare yourselves in battle."

All the Lombards were happy about that. "Then we will gladly fight," they said, "if that is so."

[360] They followed the wondrous sign, and all took notice of it. Each of them said, "When will we arrive?"

The courageous men rode up onto the field. The little one cried out loudly, "Set up your tents here! [361] If you want to see the town, then come here, Otnit. I'll show you where Mount Tabor is situated. Hand the banner over to the Russian's hands. Now you can see the heights and the rock wall."

[362] The strong Russian angrily grabbed the banner. They were all glad now that they saw the town. The Russian, filled with anger, didn't want to stop. He carried the banner right up to the town moat. [363] He planted the flag on the town wall. He ordered the Lombards to set up camp there. The marshal[96] allowed them to use the field next to the town. There they filled the grounds with many splendid pavilions, [364] which they had been given by the wealthy Muslim in Messina. Two of them were stitched and woven with gold. Whenever they were spread out, the roof provided enough shade for a hundred knights in the space underneath. [365] The poles were made of ivory, clear as a mirror. At the tip of the poles was the tent's finial, in which was set a carbuncle stone that shone in the king's palace[97] as if it were a candle.

[366] They had set up their pavilions too close to the town. The Muslims wanted to force them to retreat with their arrows.

"We're much too close," said the mighty king.

"I think I can fix that," replied Alberich. [367] "Just stay here quietly under cover of the town wall. I'll make sure today that their arrogance comes to an end. Wherever they may have weapons on the town wall, I'll destroy them all and throw them into the moat. [368] I'll take care of it tonight," replied the dwarf.

He took his leave of the king and climbed up the hill. There he looked on the wall for whatever weapons he could find. He promptly destroyed them and threw them off the wall.

---

96. This was generally the field commander, usually one of the king's ranking nobles. Here it appears that the marshal is more akin to a deputy commander or executive officer, i.e., responsible for the details of logistics and organization. Ilias seems to be the actual commander of the army.

97. It is uncertain whether Machorel's palace in Mount Tabor is meant, i.e., that the light shines all the way into the enemy castle, or if the pavilion described here is King Otnit's traveling "palace" or pavilion. Manuscript W reads: *in dem palas*, indicating that the light shines inside Otnit's pavilion, not into Machorel's hilltop palace.

Chapter 5: How the Town Surrendered and [They] Went On to the [Next] Town [347–483]

[369] Then King Otnit of the Lombards said, "Take a look at how the Muslim weapons are lying in the fosse. Now we can sleep in peace until tomorrow morning. We needn't be afraid that anyone will harm us."

[370] The Muslims called out loudly, "The devil's been here! What we needed to defend ourselves has been taken from us. You should willingly give this king your daughter. If he gains the upper hand, he'll surely kill us all."

[371] Then the king's wife, that virtuous Muslim, said, "You might well give your daughter to the king. You might well have to pay if you deny him your child. He razed Suders and slaughtered the people within."

[372] He raised his hand and slapped her mouth. "If you say that one more time, you'll be sorry."

The queen said, "May his god give him strength that he might still achieve victory over us both."

[373] Then a wise Muslim[98] said to the king, "Accept this counsel, since your town's defenses are weak."

The Muslim said angrily, "Since there are forty thousand of us, we will engage them tomorrow in front of the town moat."

[374] Alberich heard what they had decided. He said to the old Muslim, "Sire, I think you've gone mad. All those now living here can't help you. He'll string you up on the ramparts unless you give him your daughter."

[375] The Muslim said angrily, "Who brought you here now? I'm not the least bit interested in your opinion. You'll regret before God that you've come this close to us. My town wall will soon display all your heads."

[376] "You'll find out soon enough," replied Alberich. "If the mighty Lombard weren't in front of your town, you'd have to give your daughter to me instead. No one could protect you if I wanted to take your life."

[377] He threw sticks and stones at the little one. Alberich wasn't the least bit afraid; he had quickly removed himself. He wanted to hit him, but since he couldn't see him, he became so enraged again that he tore out his hair.

[378] Then the little one climbed down the rock wall to the ground, where he found Otnit. "The Muslim actually wants to meet you in open combat."

"Then I want nothing else," said King Otnit.

[379] Amid the danger he slept through the night until day. How quickly he awoke; how well he had slept! He cried out loudly in a manly voice to the king of the Russians, who was still asleep next to him, [380] "How much longer are you going to sleep, Ilias of Russia? We will water the green grass with blood. They want to fight us at the town moat. Let's make our preparations quickly, so we can take the mountaintop."

---

98. Manuscript A reads: *ein weiser haiden* (373,1a); manuscript W reads: *ein wilder haiden*, "a fierce heathen."

[381] They put on their bright battle armor. They carried Otnit's flag, which the strong Russian aggressively carried, up to the gate. My, how many Muslims the Lombard laid low!

[382] The Muslims all cried out, "Let's defend ourselves! The king and his army are storming the town."

Inside the walls the uproar grew ever louder. The Muslims wanted to fight; the gate was opened. [383] Then the battle-hungry men collided. They wanted to test them; no one separated them. The invaders defended themselves against the fearless townsfolk.[99]

The lovely maiden beat her own breasts. [384] She tore her hair, soft as silk, out by the roots. She feared for her father's death as she watched the battle. The mother took her daughter by the hand in anguish and went to her place of worship, where the shrines were located. [385] She prayed to her two false gods. She beseeched Apollo and Muhammed again and again.[100] Her hair fell from her head down to her feet, tousled and unkempt. Her prayer[101] was mournful. [386] Then her neck shone through her braids as white as snow. Alberich was moved by the maiden's anguish. Where the small neck shone through her braids, it was as if a carbuncle stone were burning brightly. [387] Her mouth glowed just like a rose, and like a ruby. Both her eyes shimmered like the full moon. She had the right proportions, with slender hips, tall and slim like a candle from her arms down. [388] Her arm was smooth, her hands, nothing was not beautiful. Her nails were so clear that you could see yourself in them. Her cheeks were both wet with tears, as if they were pearls. The maiden was bereft of joy. [389] Then the maiden's sorrow became almost unbearable. They implored both their gods and fell down before the shrine. The lovely woman scratched and tore at herself. Little Alberich took hold of her hands.[102] [390] He gently held her hands in his.

The lady said to her mother, "Who is here beside me? Who is it that grabs[103] me and holds me fast? His behavior is uncourtly; he won't let go of me." [391] Then the fair maiden said, "Let me go, I beg of you. Is it you, Apollo, or is it you, Muhammed? Help me in my time of trouble, if it is you, my idol."

"No, it is not," said the little one. "I am a messenger from heaven."

---

99. Manuscripts AW read: *da werten sich die geste den wirten unverzait* (383,3). This employs the metaphor of "guests" and "hosts," an image similar in martial humor to the terms "home" and "away" teams.

100. Manuscript A reads: *si flehte harte dicke* (385,2a); manuscript W reads: *si volgten nach der diche*, "they were attentive again and again."

101. The Middle High German technical term *gruos* (Latin *incipit*) designates the opening to a prayer or liturgical text.

102. This line and the first half of the next line (389,4a–390,1a) are missing in manuscript W.

103. Manuscript A reads: *wer ist der mich da vahet* (390,3a); manuscript W reads: *wer ist, der mich da wechet*, "who frightens me."

Chapter 5: How the Town Surrendered and [They] Went On to the [Next] Town [347–483]

[392] "How dare you touch me in front of my gods! You should let me go now!" replied the maiden. "They will easily overpower [you],[104] now that they are here with me."

"Take care," said the little one. "I'm more powerful than they are."

[393] "Tell me what you want," said the fair maiden.

The little one said politely, "It will be revealed to you. My master in heaven has sent me to you. You shall be queen over all of Italy."

[394] Then the noble maiden said, "What you say is not true. I was born and raised a Muslim. That's how I will die," said the queen. "I want to stay with my mother and with my father."

[395] Then the little one replied, "This talk won't help you. Since you're being so defiant to your creator, a great scourge will afflict your beautiful body, which you won't be able to overcome as long as [you] live."

[396] Then the young woman said, "I don't know who created me."

He said, "He is called Christ. He has authority over the earth and the kingdom of heaven, and over all creation," said Alberich. [397] "Everything you can think of is subject to him. If you won't take the Lombard as your husband, if you won't bow to his will, then you seem foolish to me. He will make you lame in your hands and your feet. [398] He will take away your beauty and make you blind as well. You should believe in him. After all, you are his child. From him you have received beauty and a fair complexion."

The young woman said, "I'm not afraid of your god."

[399] He had little success, whatever he offered her. He wanted to see the battle, so he went up to the window and looked to see who was winning the battle. The Christians were pushing the Muslims forcefully back across the moat.[105]

[400] The Lombard was carving a breach on both sides. Behind him the Russian forcefully carried the flag up to the town gate and planted it next to the wall. They both took their swords in both hands.

[401] Then little Alberich said to the young woman, "Don't you want to see the battle, mighty queen? If you don't consent to everything my God demands of you, you will see your father die in this battle."

[402] Then the young woman said, "There are many Muslims."

"Then I'll support my friend in every way I can."[106]

---

104. Manuscript A reads: *sie handelt leicht übele* (392,3a). This is emended in the Reclam edition to *sie handelnt dich leicht übele*. This emendation is based on the manuscript W reading: *si handelnt dich leicht ubel*. The manuscript A text would be (not in quotation marks, but rather as narration): "She is quick to act badly."
105. Most town or castle moats during the Middle Ages were not filled with water. They were deep, broad ditches in front of the walls that made storming the walls with machines or men more difficult, as the attackers would first have to climb out of the moat or fill it in.
106. Most likely spoken by Alberich.

199

The young woman and the old woman went up to him there. As they watched the battle, they both lost heart.

[403] "Do you see," said the little one, "my God's wrath? If you don't change your mind quickly, your father will be lost. You can still choose the Lombard as your husband before a great catastrophe befalls all of you today."

[404] Then the maiden said politely, "Husband? But what is that? I'll never promise you this unless you explain it to me."

"You will very quickly come to know," said her mother, "what a husband is. Before your father is killed, do what he asks of you."

[405] The little one said politely, "A husband is a good thing. If you want to submit to men, you must become a woman. Once you become used to it, through the night until the day, you may find it so pleasant that no one can keep you from it."

[406] "However it may be for me, good or bad, I won't put any faith in your falsehoods. I will never assent to your request or your command unless I see that you are stronger than my god. [407] I haven't seen you so powerful or so strong today that you could even touch my gods or their shrine."

In no time at all the little one picked up the shrine. He smashed [it] against the wall and flung it into the moat.

[408] "Take a look," said the Russian, "what an amazing battle that little Alberich is fighting up there on the wall. I don't know who might be helping him; he's raised this fight to another level.[107] All the Muslims' deities are lying in the moat."

[409] Then there were only a few Muslims left outside. The Christians drove them back through the town gate. The young woman said, "May you be his shield of protection, so that I don't lose my father. I will do whatever you want."

[410] The little one said cleverly, "You must stop resisting. If you want to save the Muslims and your father, if you want me finally to make peace, if you want to have the king, send him your ring."

[411] "I promised him I would, and now it must be done. If I'm to have him as my friend, then let me see him first."

The little one replied, "Do you see who's standing there, the one who has defeated so many Muslims by himself? [412] His armor shines out among all the rest, just as a candle is seen in a dark house. He fights in the front ranks; his sword is bloody."

"Truly," said her mother, "he is worthy of an excellent woman."

---

107. Manuscripts AW read: *er hat den streit <u>erhaben</u>* (408,3b). Thomas translates: "it was surely he who began it" (29). The Reclam edition translates: "he has turned the battle into something sublime" ("er hat den Kampf zu etwas Erhabenem gemacht"). I have followed this more figurative sense of "raising up," given the context and Ilias's approval.

Chapter 5: How the Town Surrendered and [They] Went On to the [Next] Town [347–483]

[413] Then the young woman said, "Take my gold ring to him. Tell the Lombard that I am faithfully beholden to him. Please ask him to withdraw from the town with his army. I will do as he commands, so that he might spare my father."

[414] Then the worthy little man was especially glad of her declaration. He took the ring and hurried to see the king. "May this news please you, King Otnit, that a beautiful young woman will lie in your arms."

[415] The king was so relieved that he forgot all about the battle. The Lombard said, "So tell me more—what does my lady confer on me, that noble queen?"

"The Ace,[108] her true love. And she sends you this ring. [416] Now tell the Russian to stop; you've fought enough now. Your lady and her mother have asked you to withdraw from the town and let the Muslims live. She wishes to surrender her beautiful body to your mercy."

[417] Then the Lombard said, "Truly, then it will be done. If only I were so lucky now that I might see her."

The Russian said angrily, "Don't make peace yet; you'll have the lady as it is. Help me get through the gate."

[418] The little one said angrily, "How will a beautiful woman find happiness with the man who took her father's life? He can well do with honor what the lady asked of him. In the name of the Lord![109] You never will get enough of fighting."

[419] Then the Lombard said, "I will not deny her anything."

By then the Muslims had closed the gate.[110] They didn't want to fight anymore. They slammed the gate shut, leaving Otnit and his men standing outside. [420] Then the mighty king sounded his small[111] battle horn. He had already lost a good many of his heroes. Of his thirty thousand heroes he had only six thousand[112] men left, but still the Muslims did not dare face the Christians.

[421] Then the worthy and mighty king withdrew from the fortress. "We should now conceal ourselves," replied Alberich. "I know a stream by a green meadow where no one will find us; there we can get some rest."

---

108. Manuscript A reads: *daz dus, ir holde minne* (415,4a); manuscript W reads: *daz tut si ir holdeu minne*, "she offers this, her loyal love." According to the Reclam edition (635n415,4), *dus* (two) comes from the southern French *daus*, the number two and the name of the highest playing card. The metaphor of the game would be that she will give Otnit her highest card, i.e., all her love. The manuscript W reading is more straightforward.

109. Manuscripts AW read: *(in) nummer dummer namen* (418,1a). This kind of nonsense phrase is found elsewhere in the Middle High German corpus (e.g., Walther von der Vogelweide, *L* 31,33). Pannier translates it as a corruption of the Latin *in nomine domini*. Thomas follows by (not) translating: "*In nomine domini amen*" (30).

110. This line is missing in manuscript W.

111. The manuscripts agree in this reading of "small" (*lützel*), and all translators agree on its meaning, but there seems no good explanation for why Otnit's battle horn should be characterized in this way. In *Wolf Dietrich B* there is mention of a "small horn" (*kleine horn*, 872b) that is used by Wolf Dietrich in his assault on Constantinople.

112. Manuscript W reads: *funf tausent* (five thousand; 420,3b).

[422] The Russian took the flag in his hands again and unhappily rode away from the rock wall. He turned to a remote area with a spacious heath, which the little one knew. The army encamped there.

[423] "The two of us have to go back," said the dwarf. "You should ride with me, Otnit, back to the mountain. I have faith in God and in my own guile, that we won't return from there unless we have the maiden. [424] You should command all your army to remain alert. I would take more men to the town wall, but they would notice us. We can't get close without the watchman calling us out at the town moat. [425] We'll hardly be able to return without being challenged. You should ask the bold Russian and his heroes to come to your aid when I call for them. If they delay too long, then the maiden will be lost to you."

[426] Then the battle companions rode back to the rocky mount. Without being seen they ran up to the town wall, where he told Otnit to wait at the bluff below the town. Without being seen he went up onto the town moat. [427] Then he climbed up over the town wall undetected. He found the young woman and the old queen sitting together among other Muslim women. They were sitting among the dead, mourning in pain and anguish.[113] [428] The mighty queen[s] were sitting next to each other. Alberich hid himself between the two of them. The little one said very softly to the young queen, "When are you going to fulfill your promise?"

[429] "I will do so very gladly, whenever you like. The king really caused mayhem among the Muslims. Since you won't release me, give me your advice. How can I join the hero who has paid such a high price for me?"

[430] Then the little one replied, "If you will follow my instructions, tell your mother that God has come again."

"I heard you," said the old Muslim's wife. "I'm afraid that if I help her in this, her father would kill me."

[431] "Just follow my advice, that will benefit both of you. Don't stray from my counsel; I'll tell you what to do. You should allow your daughter to go, so that she might care for her false god, Muhammed, so that he is resurrected."

[432] Then the fair maiden said in a loud voice, "If you allow me, lady and mother mine, then I will go outside the gate onto the town moat. This is what both our gods have asked me to do. [433] They have revealed to me that they want to avenge the shame of the Lombard's punishment,[114] and they say that if I beseech them they will come back."

---

113. Manuscript A reads: *und qualten sere ir leib* (427,4b); manuscript W reads: *und chlagten ser ir leip*, "lamenting greatly."

114. The Reclam edition has translated manuscript A's *des Lamparten suon* (433,2b) with "the Lombard's son" or "the son of Lombardy" ("des Lamparten Sohn"). Thomas agrees and translates: "son of Lombardy" (30). This would represent the only case where Otnit is so characterized. Kofler takes *suon* (manuscript W's *sun*) to mean "judgment" or "punishment" ([Straf]Gericht).

Chapter 5: How the Town Surrendered and [They] Went On to the [Next] Town [347–483]

"You have permission to go," said the old queen.

[434] "Mother and lady, they have also told me that I should go outside the gate by myself, that I alone should look upon them and no one else."

"No one will follow you."

[The] maiden was glad of that. [435] She refused an escort, as much as she was urged otherwise. She walked out beyond the town wall by herself. The wild little man took the maiden by the hand and led her down to the bluff where Otnit was waiting. [436] By then Otnit had wielded his sword the entire day in battle. He had fallen asleep from exhaustion on his saddle bow. The little one called to him softly. After being very patient, when he still wouldn't wake up, he hit him with his fist.

[437] "You will lose your honor and your life with sleep! Wake up,[115] Lombard, I bring you the queen!"

The Lombard awoke from his slumber and said, "Oh joy, that I have lived to witness this day. [438] If I were near death, I would still be well again."

He embraced the lady and kissed her more than a hundred times.

"I will allow you to do this," said Alberich then, "to embrace and kiss the mighty queen. [439] But you will not make the maiden your wife until she is baptized. She's still a Muslim. Now, friend, my advice is that you get away from here quickly."

He jumped into his saddle and set the maiden in front of him. [440] They both rode down the hill away from the town. Their horse ran at a gallop; they waited for no one. He wanted to misdirect the Muslims; Alberich was smart. He carried one of the idols into the town. [441] He did this on account of the Muslims; he was mocking them. They thought their god, Muhammed, could speak. He called out beside the shrine, since no one could see him. He wanted to make fools of the Muslims.

In a loud voice he said, [442] "Get down on your knees and say your prayers. Thank the young woman. Here am I, Muhammed. You should all thank the young queen. She beseeched me and my companion [443] that we should return to our rock wall. Look here, I have set myself up here against the wall. No one should disturb the maiden; this she requests of all of you. She knows how to appeal to us according to Muslim rites."

[444] In this way he made fools of all the Muslims alike. Alberich got up to go look for the Lombard, through the mountains and the rocks, to where he found Otnit, whose horse was exhausted. He had driven him too hard.[116]

---

115. Manuscript A reads: *nu wache, Lamparte* (437,2a); manuscript W reads: *nu lache, ich pringe dir...*, "Now laugh, I bring you...," which is clearly the inferior reading in this context.

116. Manuscript A reads: *darzuo het ers verrant* (444,4b); manuscript W reads: *het er sich verrant*, "he rode (himself) the wrong way," i.e., he got lost.

[445] The Muslim sat locked inside a room. He tore at his beard out of anger and spite, because he had to accept being shamed by the Lombard.

"Open up," said the chamberlain. "I have good news for you."

[446] Then the Muslim replied, "Tell me then, if it's good news."

"I want to ease your burden and your despair. Muhammed and Apollo have come back, and the young queen implored them to do so."

[447] The Muslim said angrily, "So then, where is my child?"

"She's still outside the gate, where her gods are."

"Ah, woe," said the old man, "I'm cursed. To the horses! My daughter is lost!"

[448] Then the Muslims quickly prepared for battle. He gathered twelve thousand[117] Muslims around him. Otnit was still riding as fast as he could, but the Muslim was hard on his heels, following his tracks. [449] The Muslims pursued him with their fastest horses, and the Lombard raced to escape them. They saw him riding ahead in the distance; the moon gave them light. Otnit's horse was exhausted; it could go no further.

[450] "Now help the two of us as best you can, dear Alberich. Ah, woe, with whom should I leave this wonderful maiden? Now bright mail rings will be made red with blood. Before I part company with her, I would rather lie dead at her side."

[451] "God alone knows," said the little one. "I haven't figured out how to get you away from here. Ride as best you can. I know of a spring and a swamp near here; there is no horse that can get across it."

[452] Then the queen said, "I thought you were joking. Why have you completely lost faith?[118] Your god will help you now. How could I have run away from the one who raised me? I was betrayed by deception and lies.[119] [453] The best thing I can advise you," said the maiden, "is that you get away from my dreadful father as fast as you can. He'll rip out your insides if he catches you. I can't go with you; put me down here on the ground. [454] I've lost my honor, but please don't hurt me.[120] Still, I would grieve forever if you came to harm on my account."

The Lombard said, "I will not do as you say. Before I leave you today, I will lie slain next to you."

---

117. Manuscript W reads: *zwelf hundert* (twelve hundred; 448,2a).
118. Manuscript A reads: *waz <u>vertrawest</u> du so sere* (452,2a); manuscript W reads: *wez <u>traurest</u> du so sere*, "Why do you grieve so much?"
119. Manuscript A reads: *es ist <u>trügene weise</u> das mich hat betrogen* (452,4). Thomas translates Amelung's emendation to *trügenwise* as "delusion of the devil" (32).
120. Manuscripts AW read the same for the second half-line: *und tuot mir an dem leibe nicht* (454,1b), but translations vary widely. Kofler translates: "but he (my father) won't kill me" ("doch wird er [mein Vater] mich nicht töten"). Thomas translates: "I shall not be harmed" (32). Pannier translates: "even if I am still alive" ("bleibt auch das Leben mir"). Simrock simply leaves out the first two lines of the strophe from his translation.

Chapter 5: How the Town Surrendered and [They] Went On to the [Next] Town [347–483]

[455] His horse carried him well enough until he reached the stream, and he jumped to the ground once he saw the water. He let the steed go; it had had enough of the journey. He carried the maiden in his arms across the deep water, [456] away from the stream, and set her down on the ground. He threw his shield on his back; he took his sword in his hand. Regardless of how many enemies there were, he defended himself. The little one had left him to retrieve his entire army. [457] Finding the water was advantageous to both of them. They couldn't ride up on him; they had to wade over toward him. The Muslim angrily dismounted onto the grass, and so did the large force that had come with him. [458] Then the Muslim and his contingent raised their swords. The Lombard fought with stroke and counterstroke.[121] He really had to fight; he had no choice. He killed so many Muslims that you could walk over them and still stay dry.

[459] But he was overcome by fatigue, since he had fought so long. The strength and power ebbed from his arms. "I can't fight on. Ah, woe, where can I go now?"

The Saracens moved in on all sides.

[460] Then the Lombard said, "My body needs rest. If you would spare me, Muslim lord, I will hand over my sword. I don't care if you take me prisoner, as long as you let me live. I will give it to you on your word of honor and on your mercy."

[461] "For my daughter's sake I will take your life."

"I don't know what you accuse me of; she's not been made my wife."

"All those still alive can't save you now."

"Then I will," said the unfortunate man, "defend myself a while longer. [462] I will defend myself, unfortunate man, as long as I am able."

He saw men on horseback and heard the sound of hooves. His heart grew hopeful and a bit stronger. "Now defend yourself, dear nephew!" said Ilias of Russia.

[463][122] The Turkish horses were running at full speed, not walking. The Russian was in the lead and dismounted on the field alongside his sister's son, who was in dire straits. Ilias of Russia took his sword in both hands.[123]

---

121. Manuscripts AW read: *ze schlage und ze gebot* (458,2b). Kofler's note translates: "most quickly and fittingly" ("auf das Schnellste und nach Wunsch"). Thomas simply translates: "the Lombard fought as a true warrior should" (32). My translation follows the Reclam edition ("mit Schlag und Gegenschlag").
122. Strophe 463 is not in manuscript W.
123. Manuscript A reads: *das schwert gab do zu den handen von Reussen Ylias* (463,4). Since the strophe is missing in manuscript W, Amelung reconstructs the line differently: '*nu wer dich, lieber œheim!*' *sprach von Riuzen Yljas*. Thomas follows Amelung's emendation: "'Fight on, dear nephew!'" (32).

[464] Then the Lombard said, "I'm not fit to fight. You heroes, you can help me; you're well rested. I've never despaired so in all my years. Uncle, you take Rose. I can't fight anymore."

[465] The Russian was glad to receive Rose. He took the sword out of the Lombard's hand. Now there arose a great suffering and a truly massive battle. The Lombard collapsed in the lady's lap.

[466] She said, "This makes it difficult for me, since you're lying in my lap.[124] You may well die as a result, if my father defeats you."

He said, "I regret that I haven't yet been able to lie closer to you. Whatever happens to me, it is God's will. I have resigned myself to that."[125]

[467] He was barely able to ask her to take off his helmet. She wiped his brow with her sleeve and with her white hand. When the old Muslim saw him lying in her lap, he collapsed with rage and was unable to speak. [468] Meanwhile, the Muslims fought fiercely against the Christians. They advanced by walking and riding over the dead.

"Forward!" said the Russian. "It's time once more! If you can fight at all, get up and get back in the battle."

[469] Then the Lombard said, "That's how it has to be. Now wish us both luck, my dear lady. I know exactly what they want, and they shall have it." The Lombard said, "Give me back my sword."

[470] They ran at each other; many Muslims were laid low. Countless Christians also lay at their feet.

The Lombard said, "Now the real struggle begins. At least four thousand of my heroes lie dead before me."

[471] "We will avenge them," said Ilias of the Russians.

They both pressed on to where the old Muslim was standing. He and his battle flag began to give ground to them. The Lombard heartily encouraged his own men. [472] The Muslims had to retreat; their army was too small. They didn't dare defend themselves against the Christians. They all feared Otnit's savagery. The banner was thrown down; the old king took flight. [473] Otnit then angrily pursued his father-in-law, and if he had caught him he would have gladly killed him. He was chased all the way to Mount Tabor, up to its gate. The Muslim escaped within; Otnit stayed outside.

[474] The enemy had been completely wiped out in the battle. The Christians took a great haul in horses and ringed armor. Little Alberich said to the young woman, "Now your father will have to die, mighty queen."

---

124. Manuscripts AW read: *si sprach 'mir ist vil schwäre, daz ir in meiner schos liget'* (466,1). Thomas translates: "I am frightened at your lying in my lap" (33).

125. The Reclam edition, Simrock, and Pannier assign the line to Otnit. Amelung and Thomas believe the speaker in line 466,4 to be the princess. Thomas translates: "Well, I have given him up. God's will be done" (33).

Chapter 5: How the Town Surrendered and [They] Went On to the [Next] Town [347–483]

[475] Then the young woman's distress grew even greater. Tears fell from her eyes onto her lap. "If my father is to die, then it must be decried before God. But I would not blame him,"[126] said the beautiful maiden. [476] "He may never be saved; he is so embittered. He does deserve it, too. I don't care what he does to him."

The Lombard came riding back to them. By now he had won a complete victory over the Muslim. [477] He said to the young woman, "Tell me, how are you, my friend and lady? Get up and kiss me."

"I will never do so until you have first told me, king, on your honor, did you kill my father?"

[478] "I did not," said the bold man. "You should be glad, and all the more beholden to me. Your father is safe. If he had not escaped me, I would have taken his life."

The fair maiden said, "Then I welcome you."

[479] They took many of the horses and other battle gear. Those he found alive among the wounded Christians, those who could still recover, he took away with him. He had nine[127] thousand men altogether, hale and wounded. [480][128] Then he set the young woman on a Castilian horse. They rode out in the open without concealing themselves; those who were in the fortress of Suders could not prevent it.[129] He wanted to ride with his lady to the ships. [481] They gladly conceded this journey to him. He traveled by sea, where he no longer had to fear the Muslims. There on the waves he was safe from battle. Alberich and the Russian baptized the queen for him. [482] Before they had reached land, the maiden was made a woman. She forgot all about her father and her mother because of him. On the nineteenth morning they sailed into Messina, where the Muslim heartily welcomed him back in God's name. [483] King Otnit was splendidly received there. He celebrated his wedding festival with his lady at Garda. The nobility came to meet him, free men and liegemen.

So ends this chapter; another is about to begin.

---

126. In this line, it is unclear to whom the "him" (*im*) refers (475,4a), whether Otnit, for killing her father, or her father, for being embittered and trying to kill Otnit. The latter option is dispelled in the following line, assuming that lines 476,1–2 are still spoken by the princess. Kofler believes that lines 476,1–2 are spoken by Alberich in response. Another option could be that the pronoun refers to God, i.e., that she would not blame God if he allowed her father to be killed. Likewise, in 476,2b the "he" could be Otnit or God, while the "him" is Machorel. Thomas translates these lines (475,3–476,2): "'I would lament to God the death of my father,' she replied, 'but I should not blame the deed. He has such a frightful temper that he can never survive, but he well deserves what happens to him and it will make no difference to me.'"
127. Manuscript W reads: *wan tausent*, "only one thousand" (479,4b).
128. Strophe 480 is not in manuscript W.
129. This is an odd and inexplicable statement. Suders (Tyre) had already been captured and occupied by Otnit's forces. The enemy was, however, still in control of Mount Tabor. It could be that Otnit had withdrawn all his forces in preparation for his journey home, including those in Suders.

Chapter 6: How the Muslim Sent Dragon Eggs to His Son-in-Law Otnit [484–526][130]

[484] The Muslim locked himself away in a palace, so that no one in the world was with him inside. This is how he kept hidden for three whole days. Out of spite he had nothing to drink or eat. [485] No one dared call him; no one dared see him. Anyone who angered him would have suffered for it. No one dared offer him anything to eat or drink, or that he should sleep.

Then the huntsman came riding up. [486] He asked where his dear lord was. He was told that he was locked away and would see no one.

The shrewd huntsman said, "I really must see him, even if he's buried himself underground, away from people."

[487] Still, he was directed to the chamber's door. He said to the king, "Sire, come out now. Your child is well cared for; you don't need to mourn anymore. If you show yourself to be grateful, I have good news to tell you. [488] Since you're so depressed that you've lost that woman, and if you want to take the Lombard's life, if you show yourself to be grateful, then I have discovered something that will make the Lombard's life forfeit. [489] It will take his life without delay."

Joyfully the Muslim said, "May you always profit from it." He opened the door and let the huntsman enter. He said to the hunter, "So tell me, what is it [490] that will cause the Lombard such grave harm? If it will kill him, the reward will be great."

"I had followed the hounds too far and became disoriented, and unwittingly I came upon a rock wall. [491] I saw a gigantic dragon moving around on it. If I had the strength of a thousand men, I wouldn't want to face it. It would have swallowed me whole had it known I was there. I let it creep off into the forest and went to see its nest. [492] I found an egg there bigger than my head. I looked for more,[131] but I could only find two of them. They were incredibly big and heavy, so that I could hardly carry them back to my house. [493] I was afraid they would go bad and put them in a warm hole. What's inside is alive. I still have the eggs that will bring the dragons to them in their own land. Whoever fights with the devil will forfeit his life. [494] I'll take the eggs to the land of the Lombards and raise the dragons inside a rock wall. When they start to grow they'll get hungry. I don't think anything in the land will be safe from them. [495] That's how it will be for animals and people alike. Otnit is bold enough that he'll face the dragons. He won't be able to defend himself against even one of them. It will drag whoever challenges it into its cave.[132] [496] He'll have to lose his life to the dragons."

---

130. Manuscript W has no chapter title or marking.
131. The first half-line (492,2a) is missing in manuscript W.
132. Manuscript A reads: *wer in bestreife,* . . . (495,4a); manuscript W reads: *daz er in begreiffet,* . . . , "if it grabs hold of him, . . ."

Chapter 6: How the Muslim Sent Dragon Eggs to His Son-in-Law Otnit [484–526]

The Muslim said this: "For this I will give you anything you want. I'll give you a thousand marks for killing that powerful man with the dragons."

[497] Then the shrewd huntsman said, "I will help you and explain everything to you, since God has willed it. You should have two pack mules loaded with costly silks and precious stones and send me off to those distant shores. [498] Load up a chest with cotton and silk goods for me. The eggs will be kept inside at the right temperature and warmth; otherwise they won't survive. I can tell you this much. The Christians will suffer because of the dragons. [499] You should send letters to your dear daughter, that you want to be on good terms with her husband and your child. Along with precious stones send them large amounts of gold. They'll want to believe that you think highly of them both."

[500] The Muslim did what he asked. He loaded onto a ship leather sacks filled with gold and gems. Everything had to be loaded just as the huntsman wanted. He sailed on with the ships to Roman shores. [501] There he was given an escort in the land of Lombardy all the way to the castle in Garda,[133] where he found the king. He rode behind the pack animals just like an ambassador would. One of the travel chests' contents was regrettably counterfeit.[134] [502] When the shrewd Muslim went to the castle and up to the castle gate, the guard hailed him. No one there could understand his language. Without Otnit's permission, no one would let him enter.

[503] Then the king was told that an emissary had arrived. They had in all their years never heard such a language. "He's bringing along two pack animals that are carrying heavy loads. What he's trying to say, that we can't tell you."

[504] "Bring the pack animals to me along with the foreigner." He was ushered through the gate and told to go on ahead.

"What is your business here?"

The Muslim replied, "Your Majesty, I bring you news that will make you glad."

[505] Then he related various things and handed him a letter. When the king looked at it, he cried out in joy, "That he has changed his ways, may God be forever praised, that this evil Muslim won't stay raving mad forever."

[506] He directed the envoy to where the queen was. He gave the letter to the lady. After she had read the writing, "He brings good news," said the queen then. "My dear father has extended to us his goodwill. [507] He sends us both his love and friendship. He highly praises your good fortune and your power. As long as he knows you to be alive, he will be glad of it. He declares that no one in

---

133. Kofler's gloss on line 501,2 takes this to mean that Machorel had given the huntsman letters of introduction that allowed him to travel through Lombardy all the way to Garda.

134. Manuscript A reads: *was laider kunterfet* (501,4b); manuscript W reads: *waz im der tot berait*, "which would bring about his [Otnit's] death." Amelung opts for the manuscript A reading instead of manuscript W; Kofler chooses manuscript W. Thomas translates: "the contents of one pack chest was deceptive" (35).

the world is dearer to him than you. [508] He wants to be baptized and wants to come to your land. Now don't think unfavorably of what he has sent you. You should believe what you've heard said in the letter."

"I want to let you," said the Muslim, "see his gifts."

[509] He presented four heavy leather sacks to him. Inside were a great many gold pieces and precious stones. There he saw lying before him brooches and rings. The noble queen thanked her father profusely.

[510] The Muslim said, "One sack before you is still full. This gift, which is meant for you, is not yet fully grown. It will bring you precious stones. I tell you," said the envoy, "it is a frog from the garden of Abraham. [511] When it has matured, it will produce a stone finer than any the sun has ever shone upon in all the world.[135] I will tell you something else that has been sent to you. I am commanded, sire, to raise an elephant for you. [512] He can't survive outside of the mountains. I will present both of them to you soon. Just direct me to a cave."

"I will provide you with a mountain and all that you need, and will order my magistrate[136] to take good care of you."

[513] Then he ordered that he be taken to a rock wall near the town of Trento, where the mountain was located.[137] He carried his deceitful brood inside the mountain. Whatever he needed there he was given in abundance. [514] Then he spent twelve months or more inside the mountain. There he had difficulties enough with the dragons. Before he could raise them properly, he had plenty of trouble. My goodness, what grief he suffered on account of the dragons! [515] In half a year the dragons had grown so large that their master's life became unbearable, as they were constantly lying in wait to kill him. The magistrate didn't want to give them any more food either.

[516] It wasn't enough for them if they were given a cow a day. The magistrate said, "It must be the devil's spawn! My lord [would] rather not have this elephant, before it eats up a town or an entire country."

[517] Then the huntsman gave the dragons nothing to eat, and they were near death from starvation. Hunger pained them greatly; they craved the man himself. He lured them out into the light, he barely escaped. [518] Where a good man breeds evil, he will be betrayed, and so with the dragons he had raised his own enemies. Once they were on their own, they paid him no heed. He left [them] to fend for themselves and showed them the way to daylight. [519] Because of their great hunger the dragons were enraged. Whatever they set their sights on was

---

135. This refers to the so-called toadstone (*krotenstein*), which supposedly grew in the heads of frogs and was believed since Pliny the Elder to protect against poisons and to have other healing qualities.

136. Manuscripts AW read: *potestat* (Italian *podestà*), which was the highest civil office in the cities of central and northern Italy during the Middle Ages.

137. Manuscripts AW read: *da er den berg vant* (513,2b). The Reclam edition translates: "where he could keep/save himself" ("wo er sich bergen konnte").

completely destroyed. Whatever they found in the land they devoured completely. They went about their [malevolent ways][138] for more than a year. [520] In the forest and in the fields nothing was safe. They had likewise wreaked havoc across the entire world. They afflicted the people with a suffering most severe. Because of them, no one ventured out or traveled on the roads. [521] It[139] devastated the land all the way up to the castle at Garda. The people had to avoid them as best they could. They didn't dare plant their crops on the fields, nor did they dare mow their meadows by the woods. [522] Bold knights stood up to them, because of their pride and for the sake of fame,[140] but it did none of them any good. They killed hunters and farmers. The dragons were determined to leave no one in peace.

[523] Then the clergy were heard complaining about them in church. The Lombard said, "It will never be destroyed; it will regrettably never die unless I face it in battle. I must save us from it," said King Otnit.

[524][141] One night he was lying next to the queen.[142] He began to ponder his worries and cares. "If I'm unsuccessful, I will lose my life. Ah, woe, to whom will I leave my homeless wife then, [525] who gave up her father and mother on my account? I well know that even if I alone should die, we are both lost. Ah, woe, now I have to lament my cares all alone. I don't dare say anything to my wife in my distress. [526] Truly, I don't lament for towns or lands. I lament for my wife, who has been so faithful to me. I don't dare tell her anything, and yet I must face the dragon."

Another chapter of Otnit's misfortunes is about to begin.

Chapter 7: How Otnit Was Killed by the Dragon [527–75][143]

[527] Now he pondered his misfortunes again. He thought no one had heard him, but then the queen awoke. Her heart was breaking. Her anguish was so great that she cried a rain of tears onto his chest.

---

138. Manuscript A reads: *sunst heten si ir ay mer dann ein ganz jar* (519,4). The editors have taken the manuscript W reading of *erge* (wickedness) over the reading of *ay* (egg), although the Reclam edition in a note finds neither solution very convincing (640–41n519,4).
139. The text is inconsistent as to the number of dragons, sometimes using a singular, sometimes a plural pronoun (*er/si; im/in*). As of line 523,2, there seems to be only one mature dragon (with one exception, 537,4) in manuscript A. Manuscript W is more consistent with "the one" (*der ain*, 521,1) and "it/him" (*im*, 521,2), but then goes over to the plural *si* in line 522,1.
140. Manuscript A reads: *und auch durch ruomes willen* (522,2a); manuscript W reads: *durch des chuniges willen*, "because the king willed it." Amelung opts for the manuscript A reading, and Thomas follows. Kofler adopts the manuscript W reading.
141. Strophes 524 and 525 are not in manuscript W.
142. This scene is similar to bedroom scenes for couples in other romances, including Erec and Enite, Mark and Isolde, and Kriemhild and Etzel, where either a secret is unwittingly revealed or a desire made known to a sleeping partner.
143. Manuscript W has a large uncial initial "N" (*Nu*; three lines tall) to mark the start of the chapter at 527,1.

[528] She clutched him to her breasts and kissed him a thousand times. "Lord, God in heaven, what have I just heard? Ah, woe is me, poor woman, what will happen to me? A curse on my eyes, with which I first saw you. [529] And a curse on my arms, with which I embraced you. King and sovereign, to whom will you leave me now? I have abandoned," said the queen, "my father and mother for your sake, [530] along with all my family," said the mighty queen. "Should I lose you, I will have no one else. I abandoned all my family, sire, for you. Mighty, noble king, to whom will you leave me?"

[531] Then the Lombard said, "I will place you in God's care and place myself, lady, at your[144] command. However it may turn out for me, if I lose my life or perhaps keep it, there was never a woman I loved more."

[532] Then she said pitifully, "Are you in your right mind? You should reconsider this. Otnit, where are you going? You can ask counts, free men, liegemen for support."

"No," said the Lombard, "I will face the dragon. [533] The dragon came to this land because of your father's deceit. May God have mercy, that I didn't kill him with my own hand, that I ever spared him for your sake."

"May God have mercy," replied the queen.

[534] "He dispatched the dragons to kill me."

"God will have to judge him for us," said the beautiful woman, "that so many Christians were killed because of him. That he ever came to Lombardy,[145] that I lament before God."

[535] "You should console yourself," said the mighty king. "I will quickly return to you, my beloved wife. I have faith that I can avenge my wrath on the dragon."

She said, "I'm filled with fear that you will lose your life, [536] because the dragon is so evil and unholy that no one can survive his malevolence. You have often proven, sir, how skilled you are, but this challenge may bring you years of suffering."[146]

[537] "Here are the precious stones your father sent me. Now he has destroyed my people and my land. He must pay for the destruction he has caused. Wish me luck. I must find the dragons. [538] Don't shed so many tears, my dear wife."

"How can I do otherwise?" said the queen.

---

144. Manuscripts AW read: *in dein gebote* (531,2b). Amelung and Kofler both emend *dein*, "your" to *sin/sein*, "his," i.e., Otnit also places himself "at his [God's] command."

145. Manuscript A reads: *daz er ie kam in Lamparten* (534,4a); manuscript W reads: *daz ich ie chom in Lamparten*, "that I ever came to Lombardy."

146. Manuscripts AW read: *dich möcht wol verdriessen jarlang der arbait* (536,4). Thomas translates the line: "[you] might well avoid this task now" (38).

"The people will know something is wrong if you lament too much. My beloved,[147] my wife, you should tell no one about this."

[539] "So you won't let it be—you are determined to go there, sire?"

The Lombard said, "That is my sole intent."

The queen said, "I must give you up then. I can count the years that I've been lying at your side. [540] It's been six years since I first knew you. My heart has been wounded, not with a sword or a knife. Now that I can enjoy having you, my dear husband, you want to leave me," replied the queen. [541] "May God have mercy that I ever laid eyes on you." He could hear her heart breaking inside her. The queen said, "Sir, stay now. This journey will go badly for you," said the beautiful woman.

[542] "Now you should console me; instead you've given me up for dead."

She said, "You are too intent on realizing your own death."

Just then the morning light shone through the window.[148] He wanted to get out of bed, but she wouldn't let him leave her. [543] As bold as his heart was, he forgot his anger. His eyes teared up because of his great distress. As his beautiful wife took him in her arms, they both started to cry. The tears streamed down their breasts.

[544] "My lady, I beg your leave. I cannot go without it."

"As much as I hate to do so, I must grant it to you. You won't stay here. May God protect you."

"Now let me go, my beautiful wife, with your blessing."

[545] Then he jumped out of bed, put on his clothes, and opened the window above him. The Lombard said, "Whatever people say to you, don't believe it. You should not grieve too much. [546] Queen and wife, give me your ring. Whoever brings this back to you, believe him that I am dead. Whoever brings you this ring has been successful. He will take more of what is mine[149] and has seen me dead. [547] Whoever brings the dragon's head has slain the dragon, or the severed tongue that it carried in its mouth. Whoever brings the head without the tongue has deceived you. Whoever also has the tongue has not lied to you.[150]

---

147. The term here is *freundinne*, which has a range of meanings from friend, to companion, to partner and lover. I have translated the term throughout as seemed best depending on the context. In this intimate moment, both husband and wife look back on their relationship as lovers.

148. Recreated here is a typical scene of a dawn song, *alba*, or *Tagelied*, with the lover leaving at the break of day, and the woman asking him not to go. The main difference here is that the couple are husband and wife and not illicit lovers, and the man is not leaving because he fears discovery by the woman's husband.

149. Manuscript A reads: *der nimet mir etwas mere* (546,4a); manuscript W reads: *der pringet dir diu mær*, "he will bring you the news."

150. This assertion seems to be taken directly from Gottfried von Strassburg's *Tristan and Isolde*. Tristan killed the dragon and cut out his tongue as proof. The cheating seneschal brought the dragon's head to court but could not produce the tongue and so was revealed to be a fraud. Tristan produced the tongue and was hailed as a hero and the true dragon slayer.

[548] Don't believe both of them, most noble queen. Whoever brings you Rose and my bright chain mail armor, along with the dragon's tongue and this little ring of gold, then know that he has avenged me. Stay true to him. [549] He may also bring my helmet and sword. He should by rights be rewarded with your hand. Promise me that you won't take any other husband, no matter how much he bullies you, unless he's killed the dragon."

[550] He donned his battle armor, driven by righteous anger. The woman wept terribly as she fastened his bindings. There at the foot of his bed always lay a small dog that went with him into the forest when he wanted to be alone. [551] He took his leave of the lady, quickly left his chambers, and went to where his saddled horse awaited. His shield was at his side; the dog was behind him.

She said pitiably, "God bless you."

[552] After he had ridden some distance from the castle, he regretted that he had forgotten something. He thought, "I have to go back to the queen. I won't be able to find Alberich unless I have the ring."

[553] She was still standing on the battlement looking after him. She was happy when he returned from such a short journey. She thought he might stay and went to meet him at the moat.

"You think I might dismount. You shouldn't think that will happen. [554] I completely forgot it; give me my ring."

Then the lady said sorrowfully, "With what shall I remember you?"

"You can remember me on many a pleasant night."

The woman cried bitterly and gave him his gold ring. [555] Then he turned away from the castle toward the wild mountain. Underneath the green linden tree he found the dwarf. "Where are you going like that?" replied Alberich.

"I'm headed again into danger," said the mighty king.

[556] "Against whom will you fight? Who has offended you?"

Then the Lombard said, "I'm going to face the dragon."

The little one said angrily, "You must have a death wish. Why is it that you're so intent on hastening your own death? [557] If you want to fight against it, you'll do so without my help. By my faith, whoever goes up against the dragon is a fool."

The Lombard said, "I've made my decision. Whatever happens to me is God's will, for better or for worse. [558] Now I ask you for your help. Give me some hopeful advice. How can the monster be killed?"

"Now grieve," said the little one, "what it will do to you. You'll soon realize what God has presented you with there. [559] But I can reassure you concerning one thing. If you can meet it in battle, you will definitely defeat the dragon. I'm afraid, though, that you won't profit much from this, and if it finds you asleep, it will most surely carry you off. [560] I forbid you one thing. Do not fall asleep! Then I can assure you that you will survive the encounter. May God bless you. Give me my ring, and if God sends you back, it will be yours again."

[561] The Lombard threw the ring down to him on the ground. Alberich's heart was broken over this quest. He said, "Much pain and effort attend to such a thing."

"God bless you," said the big man as he rode away from the little man.

[562] Then he rode aimlessly through the mountains, directed by his intuition and his will to fight. He rode without rest throughout the day and into the night. Even then he didn't think about sleep. [563] Then he dismounted to the ground. He made a fire; he gathered random branches from fallen trees. This made the fire all the more visible[151] to the dragon. He took food and wine from his saddlebag. [564] Then he sat down on the grass. He drank and ate and gave some of it to the dog sitting in his lap. There he had no one else; he was all alone. He sat by the fire until the moon appeared.

[565] Then, wanting to ride on, he quickly untied his horse, and it distressed [him] that he hadn't found the dragon yet. So he rode on without rest through the night until the next day, when he came upon a meadow covered with roses. [566] The warrior dismounted underneath a green tree and would have gladly rested there awhile. Unfortunately he didn't have anything to eat or drink. He had neither food nor wine left in his saddlebag. [567] He had a heavy heart; his body was utterly exhausted. He sat down a bit in order to rest; he wanted to rest just a short while. He was overcome by sleep, so that his head sank down to the green grass.

[568] Sleep posed a grave danger for him; he couldn't stay awake. The dog lay down on the Lombard's lap. Because he was sleeping, he failed to see the dragon. This would cause the Lombard grave harm. [569] It broke through the thick underbrush; it leveled the trees. The dog ran toward the dragon and then back to his master. Even though he barked loudly, the slayer[152] kept on sleeping. The tired man paid no attention at all to the dog's barking. [570] Even as the dog scratched him and bit into the armor rings, he lay there like a dead man,[153] completely unawares. Once the dragon detected the human's scent, it lumbered over in the direction where the tired man lay before him. [571] The dog tried to bite him, since it had seen the dragon. Because of his helmet, it couldn't get to his head. The monstrous dragon stretched its beak forward; its mouth was open wider than a midsized door.

---

151. Manuscript A reads: . . . *ersach*, "saw" (563,3a), which is indicative; manuscript W reads: *sehe*, "would see," which is subjunctive. Kofler and Amelung emend to *ersæhe*. Thomas translates: "so that the dragon could more readily see its light" (39).

152. The original term is *gast*, which can have a broad range of meanings from guest, foreigner, invader, or enemy, to warrior or fighter. The meaning can also be ironic when implying that a certain "guest" is unwelcome. This translation tries to capture his role as warrior and hero given his specific intent to become a dragon slayer within his role as a "guest" in the dragon's territory.

153. Manuscript A reads: . . . *als ein todte* (570,2a); manuscript W reads: . . . *als ein tor*, ". . . like a fool."

King Ontit's Book

[572] [It] swallowed the knight up to both his spurs. That was because it found him there asleep. It wanted to do the same to the little dog. It aimed at it with its tail; the dog barely managed to escape. [573] The dragon hurried to get from the tree back to the rock wall. Out of loyalty to its master, the dog followed it up to the base of the mountain, where it lived with its nest. The dog was afraid and didn't dare go any further. [574] The young dragons inside were extremely hungry. Even though he hadn't been wounded, he was still destined to die. It carried him into a cave to its young. They couldn't get at him and so sucked him out of his armor. [575] Then the Lombard sadly lost his life. His dear wife knew nothing about this in Garda. He was lamented for the honor he had won for the land.

This is the chapter in which Otnit died.[154]

Chapter 8 [576–97]

[576] The dog made its way back home. When the queen saw the dog, she didn't dare show her grief publicly, but she thought to herself, "My lord has been killed."

[577] Those who saw the dog and knew its habits were praying their lord would come riding up behind it. He had to stay where he was, compelled by great misfortune. They would have to wait a long time for him. He lay dead inside the mountain.

[578] They all asked, "Where has our lord gone to? The dog came back alone; maybe he's been killed. He was probably betrayed by the noble queen. She's most likely guilty of his death."

[579] "Good God in heaven," said the beautiful woman. "If you really believe that, then kill me now."

The most prominent men said, "If you mourned his death, you would show us where he is. You know very well where he went."

[580] "What can I say?" replied the queen. "I don't dare show you the way; I gave my word. But before you are angered, and if you won't relent, then I'll tell you where he went. He intended to confront the dragon."

[581] Then all the Lombards began to lament their lord. They all said, "The dragon carried him off. Whoever wants to avenge him should do so quickly. There will never be another Otnit in Lombardy, [582] so worthy and so bold, who could govern the land so well. Our hope and our joy rested in him."

---

154. This typical chapter ending is not followed in manuscript A by a chapter heading or "title" or large initial. Manuscript W, however, does mark the beginning of a chapter at 576,1 with a large initial "S" (*Sich*; three lines high), as it does other chapter beginnings. Thomas and Pannier mark this as Chapter 8 in their translations (for Simrock it's Chapter 9), but of the text's editors, only Amelung indicates an eighth chapter.

They saw how sad the dog was there, and that it tugged at everyone's robes. [583] Whenever someone followed it, it pulled him to the gate. It wanted to point them all to the terrible dragon's tracks.

"It knows exactly where my lord is," said a liegeman from Garda. "Hand me my mail rings. I will arm myself [584] and follow the dog until I can see the path for myself. But as dear as my lord was to me, I still won't face the dragon."

He followed the dog, which knew the way very well. So the dog led the bold man very near to the cave. [585] When he saw how bloody the dragon's footprints were, he decided against riding any further and quickly turned around. He passed on the terrible news that his lord was dead. Sorrow and anguish filled Garda. [586] On account of the great sorrow the queen suffered, and because of her son's death, his mother died as well. She died from the grief of not being able to see him ever again. The noble queen was also bereft of any friends and allies.[155] [587] So they lived[156] in mourning until the third year, and the Lombards took no further notice of her. The handsome lady lost all her fair coloring. They wanted to force her to take a husband [588] who would care for her people and her land, by whom the kingdom might be well governed.

The queen said, "You shall not give me to anyone. I will not take a husband unless he first kills the dragon."

[589] When she refused to submit, the lady was banished. She was left with nothing from her kingdom to support herself except a hundred pounds in copper, that was her annual allowance. Then she learned what misery really is. [590] At the castle in Garda there was a spacious tower filled from top to bottom with treasure. Because she didn't want a husband, they were angry with her. She could make no use of any of it; they took the keys away from her. [591] No matter how much they abused her, she remained steadfast. She made her living with her hands, as many women do. In this she was helped by her maidens and ladies-in-waiting. They worked with their hands in order to support her. [592] The lady lived in constant sorrow day and night. No one cared about the people and the land. Everyone seized whatever he could take for himself. This caused the land to decline in prominence and honor.

[593] Then the margrave said to the queen, "I'm very sorry for your suffering, my lady. Do you want to come live with me?"

The woman said sadly, "I don't care what happens to me. I'm obliged to endure it all, but I won't leave Garda."

---

155. Manuscript A reads: . . . *nimmer freunde* (586,4a); manuscript W reads: *nicht mer vreuden*, "bereft of joy."
156. Manuscript A reads: *sunst lebtens* . . . (587,1a); manuscript W reads: *sust lebet si* . . . , "so she lived . . ."

[594] Then the margrave said, "Your suffering pains me. I want to avenge my lord's death for your sake. I must bide my time until my son grows to manhood, so that I know for certain to whom I can leave my estate."

[595] The nobleman and the margravine[157] cared for her. They sent food and wine to her in Garda, clothing on festive occasions, silver and gold. They remained faithful to the lady all the days of their lives. [596] So the poor woman had to live with grief and sadness. For the one to whom the queen of Lombardy was later given, and who killed the dragon that caused Otnit's death, you'll have to wait a long time still,[158] for he is not yet born. [597] He will have an ill-starred childhood, the one who will kill the dragon. I will tell you his lineage and his father. You see, he was the distant ancestor of Sir Dietrich of Verona.[159]

If you want to hear the story,[160] it will begin straightaway.[161]

---

157. This is the feminine form of margrave, the margrave's wife. An equivalent would be countess.
158. Manuscript A reads: *des müesset lange beiten* (596,4a); manuscript W reads: *des must si lange peiten*, "she will have to wait a long time."
159. Dietrich of Verona, known in German as Dietrich von Bern, was a popular hero of medieval German epic and the subject of many heroic stories. His character is based loosely on the historic Theoderic the Great (454–526), a Migration Era king of the Ostrogoths in Italy and parts of western Europe.
160. Manuscript A reads: *ditz lied das höret gerne* (597,4a); manuscript W reads: *dise leute horent gern*, "people like to listen to this." Amelung emends to the manuscript A reading. Thomas translates *lied* as "story" (42). A *lied*, or song, is not necessarily sung, but can refer to an epic text once oral but later in written form. This is most evident in the two variant endings of the *Nibelungenlied*. Manuscripts AB refer to the *nôt* (downfall, suffering) of the Nibelungen: *diz ist der Nibelunge nôt*; manuscript C refers to the text as a whole: *daz ist der Nibelunge liet* (epic story).
161. In manuscript A, the story of Wolf Dietrich begins immediately following strophe 597 in the middle of the page (fol. CCVvb). Manuscript W ends the *Otnit* text in the middle of the third column (f. 85rc), with thirty lines left blank. A new text by a later hand begins at the upper left of folio 85v, with an excerpt from the *Siebenschläfern* (f. 85va–88va). The first hand picks up again at f. 91r. It is possible that the original intent was to add a *Wolf Dietrich* text through f. 90v directly following *Otnit*, as is the case in all other manuscripts, but in fact manuscript W does not include the story of Wolf Dietrich.

THIS IS THE BOOK OF WOLF DIETRICH

HOW HE WAS BORN AND TOOK THE LADY WHO WAS OTNIT'S WIFE AS HIS OWN[1]

Chapter 1 [1–33][2]

[1] At Constantinople, in Greece, there ruled a mighty king, in whom neither virtue nor honor nor courage was forgotten by his master and creator who brought him into the world. In him there was nothing lacking, except that he was a heathen. [2] The Bulgarian forestland served him because of Greeks. His might had seized it from the Hunnish borderland. Greek kingdoms served him with their might. He reigned at Constantinople and was named Sir Hug Dietrich. [3] Botelung's sister, of the Huns, was his wife. She was astute and a virtuous person, free from all duplicity and falsehood. She gave the Greek three handsome sons. [4] They were loved by the lady and by the mighty [king].[3] For the sake of this great love, they were all named Dietrich. After she had given birth to two sons by the king, an impending military campaign lay ahead for the mighty king. [5] This he completed with honor and gained many heroes. The Greek didn't know at the time that she was carrying the third. He had sworn to undertake the campaign with Berchtung of Meran, who was his faithful counselor and rightfully accompanied him. [6] At the time he wanted to punish his friend, a king, Fruote of the Danish March, his sister's son.[4]

---

1. The book's title heading in manuscript A, in red ink, confirms that the text was meant to be completed. The fragment as it exists in manuscript A, however, ends before Wolf Dietrich marries Otnit's widow, whose name is Liebgart, a fact not revealed until near the end of the story with the heading for Chapter 13, between 523 and 524. She is not named at all in *Otnit* but referred to only as Machorel's daughter or queen or lady. The function of the story as a continuation of the Otnit tale was well established, as was its ending.
2. There is no chapter title, but the text starts with a large illuminated initial "A" (*Auf*) of seven-line height.
3. Manuscript A reads: *der künigin* (the queen; 4,1b), which would make little sense here, given the *auch* (also) in the text. All editors, with the exception of Fuchs-Jolie et al. (Reclam), have emended to *dem künege*. This asserts at the beginning of the story that the king loved all three of his sons, including the youngest who was to become Wolf Dietrich.
4. The motivation for this campaign against a close relative, much less the famous Fruote, who is characterized here both as a *freund* (meaning friend, supporter, ally, or relative) as well as the intended target of an attack (*laid tuon*), is unknown. It plays no further role in the narrative, and the circumstances of the feud are not explained. Fruote is an important figure in *Kudrun*, as a vassal

The mighty king said to Berchtung of Meran, "To whom should I leave my people and my towns, [7] my land and my inheritance, and my kingdom and my dear wife?" said Hug Dietrich.

That most loyal man said, "Who could protect them better? Entrust them to my friend, Duke Saben, [8] all the kingdoms that are subject to you, along with my lady[5] and your dear children."

He summoned mighty Duke Saben to appear. Everything that he had, he put under his authority. [9] Children and kingdoms, his wife and all his land he entrusted to him on his loyalty. That turned out badly. As soon as his dear lord had departed, he appeared respectfully before the queen.

[10] He said to his lady, "Now that my lord has gone, please don't be angry; I want to ask something of you."

She said courteously, "I'm not angry with you. If what you request is appropriate, it shall be done. [11] Should you, however, by my faith, ask for something that would make me angry with you, then I will deny you."

He said deviously, "The request is then withdrawn. I don't dare approach you if you won't promise to refrain from anger."

[12] Then the well-mannered woman said, "The request is allowed. I know you are so faithful that I won't be demeaned by you. My lord entrusted me to you on your loyalty. I know you are so faithful that you won't dishonor me."

[13] Then that most deceitful man said, "I will tell you what I want. You have the right to be angry with me, but I'm not asking for much. I've given up my lord for lost on this journey. He'll certainly never return. So then, let me sleep with you."

[14] The [lady's][6] heart burst with anger. A flood of tears streamed from her eyes onto her breast. She said, "You have broken your faith with me, and should God send him back, I will report this to my lord."

[15] When he heard how upset she was, he acted like a man who can easily turn his speech around with deceit. He said politely, "I didn't want that at all. Don't be angry, my lady. I was only testing you with this. [16] I was testing your fidelity and your virtue. You have a heart filled with chastity and every virtue. What I did with you as a trick you should forgive me. Please don't tell my lord about any disloyalty of mine."

---

and relative of King Hetel who, along with Horant and Wate, rules in Daneland, specifically in the Danish March. He is a fearsome fighter, advanced in years, and a key leader in both bridal quests as a military commander and advisor.

5. This refers to Hug Dietrich's wife, who as queen is by feudal rank Berchtung's lady. See 147,2, where this is explicitly affirmed.

6. Manuscript A reads: *die fraw* ... (14,1a), which is the subject, i.e., she breaks her own heart. Editors (Amelung, Schneider, Kofler, but not Reclam) have emended to *der frouwen*, making the lady the object. This translation adopts the emendation in principle, with her heart as the subject of the verb form *brach* (broke/burst).

[17] She said, "If you said this to fool me, then my lord won't hear about it from me. I promise you this on my faith and my honor as a woman. If you ever say something like this again, it will cost you your life."

[18] Then he could tell from her words that she was not pleased. He thought, "I've just heard that she would never do such a thing. I don't dare make this beautiful woman angry again, and if she tells my lord, it will cost me my life."

[19] Then the time approached when the third child was to be delivered by the noble queen. She was a heathen but still believed in God. When she could, in reverence, she followed his commandments.

[20] She was lying one night in her bed and slept. She hadn't quite fallen asleep when a voice called out to her. "Lady, please wake up, and forgive me for this fright. Since you believe in God, I bring you good tidings. [21] You and your husband are heathens, but you are with child. God's will is that you obey and make the child a Christian."

She said, "How gladly I obey his decree and his command. I place myself in your hands and in your God's."

[22] He said, "These tidings are true, such that you, lady, will bear a child in five days, which your creator has given you beneath your heart. You should not fail to do this, when it comes into the world. [23] About a half mile from here there is a devout man. You should take your child and go to this hermit. You should bring it to him early in the morning, and don't interfere with what he does with the child."

[24] On the fifth morning she was delivered from her distress. When she was able, she did what he had commanded. She secretly carried her little child out of the town and went to the recluse, veiled and unrecognized. [25] She didn't know where to go but still found the right way. He had been living there for more than forty years. When the queen went up to the little hut, this same recluse greeted her kindly.

[26] He eagerly declared her welcome before God. "Your son is to become a Christian. Give the child to me."

She hesitated a long time before handing the child over to him. She was unhappy to see that he was dipping him into the water. [27] Then she saw the glow of candlelight above the water. Unfortunately [she] couldn't see who was helping him with the baptism.[7] He carefully wrapped the child in a silk cloth and gave him back into his mother's hands.

[28] Then he said to the lady, "If you love this child, keep this baptismal gown until he has grown up. I will tell you, lady, what will happen to him because of it.

---

7. Amelung points to the *Dresdener Heldenbuch* (k 8) to explain that she can't see the lights because she is not Christian: *Er sach im wasser scheinen manig kertzen lieh, sie was ein heydeneynne mocht der licht gesechen nicht* ("he could see the light of many candles shining in the water; she was a heathen and could not see the light").

And if you love the child, then do not lose this cloth. [29] When you send him into danger, put this on him."

"But it will be too small for him, I fear," said the woman.

"He will become, when he is grown, a most extraordinary man.[8] However small you might think it is, when he puts it on it will fit. [30] When he wears it into battle, his body will remain unharmed. He will never be wounded by any weapons of war. He will never be killed by water or by fire."

"Then I will gladly keep it for him," replied the woman.

[31] "I will tell you more, which is, how long he will live. Every year I shall confer on him the strength of one man.[9] By God's grace he will live to be fifty years old, and his body will have the strength of fifty men. [32] You should not worry about him. He will often be in danger, and many times it will happen that he will be close to death. And I will tell you more, that he will by his own hand fight for and win a beautiful queen and a land."

[33] She would have gladly worn better clothing, but she was afraid that she would be recognized. This is the first chapter in the story of the dragon's enemy.

The poor queen is living still in Garda in her misfortune.[10]

Chapter 2: How the King Returned and Saw the Child [34–58]

[34] Then the young prince began to grow. His mother cared for him with maternal devotion, as a woman should with her child. As dear as their young children are to women, this one was loved more by her than her other children. [35] She had given him to God and denied him to the devil. The year soon came when the king was to return. He didn't yet know about the young son he had at home. The dear little child grew more and more.

[36] Envoys quickly went out to meet the mighty king. They told him the news, which was marvelous. "Now give us, sire, a reward.[11] You have a handsome son."

The Greek said happily, "I will gladly do so."

---

8. Kofler assigns this line to the queen, not the hermit.
9. Manuscript A reads: *ich wil immer zum jare eines mannes sterke geben* (31,2). This does not include an object, but editors have made emendations to add one. Amelung and Schneider read: *ich wil im ie zem jâre* . . . , and Kofler reads: *ich wil im ymmer zum jare* . . . , both providing a dative pronoun as an indirect object. The Reclam edition translates the added pronoun without including it in the original text.
10. A similar formula, referring to Otnit's widow, appears in two other early chapter endings: 58,4 (ch. 2) and 162,4 (ch. 4).
11. This reward, or *miete*, is the typical messenger's claim to payment for being the first to deliver (good) news.

Chapter 2: How the King Returned and Saw the Child [34–58]

[37] He was loving to his wife and to the child, as was proper. That marvelous little boy was then presented to him. The child was so beautiful that he beheld him gladly, and his heart was filled with joy over what his mother told him. [38] Then the little boy was left standing near the table, where he could run around, as children still do. There out of affection he was handed some bread. Any dog that took it away from him he slammed against the wall. [39] When people saw this, they all crossed themselves.

The old people all said, "May God protect me. Your three and a half years have given you incredible strength."

Many people came there to see that marvelous child. [40] Anyone who saw the child's strength along with his beauty would make the sign of the cross in wonder.

Some said things to the king, as people will talk, that are total rubbish. "Your Majesty, have him put to death. He is a child of the evil devil. [41] You must believe it; he has come from the devil. Where else could he have gained such strength? If you allow the devil to grow up, you will know what trouble is. If he grows to maturity, he will ruin the people and lands."

[42] The king did not want to hear such talk, but then he began to find fault with the child's handsome appearance and wanted to kill him. This put the child's life at risk. Because of these atrocious charges, he wouldn't grant the child his peace.

[43] Then he secretly sent for unfaithful Saben. The king said, "I think that we have not been vigilant. I will lose my honor and the child. Everyone is saying that he's not mine."

[44] Then Saben, that unfaithful man, thought to himself about how he had lied and how that had enraged the woman. His heart had for a long time been filled with thoughts about how he could get back at her for not sleeping with him.

[45] Then he said to the king, "Sire, I will tell you this, what I heard one night as I was sitting with my lady." He said,[12] "'If only the devil would come be with me always!' That very exclamation produced the little child." [46] Then he thought again, "Since I've lied about her, should she tell the truth, I may yet be betrayed."

"You shouldn't mention me in this, that she was so deranged. I shouldn't have said anything; I promised her I wouldn't."

---

12. Manuscript A reads: *er sprach* . . . (45,3a). This is emended in some editions (Amelung, Schneider, Kofler) to *si sprach* (she said), to make it clear that Saben is quoting the queen. This entire passage (45,1–46,4) features clumsy insertions of interior speech in the middle of Saben's direct address to the king.

[47] Then the king said, "I believe the woman to be innocent. But advise us, Lord Saben, how we may take his life. Tell me how the child might forfeit that handsome body, so that [he] goes back to where he came from."

[48] Then that deceitful Saben said, "I can well advise you. Have Berchtung of Meran appear before you. You don't have anyone anywhere more loyal to you. Order him to kill the little child in secret. [49] If it should happen in the open, people are so worthless that they might accuse you of killing the child. You must order him to take his life in secret."

He said, "I will do as you say. You have given good advice."

[50] Then Saben replied, "I withdraw myself from this counsel. You should not accuse me of providing you with this counsel."

He distanced himself from this same counsel because he wanted the two loyal men to come to resent each other.

[51] Berchtung was secretly brought to see the king. The wise old man said, "What sort of scheme is this? Lord, let me hear what's being planned."

The Greek said miserably, "You must kill my child for me, [52] secretly and so stealthily that no one finds out."

The loyal man said, "See here, I refuse any part in this. I will have nothing to do with his death. I would be devastated if anyone should kill my future lord."

[53] The king said, "Now consider this, Berchtung of Meran, that I have no one in my kingdom as faithful as you. Let me profit from the fact that you are known for your loyalty. You must kill the child."

He said, "I will not kill him. [54] The loyalty we have to each other can never be broken."[13]

"You have sixteen beautiful children in Lilienport, hardly yet young men, and a beautiful wife. I will have them all killed unless you kill this child. [55] They should all, of course, by rights be dear to you. I will have them all hanged on your walls, but first and foremost among them I'll kill you."

"I won't give up so much for just one [child]."

[56] The loyal man thought to himself, "It's not worth it. I will do as he commands. He is dead set on this. Before he hangs me, my children, and my wife, if he won't release me from this, I will take his life myself."

[57] Then he said to the king, "If you won't release me from this, then I will surely kill him," said Berchtung of Meran. "Since you won't relent unless it's done, you should command me to do it without witnesses."

[58] There they swore loyalty to each other. Berchtung, however, would rather have been anywhere else. This is the second trouble that beset the child.

The noble queen is living still in Garda in her misery.

---

13. It is unclear who the speaker of line 54,1 is. Amelung has the king speaking the line, but Kofler attributes it to Berchtung as a continuation of 53,4. The Reclam edition does likewise, as does this translation.

Chapter 3: How the Child Was Rescued and Secretly Given Refuge [59–120]

[59] The king said to Berchtung, "I have carefully considered how we can get the child. You will lead the watch tonight. The gate guard will be at your command. He'll let you come and go as you please. [60] I won't allow a chamberlain to remain at the door. When the child has fallen asleep, you should be standing outside. When everyone has fallen asleep in the castle, and my wife is sleeping, then I'll give you the child."

[61] Then that most faithful man did as the king commanded. He made sure that the guard would let him come and go. That most faithful man did as his lord ordered. When everyone in the castle fell asleep, he went up to the bedroom.

[62] There the man and the woman were talking to each other. They were greatly upset because of the child's appearance.

The king said to the lady, "Where did you get this child? You got it from the devil."

"No!" said the queen.

[63] Then the king said angrily, "He should not be left alive. I will disinherit him from receiving even half a town. He will receive from me neither castle nor land. Anything I might leave him would be used for evil."

[64] Then the lady said in anger, "That is as you wish. There are many high-born men who never hold a shield.[14] He will easily console [himself] with regards to your giving. The one who created him will protect the child."

[65] "He will plow and plant, that is his station. Who would leave him his kingdom? He can't even be a king's squire[15] with the way he looks. He doesn't have the character to be king. He'll have to murder people in the forest for their belongings."

[66] Then the lady said in anguish, "Perhaps he'll have a better fate. What God wants to give him, let no man take from him. What will become of him is unknown to you. He will, on his own, fight for and win a queen and a land."

[67] "Do you really believe that?" he said to the queen.

She said, "I had a dream that it will be so."

Then the Greek replied, "If he should be so fortunate, then he can leave all of his third share to his brothers here. [68] He will always have enough land for a kingdom, and if he can win it in battle, then he is certainly clever. By my faith I swear to you and so it shall be, that he will never benefit from an inch of my

---

14. The following debate as to what constitutes nobility pits the notion put forward by the king that nobility is inherently physical in its manifestation, in terms of both property and individual appearance, against the queen's assertion that nobility can be expressed, even earned, through individual action and God's intervention.

15. Manuscript A reads: *er mag nicht küniges knecht | gesein mit seinem leibe* (65,2b–65,3a). Kofler, in a note on 65,2, claims that *kuniges knecht* is a circumlocution for king. This seems doubtful.

lands, [69] nor will he ever receive any part, even if he should live forever. I also forbid my children to give him any part of my land when I die."

"Then God will have mercy on him," replied the queen.

[70] In those days no king would swear an oath which, whatever he pledged in faith, was nothing but the truth.

The lady turned over and fell asleep, and he snuck out from under the blanket. He called softly to Berchtung. [71] He whispered through the door, "Berchtung, are you there?"

The loyal man said quietly, "Yes."

"Do you know if the people in the castle are asleep?"

"Lord, no one is awake. Now hand me the child."

[72] The king was still afraid that his wife would wake up. He reached under the blanket, to her mouth and her body. His hand touched everything that is seen on women. No matter how much he touched her, regrettably she did not stir. [73] Then he went to the bed where the child lay, which he wanted to steal from his dear mother. But he didn't dare touch the little child. He was afraid that if he woke up he would wake his mother.

[74] He thought to himself, "And if the child cries out, then the mother will also start to scream, since she loves her darling, and I will be disgraced. I would rather die. I will kill him right here and give him the dead child." [75] At the head of his bed he looked for his belt, made in the Italian style, and drew out a knife. He said, "If you cry, you wicked child, I will thrust this knife into your heart up to the hilt."

[76] Then he plucked the child out of the bed where he lay. He had the knife in his hand to kill him. God protected the child by letting him sleep; otherwise he would have killed him.

Berchtung called out to him, [77] "How much longer are you going to delay? It's almost day. Give me the child now so that I can take him away before the lady awakens and the morning light betrays us."

The Greek said softly, "Go ahead, take the child."

[78] Loyal Berchtung received his lord and very quietly walked away from the chamber. When he came to the gatehouse, he went on up to the castle gate, where he mounted his horse. [79] He wrapped the child in his rain cloak.

He said to the guard, "If you say anything about me, I will cut off your head and throw you into the moat. If you stay quiet about my departure, that will be to your advantage."

[80] As soon as he was in the saddle, he regretted leaving. The guard placed the child in his lap. He rode across the bridge; the morning light was shining on him. The child awoke right at the castle bluff.

[81] Then he cried out in distress, as a child that doesn't want such a death will do. He said pitifully, "Mother, cover me up."

Chapter 3: How the Child Was Rescued and Secretly Given Refuge [59–120]

The old man said angrily, "I will not, even if you freeze."

[82] Once the morning light and the sun shone on him, he thought about his fealty. He was all alone. When the sun's rays broke through the bright clouds, he had already ridden so far that no one could see him. [83] He avoided the paths and the main road out of fear; he rode with him like a thief through the forest and the fields. By that time the child was fully awake. He forgot about the cold and played with Berchtung's chain mail rings.

[84] As the little child forgot all about his cares, he grabbed at the mail rings and said, "What is that?"

The child never tired of the armor's beauty. The Greek saw this, and his anguish grew even greater. [85] The child's body shone in his eyes like snow. Whenever the child laughed, it grieved the old man. He thought, "If I should kill you, it will never turn out well for me. My heart is so distraught, I think I'll have to die with you."

[86] He took the child to the heath, to a green meadow in an unfamiliar wilderness, where no one was near them. He put him down on the grass, then he drew his sword. For his lord's sake he was prepared to kill the child. [87] He started to look at the sword, and his heart wavered. You have surely heard it and often said it as well: the life God wants preserved, to him will come no harm. His hands wanted to kill him, but his heart would not allow it.

[88] Then he argued with himself: "What's happened to me? I've easily seen a hundred men before me, all of whom I've killed and struck down by my own hand. I must cry out to God that I am now so weak. [89] That I don't dare kill you, where does that come from?" He angrily took the child away from there. He thought in his heart, "God has given you this much. You may be so blessed that you should keep your life. [90] But before I leave you, still you will forfeit your life. I will go to a well to bring about your death. You will have to drown yourself in the water, dear child. The cause of that will be the dazzling roses inside the well. [91] I know that your young age will betray you, that your childishness will cause you to fall in. The well is deep all around, and [if you want], little child,[16] to break off the roses inside, you will certainly fall in. [92] So then I'll watch how death comes to you. If your father is a devil, he will quickly save you."

With grim determination he ran up to where he found the well in a green meadow. [93] With a heavy heart he dismounted to the ground. Still it was very hard for him that the child should die. He set him on top of the well. If the child had reached for the roses, he would have fallen in. [94] It came from being blessed that he shunned the roses. He went from the well down to the

---

16. Manuscript A reads: *der brunne ist tief alumbe und* <u>wilde</u>, *kindelein* (91,3). Editors emend *wilde* differently: Amelung to *wil du*; Schneider to *wilt du*; and Kofler to *wildu*, which is accepted in this translation. The Reclam edition's alternate interpretation of the original text is: "The well is certainly deep, and <u>overgrown</u>, little child" ("Der Quell ist überall tief—und wilde, kindelein").

broad meadow, where he fell down on the green grass just for fun. He paid little attention to the fact that he was there all alone.

[95] Loyal Berchtung was both clever and intelligent. He hid himself and his horse in the thick underbrush. He said, "I'd like to spend the entire day with you, but I'm afraid that if you get bored you'll come running back to me. [96] Still, I'll stand guard with you this one night. You'll most certainly die, now that I've brought you this far. I want to see what great miracle might befall you tonight, and if you survive until morning, then it may likely stay that way."

[97] The child was completely alone, without a care in the world. He was protected by the grace present in many a miracle. He cared for him faithfully; his help did not abandon him. The woman whose breasts he sucked was far away from him. [98] He sat there until evening; the sun had completely disappeared. Promptly the bright moon broke through the clouds. Numerous wild animals went to the well because of the heat. There was no one there to protect the child. [99] Any wild animals that eat food must also have water. If the little child were to survive, then God would have to make it so. Lions, bears, and wild boar ran up to the well. The child sat there in the middle of the field.[17] [100] Whatever animals wanted water, they all had to go there. Last of all a large pack of wolves came running up, as they are known to run when driven by great hunger. They felt hunger pangs but still did not harm the child. [101] They became aware of the child through his human scent. Because of their great hunger, each of the wolves' mouths was gaping at the child. He just sat there among them. Each one of them satisfied its hunger and so didn't eat the child.

[102] They sat in a circle around the child on the grass. Berchtung crept up even closer because of this miracle. He said, "Now I must witness something I've never seen before. I'm amazed that the wolves do you no harm."

[103] The eyes in their heads lit up like candlelight. The poor child was naïve and had no fear of his enemies. He went around to each one and grabbed it with his hands, wherever he saw their bright eyes in their heads. [104] Whatever he did to them, they tolerated. This is how he went around in their midst until dawn. Whichever one tried to resist, he just smacked it down. Berchtung laughed at these marvels through the night until day.

[105] The wise man said sadly, "You have been spared life and limb. These signs must come to you from God's grace. I certainly believe that if you were the devil's spawn, you would have been killed and slain by the wolves. [106] If I was still of a mind to kill you, then I don't want to anymore. I'm afraid I would be

---

17. Manuscript A reads: *mitten under dem geuilde sass das kindelein* (99,4). Editors (Amelung, Schneider, Kofler) emend to *gewilde*, or "in the middle of the wild animals." The Reclam edition and this translation accept the manuscript's *gevilde* (field, countryside).

Chapter 3: How the Child Was Rescued and Secretly Given Refuge [59–120]

sorry, since the vicious wolves have left you in peace. What would I blame you for, that I wouldn't let you live?"

[107] As the morning grew brighter, his reward grew even greater, that is, the poor child on the heath. The wolves went away.

That good, decent man said, "I will spare your life. I will risk my own children and my wife for your sake." [108] He said, "I'd really like to know who protected you. I want to put you to the test, as they do with Christians." He made a cross out of wood and stuck it in the ground. He said, "If you are a devil, then you will break it with your own hand."

[109] He stuck the cross in the earth in front of him. The child was so innocent that he pulled it up. He looked at it from every angle, gazed at it for a long time, and held it in his hands without breaking it.

[110] "I can see the devil will have nothing to do with you. I think you must be a Christian, and that Christ has created you. But if you are a heathen, then I leave that as it is. I will let you live, dearest child. [111] Today we are reconciled; yesterday I bore you ill will."

He picked up the child from the ground and held him in his arms. "Since you stayed alive among these wolves," he said, "you will live a long life," and kissed him on the mouth. [112] "For your sake I will allow myself to be banished, and for you I will risk everything I have. For your sake I will risk my wife and my children, the towns and castles that are under my authority. [113] I well know that this sign is evidence of good things, that you kept your life among these wolves. Even without your father's support, you'll still become a mighty king. From now on you will be called the Wolf Lord Dietrich."[18]

[114] He carried him to his horse, which he mounted with him. His eyes teared up out of fear for his lord. He said, "I would still prefer that you alone should die, rather than that my entire family should forever suffer."

[115] He rode on with these troubles and took his lord to a ranger, who had a little hut where his hunters often had a place to rest when they stayed out too long and overnighted in the forest. [116] Then he rode up to the house and knocked on the wall. The ranger immediately came out to the road, where he dutifully welcomed that most loyal man, since he had often happily lodged in that house.

[117] He said to the ranger, "Good man, where is your wife? I'm going to put both of you to the test. I came to you on account of both your faithfulness. I

---

18. This translation renders both name and epithet as they appear in the manuscript (*der Wolff herr Diettreich*), even though the word order may seem at times awkward or unusual in English. This peculiar word order, with the use of a definite article, may originally have served the purposes of meter or rhyme, but maintaining these variants helps illustrate the variability in the use of the hero's name and byname. It also emphasizes the fact that Dietrich is named "the wolf" because of his affinity with these animals.

want to ask you to do me a favor, and I'll pay handsomely. [118] You can keep this homestead where you've lived as your own, and with whatever you can use from the forest. And the village that goes with it, that will be yours as well, if you keep this handsome child for me. [119] When people ask you where you got the child, I mean, if you found him, don't let anyone know that I brought him here. You must tell no one. You must swear a solemn oath that your wife gave birth to him. [120] You should share with him all the best that you have. My lady, I will reward you if you keep him alive."

They took the child in, and the mighty nobleman rode off.

Now the Wolf Dietrich's third trouble has ended.

Chapter 4: How the Lady Lamented Her Child, Not Knowing Where He Was [121–62]

[121] As the day dawned with great anguish for the lady, she reached into the bed where the child had been lying. The beautiful bright morning cast on her a light of anguish. She searched for her dear child but sadly could not find him. [122] She threw on a robe and jumped out of bed. She looked for her child under the bed and under the bench.

The lady said in anguish, "Ah, woe, that I was ever born! Where am I, God's poorest, to go? I've lost my child." [123] The woman fell down on the floor in agony. Her cries and her weeping were absolutely pitiful. She said, "Where am I, poor woman, to go? How miserable I am! What use is living now? Death, take me away!"

[124] She cried loudly, so that people took notice. Those who were in the castle all came running. Those who grabbed her could not hold onto her. She collapsed between them; they had to give her some water.

[125] She said, "If only I dared blame you, you faithless man, you bastard of a king's bastard. What did you do with my child? Surely he's dead, and it was your doing! You deceitful monster, you know full well who killed him."

[126] "You accuse me falsely," said the mighty king. "Would I have killed my own child? That would be impossible. But if you won't desist, I'll tell you exactly where he went. The one from whom you received him has taken him back."

[127] "What you say is true," replied the queen. "I didn't receive him from just any man. He was yours. You robbed me of him, may God have mercy. When the world finds out, you'll become a laughingstock, [128] and you won't be fit to be king anymore. Where other kings are praised, you will be denounced. And by my faith, because you've taken him from me, for that I will never again come into your bed."

[129] The king then had regrets; the lady was in great pain. He understood her grievance; the woman was enraged. He secretly said to Saben in counsel, "May God have mercy, that I ever saw that child."

Chapter 4: How the Lady Lamented Her Child, Not Knowing Where He Was [121–62]

[130] Saben said angrily, "Berchtung of Meran, he committed a crime against you and the child; he murdered him and took his life. And if you're smart, you will never forgive him for it."

[131] "Ah, woe," said the Greek, "why do you say that? I could barely ask him to do it. If I now became his enemy, that would be a great betrayal. And if you accomplished that, I would gain little honor, whatever I do to him on that account."

[132] "Well, I want to set you straight there," said unfaithful Saben. "He could have spared both of you in this; he could have let him live at least another half a day. No one can speak well of such disloyalty. [133] I give you my word: Berchtung bears you ill will. As much as he may have resisted, he acted as your enemy. He is so unfaithful, Lord Hug Dietrich, that he will never rest until your kingdom is his own."

[134] Then the king said angrily, "Since he proved his disloyalty with my child and aims to do even more, give me your advice on how I might avenge myself and ruin him so he can do no harm."

[135] "I will give you this advice. Send a messenger to him; tell him it is your command that he appear at court. Tell him you want to invest men into knighthood—that's my counsel. He will quickly bring with him the best people he has."

[136] The messenger was sent off to Berchtung in Lilienport. Berchtung agreed on the spot to make the journey to court. He said, "We will be present at my lord's festivities. Come with me, young squires, if you want to be made knights."

[137] He gave away different colored cloth: red, yellow, and blue. He had a hundred warriors he wanted to be knighted. At court he was known as the loyal one, and generous as well, because he would let no one outdo him in this.

[138] Then the wise man thought to himself, "This won't do. If my lord starts to ask questions about his child, then I must have it written down, how he survived, if he should want to be more caring to his child."

[139] Then he found a loyal man who wrote all this down for him, about the circumstances that kept the child alive, from the beginning to the end, every detail, and that he had been named the Wolf Lord Dietrich. [140] Then that nobleman arrived at court and was well received, as a king should always welcome a worthy man. He arrived with such distinction that he pleased everyone.

The king said to Saben, "Berchtung has arrived. [141] Now tell me how we can deceive him in such a way that we can arrest [him]. Berchtung has a great reputation with the people at court."

"Don't allow him to carry any kind of weapon into the hall. [142] Berchtung is so strong, if he defends himself before he's arrested, he will humiliate you and your entire army. And one more thing I will tell you. When he goes to eat and sits down with your steward standing in front of him, [143] tell the queen that she should cry out in front of Berchtung that he killed your child. Both of you

The Book of Wolf Dietrich

should cry out 'To arms!'[19] three times. You should shout it out and make it known to everyone. [144] She should process around the hall at your side. In front of Berchtung's table, cry out for the third time: 'To arms against Berchtung, he killed the child!' Order sixty men in armor to enter and form up next to you."

[145] In the spacious hall the large tables were set up. Fine white tablecloths were spread out on them. Berchtung, the Lord of Meran, was told, along with all his men, to go to the hall to eat. [146] Chamberlains were positioned there to prevent the heroes from having their swords carried in behind them. As soon as each one had found a place to sit, the king, with treacherous intent, asked Berchtung to be seated.

[147] He said, "Berchtung, sit down, noble lord, and serve me. I will have your lady, the queen, seated next to you."

Berchtung thanked him for that. The king quickly went to a room where he found the queen.

[148] He said, "You must avenge yourself, most noble queen. I will point out to you who murdered your child."

The lady said miserably, "Yes, lord, who is that? Truly, both of us have reason to hate him. [149] Will you reveal the truth about who caused my suffering?"

He said, "I will tell you his name. It is Berchtung of Meran. We will arrest him today and then execute him for this."

"You do him a great injustice," said the virtuous woman. [150] "They have given little thought to your honor, those who led you to that nobleman with lies and untruths. You take Saben's lead in everything; he cares nothing about you two. You should not accuse loyal Berchtung of this. [151] Do you know what Lord Berchtung of Meran has done for you in terms of honor and good and every kindness? If he had done nothing more than give me to you, then you should be forever grateful to your dying day. [152] Out of courtesy he came to me in my chambers. He was able to win me from my brother, Botelung. He won me for himself, you see, and then gave me to you. If you won't acknowledge that, why then [153] won't you give Berchtung credit for the fact that you [have] land and castles and your honor from him? If Berchtung and his loyalty alone are lost to you, know that all your honor will come to an end."

---

19. The cry *wafen!* (lit. weapons or arms) was commonly used as a term to alert a military force to impending danger, somewhat similar to English "To arms!" or "On guard!" It was also used in legal terminology as a term for the discovery of a crime, i.e., an announcement to the community that a crime had been committed, as well as for the accusation of the alleged perpetrator at court. Here it could also be translated: "I accuse!" Grimms's *Deutsches Wörterbuch* has numerous examples of this usage in medieval German literature and court proceedings (1902, vol. 27, col. 292, s.v. "waffen, interjection" #3). Further examples can be found at 253,2 and 263,4. It can also be used to impugn or denounce someone, or to curse them (186,1b).

[154] Then the king said angrily, "He committed this murder. No matter how much you've taken his side today, you must exclaim in front of him that he took your child from you."

"No, I will not, by my faith," replied the queen. [155] "I won't do anything that harms his honor or his life. If you're to blame for the child, I will forgive you, so that Berchtung is not harmed in his honor. I will sleep in your bed as before for his sake."

[156] Then the mighty king said, "You can't refuse me in this. I heard you grieving miserably for your dear child. If you won't cry out in front of him, I will take your life."

"I would rather cry 'To arms' five times," said the gracious woman.

[157] Then the king said to the lady, "Prepare yourself accordingly."

"May God know that I do it most unwillingly."

Then [she] tore off her hair bands and tousled her hair. Her coloring was frightful on account of this dreadful burden.

[158] The king exclaimed loudly, and with him the queen, as they entered together through the door into the hall, "To arms against Berchtung! He murdered our child! We cry out to God in heaven and to all those who are here."

[159] The third loud cry occurred in front of Berchtung. The men in armor could be seen forming up next to the king. Everyone sat there and looked at each other. The king had Berchtung arrested along with all his men.

[160] Once Berchtung, that decent man, had been seized, that good man said straightaway, "I am ill-treated here. I believed that my service and my loyalty would serve me, but neither one has helped me in any way here. [161] I must suffer what there is to suffer for my loyalty. Even as loyalty has been broken with me, I will not break mine. Now everyone believes that I killed my lord, but even if I had good news to report about him, I would not tell you."

[162] Loyal Berchtung was thrown into a dungeon. There were none of his men who were not also arrested. Now Berchtung was rightly troubled on account of his dearest lord.

And the poor queen is living still in Garda.

Chapter 5: How the Captive Berchtung Was Brought to Trial [163–215]

[163] Berchtung was held captive along with his heroes. The good queen did her best to take care of them, against the king's will. They had plenty of what was brought to them at table to eat or drink. [164] So they were held captive for four months or more. Berchtung suffered on account of his loyalty. The king commanded throughout his land that everyone who had legal standing should come to court, [165] there at Constantinople, to the plain in front of the city. There he

would convene a tribunal against Berchtung of Meran. He ordered all the lords to travel there, but not to bring any weapons with them. [166] They had to fear the king because he ruled over them. They dismounted to the ground in their silk attire. No one wore any chain mail rings, except for bold Baltram, Berchtung's brother-in-law. The king despised him. [167] He was there secretly, so that no one saw him, to support and comfort Berchtung. The king had asked that he be judged mercifully. Unfaithful Saben was deputized by the king to take his place.

[168] He sat there on his high seat; he had lent him the crown. The king had renounced his royal authority to judge Berchtung.

Saben, that most unfaithful man, motioned with his hand and whispered in the king's ear, "Now pay close attention. [169] If you let him testify, Berchtung may well survive. He's already picked out the best witnesses himself."

The king ordered and commanded his men that no one should help Berchtung with his testimony. [170] Then the men elected to render a verdict sat in the tribunal. Saben told the king to have Berchtung brought forward, with calls and with shouts, as he had done before, and that he should have the queen accompany him. [171] The king wasted no time and rode up to his castle. He quickly ordered the guards in Constantinople to bring the prisoner out into the light, and to bring him to his tribunal in chains.

[172] Then the noble queen said to the king, "Give him credit for his great loyalty. He served you well; you should give him credit for that. Let me talk to Berchtung. I want to see him alone."

[173] Then the king said angrily, "My lady, I will grant you that."

The queen went to see him in the dungeon. Berchtung was brought out of the darkness into the light. The lady greeted him kindly, but he didn't answer her.

[174] "Don't you want to thank me?" replied the queen.

"Why would I want to do that, my dear lady? If I had brought down the whole world I couldn't have been denounced any more harshly. Now I can well see, my lady, that you are unfaithful."

[175] "You should not hold that against me; I did it against my will. Sadly you don't know that your lord compelled me to do this. Whatever I've done, you should forgive me and give me news of whether the child is alive."

[176] He turned his back and offered her no greeting. She said, "If it would honor you, I will fall at your feet."

The lady wanted to fall down on the ground. The old man said, laughing, "I won't leave you lying there. [177] See what you can give me in payment for this: I give you my word that your child is still alive."

She embraced and kissed him [more] than a thousand times. She said, "By your faith, but is he still in good health?"

[178] "You may lament other woes, but you needn't grieve for the child. My lady, I left him alive. But you must not tell anyone. I was able to sleep all the

Chapter 5: How the Captive Berchtung Was Brought to Trial [163–215]

better in my captivity knowing that he was alive. Take this letter. [179] You must keep it for me whether I die or live. And when I remind you of your loyalty, then have it read out loud."

The king called out loudly, "Has he not yet arrived from the dungeon?"

His hands were bound tightly behind his back.[20] [180] He said, "Am I to be bound like a thief caught in the act? As poorly as I'm being treated, it must please my lord. I'm being punished for nothing other than my loyalty. Anything I ever did wrong, I did in his service."

[181] The lord of Meran was led in front of the tribunal. There he had to stand before Saben with his hands tied. They cried out, as they had before, about their child. Though she had cried before, the queen laughed now. [182] The lady was asked to take her seat. The king accused the loyal man of having killed his child.

That unfaithful man, the king's judicial advocate, said, "Do you deny or admit this, Berchtung? Tell us now how you plead."

[183] The old man said shrewdly, "Ah, woe, Saben, my friend, you have risen to the position of king; you should show me mercy. Of what my lord has accused me, I am innocent. I don't dare say anything else. Now give me a man [184] who can be my advocate today with his speech."

Then Saben replied, "Take whomever you like."

He was heartbroken that his hands had been bound. He looked around at all of them. He saw no one [185] who dared stand up for him. He brought no one forward.

They said secretly, "We have been strictly forbidden to do so."

He stood before the tribunal as if he were a foreigner.[21] He said, "As much as I can advocate for myself, [186] no one wants to hear it. Damn[22] my friends, that they leave me alone in my hour of need."

Lord Baltram quickly appeared as an advocate. He was followed by a hundred knights, all in full armor. [187] He dismounted to the ground with a hundred suits of armor. The king was sorry to see Baltram there with so much force. His armor rattled on his body out of anger. He pushed through the crowd in front of the tribunal to get to Berchtung.

[188] He said, "Have you already been found guilty, Berchtung of Meran?"

"No, I stand here bound like a helpless man."

---

20. This is a sign of Berchtung's mistreatment by Saben and the king, as well as the illegitimacy of the tribunal. As will become clear from Berchtung's complaints, noblemen were not supposed to be bound at court. They were honor bound not to escape and to surrender to the final judgment.
21. Berchtung is described appearing before the court as a *vil ellender man* (185,3b). Here the meaning of *ellende* is closer to "foreigner" than "exiled" or "miserable," which is to say that he has no rights to witnesses or support from friends and family.
22. The original is *wafen*, as discussed in the note to 143,3, here as a kind of accusation and condemnation.

He said, "You've been bound, and you didn't tell me? Like a common thief? What is it that you've stolen?"

[189] Then the most loyal man said, "They accuse me of murder. I would like to defend myself, but no one will take my side."

"Ah, woe," said the bold man. "Why then since days of old have noblemen had land?"[23]

Baltram angrily cut Berchtung loose from his bonds. [190] Then bold Baltram of Bulgaria cried out, "Noble lords should forever be cursed and ashamed, that they would allow a decent lord to be ruined." He said, "And if they do this to him today, they will do it to you tomorrow."

[191] They were all happy that someone was willing to help him. They now all stood together with Baltram, who said, "Whoever wants may now accuse me of killing kings and emperors, one and all."

[192] Then bold Baltram said angrily, "From all I've heard about royal tribunals, no trial seems to me as unjust as this one. Your Majesty, no knight or even squire should allow [193] you to defer to Saben, an unfaithful man, who never rose to noble office under Botelung. He never even held the rank of count among the Huns. [That] you should elevate him here above us all is an utter disgrace. [194] Truly, you must listen to my brother-in-law's defense. [. . .][24] You must either bring witnesses against him or defend yourselves. One of you must stand against him, either you or Saben. [195] He will defend himself with sword and shield against the murder charge. Whoever accuses him of this today must prove in mortal combat either that he never intended any such thing or that he is guilty on all counts."

The high and the low ranking alike said, "He is right."

[196] The king whispered, "Are you going to fight him, Saben?"

"No, lord, the child is yours; you must prosecute the murder."

The king said angrily, "These counsels are worthless. I told him to kill the child. I'm not going to fight him over it."

[197] Then Saben replied, "Then you must free him from the charge. We can't lawfully take the man's life. You must say that you declare him to be innocent, even if he did murder the little child."

---

23. Manuscript A reads: *warzuo sol vor zeiten fürsten lant* (189,3b). Amelung and Schneider emend by deleting *vor zeiten*. Schneider goes further by emending *lant* to *hant*. In the feudal system, owning land implied having vassals assigned to hold the property in fealty, with an obligation to support the lord with military, legal, and economic resources or service. Landownership also conferred certain legal rights on the nobility, to include not being treated as a common thief in court.

24. Line 142,2 is missing in manuscript A. Amelung emends the lacuna with the help of the *Dresdener Heldenbuch* to add: *mit swerte muoz er rechen daz ir in zîhet mort* (k 73,2), "he must avenge with swords that you accuse him of murder."

Chapter 5: How the Captive Berchtung Was Brought to Trial [163–215]

[198] Then the king said shrewdly, "Berchtung, I'm very sorry that I've caused you such distress. I don't know if you are guilty, but I will let you go free. Whatever I might do now, the child is lost in any case."

[199] Berchtung cried out loudly, "May God be praised, Your Majesty, that you have thought it over and come to your senses. Unfounded accusations harm those who are loyal. My lady and queen, now let it be known what is in your letter."

[200] Then she looked for it in her sleeve.[25] When she found the letter, she put it in the hands of a chaplain. After he had looked at the letter and broken it open in front of her, he gave it back to the lady once he saw what was written in it.

[201] The lady said angrily, "You're a tiresome man. Now that you've seen the letter, tell us what is in it."

"My eye sees marvelous intrigues therein. Do with me what you will, my lady, but I will not read the letter for you."

[202] The clergy to whom she showed it all did the same, and because of that they resented the king. They did not dare read the letter in front of the king. They thought, "He's angry and would not let us live."

[203] The lady gave the letter to another chaplain there. She said, "Take this letter for my sake." She said, "Come sit here right next to me. Sir priest, now tell me exactly what is written here. [204] And if you don't tell me exactly what is in the letter, I will take away your parish and do you great harm. And you should read it loudly so that it can be easily heard, so that if someone has done wrong, he may be ashamed today."

[205] Then the priest said loudly, "In this letter it is written that our young lord is still alive. Never before has a little child so narrowly escaped with his life."

"That's wonderful news!" replied the queen.

[206] "My lady, it was ordered by our lord, the king, that the little child be killed. He ordered Berchtung to take his life, or else he would hang his children and his wife at Lilienport. [207] My lord stole the child from his bed and gave him to Berchtung, who carried him through the hall. He took him out of the castle. When he went to kill him, he was unable to do so on account of his heartfelt loyalty. [208] He took him to a well with roses growing inside it. He wanted him to drown himself, but he did not do so. If he had reached out for the roses, he would have fallen in. The little child then got up from the top of the well. [209] Without food or drink he sat for an entire day in the rain and wind, and regrettably no one cared for him. Without help of any kind, he sat there like a little orphan."

"May God repay him for that," said the queen.

---

25. It was fashionable in the thirteenth century for ladies to wear dresses with long, voluminous sleeves (*stûche*), such that items could be placed in the folds or inside the sleeve.

[210] "There he sat among the wolves, my lady, all night long. If God had intended for him to die, he would have perished there. The wolves did not harm him. As hard as it is to believe, he still enjoys life.[26] [211] Berchtung was standing close enough to witness these miracles, that these signs were conferred on the child. He picked up the little child from the ground and kissed his dear lord again and again. [212] He said, 'Whatever happens to me, your life is secure. I well know that this sign is evidence of good things. You will not die; you will win a kingdom.' This is why he was called the Wolf Lord Dietrich."

[213] Things began to get hot for Saben under the crown, so that sweat ran down his forehead out of fear. He would have rather been anywhere else.

"My lady, by your leave, the reading of the letter is concluded."

[214] Then the king said shrewdly to Berchtung of Meran, "I arrested you without cause; I alone am guilty of that. I alone am guilty with regard to my dear son. Now avenge yourself as you see fit. Saben told me to do it. [215] Should I live a thousand years in this world, I would not count on Saben for even the slightest thing. He will never again hold my esteem."

Berchtung is once again relieved of his great troubles.

Chapter 6: How Saben Quit the Land on Account of His Great Disloyalty [216–50]

[216] Then the king said angrily, "Now avenge yourself on this man and make him pay for what he did to us. He had three deaths made ready for you. According to the law he should receive in turn what he did to you."

[217] "You should avenge yourself on him," said the queen. "He dug your grave for you; now he should lie in it. Breaking on the wheel or hanging or being burned at the stake,[27] he would have submitted you to all these forms of torture."

[218] Berchtung took hold of Saben and led him away. He was mourned by some only because he was handsome. He showed him the gallows, the stake, and the wheel. He was so unfaithful that no one spoke up for him there. [219] Then Berchtung, that good man, said, "What now, friend Saben? Now you must lie in the grave you dug for me. Your disloyal conduct has landed you there. You don't deserve to have someone plead for you."

[220] Then the unfaithful man said, "If you won't have mercy on me, then I don't care what happens to me. But if you are loyal, then you can easily show mercy. Friend and lord, have mercy on me."

---

26. Schneider attributes this line to either the queen or a third person.
27. All three of these types of execution, or torture until death, were generally reserved for commoners in the Middle Ages. The nobility usually had the option of beheading, which is not mentioned here.

Chapter 6: How Saben Quit the Land on Account of His Great Disloyalty [216–50]

[221] "We have been friends since childhood, and if my lord would allow me, I would gladly let you live," replied loyal Berchtung of Meran. "I would also forgive what you've done to me."

[222] Then Saben replied, "Friend, if you would spare me for the sake of friendship and loyalty, let me swear to leave this land, never to return as long as you live, that on account of your faithfulness you might forgive me for this murder. [223] Do this out of the goodness of your heart and let me live. Take my royal office for yourself, let me and my wife walk away from all my property with nothing but a staff."[28]

"Yes," said the good man, "but your wife has done me no harm."

[224] Then he took his friend and led him by the hand to where he found the king and other noblemen present.

He said to the king, "Let my friend live. I have put my anger behind me; now you should forgive him as well."

[225] Then the king said angrily, "I don't care what you do with him. I say to you that you should be wary of him always. However much longer you let him live will be to your detriment."

"By my faith, he must hang," said the queen.

[226] Then Berchtung said politely, "My lady, forswear your anger. I will restore what you have lost on his account. Grant me this favor, mighty and noble queen, and let my friend live, as much as you love Wolf Lord Dietrich."

[227] Then the queen said, "If you want that I should let him live, then you must command him to quit this land, and to relinquish any role at court. Otherwise it cannot be. I don't want to set eyes on him ever again."

[228] Then the king said angrily, "He must leave this land. [. . .][29] You shall take his lands in fief,[30] along with all the people in them."

"No," said the loyal man. "His wife is expecting a child. [229] I will take responsibility for the lady as long as she lives, and I ask that you not give the child's inheritance to anyone else. I will look after them both. But if the child should die, then I will share with the mother; the other part will be mine."

[230] The deceitful man thanked him for that. He then left the land. He took his leave of the nobility; he left to join the Huns. All of them alike thanked Berchtung of Meran for dealing so well with his friend. [231] Berchtung made preparations and went home to his own land. He gathered up his young lord there where he had left him. He dressed his dear lord in bright clothing, just as

---

28. This could be either a pilgrim's or a penitent's staff, or more generally a peasant's staff. The point is that Saben and his wife will not be riding a horse but rather walking as commoners.
29. Line 228,2 is missing in manuscript A. None of the editors make any emendations to fill the gap but rather point to a similar passage in the *Dresdener Heldenbuch* (k 84,4).
30. The king is essentially taking control of the land and giving it to Berchtung as his vassal, denying Saben his previous position as the king's vassal. Berchtung refuses so that Saben's unborn child might still make a claim to the vassalage when he or she comes of age.

he did with his sixteen other children. [232] Then he returned to court with joy, as noblemen were used to doing then, in noble fashion. The noise and praise for other nobles was nothing in comparison, as he brought the seventeen children back to Constantinople.

[233] The queen received them with great delight. She said, "Now tell me, for goodness sake, where is my child?"

Then the loyal man said, "Look, there he goes, the tallest and the strongest of them all. [234] The others are all at your service and are my children. They're at least nine years older than he is. He's spent his tender years in such a way that he can dare to roughhouse with any of them. [235] I want to tell you, my lady, a poor man raised [him], someone he fought with a lot, so that he fled from him into the forest. When he angered him he would hit the man so hard that, if he could catch him, he would knock him to the ground. [236] The poor man's wife also often had to hide from him. They complained to me that they barely survived. They were never angrier with the devil from hell. They kissed me lovingly when I took him away from them."

[237] His father wanted to give him a hug; he liked him well enough, but the child didn't recognize him. He pushed his father away from him and gave him a firm kick with his foot.

"You're certainly never," said the father, "sitting on my lap again."

[238] Berchtung was thinking about his first journey to court. He gathered together his heroes, with whom he had been held captive.

He said, "Sire, compensate these guests for their injury. They were held captive with me, and I brought them together here. [239] They would very much like to be made knights."

"I will compensate them for their injury," replied the queen.

Whatever knights should have was prepared for them, saddles and shields and three sets of clothing. [240] Sturdy Castilian horses were given to each of them, along with squires, clothing, and forty marks a piece. The festivities lasted a good fifteen days. With this the queen forgot her anguish and lament.

[241] On the fifteenth morning the mighty queen said, "To whom should we give the one named Wolf Dietrich into fosterage?"[31]

Then the king said sensibly, "You should ask Berchtung to foster the boy. He suffered much on his account [242] when he remembered his chief loyalty to him. We should both thank him for that, since no one can foster him better."

---

31. Children of nobility, especially royals, were often given over into fosterage for instruction and tutelage to a relative at around the age of seven. A prime candidate for foster father was the mother's brother, the child's uncle. This would seem to be Baltram in this case, but the king makes a case for Berchtung instead.

"I delivered the young lord back into the queen's hands."[32] That most loyal man said, "Why would he come to me without lands? [243] Whatever you entrust me with on his behalf will not be lost."

The king said, "Truthfully, Berchtung, I have sworn against this. I would gladly give him his third, but I dare not break my oath. That I solemnly swore an oath against it, that is his mother's doing. [244] She said he would win a queen and a land. 'What good is my land to him then?' I said right away."

The lady said angrily, "If he lives until then, he will easily take for himself what we do not want to give him."

[245] Then the king said astutely, "What he might achieve, that should be your concern, Berchtung of Meran. When he comes of age and is ready to fight, I've saved for him a set of armor and a good sword, [246] so he can well defend himself against his enemies, along with a horse that not even the fastest can catch. And if his brothers don't give him what he is rightfully owed, and if he's worthy, then he'll take his part from them. [247] You should help him in this; I place him in your hands for this. Ask him not to be resentful toward his brothers. Ask them that they willingly give him his third part, or perhaps he'll gain all of it, if he's fortunate. [248] After my death I entrust you with everything I have, dear loyal lord. It will be subject to you, so that you can divide it properly between my children. And I commend your lady to your loyalty."

[249] Then Berchtung said astutely, "I will entrust him with my children, the ones I and my wife have by God's grace. My dearest young lord, they will serve you, and I will serve you as well until you have grown to manhood."

[250] Berchtung asked to take his leave, which was granted. He went home with his children to his land and was happy to have saved the mighty king's life.

Now the Wolf Lord Dietrich is freed from one of his troubles.

Chapter 7: How Hug Dietrich Died and Saben Gained Favor [251–309]

[251] Berchtung faithfully took in the dear child and entrusted him to his dear wife, upon her life. He said, "You shall always benefit from the faithfulness you show our future lord as your own child."

[252] Then Berchtung was also very satisfied with all this. He often laughed heartily at his lord's behavior, that he would abide no one in the castle, that he

---

32. Manuscript A reads: *ich gab der künigin den junkhern an die handt* (242,3). All editors (Amelung, Schneider, and Kofler) emend to *im gab diu küniginne*, "the queen delivered the young lord to him." This emendation seems logical, although the note in the Reclam edition (657–58) indicates that the line could be understood as an interjection by Berchtung, since he did indeed give the queen back her son, with 242,4 continuing Berchtung's direct speech, since he appears to be present at the king's and queen's conversation, as is young Wolf Dietrich.

would tussle with and beat even strong men. [253] He was so irritating and tiresome in the castle that they all cried "to arms" against the Wolf Dietrich. Whenever Berchtung wanted to punish him for his misbehavior, [he] actually had to catch him and tie him up. [254] When they tied him up, he only hit him for his own good, so that he had to give up his disobedience all the sooner. He hit him often and hard; the blows hurt him. Whatever he then promised him, he never broke his word.

[255] Death was approaching, as it still often does, meaning everyone must die, whether evil or good, poor beggars or mighty and noble kings. So Hug Dietrich, too, was near his end. [256] Then he entrusted Berchtung with towns and land; all three of his sons and his wife he committed into his loyal hands.

Berchtung of Meran said courteously, "I will have nothing to do with anyone who does not obey me."

[257] So the king was quickly mourned and soon forgotten. Because of that many lands lay in ruins after him. Once the land's solace and support had died and gone, unfaithful Saben tried to regain his lady's favor. [258] Then the land began to suffer trials and mayhem. Ah, woe, that women can so easily be persuaded. She asked Berchtung if he should have her favor. It was to his lady's favor that unfaithful Saben tried to return.

[259] Then Berchtung said angrily, "Do you now want to forgive him, and before you didn't want to let him live? My lady, should he regain your esteem, he will ruin you and your child. He will ruin me and all those who are loyal to you."

[260] Then the queen said, "Should I go against you?[33] The highest men in the land have spoken to me about him and asked that I grant him my favor, if you think it is right."

"You will [regret] it straightaway, my lady, if you do this."

[261] "Since you won't allow me, then I will not do it."

"And if you do it anyway, he will ruin you and your son."

She promised him this and yet still granted him her favor. For that she was forced to give up her staff and guide.[34] [262] After the unfaithful man had regained her favor, he began to direct his attention to Berchtung of Meran, and he began to think about the noble queen, how he could banish her and her dear child.

[263] Then the loyal man said, "Ever since she granted him her favor, he's interested in seeing that I pay with my life. Well, one should never believe a woman. To arms against myself! Why did I not take his life? [264] Whoever

---

33. Manuscript A reads: *sol ich da von ew getreten* (260,1b). Kofler translates in his gloss: "(should I) distance myself for your sake" ("euretwillen Abstand nehmen"). Amelung solves the line by deleting *ew*, essentially meaning "should I step away [from this decision, from his advances]."

34. The term *rechten laid stab/leitestap* (261,4b), or literally "proper guide staff," can refer figuratively to a leader or leading figure, in this case most likely Berchtung.

Chapter 7: How Hug Dietrich Died and Saben Gained Favor [251–309]

spares common thieves and the unfaithful, they rarely change, something I should have considered. Why did I want to save the man who was so unfaithful to me? Now may God have mercy, that I ever spared his life."

[265] Berchtung was quickly banished from the royal counsel. Saben focused his attention on the lady and the children. He conspired with the nobles day and night about how he could manage things, which he quickly did.

[266] He constantly said to the young princes, "You have the right to know, my lords, who you are. Because of your mother's deceit, the third king is a fraud. The one she claims to be your brother is not your brother at all. [267] Day and night she plots against your honor and is constantly thinking of how she might ruin you. Banish her from the castle; she is here to do you harm. And take away everything she inherited from your father. [268] This is why you are hated by the people in the land. The one she claims to be your brother is a bastard. With this your father's honor has been destroyed. May God grant that you succeed in making her suffer."

[269] Both the young princes thought he was telling the truth, and so the woman was utterly ruined by his lies. He also cheated the poor child out of his kingdom. The queen was banished along with her son Wolf Dietrich.

[270] The young princes both said to their mother, "We are most unhappy about one thing in particular. Isn't the Wolf Dietrich supposed to be our brother?"

"Yes, he is, by my faith," replied the queen.

[271] "He is, mother, on his father's side not my father's child. This is what people tell us, those who know about this. We are not able, truly, to stand up for ourselves against you."

The eldest brother said, "You must leave this house. [272] What good is the king's inheritance to you? You are not a queen. That you, despite all this wealth, cuckolded my dear father and us will not be to your benefit. So take up now with the man you took up with before."

[273] The lady said sadly, "Now may it be decried before God that you should accuse me of this. Who told you this? Ah, woe is me, that Saben ever gained my goodwill, and that I didn't listen to Berchtung of Meran."

[274] "God have mercy," said the young man, "that our mother is so immoral and that we ever became your children.[35] If you did not follow him before, then that can now be rectified. Get up and go to Lilienport and follow Berchtung of Meran."

---

35. Manuscript A reads: *Got erparme, sprach der junge, daz unnser* <u>muter</u> | *ist also recht unraine und daz wir ye wurden ewr* <u>kind</u> (274,1–2). Lines 274,1 and 274,2 do not rhyme. Either line, or both, is therefore defective in some way, and the editors have tried to emend appropriately. Amelung: *daz ir unser muoter bint* (274,1b); Schneider: *daz ir, muoter, sint* (274,1b); Kofler retains the manuscript's reading. None of the emendations, however, changes the basic meaning in any significant way.

[275] The lady said sadly, "Ah, woe, my son, let me stay here with you, and with the inheritance that your father left me. If I had had another man while he was alive, I would be deeply ashamed. Even after his death I will not take another man."

[276] Then the king said angrily, "I will tell you what you will do. You will stay here no longer than tomorrow morning. Your valuable dowry belongs to my brother and me. You will never again be queen in this city."

[277] "Now may God have mercy that I ever saw Saben, that I have this struggle and strife because of him."

Anyone she might have turned to, that was now futile; the young princes would not relent in their anger. [278] She was barely able to keep her horse and clothing. Whatever valuables were found in her room, the lady was left with hardly a single mark's worth. She had to travel to Berchtung of Meran as a penniless woman.

[279] She rode pitifully up to the gate entrance. Berchtung was told, "The queen is coming."

He said, "Everything we have inherited is now lost. I believe unfaithful Saben has banished her."

[280] Nevertheless, he went out with his heroes to meet the lady, and along with his wife he welcomed the queen.

He said to the child, "Come here, my lord. You should greet your dear mother along with me."

[281] Then the young lord said, "But my mother is here. She hasn't left Lilienport for a whole year."

He thought Berchtung's wife was his mother; his life was burdened by this notion.

[282] Then the loyal man said, "Truly she is not your mother, and still serves you most gladly wherever you might need it. Truly I also do the same, wherever you have the need. The man who by rights should be called your father is dead."

[283] So both of them remained silent out of sadness. The joy they had felt in their hearts was gone. He had much grief even though he was only a child. He then ran up to the gate and greeted his mother.

[284] Berchtung said courteously to the lady, "What is it that you want, Your Majesty, in my humble abode?"

She said, "We must seek out those friends as we have them. Mine have banished me as Saben told them to."

[285] "May God in heaven reward him for banishing you. He has done to you as you deserve, since you rejected my advice. 'For those guided by loyal friends, that guidance will end happily.'[36] Who relies on someone whose heart is without loyalty?"

---

36. This line (285,3) could be proverbial, and it may include the following line as well.

Chapter 7: How Hug Dietrich Died and Saben Gained Favor [251–309]

[286] "I've been treated badly," replied the queen. "Be mindful of your loyalty and let me stay with you, and let me suffer along with you, sir, whatever happens to you."

"Truly," said the old man, "you will not stay with me. [287] Both your sons have more than I do. Saben has the kingdom; there is little that belongs to me. You didn't listen to me, and now you've suffered the consequences. The one who always saw me as an enemy, you invited him into your home."

[288] Then the noble queen said pitifully, "So do with me as you will; I have no one else."

The old man said politely, "Then you are welcome in God's name. May you be the lady and queen in my own land."

[289] Then the young man said politely, "Lady, you are welcome in my father's house. Whatever I can do for you and however I may serve you, I will do so at any time. I serve you all the more gladly because you are my mother."

[290] The lady fell silent out of sadness and said nothing more. The old man consoled her and took her to her room. The lady was cared for and treated well. The young man could hardly wait until the next day. [291] The old man obliged him to respect him, so that he had to help him get dressed every morning. Whenever he lost his temper with him, he did so out of love, so that service in foreign lands would be all the more appealing to him. [292] On this occasion, in the morning, he stood next to his bed and served him as chamberlains do, until he had made everything ready to go to church. Everything that he needed he had put on.

[293] He wanted to leave the room ahead of him. The young man said courteously, "Sir, please stay here. You will have to do without my services from now on, unless you tell me who I am and from what family I come."

[294] The old man said laughing, "But you are my child. You are surely more loved by me than are your brothers."

"Be still," said the young man. "This is no joking matter. Today you are my father, but yesterday you were not? [295] I wish to ask you, sir—please tell me everything—to what land I should rightly journey to see my father, or where I will find him dead. I want to leave as soon as possible. If I am from a noble house, then I wish to act accordingly."

[296] The old man granted this; otherwise he would have been dead, given that he[37] carried a nobleman's sword under his arm. [Berchtung] said, "Go ask the lady who arrived here yesterday. She knows your family and will tell you the truth."

---

37. This is Wolf Dietrich.

The Book of Wolf Dietrich

[297] He started to leave; he asked nothing more of him. The old man was glad the young man had left him. He left the chamber and departed from his master, but still he[38] said fearfully, "Leave the sword here."

[298] "Truly," said the youth, "I refuse you in this. Find yourself another sword; this one I will carry myself."

He angrily carried the sword in his own hand and went into the church where he found his mother.

[299] He said, "Now tell me, lady, if you are a queen, do you think you know who my father is? Since you are my mother, and I am your child, you should tell me where my friends and relatives are."

[300] "You are so filled with anger," said the good woman, "but still I believe that you won't harm me. I can no longer tell you who your friends and relatives are, except that I am your mother and you are my child."

[301] "But can a child come from a mother without a father?"

"Truly," said the lady, "I've never heard such a thing. A child is of course born with a father and a mother. The father whom you had, though, you have unfortunately lost."

[302] "So tell me where he died or where he lived. And if you don't tell me the truth, I won't let you live."

She said, "Dear sir, you shall do me no harm. You are a king's son on all four sides. [303] Your father and your mother were king and queen. You should also be a powerful king by rights. Your father was a powerful and mighty king in Greece. He ruled at Constantinople and was named Hug Dietrich." [304] She said, "You are educated, so take this letter in your hand."

He found written in it his life and his death, how Berchtung saved him. He read in the letter how he was betrayed and how he was saved. [305] Then he lay his head in his mother's lap. Both of them cried and were deeply saddened. He embraced and kissed her; her clothes became wet. Because of his love for his master, he forgot about the sword. [306] He gave the letter[39] back into his mother's safekeeping and went looking for Berchtung. He left the sword lying there and offered his master the greeting he craved. He kissed his hands and bowed down at his feet.

[307] "May God recompense you, Lord of Meran, my master and lord, for what you have done for me. I have my honor and my life by your goodwill. I want, dear master, to place myself in your benevolent hands. [308] I have properly inquired as to where I come from. It was not right that my inheritance was

---

38. This is Berchtung.
39. The Middle High German term is *tavel* (306,1a), or tablet. This evokes the idea of a wax tablet, such as was still in use in the Middle Ages for taking notes, or, as in this case, writing a letter. However, the previous description (200,3) talks of breaking the letter open, implying a seal, and so we imagine the letter to be written on parchment.

taken from me. God knows, Saben will pay me for his unfaithful deeds, that he banished me and my mother in this way. [309] Now I, too, have grown up and become a strong man. My rightful inheritance must be given to me. I will surely never rest until I win a kingdom."

Now Wolf Lord Dietrich will surely have more troubles.

Chapter 8: How Wolf Dietrich Fought Against His Two Brothers and Defeated Them [310–66]

[310] The old man said sadly, "You have manhood and virtue, but you have too little youth to go with your grown body. It will harm your heroes[40] and your childhood that you strive all too soon for longing and hardship."

[311] The young man said politely, "Whoever wants comfort will seldom seek out distant lodgings. But whoever wants to enjoy a life of comfort in old age will have to strive for prosperity in his youth. [312] You will not dissuade me as long as I am fit. I will endeavor in my youth to achieve what I can. My brothers will be my enemies, unless they hand over our inheritance to me and my mother."

[313] The old man said sadly, "What I say is the truth. I have not been burdened by war for forty years, but now in my old age I must suffer hardship with you. May God have mercy that I ever set eyes on Saben. [314] I will help you against him and your brothers, until they do what is right by you and my lady. If you don't want help, and if you go looking for a fight before you're ready, promise me this, [315] that you won't fight when we go into battle. I would be happy to see it, but it is not yet time. In Greece we have the custom that a man must be fully grown to be allowed to wield a sword, when he is twenty-four years old."[41]

[316] "Be still," said the young man. "If I see you in danger, I would sooner lie dead before you than let you die. I will fight by myself for my kingdom. I give myself permission to do so," said Wolf Dietrich.

[317] "Truly," said the old man, "I don't dare deny you. We will surely return, if God in heaven wants to protect us. The land of Greece will serve us, or we will lose our lives. First you must hear what I will give you in service. [318] Sixteen young men, the dearest I have, they are all my sons and are your subjects. They will all be outfitted in full battle armor as are you, each one of them leading a thousand knights with a banner in hand. [319] I myself will also, dear lord, increase your army with a thousand men in snow-white chain mail rings. I will

---

40. This will be Wolf Dietrich's army, including his liegemen, Berchtung's sons.
41. Manuscript A reads: *er muest volwachsen gar, | daz in iemand schwert erlaube, er hab dann vierundzwainzigk jar* (314,3b–314,4b). Amelung emends to: *. . . ern hab vier und zweinzic jâr*. It remains unclear what *volwachsen* (fully grown) means or how it could be determined, or indeed why twenty-four is the age of maturity for wielding a sword, an age that seems somewhat advanced in terms of a young man's fighting abilities. Most men were knighted by their early twenties.

give you these heroes and a bright banner. They have been carefully selected, and they will not abandon you. [320] They will be ready for you in twelve weeks. Then we will both avenge our injury in anger. It would be unlucky indeed if we could not win a kingdom."

"May God reward you for this contribution," said Wolf Dietrich.

[321] Then the warriors had to prepare for danger. They came to Lilienport on that day as he had ordered, the noble and the bold men whom Berchtung greeted gladly. None of them were missing even one metal ring or one strap.

[322] The young man said happily, "They have come with joy, and should I become their lord, they will all reap the rewards. What any one of them desires, I will not deny him. So which suit of armor will I wear?"

[323] He said, "I would gladly give you your father's sword. Then you would be well protected in battle, but you must release me from this, for it is not possible. God might strike you down if you wielded it against your brothers."

[324] "Truly," said the Greek, "I am also my father's son. But I don't want to inflict any harm on them with the sword."

He ordered that they bring him another bright blade and a good suit of chain mail, which was, however, not quite so strong. [325] He donned the chain mail rings and took leave of his mother.

The queen said, "Please spare your brothers. Don't make them suffer when they are unfaithful. All three of you are children from the same two people. [326] What I have kept for you is not yet right for you, since you are intent on waging war against your brothers."

He said, "If we can defeat them, that would do my heart good. I'm fortunate," said Wolf Dietrich, "that I can fight against them. [327] Nonetheless I will gladly comply with your wishes, mother."

She kissed her dear son and repeatedly commended him to God.

The young lord cried out loudly, "Come out of your hovel.[42] What are you doing inside all day? Are you still caring for your mothers? [328] I have publicly declared war on your brothers. They are gathering enemy forces along the entire border. We are fighting on the side of right; may God reward us for that. They want to deny us the border march with thirty thousand heroes. [329] Now let the flags fly with joy across the field. My lands will be recompensed with dead men. If God grants me good fortune, I will win a kingdom. May we now go on to fight with joy!" said Wolf Lord Dietrich.

---

42. Manuscript A reads: *vil laute rüefte der junkherre* . . . (327,3a). Amelung, Schneider, and Kofler change the speaker to Berchtung by inserting a word: *viel laute rief* (Amelung, Schneider) or *rüeffet* (Kofler) *der alte, "juncherre, . . . ,"* ("the old man cried out loudly, 'young man', . . ."). Presumably Berchtung is addressing Wolf Dietrich. In the Reclam edition and this translation, Wolf Dietrich's speech continues from 327,3 through 329,4 and is addressed to his warriors, although the possibility remains open that strophe 328 is spoken by Berchtung, as an interjection without attribution.

Chapter 8: How Wolf Dietrich Fought Against His Two Brothers and Defeated Them [310–66]

[330] Beautiful Castilian horses were brought out to the men, and flags waved mightily over the heath. There was a great throng there at that place. The spears' shadow could be seen a long way off. [331] They rode with a great force into the middle of Greece. No one deterred them; they went unchallenged.

"Truly," said the Greek, "no one need give me a kingdom. I will burn my part to the ground," said Wolf Dietrich.

[332] They marched openly through the land of Greece. The evening and morning were marked by pillage and fire, up until the fourth day around early morning, when the kings also appeared with a great host. [333] Their army was powerful and strong. They led at least thirty thousand men, at closed ranks, toward the morning star as the day dawned. Both their advanced guards protected them; they saw the two sides moving toward each other.

[334] "You see," the unfaithful Saben said to the kings, "what we have facing us here with Berchtung? He never served your father with such a large army. And should he live long enough, he will cause us great harm."

[335] Then Berchtung of Meran, with exceptional determination, said, "Now we will hold the Greeks accountable. Knights and squires alike may take comfort in this today, that God will always sustain us. We fight for a righteous cause."

[336] The armies on both sides turned to face each other. Those looking for a fight were all made miserable.[43] They crashed into each other; they broke all their lances. They sang their songs of war in both armies. [337] Then fear and desperation grew on both sides. Bright mail rings were turned red with blood, as armies became entangled in confusion. The Wolf Lord Dietrich fought in front of Berchtung. [338] Splinters flew from their hands up into the sky. After the lances were shattered, they drew their keen blades and dismounted from their horses to the ground. They all had to give way wherever Wolf Dietrich was. [339] He slashed an opening and path on both sides. They all met their end, those the young man encountered. The Greek and Berchtung broke through the enemy three times, and whoever he didn't kill was still gravely wounded. [340] He struck some through the helmet down to the sword belt. The ground was drenched with the blood of men.

"Now we must flee," said Saben to the mighty king. "That's the wicked devil; it could never be Wolf Dietrich."

[341] Then bright mail rings turned red from blood. The mighty army had to give way to him because of it, but first he avenged his anger with steely resolve. He waded through dead bodies up to his spurs in blood. [342] Then the heath was empty of all those still alive. Blood poured onto the ground through the bright

---

43. Manuscript A reads: . . . *die wurden alle <u>unfro</u>* (336,2b). Amelung, Schneider, and Kofler emend *unfro* to *fro* (with support from the reading in manuscript k), i.e., the knights and squires are happy to be engaged in battle, whereas the original indicates that they will all suffer from the real brutality of war, stripped of its imagined glory.

mail rings. Many cried out over the young Greek. On that day Wolf Dietrich split the heads of many a man. [343] Berchtung and his lord ran across the field. They wanted to find Saben, but his pavilion was empty. When they couldn't find him they went berserk. They tore down the pavilions and slashed the horses' legs.[44] [344] Of those they found trying to escape, not one survived. They enriched the soil and grass with the dead. Berchtung of Meran himself hunted down the enemy, along with ten of his sons. These were his eleven liegemen.

[345] As both sides fought intensely against each other, Saben rode onto the field along with the kings. They were waiting to see how the grand army would fare, but they could both see that it fled without further resistance. [346] The two mighty kings halted there on the heath.

"Now who are those three," said Wolf Lord Dietrich, "the ones I see standing together there on the lookout?"

"Those are your brothers and the unfaithful Saben."

[347] "They won't get away from us," he said. "After them!"

"You won't be able to catch them," said Berchtung of Meran.

"If only I could get my hands on Saben," said Wolf Lord Dietrich. "For that I would give up the kingdom of Greece."

[348] Even though they tried to stop him, he still rode across the field. The other three then rode away from him at a fast clip.

Wolf Dietrich called out loudly, "Unfaithful Saben, I want to offer you a truce. Stay where you are."

[349] Then the unfaithful man said, "That's not going to happen. I'm afraid of Berchtung and your own unfaithfulness."

The Greek said angrily, "Who gave you the right to deny me my lawful inheritance? [350] Or who gave you authority over my mother? You'll be made to atone for that, and running away won't help you."

Saben replied, "You've been well armed. The [. . .][45] has equipped you with his armor and his good sword. [351] With these, murderer, you will always have what you need. In addition the horse that carried him is intended for you. This bequest is more useful to you than any kingdom."

"I shall have more than that," said Wolf Dietrich.

[352] Then Saben replied, "So ride then, on our life.[46] We offer you and Berchtung a truce and want to share with you, so you receive the best part."

---

44. A cruel tactic that would have made it impossible for the enemy to escape on horseback.
45. Manuscript A reads: *dir hat der* [. . .] *geschaffen* . . . (350,4a). Apparently the line lacks a subject. Editors (Amelung, Schneider, Kofler) insert *künic*, referring to Wolf Dietrich's father.
46. Manuscript A reads: <u>reyte dan</u> *auf unnser leben* (352,1b). Schneider emends to: *rît dar, ûf unser leben*; Amelung to: *reit dan, ûf unser leben*. Kofler retains the manuscript reading. Schneider clearly objects to Amelung's emendation from *reyte* to *reit*, commenting with a *so!* in parentheses (1930/1968, xxviii), and inserting the imperative form instead (*rît*).

Chapter 8: How Wolf Dietrich Fought Against His Two Brothers and Defeated Them [310–66]

Berchtung said, "What arrogance![47] He doesn't want your truce."

[353] There followed a long, heated argument between them. The one side then turned around and the others rode off. Saben called out loudly, "I'll tell you what you should do. Hero, if you're bold enough, wait here for us until morning."

[354] "Truly," said the Greek, "that I will not do."

He gave his horse free rein but couldn't catch them. When he couldn't overtake them, even though he was a mighty king,[48] the Wolf Lord Dietrich shed tears of anger.

[355] Then the brothers-in-arms returned to the field of battle and finished off the enemies they found there. The young man said angrily, "And if you agree, my master, we should wait here for the enemy until tomorrow."

[356] "I would advise against that," said Berchtung of Meran. "In the morning they'll bring an army of more than a thousand men, who are all in armor and will cause us great harm. I believe that we're both in for a great deal of misery."

[357] "Don't lose your courage so quickly," said the Wolf Lord Dietrich. "I will either lose my life, or I will win a kingdom."

The old man said angrily, "Shall I tell you the truth? Those we brought to this battle have all been killed. [358] I led sixteen of my children into battle for you. They died at your side; there are only ten left. Do you want to face an entire army with only twelve men? Fight with whomever you want, but I think you have only eleven liegemen left."

[359] "May God in heaven forbid," said Wolf Dietrich, "that they paid such a heavy price for my poor kingdom. Such great injury should not befall my subjects. I won't believe they're dead unless you show me first."

[360] Then the wise man took his lord by the hand, and there he saw the dead men. He recognized them right away. When he saw how disfigured their faces were, he fell down on each one. He could not speak out of anguish. [361] Then he took off their helmets; they had been mortally wounded. Overlooking none of them, he kissed each one on the mouth. His heart was broken; his eyes were moist. Berchtung totally forgot his own children because of his lord.

[362] Then he pulled the young man away from his children and said to his lord, "Where is your self-control? Do you want to weep over the men who have been taken from me? They were my children; let me lament them myself."

[363] The Greek said sadly, "I regret that I am still alive. As long as I was alive, you would have given your life for mine.[49] I would give up Greece and every

---

47. Amelung, Schneider, and Kofler emend the original *hoffart* (pride; 352,4a) to *hovewart/hofwart*, which Kofler translates as "court dog" or "courtyard dog" (Hofhund).
48. Manuscript A reads: *Da ers* nicht mocht erreiten noch der *künig* reich (354,3). Amelung and Schneider emend to: *dô er sîn . . . noch der künege*, meaning "He couldn't overtake him or the mighty kings." Kofler agrees with half of this emendation by adding the plural *e* to *künig*.
49. Manuscript A reads: *hest du mirs gegeben* (363,2b). Kofler explains in a note that *mirs* should be expanded to *hetest du mir si gegeben*, which could translate to: "you would have sacrificed them

other kingdom if my brothers-in-arms were still alive," said Wolf Dietrich. [364] "Since you lost these noblemen because of me, Berchtung, dear master, avenge your anger on me. It's my fault that you lost your children. You have permission before God to take my head. [365] You should kill me for God's sake, since I wish that it be done."

He wanted to plunge his own sword into himself. The old man quickly saw that he was dead serious. He grabbed the sword away from him and threw it to the ground.

[366] He said to his lord, "Enough of this grieving. Let the woman who carried them inside her weep over them."

The young man said, "There is no lament that can equal my pain. Now I really do have troubles," said Wolf Lord Dietrich.

Chapter 9: How Wolf Dietrich Lamented His Liegemen, Berchtung's Sons [367–96]

[367] The old man said angrily, "Let your grieving be. The children belonged to me and my wife. Help me now look after myself, and let's let the anger be. Whatever we might do about it, they'd still be lost. [368] Help for us both is not completely lost without them. Other people will come of age for us, and other years will come. It does us no good to cry over the children. They will not come back to life, those who have died. [369] I tell you," said the old man, "if you want to follow me, then follow me with all your resolve. I will advise you best. I will be ruined along with you, or you will win your kingdom."

"I will do as you command," said Wolf Dietrich.

[370] "I tell you," said the old man, "if you cry over the children who have fallen here in your service, if you continue to cry over them, I will no longer serve you."

"So then I will laugh with you instead," said the noble king.

[371] "We must abandon this field of battle," said Berchtung of Meran. "You have only eleven liegemen left in this world. We must retreat with them; it is time to flee. A thousand knights are coming for us; we can't match them."

[372] The young man said sadly, "Must I leave your children unavenged, those who died alongside me? To whom should I leave my comrades and my liegemen then?"

"We can't constantly boil with rage," said Berchtung of Meran. [373] "I tell you," replied the old man, "if we stay here until morning, there will be so many

---

[Berchtung's children] for me." The Reclam edition is a bit less clear on its meaning, translating the passage literally as "you would have given yours for me" ("hättest du deins für mich gegeben").

Chapter 9: How Wolf Dietrich Lamented His Liegemen, Berchtung's Sons [367–96]

of the enemy that no one could escape them. Now we must retreat to our castle; that is the sensible thing to do."

"I retreat most unwillingly," said Wolf Dietrich.

[374] "It is essential that you retreat; we have no defense. You've probably heard the saying: 'two are masters against one.' There may be a thousand coming, and they will all fight against you. So why do you want to kill yourself and me? [375] We must retreat into the forest," said Berchtung of Meran. "You can't survive with eleven comrades against a thousand men, and besides we don't even have a single undamaged shield."

The Greek said sadly, "I will do as you wish."

[376] "Then we should go," said the old man, "to the castle in Lilienport. We perpetrated a great slaughter among the Greeks."

"I don't care," replied Wolf Dietrich. "Even if they never bend the knee, Constantinople and all the Greeks' gold would still belong to me."

[377] "I tell you," said the old man, "I have enough to sustain a hundred knights at table. I can give you plenty of that for five years at Lilienport. If you want more than that, you'll have to provide it yourself. [378] As long as the rations last, the food and the wine, we'll be safe from being taken by storm by the enemy. If they don't besiege us, then we'll foray into the kingdom."

"On the castle walls is where I want to die," said Wolf Dietrich.

[379] They stayed off the roads[50] throughout the night until the next day. The old man led the way; he took care of his children. They climbed up the mountains, which were fairly high, and Berchtung was plagued by the mail rings he wore.

[380] "You can't keep up with me," said Lord Dietrich.

"I wouldn't care about what happened to me, if only you had a kingdom."

"Be still," said the young man, "and look closely. I see a fire flickering. I think that's the enemy army. [381] Before I ride into Lilienport, if they aren't good friends, then they'll have to be attacked."

"Truly," said another, "I see a light there, too. If that really is the enemy, then not one of them will survive."[51]

[382] "In fact, I will die unless I see who they are."

He leaped into his armor as if it were child's play, climbed down from the high bluff and was off, so that his eleven liegemen could hardly keep up. [383] The tree stumps and the ditches seemed to him like nothing. He started the battle

---

50. Manuscript A reads: *si bewagen sich der genge* (379,1a). Kofler glosses the half-line "they avoided the paths" ("sie mieden die Wege"). The Reclam edition translates: "they took the road" or "they went on their way" ("Sie begaben sich auf den Weg"). The infinitive form is *bewëgen*, a strong Class Va verb, meaning "to avoid" or "to give up" (see, e.g., 393,2).

51. It is possible that Wolf Dietrich speaks this line, but only Hagen's edition (1855, 121) indicates this.

before they could arrive to help. Berchtung's sons all together jumped down from the bluff after him. The enemy feared him as many a mail coat rang out. [384] Even before they all joined up to do battle together, Wolf Lord Dietrich had already given them a terrible fright. They abandoned their armor and their horses by the campfire. They feared for their lives and escaped through a marsh. [385] They found fifty Castilian horses left standing there, and the eleven liegemen took eleven of them. Wolf Dietrich took the twelfth one there, but they left some marvelous suits of armor to the enemy.

[386] The old man said sadly, "We should ride toward the castle. Tomorrow we'll find guests[52] there; we won't be able to prevent that. I won't be able to make use of any of my lands. We'll be surrounded in the castle before daylight tomorrow."

[387] They were set upon that same day,[53] but still they arrived in Lilienport. The guard instantly recognized his master's voice, and his lady could hear him from the ramparts. She counted only ten children on the other side of the gate.

[388] She asked the eleventh one, "Berchtung, where is our lord?"[54]

The old man said sadly, "This is all that is left to us. The ones who have died can't be lamented enough. Keep your composure, my lady. Wolf Dietrich is still alive."

[389] She said most pitifully, "Where are my children?"

The old man said angrily, "I know very well where they are. They've paid for the heartbreak their deaths have caused. I'll throw you off the wall if you ever think of them again. [390] What the two of us ought to lament, he will do so by himself. Now comfort my lord. We must care for him, so that he can forget the children's death with our help. I'm still beset with grief that he cried out so loudly over them."

[391] So the lady obeyed him and forgot the children, but hidden away in secret her eyes would shed tears. The lament in the castle became unbearable, and no one lamented more than Wolf Dietrich. [392] So everyone's grief lasted until the fifth day. Finally they stopped lamenting the dead, whom no one can awaken.

---

52. This is a good example of Berchtung's dry humor, casting the inevitable enemy siege as the arrival of "guests."
53. Schneider and Kofler emend the original *heute* (387,1a) to *harte*, meaning "vigorously."
54. Manuscript A reads: *Berchtung wo ist unser her(r)* (388,1b), written with a line or backward hook over the "r." This should be read as a suspension mark, i.e., a sign for a missing letter (see Bäuml, 30; Reclam, 683). The mark indicates a correct reading of *herr* (lord), as it appears in the Reclam edition. Amelung, Schneider, and Kofler have written the word as *her* (Kofler notes *her'* in the manuscript apparatus). The manuscript consistently writes *her(r)* for "lord" and *heer* for "army." Amelung and Schneider consistently write *hêr* for "lord" and *her* for "army." Kofler and the Reclam edition consistently write *herr* for "lord" and *heer* for "army." This would seem to indicate that Amelung and Schneider take the word to mean "army," i.e., "Where is our army?" Kofler hedges and is undecided, since he writes neither *herr* nor *heer*, but in this case *her*.

On the fifth morning there arose a loud noise. The mountains and valleys were occupied and filled [393] with the terrible enemy; the castle was surrounded. They had to abandon hope of finding any way out of the castle.

The guards cried out loudly, "Wake up and be on guard. The fields and mountains are full of the enemy."

[394] Then the lord of Meran shuddered in his bed. He went to the window and recognized some of the men. Many of the attackers were wearing foreign helmets. He was shocked when he saw so many foreign guests.

[395] Then he went over to the bed where his lord was lying, and he wakened him gently. "Get up, it's daytime. Your brothers have surrounded us; now we will suffer. Five thousand or more are encamped in front of my castle."

[396] Then he threw a blanket around his bare chest. They stepped up to the window and saw the great force encamped outside the walls, the two mighty kings.

"Now I really am troubled," said Wolf Dietrich.

Chapter 10: How He and His Eleven Sons[55] Were Besieged [397–445]

[397] "Be still," said the old man, "and keep your composure. No one should behave badly because of his misery. A man should also not be overjoyed by his blessings. No matter what we might do, it will be what it will be."

[398] The young man said angrily, "Since God has granted that they come so close, I will risk my life and honor for my kingdom. God will not let me perish," said Wolf Lord Dietrich.

[399] Those in the castle prepared themselves for battle, but their gate remained unbarred the entire time. They let down the drawbridge and went out past the gate. What they had craved inside the castle they found outside. [400] As large as their force was, the numbers were still uneven. Wolf Dietrich was often victorious. There was a great deal of agony from the heavy fighting. The enemy rarely fought without leaving twenty dead. [401] In this way many of the guests were brought low by the hosts. I[56] won't even count those who were wounded. The hosts beat back the invaders completely, and none of them came close enough to storm the castle.

[402] Then a truce was arranged, as well as a day for negotiations. Saben and Master Berchtung were the mediators.

---

55. Kofler emends the original *sune* to *dienstman*, since it is Wolf Dietrich who has eleven liegemen, not Berchtung, who has ten sons.

56. The only first-person narrator's "I" in *Wolf Dietrich A* until strophe 507, after which it is quite frequent.

"I will give you the best advice," said unfaithful Saben. "You should follow it if you want to stay alive. [403] Berchtung, I advise you, if you value your life, to surrender your young lord and the castle to the kings."

"May God in heaven prevent that," said Berchtung of Meran. "He has relied on my loyalty for much too long."

[404] Saben said, "The two kings have both sworn an oath that they will not quit the field until the castle has been taken. You and your lord and all your children will be hanged on the walls, along with everyone else in the castle."

[405] The old man said sadly, "I have to be prepared for that. Still, I will lie dead with my loyalty and honor intact."

The truce came to an end. He rode back inside and reported the conversation to his dear lord. [406] What the kings had sworn they carried out. They besieged the castle up until the fourth year. The young man's regrets grew along with his suffering, that he should die this way. He was tired of being so inactive.

[407] He grew wiser from his troubles, as intelligent young people do. Early one morning he stood in front of Berchtung. Wolf Lord Dietrich said most pitifully, "No one can win honor or a kingdom with idleness."

[408] "So tell me," said the old man. "What do you want me to do now? If I knew how I should accomplish it, I would gladly help you."

The Greek said sadly, "May God protect you. It will be as God wills it. Sadly I must leave you."

[409] The old man said angrily, "You don't know where to go. If you come up with such schemes I can't support you. The bird that leaves its nest too soon may well not succeed, and so it will be with you, my lord."

[410] The Greek said politely, "My feathers are long and have grown; they don't seem weak to me. I'm the strongest and biggest of all of you. As my troubles bear down on me, I easily grow in awareness. [411] Permit me to go."

"Why are you doing this?"

"Am I to perish here with you?"

"What would you rather do?"

"I want to save you and your children, who have suffered trouble and fear because of me."

[412] Then the loyal man said, "What were you thinking, that you should want to start something you can't finish? And that you're considering this, that really is unwise."

"What good is something left untried?" said Wolf Lord Dietrich. [413] "I want to ride across the world, to every land, until I hear of a king somewhere on this earth so renowned and mighty, in whose service I will enter, that he can help me assert my rights against my wicked brothers. [414] If he helps me defeat them, then I will be his liegeman. I want to receive a share of the land from his good graces."

Chapter 10: How He and His Eleven Sons Were Besieged [397–445]

"God only knows," said the old man, "you will ride for many a day. I don't know of any king who would be able to help you."

[415] "Stop," said the Greek. "How can that be? I won't believe it until I've seen it for myself. What good is life to a child without free will? If you know of anyone, tell me where he might be."

[416] "Since you won't let it be," said Berchtung of Meran, "if you want to look for help, then I know a man who, if he weren't so far away, would save us here with an army."

"He's the one I will look for, even if he is across the sea. [417] You should tell me about him and where his land lies."

"It is called Lombardy, and he is called Otnit. There is no king his equal; that's how mighty his army is. He took a wife by force from a king across the sea. [418] He knows about everything in valleys and mountains. A dwarf helped him win that same queen.[57] Whatever the king wants must be done. Whatever he opposes cannot withstand him."

[419] The Greek said politely, "So allow me to go. Even if I did not have to do this, I would still want to go there, to see the king of whom I hear such marvels told."

They regrettably didn't know that the dragon had carried him off.

[420] The old man said astutely, "This journey is too difficult for you. You won't find a road or a clear path anywhere. You'll often come to see that I'm telling the truth. You'll have to ride for six weeks without seeing any lands or people. [421] It is called the Romanie and has neither lands nor people. You will find neither acreage nor fields that have been sown. If you go down this road, my child, you will regret it."

The young man replied, "Lord and master, help me."

[422] "That's why I must," said the old man, "refuse to let you go. You won't be able to feed yourself along the way. Wild lions roam around like shepherds of the flocks."

"You can't frighten me," said the young man, "with animals."[58]

[423] "Since you don't want to stay," said Berchtung of Meran, "then I will gladly give you what I've been keeping for you: Falcon, the very best horse your father once rode. He often fought for victory in many a great battle. [424] His helmet, his armor, his shield, and his sword, these I have kept for you, if you want to have them now."

---

57. Amelung and Schneider reverse the first two lines (418,1–2), since the knowledge of valleys and mountains applies more to Alberich than it does to Otnit.
58. This statement refers to his early trial with wolves, which is to say that Wolf Dietrich recognizes that wild animals will do him no harm.

"This shield, truly, will never be seen around my neck. Why should I carry this? I don't yet have his noble office.[59] [425] I will choose a shield myself," said the young man. "I will face all the wild animals with supreme confidence. The ones I kill will hardly be missed. I will carry the victory[60] over whichever one can defend itself the longest. [426] I want to swear oaths to this effect, or lie dead instead. For the sake of its honor, I will always help its fellow species out of every danger, and swear loyalty to them."[61]

The old man said sadly, "May God keep you for me. [427] And if you don't want to stay, my dear lord, go quickly and take leave of your dear mother."

Then they both went to where he found his mother. The old man said sadly, "Your son wants to venture out into the world."

[428] "May God in heaven prevent that," said the queen.

"A man should travel far and wide,[62] my dear mother."

She said, "My son and lord, to whom will you leave me then?"

"I will entrust you to my master, Berchtung."

[429] "May God preserve your life, my dear child. What I have kept for you, I will give you now. Now I must forever bewail my suffering, to my great injury." She said to the young man, "Hand me my coffer." [430] Her heart was filled with emotion as she found the clothes. She said to her dear child, "Now take this gown."

As much as she cried there, his eyes did not shed tears. He looked at the gown. He said, "Mother, what am I to do with this? [431] I would much rather take a hard, bright suit of armor. Give it to whomever you like, mother. I don't want it."

"You should have faith in it, son. It's for your own good, since you want to ride out all alone. You're still so childish."

---

59. By the middle of the thirteenth century heraldic devices had become fairly common on shields, banners, surcoats, and to some extent helmets. These emblems represented the bearer's identity, either by family name, region, or affiliation with a particular institution, such as the military orders during the Crusades. In Wolf Dietrich's case, he cannot yet carry his father's shield presumably because it carries the heraldic emblem of the king of Constantinople.

60. Manuscript A reads: *des sigk wil ich tragen* (425,4b). Amelung, Schneider, and Kofler emend to *sigel* (sign), i.e., the heraldic crest he will choose for his shield.

61. This animal turns out to be, somewhat predictably, the lion. Perhaps the most famous knight to have developed a special bond with a lion is Yvain, or Iwein in German. In Chrétien de Troye's story, Yvain rescues a lion from a dragon, and the lion goes on to become the knight's faithful companion, much like a loyal hunting dog. It seems quite likely that this theme is borrowed here, but the lion is not further developed in any way in *Wolf Dietrich A* (see 600–601).

62. Manuscript A reads: *er sol vil vast wallen* (428,2a). It is unclear whether the referent of *er* is God or some unspecified person or man, or Wolf Dietrich himself. Kofler translates: "a man must travel a lot" ("der Mensch muss viel reisen"). Schneider emends *er* to *ich*, thus alleviating the referent problem. The Reclam edition takes a different approach, interpreting *er* as referring to God: "He (God) should vigorously desire [it] and travel along" ("Er soll kräftig wollen und mitwallen"). There is in any case a strong possibility of a play on the words *welle* and *wallen* in 428,1–2.

[432] "But I'm much too large a man for the gown. It won't fit me anywhere, in length or width."

She said, "So give it back to me if it hurts you anywhere. If you've ever loved me, then let me see how it fits you."

[433] Then he minded his mother and took it in his hands. He thought it would be too small for him, the gown. He slipped into the outfit, and it became larger for him. He said, "So tell me, mother, is it any good for fighting?"

[434] She said, "It wouldn't have been in my coffer for so long otherwise. Neither fire nor water nor anything else can do you harm. Wherever it reaches you can never be wounded, and you will be kept safe and sound from all weapons. [435] You have put on over your heart the protection of grace. This is the same gown in which you were baptized. You should believe in God, then you will win your kingdom."

"May he see fit to protect me," said Wolf Lord Dietrich.

[436] Then he had his father's battle armor brought to him. His mother wept as she fastened the straps for him. They all despaired of the bold and noble warrior and believed that they would never see him again. [437] When everyone in the castle sadly became aware that the young lord intended to go on this questing [journey], old and young alike could not stop crying. No one was more saddened by it, though, than his eleven liegemen.

[438] The old man said to the young one, "Think about our years together. Once you are among strangers you will forget all about us. In your innocent youth you may fall in love with a woman. Then you will care little if we lose our lives."

[439] "You have little faith in me," said Wolf Dietrich. "If someone gave me the most beautiful woman and a thousand kingdoms, along with all the lands and castles in the world, I would never marry before I rescue you and your children."

[440] "Give me your promise on this," said Berchtung of Meran, "that you won't break it."

He swore an oath, which he pledged on his sword, an oath he kept always. As often as he might have done so, he never broke his oath.[63]

[441] "I tell you," said the old man, "I'm very poor, but I have saved thirty marks of gold for you. If God sends you to some proprietor's lodgings, you will at least have some comfort at first. [442] Don't stray from the right path. Your horse is incredibly fast. On your saddle hang two flasks, and on the other side a bag full of hunter's provisions. When all that is gone, then may God provide for you. [443] I can't come to your aid on the other side of the gate. Ride as God shows the way; you alone have taken this on. When they ask you for information as you ride past the gate, say, 'I'm a guard who is supposed to stand watch here

---

63. This refers to his future meeting with the sea queen (470–505).

The Book of Wolf Dietrich

tonight.' [444] They might want to seize you, but weak you are not. You can defend yourself against all of them."

When his horse had been brought to the courtyard, everybody there ran away because of their great grief. [445] Out of grief no one wanted to look at anyone else. His eleven liegemen kissed him often. They threw open the gate; their grief was immense. So he rode across the drawbridge, his little children left unprotected.

Chapter 11: How His Sword Broke on the Dragon, and It Carried Him into the Mountain [446–505][64]

[446] As he quickly rode away from the castle, his people looked out after him. They were heartbroken. He turned toward the enemy like a noble warrior. Wolf Lord Dietrich will now definitely have his troubles.

[447] There were a lot of questions about who he was and where he came from. He said to the watchmen, "I'm guarding the entrance to the castle. It was just now opened; Wolf Dietrich and his eleven liegemen are trying to escape."

[448] Then he rode past the enemy, and no one seized him. Whoever got in his way anywhere along the path, however, was gravely wounded and asked him nothing more. He was dead and carried away, having never moved from his post. [449] Then he rode alongside the forest the whole night through. He kept watch against the enemy by himself, alone. That day he sent them at least twenty dead men back to the army. When they realized this, they fled without offering any resistance.

[450] "May God have mercy," said unfaithful Saben, "that we were all so terrible at keeping watch that Wolf Dietrich escaped from us. He may yet win his kingdom on his own."

[451] Then he returned to the road the next morning. He wanted to head to Lombardy; that is the direction he took. He rode on briskly the whole day until evening, but suddenly he became disoriented, which he would come to regret. [452] Then the evening forced him to stop from going on. Of what he had taken with him, he ate only a little bit. He could do no more out of exhaustion, as still happens to some. As much as sleep tormented him, though, he got no sleep at all. [453] Then he made a fire, which cast its light throughout the forest. He gathered the scattered tree branches by himself. In his inexperience he tried to

---

64. This chapter division is likely misplaced and would more properly fit after strophe 446 and its formulaic final line. Amelung and Schneider both emend the manuscript to place the heading there. The substance of the heading is also incorrect, as it refers not to the following section but rather to the final episode in Chapter 17, beginning with strophe 596. In fact, the headings for Chapters 11 and 17 are virtually identical. The manuscript's illustrator painted a dragon with a broken sword on its back in the margins here (fol. 212v), based on this incongruous heading.

Chapter 11: How His Sword Broke on the Dragon, and It Carried Him into the Mountain [446–505]

catch some wild game. He would have gladly stalked something, but nothing came into view.[65]

[454] On the third day he continued on. As much as he suffered on the journey, he never forgot to think of Berchtung, his master from Meran. He often commended his eleven liegemen to God. [455] The royal[66] warrior rode until the fifth morning. He avoided taking the road and path entirely. He saw plenty of game in large herds, but his horse began to tire, which distressed him greatly. [456] Then his great hardship began to affect him. He was denied all the things that brought him joy. He was burdened by a great weight, which he couldn't avoid, because he had to travel through the wilderness, absent any path.

[457] "May God have mercy," said the Wolf Dietrich. "I'm squandering my entire kingdom here in this forest."

He took off his armor and threw it down on a tree stump. With a sad heart he departed from there.

[458] "Ah, woe," said the Greek, "how can I save myself? Exposed like this, how can I protect myself against the enemy? My father's inheritance is of no use to me anymore. To whom shall I leave you now?" said the noble king.

[459] Most pitifully he fled from the bewildering terrain.[67] Over tree stumps and rocks he pulled his horse along. He would have gladly found some relief from his fatigue. He traveled several long stretches[68] next to his horse on foot. [460] He hit it several times with sticks and switches, but the horse collapsed from hunger and exhaustion. He wasn't able to revive it, no matter how much he struck it. His horse was so precious to him that he carried the saddle himself. [461] He fastened it securely on his own back. He came to a mountainous area, where the sun shone down on him. There he heard a voice that sounded out loudly, and mountain and valley echoed in reply. [462] There has never been such a ghastly call.

"I believe this must be hell," said Wolf Lord Dietrich. "But regrettably I don't have anyone who can tell me more about it. It will be as God wills it. I'll just have

---

65. Manuscript A reads: *da versuochte er vil des wildes durch seinen tumben sin | vil gern het ers bestanden, dhaines bestuond aber in* (453,3–4). Kofler takes this to mean that he is searching for an animal as his armorial crest. This is doubtful. It is just as likely that this refers to some attempt to kill an animal for his meal that night.
66. The Reclam edition keeps the original *künig degen* (455,1b), translated as "king's offspring and warrior" ("Königsspross und Krieger"). Amelung, Schneider, and Kofler emend to *küene degen*, or bold man/warrior.
67. Manuscript A reads: *hart barmikliche er von dem geswerbe floch* (459,1). Amelung, Schneider, and Kofler emend original *geswerbe* to *geserbe/geserwe* with the meaning "armor," i.e., Wolf Dietrich is leaving his armor behind (which he somehow later has with him again). The Reclam edition translates the original *geswerbe* with "confusion" or "turmoil" (Geschwurbel).
68. Manuscript A reads: *wol dreier raste lange* (459,4a). The term *raste* denotes stretches between rests. The phrase would literally mean "three long stretches of travel between rests," with long being an indeterminate time or distance.

to go there myself. [463] I believe the devils are here beside me; I hear Lucifer crying out along with all his children."

He led his horse down the bluff to the valley below. They both fell down several times on account of their hunger and thirst.

[464] The Greek said sadly, "May God grant me a path to find the devil. As meager as my defenses are, believe me, I will face the devil. If I must die, then it will be here."

[465] He climbed down the bluff; he saw some water there. "To arms!" said the Greek. "What a monstrous stream."

The monstrous hell and the devils he found there were the waves of the sea pounding against the cliffs. [466] He made it down to the beach, with falls and tumbles, to the even ground down at the shore. There stood a green linden tree; underneath it was a meadow, where the flowers and grass were as high as his belt. [467] The roses and the clover gave off a sweet fragrance.

"Ah, bless me," said the Greek. "No matter what happens to me, God has provided a pasture all around here for my horse. I'm relieved now that it has something to eat. [468] We're not going to leave this meadow. Now I want to sleep here, on my saddle bow. Should I die of hunger, I'd rather lie dead here than on the bare ground. This grass is as red as roses. [469] Since I've found this green linden and the meadow, and I can hardly ride or walk on account of hunger pangs, where better to die? It's so wonderful here."

The Wolf Lord Dietrich fell asleep amid longing and troubles. [470] Thirst and hunger almost cost him his life. A monstrous woman, with skin made of scales, came up from the ocean depths. She looked just as if she were the devil's bride, [471] completely covered with long strands of seaweed, the kind that grows in the water like a strange grass. She had a long beard hanging from her chin to her feet. As ugly as she was, still she offered a tender greeting. [472] She was covered in slime and wet all over. Her hair went down to her ankles and beyond. Her eye sockets were far apart and as deep as two fingers, to where the eyes are. [473] Her mouth was like a large vat, her teeth elongated. Her feet were like a shovel; her walk was grotesque. Her forehead was long and broad. When she awakened the noble man, he would suffer for it.

[474] She stepped over the Greek and took his sword from him. She said, "Now no one knows what it is you wanted. You quest for adventure," said the wild woman. "It would be a wicked person indeed who took your life now. [475] Being so young, you have wonderful arms and legs. If I knew you were a nobleman, I would gladly give you peace."

She quickly hid his sword—she was good at that—and then she hid herself in the hollow of a tree.

[476] When the Greek awoke and didn't see his sword, he wrung his hands and said pitifully, "God knows, thieves were here, right next to me. If I came upon something that wasn't monstrous, I might still survive."

Chapter 11: How His Sword Broke on the Dragon, and It Carried Him into the Mountain [446–505]

[477] Then he sadly took his letter into his hands. All his troubles he found written there. The woman listened quietly until he had finished reading everything written about him in the letter.

[478] After the Wolf Lord Dietrich had read about all his troubles, the mighty queen spoke from inside the tree. With a serious demeanor the queen said, "Who gave you permission to lie here and make yourself comfortable?"

[479] He quickly looked around. When he spotted the lady, he dropped the letter from his hands out of fear. The Greek said fearfully, "What harm is it to you? I was completely exhausted when I was attracted to this place. [480] You may speak to me with gentle words, and give me credit for doing you no harm. Is this green linden tree and this meadow yours?"

"Yes, it is mine," said the queen.

[481] "Don't be angry that I slept here, and help me regain what's rightfully mine. I've lost my sword. It was taken out of its sheath while I was lying here."

She said, "I'll gladly help you however I may be helpful. [482] If you had a friend, that might improve things for you. I can well see," said the woman, "that you are somewhat confused. Now tell me," said the woman, "what is it that troubles you so? You have a stout heart but yet you [lie] here practically dead. [483] It would be a real sin if you were to perish. I trust I could help you if only you thought more highly of me."

"I'm not confused, not in mind or in body. Hardship is to blame that I appear so feeble. [484] God, if I'm to die, then please make it quick. I might recover, however, if I had some food and wine. It wouldn't take much expertise to cure me. Thirst and hunger have taken away my strength."

[485] "I know very well what sort of balm your heart needs. I could easily cure thirty thousand knights myself."

The Greek said sadly, "She's a friendly woman.[69] And if you believe in God, then restore my health."

[486] "I really don't care if you lie here dead. You'll have very little help from me unless you tell me who you are."

"My father was a Greek and a mighty king. He ruled at Constantinople, and his name was Hug Dietrich. [487] My wicked brothers have now banished me."

"I have in fact heard this," said the queen.

"I've lost all my heroes because of them. They have also besieged my eleven liegemen. [488] I will never recover if they're killed in Greece."

She said, "If you follow my advice, they will be delivered from danger. What your friends counsel you will not lead to ruin. If you want to be revived, do what I ask of you. [489] Take me as your wife, and I will give you three kingdoms."

---

69. Manuscript A reads: *si ist* ein gehewr weib (485,3b). Schneider emends to *sist du*; Amelung to *sistu*. Both would mean: "if you were a friendly woman," thus solving the clumsy shift in address from the second to the third person and back again.

"No, I cannot, by my faith," said Wolf Dietrich. "Let me die here now; I don't care what happens to me. The evil devil's mother will not enjoy my embrace. [490] Don't be angry that I so quickly refuse you. I've forsworn you and all women till the day I die. If you become angry, how will I then be saved? Even if I took every woman, I would still have to refuse you. [491] The devil from hell would probably come to the wedding."

Her little mouth grew three times larger out of joy. She stepped back, and the lady became more beautiful. She slipped out of the scales and threw them on the ground. [492] She outshone all other women like the light of the sun. The beauty of all young women was nothing compared to her. He forgot hunger and thirst on account of her beauty.

"I think," said the Greek, "that a woman has never pleased me more. [493] My spirits have been raised, you please me so much. Now may God in heaven have mercy that I can't have you. Please sit down, my lady, for God's sake, and comfort me."

She said tenderly, "Tell me, what is the matter?"

[494] "I have sworn an oath, oh lovely lady, that I would never take a wife until I rescue my eleven liegemen."

"I tell you," said the lady, "if you value your life and if you defeat your brothers, then you must give me one of them. [495] If I only asked for you, my lord, then God would not allow it. You will take another wife. But let me take your brother with me down to the ocean floor. I will show him a thousand wonders every day. [496] Everything the sea covers is under my authority, in addition to some thirty lands above the waves. I will give him power over all goblins on land and in the sea, along with all the wonders of the sea. What better life could he have?"

[497] "Truly," said the Greek, "I will give you my brother. You can rely on my loyalty without any doubt, that is, if I can defeat him, noble and beautiful lady."

The queen said, "I ask nothing more of you. [498] I know of something edible that's useful and beneficial, and it will do your body and your mind good. You can easily take it with you in your satchel. It won't be a burden to you; it is neither food nor wine. [499] If you promise me faithfully, then you'll remain free from troubles. Don't give this nourishment to anyone unless they are faithful. I will tell you about this root. It has such wonderful properties that when you consume it, you will be as strong as a lion. [500] Your head was lying on it. There is much of it in the world, but one should be careful with it."

She led him to the tree where she had seen the root. She taught him how to recognize it, wherever he might see it.

[501] After he had put a bit of the root in his mouth, "Ah, how wonderful," said the Greek. "Now I'm well again. There is not even an ounce of infirmity left in my body. All my strength, my lady, I have back again. [502] You must advise

Chapter 12: How He Defeated the Robbers in the Forest [506–23]

me, my lady, since you are so faithful, how I can restore my mount to its full strength."

She said, "You can give it a piece of the same root, and it will regain its strength and be cheery and hale."

[503] This was done immediately, and his horse regained its strength. He saw that his steed was once again in a spirited mood. As thin as it was, it still carried him away from there.

The helpless man was delivered from his troubles.[70]

[504] The Greek said courteously, "My lady, do you perhaps know what road to take to get to the land of Lombardy?"

"You won't find any road. Ride along the seashore and you will soon see Lombardy. May God grant you good fortune there. [505] Take care of yourself, my lord. There is no peace in that land, where once there were courts that could hang and execute. You won't lose your way again," said the mighty queen.

Now the Wolf Lord Dietrich is relieved of his troubles.[71]

Chapter 12: How He Defeated the Robbers in the Forest [506–23]

[506] From there he proceeded through the green forest as the lady had instructed him, on the various paths close to the sea through the wild land. The paths and roads were completely unknown to him. [507] That's why he often got lost, as I have gathered.[72] On the fourth morning the bold man entered a dense wilderness. There he heard a loud weeping; a beautiful maiden had been taken there by force. [508] There were fifty robbers in the area, who had caused a great deal of destruction in the forest. They plundered the land across the fields and on the roads. The people of the land knew all about the harm done. [509] The bold man

---

70. Hermann Schneider's edition (1930/1968) ends here, with what he considered in his edition's subtitle to be the "true" text (*Der echte Teil des Wolfdietrich der Ambraser Handschrift 'Wolfdietrich A'*).
71. The Reclam edition notes that this may be the end of the original fragment, with a continuator taking over at this point who added another 101 strophes. The style differences are clear and obvious, including much shorter chapters, greater use of formulaic fillers (especially with authorial comments; see next note), and a gross lack of concern for narrative logic.
72. Here begin the many authorial "I/we" interjections unknown either in *Otnit* or *Wolf Dietrich* (with only two exceptions: O 597,2a; WDA 401,2b). The use of the authorial first-person singular or plural is formulaic and repetitive: *als ich(s) vernomen han; als wir das han vernomen; als uns das ist gesait, als uns das ist bekannt; als wir hören sagen*, etc., almost always in the second half-line, and interchangeable as required by rhyme.

The Book of Wolf Dietrich

arrived there all by himself. Ah, woe, there was courageous fighting here among the combatants.[73]

When the robbers saw him coming their way, each one of them said, as we have gathered, [510] "There's a man coming who's wearing a suit of armor. You should all know that I want it for myself."

Then another one replied, "As strong as he may think he is, here in the wilderness he'll have to give up his horse."

[511] "So give me the helmet," said the third one there.

The fourth one said, "Then I'll be happy with the sword."

Whatever anyone wanted to have was divided up this way. When the bold man saw them, he charged through the woods. [512] The noble man was eager to go after the robbers. Sword, shield, and spear were quickly made ready. Those who sat by the campfire and had made the maiden scream, he slew twenty-four of them, as we have been told.

[513] The others ran away, but they had been wounded. The maiden was set free that very minute. She ran up to the bold man and thanked him.

She said, "May God repay you, you wonderfully bold man."

[514] Then he dismounted, that wonderfully bold, strong man. He lifted the noble maiden up on the horse in front of him. He proceeded through the wilderness, as far as we know, to a peasant farmer whom he found nearby.[74] [515] He gave the lady over to him, as we have gathered. The bold man proceeded onward from there. No one told him anything; he knew nothing about what the people and the land were like. [516] Wherever he rode among other people on the roads, they were so miserable that no one asked him anything. No one asked anything.[75] This is how he entered the land. King Otnit's death was unknown to him.

[517] Early one morning the bold man happened upon a very narrow path that took him into the woods. He was troubled by that. The forest was very dense, since there was virtually no open ground or grass there. [518] This is why he often got lost, as still frequently happens. The noble and bold lord had nothing to eat. Throughout the land, wherever he made camp for the night, he was always cared for, as we have gathered. [519] Then the bold man rode all day, so that he ate very little in the forest. As evening was approaching, the bold man found a peasant farmer, as I have gathered. [520] He helped him with some food

---

73. Amelung alone changes the original (plural) *von den recken* (509,2a) to the singular *von dem recken*, meaning that the courageous fighter was Wolf Dietrich alone, as robbers would not normally be referred to either as *recken* or as courageous fighters.

74. This passage is reminiscent of the formulaic scene where Berchtung takes Wolf Dietrich to peasants in the forest for safekeeping (115–20), and it will be repeated at the end with a lady who has just given birth (573–76).

75. Amelung emends the original *da fraget auch niemand* (516,3a) to *dô fragete er . . .* Kofler emends to *da fraget er . . .*, the insertion of *er* (he) meaning that no one asked Wolf Dietrich anything (516,2), and he didn't ask them anything either.

and asked the bold man what he'd been doing in the forest all day, that he had come to him so late. For the first time he told him the story, as we have gathered.

[521] He said, "I came from Greece into this land, and I wanted to get to Garda. So tell me now where I can take the right road from you to there."

He said, "My dear lord, I can easily show you."

[522] The peasant went out with him into the woods. He pointed out the road to him, that exceptional man. Then it got dark. That he didn't stay there will always make me wonder what drove him on. [523] But he proceeded through the wild terrain and the mountains. He began to make his way to the Garda lake and anxiously rode through the forest the whole night.

Now the Wolf Lord Dietrich is relieved of one of his troubles.

Chapter 13: How He Heard Lady Liebgart[76] Lament Her Dear Husband [524–55]

[524] He could hear the sound of the Garda lake; the night was dark. He heard the watchmen making noises and a queen grieving woefully. He hurried along, before the new day dawned. [525] Then he dismounted from his horse and led it through the woods. The bold man heard the grieving again. He thought, "If you are being held captive, I will save you."

It was Otnit for whom his beautiful wife grieved. [526] At that time he was unfamiliar with the castle and the land. The noble man suddenly rode up to Garda. He quickly tied up his horse, as we hear it told. He made his way to the wall and heard the lady grieving.

[527] She grieved pitifully; her grief was great. "Now I'm here in Garda, bereft of all happiness. Heavenly emperor, what did I do to you, that you took my dear husband from me? [528] He won me by force far away in Muslim lands. I know nothing about any of my kinsmen.[77] I was a Muslim woman and he a Christian man, until I accepted holy baptism for his sake. [529] Now I have to be without him; this I lament to Christ, who has power over all the world."

Here the mighty queen lamented lamentably; Wolf Lord Dietrich heard it next to the wall.

[530] "Since I've lost my dear husband, and God has conferred such suffering on me, I will throw myself down."

Here Wolf Lord Dietrich was standing ready with his shield, when a lady-in-waiting held the mighty queen back. [531] She had secretly followed her there. She was devoted to the queen and completely loyal.

---

76. This is the very first mention of Otnit's wife's name in either *Otnit* or *Wolf Dietrich A*.
77. In manuscript A these two long lines (528,1–2) do not rhyme.

The Book of Wolf Dietrich

"Lament your dear husband modestly, my lady. Almighty God lives still, and he can well recompense you."

[532] "How can I be recompensed for my dear husband? I think there could be no more worthy man in all the world. He said that in all the world there was no one his equal, except for one man from Salneck whose name is Wolf Lord Dietrich. [533] He is a powerful man there in Greece. He is served mightily by fields and many forests. When Otnit, my lord, last rode away from me, what great tales he told about that bold man."

[534] Wolf Lord Dietrich spoke first there at the wall. "Moderate your lament, mighty queen."

The worthy woman was ashamed and wanted to leave. He asked her to stay, for the good name of all women.

[535] "You should let me know for whom you grieve. Who was that most courageous man whom you lament so much?"

She thought it might be her lord, Otnit, her dear husband, who had asked this in order to test her. [536] Tears from her eyes fell down to the ground. They wet his hands there in front of the wide hall. The night was not so dark; she saw the bold man below. The queen felt immense joy.[78]

[537] "Is it you, my dear lord?" said the good woman. "It is because of my poor service to you that you test me so.[79] It's time you show yourself and save me from my suffering, mighty King Otnit. [538] Now Count Hermann wants to make me his wife, but in your days he was subordinate to you. Think, sire, how that would make you look, and save me from this menace, most virtuous man. [539] Now I must suffer great adversity daily, so that in the end I would much prefer death. Someone wants me as his wife who once held office under Otnit. Almighty God in heaven, may this be lamented before you.

[540] "Since my Lord Otnit last left me, I've had no one who has supported me. So I'm always beset by sorrow and sadness. They give me only a hundred pounds in copper of my money.[80] [541] Then with difficulty I have to make do for the year. What my ladies and I can earn with our hands is my annual income

---

78. Manuscript A reads: *da het die küniginne sich freuden gar <u>bewegen</u>* (536,4). Kofler glosses the passage: "(the queen) lost all joy" ("alle Freude verloren"). This is exactly the opposite of the Reclam edition translation ("da begann die Königin, sich maßlos zu freuen"), which is adopted here. The question hinges, as before (379,1a), on the correct meaning of the verb *bewegen*. The weak verb basically means "to move" an accusative object, whereas the strong verb can mean either "to choose" or "to give up on" someone or something (see *Mittelhochdeutsches Wörterbuch*, eds. Gärtner et al., 2007, vol. 1, col. 749–50, "bewegen, swV." and "bewëgen, stV.").

79. Manuscript A reads: <u>das</u> *hat mein armer dienst getan wider deinen leib | daz du mich so versuochest* (537,2–3a). Amelung and Kofler emend *das* to *was*, making this a question: "What was it about my poor service . . . that makes you test me so?"

80. The measure of weight was consistent, but value depended on the material: gold, silver, or copper. The amount is the same as stated in *Otnit* 589,3b.

Chapter 13: How He Heard Lady Liebgart Lament Her Dear Husband [524–55]

from which I must live. Sweet God in heaven, may he soon relieve my suffering. [542] Remember, sire, when I first lay with you. How your bold body gently took mine. For your sake I undertook a most arduous journey. You should remember this, scion of noble lords."

[543] "I am not your lord. I am an exiled man, who has never had a land or people or inheritance. I was banished through no fault of my own. Nothing was left to me except my shield and spear, [544] along with my horse and saddle. With this I must make do. I am an exiled man in this land. I would gladly lament my great adversity to you, lady, but your grief for your noble husband's death is much greater."

[545] "Why should [you],[81] courageous one, complain to me about your suffering? In many lands they have much to say about me. They say in this land that my husband is dead. This is why I endure sorrow and privation here in Garda."

[546] "So tell me, queen, how do things stand with him?"

"Sir, I sent a well-armed man out of this house to avenge his righteous anger on the dragons. Because of that I have lost my dear lord."

[547] He said, "I have come here on a quest for adventure. I have properly heard your lament, my lady. I will avenge you against the dragons, or like him they will have to carry me off. Your grief moves me to great compassion."

[548] "I would advise against that," said Lady Liebgart. "My Otnit, that gentle man, had the strength of twelve men. One of the dragons pulled him into a cave. You should stay here and let me alone grieve for him. [549] How do I deserve," said the good woman, "that you should risk your life on my behalf? The journey to the dragons through the woods is difficult. I want to advise you, noble sir, to stay here."

[550] Then the noble knight said, "That will not happen. I will prevail over them in the end, if I find them in the woods. Since [they][82] commit murder, they will have to pay with their lives. You should wait for this news, most virtuous woman."

[551] He then requested leave to go; she asked him to stay. "Tell me, noble knight, by what name are you called? Reveal yourself, bold man, for the sake of your virtue, so that I can better pray to God for your honor."

[552] He said, "My queen, that cannot be. I must first go to the forest to live or die."

He went to his horse; may he always be praised for that. Fully armed, he jumped into the saddle without using a stirrup.

---

81. Manuscript A reads: *was möcht ich, ellensreicher* (545,1a). Amelung and Kofler emend the original *ich* (I) to *ir* (you), i.e., the queen questions why Wolf Dietrich should lament his own suffering, as opposed to Liebgart questioning her own complaint, which she continues. I have adopted this emendation. The Reclam edition retains the manuscript reading.
82. This word is not in manuscript A. All editions insert *si* (550,3a).

[553] Lady Liebgart said through many tears, "Ah, woe is my lord; this is the same as his journey. Are you trying to test me even more?" replied the good woman. "May God in his mercy preserve your life."

[554] He paraded with his horse in front of the moat, and without delay, as we have gathered, he bowed before the queen and hurried to depart. The virtuous woman sent many a blessing his way. [555] Then he turned away from the castle, to the deep woods down toward the Etsch. There the bold man found the right road, which he took.

Another chapter of Wolf Dietrich's quest is now completed.

Chapter 14: How He Found a Dead Knight Who Had Been Left by the Dragon [556–72]

[556] Along the Etsch he rode into the mountains as fast as possible toward Trento. There were miners located there at the time, and the poor men informed him of their great suffering.

[557] "May God welcome you, sir, here in this land, if God in heaven has sent you to help us. A wild dragon has done us much harm. It has killed at least five hundred men here. [558] You should help make things right, highborn hero. May you be chosen as the ruler and lord of us all. It took King Otnit away from us. He was still young in years; he was praised far and wide."

[559] There were shields brought forward, truly, laden with treasure for the bold man, as we heard tell.

"You can keep your riches," said the worthy man. "It is God's will that made me undertake this journey."

[560] The noble knight stayed there until the third day. He and his horse were well cared for there. They served him diligently; that was certainly proper. Many a knight and squire did so with goodwill.[83] [561] One day around *none*,[84] the man was now rested,[85] he began to inquire about the wild forest. He asked them to show him the dragon's tracks. They pointed him to the rock wall in the sea lake.[86] [562] Wolf Lord Dietrich took his leave of Trento, and the praiseworthy

---

83. It is unexplained how knights and squires came to be among the miners.
84. This is a Latin term used in canonical time. It is the ninth hour of the day after dawn, or sometime around 3 p.m.
85. Amelung emends manuscript A's *man* (561,1b) to *mân* (moon), meaning that it was the afternoon and the moon was resting, i.e., not seen. Kofler does not comment on or note this emendation. It is noted in the Reclam edition, but without comment.
86. The word *Mersê* (561,4a) is capitalized in manuscript A, but it does not correspond to a known place-name. It could simply mean "lake by the sea" or "sea lake." All editions capitalize the word. Amelung emends . . . *in dem Meersee* to *bî dem Mersê*, indicating that the cave is near the lake but not in or on it.

Chapter 14: How He Found a Dead Knight Who Had Been Left by the Dragon [556–72]

hero quickly rode across the heath. He turned onto a road into the wild forest. There, in fact, he found a dead man.

[563] He had just before been left by the dragon. He dismounted to the ground; he was deeply saddened.

He said, "Ah, woe, sir, your plight troubles me greatly. You are most likely of noble birth; your clothes are made of silk. [564] You are certainly from a princely family."

He found two small, precious rings on his hand. Pieces of clothing were lying all around in a circle. The path was bloody; he was drenched in a fearful sweat. [565] He heard a woman's voice in painful lament; at the time she was overwhelmed by cares. She was a countess. How could she have suffered more? The lady had given birth to a little boy. [566] The one who lay dead before him, he was her husband. She had run into the forest to hide from the people, which is where the stranger now ran to. In her weakness she reached out to him with her white hand. [567] She was so weak she could not speak. That excellent man felt compassion for her. In a short while the lady regained her faculties and began to ask questions of the handsome knight.

[568] Then the proud lord said courteously, "Tell me, noble lady, who brought you into these woods?"

"Sir, a dragon took away the dearest husband a woman ever gained in this world. [569] It happened in an orchard this morning. Because of it all my joy is truly destroyed. He was generous with wealth and a most worthy man. I ran away to hide from people here in this forest. [570] My joy has been torn from me, now I have found misery." The virtuous woman said, "I am now near death."

The noble knight said, "My lady, you will surely recover, if God desires it. I will be your nurse."[87]

[571] Then in her weakness the praiseworthy lady said, "Ah, woe, noble knight, I'm embarrassed in your presence."

"Embarrassment is out of place here," said Wolf Lord Dietrich. "I will help you overcome your troubles, if I have my wits about me."

[572] He began to walk away from the rock wall and soon brought some water in his helmet. The woman refreshed herself. This I make known to you: the noble's actions helped her recover from her weakness.[88]

---

87. The Reclam edition (669) comments extensively on this passage, where Wolf Dietrich takes on the exceptional role of nurse to a woman who has given birth.
88. This strophe does not have the usual final transitional line between chapters about cares or troubles (*sorge*), even though it does offer a kind of positive resolution to the woman's plight.

Chapter 15: How He Brought the Dead Knight's Wife to a Peasant and Gave Her Over to Him, Along with the Child [573–79]

[573] His armor was removed; his fur cloak was taken off him.[89] She had not been denied the bold man's help. Along with the child, he carried her right then to a peasant farmer, whom he found near there.

[574] "Take care of the lady for me," said Wolf Lord Dietrich, "with all due honor. I will pay you handsomely for it."

The host said to the guest, "Everything I have will be at my lady's service."

[575] Then the bold man said to the peasant, "Landlord, by your faith, you should know this. You are to baptize the little child. Do so reverently, and name him after my father, Hug Dietrich."

[576] He[90] was honorably cared for by the landlord. He took his leave of both of them there, that worthy man, and quickly returned to the dead man. The noble knight found his horse still tied up there.

[577] He said, "Ah, woe, sir, your life fills me with regret. May God grant your soul a light punishment."[91] So he sadly grieved for the noble count. He said, "I found your beautiful wife today in distress."

[578] He brought both greenery and grass to cover the dead man. He rushed off after the dragon, which he loathed. The excellent lord felt the strong effects of the night; he certainly had to forego any sleep. [579] So the bold man rode through the night. He heard sweet birdsong in the forest. The night was pitch black; he rode on with trepidation.

Now Wolf Lord Dietrich really is in trouble again.

Chapter 16: How the Horse Drove the Dragon Away While He Slept [580–95]

[580] He rode through a gorge up toward a rock wall. He was in great need of sleep—this I make known to you. The day dawned to him, as we have now gathered, as the bold lord came upon a heath. [581] Then he dismounted from his horse to the ground and lay down on his shield's edge to sleep. The bold lord slept well into the light of day. The dragon crawled out of its cave and went to hunt for food. [582] It left the nest to feed its great maw.

---

89. This refers to the dead knight.
90. Amelung and Kofler emend the original *er* (he; 576,1a) to *ir* (they), with reference to the newborn child and the lady.
91. This is a reference to a limited time in Purgatory. The Middle High German word *wize* (manuscript A: *weitze*, 577,2b) refers to punishment or torture, especially in Purgatory or Hell. It glosses Latin *supplicium* and *tormentum*.

Chapter 16: How the Horse Drove the Dragon Away While He Slept [580–95]

A dwarf[92] called out from the rocks, "Wake up, famed lord, it is time. You remind me of the great tragedy with King Otnit. [583] He came here into this forest because of the dragon. Here that excellent man lost his life as well. Otnit, the noble, lost his life here. Liebgart, his beautiful wife, cried[93] for him still in Garda."

[584] Still the wonderfully bold man was sleeping under his shield. The dragon quickly moved toward him through the forest, and still the scion of noble lords slept soundly. The dwarf started to pull at his hair and beard.

[585] "Ah, woe, why don't you wake up, you wonderfully bold man? No one in the world acts this way, if he dares to stand up to dragons. Ah, woe, if you won't wake up, who will secure peace for us, or who will avenge the poor, if you lose your life?"

[586] Still the bold, proud man slept on his shield. The dragon quickly came up on him through the thicket. The horse broke free of its reins and charged at the dragon. It attacked the dragon and drove it away from the lord into the woods. [587] After it had driven the ferocious dragon away from there, it ran back to that lord, as I have gathered, and wanted to wake him—this I make known to you. It struck him at the shield's edge with its hooves. [588] It suffered great and uncommon harm from the dragon. This you should believe: it was very close to death. The dragon had already begun to rip at its beautiful coat, but at that moment it was still bold and quick. [589] It had driven the great dragon far away. Now the bold man was left there all alone. He finally awakened. Listen to what he said when he saw his fine horse wet with blood.

[590] "Woe, that I did not stay awake," said the bold man. "I would have helped you, as you did me. I can see from your wet coat that you were in distress. If it had not been for God's and your help, we would both be dead. [591] Now I have your faithfulness and your help to thank that I'm still alive today. I can see from your appearance that the dragon has been here. Now God has helped us survive."

[592] He got up from the ground, as I have heard. He gathered the reins and put them back on the horse. He measured the dragon's footprints, and its stride was terrifying. The claws in front of the instep were as long as someone's forearm.[94]

[593] Then the noble knight said, "Look, what is this? The devil straight out of hell. Who could ever survive that? If I had remained behind in this forest a dead man, who then would have rescued my eleven liegemen? [594] I left them there in Greece in grave danger. They struggle every day with nothing less than

---

92. This is probably not Alberich, but a typical "stone" or mountain dwarf.
93. Amelung and Kofler emend the original past tense *bewainte* (583,4a) to the present tense *weinet/bewainet*, meaning that she cries for him still.
94. Middle High German *dûmelle* (manuscript A: *daumelle*, 592,4b) is the distance between the elbow and the tip of the thumb. We might say something like "arm's length."

death. Lord God in heaven, let me live long enough so that I might still give them comfort and joy."

[595] Then he quickly tightened his horse's saddle girth. He mounted it with determined resolve, and the praiseworthy man headed toward the dragon.

Now Wolf Lord Dietrich is headed for trouble.

Chapter 17: How His Sword Broke on the Dragon, and It Carried Him into the Mountain [596–606]

[596] Then he turned toward the wilderness, through the mountains toward the rock wall, as I have gathered. The noble knight dismounted to the ground and quickly tied his horse to a tree. [597] The bold man went toward the mountain; he was certainly committed to doing battle. By the time he came to the cave, as you have certainly gathered, the hero had arrived there with determined resolve.

[598] "Sir landlord, are you home?" said the bold man. "The guests out here want to face you in battle. Defend yourself like a man," said the bold lord. "You'll repay me for all the dead who have lain before you."

[599] There were five young ones; they bared their teeth at the knight. The old one was not at home; it had gone out to get food. "What kind of honor can I gain here with you whelps? I want to get at the old one; it has caused us great suffering."

[600] Then he turned away from the young ones, left the rock wall, back toward the forest [. . .] [. . .]⁹⁵ a terrible battle fought by a wild lion, the other was the dragon. [601] There he carried the lion in red gold on his shield. He saw the wild beast there in considerable difficulty.

"If I can't help you, then I will give you up and never again carry you painted on my shield."⁹⁶

[602] The bold man took hold of the spear in his hand. He ran toward the dragon in a mighty joust. The spear burst into pieces out of his hand. He could not defeat him, which the guest greatly regretted. [603] Then the noble knight dismounted to the ground and quickly tied his horse to a tree, took his sword in both hands, and attacked the dragon. He could not defeat him. The guest continued the assault.

[604] The sword broke into three pieces, split like an apple. Many thoughts went through the noble knight's mind.

---

95. Two half-lines are missing, although there is no gap in the manuscript. Amelung fills the gap with *dô hôrte er zehant* | *vor im in dem walde* (600,2b–600,3a), or "there he suddenly heard in front of him in the forest . . ." This reconstruction is based on a similar passage in version B (512,1–2).
96. This refers back to Wolf Dietrich's oath to help the particular animal that could best defend itself against him (see 425–26), which naturally turned out to be a lion. This passage seems inserted for the sole purpose of allowing him to fulfill that oath.

Chapter 17: How His Sword Broke on the Dragon

He stretched out his hands: "Oh merciful God, you can help me. I'm in great danger here. [605] Help me, God in heaven, merciful Christ, help me now, since you are all powerful. And if I remain in this forest a dead man, then protect my eleven liegemen [for me] [in] Greece. [606] They are lost as well, if I lose my life here. Sweet Christ in heaven, I have surrendered myself to you. At this point things look bleak for me."

Now Wolf Lord Dietrich really is in danger.[97]

---

97. In manuscript A the story of Wolf Dietrich ends here, a fragment. In the third column of folio 214v, the remaining nineteen lines to the bottom of the page are left blank. Aside from the formulaic last line, there is no indication that another chapter was to follow. The next text, *Das puech von dem ubeln weibe*, begins at the top of the following page, folio 215r.

THE ENDING OF WOLF DIETRICH A

according to the Dresdener Heldenbuch (k)[1]

235–51 Conclusion of the fight with the dragons. After Wolf Dietrich's sword breaks, he is carried off by the dragon to its lair, to be fed to its young. He is, however, protected by his baptismal shirt. When the dragons go to sleep, he dons Otnit's armor and takes possession of the sword Rose. Although he is then swallowed by the older dragon, Wolf Dietrich cuts himself out of its belly and goes on to kill the young as well. He cuts off their heads and takes the tongues with him. Otnit is buried, and Wolf Dietrich takes his magic ring.

252–89 A Saracen lord and his daughter. A dwarf gives Wolf Dietrich much-needed sustenance and tells him of a Saracen lord who rules there in the land. He rides to the magic castle Walledeisse, where the ruler and his sorceress daughter welcome him. Wolf Dietrich refuses to reveal his identity, however, which angers the lord. The two are at first reconciled by the daughter, but when the Saracen lord attempts to poison his guest, his daughter intervenes to prevent it.

After refusing to sleep with the daughter despite her father's permission, Wolf Dietrich is challenged to a trial by combat in which each man has a throw of three knives. Wolf Dietrich narrowly avoids his opponent's throws and then kills the lord with his three.

The daughter employs various spells to prevent Wolf Dietrich's escape. First the castle spins like a wheel, then a lake is created around the castle. Forced into the lake along with him, the sorceress conjures a glass bridge, which promptly collapses once he rides onto it. Wolf Dietrich eventually makes his way out of the lake, only to be surrounded by a burning forest, while the sorceress flies away in the guise of a magpie. Lastly, he finds himself trapped in a great ravine between glass mountains until the magic finally wears off on the fourth day.

290–99 More magic and resistance. Exhausted and famished, Wolf Dietrich falls asleep, only to be carried off by twelve magical goddesses into their mountain domain. After sleeping for three days and feasting lavishly to restore himself, Wolf Dietrich becomes the object of desire of the most beautiful of the twelve. Resisting their entreaties, he and his horse manage to escape from a golden cage after three days. He is immediately confronted by twenty-four goddesses, and again is lavishly served at a magic table. These ladies, too, want him to stay. While riding off, he is enveloped by a large snake, which stays with him for three days until its magic dissipates.

---

1. This synopsis covers strophes 235–334 of the manuscript k text and is based on the Reclam edition (2013), 584–611, which itself is based on the text edited by Amelung (1871), 153–63.

The ending of Wolf Dietrich A

300–306   False claims and justice. A knight named Vordeck discovers the dragon heads and, bringing them to Garda, claims to have slain them. He furthermore claims as his reward the hand of Queen Liebgart. Wolf Dietrich attends the wedding festivities in disguise as a poor pilgrim. He secretly reveals the magic ring to the queen, who recognizes it as Otnit's. Wolf Dietrich examines the dragons' heads in public, asking where the tongues might be. He reveals the tongues and his true identity as the proper claimant to the queen. Vordeck is immediately executed, and Wolf Dietrich and Liebgart are wed.[2]

307–14   First return to Greece. Wolf Dietrich is crowned king of Lombardy, but, remembering Berchtung and his sons, he leaves for Greece after twelve weeks. Promising to return, he travels to Constantinople, again in the guise of a poor pilgrim, where he learns from a gate guard named Ortwein that Berchtung has died and his sons have been imprisoned. Wolf Dietrich visits the grave site where the spirit of Berchtung speaks to him, imploring him to forgive his own brothers, who are not to blame for his death, and to help his ten sons in their suffering. Wolf Dietrich returns to Garda.

315–21   Search for the queen. On his return he finds that Liebgart has disappeared, having been lured by an unknown dwarf to a bucolic spring. Wolf Dietrich searches for her, as does Alberich, the queen's father-in-law. After a year's time, Alberich finds the queen and keeps her safe in his mountain retreat. Alberich then searches another three months for Wolf Dietrich, and on finding him leads him to the mountain where he is reunited with Liebgart. Before they can make their way home, he must fight an army of dwarves. With their defeat, all are happily reunited in Garda.

322–25   Second return to Greece. Wolf Dietrich again requests leave to free Berchtung's sons, his ten liegemen in Greece, and to avenge himself on his two brothers. He returns to Greece with an army of sixty thousand and destroys Constantinople. Wolf Dietrich captures his brothers, has Saben killed, and turns the Greek lands over to Berchtung's sons.

326–33   Happiness and regret. Wolf Dietrich lives happily with Liebgart in Garda for twelve years. He then secretly enters a monastery named Tischzung to do penance for his sins. The abbot tells him he can atone for his sins by spending the entire night on a bier, but he must not get up for any reason. He accepts the challenge and is tempted and assaulted the entire night by evil spirits. Wolf Dietrich resists but dies that night nonetheless, absolved of his sins. Meanwhile, Liebgart, who has been searching for her husband, blames the monastery for his death. Having heard the true story of Wolf Dietrich's death, however, she joins the convent herself, endowing it with great wealth to her honor and that of her

---

2. Much of this episode is very similar to a scene in Gottfried's *Tristan and Isolde*, in which the cowardly seneschal attempted to take credit for killing the dragon that Tristan had vanquished (*T* 10,803–11,366).

The ending of Wolf Dietrich A

two husbands. She dies a year later and is laid to rest next to Otnit and Wolf Dietrich.

334 The poet justifies himself for shortening the old poem from 700 to 333 strophes, as it can now be heard in a single sitting.

PLACENAMES
Kudrun

Textual variations of a name are provided in parentheses, to include those variants that may be identical to the (English) spelling used in the text. All occurrences in the text are noted with a line number, except in those few cases with fifty or more instances. Line numbers in square brackets (e.g., [561,3]) refer to the Bartsch/Stackmann numbers when they differ from the manuscript's (and translation's) strophic order.

Abakie (*Abakie*; *Albakine*), one of Siegfried's lands, presumably part of his African kingdom (673,2; 829,4)

Abalie (*Abalie*; *Abaly*; *Agaby*; *Abagy*), an eastern land known for its silks (for sail making), gold, and precious jewels; also mentioned in *Biterolf* 1155 (267,3; 864,4; 1248,2; 1684,3)

the Alps (*von den Alben*), or mountains in general; in reference to strong winds (861,2)

Alzabe (*Alzabe*; *Azzabe*), Siegfried's crown land; a part of Siegfried's African kingdom, but separate from Moorland (579,1; 667,4; 670,2; 673,2; 698,4; 706,2; 719,2; 728,2; 836,1; 1696,2)

Amile, an eastern land named as the place of origin for one of Horant's melodies (397,1)

Arabia (*Arabi*; *Arabe*; *von Araben*), source of rare silks and ropes (anchor lines) (266,1; 1326,1; 1588,4; 1616,2)

Baghdad, from the placename *Baldac*, both the source of and a kind of precious silk (*baldekin*); until the middle of the thirteenth century, one of the largest cities in the world (301,3)

Balian, capital of Ireland; Sigebant's, and then Hagen's main castle and town; from the Irish word *baile* (town) (161,2; 288,2; 293,1; 441,1; 559,4)

Campalie, a source of robes or cloaks (*röcke*); possibly present-day Champagne (332,2)

Campatille, a castle or town in Hegelingen; a residence of Hetel (235,2)

Cassiane, King Ludwig's and Hartmut's main castle in Ormanie; taken by Herwig and his allies in the final battle (1534,2 [1535,2]; 1541,2; 1543,3; 1692,2)

Daneland, **land of the Danes** (*Tennelant*), one of the lands in Hetel's kingdom; place where Hetel grew up; homeland of Horant, Fruote, and Irolt (204,1; 216,1; 221,2; 320,4; 331,1; 415,2; 466,1; 488,1; 509,3; 571,4; 576,4; 602,2; 696,3; 715,2; 722,4; 723,1; 1111,2; 1112,2; 1370,1; 1414,1; 1532,1; 1541,1; 1546,1; 1549,4; 1612,4; 1613,2; 1668,3); of the **Danish kingdom** (*von Tennereiche*), an appellative for Horant; historically by the twelfth century, the Danish kingdom included what is present-day Denmark and parts of southern Sweden; it saw territorial gains in the early thirteenth century in the south that included most of the German Baltic coast; these territories were lost again to northern German nobles following the Battle of Bornhöved in 1227 (354,3)

Placenames

Danish March (*Tennemarch*), border region, or march, near or part of Daneland; near Walays; ruled by Horant; where Kudrun spent her youth; historically a march established north of the Eider river by Charlemagne around 810, the march became Danish in 1035 (200,1; 206,1; 219,4; 242,4; 263,3; 272,1 [271,1]; 292,3; 341,4; 349,3; 372,2; 378,4; 381,4; 439,4; 537,1; 549,4; 552,2; 564,2; 571,1; 575,3; 600,2; 634,2; 689,1; 711,1; 814,1; 884,2; 886,1; 898,2; 938,2; 1083,2; 1086,4; 1089,4; 1139,1; 1180,2; 1181,1; 1399,1; 1497,1; 1611,4; 1644,3; 1691,3; 1644,3; 1686,3; 1691,3; 1694,4)

Dark Sea (*vinster mer*), Middle High German rendering of Latin *mare caligans*; a dangerous ocean because of its association with a magnetic mountain; originally located in northern Europe as a polar sea, but transferred to a Mediterranean setting in *Herzog Ernst* (1126,2; 1128,2)

Diethmers, part of Hetel's kingdom; probably the present-day Dithmarschen, a district in Schleswig-Holstein on the North Sea (208,2)

Frideschotten, home of Queen Uote, Sigebant's wife, Hagen's mother; one-time seat of Ludwig's realm; somehow connected to Norway; possibly a part of present-day (northern) Scotland, including the Hebrides, Orkney, and Shetland Islands (9,3; 30,1; 611,1)

Frisia (*Friesen*; *Fryesen*; *Friesen lanndt*), part of Hetel's kingdom, ruled by Irolt; home of Morunc; present-day Frisia or the Frisian Islands in the North Sea (208,1; 231,4; 272,1 [271,1]; 481,1; 938,1)

Galays, distant land subject to Herwig; an army is located here at the foot of a mountain; not likely the same as Walays, since both occur in the same strophe (641,3)

Galicia (*Galizen lant*; *Galitzen lannde*), home of Hildeburg; associated with Portugal; present-day autonomous community in northwestern Spain (1009,1 [1008,1]; 1196,3)

Garadie (*Garadie*; *Karade*; *Baradie*; *Gradie*; *Garadine*; *Garaday*; *Garadi*), home of the count who rescues Hagen and the young women from the griffins' island; perhaps near Ireland; not the same as Karadie (see below), despite orthographic similarities (108,3; 116,4; 126,1; 130,3; 136,2; 144,3; 150,4; 158,2)

Givers (*Gyfers*; *Giuers*; *Giners*), magnetic mountain or town near or in a magnetic mountain; Hilde's fleet was drawn to and held by a magnetic mountain near Givers. According to an old story told by Wate, it was the location of a fabulously wealthy kingdom. A rising westerly wind saved the fleet and moved it out of reach of the magnetic effect. It may have been in or near the "Dark Sea" (*vinster mer*), which could have been in the north. It has been connected to *mons Gyber*, or Mount Etna (Monte Gibello), in Sicily, but the southern locale would make little sense in this context (1126,1; 1128,4; 1135,2; 1138,2)

Gyfers, a town or land on the coast subject to Horant, near or in the Danish March; possibly present-day Jever, the capital of Friesland, Lower Saxony (564,2)

Gustrate, unidentified landmark west of Ormanie, where the sun sets as the Hegelingen prepare for battle; possibly Golstert, present-day Start Point, a prominent peninsula and navigational landmark on the southwestern English coast between Dartmouth and Plymouth (1164,3)

Placenames

Hegelingen, Hetel's kingdom and crown land; somewhere near Ortland; its capital is Matelane; given the *-ingen* suffix, the name would have originally meant the "land or descendants of Hegel" (207,1; total of 104 occurrences)

Holzanland (*Holzane lanndt*), land belonging to Morunc and perhaps Irolt, held in fief from Hetel; near Frisia; probably present-day Holstein (1089,1)

Ikaria (*Ykaria*), land belonging to King Siegfried; possibly a Greek island (Icaria) in the southern Aegean Sea (581,1)

India (*India*; *Yndia*), homeland of Hilde, Kudrun's grandmother, Hagen's wife; imagined as a fabled land in the East (118,3; 170,1; 177,3; 197,2)

Ireland (*Eyerlannt*; *Eyrlant*), kingdom belonging to Hagen; inherited from his father Sigebant, and his father Ger; present-day Ireland, either in part or whole (1,1; 15,4; 20,1; 35,1; 37,3; 40,3; 52,2; 59,4; 65,2; 70,3; 110,3; 129,3; 134,4; 136,4; 159,4; 183,1; 194,1; Ch. 5 heading; 212,2; 226,3; 230,2; 238,4; 256,2; 317,2; 354,1; 378,2; 429,3; 440,4; 455,1; 472,3; 490,1; 495,2; 498,4; 551,2; 593,2; 1009,3 [1008,3]; 1267,1; 1650,1; 1680,2); **kingdom of Ireland** (*Eyrich*; *Eyrreiche*), historically, much of Ireland was controlled by Anglo-Norman nobility throughout the thirteenth century and into the fourteenth (124,3; 139,3; 229,3; 357,3; 508,3; 578,3; 1339,3)

Iserland (*von Yserlannde*), homeland of Hilde's (unnamed) youngest female companion; she is later married to an (unnamed) king in Norway (120,3; 191,4)

Karadie (*karadie*; *karady*; *karadine*; *karade*; *karadi*), Siegfried's homeland; it is unclear how this is related to a land of the same name that belongs to Hagen: Hagen gives Ludwig castles in fief in **Karadine** (610,3), making Ludwig Hagen's vassal (702,1; 719,1; 731,3; 733,3; 833,4; 1120,2; 1139,4; 1368,1; 1540,4 [1534,4]; 1589,2; 1643,4; 1651,4; 1654,2; 1663,1; 1695,4)

Matelane (*Matelane*; *Motelane*; *Matalane*; *Macelane*), Hetel's main castle in Hegelingen; home of Hilde and Kudrun (760,3; 763,3; 764,4; 771,3; 777,3; 798,3; 852,1; 881,1; 937,2; 1118,4; 1569,1; 1570,3; 1572,1; 1573,3; 1592,2; 1609,2; 1667,4; 1669,4; 1700,3)

Moorland (*Morlant*), Siegfried's kingdom; probably meant to represent the lands of the "Moors" in the Near East, Mediterranean, or North Africa (580,1; 582,3; 584,4; 668,1; 683,3; 703,2; 705,1; 712,3; 728,2; 826,3; 831,2; 832,1; 835,1; 947,1; 1589,3; 1677,2); **Moorish kingdom** (*von Morenreiche*) (729,3; 1459,3)

Nifland (*Nifland*; *Nyflant*), land belonging to Morunc (211,1; 564,1)

Norway (*in Horwage*; *gegen Norwagen*), the homeland of Queen Uote (Sigebant's wife); part of present-day western Norway, including the northern Scottish islands, most likely along the North Sea coast (8,4; 193,3)

Ormanie (*Ormanie*; *Ormenie lant*; *Ormanie lant*; *Ormandin*; *Ormandinen*), Ludwig's kingdom; Hartmut's home; some considerable distance from Daneland and Hegelingen (599). Given the orthographic variations in Ried's manuscript, it is difficult to make any distinctions between Ormanie and a land possibly identifiable as Normandy. The names are interchangeable and either one can be taken as the home seat of Ludwig's kingdom. There is no evidence in the text that links this kingdom with a historical area called Normandy, although it has been suggested that the Norman kingdom of Sicily might fit this criterion (Blamires, 444). There has been some speculation that the name was originally *Romanie* by way of metathesis of "o" and "r," another name

Placenames

for Byzantium (there is mention of a nonspecific Romanie in *Wolf Dietrich A* (*WDA* 421,1). See also Störmer-Caysa, 645; Gibbs/Johnson, 174 (587,1; 82 occurrences); **Normandie** (*Normendi*; *Normandin*; *Normandie*; *Normande lanndt*; *Normanie lant*) (588,3; 604,1; 1618,1; 1630,1; 1693,1; 1703,3); **Hormandin** (*Hormandin*; *Hormandine*) (739,1; 751,1)

Ortland (*Ortlant*; *Ortlannde*), land adjacent to or near Hegelingen, at times synonymous with it; part of Hetel's kingdom near Frisia; ruled by Irolt as Hetel's vassal; also home of Ortwin; almost universally emended to Nortland, Nordland, or Northland by editors and translators, although no such historical place can be located (Piper, Martin, and Armour retain Ortland); as with Ormanie/Normandie/Hormandin or Horwage/Norwage, the orthographic variation between Or-, Nor-, and Hor- seems not to distinguish different geographic locations (204,4; 207,2; 273,1; 565,1; 716,1; 920,1); **Nortland** (*Nortlant*; *Nortlande*) (371,3; 1096,1; 1103,1; 1704,2); **Hortland** (*Hortlant*; *Horlant*) (466,4; 520,1; 749,3; 884,3; 939,1; 1154,1; 1173,3; 1235,1; 1404,1; 1417,4; 1515,2 [1513,2]; 1531,1; 1573,1; 1642,2; 1676,1); **Hortrich** (*Hortriche*; *Horriche*; *Hortreichen*), kingdom of Ort (481,1; 634,3; 1367,3; 1371,3)

Poland (*Polay*; emended to *Polan*), land supposedly belonging to Hagen, which the narrator disputes (288,3)

Portugal (*Portegale*; *Portigal*), homeland of Hildeburg, Hilde's companion; supposedly hostile to the Danes, a place in conflict with Horant and Fruote; possibly present-day Portugal, although its location makes no sense in this context; it is simply a far-off kingdom; historically Portugal became an independent kingdom by the middle of the twelfth century (119,2; 222,2; 485,3; 1009,2 [1008,2])

Salme, home of the ship's captain who rescued Hagen from the griffins' island; near Ireland and somehow related to Garadie (110,1)

Seeland (*Seelant*; *Sebelandt*; *Sewenlandt*), Herwig's kingdom; possibly Dutch Zeeland or Danish Zealand (669,3; 671,1 [emended from *land*]; 675,1; 718,3; 726,3; 733,3; 934,1; 1241,3; 1373,3; 1486,1); **Sewen** (*Sewen*; *Seben*; *Seeben*), variation of the name (706,1; 867,1; 1214,1; 1257,1 [1260,1]; 1484,4; 1674,1)

Spain, contained in a reference to Spanish brass, used by Hilde's fleet to build ships that were not susceptible to magnetic effects (*Spanischem messe*, 1109,3)

Stormarn (*Sturm*; *Sturmen*), a march bordering Daneland; Wate rules here as Hetel's vassal; birth place of Hetel; part of Hetel's kingdom; possibly present-day Stormarn, a district in Schleswig-Holstein, Germany (204,2; 223,3; 231,2; 232,1; 257,4; 270,1; 331,3; 358,1; 564,1; 688,1; 728,1; 908,3; 925,1; 1092,3; 1182,2; 1183,2; 1411,3; 1510,4 [1508,4]; 1546,1; 1577,3; 1682,1); also known as **Stormland** (*Sturmlant*) (263,1; 362,2; 465,1; 506,3; 516,2; 634,1; 830,3; 910,1; 938,1; 1091,1; 1367,3; 1392,1; 1611,3)

Swabia (*ze Swabe*), a wealthy medieval duchy in southwestern Germany, perhaps standing in for German-speaking lands in the south or as a whole (744,2)

Walays (*Walays*; *Waleis*; *Walayss*; *Valays*; *Walais*; *Waylais*), a land near the Danish March, west of Ormanie, part of Hetel's realm; a march and seat of Morunc (208,2; 465,2; 466,2; 493,3; 497,2; 641,4; 697,1; 799,4; 884,1; 938,3; 1087,2; 1102,1; 1370,3; 1415,3); seemingly unrelated to this, the home of one of Kudrun's (dead) admirers (200,2)

Wulpensand (*Wulpensannde*; *Volpen sannt*; *Fulpen sant*; *Wlpensannde*; *Wlpensant*; *Vlpensande*; *Volpensant*), "Wolf" island, where King Hetel and his allies engage in a battle with King Ludwig's forces; the mission to free Kudrun and her ladies fails, as Hetel is killed in the battle and Ludwig and his army escape; site of a great monastery and hostel built in memory of the fallen Hegelingen warriors; possibly present-day Wulpen, an island in the Dutch Scheldt estuary (809,4; Ch. 17 heading; 848,1; 871,4; 900,2; 918,3; 949,2; 950,4; 1122,1; 1434,4); **Wulpen Island** (*Vlpenwerde*; *Wlpen werde*), variation of the name (883,4; 897,4).

Otnit and *Wolf Dietrich A*

Textual variations of a name are provided in parentheses, to include those variants that may be identical to the (English) spelling used in the text. All occurrences in the text are noted with a line number, except in those few cases with fifty or more instances. All textual variations of a name are included in parentheses, with an annotation of A or W or AW depending on the manuscript(s) in which the variant occurs.

Apulia (AW: *Pulle*), southern Italian region subject to the Muslim nobleman Zacharis; after 1130 a duchy within the Norman kingdom of Sicily; ruled by the Hohenstaufen dynasty from 1194 to 1266 (*O* 61,2)

Arabia (A: *Arabi*; W: *Arabei*), land from which Alberich takes his golden chain mail; traditionally associated with a fabulously wealthy Arabic land that is not specifically localized (*O* 114,2)

Benevento (A: *Bonefente*; W: *Bonavent*), town or region subject to Duke Gerebart of Troia; present-day town in southern Italy, north of Apulia; historically subject to papal rule since the middle of the eleventh century (*O* 48,3)

Brescia (A: *Breyssen*; W: *Brisen*), part of Otnit's kingdom; present-day city in Lombardy; the town of Brixen/Bressanone in the southern Tirol is also a possible match (*O* 5,3)

Bulgaria (*Bulgerie*), Bulgarian realm subject to Baltram, part of which is beholden to Hug Dietrich; historically the Second Bulgarian Empire was a regional power in the thirteenth century, but declined by the end of the fourteenth under pressure from Mongols and the Byzantine Empire (*WDA* 2,1; *WDA* 190,1)

Caucasus (A: *Caucasas*; W: *Kaukasas*), name of a mountain, supposedly in or near Arabia, that was the source of the gold in Alberich's chain mail armor (*O* 114,4)

Constantinople (*Kunstenobl*; *Chunstenopel*; *auf Kunstenobele*; *auf Chunstenobele*; *zu Chunstenopele*), residence and capital city of the Greek king; historically one of the great cities of late antiquity and the Middle Ages; Constantine's capital of the Eastern Roman Empire and Byzantium; briefly capital to a Latin Empire (1204–61) following the Fourth Crusade (*WDA* 1,1; 2,4; 165,1; 171,2; 232,4; 303,4; 376,4; 486,4)

Placenames

Danish March (*Tennemarche*), homeland of Fruote, opponent of Hug Dietrich's military campaign; borders on Daneland and features prominently in *Kudrun* (*WDA* 6,2)

Etsch (*Etsche*), river near Garda, presumably the present-day Etsch/Adige River in northern Italy (*WDA* 555,2; 556,1)

France (A: *Karlinge*; W: *Cherlinge*), all or part of the former Carolingian Empire (*O* 253,1)

Garda (AW: *Garte*; W: *auf Garten*; *Gart WDA*), Otnit's capital city; probably near or on present-day Lago di Garda in northern Italy (*O* 5,4; 30,1; 34,2; 35,2; 38,3; 52,3; 60,2; 83,1; 86,2; 166,4; 193,3; 195,2; 196,3; 214,3; 483,2; 501,2; 521,2; 575,2; 583,3; 585,4; 590,1; 593,4; 595,2; (*WDA* 33,4; 58,4; 162,4; 521,2; 526,2; 527,2; 545,4; 583,4)

Garda lake (A: *Gartensee*; W: *Gartese*; *Gartsee WDA*), lake near Garda, presumably present-day Lago di Garda, Italy (*O* 88,1; *WDA* 523,2; 524,1)

Greece (*ze Kriechen*; *Kriechen lanndt*), the kingdom of Hug Dietrich and his sons; presumably meant to represent the Byzantine Empire (*WDA* 1,2; 2,1; 303,3; 315,3; 317,3; 331,1; 332,1; 347,4; 363,3; 488,1; 521,1; 533,1; 594,1; 605,4)

Italian lands (AW: *ze Walhen*; A: *in walhischen reichen*; W: *in welhischen richen*), Romance-language–speaking lands; in this context usually Italian areas (*O* 3,3; 253,2; 353,2; 393,4)

Jerusalem (A: *Iherusalem*; W: *Jerusalem*), part of Machorel's territory, where he wears the king's crown; presumably identical with the historical city in Judea; Jerusalem was captured by crusaders in 1099 and then lost to Saladin in 1187; for a brief time under Frederick II, the city was again administered by European nobles between 1229 and 1244 (*O* 13,4)

Lateran (A: *Latron*; W: *Lateran*), the traditional residence of the pope in Rome; the archbasilica of St. John Lateran is the official ecclesiastical seat of the pope (*O* 6,4)

Lilienport, Berchtung's home town and castle; presumably in the Meran region, but located in Greece according to 488,1 and 594,1 (*WDA* 54,2; 136,1; 206,4; 274,4; 281,2; 321,2; 376,1; 377,3; 381,1; 387,1)

Lombardy (AW: *Lamparten*; A: *von Lamparte*; *der Lamparten lant*; W: *Lanparten*; *Lamparten lant*), Otnit's home and crown land; presumably related to the present-day region of northern Italy (*O* 2,3; 3,1; 7,4; 12,4; 16,1; 20,2; 51,2; 58,1; 118,4; 144,1; 161,2; 294,3; 369,1; 494,1; 501,1; 534,4; 581,4; 596,2; *WDA* 417,2; 451,2; 504,2; 504,4)

London (A: *Lunders*; W: *Suderz*), only in manuscript A, town where the book of Otnit is discovered; manuscript W reads *Suderz* (Tyre) (*O* 1,1)

Meersee, literally "sea lake"; possible place-name of a lake near Trento and near the dragon's cave; capitalized in the manuscript; not identifiable with any actual place (*WDA* 561,4)

Meran, Berchtung's crown land; used exclusively as Berchtung's toponymic byname; presumably identical with the northern Italian city, but also possibly relocated within the Greek kingdom (*WDA* 5,3; 6,3; 48,2; 53,1; 57,2; 130,1; 145,3; 149,2; 151,1; 165,2; 181,1; 188,1; 214,1; 221,3; 230,3; 245,2; 256,3; 262,2; 273,3; 274,4; 278,4; 307,1; 335,1; 344,3; 347,2; 356,1; 371,1; 372,4; 375,1; 394,1; 403,3; 416,1; 423,1; 440,1; 454,3)

Messina (AW: *Messin*; W: *Messyn*; *Messein*; *Messen*), town and port in northeastern Sicily; point of departure for Otnit's fleet, provided to him by Zacharis; important medieval port for crusading forces (*O* 65,2; 215,4; 364,1; 482,3)

Mount Tabor (AW: *Montabur*; A: *Muntabur*; W: *Montaborur*; *Montabaur*; *Montabour*), Machorel's birthplace and residence; historically a fortress in Lower Galilee held by Sultan Malek al-Adel, Saladin's brother; built in 1212 and unsuccessfully besieged in 1217 by a crusader army (Fifth Crusade); occupied by Christians in 1229 until defeated by the Mamluk ruler Baibars in 1263 (*O* 13,2; 19,1; 123,3; 266,4; 348,4; 354,3; 358,4; 361,2; 473,3)

Nocera (A: *Stutschir*; W: *Nutschir*), town or region subject to Duke Gerebart of Troia; possibly present-day Nocera in southern Italy (*O* 48,3)

Roman shores (*römischen staden*), presumably Italy; the destination given for the huntsman's voyage to kill Otnit with the dragon eggs (*O* 500,4)

the Romanie, a region on the way from Lilienport to Lombardy, apparently devoid of people or cultivated land (*WDA* 421,1)

Rome, the seat of all secular power; representative of the glory of the former (western) Roman Republic and Empire (*O* 6,4)

Russia (A: *Rewssen*; *Reussen*; W: *Reuzzen*; *Ruzzen*), homeland and kingdom of Ilias, Otnit's uncle; used almost exclusively as a toponymic byname, with one exception (67,1) that refers to travel to a place (*O* 17,1; 23,1; 28,2; 46,1; 61,3; 64,1; 67,1; 223,4; 230,4; 237,2; 294,3; 305,1; 312,4; 324,4; 352,2; 380,1; 462,4; 463,4)

Salneck (*von Salnegge*), according to Otnit's wife, Wolf Dietrich's hometown or region; possibly Saloniki, Greece (*WDA* 532,4)

Sicily (AW: *Cecilie*), home of Zacharis, a Muslim vassal of Otnit (*O* 41,1)

Suders (A: *Suders*; *Syders*; *Suder*; W: *Suderz*; [D]*aderz*; *Sauders*), town and castle in Syria; Machorel's capital city; probably the historical fortress of Tyre in present-day Lebanon (Arabic صور, Ṣūr; Greek Τύρος, Tyros; French Tyr or Sour) (*O* 1,1 [in manuscript W, not A]; 14,1; 217,4; 218,3; 221,1; 221,4; Ch. 4 heading; 371,4; 480,3)

Syria (AW: *Surie*; A: *Syrie*; W: *Syureie*), land subject to Machorel, with Suders as its capital (*O* 14,1; 218,2; 220,2)

Trento (A: *ze Triente*; W: *Trient*; *Triendte*; *Triende WDA*), town in northern Italy near the cave in which the dragons are hatched and raised (*O* 513,2; *WDA* 556,2; 562,1)

Troia (A: *Troyen*; W: *Troyn*; *Tryn*), land subject to Duke Gerebant; possibly the southern Italian town of Troia in Apulia (*O* 39,1; 48,2)

Tuscany (AW: *Tuscan*; A: *Tuschon*; *Tuschan*), land belonging to Margrave Helmnot (*O* 10,1; 36,1; 47,1)

Verona (AW: *Perne*; W: *Pern*), capital city of the epic hero Dietrich of Bern; Bern is the medieval variation of the city's name; part of Otnit's kingdom; present-day city in northern Italy (*O* 5,3; 597,3)

PERSONAL NAMES
Kudrun

Textual variations of a name are included in parentheses. Line numbers refer to the first (or single) mention in the text.

the Count of Garadie (*Graue von Garadie*), otherwise unnamed ruler of Garadie, a land close to Ireland; probably identical with the ship's captain, who is from Salme (110,1); rescued Hagen and the three princesses from the griffins' island; plan to take young Hagen hostage foiled; taken to Ireland and reconciled with his former enemy, Hagen's father Sigebant (116,4)

the Danes (*Tenen*), people subject to Hetel and his vassal Fruote; inhabitants of Daneland and the Danish March; Horant and Morunc were also considered Danes (333,4)

the Franks (*Francken*), mentioned as an example of particularly ferocious fighters (366,4)

the Frisians (*Friesen*), Irolt's subjects and warriors (1374,2)

Fruote of the Danes; of the Danish March (*von Tenen*; *von Tennemarche*), elderly ruler of the Danish March and, along with Wate, a prominent military leader and royal counselor; the name means "wisdom"; characterized as experienced and clever; in *Kudrun*, a relative of Hetel, possibly an uncle; often paired with Horant; close friend and relative of Wate and about the same age (355,2); mentioned only once in *Wolf Dietrich* as a king and Hug Dietrich's enemy, Hug Dietrich's sister's son (219,4; *WDA* 6,2)

Ger, early king of Ireland; the first of five generations portrayed in *Kudrun*; Sigebant's father; Hagen's grandfather; Hilde's great-grandfather; Kudrun's great-great-grandfather; Ireland was also called Ger's land (1,2)

Gerlint, queen of Ormanie; Ludwig's wife; Hartmut's mother; tormented Kudrun and Hildeburg; executed by Wate; known as "wicked" (*ubel*) (588,1)

Hagen, king of Ireland; Hilde's husband; father to their daughter Hilde; Kudrun's grandfather; abducted as a child by a griffin; survived on a desert island along with three young women; rescued and restored to his parents in Ireland, he married Hilde of India, one of his three companions; his daughter Hilde abducted by kinsmen of Hetel; pursued the Hegelingen and fought them to a draw on the shores of Walays, recovering Hilde and reconciling with Hetel; known as "fierce" (*wild*) and "Terror (or devil) of all Kings" (*valant aller künige*) (22,4)

Hartmut (*Hartmuot*), lord in Ormanie and future king; son of King Ludwig and Queen Gerlint; unsuccessful suitor of Kudrun who then abducted her and left her in his mother's care; captured by Herwig's forces; eventually married to Hildeburg as part of a general amnesty and reconciliation (587,4)

the Hegelingen, people of the kingdom of Hegelingen; subjects of King Hetel (207,1)

Heregart, a lady in Kudrun's household, taken with her to Ormanie; had a relationship with an official in Hartmut's court in the hopes of gaining a high position and security through marriage; later killed by Wate (1007,4)

Herwig (*Herwig; Herwigk*), king of Seeland; rejected as Kudrun's suitor by Hetel; attacked Hegelingen in force and nearly defeated Hetel's troops; reconciled and betrothed to Kudrun, but forced to leave her in her mother's care; attacked in his own land by Siegfried and his Moorish army; supported in defense by Hetel and his army; led the expedition to free Kudrun in Ormanie, where he killed King Ludwig in battle; married to Kudrun in the end; his unnamed sister married to Siegfried (586,4)

Hetel, young king of Hegelingen; an orphan, raised by his kinsman Wate; husband to Hagen's daughter, Hilde; Kudrun's and Ortwin's father; lord of seven lands; ruled over Ortland, Frisia, Holzan, Diethmers, Nifland, Stormarn, Walais, Daneland, and the Danish March; sent an expedition to Ireland to win Hilde; battled Hagen's army to a draw on the shores of Walays; reconciled with Hagen, then married to Hilde; denied petitions by Siegfried, Hartmut, and Herwig to marry his daughter Kudrun; eventually granted Kudrun's hand in marriage to Herwig; led an expedition to Seeland to support Herwig against Siegfried; killed by Ludwig at the Battle of Wulpensand (206,3)

Hilde, princess from India; shared exile with Hagen and two other princesses on the griffins' island; Hagen's wife; Kudrun's grandmother (170,1)

Hilde, queen of Hegelingen; Hagen and Hilde's daughter; Hetel's wife; Kudrun and Ortwin's mother; voluntarily left Ireland with Wate and his company; married to Hetel after the Battle of Walays; known as "fair" or "beautiful" (*diu schoene*) (197,4)

Hildeburg (*Hyldeburg*), princess from Portugal; shared exile with Hagen and two other princesses on the griffins' island; faithful companion to Kudrun, especially in captivity in Ormanie; later married to Hartmut (485,1)

the Holz men (*Holtzsæssen; Holtzsassen*), warriors from Holzanland (1374,3)

Horant of the Danish March, of the Danes (*Hor(r)annt; von Tennemarche; von Tenen*), young lord in the Danish March with Fruote; Wate's sister's son, that is, Wate's nephew; probably Hetel's cousin, although in 1112,3 Horant's mother is described as Hetel's sister, that is, Horant was Hetel's nephew; gifted singer, musician, and warrior; a senior commander in the final battle (206,2)

Irolt (*Yrolt*), young ruler of Ortland, including Holzan and Frisia; part of Hetel's extended family (*künne*); related to Wate; often paired with Morunc; took part in the expedition to Ireland to win Hilde, as well as the military campaigns to Seeland and Ormanie (231,4)

the Irish (*den Eyrlande*), inhabitants of Ireland; subjects of Hagen (496,4)

Kudrun (*Chutrum; Chautrum; Chautruomb; Chutron; Chautrun; Chaudrun; Chautruon*), King Hagen's granddaughter; King Hetel's daughter; King Herwig's bride and in the end queen of Seeland; raised in the Danish March by relatives; admired by suitors from many lands; enlisted her father's aid to save Herwig and Seeland from Siegfried's attack; abducted by Hartmut, brought to Ormanie, and tormented in captivity for fourteen years by Hartmut's mother; freed by a Hegelingen military invasion sent by her mother; reconciled warring parties through arranged marriages; known as "fair" or "beautiful" (*diu schoene*), like her mother (575,2)

Ludwig, king of Ormanie; Gerlint's husband; Hartmut's father; former or current vassal of Hagen; killed Hetel in the Battle of Wulpensand; himself killed by Herwig in the final Battle of Cassiane (588,3)

Personal Names

the Moors (*Mæren; Moren*), people subject to Siegfried; presumably inhabitants of Islamic North Africa or the Near East (670,3)

Morunc (*Morungk; Horung; Morung*), young nobleman from Frisia; lord of Nifland and margrave of Walays; vassal of Hetel; close friend of Irolt; part of Hetel's extended family (*künne*); participated in all the expeditions of the Hegelingen (211,1)

Ortrun, daughter of King Ludwig and Queen Gerlint; Hartmut's sister; supported Kudrun in Ormanie; later married to Ortwin, Kudrun's brother (973,2)

Ortwin (*Ortwein*), son of Hetel and Hilde; Kudrun's brother; king of Ortland; raised by Wate. In the Battle of Wulpensand, he was a young warrior. Some fourteen years later at the Battle of Cassiane he was an inexperienced twenty-year-old; married to Ortrun after the Battle of Cassiane (574,1)

Otto (*Otte*), king of an unnamed land; his brother was supposedly Hagen's vassal and involved in a feud with Ludwig (611,2)

the Saxons (*Sachsen*), mentioned as an example of particularly ferocious fighters (366,4)

Siegfried (*Seyfrid; Sifrit; Sivrit*), king of the Moors and Moorland; ruled over seven kings; his kingdom included Karadie, Alzabe, Abakie, and Ikaria; rejected suitor of Kudrun; attacked Herwig in retaliation for his betrothal to Kudrun; participated in the battle to gain Kudrun's freedom in Ormanie; later married to Herwig's unnamed sister (580,1)

Sigebant, king of Ireland; Ger and Uote's son; Hagen's father; Uote of Norway's husband (1,2)

the Stormarn, the men from Stormarn; Wate's subjects (1682,1)

Uote, early queen of Ireland; Ger's wife; Sigebant's mother; Hagen's grandmother; Kudrun's great-great-grandmother; ruled alone after Ger's death (1,3)

Uote (*Uote; Ute*), queen of Ireland; Sigebant's wife; Hagen's mother; originally from Norway and Frideschotten (42,4)

Wate, aged ruler of Stormarn; legendary warrior and military leader; related to Hetel and the Hegelingen clan; raised Hetel as a boy and also raised Hetel's son, Ortwin; close advisor to the king; often paired with Fruote; led the bridal quest to Ireland and the military expeditions to Seeland, Wulpensand, and Ormanie; robbed pilgrims of their ships and soldiers, for which he was rebuked; executed Heregart and Gerlint after the Battle of Cassiane; known as "old" Wate, reputed to be quick to anger, ruthless in battle, and merciless to his enemies; also known for his skill in healing (205,1)

Wigaleis (*Wygolays*), Hetel's vassal and counselor; the name is borrowed from Wirnt von Grafenberg's work *Wigalois* (582,2)

Unnamed Persons

Herwig's sister, Siegfried's bride from Seeland; brought to Hegelingen with her entourage to marry Siegfried (1643,4)

Hilde's chamberlain, a cousin of Horant; exiled in Ireland; served at Hagen's court (392,1)

Horant's mother, also Hetel's sister (1112,3)

Princess from Iserland, unnamed and youngest companion to Hilde of India and Hildeburg of Portugal on the griffins' island; she later marries an unnamed nobleman from Norway (120,1)

Personal Names

Otnit and *Wolf Dietrich A*

Textual variations of a name are included in parentheses, with an annotation of A or W or AW if the name occurs in both manuscripts.

Alberich (AW: *Alberich*; *Albereich*; A: *Albrichen*; W: *Albreich*), a dwarf king over five hundred years old; Otnit's biological father; raped Otnit's mother; only visible to the owner of a magic ring; provided chain mail armor made of gold and other weapons to Otnit; pledged to support him in his quest for a bride; participated in the Battles of Suders and Mount Tabor; led Liebgart out of her father's fortress to Otnit; advised Otnit against his fight with the dragon; mentioned but not named in *Wolf Dietrich A* (*O* 119,2; *WDA* 418,2)

Apollo (AW: *Appollen*; A: *Appollo*; W: *Appolle*), a Greek god, but in the context of the crusader era, a pagan object of worship for Muslims, along with Muhammed (*O* 271,2)

the Apulian (A: *Pulleschar*, W: *Pullicher*), Zacharis, the man from Apulia, Otnit's Muslim vassal (*O* 66,1)

Baltram, Berchtung's brother-in-law and ally; from Bulgaria in the east; supported Berchtung during his trial (*WDA* 166,3)

Berchtung of Meran (A: *Berchtung*; *Bertung*; *Berchtunge*), elderly lord of Meran; Hug Dietrich's faithful counselor and vassal; Wolf Dietrich's foster father and mentor; ordered by the king to kill Wolf Dietrich, he set him free instead; arrested and tried on his return for murder; freed with Baltram's support; exiled Saben as punishment for his treason; banished from court on Saben's return; supported Wolf Dietrich in his fight against his brothers; known as "the loyal" (*der getrewe*) (*WDA* 5,3)

Botelung, brother of Hug Dietrich's wife; lord among the Huns (*WDA* 3,1)

Dietrich (*Diettreich*), the name given to all three sons of Hug Dietrich; only Wolf Dietrich is further qualified in the text with the sobriquet "the Wolf" (*WDA* 4,2)

Dietrich of Bern (A: *Diettrich*; W: *Dietreich*), Dietrich of Verona; great hero of Germanic legend; mentioned as a descendant of King Otnit of Lombardy (*O* 597,3)

Engelwan (A: *Engelwan*; W: *Engelman*), Burgrave of Garda; Huteger's son; Helmnot's brother; Otnit's vassal and advisor (*O* 30,1)

Falcon (*valke*), Wolf Dietrich's incredibly fast horse, given to him by Berchtung; previously owned by his father, King Hug Dietrich; saved Wolf Dietrich from the dragon (*WDA* 423,3)

Gerebant (A: *Gerebant*; *Gerebart*; W: *Gerwart*), duke of Troia; Otnit's vassal (*O* 39,1)

the Greek (*Krieche*), toponymic epithet for both Hug Dietrich and Wolf Dietrich (*WDA* 3,4; 324,1)

the Greeks (*Kriechen*), subjects of King Hug Dietrich and his sons; essentially Greek inhabitants of the Byzantine Empire (*WDA* 335,2)

Helmnot (AW: *Helmnot*; W: *Lemnot*), margrave of Tuscany; Huteger's son; Engelwan's brother; Otnit's vassal (*O* 10,1)

Hermann, count in Lombardy and suitor of Otnit's widow; former vassal of Otnit (*WDA* 538,1)

Personal Names

Hug Dietrich (*Hugdiettreich*; *Hugediettreich*; *Hugediettrich*; *Hugediettereich*), king of Greece; reigned at Constantinople; father of three sons, including Wolf Dietrich; Fruote's uncle (*WDA* 2,4)

Hug Dietrich (*Hugediettreich*), baby boy of a (deceased) count and countess; rescued by Wolf Dietrich, who chose to name the child after his own father (*WDA* 575,4)

the Huns (*Hunen*), Botelung's subjects; people of the mighty Hunnish kingdom (*WDA* 3,1)

Huteger (A: *Huteger*; W: *Leutiger*), seneschal, or high steward, at Otnit's court in Garda; father of Helmnot and Engelwan (*O* 33,1)

Ilias (AW: *Ylias*; W: *Ilias*; *Yliaz*), king of Russia; Otnit's uncle, advisor, and vassal; great warrior and military leader; was first to mention Liebgart to Otnit; led the bridal quest and crusade to Machorel's kingdom of Syria; massacred innocents after the Battle of Suders (Tyre); came to Otnit's rescue at the final battle of the marsh (*O* 11,1)

the Italians (*Walhen*), Otnit's subjects in Italy (*O* 357,1)

Liebgart (*Liebgart*; *Liebegart*), Machorel's daughter; Otnit's wife and widow; queen of Lombardy in Garda; unnamed in the entire *Otnit* text; baptized by Alberich and Ilias; Wolf Dietrich's future wife (*O* 11,3 [not mentioned by name]; *WDA* 548,1)

the Lombard (AW: *Lamparte*; A: *Lamparthe*; W: *Lampart*), Otnit's toponymic epithet (*O* 29,1)

the Lombards (AW: *Lamparten*; A: *Lamparde*; *Lamparte*), citizens of Lombardy; Otnit's subjects (*O* 23,3)

Lucifer, a name for the devil (*WDA* 463,2)

Machorel (A: *Nachorel*; W: *Marchorel*), king of Syria, which included Jerusalem, Mount Tabor, and its capital, the town of Suders (presumably Tyre); father of Liebgart; fought unsuccessfully against Otnit to keep his daughter for himself; escaped back to Mount Tabor; sent dragon eggs to Otnit's kingdom for revenge; corruption of the name al-Malik al-Adil, Saladin's brother, heir, and sultan of Egypt and Syria from 1200 until his death in 1218 (*O* 13,1)

Muhammed (AW: *Machmet*), the Prophet; depicted in *Otnit* and other medieval texts as one of the pagan gods worshipped by Muslims (*O* 271,2)

Otnit (A: *Otnit*; *Ottnit*; *Otneit*; W: *Ortnit*; *Ortneit*; *Ortneid*; A: *Otneidt WDA*), young king of Lombardy; lord of seventy-two liegemen; Alberich's biological son; Liebgart's husband; reputed to have the strength of twelve men while gaining one strength every year; discovered Alberich, his father, while in search of adventure; sailed with an army and his supporters to Syria to win the hand of Liebgart, the Muslim king's daughter; often despairing, he succeeded in his quest with Alberich's and Ilias's support; married to Liebgart in Garda; slain by a dragon sent by his father-in-law, Machorel (*O* 5,2; *WDA* 417,2)

Rose, Otnit's sword, given to him by his father, Alberich (*O* 116,3)

the Russian (A: *Reusse*; W: *Reuzze*), Ilias's toponymic epithet (*O* 56,1)

the Russians (A: *Reussen*; *Rewseen*; W: *Reuzzen*; *Ruzzen*), inhabitants of Russia; Ilias's subjects (*O* 11,1)

Saben (*Saben*; *Sabene*; *Sabenn*), duke; counselor to Hug Dietrich and his sons; Berchtung's former friend; attempted to seduce the queen; plotted to kill young Wolf Dietrich; accused Berchtung of his murder; banished by Berchtung from the court; after the king's death, returned to the queen's favor, assumed power and acted as regent; banished the queen, Berchtung, and Wolf Dietrich; fought in support of Wolf Dietrich's two brothers; known as "the unfaithful" (*der ungetrewe*) (*WDA* 7,4)

Saracens (A: *Sarratine*; W: *Sarrazzen*), general term for Muslims or Arabs (*O* 326,4)

(the) Wolf Dietrich (*Wolf(f) her(r) Diett(er)reich; Wolf(f)diett(er)reich; Wolf(f)diettrich*), youngest son of Hug Dietrich, king of Greece; brother of two Dietrichs; future husband of Liebgart, Otnit's widow; ancestor of Dietrich of Bern; spared from an early death by Berchtung; given the epithet "the Wolf" by Berchtung and later fostered by him; disowned and banished by his brothers; invaded Greece with an army to restore his rights; defeated his brothers and Saben in battle, but retreated to Berchtung's castle because of heavy casualties; escaped from the siege to seek Otnit's support in restoring his crown; eventually arrived in Garda, where he pledged to Liebgart that he would defeat the dragon; mentioned but unnamed in *Otnit* as a dragon slayer and future husband of Otnit's widow (*O* 596,4; *WDA* 113,4)

Zacharis (A: *Zachareys*; W: *Zacharise*), Muslim king of Sicily; lord of Apulia; vassal to Otnit; provided Otnit with provisions and a fleet for his army at Messina; possibly a reference to Abu Zakariya Yahya, the Almohad governor of Gabès and then of Tunis, a diplomatic interlocutor of Emperor Frederick II (*O* 41,1)

Unnamed Persons:

Count and Countess, after her husband was killed by the dragon, the Countess gave birth to a baby boy, whom Wolf Dietrich had baptized as Hug Dietrich; both were handed over to the care of a peasant (*WDA* 562,4; 565,1)

King of Lombardy, Otnit's putative father; his mother's husband (*O* 169,1)

the Margravine, Margrave Helmnot's wife, who along with him cared for Otnit's widow, Liebgart, in her exile in Garda (*O* 595,1)

Queen of Greece, Botelung's sister; wife of Hug Dietrich; mother of Wolf Dietrich (*WDA* 3,1)

Queen of Lombardy, Otnit's mother; gave Otnit a magic gold ring with which to see his father Alberich; died after the news of his death (*O* 70,1)

Queen of Syria and Jerusalem, Liebgart's mother, the wife of Machorel (*O* 21,4)

Sea Queen, saved Wolf Dietrich from hunger and exhaustion; demanded in return to become his wife; agreed to help him if he gave her one of his brothers (*WDA* 470,2)

FAMILY TREE FOR MAIN CHARACTERS IN KUDRUN

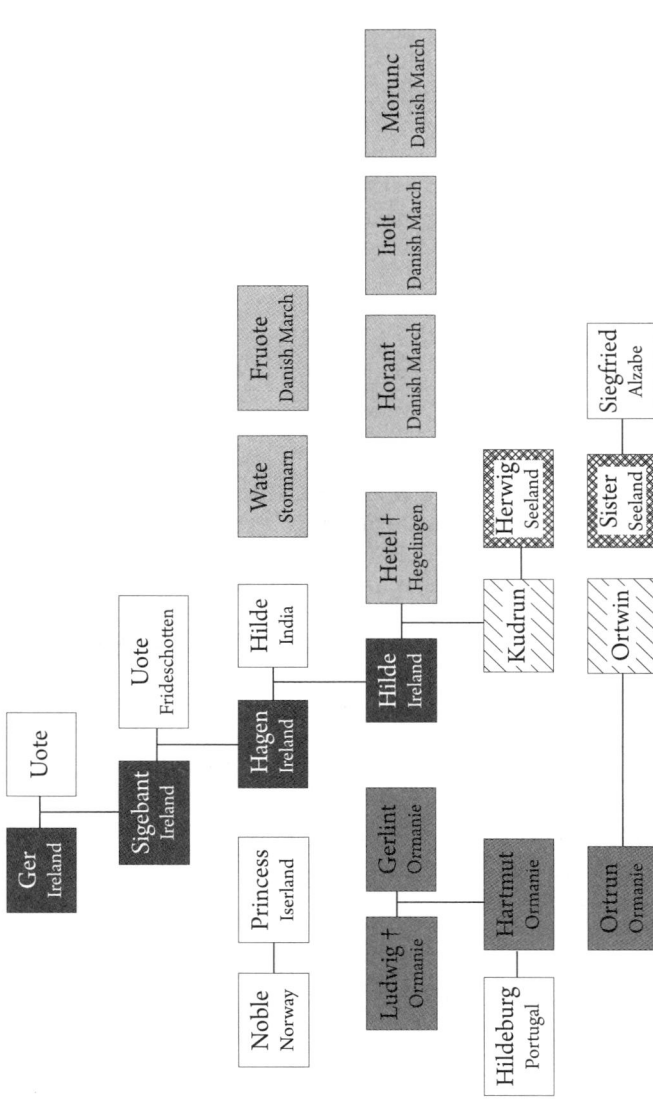

Kudrun is a multi-generational saga, and this chart arranges its five generations according to the main royal houses, their offspring, and seats of power: Ireland, Hegelingen, and Ormanie. King Hagen of Ireland, his daughter Hilde, who marries into the Hegelingen clan, and her daughter Kudrun are at the nexus of three generations that interact in ways that prompt a reassessment of what it means to be heroic.

MANUSCRIPTS CONTAINING KUDRUN AND VERSIONS OF OTNIT AND WOLF DIETRICH

The only manuscript that contains the *Kudrun* text is the so-called *Ambraser Heldenbuch*, which was copied in Tirol by Hans Ried, begun in 1504 at the behest of Emperor Maximilian I and completed in 1515 or 1516.[1] This collection of twenty-five works written in the late twelfth and thirteenth centuries is distinctive in that fourteen[2] are extant only in this one sixteenth-century manuscript. In the manuscript, the text of *Kudrun* follows the *Nibelungenlied* and its epilogue, the *Nibelungenklage*, and is itself followed by *Biterolf*, *Otnit*, and an unfinished exemplar of *Wolf Dietrich A*. These texts were copied in a southern Bavarian dialect of early New High German and have mostly been edited in a normalized Middle High German. Various versions of *Otnit* and *Wolf Dietrich* are transmitted either together or separately in sixteen other manuscripts dating from the mid-fourteenth to the late fifteenth centuries.

This inventory arranges the manuscripts by content, that is to say, it focuses primarily on the transmission of the *Kudrun* text and the four different redactions of *Otnit* and *Wolf Dietrich*. The descriptions include the commonly assigned manuscript designator, current location, shelf number, and folio span of each work in order of appearance along with an indication of the time of manufacture. The numbers at the end of each description in square brackets refer to the online *Handschriftencensus*, which lists manuscripts alphabetically by current location, and the numbering given there to each manuscript under the first work listed. Digital copies of several of the manuscripts can be found online, while a diplomatic and allographic transcription along with full-color images of the entire *Ambraser Heldenbuch* is now available in eleven volumes, published in 2022 by Mario Klarer.

---

1. Hans Ried completed the written text before his death in 1516, but the illumination and illustration of the codex were likely completed in 1517.
2. In some cases, Hartmann von Aue's *Erec* is included, for a total of fifteen texts. However, *Erec* is also partially transmitted in another three manuscript fragments, unlike the fourteen other works that have no other manuscript transmission whatsoever outside of the *Ambraser Heldenbuch*.

Manuscripts Arranged by Content

Kudrun, Otnit, and *Wolf Dietrich A:*
A, Vienna, Österreichische Nationalbibliothek, Cod. Ser. nova 2663, 140r–166r; 196r–205v; 205v–214v (parchment; 1504–16; *Ambraser Heldenbuch*) [1]

Otnit:
W, Vienna, Österreichische Nationalbibliothek, Cod. 2779, 71v–85r (parchment; first half, fourteenth century; *Windhagen* manuscript) [10] Linz, Landesarchiv, Buchdeckelfunde Sch. 3, II/4e (fragment, two double leaves)

Otnit and *Wolf Dietrich A:*
k, Dresden, Landesbibliothek, Mscr. M 201, 1r–43r; 44r–91r (paper; 1472; *Dresdner Heldenbuch*; heavily redacted and shortened; includes ending to *Wolf Dietrich A*) [2]

Wolf Dietrich B:
B, Vienna, Österreichische Nationalbibliothek, Cod. 2947, 1r–48v (paper; about 1470) [14]
H, Berlin, Staatsbibliothek, mgq 761, 1r–57r (paper; first half, fifteenth century) [2]
K, Heidelberg, Universitätsbibliothek, Cpg 109, 3r–76v (paper; 1516–27) [6]

Otnit and *Wolf Dietrich C:*
C, Berlin, Staatsbibliothek, mgf 844 (parchment; first half, fourteenth century; fragment, two double leaves and two separate leaves) [1] Wolfenbüttel, Herzog August Bibl., Cod. A Novi (6) (fragment, remainder of a double leaf and three separate leaves)

Otnit and *Wolf Dietrich D:*

Variant a:
a, Heidelberg, Universitätsbibliothek, Cpg 365, 1r–36r; 36r–186v (paper; about 1420) [4]
b, Frankfurt a. M., Universitätsbibliothek, Ms. Carm. 2, 1r–40r; 40v–226v (paper; about 1420) [3]
c, Strasbourg, Seminarbibliothek, Heldenbuch (n.s.), 13r–50v; 53r–201r (paper; 1476–79; *Strassburger Heldenbuch*, Diebolt von Hanow) [7]
d, Strasbourg, Stadtbibliothek, Cod. B 81, 173r–195v; 1r–110v (paper; 1476) [8]
h, Dortmund, n.s. (lost; paper; fifteenth century; fragment, three leaves; only *Wolf Dietrich*) [3]

Variant e:
e, Heidelberg, Universitätsbibliothek, Cpg 373, 1r–25v; 25v–131r (paper; about 1420) [5]
e^2, Wernigerode, Fürstliche Stolbergische Bibliothek, Cod. Zb 4m, 218v–220r (paper; last quarter, fifteenth century to first third, sixteenth century; only twenty-four lines of *Wolf Dietrich D* are transmitted in this codex) [13]
f, Stuttgart, Landesbibliothek, Cod. poet. et phil. 2° 91, 1r–29v; 30r–189v (paper; 1469–71) [9]
g, Karlsruhe, Landesbibliothek, Cod. Donaueschingen 90, 1r–25v; 26r–148r (paper; 1452) [6]

Variant y:
y, Vienna, Österreichische Nationalbibliothek, Cod. 15478, 160r–183v; 184r–290r (paper; about 1480–90; formerly Piaristencollegium Wien) [11]

(Variant z):
z, *Heldenbuch*, printed by Johann Prüss, Strasbourg, about 1479–84 (GW 12185)

LIST OF TEXTS IN THE *AMBRASER HELDENBUCH*

(Vienna, Österreichische Nationalbibliothek, Cod. Ser. nova 2663)

*denotes a text that is extant in this manuscript alone

Courtly Works
1. *Frauenehre*, Der Stricker
2. *Moritz von Craon**
3. *Iwein*, Hartmann von Aue
4. *Das (erste) Büchlein* or *Die Klage*,* Hartmann von Aue
5. The so-called *zweites Büchlein**
6. *Der Mantel*,* Heinrich von dem Türlin (?)
7. *Erec*[*], Hartmann von Aue (the only mostly complete manuscript)

Heroic Epic
8. *Dietrichs Flucht*
9. *Die Rabenschlacht*
10. *Das Nibelungenlied*
11. *Die Nibelungenklage* (incomplete)
12. *Kudrun**
13. *Biterolf und Dietleib**
14. *Otnit*
15. *Wolf Dietrich A**

Short Narratives
16. *Die böse Frau**
17. *Die getreue Ehefrau*,* Herrant von Wildon
18. *Der verkehrte Wirt*,* Herrant von Wildon
19. *Der nackte Kaiser*,* Herrant von Wildon
20. *Die Katze*,* Herrant von Wildon
21. *Frauenbuch*,* Ulrich von Liechtenstein
22. *Meier Helmbrecht*, Wernher der Gartenaere
23. *Pfaffe Amis*, Der Stricker
24. *Titurel*, Wolfram von Eschenbach (fragment)
25. *Der Priester Johann** (fragment)

SELECTED BIBLIOGRAPHY
Kudrun

Editions and Translations into German (listed by date)

Der Helden Buch in der Ursprache. Edited by Friedrich von der Hagen and Anton [*sic*] Primisser. Vol. 1. Deutsche Gedichte des Mittelalters 2. Berlin: Reimer, 1820. [includes *Otnit* and *Wolf Dietrich A* from the *Dresdner Heldenbuch*]

Kutrun: Mittelhochdeutsch. Edited by Adolph Ziemann. Bibliothek der gesammten deutschen National-Literatur 1. Quedlinburg: Basse, 1835.

Gudrun: Nordseesage, Nebst Abhandlung über das mittelhochdeutsche Gedicht Gudrun und den Nordseesagenkreis. Translated by Albert Schulz. Berlin: Mittler, 1839.

Gudrun: Aus dem Mittelhochdeutschen übersetzt. Translated by Adelbert Keller. Stuttgart: Ebner & Seubert, 1840.

Gûdrûnlieder. Nebst einem Wörterbuche. Edited by Ludwig Ettmüller. Zürich: Verlag des literarischen Comptoirs, 1841.

Gudrun: Deutsches Heldenlied. Translated by Karl Simrock. *Das Heldenbuch*, vol. 1. Stuttgart: Cotta'scher Verlag, 1843.

Kudrun: Die echten Theile des Gedichtes, mit einer kritischen Einleitung. Edited by Karl Müllenhoff. Kiel: Schwerssche Buchhandlung, 1845.

Gûdrûn. Edited by Alexander Vollmer. Dichtungen des deutschen Mittelalters 5. Leipzig: Göschen'sche Verlagshandlung, 1845.

Gudrun: Nach der Müllenhoff'schen Ausgabe der echten Theile des Gedichts. Translated by Friedrich Koch. Leipzig: Wiegand, 1847.

Kudrun: Übersetzung und Urtext, mit erklärenden Abhandlungen. Edited and translated by Wilhelm von Ploennies. Leipzig: Brockhaus, 1853.

Echte Lieder von Gudrun nach Müllenhoffs Kritik. Edited by Karl Hahn. Vienna: Braumüller, 1853.

Gudrun: Altdeutsches Heldengedicht. Translated by Adolf Bacmeister. Stuttgart: Palm, 1860.

Kudrun. Edited by Karl Bartsch, 1865; revised and introduced by Karl Stackmann. 5th ed. Deutsche Klassiker des Mittelalters 2. Wiesbaden: Brockhaus, 1965. Reprinted in Altdeutsche Textbibliothek 115. Tübingen: Niemeyer, 2000.

Kudrun. Edited by Ernst Martin. Germanistische Handbibliothek 2. Halle: Waisenhaus, 1872; 2nd edition, 1902.

Gudrun: Ein mittelhochdeutsches Heldengedicht. Translated by Hermann Junghans. Universal-Bibliothek 465–66. Leipzig: Phillip Reclam jun., 1873.

Kudrun. Edited by Barend Symons, 1883; revised by Bruno Boesch. 4th ed. Altdeutsche Textbibliothek 5. Tübingen: Niemeyer, 1964.

Gudrun: Übersetzt und mit erläuternden Anmerkungen versehen. Translated by Ludwig Freytag. Berlin: Friedberg & Mode, 1888.

Kudrun. Translated by Hans Löschhorn. Halle: Waisenhaus, 1891.

Kudrun. Edited by Paul Piper. Kürschners Deutsche National-Litteratur 6. Stuttgart: Union Deutsche Verlagsgesellschaft, 1895.

Kudrun: Monumentalausgabe. Eins von 1400 numerierten Exemplaren. Edited by Ernst Schulte-Strathaus. Munich: Hyperion Verlag, 1911.

Der Nibelunge Not. Kudrun. Edited by Eduard Sievers. Leipzig: Insel-Verlag, 1921. Reprint 1955.
Warnlieder. Edited by Henrik Becker. Vol. 2: *Hildebrand, Dietrich, Kudrun.* Leipzig: VEB Bibliographisches Institut, 1953. 190–273.
Gudrun: Deutsches Heldenlied. Translated by Karl Simrock, updated by Friedrich Neumann. Reclams Universal-Bibliothek 465–67. Stuttgart: Reclam, 1958.
Kudrun: Ein Heldenepos, eingeleitet, übersetzt und mit Anmerkungen versehen. Translated by Siegfried Colditz. Leipzig: Philipp Reclam jun., 1962.
Kudrun: Die Handschrift. Edited by Franz Bäuml. Berlin: de Gruyter, 1969.
Kudrun: Ein mittelalterliches Heldenepos. Translated by Joachim Lindner. Berlin: Verlag der Nation, 1971.
Das Nibelungenlied. Kudrun: Text, Nacherzählung, Wort- und Begriffserklärung. Edited and retold by Werner Hoffmann. Darmstadt: WBG, 1972.
Ambraser Heldenbuch: Vollständige Faksimile Ausgabe im Originalformat des Codex Vindobonensis Ser. nova 2663. Edited by Franz Unterkircher. Graz: Akademische Druck-und Verlagsanstalt, 1973.
Kudrun. Translated by Bernhard Sowinski. Reclams Universal-Bibliothek 466. Stuttgart: Reclam, 1995.
Kudrun: Mittelhochdeutsch/Neuhochdeutsch. Edited and translated by Uta Störmer-Caysa. Reclams Universal-Bibliothek 18639. Stuttgart: Reclam, 2010.
Kudrun. Edited by Mario Klarer. Ambraser Heldenbuch, Gesamttranskription mit Manuskriptbild, vol. 8. Berlin: de Gruyter, 2022.

Translations into English (listed by date)

Gudrun: A Medieval Epic. Translated by Mary Pickering Nichols. Boston: Houghton Mifflin, 1889. [verse translation]
Gudrun: Translated from the German of Ferdinand Schmidt. Translated by George P. Upton. Life Stories for Young People. Chicago: McClurg, 1906. [a loose prose retelling]
Gudrun Done into English. Translated by Margaret Armour. New York: E. P. Dutton, 1928. Also in Everyman's Library 880. London: Dent, 1932.
Kudrun. Translated by Brian Murdoch. Everyman Classics. London: Dent, 1987.
Kudrun. Translated by Winder McConnell. Columbia, SC: Camden House, 1992.
Kudrun. Translated by Marion Gibbs and Sidney Johnson. Garland Library of Medieval Literature 79. New York: Garland, 1992.

Other Primary Texts and Anthologies, Along with Translations in English (listed alphabetically)

Deutsche Gedichte des Mittelalters. Edited and translated by Ulrich Müller, with Gerlinde Weiss. Reclams Universal-Bibliothek 8849. Stuttgart: Reclam, 1993.
Freidanks Bescheidenheit: Auswahl. Edited by Wolfgang Spiewok. Leipzig: Reclam, 1991.
Gottfried von Strassburg. *Tristan und Isold.* Edited and translated by Walter Haug and Manfred Scholz. Berlin: Insel Verlag, 2012.
Gottfried von Strassburg. *Tristan and Isolde: With Ulrich von Türheim's Continuation.* Edited and translated by William Whobrey. Indianapolis/Cambridge: Hackett Publishing, 2020.
Kreuzzugsdichtung. Edited by Ulrich Müller. Tübingen: Niemeyer, 1969.
Medieval German Lyric Verse in English Translation. Translated by J. W. Thomas. UNC Studies in the Germanic Languages and Literatures 60. Chapel Hill: University of North Carolina Press, 1968. [Walther von der Vogelweide, 107–25]

Selected Bibliography

Neidhart von Reuental. *Lieder*. Edited and translated by Helmut Lomnitzer. Reclams Universal-Bibliothek 6927. Stuttgart: Reclam, 1984.

Neidhart: Selected Songs from the Riedegg Manuscript. Edited and translated by Kathryn Starkey and Edith Wenzel. TEAMS Medieval German Texts in Bilingual Editions 5. Kalamazoo: Western Michigan University Press, 2016.

Das Nibelungenlied und die Klage: Nach der Handschrift 857 der Stiftsbibliothek St. Gallen. Edited and translated by Joachim Heinzle. Berlin: Deutscher Klassiker Verlag, 2015.

The Nibelungenlied: With the Klage. Edited and translated by William Whobrey. Indianapolis/Cambridge: Hackett Publishing, 2018.

Ovid. *Metamorphoses*. Translated by Brookes More. Boston: Cornhill, 1922.

Rudolf von Ems. *Alexander: Ein höfischer Versroman des 13. Jahrhunderts*. Edited by Victor Junk. Leipzig: Hiersemann, 1928/1929. 2 vols. Reprint, Darmstadt: WBG, 1970.

Rudolf von Ems. *Willehalm von Orlens*. Edited by Victor Junk. Berlin: Weidmann, 1905. Deutsche Texte des Mittelalters, vol. 2. Reprint Dublin: Weidmann, 1967.

Tannhäuser: Poet and Legend. With Texts and Translations of His Works. Translated by J. W. Thomas. UNC Studies in the Germanic Languages and Literatures 77. Chapel Hill: University of North Carolina Press, 1974. 164–69.

Walther von der Vogelweide. *Werke*. Vol. 1: *Spruchlyrik*. Edited and translated by Günther Schweikle. 3rd ed. edited by Ricarda Bauschke-Hartung. Reclams Universal-Bibliothek 819. Stuttgart: Reclam, 2009.

Walther von der Vogelweide. *Werke*. Vol. 2: *Liedlyrik*. Edited and translated by Günther Schweikle. Reclams Universal-Bibliothek 820. Stuttgart: Reclam, 1998.

Secondary Literature in English (listed alphabetically by author, with a few of the more important references in German)

Bäuml, Franz. "Some Aspects of Editing the Unique Manuscript: A Criticism of Method." *Orbis litterarum* 16 (1961): 27–33.

Bäuml, Franz. "The Gabilûn-Episode in *Kudrun*: Some Palaeographic Implications." *Manuscripta* 9 (1965): 67–78.

Becker, Peter Jörg. *Handschriften und Frühdrucke mittelhochdeutscher Epen*. Wiesbaden, 1977. 61–64, 153–55.

Begriffsglossar und Index zur Kudrun. Edited by Klaus Schmidt. Indices zur deutschen Literatur 29. Tübingen: Niemeyer, 1994.

Bennett, J. A. W. "Concerning Wade . . ." *Modern Language Review* 31 (1936): 202–3.

Blamires, David. "The Geography of *Kudrun*." *Modern Language Review* 61 (1966): 436–45.

Bostock, John. "The Structure of the *Kudrun*." *Modern Language Review* 53 (1958): 521–25.

Bowden, Sarah. *Bridal-Quest Epics in Medieval Germany: A Revisionary Approach*. MHRA Texts and Dissertations 85. Cambridge: Modern Humanities Research Association, 2012.

Campbell, Ian. "Kudrun's wilder Hagen, Vâlant aller Künige." *Seminar* 6 (1970): 1–14.

Campbell, Ian. *Kudrun: A Critical Appreciation*. Anglica Germanica Series 2. Cambridge: Cambridge University Press, 1978. Reviewed by D. H. Green, *Medium Ævum* 49 (1980): 133–35, and Ernst Dick, *Journal of English and Germanic Philology* 80 (1981): 293–96.

Claasen, Albrecht. "Poetic Reflections in Medieval German Literature on Tragic Conflicts, Massive Death, and Armageddon." In *The End-Times in Medieval German Literature: Sin, Evil, and the Apocalypse*, edited by Ernst Ralf Hintz and Scott Pincikowski. Martlesham, UK: Boydell & Brewer, 2019. 72–97.

Domanski, Kristina. "Zwischen Naturstudium und Dekor." In Klarer, *Kaiser Maximilian I. und das Ambraser Heldenbuch*, 145–69.

Selected Bibliography

Ertzdorff, Xenja von. *Rudolf von Ems: Untersuchungen zum höfischen Roman im 13. Jahrhundert.* Munich: Wilhelm Fink Verlag, 1967.
Frakes, Jerold. "Feudal Bridal Quest Turned on Its Jewish Head." In *The Emergence of Early Yiddish Literature: Cultural Translation in Ashkenaz.* Bloomington: Indiana University Press, 2017. 151–90.
Frakes, Jerold. "Women, Sovereignty, and Class in *Kudrun*." In *Brides and Doom: Gender, Property, and Power in Medieval German Women's Epic.* Philadelphia: University of Pennsylvania Press, 1994. 182–218.
Glier, Ingeborg. *Artes amandi: Untersuchungen zur Geschichte, Überlieferung und Typologie der deutschen Minnereden.* Munich: Beck, 1971.
Hoffmann, Werner. *Kudrun: Ein Beitrag zur Deutung der Nachnibelungischen Heldendichtung.* Germanistische Abhandlungen 17. Stuttgart: Metzler, 1967.
Kerth, Thomas. "Minstrels and Bridal Quests." In *King Rother and His Bride: Quest and Counter-Quests.* Columbia, SC: Camden House, 2010. 1–20.
Klarer, Mario, ed. *Kaiser Maximilian I. und das Ambraser Heldenbuch.* Vienna: Böhlau, 2019.
McConnell, Winder. *The Epic of Kudrun: A Critical Commentary.* Göppinger Arbeiten zur Germanistik 463. Göppingen: Kümmerle, 1988.
McConnell, Winder. "Hagen and the Otherworld in *Kudrun*." *Res Publica Litterarum* 6 (1983): 211–21.
McConnell, Winder. "Kudrun." In *Medieval Germany: An Encyclopedia*, edited by John Jeep. New York: Garland, 2001. 430–31.
McConnell, Winder. "Marriage in the *Nibelungenlied* and *Kudrun*." In *Spectrum Medii Aevi: Essays in Early German Literature in Honor of George Fenwick Jones*, edited by William McDonald. Göppingen: Kümmerle, 1983. 299–320.
McConnell, Winder. "The Passing of the Old Heroes: The *Nibelungenlied, Kudrun,* and the Epic Spirit." In *Genres in Medieval German Literature*, edited by Hubert Heinen and Ingeborg Henderson. Göppinger Arbeiten zur Germanistik 439. Göppingen: Kümmerle Verlag, 1986. 103–13.
McConnell, Winder. "Wate and Wada." *Modern Language Notes* 92 (1977): 572–77.
McConnell, Winder. *The Wate Figure in Medieval Tradition.* Stanford German Studies 13. Bern: Peter Lang, 1978.
Müller, Jan-Dirk. *"Episches" Erzählen: Erzählformen früher volkssprachiger Schriftlichkeit.* Philologische Studien und Quellen 259. Berlin: Erich Schmidt Verlag, 2017.
Müller, Stephan. "Prominente Unikate: Zu den (verlorenen) Vorlagen des Ambraser Heldenbuchs und dem heldenbuch zu Runkelstein." In Klarer, *Kaiser Maximilian I. und das Ambraser Heldenbuch*, 88–98.
Murdoch, Brian. "Interpreting *Kudrun*: Some Comments on a Recent Critical Appreciation." *New German Studies* 7 (1979): 113–27.
Nibelungenlied und Kudrun. Edited by Heinz Rupp. Wege der Forschung 54. Darmstadt: Wissenschaftliche Buchgesellschaft, 1976.
Nolte, Theodor. *Das Kudrunepos: Ein Frauenroman?* Tübingen: Niemeyer, 1985.
Panzer, Friedrich. *Hilde-Gudrun: Eine sagen- und literargeschichtliche Untersuchung.* Halle: Niemeyer, 1901.
Pearson, Mark. "Sigeband's Courtship of Ute in the *Kudrun*." *Colloquia Germanica* 25 (1992): 101–11.
Poor, Sara. "Gender Studies and Medieval Women in German." *College Literature* 28 (2001): 118–29.
Rasmussen, Ann Marie. *Mothers and Daughters in Medieval German Literature.* Syracuse, NY: Syracuse University Press, 1997.

Selected Bibliography

Roland, Martin. "Cod. 2779." In *Mitteleuropäische Schulen I (ca. 1250-1350)*, edited by Martin Roland and Andreas Fingernagel. Vienna: Verlag der Österreichischen Akademie der Wissenschaften,1997. 266–68.
Sandbach, Francis. *Nibelungenlied and Gudrun in England and America*. London: David Nutt, 1904.
Schneider, Karin. *Paläographie und Handschriftenkunde für Germanisten*. Berlin: de Gruyter, 2014.
Symons, Barend. "Zur Kudrun." *Beiträge zur Geschichte der deutschen Sprache und Literatur* 9 (1884): 1–100.
Torrance, James. *A Concordance to the Middle High German "Kudrun."* PhD diss., University of California, Los Angeles, 1993.
Wailes, Stephen. "The Romance of Kudrun." *Speculum* 58, no. 2 (1983): 347–67.
Walshe, Maurice. "Kudrun in the Balkans?" *Slavonic and East European Review* 26, no. 67 (1948): 484–93.
Walshe, Maurice, Branislav Krstić, and Vera Javarek. "The Kudrun Story in the Balkans." *Slavonic and East European Review* 28, no. 71 (1950): 451–65.
Ward, Donald. "The Rescue of Kudrun: A Dioscuric Myth?" *Classica Mediaevalia* 26 (1965): 334–53.
Willson, H. Bernard. "Dialectic, 'Passio' and 'Compassio' in the *Kudrun*." *Modern Language Review* 58 (1963): 149–203.
Wisniewski, Roswitha. *Kudrun*. Sammlung Metzler 32. 2nd ed. Stuttgart: Metzler, 1969.

Otnit and *Wolf Dietrich A*

Editions and Translations into German of Otnit *and* Wolf Dietrich *(listed by date)*

Otnit. Edited by Franz Joseph Mone. Berlin: Reimer, 1821. [Manuscript a]
Künec Otnídes Mervart unde Tôd. Edited by Ludwig Ettmüller. Zürich: Höhr, 1838. [Manuscript W]
"Ortnit: Aus der Ambras- und Windhag-Wiener Handschrift." Edited by Friedrich von der Hagen. In *Heldenbuch: Altdeutsche Heldenlieder aus dem Sagenkreis Dietrichs von Bern und der Nibelungen*. Vol. 1. Leipzig: Schultze, 1855. 1–69. Reprint, Hildesheim: Olms, 1977. [Manuscripts AW]
"Wolfdietrich: Aus der Ambraser Handschrift." Edited by Friedrich von der Hagen. In *Heldenbuch: Altdeutsche Heldenlieder aus dem Sagenkreis Dietrichs von Bern und der Nibelungen*. Vol. 1. Leipzig: Schultze, 1855. 73–151. Reprint, Hildesheim: Olms, 1977. [Manuscript A]
"König Ortnits Meerfahrt und Tod." Translated by Karl Simrock. In *Das kleine Heldenbuch*. Stuttgart: Cotta'scher Verlag, 1859. 369–505.
"Hugdietrich und Wolfdietrich." Translated by Karl Simrock. In *Das kleine Heldenbuch*. Stuttgart: Cotta'scher Verlag, 1859. 509–725. [*Wolf Dietrich B*]
Der Grosse Wolfdieterich. Edited by Adolf Holtzmann. Heidelberg: Mohr, 1865. [*Wolf Dietrich D*]
Jacobs, Eduard. *Die ehemalige Büchersammlung Ludwigs, Grafen zu Stolberg, in Königstein und Mittheilungen zur deutschen Volksdichtung aus einer dorther nach Wernigerode gelangten Handschrift*. Wernigerode, 1868. 21–23. [Manuscript e^2]
Deutsches Heldenbuch: Ortnit und die Wolfdietriche nach Müllenhoffs Vorarbeiten. Edited by Arthur Amelung and Oskar Jänicke. Vol. 1. Deutsches Heldenbuch, vol. 3. Berlin: Weidmannsche

Buchhandlung, 1871; reprint, Dublin: Weidmann, 1968. [*Wolf Dietrich A* and *B*; vol. 2, 1873, contains *C* and *D*]

"Dortmunder Bruchstücke einer Handschrift des Heldenbuchs aus dem 15. Jh." Edited by Wilhelm Crecelius. *Zeitschrift für deutsches Altertum und deutsche Literatur* 19 (1876): 468–70. [Manuscript h]

Ortnit: Ein Heldengedicht. Translated by Karl Pannier. Reclams Universal-Bibliothek 971. Leipzig: Reclam jun., 1877.

Ortneit und Wolfdietrich nach der Wiener Piaristenhandschrift. Edited by Justus Lunzer von Lindhausen. Tübingen: Laupp, 1906. [Manuscript y]

Wolfdietrich: Der echte Teil des Wolfdietrich der Ambraser Handschrift (Wolfdietrich A). Edited by Hermann Schneider. Altdeutsche Textbibliothek 28. Halle: Niemeyer, 1930. Reprint 1968. [Manuscript A]

Studies in the Dresdener Heldenbuch: An Edition of Wolfdietrich K. Edited by Edward Fuchs. Louisville: Fetter, 1935. [Manuscript k]

Das Strassburger Heldenbuch: Rekonstruktion der Textfassung des Diebolt von Hanowe. Edited by Walter Kofler. 2 vols. Göppingen: Kümmerle, 1999. [Manuscript c]

Ortnit und Wolfdietrich D: Kritischer Text nach Ms. Carm. 2 der Stadt- und Universitätsbibliothek Frankfurt am Main. Edited by Walter Kofler. Stuttgart: Hirzel, 2001. [Manuscript b]

Das Dresdener Heldenbuch und die Bruchstücke des Berlin-Wolfenbütteler Heldenbuchs. Edited by Walter Kofler. Stuttgart: Hirzel, 2006. [Manuscript k and the C fragments]

Wolfdietrich B: Paralleledition der Redaktionen B/K und H. Edited by Walter Kofler. Stuttgart: Hirzel, 2008. [Manuscripts BHK]

Ortnit und Wolfdietrich A. Edited by Walter Kofler. Stuttgart: Hirzel, 2009. [Manuscript W as *Leithandschrift* for *Otnit*; manuscript A for *Wolf Dietrich A*]

Otnit. Wolf Dietrich: Frühneuhochdeutsch/Neuhochdeutsch. Edited and translated by Stephan Fuchs-Jolie, Victor Millet, and Dietmar Peschel. Reclams Universal-Bibliothek 19139. Stuttgart: Reclam, 2013. [Manuscript A]

Ortnit. Wolfdietrich A. Edited by Mario Klarer. Ambraser Heldenbuch, Gesamttranskription mit Manuskriptbild. Vol. 10. Berlin: de Gruyter, 2022. [Manuscript A]

Translations into English (listed by date)

Das Heldenbuch—The Book of Heroes: Illustrations of Northern Antiquities from the Earlier Teutonic and Scandinavian Romances, Being an Abstract of the Book of Heroes and Nibelungen Lay. Translated by Henry Weber, Robert Jamieson, and Walter Scott. Edinburgh: Longman, 1814. 45–136. [prose translation of *Wolf Dietrich A*, with some passages of verse]

Epics and Romances of the Middle Ages: Adapted from the Work of Dr. W. Wägner. Edited by W. S. W. Anson and M. W. MacDowall. London: Sonnenschein, 1883. 55–114. [a loose prose retelling of *Otnit* and *Wolf Dietrich*]

'Ortnit' and 'Wolfdietrich': Two Medieval Romances. Translated by John Wesley Thomas. Studies in German Literature, Linguistics, and Culture 23. Columbia, SC: Camden House, 1986. [translation of *Otnit* and *Wolf Dietrich B*]

Secondary Literature in English (listed alphabetically by author, with a few of the more important references in German)

Bornholdt, Claudia. *Engaging Moments: The Origins of Medieval Bridal-Quest Narrative*. Berlin: de Gruyter, 2005.

Dinkelacker, Wolfgang. *Ortnit-Studien: Vergleichende Interpretation der Fassungen*. Berlin: Schmidt, 1972.

Selected Bibliography

Fichtner, Edward. "Ortnit, or the Failure of Patriarchy." *Neophilologus* 93 (2009): 659–74.
Firestone, Ruth. "A New Look at the Transmission of Ortnit." *Amsterdamer Beiträge zur älteren Germanistik* 18 (1982): 129–42.
Haymes, Edward. *Ortnit und Wolfdietrich: Abbildungen zur handschriftlichen Überlieferung spätmittelalterlicher Heldenepik*. Göppingen: Kümmerle, 1984.
Haymes, Edward. "*ez wart ein buoch funden*: Oral and Written in Middle High German Heroic Epic." In *Comparative Research on Oral Traditions: A Memorial for Milman Parry*, edited by John Miles Foley. Columbus, OH: Slavica, 1987. 235–43.
Haymes, Edward. "*Wolfdietrich* and *Ortnit*." In *Medieval Germany: An Encyclopedia*, edited by John Jeep. New York: Garland, 2001. 821–22.
Schmid-Cadalbert, Christian. *Der "Ortnit AW" als Brautwerbungsdichtung: Ein Beitrag zum Verständnis mittelhochdeutscher Schemaliteratur*. Bern: Francke, 1985.
Schröder, Edward. "Der Ambraser Wolfdietrich: Grundlagen und Grundsätze der Textkritik." In *Nachrichten von der Gesellschaft der Wissenschaften zu Göttingen, philol.-histor. Klasse*. Berlin: Weidmann, 1931. 210–40.